AND A WOMAN SHALL LEAD THEM . . .

As the Hovertanks charged, the Aliens led by the red Bioroid swooped at the Veritechs who stood their ground, firing, in Battloid configuration. The Bioroid blew away two of the VTs, easily avoiding most of their fire and shrugging off the rest.

"Switch to Gladiator mode!" Dana called over the tac net. In midair the tanks shifted, reconfigured, *mechamorphosed*. When they landed, they were squat, two-legged, waddling gun turrets the size of houses, each with a massive primary-battery cannon.

Dana hopped her Gladiator high, landing to one end of the Bioroid firing line, to set up an enfilade. But an alien had spotted her and swung to fire. Dana got off the first round and holed the outworld mecha with a searing energy bolt that left glowing, molten armor in its wake.

"Gotcha!"

By Jack McKinney
Published by Ballantine Books:

THE ROBOTECH™ SERIES:
GENESIS #1
BATTLE CRY #2
HOMECOMING #3
BATTLEHYMN #4
FORCE OF ARMS #5
DOOMSDAY #6
SOUTHERN CROSS #7
METAL FIRE #8
THE FINAL NIGHTMARE #9
INVID INVASION #10
METAMORPHOSIS #11
SYMPHONY OF LIGHT #12

THE SENTINELS™ SERIES:
THE DEVIL'S HAND #1
DARK POWERS #2
DEATH DANCE #3
WORLD KILLERS #4
RUBICON #5

ROBOTECH: THE END OF THE CIRCLE #18
ROBOTECH: THE ZENTRAEDI REBELLION #19
ROBOTECH: THE MASTERS' GAMBIT #20
ROBOTECH: BEFORE THE INVID STORM #21

KADUNA MEMORIES

THE BLACK HOLE TRAVEL AGENCY
       Book One: EVENT HORIZON
       Book Two: ARTIFACT OF THE SYSTEM
       Book Three: FREE RADICALS
       Book Four: HOSTILE TAKEOVER

ROBOTECH:

SOUTHERN CROSS
METAL FIRE
THE FINAL NIGHTMARE

Jack McKinney

A Del Rey® Book
BALLANTINE BOOKS • NEW YORK

A Del Rey® Book
Published by Ballantine Books
Copyright © 1987 by Harmony Gold U.S.A., Inc. and Tatsunoko Production Co., Ltd.

This work was originally published in three separate volumes by Ballantine Books in 1987.

http://www.randomhouse.com

ISBN 0-345-39184-5

Printed in Canada

First Edition: April 1995

10 9 8 7 6

SOUTHERN CROSS

DEDICATED TO ALL
ROBOTECH FANS AND READERS

CHAPTER
ONE

Those who were surprised at Dana Sterling's choice of a career in the military displayed not only a lack of understanding about Dana but also a failure to comprehend the nature of Protoculture, and how it shaped destiny.

After all, as a mere babe in arms Dana had played a pivotal part in a vital battle in the First Robotech War, the attack to take the Zentraedi's orbital mecha factory; with two of the greatest fighters in history as parents, is it any surprise that she would follow the warrior's trade?

But more important, Dana is the only offspring of a Human/ Zentraedi mating on Earth, and the Protoculture was working strongly through her. She is to be a centerpiece of the ongoing conflict the Protoculture has shaped, and that means being a Robotech soldier in excelsis.

> Dr. Lazlo Zand, notes for *Event Horizon: Perspectives on Dana Sterling and the Second Robotech War*

I T WAS A DATE THAT EVERY SCHOOLCHILD KNEW, THOUGH FOR some its significance had become a bit blurred.

But not for the people gathered in the auditorium at the Southern Cross Military Academy. Many of the veterans on the speakers' platform and among the academy teaching staff and cadre knew the meaning of the date because they had lived through it. Everyone in the graduating class revered it and the tradition of self-sacrifice and courage it represented—a tradition being passed along to them today.

"Today we celebrate not only your achievements as the first graduating class of the Academy," Supreme Commander Leonard was saying, glowering down at the young men and women seated in rows before him. "We also celebrate the memory of the brave people who have served in our planet's defense before you."

Leonard continued, summarizing the last great clash of the Robotech War. If he had stopped in mid-syllable, pointed at any one of the graduating cadets, and asked him or her to take the story from there, the graduate would have done it with even more detail and accuracy.

They all knew it by heart: how Admiral Henry Gloval had taken the rusting, all-but-decommissioned SDF-1 into the air for a final confrontation with the psychopathic Zentraedi warlord Khyron, and died in the inferno of that battle.

They also knew the high honor roll of the women of the bridge watch who had died with him: Kim Young; Sammie Porter; Vanessa Leeds—all enlisted rating techs scarcely older than any of the cadets—and Commander Claudia Grant.

Sitting at the end of her squad's row, Cadet Major Dana Sterling looked down the line of faces beside her. One, with skin the color of dark honey, stared up into the light from the stage. Dana could see that Bowie Grant—nephew of that same Commander Claudia Grant and Dana's close friend since childhood—betrayed no emotion.

Dana didn't know whether to be content or worried. Carrying the name of a certified RDF hero could be a tough burden to bear, as Dana well knew.

Leonard went on about unselfish acts of heroism and passing the torch to a roomful of cadets, none of whom had yet reached twenty. They had had it all drilled into them for years, and were squirming in their seats, eager to get moving, to get to their first real assignments.

Or at any rate, *most* felt that way; looking down the line, Dana could see a withdrawn look on Bowie's face.

Leonard, with his bullet-shaped shaved head, massive as a bear and dripping with medals and ribbons, droned on to the end without saying anything new. It was almost silly for him to tell them that the Earth, slowly rebuilding in the seventeen years since the end of the Robotech War—fifteen since Khyron the Backstabber had launched his suicide attack—was a regrettably feudal place. Who would know that better than the young people who had grown up in it?

Or that there must be a devotion to the common good and a commitment to a brighter Human future? Who had more commitment than the young men and women sitting there, who had sworn to serve that cause and proved their determination by enduring years of merciless testing and training?

At last, thankfully, Leonard was done, and it was time to be sworn in. Dana came to attention with her squad, a unit that had started out company-size three years before.

Dana stood straight and proud, a young woman with a globe of swirling blond hair, average height for a female cadet, curvaceous in a long-legged way. She was blue-eyed, freckled, and pug-nosed, and very tired of being called "cute." Fixed in the yellow mane over her left ear was a fashion accessory appropriate to her time—a hair stay shaped to look like a curve of instrumentation suggesting a half-headset, like a crescent of Robotechnology sculpted from polished onyx.

The graduating class received their assignments as they went up to the stage to accept their diplomas. Dana found herself holding her breath, hoping, hoping.

Then the supreme commander was before her, an overly beefy man whose neck spilled out in rolls above his tight collar. He had flaring brows and a hand that engulfed hers. But despite what the UEG public relations people said about him, she found herself disliking him. Leonard talked a good fight but had very little real combat experience; he was better at political wheeling and dealing.

Dana was trying to hide her quick, shallow breathing as she went from Leonard's too-moist handshake to the aide whose duty it was to tell the new graduates their first assignments.

The aide frowned at a computer printout. Then he glanced down his nose at Dana, looking her over disapprovingly. "Congratulations. You go to the Fifteenth squad, Alpha Tactical Armored Corps," he said with a sniff.

Dana had learned how to hide emotions and reactions at the Academy; she was an old hand at it. So she didn't squeal with delight or throw her diploma into the air in exultation.

She was in a daze as she filed back to her seat, her squad following behind. The ATACs! The 15th squad! *Hovertanks!*

Let others try for the soft, safe, rear-echelon jobs, or the glamourous fighter outfits; nowadays the armored units were the cutting edge of Robotechnology, and the teeth and claws of the United Earth Government's military—the Army of the Southern Cross.

And the 15th had the reputation of being one of the best, if not *the* best. Under their daredevil leader, First Lieutenant Sean Phillips, they had become not only one of the most decorated but also one of the most court-martial-prone outfits around—a real black-sheep squad.

Dana figured that was right up her alley. She would have been graduating at the top of her class, with marks and honors succeeding generations would have found hard to beat, if not for certain peccadillos, disciplinary lapses, and scrapes with the MPs. She knew most of it wasn't really her fault, though. The way some people saw it, she had entered the Academy with several strikes against her, and she had had to fight against that the whole way.

Cadets who called her "halfbreed" usually found themselves flat on their faces, bleeding, with Dana kneeling on them. Instructors or cadre who treated her like just one more trainee found that they had a bright if impulsive pupil; those who gave any hint of contempt for her parentage found that their rank and station were no protection.

Cadet officers awakened to find themselves hoisted from flagpoles . . . a cadre sergeant's quarters were mysteriously walled in, sealing him inside. . . . The debutante cotillion of the daughter of a certain colonel was enlivened by a visit from a dozen or so chimps, baboons, and orangutans from the Academy's Primate Research Center . . . and so on.

Dana reckoned she would fit into the 15th just fine.

She realized with a start that she didn't know where Bowie was going. She felt a bit ashamed that she had reveled in her own good fortune and had forgotten about him.

But when she turned, Bowie was looking up the row at her. He flashed his handsome smile, but there was a resigned look to it. He held his hand up to flash five outspread fingers—once, twice, three times.

Dana caught her breath. *He's pulled assignment to the 15th, too!*

Bowie didn't seem to be too elated about it, though. He closed the other fingers of his hand and drew his forefinger across his throat in a silent gesture of doom, watching her sadly.

The rest of the ceremonies seemed to go on forever, but at last the graduates were dismissed for a few brief days of leave before reporting to their new units.

Somehow Dana lost Bowie in the crush of people. He had no family or friends among the watching crowd; but neither did she. All the blood relatives they had were years-gone on the SDF-3's all-important mission to seek out the Robotech Masters somewhere in the far reaches of the galaxy.

The only adult to whom Dana and Bowie were close, Major General Rolf Emerson, was conducting an inspection of the orbital defense forces and unable to attend the ceremony. For a time in her childhood, Dana had had three very strange but dear self-appointed godfathers, but they had passed away.

Dana felt a spasm of envy for the ex-cadets who were surrounded by parents and siblings and neighbors. Then she shrugged it off, irritated at herself for the moment's self-pity; Bowie was all the family she had now. She went off to find him.

Even after three years in the Academy, Bowie was a cadet private, something he considered a kind of personal mark of pride. Even so, as an upperclassman he had spacious quarters to himself; there was no shortage of space in the barracks, the size of the class having shrunk drastically since induction day. Of the more than twelve hundred young people who had started in Bowie's class, fewer than two hundred remained. The rest had either flunked out completely and gone home, or turned in an unsatisfactory performance and been reassigned outside the Academy.

Many of the latter had been sent either to regional militias, or "retroed" to assorted support and rear-echelon jobs. Others had become part of the colossal effort to rebuild and revivify the war-ravaged Earth, a struggle that had lasted for a decade and a half and would no doubt continue for years to come.

But beginning with today's class, Academy graduates would begin filling the ranks of the Cosmic Units, Tactical Air Force, Alpha Tactical Armored Corps, and the other components of the Southern Cross. Enrollment would be expanded, and eventually all officers and many of the enlisted and NCO ranks would be people who had attended the Academy or another like it.

Robotechnology, especially the second-generation brand currently being phased into use, required intense training and practice on the part of human operator-warriors. It was another era in human history when the citizen-soldier had to take a back seat to the professional.

And somehow Bowie—who had never wanted to be a soldier at all—was a member of this new military elite, entrusted with the responsibility of serving and guarding humanity.

Only, I'd be a lot happier playing piano and singing for my supper in some little dive!

Sunk in despair, Bowie found that even his treasured Minmei records couldn't lift his spirits. Hearing her sing "We Will Win" wasn't much help to a young man who didn't want anything to do with battle.

How can I possibly live this life they're forcing on me?

He plucked halfheartedly at his guitar once or twice, but it was no use. He stared out the window at the parade ground, remembering how many disagreeable hours he had spent out there, when the door signal toned. He turned the sound system down, slouched over, and hit the door release.

Dana stood there in a parody of a glamour pose, up on the balls of her feet with her hands clasped together behind her blond puff-ball hairdo. She batted her lashes at him.

"Well, it's about time, Bowie. How ya doing?" She walked past him into his room, hands still behind her head.

He grunted, adding, "Fine," and closed the door.

She laughed as she stood looking out at the parade ground. "Su-ure! Private Grant, who d'you think you're kidding?"

"Okay! So I'm depressed!"

She turned and gave him a little inclination of the head to acknowledge his honesty. "Thank you! And *why* are you depressed?"

He slumped into a chair, his feet up on a table. "Graduation, I guess."

They both wore form-fitting white uniforms with black boots and black piping reminiscent of a riding outfit. But their cadet unit patches were gone, and Dana's torso harness—a crisscross, flare-shouldered affair of burnt-orange leather—carried only the insignia of her brevet rank, second lieutenant, and standard Southern Cross crests. Dark bands above their biceps supported big, dark military brassards that carried the Academy's device; those would soon be traded in for ATAC arm brassards.

Dana sat on the bed, ankles crossed, holding the guitar idly. "It's natural to feel a letdown, Bowie; I do too." She strummed a gentle chord.

"You're just saying that to make me feel better."

"It's the truth! Graduation Blues are as old as education." She struck another chord. "Don't feel like smiling? Maybe I should sing for you?"

"*No!*" Dana's playing was passable, but her voice just wasn't right for singing.

He had blurted it out so fast that they both laughed. "Maybe I should tell you a story," she said. "But then, you know all my stories, Bowie." *And all the secrets I've ever been able to tell a full-breed Human.*

He nodded; he knew. Most people on Earth knew at least something of Dana's origins—the only known offspring of a Zentraedi/Human mating. Then her parents had gone, as his had, on the SDF-3 expedition.

Bowie smiled at Dana and she smiled back. They were two eighteen-year-olds about to take up the trade of war.

"Bowie," she said gently, "there's more to military life than just maneuvers. You can *make* it more. I'll help you; you'll see!" She sometimes thought secretly that Bowie must wish he had inherited the great size and strength of his father, Vince Grant, rather than the compact grace and good looks of his mother, Jean. Bowie was slightly shorter than Dana, though he was fierce when he had to be.

He let out a long breath, then met her gaze and nodded slowly. Just then the alert whoopers began sounding.

It sent a cold chill through them both. They knew that not even a martinet like Supreme Commander Leonard would pick this afternoon for a practice drill. The UEG had too much riding on the occasion to end it so abruptly.

But the alternative—it was so grim that Dana didn't even want to think about it. Still, she and Bowie were sworn members of the armed forces, and the call to battle had been sounded.

Dana looked at Bowie; his face registered his dismay. "Red alert! That's us, Bowie! C'mon, follow me!"

He had been through so many drills and practices over the years that it was second nature to him. They dashed for the door, knowing exactly where they must go, what they must do, and superlatively able to do it.

But now, for the first time, they felt a real, icy fear that was not for their own safety or an abstract like their performance in some test. Out in the corridor Dana and Bowie merged with other graduates dashing along. Duffel bags and B-4 bags were scattered around the various rooms they ran past, clothing and gear strewn everywhere; most of the graduates had been packing to go home for a while.

Dana and Bowie were sprinting along with a dozen other graduates, then fifty, then more than half of the class. Underclassmen and women streamed from other barracks, racing to their appointed places. Just like a drill.

But Dana could feel it, smell it in the air, and pick it up through her skin's receptors: there was suddenly something out there to be feared. The cadet days of pretend-war were over forever.

Suddenly, emphatically, Dana felt a deep fear as something she didn't understand stirred inside her. And without warning she understood exactly how Bowie felt.

The young Southern Cross fighters—none older than nineteen, some as young as sixteen—poured out of their barracks and formed up to do their duty.

CHAPTER TWO

It seems an imprecise thought or ridiculously metaphysical question to some, I know, but I cannot help but wonder. If the Robotech Masters rid themselves of their emotions, where did those emotions go?

Would there not be some conservation-of-energy law that would keep such emotions from disappearing completely but would see them transmuted into something else? Were they all simply converted to the Masters' vast longing for power, hidden knowledge, Protoculture, immortality?

And is that the by-product of stepped-up intellect? For if so, the Universe has played us a dreadful joke.

Zeitgeist, *Insights: Alien Psychology and the Second Robotech War*

COLD LUNA SWUNG IN ITS AGES-OLD ORBIT. IT HAD WITnessed cataclysms in epochs long gone; it had watched the seemingly impossible changes that had taken place on Earth through the long eons of their companionship.

In recent times the moon had been a major landmark in the war between Zentraedi and Human, and looked down upon the devastation of Earth, fifteen years ago.

It was into the moon's cold lee that Captain Henry Gloval attempted to spacefold the SDF-1 at the outset of the Robotech War. There was a grievous miscalculation (or the intercession of a higher, Protoculture-ordained plan, depending on whether or not one listened to the eccentric Dr. Emil Lang), and the battle fortress leapt between dimensions to end up stranded out near Pluto.

But Gloval's plan, using Luna as cover and sanctuary, was still a sound one. And today, others were proving its worth.

Six stupendous ships, five miles from end to end through their long axes, materialized soundlessly and serenely in the dawn. They were as strong and destructive and Robotechnologically well-equipped as the Masters could make them.

10

Still, they were wary. Earth had already provided a charnel house for mighty fleets; the Robotech Masters had no more Zentraedi lives to spend, and had no intention of risking their own.

The voice of one of the Robotech Masters echoed through the command ship. He was one of the triumvirate that commanded the expedition, that ruled the ships, the Clonemasters, soldier-androids, Scientist Triads, and the rest.

He had sprung from the humanlike inhabitants of the planet Tirol, creatures who were virtually Human in plasm and appearance. But the Robotech Master's words came tonelessly, expressionlessly, and without sound; he was in contact with the Protoculture, and so spoke with mind alone.

He sent his thoughts into the communications bond that linked his mind with those of the transformed overlords of his race, beings like him but even more elevated in their powers and intellect—the three Elders.

The disembodied words floated in the chilly metallic passageways. *We are in place, Elders—behind the moon of our objective, the third planet. All monitoring and surveillance systems are fully operational. You will begin receiving our primary transignal immediately.*

The technical apparatus of the ships pulsed and flowed with light, and the power of Protoculture. Some parts suggested blood vessels or the maze of a highway system, where pure radiance of shifting colors traveled; others resembled upside-down pagodas, suspended in the air, made of blazing materials like nothing that had ever appeared in the Solar System before.

The enigmatic energies opened a way across the lightyears, to a sphere like a blue sapphire fifteen feet across. It threw forth brilliance, the glare splashing off the ax-keen, hawk-nosed faces of the three Elders who sat, enthroned in a circle, staring up at it. From far across the galaxy the Elders reached out with their minds to survey the Robotech Masters' situation.

The Elders were of a type, fey and gaunt, dressed in regal robes but looking more like executioners. All three had bald or shaven pates, their straight, fine hair falling below their shoulders. Under their sharp cheekbones were scarlike creases of skin, suggestive of tribal marks, that emphasized the severity of those laser-eyed faces.

They studied the images and data sent to them by their servants, the Robotech Masters.

One of them, Nimuul, whose blue hair was stirred by the air

currents, mindspoke. His disembodied voice was thick as syrup. *The first transignal is of the area where the highest readings of Protoactivity have been recorded. Preliminary inspection indicates that it is unguarded.*

That pleased the other Elders, but none of them evinced any emotion; they were above that, purged of it long ago.

Hepsis, of the silver locks, cheek resting on his thin, long-fingered fist, forearm so slender that it appeared atrophied, watched the transignal images balefully. *Hmm. You mean those mounds of soil and rock?* His voice was little different from Nimuul's.

Yes.

The three were looking at the transignal scene of the massive artificial buttes that stood in the center of what had once been the rebuilt Macross City. The transignal was showing them the final resting places of the SDF-1, the SDF-2, and the flagship of Khyron the Backstabber.

All three ships had been destroyed in those few minutes of Khyron's last, suicidal attack; all had been quickly buried and the city covered over and abandoned due to the intense radiation, the last place ever to bear the name Macross.

Nimuul explained, *Zor's ship is probably—Wait!*

But he didn't have to draw their attention to it; Hepsis and Fallagar, the third Elder, could see it for themselves. For the first time in a very long time, the Elders of the Robotech Master race felt a misgiving that chilled even *their* polar nerves.

Three night-black figures wavered in the enormous transignal globe, defying the best efforts of the Masters' flagship's equipment to bring them into focus. The entities on the screen looked like tall, sinister wraiths, caped and cloaked, high collars shadowing their faces—all dark save for the light that beamed from their slitted eyes.

Three, of course—as all things of the Protoculture were triad. *The area* is *guarded by a form of inorganic sentry,* Nimuul observed. *Or it could be an Invid trap of some kind.*

Fallagar, his hair an ice-blue somewhere between his comrades' shades, gave mental voice to their misgivings. *Or it might be something else,* he pointed out. *Something to do with the thrice-damned Zor.*

The images of the wraiths faded, then came back a bit against a background of static as the transignal systemry struggled to maintain it. It seemed that the ghostly figures *knew* they were under observation—were toying with the Masters. The lamp-bright eyes seemed to be staring straight at the Elders.

Then the image was gone, and nothing the Scientist Triad or Clonemasters could do would bring the Protoculture specters back into view. White combers of light washed through the blue globe of the transignal imager again, showing nothing of use.

By a commonality of mind, the Elders did not mention—refused to recognize—this resistance to their will and their instrumentality. The guardian wraiths would be discussed and dealt with at the appropriate time.

What do you wish to view next, Elders? asked a deferential Clonemaster.

Nimuul was suddenly even more imperious, eager to shake off the daunting effects of the long-distance encounter with the wraiths. *Show us the life forms that protected this planet from our Zentraedi warriors and now hold sway over the Protoculture Matrix.*

Yes, Elder, the Clonemaster answered meekly.

Hepsis told the other two, *The Humans who obliterated our Zentraedi are no longer present, according to my surveillance readings, my Brothers. But their fellows seem ready to protect their planet with a similar degree of cunning and skill.*

The transignal was showing them quick images of the Southern Cross forces: Cosmic Unit orbital forts and Civil Defense mecha, ATAC fighting machines, and the rest.

One intercepted TV transmission was a slow pan past the members of the 15th squad, monitored from a Southern Cross public information broadcast. The Elders saw Humans with a hard-trained, competent look to them, and something else . . . something to which the Elders hadn't given thought in a long, long time.

It was youth. The camera showed them face after face—the smirking impertinence of Corporal Louie Nichols; the massive strength of Sergeant Angelo Dante; the flamboyance of their leader, the swashbuckling ladies' man, Lieutenant Sean Phillips.

The Elders looked at their enemies, and felt a certain misgiving even more unsettling than that of the wraiths' image.

The three rulers of the Robotech Masters, privy to many of the secrets of Protoculture, were long-lived—would be Eternal, if their plans came to fruition. And as a result of that, *they feared death,* feared it more than anything. The fear was controlled, suppressed, but it was greater than any child's fear of his worst nightmares, more than any dread that any mortal harbored.

But the young faces in the camera pan didn't show that fear, not as the Elders knew it. The young understand death far better than their elders will usually acknowledge, especially young people in the military who know their number could come up any time, any day. The faces of the 15th, though, told that its members were willing to accept that risk—that they had found values that made it worthwhile.

That was disturbing to the Elders. They had clones and others who would certainly die for them, but none who would do so of their own volition; such a concept had long since been ground mercilessly from their race.

There was once more that unspoken avoidance of unpleasant topics among the Elders. Nimuul tried to sound indifferent. *It is hard for me to believe that these life forms could offer any resistance to us. They are so young and lack combat experience.*

He and his fellows were purposely ignoring an unpleasant part of the equation. If, in war, you're not willing to die for your cause but your enemy is willing to die for his, a terrible weight has been set on one side of the scales.

The Elders shuddered, each within himself, revealing nothing to one another. *I've seen enough of this,* Fallagar said, gathering his cloak like a falcon preparing to take wing, letting impatience show.

What images would you view now, Elders? asked the unseen Clonemaster tentatively.

Fallagar's silent voice resounded through the viewing chamber. *I think we have enough information on* these *life forms, so transmit whatever else you have on line. No matter how interesting these abstractions may be, the time has come for us to deal with the problems at hand!*

The globe swirled with cinnamon-red, came back to blue, and showed the headquarters of the Army of the Southern Cross.

It was a soaring white megacomplex in the midst of Monument City. The countryside was marked with the corroded, crumpled miles-long remains of Zentraedi battlecruisers. They were rammed bow-first into the terrain, remnants of the last, long-ago battle.

The headquarters' central tower cluster had been built to suggest the white gonfalons, or ensigns, of a holy crusade hanging from high crosspieces. The towers were crowned with crenels and merlons, like a medieval battlement.

It all looked as if some army of giants had been marshaled. The architecture was meant to do just that—announce to the planet and the world the ideals and esprit of the Army of the Southern Cross.

The name "Southern Cross" was a heritage of those first days after the terrible Zentraedi holocaust that had all but eliminated Human life on Earth. Less damage had been done in the southern hemisphere than in the northern; many refugees and survivors were relocated there. A cohesive fighting force was quickly organized, its member city-states all lying within view of the namesake constellation.

Yes; we are through studying this planet for now, Fallagar declared. *Now establish contact with our Robotech Masters.* It was time for decisions to be passed down, from Elder to Robotech Master, and so on down the line at last to the Bioroid pilots who would once more carry death and fire to Earth in their war mecha.

Signals sprang among the six ships' communications spars, which looked for all the world like huge, segmented insect legs.

What you have shown us has pleased us, Fallagar said with no hint of pleasure in his tone. *But now we must communicate with the inhabitants of this planet directly.*

While the Robotech Masters were being alerted to hear their overlords' word, blue-haired Nimuul said to his fellows, *I would make a point: these invisible entities who guard the Protoculture masses within the mounds on Earth may require special and unprecedented—*

Another voice came as the globe showed the gathered Robotech Masters. *Elders! We hear and serve you, and acknowledge your leadership and wisdom!*

Younger and at an earlier stage of their Protoculture-generated personal evolution, the Robotech Masters looked in every way like slightly less aged versions of the Elders. The Masters had the gleaming pates, the chevronlike skin seams under each cheekbone, the fine, straight hair that reached far down their backs and down their cheeks in long, wide sideburns. Their mental voices had been given that eerie vibrato by direct exposure to Protoculture. They wore monkish robes with sash belts, their collars in the shape of a blooming Invid Flower of Life.

Like virtually everyone in their culture, the Robotech Masters were a triumvirate. The slight differentiations among members of a triad, even differences of gender, served only to emphasize their oneness.

The Masters stood each upon a small platform, in a circle around their control monitor, an apparatus resembling a mottled technological mushroom five feet across, floating some five yards above the deck. It was the Protoculture cap, source of their power.

Nimuul held his perpetual scowl. *Your transignal images were sufficiently informative, and you have reported that your war mecha are prepared. But now we must know if you are ready for us to join you.*

Twenty years earlier, the race that called itself the Robotech Masters had sensed the enormous discharge of Protoculture energy in the last battle on Earth. But their instrumentality was depleted because the rebellious genius Zor had sent the last Protoculture Matrix away in the SDF-1, and the Zentraedi's destruction and the endless war against the Invid had made great demands on the remaining reservoirs.

The Masters lacked the Protoculture power to send their armada to the target world by the almost instantaneous shortcut of hyperspace-fold generation. Therefore, the Elders had dispatched the six enormous mother ships, with their complements of assault craft and Bioroids, on a twenty-year voyage by more conventional superluminal drive. Now that the journey was over, the Elders meant to rejoin the expedition by means of a small spacefold transference—of themselves.

But Shaizan, who most often spoke for the Robotech Masters, answered, his blue-gray hair flowing with the movements of his head. *No, Elders! We are very close to regaining the lost Protoculture masses and recovering secrets that Zor attempted to take to the grave with him. But we must not make the same mistakes the Zentraedi made!*

We must know more about their strengths and weaknesses, added Dag, another Master, gazing up at the Elders' image.

Nimuul's frown deepened. *You must not fail.* The Robotech Masters all bowed deeply to their *own* Masters, the Elders.

When the Elders broke contact, the Robotech Masters looked in turn to the Clonemasters and the other triumvirates gathered below the hovering Protoculture cap. Shaizan, gathering his blue robes about him, his collar hanging like an orange flower around his neck, snapped, "Now, do you understand the plan, and do you anticipate any problems, group leader?

The Clonemasters and the rest looked in every way like Human males and females, fair-skinned for the most part. They tended toward an aesthete slimness, with long hair and form-fitting clothing that might have come from the early renaissance, draped with short capelets and cloaks. Among their triumvirates there was little differentiation in appearance or clothing.

The Clonemaster group leader replied in a voice somewhere between that of a Human and that of a Robotech Master. "Master, every Bioroid pilot is briefed and prepared to execute the first phase exactly as you have decreed. The only problem is in keeping our operators functional; our Protoculture supplies are quite minimal."

Shaizan frowned at the group leader as the Elders had frowned upon the Robotech Masters, with that same angry ruthlessness. "Then double the numbers of Bioroid fighting mecha assigned to the attack. You may draw additional Protoculture from the ships' engines only if it proves absolutely indispensable to success of the mission."

Dag, more lantern-jawed than his triumvirate-siblings, the most intellectual of them, added, "If possible, I would like some Human captives for experimental purposes."

Bowkaz, the most military of the three Robotech Masters, contradicted, as was his prerogative in tactical matters. "No," he told Dag. To the group leader, he added, "You will proceed, but only as per our original orders. Understood?"

The group leader inclined his head respectfully. "As you will."

Shaizan nodded, inspecting the Clonemasters and the other triumvirates coldly. "Then we look forward to your success and trust that you will not fail."

The group leader said emotionlessly. "We understand the consequences of failure, Master."

As did everyone on the expedition, the Robotech Masters' last desperate throw of the dice. The group leader met their scowls. The Bioroid war machines were waiting to bring destruction to the unsuspecting Humans.

"We will not fail you," he vowed.

When the clone triumvirates had hurried away to execute the probing attack, the Robotech Masters summoned up an image of the maze of systemry in their flagship. The living Protoculture instrumentality suggested internal organs, vascular tubes, clear protoplasmic tracts strobing with the ebb and flow of energy.

Dag bespoke his fellows. "If we could capture a Human, our mindprobe would reveal whether they've discovered any hint of the existence of the Protoculture Matrix."

"Not necessarily," Bowkaz replied.

They all looked at the shrunken mass of Protoculture left to them. The secret of making a Matrix had died with Zor, and there was no other source of Protoculture in the known universe. This Matrix was the Robotech Masters' last chance for survival.

"There will be time to interrogate the Humans once they lie defeated and helpless beneath our heel," Shaizan said.

CHAPTER THREE

I couldn't really tell you who said it first—commo op, Black Lion, cruiser crewmember—but somebody did, and, given the circumstances, everybody just naturally picked it up, starting then and there: the Second Robotech War.

Lieutenant Marie Crystal, as quoted in "Overlords," *History of the Robotech Wars,* Vol. CXII

 PACE STATION LIBERTY SWUNG SLOWLY IN ITS LAGRANGE Five holding place, out near Luna. It combined the functions of outpost fortress, communications nerve center, and way station along the routes to Earth's distant colonies on the moon and elsewhere. Its complex commo apparatus, apparatus that wouldn't function as well on Earth, was the Human race's only method of maintaining even intermittent contact with the SDF-3 expedition. Liberty was in many ways the keystone to Earth's defenses.

And so it was the natural target.

"Liberty, this is Moon Base, Moon Base!"

The Moon Base communications operator adjusted the gain on his transmitter desperately, taking a moment to eye the radar paints he had punched up on a nearby display screen.

Five bogies, big ones, had come zooming around from the moon's dark side. The G2 section was already sure they were nothing the Human race had even used or seen before. Performance and power readings indicated that they were formidable vessels, and course projections had them headed straight for Liberty, at appalling speed.

"Why won't they answer? WHY?" The commo op fretted, but some sort of interference had been jamming everything since the

bogies first appeared. And nothing Moon Base could get off the ground could possibly catch the UFOs.

The op felt a cold sweat on his brow, for himself as well as for the unsuspecting people aboard the space station. If Liberty were knocked out, that would leave Moon Base and the other scattered Human sentry posts in the Solar System cut off, ripe for casual eradication.

The indicators on his instruments suddenly waffled; either the enemy had been obliged to channel power away from jamming and into weapons, shields, or whatever, or the signal-warfare countermeasures computers had come up with a way to punch through a transmission. A dim, static-fuzzed voice from Liberty acknowledged.

The Moon Base op opened his headset mike and began sending with frantic haste.

"Space Station Liberty, this is Moon Base. Flash message, I say again, flash message! Five bogies closing on you at vector eight-one-three-slash-four-four-niner! You may not have them on your scopes; they have been fading in and out on ours. We didn't know they were here until we got a visual. Possible hostiles, I say again, possible hostiles. They're coming straight for you!"

In the Liberty Station commo center, another op was signaling the duty officer that a flash message—a priority emergency—was incoming, even as he recorded the Moon Base transmission.

When it was done, he turned and exercised a prerogative put in place during the rebuilding of Earth after the Zentraedi holocaust. There wasn't time for an officer to get to the commo center, evaluate the message, get in touch with the G3 staff, and have a red alert declared. Every second was critical; the Human race had learned that the hard way.

No op had ever used it before, but no op had ever faced this situation before. With the decisive slap of a big, illuminated red button, a commo center corporal put the space station on war footing, and warned Earth to follow suit.

He tried to piece together the rest of what the Moon Base op was saying just as he spied a watch officer headed his way. The op covered his mike with his hand and called out, "Red flag, ma'am! Tell 'em to get the gun batteries warmed up, 'cause we're in trouble!"

The commo lieutenant nodded. She turned at once to a secure intercom, signaling the station's command center. Klaxons and alarm hooters began their din.

"Battle stations, battle stations! Laser and plasma gunners, prepare to open fire!"

Armored gunners dashed to their posts as Liberty went on full alert. The heavily shielded turrets opened and the ugly, gleaming snouts of the twin- and quad-barreled batteries rose into view, traversing and coming to bear on the targets' last known approach vector.

Near the satellite fortress, a flight of patrol ships swung around to intersect the bogies' approach. They were big, slow, delta-shaped cruisers, slated for replacement in the near future. They were the first to feel the power of the Robotech Masters.

The five Robotech Master assault ships came, sand-red and shaped like flattened bottles. The leader arrowed in at the Earth craft, opening up with energy cannon. A white-hot bolt opened the side of the cruiser as if gutting a fish. Atmosphere and fireballs rushed from the Human ship. Within it, crewmen and -women screamed, but only briefly.

The Masters' warcraft plunged in, eager for more kills.

"I can't raise any of the patrol cruisers, ma'am," the Liberty Station commo op told TASC Lieutenant Marie Crystal. "And three of them have disappeared from the radar screens."

Marie looked up at the commo link that had been patched through to her by the commander of the patrol flotilla with which her Tactical Armored Space Corps fighter squadron was serving. She nodded, her delicate jaw set.

She was a pale young woman in battle armor, with blue eyes that had an exotic obliqueness to them, and short, unruly hair like black straw. There was an intensity to her very much like that of an unhooded bird of prey.

"Roger that, Liberty Station. Black Lions will respond." She ran a fast calculation; the flotilla had diverted from its usual near-Earth duties when the commo breakdown occurred, and was now very close to Liberty—close enough for binocular and telescope sighting on the explosions and energy-bolt signatures out where the sneak attack had taken place, beyond the satellite.

"Our ETA at your position in approximately ninety seconds from launch." He acknowledged, white-faced and sweating, and Marie broke the patch-up. Then she signaled her TASC unit, the Black Lions, for a hot scramble.

"*Attention all pilots. Condition red, condition red. This is not a drill, I say again, this is not a drill. Prepare for immediate launch, all catapults. Black Lions prepare to launch.*"

The decks reverberated with the impact of running armored boots. Marie led the way to the hangar deck, her horned flight helmet in one hand. There was all the usual madness of a scramble, and more, because no one among the young Southern Cross soldiers had ever been in combat before.

Marie boarded her Veritech fighter with practiced ease, even though she was weighted down by her body armor. The scaled-up cockpit had room for her in the bulky superalloy suit, but even so, and even after years of practice she found it a bit more snug than she would have liked.

The Tactical Armored Space Corps' front-line fighter-craft had been decreased in size quite a bit since the Robotech War because they no longer needed to go to a Battloid-mode size that would let them slug it out toe-to-toe with fifty-foot-tall Zentraedi warriors or their huge Battlepods.

Her maint crew got her seated properly and ready to taxi for launch. As Marie sat studying the gauges and instruments and indicators on her panel, she didn't realize how much like a slim, keen-eyed Joan of Arc she looked in her armor.

Strange, she brooded. *It's not like I thought it would be. I'm anxious but not nervous.*

Crewpeople with spacesuits color-coded to their jobs raced around, seeing to ordnance and moving craft, or racing to take their places in the catapult crews. They, too, tended to be young, a part of Robotechnology's new generation, shouldering responsibilities and facing hazards that made them adults while most of them were still in their teens. Even in peacetime, death was a part of virtually every cruise, and the smallest mishap could cost lives.

The Black Lions launched and formed up; the enemy ships turned toward them but altered course at the last moment, launching their own smaller craft.

"What *are* those things?" Second Lieutenant Snyder, whose callsign was Black Beauty, yelled when the enemy fighters came into visual range, already firing.

Gone were the simple numeral callsigns of a generation before; Earth was a feudal hegemony of city-states and regional power structures, bound by virtually medieval loyalties, under the iron fist of the UEG, and the planet's military reflected that. So did the armor of the Southern Cross's ultratech knights, including Marie's own helmet, with its stylized horns.

"Shut up and take 'em!" Marie snapped; she hated unnecessary chatter on a tac net. "And stick with your wingmen!"

But she didn't blame Black Beauty for being shocked. *So, the Zentraedi are back,* she thought. *Or somebody a lot like them.*

The bogies that were zooming in at the Black Lions were faceless armored figures nearly the size of the alien invaders who appeared in 1999 to savage Earth and initiate the Robotech War. These were different, though: They were Humanoid-looking, though insectlike; Zentraedi Battlepods were like headless alloy ostriches bristling with cannon.

Moreover, these things rode swift, maneuverable saucer-shaped Hovercraft, like outlandish walking battleships riding waterjet platforms.

But they were fast and deadly, whatever they were. The Hovercraft dipped and changed vector, prodigal with their power, performing maneuvers that seemed impossible outside of atmosphere. Up until today that had always been a Veritech specialty.

About twenty of the intruders dove in at a dozen Black Lions, and the dogfighting began. Fifteen years had gone by since the last time Human and alien had clashed, and the answered prayers that were peace were suddenly vacated.

And the dying hadn't changed.

The small volume of space, just an abstract set of coordinates, became the new killing ground. VT and Bioroid circled and pounced at one another, fired or dodged depending upon who had the advantage, maneuvered furiously, and came back for more.

The aliens fired extremely powerful energy weapons, most often from the bulky systems packages that sat before them on their control stems. That gave the Lions the eerie feeling that a horde of giant metallic water-skiers was trying to immolate them.

But the arrangement only *looked* funny; incandescent rays flashed from the control-stem projectors, and three TASC fliers died almost at once. The saucer-shaped-Hoverplatforms turned to seek new prey. This time they demonstrated that they could fire from apertures in the control-stem housings.

"Black Beauty, Black Beauty, two bogies on your tail!" John Zalenga, who was known as White Knight, called out the warning. "Go to turbo-thrust!" Marie spared a quick glance to her commo display, and saw Zalenga's white-visaged helmet with its brow-vanes on one side of a split-screen, Snyder's ebony headgear, like some turbaned, veiled muslim champion's on the other.

But before Snyder could do anything about his dilemma, the two were on him, their fire crisscrossing on his VT's tail. Marie heard the fight rather than saw it, because at that moment she had the shot she wanted at a darting alien Hovercraft.

VT armament had changed in a generation: gone were the autocannon and their depleted transuranic shells. Amplified laser arrays sent pulses of destructive power through the vacuum.

Armored saucer-platform and armored alien rider disappeared in a cloud of flame and shrapnel.

Marie's gaze was level and intent behind her tinted visor. "We lost Black Beauty; the rest of you start flying the way you were taught! Start flying like Black Lions!"

Outside of a few minor brushfire conflicts over borders, the VTs of Marie's generation had never flown combat before. Certainly, Aerial Combat School was nothing like this: real enemy fire and real friends being blown to rags of sizzling flesh and cinders, with the next volley coming at *you*.

But Marie's voice and their training put the Lions back in control. The survivors got back into tight pairs, covering one another as the Bioroids came back for another run.

"Going to Guardian mode," Marie bit out, her breath rasping a little in her helmet facemask. They were all pulling lots of gees in the hysterical maneuvering of the dogfight; as trained, they locked their legs and tightened their midsections to keep the blood up in their heads, where it was needed. The grunting and snorting for breath made the Black Lions' tac net sound as if some desperate tug-of-war were in progress.

Marie pulled the triplet-levers as one; her VT began changing.

None of the intricacies of mechamorphosis mattered much to the young VT leader with a sky full of bogies coming at her. All Marie really cared about was that when she summoned up her craft's Guardian configuration, the order was obeyed.

She could feel the craft shifting and changing shape around her, modules sliding and structural parts reconforming themselves, like some fantastic mechanical origami. In moments, Veritech became Guardian, a giant figure like a cross between a warrior and a space-battlecruiser, a sleek eagle of Robotechnology.

"Got you covered, White Knight," she told Zalenga. "Here they come." The Masters' battle mecha surged in at them, the flashes of their fire lighting the expressionless insect eyes of the Bioroids' head-turrets.

But the next joust of spaceborne paladins was very different from what had gone before. The Guardian had most of the speed of a Veritech, but the increased maneuverability and firepower that came from bringing it closer to anthropomorphic form. More or less the form of the Bioroids.

But more, Marie Crystal *thought* her craft through its change and its actions. The secret of Robotech mecha lay in the pilot's helmet—the "thinking cap," as it had been dubbed. Receptors there picked up thought impulses and translated them into the mecha's actions. No other control system could have given a machine that kind of agility and battle-prowess, which seemed more like those of a living thing.

Marie dodged one Hovercraft's fire, neatly missing that of the thing's companion, darting like a superalloy dragonfly. She controlled her mecha with deft manipulations of the gross motor-controls—hand and foot controls there in the cockpit—but more important, she *thought* her Guardian through the firefight. Mental imaging was the key to Robotech warfare.

The lead Bioroid was firing at a place Marie's Guardian no longer occupied. She blasted it dead center with an almost frugally short burst of intense fire, a hyphen of novafire that was gone nearly before it had begun. The Bioroid erupted outward in fireball demise.

She ducked the backup Bioroid's cannonade, too, and wove through it to fix the alien mecha in her gunsight reticle and shoot. The second Bioroid was an articulated fortress—bulbous-forearmed, bulbous-legged—one moment, and a superheated gas cloud headed for entropy the next.

The other Black Lions weren't slow to pick up on the new tactics. Some went to Guardian mode, and one or two to Battloid—the Veritech equivalent of the Bioroids—while one or two remained in Fighter mode. The Bioroids simply could not adjust to the smorgasbord of Earthly war-mecha suddenly facing them.

Tables turned, and it was the invader mecha that disappeared in spheres of white-hot explosion. Then it became apparent that they had had enough; like oily, scuttling beetles, the two or three survivors hunkered over their control stems and fled.

A controller from the Lions' cruiser got through to them just as they were preparing to mechamorphose and pursue the enemy until none were left.

"Black Lion Team, break contact! All Veritechs, break contact! Let 'em go for now, Lions, and return to the ship at once."

The ballooning explosions began to die away; Marie gathered up her unit unhurriedly, enjoying mastery of the battlefield.

But she knew that the tactics that had won the Lions this day's fight might not be as effective next time. And she knew, too, that the force her team had faced was probably a negligible number in terms of the enemy's total strength.

She thrust the thought aside. Today was a victory; embattled humanity, cast into the eye of the storm of interstellar Robotech warfare again, had to relearn the skill of taking things one moment, one battle, one breath of life at a time.

CHAPTER FOUR

It was Bowie I'd legally taken as my ward, his parents being among my closest friends, but it was often Dana who gave me greater cause for worry. With her mixed parentage and the grief she sometimes got about it, she was often torn between two distinct modes of behavior, the sternly military and the wildly anti-authoritarian.

And, none of us really know what it was Lang, and later Zand, were doing to her in those experiments when she was a baby. We suspect it had something to do with Protoculture, and activating the alien side of her nature.

But Zand knows one thing: he knows how close I came to killing him with my bare hands that day when I came to take baby Dana away from him. And if anything ever happens to her because of what he did, Zand's fears will be borne out.

From the personal journal of
Major General Rolf Emerson

LIKE MOST SOUTHERN CROSS MILITARY FACILITIES, THE PLACE was roomy. The devastating attacks of the Zentraedi had seen to it that Earth would have no problems with population density for some time to come.

This one was a large, truncated cone, an airy building of smoky blue glass and gleaming blue tile, set on a framework of blue-tinted alloy. The architecture had a nostalgic art-deco look to it. It was big even though it served only as barracks to a relatively few people; much of the above-ground area was filled with parts and equipment storage and repair areas, armory, kitchen and dining and lavatory facilities, and so on. In some ways it was a self-contained world.

Mounted on its front was an enormous enlargement of a unit crest, that of the Alpha Tactical Armored Corps, the ATACs, and beneath that the squad designation: 15.

The crest was lavish, almost rococo, with rampant lion and unicorn, crown, gryphon, stars, shields, and the rest. The viewer had to look closely to see that one element of what was supposed to be crossed machetes looked more like . . . rabbit ears. The 15th had an old, gallant, and highly decorated past but a reputation for trouble, and for deviltry as well. The origin of the rabbit ears in its heraldry had a hundred different versions, and quite possibly none of them were true.

Inside, in a unit ready-room, there was an unusual level of banter going on, with almost a celebratory air. The same alarm that had disrupted Dana's graduation day proceedings, as word came of attack from space, had taken the ATACs off a peacetime footing.

Dana and Bowie had spent a week with the 15th, getting ready for the follow-up attack that never came. But at least there was no more falling out for silly make-work details or drudge jobs from the duty roster; the 15th had made sure it was ready to go, then had been ordered to stand-to and remain in barracks pursuant to further orders.

In civilian terms, it was a little like a small lottery win. The troopers of the 15th were napping or reading or chatting amiably to one another or watching vid. Bowie Grant was fooling around at an ancient upright piano that someone had scavenged for the 15th over a decade before; by diligent work he had gotten it back in tune, and now played it with eyes closed. On his torso harness and arm brassards were the 15th's crests.

Near him, Louie Nichols listened indifferently to the music while he cleaned and reassembled a laser pistol. Totally synthesized synaptic-inductance music with enhanced simu-sensory effects was more to Louie's liking; the lanky corporal was a sort of maverick technical genius given to endless tinkering and preoccupation with gadgetry.

Still, Bowie's music wasn't too bad for primitech stuff, Louie decided. Bowie was liked well enough after a week in the 15th, but he was still a bit of an oddball, like Louie himself. A man who looked out at the world through big, square, heavily tinted goggles—few people had seen Louie's eyes, even in the shower. Louie had decided Bowie was a misfit and therefore somewhat of a kindred soul, and that Dana was a bit of the same. So he had taken to the 15th's newest troopers.

Others had accepted them, too, though there was a little coolness toward Dana; she had been assigned as the 15th's new Executive Officer since the old XO had been hospitalized after a training maneuver injury. It was all perfectly ordinary, since she had been commissioned out of the Academy, but—she was the first woman in the 15th, one of the first in the ATAC.

Two privates were killing time with a chess game. "D'you hear the latest skinny?" the smaller one asked casually. "Our CO's gonna be in stockade for a while."

His big, beefy opponent shrugged, still studying his bishop's dilemma. "Too bad Sean's such a ladies' man—too bad for *him*."

"He shouldn't've made a pass at a superior officer," the first said.

A third, who had been kibbitzing, contributed, "Sean just didn't have his mind right, or he would've known better. Ya just *don't* go grabbing a colonel's daughter like that."

No, indeed; especially when the daughter was herself a captain. But scuttlebutt had it that the grabbing had gone rather well and that initial reaction was favorable, until the ATAC Officer of the Day wandered in and found army furniture being put to highly unauthorized use, as it were, by army personnel who were supposedly on duty. It was just about then that the colonel's daughter started yelling for help.

It was a brief court-martial, and word was that Lieutenant Sean Phillips grinned all through it. A constant stream of letters and CARE packages, sent by other female admirers, was brightening up his guardhouse stay.

Sergeant Angelo Dante, engrossed in a conversation of his own, snorted, "Aw, all she is is a snotty, know-it-all teenager!" He had served under Sean for some time, and resented seeing him replaced. He was so preoccupied with it that he didn't realize the rec-room door had slid open and the replacement was standing there.

"Why, Angelo, you say the sweetest things," a lively female voice said mockingly. Everyone looked around, startled, to see Dana posed glamourously in the doorway. The brevet pips were gone from her torso harness; she had been promoted from temporary XO—a kind of on-the-job training—to the CO slot, now that Sean was going to be spending some time playing rock-hockey over at the stockade.

Bowie stood up from the piano with a smile on his face. "Congratulations, Lieutenant Sterling," he said with genuine delight, much as he disliked the military.

Nobody bothered to call attention; the 15th was a casual kind of place under Sean. But there were a few appreciative whistles and murmurs for Dana's pose, and Evans, the supply sergeant, raised a coffee mug to her from his place on a stool at the (currently dry) bar. "A toast! To the cutest second lieutenant in the ATACs!" he said, pronouncing it *AY-tacks*.

Other voices seconded the sentiment. Dana strolled over toward Angelo Dante with a seductive, swivel-hipped gait. "What's the matter, Angie? Don't think I'm tough enough?" She gave him a languorous smile and kept it there as she gave him a swift kick in the shin.

Angelo was utterly shocked, but he barely let out a grunt; he was a tall, muscular man, well known for his strength and ability to withstand punishment. Dana let the guffaws and catcalls go on for a few seconds as the 15th razzed Angelo for being taken off guard. Angelo rubbed his shin and snarled at her retreating back, but inside he was suddenly reevaluating his opinion of "Miss Cadet," as he had been calling her.

Dana crossed to the windows, then whirled on them, cutting through the hoots and catcalls. "Fall in! On the double!"

There was a confused half-second of disbelief, then the 15th scrambled to stand at attention in two precise ranks, facing her. "Now what's she trying to prove?" Angelo heard someone mutter.

Dana looked them over, hands locked behind her back. She waited a few seconds in the absolute silence, then said, "Y'know, I've been giving this a lot of thought. And I've decided that this squad is dull. Definitely cute, but dull."

She walked along the front rank, inspecting her new command. "However, I *think* there's still hope for you, so prepare to move out!"

She had come to the end of the front rank, where Angelo stood glowering at her. "Something on your mind, Angie?"

He said, tight-lipped, "I could be wrong about this, but aren't we on ready-reaction duty this week?"

The ready-reaction squad was a kind of fire brigade, ready to move at once should any trouble occur, either at the base or elsewhere. The fact that it had to be ready to move on a moment's notice meant that the ready-reaction force usually kept all personnel in or immediately around its barracks.

But Dana gave Angelo a scornful look. "What's that got to do with a training maneuver?"

It wouldn't actually be breaking a reg, but it would be bending some. "Well, we haven't gotten official clearance from regimental HQ."

If there was a funny, warm Human side to her, there was a fire-breathing Zentraedi amazon side, too. Dana's eyes narrowed and her nostrils flared. "If you're looking to be busted to buck private, Dante, just keep doing what you're doing! 'Cause *I* give the orders here and *you* obey them!"

The usually gruff Angelo unexpectedly broke into a smile. "If you say so, Lieutenant." The simplest solution would be to give the kid enough rope, and even egg her on a little without being too obvious about it.

Dana showed locked teeth and the assembled 15th wondered silently if steam was going to start coming out of her ears. "If you have a problem, *Sergeant,* maybe I ought to send you to get your Chaplain Card punched. Or do you just resent taking orders from a woman?"

That stung Angelo, who *was* what he liked to think of as a little old-fashioned, but didn't want to be branded a sexist. He drew a deep breath. "That's not it at all, Lieutenant, but with all this trouble out at Liberty and the Moon Base—what if something happens and we're not here?" He gave her a condescending smile.

Dana was furious. Dante plainly didn't think she was fit to command, to fill the shoes of the dashing, devil-may-care Sean Phillips. So the 15th respected officers with a wild streak only, officers who were daredevils? She'd show them that Dana Sterling could lead the pack!

"In that case, Sergeant," she said, smirking, "why don't *you* just sit here and twiddle your thumbs? The rest of you, get to your Hovercycles! Move out!"

She's acting like it's all just a big picnic, Angelo saw. *I just hope she doesn't get us* all *into trouble.*

But as the 15th dashed for the drop-rack, whooping and shouting, Angelo was right with them.

The drop-rack was a sort of skeletal ladder that, like a conveyor belt or pater-noster, moved downward endlessly, a modern-day firemen's pole giving quick access to the motor pools below ground level.

At the first motor pool level, the troopers jumped from the drop-rack with practiced ease, just before it disappeared through a square opening in the floor, bound for the next level down, where the Hovertanks were kept.

The 15th dashed to its Hovercycles, one-seater surface-effect vehicles built for speed and maneuverability. Dana leapt astride her saddle, taking the handlebars. "Recon patrol in G sector, gentlemen!"

She settled her goggles on her face, gunned the engine. "Let's . . . go-ooo!" The 15th shot away after her, yahooing and giving rebel yells.

Dana laughed, exulting. *Whoever said a drill couldn't be fun?*

* * *

First they barreled through Monument City on a joyride that sent civilian pedestrians scuttling for safety. The cycles roared up and around access ramps and cloverleafs, threaded through traffic, and got into cornering duels with one another. The troopers yelled to one another and howled their encouragement to Dana, who had taken the lead.

She loved it, loved setting the pace and hearing her men cheer her on. "See if you can keep up with me, guys!" She gave a burst of thruster power, leaping the railing to land on an access ramp higher up and several yards away. They were headed the wrong way, against oncoming traffic.

Somehow, nobody was killed; the cycles deftly jumped the cars with thruster bursts, and the careening civilian cars managed not to annihilate one another as they slewed to avoid the troopers. Fists were shaken at them, and obscenities hurled, but the Southern Cross soldiers were above it all, literally and figuratively.

Then it was down onto a major traffic artery, for a flat speed run into the badlands on Monument City's outskirts. Rusting Zentraedi wreckage of the Robotech War dotted the landscape. This particular area still hadn't recovered from the alien fusillade that had devastated nearly the entire planet some seventeen years before; it looked more like the moon.

"Fokker Base is only a few more miles," Dana yelled over the wind and the sound of the engines. "We'll stop there!"

As Bowie passed the word, she thought sarcastically, *All this commanding is such a lot of work.* Then she laughed aloud into the rushing air.

Marie Crystal and her Black Lions were relaxing in the squadron canteen when the shrilling of the Hovercycle engines approached. The VT pilots had just finished an afternoon of target runs.

Dana came to a stop with a blare of thruster power and a blast of dust and debris. She hopped from her cycle as the rest of the 15th drew up next to her. She looked the enormous base over; Fokker wasn't far from the Human-made mounds that covered the fallen SDF-1, SDF-2, and the flagship of Khyron the Backstabber.

The place was the home of Tactical Air Force and Cosmic Units along with the TASC Veritechs, as well as experimental facilities and an industrial complex. It was also a commo nexus and regional command headquarters.

Inside the canteen a mohawked VT pilot inspected the 15th

through a large permaplas window. "Uh-oh, looks like school's out."

Dana was gazing back at the pilots now. "Hey, the eagles are being led by a dove, huh?" said one Lion approvingly.

Marie set hands on hips and *hmmph*ed. "More like turkeys being led by a goose," she sneered.

Dana led her men in and was confronted by First Lieutenant Marie Crystal. Dana saluted, and Marie barked, "State your mission."

Dana saw that the hospitality carpet was definitely not out. There had always been rivalry between the TASCs and the ATACs; their VTs and Hovertanks had some Robotech capabilities in common and therefore at times ended up with overlapping mission responsibilities. There was strong disagreement about which mecha was better in this mode or that, and which was the all-around superior. More than a few fists had flown over the subject.

This was the first time Dana had encountered such hostility, though. She had chosen Hovertanks because, she was certain, they were the most versatile, formidable mecha ever invented, so she wasn't about to take guff from some VT bus driver.

Dana identified herself, then drawled, "It's been a hard ride an' a dusty road. Y'wouldn't happen to have a little firewater around, would yuh, pard?"

That had the 15th guffawing and the Black Lions choking on their coffee. Marie Crystal's brows met. "What'd you do, kid, escape from a western? Don't you know how a commander's supposed to behave, even the commander of a flock of kiddie cars?"

Now Dana was annoyed, too. "My squad's got more citations for excellence than you could fit into your afterburner! Number one in every training maneuver and war game it's ever been in!"

Marie smiled indulgently, maddeningly. "Games don't prove a thing; only combat does."

Dana decided things had gone far enough. The 15th and the Lions were eyeing one another, some of them rubbing their knuckles thoughtfully.

Dana turned to go, but threw back over her shoulder, "My unit would never turn its back on a *real* fight, Lieutenant."

Her troopers began to follow her, but one of the VT fliers—Eddie Muntz, a pinch-faced little guy with a reputation as a troublemaker—jumped to his feet. He called after them, "Hey, wait! Don'tcha want a cuppa coffee?"

Royce, a tall, skinny trooper wearing horn-rimmed glasses,

turned to tell him no thanks. He got most of a full cup flung into his face.

Eddie Muntz stood laughing, managing to gasp, "Nothing like a good cuppa Java, I always say!" He was convulsing so hard that he didn't see what was headed his way.

"Try *this*," Bowie Grant invited, and tagged Muntz with an uppercut that sent him crashing back across the table. Bowie didn't like the army, or violence, but senseless cruelty was something that simply enraged him.

A couple of Lions helped Muntz to his feet, one of them growling, "So, the kids want to play rough."

Muntz wiped blood from his split lip. "Pretty good for somebody in day care," he admitted. Then he launched himself through the air to tackle Bowie.

But Bowie was ready for him; the ATAC trooper caught a hold of Muntz's uniform at the same time bringing up one foot and setting it in the juncture where leg met abdomen. Bowie fell backward to the floor, rolling, pulling his opponent with him, and pushing him with the foot that was in Muntz's midsection. It was just like Bowie had been taught at Academy hand-to-hand classes; with a wild scream the practical joker went flying through the air straight over Bowie's head.

Bowie's only miscalculation was that Dana was right in Muntz's trajectory. The VT pilot crashed into her headfirst and bore her to the floor. They lay in a tangle of arms and legs, with Dana hollering at the dazed Muntz to get off her.

Dana's scrabbling hand encountered a piece of metal, a table leg that had rolled there after Muntz's first fall. She grabbed it just as the VT pilot shook his head and leapt to his feet to face Bowie again.

His luck wasn't any better this time; Bowie was just out of the Academy, young and fast and in good shape. He rocked Muntz back with a left hook, and Muntz ended up knocking Marie Crystal back onto a couch, lying across her lap. While Marie pounded his head and howled at him to get off her, the riot got going in earnest.

As chairs were flung and punches thrown, kicks and leg-blocks vigorously exchanged, Dana suddenly realized what she had gotten herself and the 15th into.

And she stood numbly, watching a mental image of her lieutenant's bars as they flew away into the clouds forever on little wings. *I wonder if Sean's got any CARE packages to spare, there in the stockade?* she thought.

CHAPTER FIVE

The occasions of the 15th's first social encounter with the Black Lions was rather less auspicious than subsequent, more cooperative military collaborations. It is a fact, though, that the ATACs ever thereafter insisted on referring among themselves to Veritech recons and penetration strikes in football-play jargon, as "Debutantes Go Long."

Zachary Fox, Jr., *Men, Women, Mecha:*
the Changed Landscape of the Second Robotech War

DANA WAVED THE TABLE LEG, SHOUTING, "STOP! STOP THIS immediately!" It didn't do a bit of good.

The brawl was a confused sequence of split-second events; time and distance seemed strangely altered. A blond VT pilot swung his forearm into the face of a 15th trooper; another of Dana's men downed the mohawked Black Lion with a dropkick.

An ATAC was on the floor with a VT pilot's head in a leg lock; Shiro had Evans down and bent the wrong way, painfully, in a "Boston crab." Marie Crystal finally got the groggy Eddie Muntz off her just in time to have Louie Nichols and a VT man with whom he was locked in combat pile into her and bear her down in a struggling heap.

Dana couldn't think of anything to do but keep yelling "Stop! Stop!" and wave the table leg. It didn't accomplish much, and she had to stop even that and duck suddenly as a Black Lion flung bodily by Angelo Dante went crashing through the big window behind her.

The broken window let in a sound that made Dana's blood run cold: police sirens. An MP carrier was coming hell-for-leather across the field toward the canteen, all lights flashing. Dana turned and bellowed, "MPs! Hey, it's the MPs! Let's get outta here!"

Other voices took up the cry, and in seconds the brawl was

over. Marie Crystal looked on as the 15th raced after its leader, hopping on Hovercycles. Dana made sure all her men had gotten out. "Split up! We'll meet back at the barracks!" The ATACs zoomed off in all directions.

Dana gunned her engine and headed off straight for the police van. It was closer now, an open surface-effect vehicle, and she could see that there was a fifteen-foot-tall police robot standing back on the troop carrier bed. Dana calmly watched the distance close; she was determined to keep the MPs busy until the rest of the 15th had time to get clear.

The MP major standing behind the open cab felt sudden misgivings as the cycle rider came straight at the van's windshield. He let out a squawk and went for his sidearm, steadying it at her with both hands over the top of the cab. "Stop or I'll shoot! *Look out!*"

The latter was because Dana had increased speed and hit her thrusters. The major dove for cover, thinking she was out to decapitate him. But at the last instant she took the cycle up in a thruster-jump, neatly tagging the police robot's head with the skyscooter's tail. The robot toppled backward like a falling sequoia as the major screamed in horror. The sound the machine made against the hardtop resembled that of several boilers being rung like gongs.

The Black Lions stood outside the canteen, watching, as Dana threw them a jaunty wave and disappeared in the distance. Marie Crystal stood with hands on hips, a feline smile on her face. "Not bad for a beginner, Lieutenant Sterling. You show real promise." *And you haven't heard the last of the Black Lions!*

The MP van slowed to a stop. The major shook his head in disgust, watching the ATAC cycles leave dust trails to all points of the compass. *Doesn't the Academy teach these hoodlums the difference between us and the enemy?*

The robot lay unmoving, but its visor lit with red flashes with each word it spoke. "Hovercycle operator identified as Lieutenant Dana Sterling," the monotone voice announced, "Fifteenth ATAC squad." It made some strange noises, then added, "Recommend immediate apprehension. I don't feel very well. May we return to headquarters now? Perhaps you could give me a hand up, sir. *Vvvt! Wwarrrzzzp! Kktppsssst!* Reenlistment bonus? Sounds good to me!"

The major gave the robot a little first-echelon maintenance in the form of a good swift kick.

* * *

On a moonlit night with the silver veins of cloud overhead, Monument City had the look of a place transported to an eldritch graveyard. The wind-sculpted crags and peaks around it, the rusting dead leviathans of the Zentraedi wreckage, the barrenness of the countryside that began at the city limits—it all suited Dana's despair precisely.

Earlier that day she had led the 15th in a triumphant joyride up a curving concrete access ramp; now she crouched in an alley beneath it, in a part of the city where, she hoped, she could pass as just one more vagrant.

Sitting near the pile of refuse that concealed her cycle, hugging herself to conserve body heat, Dana sat with her back against a brick wall and tried to figure out what to do next. Eventually, she knew, she must return to the base and face the charges that would be brought against her; she just wanted some time to think things through. She was reassessing her entire concept of what it meant to be a commander.

Dana sighed and looked up at the cold, diamond-bright moon, and wondered whether Humans—whether she—would be fighting and dying there soon. If there was a war coming, as everybody was saying, she didn't have too much to fear from the MPs or a court-martial; the Southern Cross Army would need a capable young Hovertank officer too much to let her moulder in stir for very long. Besides, there was General Emerson, family friend and unofficial guardian, and though she hated the idea of asking for help, his influence could work wonders for her.

But she would be leading men and women into battle, and possible death; she *must not make any more misjudgments*. She hated being mocked and wronged, and she longed so very much to *connect* with something—perhaps her squadmates would be like the family she had never really known.

She sighed, pulling a holobead from an inner uniform pocket. Thumbing it in the dimness of the alley, she looked again on the image she had seen ten thousand times before.

There was Max Sterling, the greatest VT pilot who had ever lived, pale and boyish, with oversize corrective glasses and blue-dyed hair. Next to him was Miriya Parino Sterling, the woman who had commanded the Zentraedi's elite Quadrono Battalion, reduced from a giantess to Human proportions by a Protoculture sizing chamber, a woman with the predatory look of a tigress, and all the sleek beauty of one as well.

But they clung to each other lovingly, and between them they held a happy, blue-haired baby. Dana.

And now they're—who knows? she thought. She looked at the stars and reflected, as she did almost every night, that her mother and father might be beyond the most distant of them. Or might be dead. No communications had been received from the SDF-3 expedition to find and deal with the Robotech Masters.

Dana pressed a minute switch, and the holobead showed its other image. An odd-looking trio stood there: Konda, tall and lean, with purple hair and an expression that said he knew something others didn't; Bron, big and broad, with such strong, callused hands and yet such a sweet, gentle nature; and Rico, small and wiry and fiery, dark-haired and mercurial.

Dana looked on them fondly; in front of them stood a Dana who was perhaps five, her hair its natural yellow color now, grinning and holding Bron's forefinger, squinting because the sun was in her eyes. The 15th's new—perhaps former, by now—CO heaved another sigh.

Konda and Bron and Rico were former Zentraedi spies, shrunk to Human size, who had fallen under the spell of Human society. Max and Miriya left with Rick Hunter, Captain Lisa Hayes, and the rest of the expedition in the SDF-3, and there was a certain lapse of time there that Dana couldn't account for and had been too young to remember—things that even General Emerson wasn't too forthcoming about. But eventually the erst-while spies, learning that for some unexplained reason Max and Miriya had been persuaded to leave her behind, appointed themselves her godfathers.

A strange upbringing it was. No other person in history had been subjected to both Human and Zentraedi attitudes and teachings from infancy. The ex-spies were really only enlisted men, not well educated even for Zentraedi, whose whole history and lore were a Robotech Masters' concoction. Still, they taught her everything they could about her mother's people, and took better care of her than many natural parents could have done, in their own slightly bumbling, endearing way.

All the rebel Zentraedi—the ones who had defected to the Human side only to turn against the Earth again—had been hunted down while Dana was still an infant, and all the rest, including her godfathers, had either gone along with the SDF-3 or exiled themselves on the factory satellite. Eventually her godfathers had passed away, almost at the same time. She was never certain whether it was from some Earthly malady or simply a vast loneliness; their three human loves, Sammie, Vanessa, and Kim, had died with Gloval and Bowie's aunt Claudia in the SDF-1's final battle. The ex-spies had never taken others.

With the trio gone, it was government youth shelters and schools for Dana once more, often with Bowie as her companion because Rolf Emerson simply couldn't have children along with him. And then, in time, there was the Academy. But when Dana heard bitter words about the innate savagery of the Zentraedi nature, she thought back on the one-time giants who had shown her such a happy family life, at least for a little while.

She deactivated the holobead with a stroke of her thumb, leaning her head back against the coarse bricks, eyes closed, taking in a deep breath through her nostrils. There were the distant lights of apartments, where families were getting together for dinner after a day of workaday life.

Dana let her breath out slowly, wishing again that she could be one of them, wishing that the holobead images could come to life, or that her parents would come home from the stars.

There was a sudden whimper and the hollow bounce of an empty can nearby. She was on her feet, reflexively ready for a fight. But there was no enemy there. It was, instead, a quite special acquaintance.

"Polly!"

She stopped to gather the little creature up, a thing that looked like a mophead, its tongue hanging out. It might have passed for a terrestrial dog until one took a closer look. It had small knob-ended horns, eyes that were hidden beneath its sheepdoglike forelock—but that were definitely not the eyes of an Earth lifeform—and feet resembling soft muffins.

It's a pollinator, Bron had told her gently the first time she was introduced to it. That's how she had given the thing its name, even though she had no idea whether Polly was male or female.

She never found out just how the ex-spies had come across the affectionate little beast; they had promised to tell her in the "someday" that had never come. But she had learned that Polly was a magical creature indeed.

For instance, Polly came and went as it pleased, no matter if you locked it in or tied it up. You would look around, and Polly would just be gone, maybe for a little while or maybe for a long time. It reminded her a little of *Alice's Adventures in Wonderland,* and later, another oldtime book title she came across, *The Cat Who Walks Through Walls.*

The pollinator was her first adult-style secret, since her godfathers told her she must never mention it to anybody, and she had kept that secret all her life. Apparently, Polly was part of some miraculous thing, but she never found out what. Polly had managed to find her for brief visits four or five times since the death of Konda, Bron, and Rico.

"Did you hear me thinking about them?" she murmured, petting the XT creature, pressing her cheek to it as it licked her face with a red swatch of tongue. "Didja know how much I can use a slobber on the face just now?" Her tears leaked out no matter how she tried to hold them back. "Looks like we're both gonna be cold tonight."

She wiped her cheek, smearing the tears and dirt. "I can't believe I let things get so far out of control."

But somehow she felt less terrible. She managed to fall asleep, the pollinator curled up warmly against her. The dark dreams that came to her at times, filled with terrors that were both nameless and otherwise, stayed away this time.

But she had her strange Vision again, as she had had on rare occasions ever since she could remember. In it, a vortex of purest force swirled up from the planet Earth like the funnel of a cyclone; only it was a cyclone a hundred miles in diameter, composed of violent energies springing from sheer mental power. The uppermost part of the mind-tornado reached beyond Earth's atmosphere, then it suddenly transformed into an incandescent phoenix, a firebird of racial transfiguration.

The crackling, radiant phoenix spread wings wider than the planet, soaring away quicker than thought to another plane of existence, with a cry so magnificent and sad that Dana dreaded and yet was held in the powerful beauty of this recurring dream. Her Vision was another secret she had always kept to herself.

As Dana stirred in her sleep, something came between her and the streetlights. That struck through to a trained alertness that had long since become instinctive; she lay utterly still, opening one eye just a crack.

Looming over her was the person of Lieutenant Nova Satori of the Global Military Police. Backing her up were a half-dozen MP bruisers cradling riot guns. Some sort of dawn was trying to get through clouds that looked like they had been dumped out of a vacuum-cleaner bag. The pollinator was no longer lying against Dana.

Nova was enjoying herself. She was turned out in the MP dark-blue-and-mauve version of the Southern Cross dress uniform, her blue-black hair fluttering and luffing against her thighs like ʻ, caught back with a tech ornament like Dana's.

In Nova's quick dark eyes and the heart-shaped face there was the canniness of both the cop and the professional soldier.

"Well, good morning," said Nova with a pleasant purr.

Funny how you run into old buddies when you least expect it, Dana reflected, and rose to her feet in one smooth move. She and Nova went back in a long way. Dana put on her best Miss Southern Cross Army smile. "Well, Lieutenant Satori! How ya been? *You're* out early!"

Dana gave a completely false laugh while looking over possible escape routes as Nova said in a Cheshire cat voice, "Fine, just fine."

Polly was nowhere in sight, and there were no avenues of escape. *Uh-oh.*

In Southern Cross HQ, high up in one of the buildings that looked like crusaders' war-standards, the army's command center operated at a constant fever pitch, a twenty-four-hour-a-day steam bath of reports, sensor readouts, intelligence analysis, and system-wide surveillance.

Scores of techs sat at their consoles while diverse duty officers and NCOs passed among them, trying to keep everything coherent. Overhead, visual displays flashed on the inverted dome of the command center ceiling, showing mercator grid projections, models of activity in the Solar System, and current military hotspots.

On one trouble-board, ominous lights were blinking. An operations tech covered his headset mike with the palm of his hand and yelled, "Cap'n? Come take a look at this."

The ops captain bent down over the tech's shoulder and examined the screen. There was a complete garble of the usual computer-coded messages.

"It ain't comin' from the space station, sir," the tech said. "It's like somebody's messing with satellite commo, but who? And from where, if you catch my drift, sir."

The captain frowned at the display and double-checked the alphanumerics. Then he spun and barked, "Get General Emerson over here ASAP!" The message was being relayed ASAP—as soon as possible—before he was done speaking.

The tech looked up at the ops captain. "What d'you guesstimate, sir? Y'figure it's those—"

"Let's hope not," the captain cut him off.

Space Station Liberty was like a colossal version of a child's rattle, hanging endlessly at Trojan Lagrange Point Five. It was manity's sole link with the SDF-3 expeditionary force that had set out either to negotiate an end to hostilities or beat the Robotech Masters into submission.

Messages had been few and far between, and some thought them bogus, but hope still thrived. Or at least it had until the Robotech Masters came.

A command center tech covered his mike and called to an operations officer, "Sir, I have a large unidentified paint."

But Major General Emerson, Chief of Staff, Ministry of Terrestrial Defense, was in the command center by then, and came to bend near the tech and the all-important screen. The ops officer, a captain, knew when it was politic to take a back seat to a flag-rank officer. Which was almost always.

Besides, this was Rolf Emerson, hero of a dozen pivotal battles in the Global Civil War and the disorders that followed the Robotech War. For all of that, he was soft-spoken and correct to the lowest-ranking subordinate. The word was that he would have been supreme commander—would have been a UEG senator for that matter—long since, except that he hated political games. In the final analysis he was a GI, albeit a brilliant one; the men and women under his command respected him for it and the politicians and supreme staff officers resented him, determining that he would never get another star.

But he was far too valuable to waste, so he was in the right place at the right time on a day when the Human race needed him badly.

"Put it up on Central Display, please, Corporal," Rolf Emerson requested quietly.

The object and its trajectory and the rest of the scanty data appeared on the billboard-size central display screen. There was a single soft whistle. "Big, bad UFO," Emerson heard a thirty-year vet NCO mutter.

"Fast, too," an intelligence major observed; she grabbed up a handset and began punching in codes that accessed her own chain of command.

"Sir, d'you think this has to do with the shootout out by Moon Base?" the captain asked.

"Still too early to tell," Emerson grated. The captain shut up.

The tech reported, reading his instruments. "According to computer_ _he UFO is a powered vehicle and it's on an Earth-_ _vector, estimated time of entry in Earth atmosphere one_ _enty-three minutes, forty seconds . . . mark. Visual_ _proximately three minutes."

"Give me a look at this thing," Emerson said in a low, even voice that people around him had come to recognize as one that brooked no failure. People jumped, babbled computer languages, typed at touchpads, made order out of chaos. Not one of them would have changed places with Emerson. The atmosphere in the command center had officers and enlisted ratings loosening their tunic collars, coming to grips with the fact that the Main Event might just be coming up during their watch.

"We need to see what they look like," Emerson said to a senior signals NCO who was standing near. She was his imagery interpretation specialist, and she went to work at once, coordinating sensors and imagery-interpretation computers.

At a Southern Cross communications and sensor intel satellite, sensor dishes and detection spars swung and focused. Information was fed and rejiggered and processed, nearly a billion and a half (prewar) dollars worth of technology going full-choke to process data that ended up in front of a reedy young man who had been drafted only eight months before.

Colonel Green, one of Emerson's most trusted subordinates, barked, "Corporal Johnson, talk to me! Haven't you got anything yet?"

Johnson had gotten used to the brass screaming at him for answers; he had become imperturbable. He had gone from being a weird technofreak highschooler through a basic training that still gave him nightmares to a slot as one of the few people who *truly* understood how Liberty's equipment worked.

So Colonel Green didn't rattle Johnson; he had had to introduce any number of brass hats to the stark facts of reality. The instruments would show what they would show, or not, and there were only limited things Humans could do about it. The first thing you had to teach officers was yelling louder rarely helped.

"One moment, sir." The female imagery interpretation NCO came over to watch.

Johnson worked at his console furiously, more a magician than a technician, and was rewarded with a raw, distorted image. The officers looking over his shoulder would never appreciate how much finesse that had taken, but the senior sergeant did.

Then it was gone again. Johnson punched up the recording of the intercept and put it up on the huge main screen. "Sir, I had a visual but I lost it. Countermeasures maybe; I dunno. Playback on screen alpha."

Something was out there all right, something enormous and blockish and headed for Earth, something with more mass than anything Humans had ever put in the sky. Something whose power levels made all the indicators jump off the scales, and made all the watching Southern Cross higher-ups clench jaw muscles.

"Wish we could see that thing better," Colonel Green muttered. Whatever Johnson had picked up, it was artificial and fast-moving; the zaggies in the sensor image kept it from telling them much more.

And it's coming right our way, Emerson contemplated.

CHAPTER SIX

The importance and power of the Global Military Police—the GMP—was directly attributable to the near-feudal nature of Earthly society at that time. The GMP constituted the only truly worldwide law-enforcement organization, and was a check and balance on those who had at their disposal the tremendous power of Robotechnology. As a result, the GMP was an organization with its own war machinery, combat forces, and intelligence network.

A career in the GMP was a possible road to swift personal advancement, but the recruit had to say farewell to all outside friendships; such things could no longer exist for him or her.

S. J. Fischer, *Legion of Light:
A History of the Army of the Southern Cross*

"**W**HAT COULD THAT THING *BE*?" COLONEL GREEN burst out. Emerson was already way ahead of him, wondering what the hell might lie in the lee of the moon.

"Accelerating," Johnson said. A fine sweat had appeared on his brow. The display symbol for the intruder was marking its progress with integrals coming much more quickly. It was coming at Earth fast; it was nearly upon Liberty.

Just then there was a tremendous surge through all the sensor/commo apparatus, after which many indicators went dead.

"Playing for keeps," Green observed.

An op near Johnson turned to yell, "Sir, we've lost commo with Liberty: voice, visual, everything on the spectrum."

"Patch in whatever you have to, but *keep that bogie in sight*," Rolf said in measured tones. He turned to Lieutenant Colonel Rochelle, his adjutant. "Get everything you've got on red alert. Get all the ready-reactions set for possible XT warfare. Prime the Hovertanks especially, and the VTs. Gimme everything, right? *Everything!*"

Oh, Dana, Bowie! God keep you . . .

43

He swung to the intel major, whom he knew to be an internal security fink. "Use whatever code you have to, Jackie, and get me a UEG telequorum, right now." She looked away from his gaze at once, unable to meet it. Then she licked her lips, resettled her glasses, picked up a handset. She cradled the phone to her, turning her back to the others there in the command center, and punched out a code.

Green came up behind Emerson to whisper harshly, "If they're the Masters, d'you *really* think we stand any chance against them?"

"Don't sweat it, Colonel."

"But sir, we don't even know who they are or what they can do to—"

Rolf Emerson whirled on him angrily, then suddenly quieted. He rapped the knuckle of one forefinger against Green's ribbons, decorations from another war and another time. Emerson wore just about as many; they were two graying men listening to alarms, knowing it was the death knell of the everlasting peace they had fought and hoped for.

"This planet's *ours*, Ted."

"But, General, isn't there—"

"*Earth is ours!* Maybe it is the Masters, but who cares? *This planet is ours!* Now go saddle up everything we've got groundside, and draw up a rapid deployment op-plan, 'cause we're gonna need one real bad."

Ten days went by, and Dana figured she had miscalculated her worth. Or else, possibly, was there to be no war? In any case, she mouldered in solitary confinement, against all expectation.

Hard rations of protein cracker and water scarcely affected her; things had been worse, *much* worse, on any number of training maneuvers; stockade was a cakewalk.

Mostly, she caught up on sleep, and worried about what was happening to the 15th, and stared out the window from her bunk. In her dreams there was a strange procession of images, and twice the haunting cry of the phoenix.

The door viewslit slid back; Dana recognized the eyes she saw there, and the limp blond hair around the face. Colonel Alan Fredericks said in a voice muffled by the door, "Accommodations to your liking, Ms. Sterling?"

Dana curled a lip at him. "Sure, it's home sweet home, sir."

Fredericks said, "I'm glad you've held up so well for ten days. Anything to say for yourself?"

Dana indicated her smudged face and rank, filthy uniform. "A hot bath and a change of clothes would feel nice. And maybe a manicure and a facial."

Fredericks allowed himself a thin smile. "No, no—we don't want you to be distracted from contemplation of your crimes, do we now?"

Dana sprang to her feet, holding her hands out to him imploringly. "Please let me return to my squad! Sir, we might be at war anytime now; I've got to be with the Fifteenth!"

"Stop your whining!" Fredericks roared at her. "If it were up to me, you would have been drummed out of the Army of the Southern Cross!"

He sniggered. "Little Dana, daughter of the great heroes, Max and Miriya Sterling! It seems blood doesn't always tell, does it?"

Actually, Fredericks was of the opinion that breeding *did* tell, and was glad that this halfbreed had proved it. But he dared not say such a thing with guards nearby as witnesses.

Dana fell to her knees, nearly in tears, facing the cold eyes in the door viewslit. "Sir, I'm begging you: give me a chance to square things, to prove myself. I'll never disgrace my family name or break a reg again. I swear it—"

"Stop sniveling!" Fredericks shouted.

The truth was, there was pressure on him from higher up to release Dana. Some of it came from her regimental commander, who needed her, and some from the Judge Advocate General's office; the JAG thought ten days was more than enough. General Emerson had said a few words on her behalf in the right ears, too.

But there was yet another source of pressure, one that Fredericks hadn't quite been able to track down. Evidence pointed toward its coming through civilian channels—from very high up indeed in the scientific and research power structure. One name he heard had him surprised and cautious: Dr. Lazlo Zand.

Zand had been the disciple of Dr. Lang, the high priest of Robotechnology. When Lang went off with Rick Hunter, Dana's parents, and the rest in the SDF-3, Zand remained behind. Now Zand's activities and whereabouts were so shrouded in mystery as to defy even Frederick's efforts at investigation.

"Since you're so repentant, perhaps I will see what I can do," Fredericks told Dana coldly. The viewslit slid shut.

Dana, back on her feet, thrust her fist high into the air. *"Yahooo!"*

* * *

It was less than an hour later when the door of her cell rolled open. Dana stepped into the corridor to find Colonel Fredericks giving her his best basilisk glare. He held a leather swagger stick that resembled a riding crop, of all things. Standing on the opposite side of the doorway was Nova Satori.

Someone else was approaching, being escorted by two rifle-toting guards. Fredericks had arranged the chance meeting to see what would happen.

"Hey, Dana!"

She whirled, and a sunny smile shone on her face. "Sean! What're you doing in solitary? No, don't tell me; you, ah, made a pass at a general's wife?"

Sean Phillips, erstwhile CO of the 15th, gave her one of his famous roguish grins. He was even more famous as a Don Juan than as a fighter, a tall, athletic twenty-three-year-old with a boyish haircut and long brown locks framing his face.

Sean gave her a wink. "Naw. They decided I needed a little privacy, I guess; you know how it is when you're a celebrity. Besides, they're springing me tomorrow."

Nova caught a subtle signal from Fredericks, and barked, "Shut up and keep moving, Phillips!" The look on her face let everyone know that she was immune to his charms; she had put Sean in his place the moment he tried his Romeo routine on her. And the second time, and the third.

Sean was shoved into the cell Dana had just vacated, and the door rolled shut. Nova told Dana, "Just screw up one more time, Lieutenant, and you won't even know what hit you."

Dana choked back the retort that came to her lips. "Yes, ma'am." She saluted the two MP officers, did a right face, and moved out.

"I don't trust either of them, Nova," Fredericks said quietly, slapping his palm with the swagger stick. "Keep me updated on her activities, and on Phillips's, too, once he's freed."

"Will do, sir."

Dana's release came just as the UEG made public the news of the aliens' appearance. It was a brief, tersely worded statement ending with the fact that the ship had taken up a geostationary orbit some twenty-three thousand miles out in space.

Of course, the entire Southern Cross Army was going to red alert; that was why she had been released. Dana soon found herself in a jeep with Nova Satori and two guards, being hustled back to the 15th. Her regimental commander wanted every Hovertank manned; there was some word that Sean might get an early release, too.

At a Southern Cross base, the silo blast doors were open and the Earth's most powerful missiles were primed. Captain Komodo, battalion commander, surveyed his instrumentation. He was a broad, powerful-looking man of Nisei descent, with a chestful of medals.

A fire-control tech looked up at him. "Sir, is there any word on who these aliens are?"

Komodo frowned. "It's obvious they're the same ones who attacked Moon Base. But now we're ready for them." Komodo had lost a brother in that raid; he hungered for revenge.

He spun to face a commo operator. "I told you to keep me informed! Well?"

The op shrugged helplessly. "No further orders, sir; we're still instructed to stand by."

"Fools!" muttered Komodo. "We have to strike *now*!" He reached down to flip up the red safety shields and expose a row of firing switches. Then Captain Komodo looked angrily into the sky, waiting.

At Southern Cross Command Headquarters, Emerson was in the eye of the storm.

"Sir, the alien's moving into a lower orbit," a tech reported.

"General, why are we waiting?" Green demanded. "With all due respect, sir, you must give the order to attack. Immediately!"

Emerson shook his head slowly, watching the displays. "It is imperative that we find out who they are and why they're here. We cannot fire first."

Green gritted his teeth. His hope that Supreme Commander Leonard or some other top brass would overrule Emerson had not come to pass. "But they killed our people, sir!"

Emerson turned to him. "I'm aware of that. But what proof do we have that Luna didn't bring the attack on itself by firing first? Do you want to start a war that nobody wants?"

Green swallowed his angry retort. He was old enough to remember the Zentraedis' first appearance and their disastrous onslaught.

So was Emerson; the general had seen enough war to dread starting one.

At the missile base the commo op looked to Captain Komodo. "Sir, the enemy spacecraft is descending from orbit—thirteen thousand miles and descending rapidly."

Komodo stood with teeth clenched, jaw muscles jumping. "Are you sure your equipment's working, Sparks? That there's been no command to open fire?"

"Affirmative, sir."

Komodo's fists shook. *If those cowards at headquarters would just work up the guts to give me the green light, I'd blow those aliens out of the sky!*

With the Earth an ocean-blue and cloud-white gem beneath it, the Robotech Masters' ship suddenly launched three sand-red objects shaped like pint whiskey bottles. Their thrusters howled, and they dove for the planet below.

"Captain, landing craft of some kind have left the mother ship and begun entry maneuvers."

Komodo looked over the fire-control tech's shoulder. "Got 'em on radar yet?"

"That's affirm, sir."

Komodo clapped a hand to the man's shoulder. "Good! I want A and B batteries to take out the mother ship first; it won't be launching any more sneak attacks. Charlie and Delta batts will target the attack craft."

The tech was looking at him wide-eyed. "What's wrong? I gave you a fire-mission!" Komodo shouted.

"But sir! HQ gave specific orders that—"

Komodo caught the hapless youngster up by his torso harness and flung him aside. "You idiot! You want to wait until they blow the whole planet away?" His fingers flew over the control console; in moments the ground trembled.

The huge, gleaming pylons—Skylord missiles—rose up in fountains of flame and smoke, shaking the base and the surrounding countryside.

The Robotech Masters proved themselves not to be infallible or invincible; though they vaporized two Skylords with charged particle beams, the other two got through, making brilliant flashes against the huge mother ship.

On Earth, Emerson and the others in the command center looked at their screens in astonishment. "Confirmed Southern Cross missile launch, sir," someone said. "Heavy damage thought to have been suffered by the enemy ship; sensors indicate they're floating dead in space."

Emerson turned on his subordinates with white-hot anger.

"Who launched those birds?" There was confusion among them and, Emerson knew, no time to waste placing blame.

Now we're committed. "Open fire! Hit 'em with everything we can throw. Inform Supreme Commander Leonard and tell Civil Defense to get on the stick!"

"War," said Commander Fredericks, savoring the word and the idea. "Just my luck to be stuck here guarding a bunch of underaged eightballs."

"Yes, sir," Nova answered. She wasn't quite as eager to kill or be killed as her superior, but knew that it would be wise to hide the fact.

"Still, little Dana should see some action," Fredericks frowned, slapping his desktop with his swagger stick. "Probably do her good, too."

He rose from his chair. "Well, let's see what we can do to guarantee that, eh?"

The Skylords were all away; Captain Komodo stared in fury as the screens showed him how, one after another, they were blown to harmless mist by the energy weapons of the descending enemy. Not surprisingly, the alien assault craft were homing in on the source of the missiles that had damaged their mother ship.

"Fire!" Komodo bellowed, and rack after rack of APC-mounted Swordfish missiles boiled away into the air, leaving corkscrewing white trails. Tremendously powerful pulsed beams from the assault ships blasted them out of the sky in twos and threes, while the aliens closed in on the base.

Komodo gulped and watched the bottle-shaped vessels come into visual range. He looked around him for a rifle or a rocket launcher; he had no intention of running and he had no intention of going down without a fight.

High above, access ports opened and enemy mecha swarmed out. Led by a red Bioroid like a crimson vision of death, the Masters' warriors dove their Hovercraft and sought targets, firing and firing.

Hwup! Tup! Thrup! Fo'!
Alpha! Tact'l! Armored! Corps!
For-git Jody! For-git Dotty!
Ay-tacks OWNS yo' student body!

Cadence chant popular among ATAC drill instructors

IN THE READY-ROOM OF THE 15TH SQUAD, ATAC, TROOPER WINston was sitting with chin on palm and gazing at his squadmates sourly. "Finally, the balloon goes up—and we're stuck here!"

Next to him, Coslow, arms folded on his chest, nodded. "Why's it always our turn in the barrel?"

Angelo Dante nodded. "All this terrific talent being wasted just 'cause both of our officers happen to be doing bad time."

They weren't even suited up in armor. Express orders from Higher Up said that no Hovertank outfit would be allowed into a combat situation without a commissioned officer—preferably an Academy-trained one—in command.

Bowie, pacing, crossed to Angelo. "Why don't they just let *you* take over, Sergeant?"

Angelo sighed philosophically and shook his head. "I'd love it, kid, but there's just no way, know what I mean?"

Any Hovertanker knew the drills and could act independently on a combat mission—could even take over command if it came to that—but the Hovertanks had to be able to do more. The knowhow to integrate with other types of mecha, with TASC units like the Black Lions and so forth; to interpret complex tactical scenarios; to understand the various commo computer languages; to see, in short, the Hovertank's mission in terms of an entire

Southern Cross op-plan, and to work to the maximum benefit of that overall plan was something that took years of study—study Angelo hadn't received.

Angelo raised his shoulders, dropped them. "This isn't one of Dana's drills. There's gonna be lives on the line this time, Bowie."

Not to mention one of the first fully operational Hovertank outfits in the Southern Cross, a huge investment of time and treasure and technology. The UEG's newest combat arm *must* serve well and protect the people who had paid its price tag.

Louie Nichols was polishing his sidearm again. Word had it that he had figured out an unauthorized modification that would triple the power of its pulses; people edged away from him when he played with the handgun, not wanting to be at ground zero in case Louie overlooked some potential glitch.

"No offense, Angelo," Louie said, "but I'm a little too busy to die right now."

"Anyhow, thanks for the vote of confidence, Bowie," Angelo finished.

Just then the door to the ready-room parted and there stood Dana, in full spit-shined combat armor lacquered white, black, and scarlet, her helmet in the crook of her left arm. The armor, all ultratech alloy, somehow had the look of an earlier day to it—a flaring at the hips and shoulders that suggested both jousting panoply and whalebone corsetry.

"Fall in!"

The 15th's collective mouth hung open. Angelo came to his feet. "I thought you were doing thirty days bad time. You're not serious, right?"

Dana beamed. "Wrong again. Crank it up, Fifteenth! We're heading for a hotspot, to stop the enemy or die trying!"

Angelo released a deep breath. "Yes ma'am." *But dying under the command of a diz-zo-max teenager—it isn't exactly the way I'd hoped to go out.*

Louie walked by, holstering the pistol, eyes hidden in the dark goggles. "Well, when the whistle blows, everybody goes, Angie, so let's get goin'!"

This time they took the drop-rack one level deeper, leaping clear amid the Hovertank parking bays as the lights came up to full brightness. All were armored now, dashing to their craft with the sureness of constant drill. The overhead lights flashed white, red, white, red, to indicate the 15th was rolling on a priority wartime deployment.

The Hovertanks were bigger than their pre-Robotech counterparts, and heavier; yet they lifted lightly on thrusters, turning end-for-end like pirouetting rhinos, very maneuverable and responsive. The 15th handled their mecha with manual controls; there was no need for the thinking caps yet.

The bulky war machines followed as Dana led the way in her command tank, the *Valkyrie*, shooting up the access tunnel, following the glowing traffic-routing arrows embedded in the pavement.

They left the base and the city behind, heading for their assigned objective. The Hovertanks took up a precise skirmishing formation behind her. The mecha's headlights, under the downward sweep of the forward cowling, gave them the look of angry crabs.

Today I show them I've got what it takes. Dana steeled herself.

"Fifteenth squad will proceed ASAP to sector Q, I say again, Q for Quebec." The order came over the command net. "Suspected alien landing site. Use extreme caution."

" 'Kay; you all know what to do," Dana told her ATACs. But inwardly she winced. *Alien!* I'm *half alien, and I'm on my way out to put my hide on the line for this planet, you sorry sack!*

Yeah, now this is where I belong, Angelo thought, the wind harsh in his face, the tank shrilling beneath him.

The Hovertanks were assemblages of heavy-gauge armor in angular, flattened shapes and acute edges, with rounded, downsloping prows, riding thruster pods. The angles, as in armor throughout history, were for deflection of rounds aimed at the tanks.

The Hovertanks kicked up huge plumes of dust as they raced to sector Quebec. Long before they got there, the members of the 15th could see that they had drawn a hotspot; explosions blossomed as detonations threw debris high in the distance, while energy beams drew angry lines through the air.

They topped a rise and looked down on a smoking battlefield. Scattered all around were blasted and burning scraps of war mecha, almost all of Earthly origin. A Civil Defense Flying Corps outfit was manning outmoded ten-year-old VTs. The aircraft had come to life and assumed Battloid configuration, but they lacked the size, firepower, and groundfighting ability to deal with the ravaging XT mecha.

A tiny part of the enemy's telemetry had been intercepted, most of it impenetrable. But using certain old Zentraedi decryption programs, the code breakers had come up with what they thought was the designation of the invaders' war machines: Bioroids.

Dana pulled on her helmet/thinking cap, which featured graceful wings at either side, and a curved crest like a steel rainbow along its center. As she made it fast to her armor, it sealed and became airtight; so protected, she could survive radiation, chemical agents, water, vacuum, high pressure—almost any hostile environment. The wings and crest gave her a look that validated the name with which she had christened her tank, *Valkyrie*.

"Here we go!"

She gunned her tank's power plant, then set off, leading the way. The 15th raced after her.

Down below, the CDs were doing badly. The enemy mecha were drubbing them terribly; as the 15th watched, two blue giants led by a red one, all riding the flying-saucer Hoverplatforms like futuristic charioteers or alien water-skiers, stooped for another kill.

As the tankers charged in, the Bioroid trio led by the red one swooped in at two VTs who stood their ground in Battloid configuration. The red Bioroid, in the lead, fired quick, accurate bursts with the gun mounted on its control stem, and blew two of the VTs away, easily avoiding most of their fire and shrugging off the rest.

The Hovertanks were in the air now. "Switch to Gladiator mode!" Dana called over the tac net. In midair the tanks shifted, reconfigured, *mechamorphosed*. When they landed, they were squat, two-legged, waddling gun turrets the size of a house, each with a single massive cannon stretching out before it. The big guns were the mecha's primary batteries, even more powerful than the tank cannon.

The Gladiators fired, shoulder to shoulder. It was like a cannonade from the heaviest artillery. Two blue Bioroids went up in furious explosions, then a third. Another jumped clear of its Hoverplatform just as the platform was blown to bits. The Bioroid fired in midair, with a Bioroid-size pistol shaped something like a fat discus held edge-on, and took cover immediately when it hit the ground.

Other Bioroids were already there, having seen what intense fire the Gladiators could throw into the air. The aliens set up a determined counter-fire with Bioroid small-arms.

Dana took a deep breath and hopped her Gladiator high, imaging the move through her thinking cap. She landed to one end of a Bioroid firing line to set up an enfilade. But an alien had spotted her, and swung to fire. Dana got off the first shot and holed the outworld mecha through and through with a brilliant lance of energy that left glowing, molten metal around the edges of the point of entry.

"Gotcha!"

The Bioroids continued a stubborn, grudging resistance, but it was clear at once that the Hovertank Gladiators had advantages the Veritech Battloids didn't. They were bigger, more powerful, and more heavily armored, and carried greater firepower. On the ground, slugging it out toe to toe, the Bioroids had met their match.

Deafening volleys of nova cannonfire hammered back and forth in the little valley; Bioroids fell, discovering that without their Hovercraft they were on an equal footing with the ATACs.

The firefight raged on, neither side gaining or losing much ground. Suddenly, the red Bioroid leapt high from its position behind the blues. Showing great dexterity, it avoided the few cannon rounds that the startled Gladiators got off at it, to land between two 15th mecha. It blasted one at point-blank range, and turned to fire at the second even as the other Gladiator swung its barrel around desperately.

The red Bioroid fired into the second Gladiator while the first was erupting in a fireball; the second Earth mecha, too, went up in a groundshaking explosion. The red jumped again, to continue its awesome offensive.

Dana shook herself to get over the shock of it; two troopers dead in seconds, two mecha utterly destroyed, and the red bounding on to attack again. *All right, Dana!* she told herself firmly. *Show 'em what you've got!* "Dante, switch your team to Battloid mode, *now!*"

She did the same, jumping her mecha to a better firing position. The craft went through mechamorphosis in mid-air, taking on the form of a huge Human-shaped battleship, an ultratech knight. Half the 15th reared up now in Battloid form, the remainder hunkered down in Gladiator to give fire support.

The blue Bioroids seemed daunted, surprised at the mechamorphosis and unsure about coming to grips with the Humaniform machines. But the red Bioroid carried the attack once more, aiming the massive disc-pistol at Dana and unleashing a raging bolt of energy.

"Oh, no, y'don't!" She jumped her Battloid high as the shot annihilated the ground where she had stood. At her command the Battloid took its plasma rifle—which was the tank's cannon now reconfigured—into its hands as it flew through the air. Dana fired on the fly, muttering, "Now it's *your* turn!"

The red ducked, then raced to meet her as her Battloid landed with a deft flip. In moments they were ducking it out in the rocks nearby, springing up to fire at each other, then diving for cover again, while the rest of the 15th engaged the invaders once more. Without the red to lead them, the blues' assault faltered.

But in the meantime, Dana was fighting a desperate duel against a very capable foe. What's more, she couldn't lose the strange feeling that she *knew* this machine, knew something all-important and fateful about it. It was stronger than mere déjà vu, more like an emphatic Vision.

She spotted Louie Nichols's Gladiator on the cliffs above her. "Gimme some covering fire, Louie!"

"Yo!" The magnification in Louie's goggles was at normal, and they were letting in all available light even though they were still opaque from the outside. He relied on his tank's range finder rather than on the one in his goggles as he swung hard on the steering grips, imaged the shot through his helmet receptors, and got ready to let one off.

The red spied him just as he took aim, and leapt. Louie was so busy trying for the shot, trying to lead his bounding target just right, he didn't realize one of the assault craft had swung in low over the battle.

The cannon round hit the craft's underbelly almost dead center, jolting it—perhaps the most bizarre event of a bizarre day. The Bioroids halted, seemed to listen to something, and began retreating.

In moments their Hovercraft came to the surviving invaders, summoning them like faithful hunting hounds. The enemy mecha jumped aboard, and raced for their ship. As it turned to go, the red Bioroid paused to look at Dana one last time. It seemed to be staring right into her eyes, thinking thoughts that were meant for her. Once more she had the strange sensation, like some impossible memory, that she and the foe had some essential bond.

"We did it, Lieutenant!" Angelo called out, elated, over the tac net. "Not bad for a baptism of fire!"

"Sir, all enemy mecha and landing craft have withdrawn," Green reported to Rolf Emerson. "They ran for it as if they weren't going to stop until they were home. The mother ship has moved back to a geostationary orbit. You were right, General; we sent them packing once before and today we did it again! All units are at yellow alert and awaiting further orders."

Emerson turned from his contemplation of Monument City.

"G2 Intelligence staff has concluded, and I concur, that the aliens are here for our Protoculture supply, gentlemen. You may be sure that we will see them again."

Lieutenant Colonel Rochelle, Emerson's adjutant, looked dismayed. Colonel Green said gruffly, "Let 'em! My boys and girls're ready, anytime!"

But it was depressing news. Protoculture was essential to the operation of Robotechnology, and the Earth's supply was limited. As far as Humans knew, all that remained of it was what was left after the Robotech War. The Zentraedi had originally invaded Earth to claim the Protoculture Matrix from Zor's crashed ship, but subsequent investigation had failed to turn up anything. It seemed the last remaining means for the actual production of Protoculture was gone forever.

Zentraedi and Humans alike were unaware of what lay beneath the three burial mounds near the ruins of Macross City—of the trio and wraiths who guarded the wreckage of the SDFs 1 and 2 and Khyron's vessel, and the unique treasure they protected.

"Damage report?" Emerson said.

"Fighting was contained to unpopulated areas," Green answered.

"Minimal losses; Fifteen ATAC squad stopped those aliens' butts *cold*, sir," Rochelle added.

Emerson nodded. "The Fifteenth, hmm? Looks like Lieutenant Phillips gets himself another commendation."

Rochelle *ahemmed*. "He wasn't there, sir; they didn't get him out of the slammer in time. Lieutenant Dana Sterling led the squad today."

Emerson permitted himself a proud smile. "Ah, Dana. Yes."

The drudgery of checking over all their mecha and equipment after the battle, preparing to go into combat again at a moment's notice, was sobering work to the 15th. They had won, but they had taken losses, too; dead and wounded who might easily have been any of those who came through unscathed.

After they got the order to stand down, they worked, fighting every instant and every portion of the battle again, over and over, among themselves; recounting and arguing, joking and lamenting.

It was still going on up in the ready-room, when the door opened and Sean Phillips walked in, escorted by Nova Satori. "Hi, guys. Life pretty boring without me around, was it?"

"We managed to keep ourselves occupied." Louie grinned.

Nova snapped, "By order of the commander, Alpha Tactical

Armored Corps, Sean Phillips is reduced to the rank of private, second class."

Everyone in the room gasped. Nova went on. "And as for you, Sterling—"

Dana snapped to attention. "Whatever I did this time, ma'am, I'm ready and willing to accept disciplinary action."

"Quiet!" Nova barked. "You've been promoted to permanent command of the Fifteenth, Lieutenant. Don't blow this chance, because I'll be keeping an eye on you." Nova turned and exited. Except for Sean, everybody there was watching Dana.

The computer-controlled bar that dispensed only non-alcoholic drinks to those on duty was ready to serve something a little stronger. Sean had already eased over to it, and was taking a long pull from a tall glass. "Private Second Class Phillips!"

Sean spat out part of his drink as Dana shouted his name. "*I'll* be watching *you*," she told him.

Sean looked startled, then gave her a dose of the famous grin. "Just give the word. I'm yours to command, Lieutenant."

There was knowing laughter and some catcalling from the rest of the 15th, but Dana was satisfied that the point was made, and that everyone accepted the change of command. She couldn't afford to have Sean second-guessing her, or having her troops expect him to.

Sean was a great soldier and a definite asset, but she didn't think much of the idea of putting a busted CO back in the outfit he had commanded. But it looked like she would have to live with it.

Later, in the shower, she ran over the things she would have to get done as soon as possible. Replacements for the casualties and the destroyed Hovertanks would be coming in, and she would have to do some reshuffling of her Table of Organization and Equipment. There would be training and more training, to make the 15th a well-integrated fighting unit once more—and little time to do it in.

In the midst of all her ruminations she suddenly stopped, standing stiffly, immobilized. As vividly as if it were actually there before her, she saw the red Bioroid again . . . felt again that strange sensation of a bond between them.

CHAPTER EIGHT

I am satisfied that I've now ended any blasphemous talk of treating with the aliens, either among my subordinates or the Council. These aliens are an abomination, a violation of the Divine Plan; we must exterminate them all. That is our holy obligation.

From the personal journal of
Supreme Commander Anatole Leonard

EASSURING MEDIA ANNOUNCEMENTS OF THE SITUATION were quickly followed by a formal declaration of war. The armored troops posted on street corners and patrolling everywhere were more for the civilians' peace of mind than any deterrent value.

But the Human race had been very much a military culture since the Global Civil War and, organized along feudal lines under the UEG, accepted the necessity that it must fight once again.

"Headquarters' thinking is that we can't sit around and wait for them to make the next move," Rochelle told the assembled officers. "The opinion is that their Robotechnology and scientific edge outweighs our numbers and home-field advantage. We've got to start calling the play—draw them out with fighters, lay in a missile barrage on that flagship. We've got to keep them off balance."

"It's just not in our blood to sit and wait for them to call all the shots," a G3 light-colonel agreed.

A G2 intel major took off his glasses, shaking his head. "But their counterattack might end up annihilating our entire defense force, don't you understand that?"

"That's right, it's insane to attack now! It's like jabbing a stick

58

into a hornets' nest—a very *short* stick," a recon captain laughed harshly.

"That will do!" Rochelle bit out the words, and the assembled officers subsided. Dana looked up and down the table, studying them.

Marie Crystal was there; so was Fredericks. So were some other ATACs people, some Civil Defense—it was odd to know that her unit's survival might depend on these people, or theirs on her.

"The decision has been made," Rochelle went on. "You in this Strikeforce will carry the war to the enemy. Lieutenant Sterling's squad will handle rear guard and provide an entrenched fall-back position. There will be additional coverage from nearby missile and artillery bases and the various ready-reaction units. Lieutenant Crystal, your Black Lions will be our spearhead."

They already knew the plan, had the briefing files before them and the tactical displays on screens around the room, but he reviewed for them one more time anyway. When he was finished, Marie said, "We'll be ready, sir."

Dana made a sour face. "Some people have all the luck. Don't get your tail shot off, Marie." Marie slipped her a wink.

"Colonel Fredericks," Rochelle was saying, "I'm putting these units and their installations on red alert as of now; I want the bases sealed and a full commo blackout imposed. This attack has to come as a complete surprise. No one enters or leaves or communicates with outsiders in any way except by my direct order, understood?"

Fredericks seemed to be savoring the idea of having his MPs coop up the Strikeforce troops and make them toe the line. "Most affirmative, sir; you can count on it."

Sean Phillips snarled, "Somebody tell me what's goin' on here!"

He stood with fists cocked by the Hovertank parking bays, glowering at Louie Nichols and a few of the others who were running maintenance.

"I d-didn't want to bring it up," Louie fumbled, familiar with Sean's tripwire temper. "That is, uh—"

"As of today, you've been assigned to a new Hovertank," Bowie intervened.

"Somebody slipped up," Louie hastened. "With you bein' in the brig and all. Guess they forgot to tell you." Sean grabbed a handful of Louie's uniform and pushed him back against a tank, growling like an angry wolverine.

Sean's tank, the *Queen Maeve*, was his pride and joy, finely tuned so that it ran like a watch, lovingly maintained in every way. That made it that much more undesirable, in Louie's estimation, to be the one to tell him what had happened.

Louie yelped, and Bowie hollered, "Cut it out, Phillips!" But before anyone could break it up, Sean dropped the lanky tech-freak and wheeled, eyes roving the bays.

"Listen, they sent in a new guy from the replacement depot when you went in the stockade," Louie confessed, rubbing his chest. "Then Dana got put in command and then they jailed her and then they sprang her and made her CO—in all the confusion, the repple-depple new guy got *Queen Maeve*. And *he* was one of the guys who didn't make it, Sean."

"Your tank's in about a thousand pieces, what's left of it," Bowie added.

"So which one's mine now?" Sean seethed. Then his eyes fell on a shrouded object in an end bay. "Ah! What's that? That mine?" He ran to it before anybody could tell him the truth.

Sean dragged the cover off, losing balance and falling on his rear. He sat, looking up in amazement. It was a new tank right off the production line, a gleaming war mecha with all the latest in Robotechnology refinements.

"Oh-hh," he breathed reverently. In another moment he was clambering aboard, laughing with delight. Bowie and Louie came dashing over.

"Beautiful, isn't it?" Louie said. He and Bowie traded resigned looks; there was going to be trouble.

"Man, this baby was built with me in mind!" Sean chuckled, running his hands over the controls, checking out the cockpit. "What a sweetheart! Nobody else in the Fifteenth could handle this darlin'—"

"But I'm afraid somebody else is going to have to try, *Private* Phillips," a voice said icily. Dana stood nearby, arms akimbo.

Sean leaned back in the pilot's seat, interlocking his fingers, staring off at the ceiling and ignoring her. "Nope."

Dana came over to stand beside the *Valkyrie*'s highsheen side. "This tank's reserved for officer use, get it? Read my lips while I repeat this, Private: you'll never fly this craft."

So the honeymoon was over and it was time to really decide who ran things in the 15th. And Dana held every ace. Recalling how much Fredericks seemed to enjoy having him as a house-guest down at Barbed Wire City, Sean resigned himself. "Damn it all, there ain't no justice in this world."

Bowie and Louie and some of the others were just barely stifling their laughter. "This tin can and me woulda been history on wheels. But—" He looked to Dana. " 'Course, there's still a chance for you and me, little darlin'.' "

She had been waiting for that. Sean had been decent enough to her as a CO, had never put any moves on her—but that was before he wanted something from her. "The only history we'll make is when I send your sorry tail back to the stockade for insubordination, hotshot."

He knew her well enough to realize she would do it. Some females just didn't know how to be friendly. Sean hopped out of the tank. "All right; lay off. I was only thinkin' of the good o' the Corps. So, what'm I supposed to use as a ride?"

She gave him an innocent expression and pointed. "Look right up there."

Sean let out a curse. "That crate? The *Bad News*? That's the oldest junker we've got!"

"And it's all yours, Private; you'd better get to work on it."

Sean heaved a deep sigh. "Thanks."

"Now, listen up, everybody," Dana went on. "Orders from High Command. We move out at thirteen hundred hours tomorrow. The brass decided it's time we whip some hurt on these invaders."

There were the usual snafus, the usual hurry-up-and-waits, but all units were in place only slightly after the scheduled zero hour.

For some reason, the Strikeforce commander changed his mind at the last moment, ordering another TASC unit to go in as first attack wave. Marie Crystal stood in the base control tower and watched the VTs of the Redhawk Team take off.

In the 15th's ready-room, the tankers waited in full armor, helmets in hand. Dana strained to catch a glimpse of the fighters rising from the distant Fokker Base. *Man, I hate this waiting in the background! This is driving me zooey.*

"What's the matter, Lieutenant?" Louie Nichols smirked. "Pulling reserve duty doesn't agree with you?"

"Sometimes it's tough to just stand pat," Angelo hinted.

Dana whirled on them. "As you were! I don't need to be reminded what my orders are!"

At that moment the PA squawked, and they got the order to move out. The 15th was among the very last units to be moved into place as Southern Cross command made some final arrangements in defensive deployment.

The tankers charged for the drop-rack, and in moments they were tearing down the highway, bound for an industrial area at the edge of Monument City. The 15th went with helmets off for the time being; manual controls would suffice for a mere drive from point A to point B.

Playing shuttlecars, is that *all we're going to get to do?* Dana fumed.

The Redhawk VTs came up in a ballistic climb, then formed up for attack and headed straight for the alien. In the command center, Emerson and his staff studied a visual image of the underside of the Robotech Masters' flagship.

It was an elongated hexagon, a huge lozenge of alloy the size of a city, its superstructural features as big as sportsdomes and skyscrapers. The blinking of its white and purple running lights—if that was what the lights were—was the only sign of activity in the ship.

"No doubt their sensors have detected the Redhawks, sir," Colonel Green said.

"Attack begins in thirty seconds," Rochelle reported. "I wonder what they'll throw back at us?"

Emerson leaned forward to call down to an officer on the operations floor below. "Are you sure you haven't picked up any reaction from the alien?"

The officer surveyed the consoles manned by his techs, and the main displays big as movie screens. "That's affirmative, sir; no response of any kind."

Few things could have troubled Rolf Emerson more, but it was too late. The screens began relaying visual transmissions from VT gunpod cameras as the fighters went in. One flight broke off to make a pass over the enemy's upper hull, to size up the objective and draw fire so that a second flight could make suppression runs on the alien batteries.

The cameras showed conical structures the size of pyramids, poking up out of a landscape of systemry. There were ziggurats, onion domes, and towers like two-tined forks. But the ship remained silent and unresponsive, inert except for the lights. Two more passes didn't change that.

Emerson knew things had gone too far to simply pull back now. If he didn't give the order, Leonard or someone else farther up the line would. "All right; we'll *provoke* a response. Commence attack immediately."

* * *

The VTs swept in, releasing dozens of Mongoose missiles. The missiles were powerful and accurate, producing brilliant explosions and lots of smoke, but when the smoke cleared, it was evident that they had caused no detectable damage, none at all.

Then someone said, "Sir, I'm getting some movement from the enemy ship."

"Right." The Redhawks' leader could see them, too, now: elongated, bulbous things like inverted teardrops, looking more glassy than metallic, gracefully grooved with spiral flutings. They reminded some Human observers of chandelier light bulbs, emerging from housings or rising up from where they had lain flat along the hull, to come to bear on the fighters.

"Everybody look sharp for antiaircraft fire," the Redhawk leader said, though he had the feeling that those were more than just some AA guns snouting out to track his squadron.

The green–white serpentine discharges of energy bolts crackled from the long muzzles, writhing and intertwining like living things. All at once they were coming from everywhere, the invader ship protected by a blazing network of interlacing streams of destruction. One VT was blown to bits, then another, and two more, before the pilots could get clear.

Someone said, "Sir, I'm picking up an unidentified craft emerging from the mother ship; ID signature indicates one of their assault craft. Correction: make that *two* assault ships."

The XT craft zoomed out together and pounced on the VTs even as the Redhawk leader was warning his men. A pair of VTs attempting to strafe a cannon emplacement was taken from behind, blown to flaming wreckage by streams of green–white energy discs.

Emerson ordered the Redhawk leader, "Break off the attack on the mother ship and get on those assault craft at once! Keep them from getting back to the mother ship or reaching any ground targets."

"I copy, sir." But the VT leader didn't sound very confident about it.

Green told Emerson, "Sensor data indicate the power in each of those landing craft is superior to that in the entire Redhawk squadron."

"I'm not surprised, Colonel," Emerson said. "But it's not just a question of raw power. If we can isolate them—who knows?" Sufficient firepower concentrated in the right place might do the trick; one torpedo could sink a carrier, after all; one rocket could destroy an arsenal.

* * *

The Redhawks caught up with one of the assault craft on its plummet to the ground; they were having a hard time spotting the second.

"Okay, we've got 'im now; keep 'im in sight," the leader said, moving into position for a shot at the invader's tail. The VTs' guns hosed green–white energy discs much like the aliens'; it was Robotechnology against Robotechnology.

But the target was gone abruptly. The Redhawk leader craned to see what had happened. "Where'd he go?"

He got his answer a moment later. The landing boat had gone into an incredibly powerful dive, looped, and come around onto the Redhawk formation's tail.

"Break and shake!" yelled the leader, but it was too late to evade. The alien picked off the rear ship in the diamond of four, and went in after the others. A second burst from the invader got another VT and sent it plowing into its wingmate.

The leader came in for a high deflection shot at the bandit, but it evaded with amazing agility and slid around onto his tail, chopping away at him. The tight packages of destructive energy holed the fighter's fuselage, and sent the Redhawk leader plunging to the Earth, trailing flame and smoke.

The fighting had brought the ships down close to the ground; there was no time to eject.

Sean Phillips watched the Redhawk leader's VT plow into the ground, off in the distance, toward the air base.

"My God! Unbelievable! A whole squadron wiped out in two-three minutes!"

Angelo Dante shook his head slowly. "Maybe we didn't beat them the other day after all; maybe they just wanted to wait for the Main Event."

"We did beat them once, and we can beat them again," Dana contradicted loudly. But a moment later she gasped as she saw the second assault ship link up with the first. They turned and began an approach on the base, the origin of the fighters that had attacked their flagship. As they went they began dropping Bioroids, the mecha dispersing and advancing on their antigrav Hovercraft for an attack.

And at the head of the mountainous, armored invaders rode the red Bioroid.

CHAPTER NINE

A WW I biplane had perhaps fifteen gauges and instruments, a WW II fighter some thirty-five or so. By the time of the Global Civil War, a front-line fighter-bomber had approximately four hundred indicators, readouts, and so forth. Robotech mecha made those planes look as simple as unicycles. Is it any wonder that the RDF, and the Southern Cross Army that took its place, had little use for people with fast reflexes and the rest of it, but who couldn't, image, couldn't think their mecha through a fight? It was the only conceivable way of controlling such an instrumentality.

And even that wasn't always enough.

Zachary Fox, Jr., *Men, Women, Mecha:*
the Changed Landscape of the Second Robotech War

THE CONVENTIONAL ARMORED VEHICLES AND SELF-propelled artillery at the base did their best to send up defensive barrages, but the Bioroids were too agile and their counterfire too devastating. The Bioroids wove down through the tracers and solid-projectile fire, and then opened up.

Blasts from the discus-shaped hand weapons sent the field pieces and battle tanks up in violent ruin. The missile batteries didn't have any better luck; more Bioroids came in at low angles, taking them out with highly accurate fire.

Pilots scrambled to their planes, horrified that they had been caught on the ground by the incredible speed of the alien attack. Men and women with one foot in the cockpit, or just lowering the canopy, or beginning their taxi, were incinerated in their exploding aircraft. Whole lines of parked ships disappeared in tremendous outlashings of energy. Armored leg infantry, bravely attempting to defend the base with small arms, were mowed down on strafing runs.

The Bioroids began cutting the base to ribbons, determined to turn it into one huge funeral pyre, beaming down communications and sensor towers, strafing barracks, savaging every target they saw.

One of the few TASC units to make it upstairs was Marie Crystal's. She formed up the Black Lions, then brought them around to do whatever they could in the face of the appalling counterattack.

They spied a flight of blue Bioroids led by the red. "Okay, nail those bastards!" she yelled; the VTs went in. But the Bioroids on their flying platforms were fearless and capable; they came head-on, knocking down first one Lion, then another.

But the VTs got on the scoreboard, too; Marie waxed a blue thoroughly, saw it fall in burning pieces along with its broken sky-sled. Another blue fell like a blazing comet, and the dogfight intensified. But Marie had a moment to notice that the red leader had disappeared, had gone on, she supposed, to direct the attack on the base.

But she couldn't break loose to give chase; just then two more blues jumped her.

Far across the valley, on the outskirts of Monument City, the 15th watched smoke rise from the airfield. It was obvious to them all now that the attack was completely concentrated there, but they received no orders to move in the midst of the turmoil. Dana could only guess what a madhouse the command center must be at the moment. Apparently nobody had stopped to think that the Hovertanks were needed. That, or the message had never gotten through.

"Those dirty, murderous—" Bowie grated.

Dana made a decision. "Let's mount up."

That left Sean and Angelo to stare at her in amazement while she scrambled aboard her gleaming *Valkyrie*. Other 15th troopers raced to get rolling.

As *Valkyrie* eased forward on its surface-effect thrusters, Angelo moved to block the way. "No! Have you gone crazy?"

Dana throttled back, the tank settling, the pitch of its engines dropping. "Outta my way, Sergeant."

"We're assigned to protect this sector, Lieutenant. Or have you forgotten those orders?"

She stared down at him from her cockpit-turret. "What, so they can rip us apart one unit at a time? The commo nets are useless, and there *is* such a thing as personal initiative."

Angelo lowered his head like a bull to glare at her. "Our orders are to wait right here."

She gunned the tank again. "Then *you* can wait here, and remind 'em of that at my court-martial, Angie."

The big sergeant had to dive aside as the 15th followed Dana, screaming off to the battle. Sean, arms folded, was watching him. "You know she's gonna end up right back in the brig," Angelo said bitterly.

"Assuming we still *have* a brig." Sean smiled. Then he was boarding the *Bad News.* "See ya later, Sergeant."

Angelo was left to scratch his head, dumbfounded, as Sean hurried to catch up with the others. Then he heard another voice, a very strident one.

"Lieutenant, you are deserting your post! Return at once! Acknowledge!"

Nova Satori was pulling up on an MP Hovercycle, her blue-black hair billowing behind her under the confinement of her goggle band. She was yelling into a radio mike. With the communications systems so completely bollixed up—both from confusion and damage done by the raiders—she had been pressed into service as a messenger.

"Get back here or face a general court-martial!" she called, but she stopped the cycle near Angie's tank; it was pointless to try to follow the 15th when they were moving at full speed—especially into the middle of a pitched battle.

Angelo shook his head in resignation. "Then you'd better draw up papers on me, too, Lieutenant." He jumped to his tank, the *Trojan Horse,* ignoring her outcries.

Big shuttles and transport ships, tiny recon fliers, hangars, and repair gantries—they were all equal targets of the blue horde. And the defenders were becoming fewer and fewer.

Trying to see through the smoke in the cockpit of her damaged VT, Marie plunged toward the hardtop. She had become an ace and more in the course of the attack, but number six had *her* number, and got a piece of her just as she finished him.

She managed to throw the switches and do the imaging that sent her VT into Guardian mode. It reconfigured just in time, foot thrusters blaring as it ground in for a standup landing.

As was often the case with Robotechnology, damage suffered in one mode was less critical in another, and the very act of mechamorphosis seemed to help the craft cope.

But she was no sooner at a standstill than enemy blasts gouged the runway all around her. The red Bioroid, like a stooping bird of prey, plunged at her. The Guardian's thrusters gushed, and she leapt it high.

Gotta take him out! They raced at each other, firing.

"I copy." Green turned from the phone to Emerson. "The airbase is putting up only scattered resistance, sir. It could fall at any time."

Emerson wondered what would happen if it did. Would the aliens try to annex it—set up ground operations? Or would they simply plunder what Protoculture they could find and torch the whole installation?

Leonard and the other higher-ups had been adamant that the Hovertanks be used to protect population centers rather than deployed to Fokker Base, where Emerson wanted them in the first place. But now the top brass were out of contact, communication virtually nil, and Emerson had room to use his *own* personal initiative.

"Bring in the Hovertanks. Get the Fifteenth over there ASAP."

"Even 'as soon as possible' isn't soon enough, sir," Rochelle observed. "It'll take too long to get a message through and redeploy them."

"Try anyway!" Emerson snapped. Rochelle rushed to obey.

"Sir, shall I inform all units to be ready to evacuate the base?" Green hazarded the question. Emerson just stared at the tactical displays.

Marie and the red Bioroid played out their deadly game of high/low hide-and-seek as Bioroids and VTs clashed, fired, and were destroyed on all sides.

Marie's Guardian landed and glanced around the repair area in which it found itself, a big pulse laser gun held like a pistol in its cyclopean fist. "Okay, where y'at now?" she murmured.

She didn't have to wait long for a reply. The red came swooping over a building at her. The Guardian sprang up to meet it; as in a joust, they passed within arm's length of each other, firing away, dodging each other's fire.

But when Marie landed, the knees of her mecha gave way, cut in half by the red's energy shots. The Guardian crashed down on its chin, dazing her. She fought back the wooziness, popping the canopy and dragging herself out.

She pulled off her helmet and shoved it aside, then froze. The red had settled its Hovercraft right in front of her, and she was staring up the barrel of the discus-shaped pistol, a barrel as big as a storm drain. Marie watched, unmoving, waiting for the end.

But it wasn't the end either she *or* the red had expected. A cannon bolt came in, a thin one at high resolution set for long-distance work. The shot didn't quite take off the end of the Bioroid's arm; it missed by only a few feet.

Still, it threw up smoke and rubble, and appeared to stagger the red. Marie hugged the hardtop, shielding her head. Then she looked up, and saw where the shot had come from.

The 15th was lined up abreast and waiting. Dana stood up in her cockpit-turret, surveying her handiwork proudly as the red Bioroid pivoted to face her. She waved. "Over here, ya big metal dink! Can't ya even tell when somebody's *shooting* at you?"

As she hoped, the Bioroid rose on its platform, forgetting Marie, and rushed at her. Dana was back in her tank in a moment, the *Valkyrie* going through mechamorphosis to Gladiator, the rest of the 15th emulating her.

Dana's next salvo missed the red but knocked it waffling off course, nearly out of control. The rest of the ATACs were shooting at the blue Bioroids that surged in at them. The massed main batteries of the 15th skeeted alien after alien out of the sky; the air shimmered with heat waves at the vast forces unleashed. Thick smoke from the burning base and the exploded mecha billowed through the air. The squat, massive Gladiators volleyed and volleyed, picking off more invaders while keeping the rest at bay with their tremendous volume of fire.

The red Bioroid dropped from its platform to the ground, and was joined by a blue, to attack on foot.

"One on your right, Lieutenant!"

"I see him, Bowie!" Looking after each other was a habit they would never break, she guessed. That suited her.

The red popped up from behind a mound of fallen concrete to stitch the side of her Gladiator with a row of shots. Any other mecha in the Earth arsenal would have been severely damaged or blown to smithereens, but *Valkyrie* was scarcely touched. Dana traversed her gun barrel and whammed away again. The shot went wide, and the red and the blue came charging at the 15th's position.

The red seemed as big as Mount Everest. It and Dana fired at the same moment, near misses that rocked each other. "Bowie, cover me!"

"You got it!" Bowie drove the red back, firing with everything his tank, the *Diddy-Wa-Diddy*, had, even though the twin barrels of the secondary batteries scarcely scratched the Bioroid's hide. The rest of the 15th was busy maintaining the shield of AA fire;

Dana went to Battloid mode, springing through the air to confront the red.

The two mecha catapulted through the air at each other. Dana protected herself from the enemy's handweapon shots with the thick curve of armor mounted along one arm like an ancient duelist's *targone*.

In the meantime she drew a bead with her own titanic battle rifle, the reconfigured tank-mode cannon. The shot pierced the red's left shoulder in a spatter of molten metal and oily black smoke, a mecha-wound that spewed sparks and shrapnel and tongues of flame. The red went reeling and flailing back through the air, hit the ground with a crash, and lay sprawled. Dana rushed at it, intending to rip loose the power couplings and tubes connected to the head area, to disable it completely.

But as Dana charged in, it resumed firing. Only the reflexes of a young professional in superb condition let her leap her Battloid out of the line of fire. The red jumped to cover and so did Dana; in another moment they were playing duck-and-shoot once more.

"Angie, lay cover for me, can you?"

"It's on the way!" The cannonade from the *Trojan Horse* sent the red bounding in retreat; Dana's Battloid launched itself after.

"Gotcha now!" She fired on the fly, scoring another hit on the left shoulder as the red twisted and flipped to avoid. The alien landed awkwardly, nearly toppling. When it spun for another blast at her, she was ready.

Dana's rifle-cannon bolt blew the discus-shaped hand weapon right out of the red's fist; it stood unmoving, as if stunned.

Dana centered it in her sights. *The war's over for you, hosehead!* At last, Earth had a POW.

Just then the Bioroid was in motion again. Straight for her. *"Huh?"*

It strode directly at her weapon's muzzle. "What the—"

She fired again, a high-resolution beam that seared a hole right through it at the waistline. The red stumbled, regained balance, and charged her like an enormous defensive tackle.

Again the visions and strangely compelling images filled her. Was it because this was how she was to die? she wondered. The wash of emotion and disorientation paralyzed her where she would otherwise certainly have cut the foe in two with as many shots as it took.

Before she could shake off the trance, though, the red dropkicked her Battloid. She shook off her stupefaction and her Battloid reached to grapple, but the red had already jumped high, its flying disc platform skimming in under it to bear it away into the air.

The alien fired at her with the weapons emplaced in the steering stem's pod; she barely rolled out of the way in time to avoid being hit. The red zipped past.

"That tears it!" The *Valkyrie* hurled itself into the air, mechamorphosing. It landed solidly on both feet, in Gladiator mode, main battery traversing, Dana's sight reticle searching. *Let's see how they like it when I clean house on their assault craft!*

She fired off a max-power round, recalling how Bowie's accidental shot of the day before had momentarily stopped the invaders. She aimed for it and hit the glassy blue dome on the upper side of its nose, presuming that to be the bridge; the shot shattered the dome and elicited a splash of secondary explosion, smoke, and flame.

The red tottered again, shaken by the bolt as much as the assault craft, and its emotionless tinted visor-face swung back for a look at Dana. She and the rest of the 15th opened up on the raiders with everything they had, primaries and secondaries hammering. Three more of the blues fell in the blaststorm, but the red and the rest wove through the fire to return to their smoking, listing ship.

The raiders dove aboard. The rust-red attack ship realigned, then dove upward out of sight at great speed, before the ATACs could bring weapons to bear on it.

CHAPTER TEN

Suddenly, a new Triumvirate
Dana, Nova, Marie,
Each zigzagging from her side toward
The center of the triskelion.

Mingtao, *Protoculture: Journey Beyond Mecha*

HE BIOROIDS WERE ALL TIED IN TO THE ASSAULT ship," Rochelle reported. "Signal Intelligence and ground observers, sensors, and after-action reports all agree," he added. "The Bioroids were forced to retreat when Sterling got a round into the ship and disrupted their command capability. At least we've got *some* idea how to handle their mecha."

But it was obvious the enemy would be much more careful next time. Emerson rubbed his face wearily, feeling the bristles and looking forward to some sleep. "At least there's a *little* good news."

"Yessir. Um—" Rochelle broached a very delicate subject. "About Lieutenant Sterling abandoning her post and disobeying orders—what d'we do?"

Everyone knew Emerson was Bowie Grant's official guardian and Dana's unofficial one, but that had never made any difference as far as the young people's treatment in the Southern Cross military. Emerson knew what he would do to *any* junior officer who had done what Dana had, and after a moment's hesitation conceded to himself that it was only just.

Dana was singing loudly and, as usual, badly off key. The shower spray came down at her steam-hot, and she massaged out bruises and sore muscles. She bit her lip once or twice, pausing in her song to fight back images of the red Bioroid.

Maybe these thoughts were some alien weapon? In any case, she mustn't fall prey to them again!

The battle had been bad enough, but there was also a row of sleepless nights ahead, repairing and running maintenance, getting in replacements and shuffling the TO&E and doing yet *more* training, to get the 15th combat-ready again in less time than it could possibly take.

There was a pounding at her bathroom door. She could hear Nova Satori's voice over the rushing water, "Just can the arias, Lieutenant, and get a move on."

Dana reluctantly left the shower, winding a towel around her, and emerged from the tiny bathroom cubicle in a cloud of steam. "What d'you think, Nova? Do I have a future in show business?"

The MP lieutenant sneered. "Sure, sweeping up after the circus parade. Now, hurry up; we're late."

Dana was perfectly content to dawdle; Nova refused to tell her where she was being taken, or why, but it seemed pretty plain. "Aw, take it easy! You'll have me back in your lockup soon enough!"

Nova was leaning against the wall with arms folded. She blurted out angrily, "The ceremony's already—" She stopped, saw that Dana had caught it, shrugged to herself, and went on. "I'm taking you to receive a promotion for valor.

"They're bumping you to first looie."

"Come in, Space Station Liberty! Space Station Liberty, Space Station Liberty, this is Earth Control, Earth Control, please acknowledge, over."

The transmission had been going out ever since the Masters appeared to begin their probings of Earthly defenses. The UEG and Southern Cross were certain that Liberty was still there in its Trojan Lagrangian point—Number Five—out near Luna's orbit. All indications were that the crew was still alive. In some way the scientists and engineers were still trying to understand, the Masters seemed to be watching everything on the spectrum out Liberty's way. An op would no sooner try a frequency than it was jammed, at least as far as Earth–Liberty links were concerned.

With the flagships' arrival in Earth orbit, even the relay telesats had gone dead, and in the wake of that first barrage from Captain Komodo, the satellites had been blasted from the sky. Earth-based commo lasers were useless, what with the distortion caused by the planet's atmosphere.

But the communications people doggedly kept trying. Radio Station Liberty, with its unique Robotech long-range commo gear, was Earth's only hope for eventual contact with the SDF-3 and Rick Hunter's expedition. More, Liberty's personnel were Human beings, cut off from their home planet; Earth must make every effort on their behalf. A rescue mission out to Liberty was impossible, though. Earth lacked the ships, equipment, and facilities to mount such an expedition in the foreseeable future, now that its main aerospace installation had been so badly ravaged by the Bioroids.

But a research team over in the encryption systems shop at Signal Security came up with a makeshift solution. Earth and Liberty could phase their equipment to jump frequencies, seemingly at random, from one to the next, in milliseconds, and get in brief communications on each one before the Masters could jam it. The result would be resumed communications with Liberty and, it was hoped, Moon Base survivors.

The only problem was, somebody had to get the word, and the meticulously worked out schedule of freq jumps, through to Liberty.

"Now, I'm not going to b-s you," the briefing officer said to the young unit commanders ranged around the big horseshoe table. "Getting a tight-beam commo laser up into orbit and punching through a signal to Liberty is going to be one hairy mission."

He looked around at the leaders from Cosmic Units, TASC, ATAC, and the rest. "Supreme Headquarters is calling for volunteers. Personally, I think it should be done by assignment, but there it is. So far, only Lieutenant Crystal of TASC has consented to go on this mission."

Dana knew very well whom he was waiting for. Along with the Black Lions, her 15th had the only real combat experience in dealing with enemy mecha, and the heavily armored Hovertanks were the most effective weapons Earth had. Like any soldier who had been around for a while, she knew that one of the basic rules of existence was never to volunteer. Still, a little something extra would be expected of the ATACs; she knew that when she applied for training, and so had everybody else in the 15th.

She swallowed and rose to her feet. "You can deal us in, sir." Marie lifted one eyebrow and gave Dana a half smile.

"Very commendable," the briefing officer nodded. "But we're going to have room for only three Hovers. You pick."

Dana got the point of what a critical assignment she had volunteered for when she discovered that the mission briefing was to be given by General Emerson himself.

He wasn't sweet, gruff Uncle Rolf then; he was all business and military precision. His only concession to their former relationship was when, shaking her hand—as he had Marie's and the others'—he gave her a short, minimal flash of smile and growled, "Good luck, Lieutenant Sterling; go get 'em."

She decided to take Angelo and Bowie. Bowie accepted it without any show of emotion, with barely a word of acknowledgment. Angelo had to put on an elaborate show, with a lot of talk about going head-on against an enemy armada single-handed, but Dana had confidence in him ever since he went along with her "personal initiative" decision to race to the rescue at Fokker Base.

The rest of the 15th showed some disappointment about being left behind, but kept it to themselves, even Sean. Dana reminded herself to be wary of the ATACs' own heartbreaker, but she was beginning to feel that she could rely on him, too.

Emerson and Green stood studying the image of the enemy dreadnaught. "Are you sure Sterling and Crystal are qualified to command this mission, sir?" Green's voice echoed through the command center. "They do seem rather young for so much responsibility."

Emerson nodded thoughtfully. "Yes, but they're the best we have at leading our most powerful mecha, and they're the only two unit commanders alive who've engaged the Bioroids. And both did it effectively."

Emerson pursed his lips for a moment, then added ominously, "If anyone can do it, they can."

A command center captain named Anderson pointed out changes in the readouts; the enemy mother ship was in motion again. "They're moving into a lower orbit again, looks like."

All the launchpads for the real heavyweights were still out of commission. There were only two left that could accept shuttles, and so the mission was built around that limit; the launchpads were reusable, of course, but not in a short enough turnaround time to be of any help. Repair to damaged pads was going on around the clock, but that was of even less use today.

The two tiled white shuttles sat like delta-winged crossbow

quarrels on the inclined launch ramps. Marie was in the pilot's seat in the number one ship, the *Challenger IV*; only a few hundred yards away sat the *Potemkin*.

Her copilot, Heideger, was an experienced captain from Cosmic Units. It was only over Cosmic's objections that a TASC officer had been given command, but Marie was glad to have Heideger as her first officer anyway; the man really knew his job.

They were completing the long preflight checklist. "We're now on internal computers," Heideger said. The flight deck door slid open and Dana and Bowie entered. They were unarmored, the expected g-load being what it was, and Dana carried—Marie couldn't believe her eyes—a *magazine*! As if this were some commuter hop!

"You're late," Marie bristled.

"We were securing the tanks—" Bowie began, taken aback.

"Stow it, Private, and get to your station!" Marie spat.

Now it was Dana's turn to bristle. "He was following my orders, *Lieutenant*. Or would you like a few dozen tons of Hovertank bouncing around during launch?"

Marie drew a deep breath. "Dana, zip your lip and siddown! We're already in pre-ignition."

Voices from launch control were talking to her and to Heideger. Marie turned back to her instrument panel and began tapping touchpad squares; Dana and Bowie got to their seats just as the main engines began firing up. All systems were green.

Dana sat at a station somewhat behind Heideger, facing outboard, at the astrogation officer's station, which doubled as a gun position. In case of attack, her field of fire would protect the shuttle's port-midships area. Bowie was the next one aft, at the communications position, which also controlled the port-stern guns. Angelo Dante was at the starboard-midships guns, and a shuttle crewman was across from Bowie at the starboard-stern guns.

Dana affected boredom with the final countdown procedures. She had been on launches before, in training, and regarded them as overdramatized and unnecessarily complicated—just the sort of thing the Cosmic Units and the TASC types loved. Tankers believed in results, not ceremony! The whole thing brought out her rebellious streak.

Heideger swung around to take care of something else, punching up revised orbital ballistics, and saw that she had opened the fashion magazine on her lap. "Lieutenant, this isn't like ATACs; pay attention, because we *work* for a living around here, and everybody has to be alert!"

He turned back to his duties at once, and Marie, though she heard it, was too busy to give Dana a chewing out. Dana, as always, reacted to somebody else's orders with stubborn defiance. She opened the magazine and thumbed through the latest looks from around the world.

What d'you know; they were wearing empire-waisted, opaque stuff down in Rio, with metallic body-paint designs underneath— very daring. The rage in Osaka was all synthetic eelskin and lace. Micronesians were going in for beaded numbers with a total coverage about equivalent to a candy-bar wrapper!

The pre-ignition burn went on as the launchpads raised the shuttles up to their correct launch angle. All systems checked out. Marie found a moment in which to hope she hadn't done the wrong thing by not arguing against Dana's presence on the mission. *The kid's got guts, but she's bullheaded. And now she's 'zoided out with this magazine riff. I just hope she can keep her mind right upstairs the way she does on the ground.*

The shuttles came vertical as their primary engines flared and alpine mounds of rocket exhaust rose. At a precise moment the gantries released them, and the two ships lifted off, slowly at first, quickly gathering speed. Dana felt herself pressed back deep into her acceleration seat.

Suddenly her magazine slipped from where she'd tucked it between her knees. It flopped open and pasted itself across her face like a determined starfish attacking a choice oyster. She struggled against it, her yells muffled by the magazine. *Has anything more embarrassing ever happened to me? Nope, can't think of any. . . .*

"Told ya," she dimly heard Heideger say in disgust. No one could help her; they were all weighted by the heavy g's. The best she could do was lever the magazine up and breathe around the edges.

Suddenly a voice said, "This is the *Potemkin*, Lieutenant Borgnine speaking—Oh!"

She realized that his transmission had somehow been routed to her console as well as to Marie's and Heideger's. So, Borgnine was looking right at her. "Um, are you all right?"

"Just a second," Dana tried to say, but it came out, "Mnff uh ff-uh." Meanwhile, at the end of an eternity, the engine burn was over, and she felt a moment's zero-g as the shuttle's artificial gravity cut in.

Dana lowered the magazine, blood rushing back into her white face in a furious blush. She had a feeling she was in for some black and blue from her close encounter with haute couture.

"I'm fine!" she tried to say brightly.

Borgnine's copilot, who looked about thirteen years old, leaned over to inform his boss, "Computers say we're coming up for a new course correction."

Borgnine frowned. "What? That's much too soon. Marie, what d'your internal computers show?"

"We'll check it out and get right back to you," she said. Ideally, they would have bucked the problem back to Earth, but the Masters' interference had already put them beyond communication range.

Marie took time out to chuckle, "Hey, Dana! How'd that facial feel?"

Both shuttles jettisoned the spent solid-fuel boosters as the crews worked to find out why Borgnine's computer was acting up. The *Potemkin*'s autopilot seemed adamant that a course correction was needed, and the overrides didn't seem to be dissuading it.

"I have more bad news," Bowie said quietly. "The invaders are comin' our way. Only this time there are two of them, two mother ships."

CHAPTER ELEVEN

At this moment my hand is bleeding; I crushed a glass in frustration because I can't find out what is going on up there—none of us can! And yet I can tell something has happened to Dana, is happening to her, by means that are my secret to guard.

Ah, the Protoculture, it demands so much in return for revealing its mysteries! My life is a tiny price to pay. And Dana's, even less.

Dr. Lazlo Zand, notes for *Event Horizon:*
Perspectives on Dana Sterling and the Second Robotech War

ARIE TURNED TO BOWIE. "HOW SOON CAN WE GET THAT transmission off?"

Bowie, who was responsible for making the actual transmission, did not think things looked very good. "I'm not picking up anything from them yet, Lieutenant." And the laser hadn't even been deployed yet. It was a very tight one, for the long shot to Liberty; it had been presumed that it would take some time to establish contact, and there didn't seem to be much of that.

"Hurry it up; we've got company coming," Marie said, and went back to her flying.

Borgnine's shuttle carried no special apparatus; it was an escort ship. Moreover, there was little he could do to help anybody now, with his computers leading a life of their own. And all the time, the alien leviathans closed in on the shuttles.

Then, despite anything Borgnine and his crew could do, his engines fired. "Cut your engines! Retrofire!" Marie hollered into her mike. It did no good; *Potemkin* accelerated, directly toward the Masters' monolith that loomed on its vector.

No one could tell whether what was happening was some explainable glitch—some damage done during the Bioroids attack, perhaps, and not detected—or something the Robotech Masters had instigated. It didn't matter; the shuttle blazed toward the invader like an interceptor missile.

Borgnine tried everything he could think of, to no effect. Engines would not shut down, retros wouldn't fire, computers wouldn't listen, and altitude jets were insistently silent.

"C'mon, girl, steady. Steady now," Borgnine implored his ship.

A separate warning system computer flashed red lights and alarm whoopers, saying in its emotionless female voice, "Danger, danger. Collision alert. Collision is imminent, repeat, imminent."

"Lieutenant Crystal, I've got a runaway here," he told Marie. "Nothing we can do." Still, they tried everything they could think of.

An invader ship—the Robotech Masters' flagship—grew huge before them as they bore down on it. "Be informed: this might be enemy-induced. You're on your own. Good lu—" The shuttle slammed into the alien supership at max velocity; the impact and the detonating weapons, fuel and power systems, made an explosion that lit the faces of Marie and her copilot hundreds of miles away.

Marie instinctively put in a transmission to Earth, to inform them of the *Potemkin*'s death, just in case they were receiving down below.

Dana stood frozen by the sudden destruction of so many men and women, hearing Borgnine's last words. *You're on your own.*

"Why . . . why couldn't we . . . help them . . ."

But even more than the shock of the crash, she was frozen by this first close look at the alien flagship. It, too, seemed a remembered thing from an impossible recollection. Superimposed on it was the blank, enigmatic vision of the red Bioroid.

She sat trembling like a leaf at her station, only partially hearing Marie's biting reply. "Nothing we *could* do, you know that. We're all volunteers, remember? To tell you the truth, Lieutenant, I expected better of you. Now, shut up and do your job!"

"Enemy's now at eight hundred miles and closing fast," Heideger said matter-of-factly. There was no point in trying to outrun the swift aliens, and besides, *Challenger IV* had a mission to perform.

"*Potemkin* appears to have been destroyed, sir," the announcement came in the command center.

"What about *Challenger IV*?" an operations officer asked.

"Information limited due to enemy jamming, but the mother ships appear to be closing on the remaining shuttle."

* * *

At a distance of four hundred miles, the flagship launched assault boats. Bowie still had no contact with Space Station Liberty.

"Lieutenant, take over fire control," Marie ordered.

But Dana could only sit, trembling, eyes frozen on her instruments and the pistol-grip fire control. Before her were overlapping images of the alien ship, of the assault craft, and the Bioroid—every moment of her combats against it came back in overwhelming detail, shutting out all other thought. And on the periphery of her awareness were emotions to which she could put no name.

Bowie looked at her worriedly, but there was no time to stop to find out what was wrong. "I show enemy craft at one hundred miles and closing."

Angelo had swung around in his acceleration chair. "Lieutenant, she said 'take command.' Dana? C'mon, snap out of it!"

"Save it, Sergeant," Marie cut him off. "I'll take fire control. Gunners select targets and fire as soon as they're within range."

The assault ships started pitching at longer range than that of the shuttle's guns, but soon the two forces were sufficiently close to each other for both to be throwing out everything they had. The shuttle had a defensive shield that protected it from immediate damage, but the shield couldn't last long under the pounding it was taking.

Marie, Angelo, and the others bent to their guns—all except Dana. The firing controls were standard Robotech setups, as familiar to the ATACs troopers as to the TASC pilot.

The assault craft spread out. "They're trying to surround us!" Marie called as the twin-barreled gun mounts swung and threw out torrents of flaring disc bolts, the enemy answering with the same. "Take evasive action," she added to Heideger.

"Trying, Lieutenant," he said evenly, but the wallowing shuttle was no match for the attackers.

"Sir, enemy vessels are surrounding *Challenger*," a command center officer relayed the news.

"Has it been hit?"

Nova Satori, watching the displays at Colonel Fredericks's side, dreaded the answer. She might have little use for Dana's and Marie's lack of discipline, but Nova was behind them one hundred percent right now, and rooting silently.

"Heavy activity out there, sir, and we're still not getting reliable sensor readings—we can't be sure."

Nova watched the screens and waited.

* * *

"One coming your way, Sergeant!" Marie yelled.

"I see 'im," Angelo said distractedly, poised over his scope and pistol-grip control stick. He led his target and got it dead center; it vanished in a cloud of superheated gas.

"Good shooting!" Marie called. At that moment another bandit drilled a line of holes along the shuttle's port side.

"Shields failing," Heideger said. "Still no contact with Liberty or ground control." Another close one shook the spacecraft.

Marie realized abruptly that Dana wasn't firing. "Sterling, what's the matter with you?" A quick look told her Dana wasn't hurt. "Come on, defend your sector! We need you!"

Got to . . . get hold of myself, Dana kept repeating as if it were an incantation. But she couldn't move, hypnotized by the visions assailing her. By sheer force of will she compelled herself to say, "Yeah. I'm okay."

All at once her trance turned to an all-engulfing fear. *I shouldn't be here! I can't handle this! I'll let everyone down!*

Marie was up, to swing Dana's chair around and slap her hard across the face. "Snap out of it! Stop acting like a coward!"

Dana sat, dazed. Marie turned to Heideger. "Get someone else up here to man these guns!" She jumped back for the pilot's seat.

Dana was staring at the firing control as if she had never seen one before, and another energy disc impact sent the shuttle lurching. "Missed him!" Angelo yelled. "Dana, he's coming around to your side."

More were doing the same; the aliens had realized that Dana's sector was a vulnerable point.

The lurch had thrown Dana against the fire-control grip, and she clung to it by reflex. She instinctively thumbed the trigger button over and over. The assault craft broke off its attack run as her fire nearly nailed it.

"It's nice to have ya back." She heard Angelo's grin in his tone as she fought to center the gunsight reticle on the assault craft.

What was I doing? I could've gotten us all killed! But she thrust the thought aside as the bogie came around for another pass. The reticle centered. *Your time's up, chump!*

She thumbed the trigger again and again. The assault boat suddenly wobbled off course, leaking flame, and explosive decompression turned the leak into a brief *whoosh*, like a blowtorch. The crippled invader disappeared beneath the shuttle.

More enemy ships had been coming in at Dana's field of fire, and thinking it a soft spot, crowded together. She picked off another, and damaged a third as they sought frantically to evade.

"Good shooting, Lieutenant," Angelo admitted.

Heideger got the shuttle back under control and stabilized the damage while the others tried to drive back the assault ships and Bowie made desperate efforts to get a bearing on Liberty.

"I think the only way we're gonna do it is to get the shuttle back on a steady course," he said.

"We're closing with the mother ship," Marie informed them. There wasn't much hope of evading. "Everybody get ready."

Dana waited at her station; it had been a good try, a good try. . . . A gallant final fight.

She wondered where the targets had gone. Then Heideger called out, "The assault ships are withdrawing. They appear to be breaking off the attack."

The shuttle's guns went silent and the crew sat stunned, not believing that they were still alive. "I don't get it," Dana blinked. Nobody else did either.

But Angelo reported, "I'm picking up a directed force field on the mother ship. I think it's a charged particle beam projector."

Suddenly, enormous hyphens of energy were blazing all around them, monster discharges like nothing the Humans had ever seen before. But it seemed the mega-volleys were so enormously powerful that they were far less accurate than the flagship's other weapons.

Or maybe they're just playing with us again, it occurred to Marie. *We'll know in a few seconds.* She hit the ship's thrusters, accelerating as quickly as she dared—straight for the flagship. "Now, if we can just get in under it before it gets us!"

The bright comets of the Masters' superweapon cascaded around the shuttle as Marie wove and sideslipped with all the skill at her command. There were shouts and objections from everybody else on the flight deck.

"There's no such thing as 'out of range' to that particle gun!" Marie cried. "We'll have to get in close, where it can't get a fix on us!" The shuttle shook and seemed to want to come apart. "Brace yourselves!"

The *Challenger IV* dove in at the flagship, homing in under its vast belly. Far above, they could make out something like an enormous fish-eye lens between the hyphens of destruction it spewed forth. Then all at once the shuttle was in an area of peace and quiet, out of the megaweapon's field of fire. The Bioroids, of course, had pulled way back once that big Sunday punch let loose. The shuttle was zooming along all alone.

"Nice move, Lieutenant," Angelo conceded.

She headed in under the gargantuan ship's belly, weaving in and out of the superstructural features. "This is just a breather! There are still those AA cannon that got the Redhawks." And, they all knew, the Bioroids probably hadn't exactly headed home for the locker rooms, either.

Marie shed most of her speed with a retro-burn, steering with extremely wasteful thruster blasts that couldn't be avoided. The shuttle zipped along with the mother ship's underbelly only a few dozen yards overhead. It wove between a stupendous grotto of the insectile communications spars, like a cruise through some eerie undersea city. It passed among upside-down tuning-forklike things as big as high-rises, and downhanging Towers of Babel.

"Looks clear through there, Lieutenant," Heideger said, pointing.

Angelo forgot to breathe for a while, looking around him at the screens, the viewports. The briefings hadn't done the vessel justice. "This thing's gigantic," he understated.

Marie nodded to herself as she wended the ship along. She murmured, "I—I've never seen anything like it. . . ." It felt more like being in a submarine than a spacecraft.

"Say again, Lieutenant?" Dana piped up.

Marie turned a scathing look on her. "Paying complete inattention to practically everything today, are we, *Lieutenant?*"

Dana looked contrite. Marie glanced beyond her. "Hey, Bowie! Any luck getting a beam through?"

Bowie worked away. "Not a chance. No line of sight. Besides, all these electronic echoes and all this energy clutter are frying the avionics."

"Any word yet, young man?" Commodore Tessel called in the command center.

A tech replied crisply, "Well, sir, we're showing *something* on the sensors, but we aren't sure what it is. We're getting sloppy images, and the interpretation computers can't sort them out."

Sean Phillips and Louie Nichols entered the command center. Nobody had invited them, but Emerson noted their entrance, did not object, and his subordinates let things stand as they were. "Anything from the *Challenger?*" Sean asked Nova Satori quietly, anxiously.

The command center was a restricted area; she had no idea what favors were called in or Phillips's wiles had been used to gain entry, but Nova knew she should be chasing the two ATACs troopers out.

It just didn't seem right, though, with so many dead and so many more, perhaps, about to die. "We're getting distorted signals, so we're not sure what's happening," she told Sean.

"There," the tech said just then. "I think that's them! But—the reason our signal's distorted is because they're so close to one of the enemy mother ships. "Hell's own bells! It's right on top of them!"

The shuttle was barely drifting along. "Staying tight as possible," Marie said, tight-lipped.

"Creepy silences. *Man,* I hate creepy silences," Dana muttered.

"I suppose you'd rather have them shooting at us again?" Angelo shot back.

"Don't worry, ground-pounders!" Marie said tartly. "There'll be lots more shooting, and soon." The three ATACs frowned at that; they were armored troopers, not leg infantry ground-pounders.

Marie hunched forward in her chair; the shuttle was coming to the end of the flagship's underbelly. "Get ready to try for contact again."

"Ready and waiting," Bowie said evenly.

"Everybody look sharp," Marie said. "I'm taking us up for a look-see."

She hit the main thrusters and zoomed up from underneath the immense flagship. Immediately, two of the chandelier-bulb cannon swung into place and sent out tangled vines of green-white destruction.

"Oh, *now* they manage to find us, now that we're not hiding." Marie laughed scornfully, taking the shuttle through evasive maneuvers. "On your toes, all of you! We'll be getting company!" Still, the fact that the enemy seemed to have lost track of the *Challenger* once the shuttle was close in underneath was not to be forgotten.

"Alien assault ship on our tail," Angelo called out.

"And I'm picking up two more coming in on our flanks," Dana added.

But the alien ships refrained from firing this time. There was still more that the Robotech Masters wished to know about these primitive Earthlings, creatures like missing links really, who had in some unfathomable manner wiped out the giant Zentraedi.

The launch bays of the assault ships opened, and Bioroids zoomed forth.

Marie had partial shields back, but she zoomed in low to the flagship's upper hull, skimming it, so that the enemy cannon couldn't be depressed low enough to hit the shuttle.

The Bioroids, on the other hand, had trouble getting a clear shot, swarming as thickly as they did; they ran the risk of hitting their own ship or one another.

"Bowie, resume contact-scan," Marie ordered.

"Roger; scanning," Bowie responded. The laser-contact with Liberty required enormous precision. That would mean that *Challenger IV* was going to have to do less maneuvering, at least for a little while. And that in turn meant that somebody was going to have to keep the Bioroids away from the shuttle; repel them perhaps, or better yet, decoy them.

"Take over," Marie told Heideger. "I'm going to suit up." She began making her way to the rear cargo bay, and her Veritech.

CHAPTER TWELVE

You can't get somebody in your sights in combat without spending a lot of time after that wondering if you're in somebody else's.

Remark made by Dana Sterling to Nova Satori

THE BIOROIDS BEGAN TO PRESS THEIR ATTACK; HEIDEGER threw in some jukes-and-jinxes as the top cargo bay doors opened to make Marie's launch less of a clay-pigeon shoot.

The VT roared out into the dark vacuum, and most of the Bioroids turned to pursue at once, leaving the others to dodge the shuttle's fire. Dana and Angelo each managed to flame a blue enemy mecha.

Then it was again all turns-and-burns for Marie, a furious dogfight in the uncaring void. She bagged three of them in harrowing, furious maneuvering much more appropriate to atmospheric fighting than airless space; Robotech craft moved very much in accordance with the pilot's imaging, and Marie was much more comfortable flying where aerodynamics and control surfaces counted.

Then a fourth alien foe got a line of shots into her fuselage, but only at a grazing angle, so that they did little damage. She turned on the blue vengefully, flamed it, and neatly avoided fire from two more.

Suddenly a shape from her nightmares swooped close, the red Bioroid aiming for her. "Oh, no, you don't!" She hit emergency power, blasting away, at the same time putting the VT through mechamorphosis. The VT reconfigured to Guardian mode. Marie

87

was about to come around for another go at the red, but two blues pounced on her before she could.

Inside the shuttle, Heideger yelled, "Marie's in trouble!"

Dana waxed another blue but missed the one behind it. "Look, we've all got our own problems. Bowie, talk to me."

Bowie was intent at his work at the commo suite. "Tentative contact. I think I've got a fix on them."

"Raise the laser-transmitter," Dana ordered; that would risk having it damaged, but there wasn't much time left, and the volunteers would just have to gamble.

Outside, Marie led the first blue along, getting it between her and the second, then zapping it thoroughly. The second came through the spherical fireball of the first, blinded a bit by it, so that she took it by surprise and peppered it with a sustained burst. It, too, was obliterated.

"Transmitter in position," Bowie said over the tactical net.

Marie spared a quick glance while maneuvering and craning for more opponents. "Roger! I see it!" The laser had emerged from an armored pod over the flight deck. It was such a fragile, unimpressive-looking device, it occurred to Marie, to have been the centerpiece of such carnage.

A blue seemed to notice the apparatus and go in for a shot at it, but Marie pounced on it from the six o'clock position and shot the alien war machine to shreds.

"Awright, Bowie, now or never," Dana said, swinging her guns to a new target.

Bowie began sending the encoded transmission in burst format; all the information was contained in a single micro-pulse that was repeated over and over. If just one pulse got through, the Liberty operators could decrypt it instantly, reprogram their transmitters, and resume contact. The pulse-message also detailed what had happened on Earth since the aliens' appearance.

The problem was that the shuttle was being battered so badly by enemy fire that not even the complex compensating gear could keep the beam well on target.

The shuttle volunteers began firing again, pressing the triggers until their thumbs grew tired, as more Bioroids came in at them to replace the ones they destroyed. Marie turned and was a split-second too late to dodge, and the red Bioroid came at her out of nowhere and scored a hit. She twisted the Guardian to avoid the worst of the blast, and smashed against the shuttle's fuselage. "I'm hit!"

"Marie!" Dana yelled over the net.

"It's that red Bioroid," Marie moaned in pain as the marauder came at her in another pass. Her Guardian barely got out of the way, but the red gave an impression of toying with her. "He's too quick for me!"

Dana looked at the scene on the external monitors, wide-eyed. *It's the same one,* she knew with a certainty she never questioned. *The one I—I'm afraid of. But why? What are these strange feelings? And now it's going to kill Marie.*

But a diamond-hard resolve came into her. *No! I won't let it!* "I'm going out there," she decided, rising from her place.

Bowie and Angelo started to object, but she was already dashing aft. "Do your best to hold them. And get that message through!"

The endless drill of the Academy and duty with the 15th served her well; in seconds she was in armor, climbing into her Battloid-mode mecha. *I know how that Bioroid thinks! I don't know how, but I do! I can beat him!*

"More bandits coming," Angelo reported as the cargo bay doors opened again. The doors swung up and out to reveal a volume of space filled with the deadly blossoms of explosions and the streaming discs of the Robotech energy weapons.

A blue saw the opening and tried to ride its Hovercraft right down into the shuttle cargo bay. Dana's Battloid brought up its heavy rifle and hosed the blue with blazing energy, sending it back in burst fragments.

She swung the rifle back and forth, driving back nearby attackers. "Hang on, Marie! I'll be right with you!"

"Thanks," Marie said, sounding harried. "I could use the help."

"Bowie! Any response from Liberty?"

Sweat ran down Bowie's face in rivulets. "Not yet."

Tessel tried to contain his frustration. "Why hasn't Liberty answered? Why?"

Like everyone else in the command center, he was afraid what the answer might be. Perhaps the whole theory behind the plan was wrong, or the equipment wasn't up to the job. Or perhaps there was no one alive at Space Station Liberty to hear.

"Sir, we can't raise Liberty *or* the shuttle. It's beginning to look like it's a wipe, sir," a G2 analyst reported.

Nova heard the sharp intake of breath at her side, Sean and Louie. The three young soldiers said nothing, fearing it might bring bad luck; they watched the screens, not blinking, not moving.

* * *

Dana added the tremendous firepower of her Battloid to that of Marie's Guardian and the shuttle's batteries. Heideger somehow kept minimal shield power, although the ship took a number of hits. The whole area around the shuttle was a crisscrossing of the heaviest firing Dana had ever seen. Bioroids came apart in mid-pounce, only to be replaced by more.

Then Marie called out, "You can't win! You're not even *Human*!" and Dana saw that the red had reappeared like a Horseman of the Apocalypse, diving at the Black Lion leader. Marie and the red chopped away at each other with intense fire until the range was very short, nearly point-blank. Then the red sheered off and came around for another try.

"Dana, he's headed your way! I'm joining you!"

In moments, Marie was in the bay beside Dana, shoulder to shoulder, muzzles aimed high as the enemy leader rushed in at them again, his oval hand weapon putting out rounds one on top of the next.

It became a collision course, the two women and the alien vying to see which side could put out a more murderous volume of fire. VT Battloid and Hovertank Battloid stood their ground as the red closed in.

"Just keep shooting, Dana, keep shooting!"

Bolts from the heavy cannon that was Dana's rifle scored at last, ripping into the edge of the red's visor, so that smoke and burning scrap spun from it. The red veered off yet again, to regain balance.

"Don't stop! He can't last long!" Marie said as the red came in at them on a new track. "You've got the angle; he's yours!"

Dana's Battloid spread its feet and stood like a metal titan flinging starflame. The red came in, and, as if events had become snarled in some kind of chrono-dimensional loop, she scored a sustained shot on the same part of the left shoulder she'd hit in the fight at Fokker Base. Once more the shoulder nearly separated; once more the red tumbled away like a seared and flailing Lucifer cast down.

Dana's mind reeled. Was this past, present, future? Was it real? "I—I got him!" she cried, bringing herself out of the disorientation.

"Good shooting, ground-pounder." Marie laughed. As before, the blue Bioroids broke off their attack as soon as their leader withdrew from the field of battle.

Inside the shuttle, Bowie activated the new frequency-jumping commo system, patching an incoming message through the tactical net so that Dana and Marie could hear it. "This is Space Station Liberty calling Earth, Space Station Liberty calling Earth. Do you copy? We have relayed your message to Moon Base. Repeat, Moon Base has resumed contact as well."

Bowie and Angelo were up, pounding each other on the back. They were about to drag Heideger into it when they saw that he was slumped, lifeless, in the copilot's seat. The joy ebbed from them.

"Oh, no . . ." Heideger had taken a fatal charge from an energy surge during the final attack. Angelo, nearly in tears, closed the man's eyes for the last time.

"They made it! Mission accomplished! *Challenger*'s heading home!" a command center tech whooped. Sean and Louie stood watching the place turn into a madhouse of celebration. Even Nova Satori was smiling, eyes shining.

Louie adjusted his dark goggles and shrugged to Sean. "With three ATACs up there—what'd they expect?"

High above the Earth, in the flagship of the Robotech Masters, all aspects of the encounter were reexamined and subjected to a coldly merciless scrutiny. The Scientist clone triumvirate had primary responsibility in this matter, though, of course, the Politician triumvirate was working in close coordination—a coordination difficult for the uncloned to imagine.

Silent discussions and debates took place, moderated through the Master triumvirate's humped Protoculture cap. The many mental voices spoke in the precision of artificially induced psi contact; they were unhampered by any emotion.

It was clear that the space station and the lunar base were in contact with the primitives below once more, in a fashion that thwarted, for the time being, the Masters' ability to jam. The Humans had millions upon millions of frequencies among which to jump, and even the resources of the Robotech Masters were finite—the more so now that Protoculture was in such short supply.

Resumed communication was of little moment, though, and the losses in Bioroids and assault ships was of scant concern. It was the *un*known that troubled the Masters. Thus far, there had been no sign of the enigmatic weapons or powers that had destroyed most of the Zentraedi race, and some five million warships.

Certainly, there had been no use of any such thing as yet. Still, though the Masters were arrogant and supremely egotistical—despite their decadence, and the blind eye they turned to their own decline—they harbored no illusions when it came to recognizing the power of giant cloned warriors they had created. Whatever had defeated the Zentraedi—had virtually swallowed the countless goliaths and their fleets and mecha like some black hole—was a force to be feared even by the Robotech Masters.

Perhaps all that had gone before was a clever Human ruse, it occurred to the cold intellects in the flagship. Perhaps all of this sacrifice and seeming vulnerability on the part of the primitives was a strategy to draw the Masters on until they met the fate of the Zentraedi.

Another body of opinion had it that whatever force had obliterated the Zentraedi—and there was evidence that that force might have been the Zentraedi themselves—it no longer existed. Therefore: press ahead; strike for the treasure beyond treasures that lay below.

And overhanging all debate was the need, the hunger, for Protoculture. Though the Masters would never have framed it so, without Zor's greatest creation they were a dying race of refugees; however, with it they would be, as they thought of themselves, Lords of all Creation.

The longing and need was greater than any mortal could ever conceive; a vampire's thirst was a mere dryness of the throat by comparison. A decision was reached in the wake of the battle; the next phase of the Robotech Masters' plan was set into motion.

CHAPTER THIRTEEN

*Of course, Dana Sterling wasn't physically isolated in her upbring-
ing; indeed, it was somewhat rough-and-tumble at times. But, while
there are indications that she was not a virgin by the time she gradu-
ated from the Academy, she seemed to have formed no strong sexual
bond of any kind—as if something were saving her as surely as
Rapunzel being kept in a tower.*

*I refer the reader to the writings of Zand, Zeitgeist, and the rest as
to what that something was; it seems certain that the events at the
mounds and thereafter bear them out.*

Altaira Heimel, *Butterflies in Winter;
Human Relations and the Robotech Wars*

TWO HOVERCYCLES HOWLED THROUGH THE NIGHT SIDE BY
side.

Dana knew there would be road grit and dust from the cinders
of the wounded Earth to wash from her hair later, but she didn't
care. Their headlights threw out cones of harsh light across the
desolation as she and Bowie barreled across the wasteland.

A night patrol would ordinarily have been a crashing bore. It
was a little like guarding the Gobi Desert; who was going to steal
this piece of real estate? But the Southern Cross Army was on
yellow alert in the wake of the *Challenger* ruckus, and everyone
who wasn't grabbing some much-needed sleep was on ready-
reaction standby. Heel-and-toe watches in the 15th's ready-room
had just about driven Dana crazy, so she had jumped at the chance
to take this patrol, to get away from the base for a while. Bowie
had naturally come along, loyal and concerned as any brother.

Besides, there was a chance, however remote, that the
Robotech Masters might try an invasion, which gave the joyride
a little added voltage.

Her hair was only partly confined by the band of her goggles
and the techno-ornament hairband she wore; Dana reveled in the

whipping of the thick, short blond waves, and the feel of the wind in her face.

When the base signaled, she let Bowie handle it; she was enjoying herself too much. Then reality caught up with her.

Bowie cut in even nearer, until they were knee-and-knee at sixty miles an hour. Both slowed a bit, so they could talk rather than use their commo link; Bowie knew Dana hated to have the base eavesdropping.

"Headquarters has been tracking us!" Bowie yelled it slowly, so that she could read his lips—lit by his instrument panel lights and the backwash from the headlight—as well as strain to hear. "They said to come about, right now!"

They both took a low hummock of sand hardened into glass by a long-ago Zentraedi blast, like a pair of steeple-chasers. Dana nodded to him. "Okay, let's go." She'd learned early in life that freedom never lasted for long.

But as they swung around, their headlights scaring up rabbits and strange radiation-bred things that had come out in the darkness, sending them scuttling for cover, Dana exclaimed in surprise, then yelled, "Hold it!"

Both cycles retroed, then came to a halt, engines at low idle. *"Hmmm."*

Bowie saw that Dana was gazing off into the distance and looked that way. "Hey!" he yelped.

Searchlights, or at least what looked like searchlights, quartered the sky over in the east. In an earlier generation someone might have said it looked like a supermarket opening.

Dana shifted her bubble goggles up onto her forehead for a better look. "That sector's been totally off limits for as long as I can remember," she pondered. Someplace over there was the decaying vessel that had at last destroyed Macross City, and the mounds in which the Human race had entombed the remains of the SDF-1, SDF-2, and the flagship of Khyron the Backstabber, the mad Zentraedi battlelord.

Entombed there, too, was whatever remained of Bowie's aunt Claudia, Admiral Henry Gloval, and the three young women whose pictures Dana's godfathers had virtually worshipped all their lives.

Bowie was poised on the balls of his feet, straddling the cycle, which bobbed gently on its surface-effect thrusters, engine humming. "Lieutenant, I dunno. And I'm not eager to find out, either." He had seen the mounds from afar, many times, but something about them made him queasy, troubled.

She had been thinking along just the opposite line, he knew; Dana turned a vexed look on him. "Say again?"

"Just a joke! Just for grins!" he fended her off.

"Not funny, Private, got me?"

"Awright! Okay!" But he saw that the squall was past. She was looking at those lights again. "What d'we do now?" he asked, as if he didn't have a sinking feeling what the answer would be.

They were the strangest mecha, or robots, or machines, or whatever they were, that Dana had ever seen. There were a dozen of them or more, like big walking searchlights the size of a Gladiator, only the round lenses had been narrowed down like a cat's iris until they were thin slits. And the slits were rotating, so there were narrow fans of light reaching into the sky, seemingly thick, then thin, then thick again when seen from one side. The rays swept back and forth across the giant cairn of the fallen SDF-1, some occasionally sweeping past, to throw up the skybeams Dana and Bowie had spotted.

Dana couldn't make head or tail of the two-legged searchlights stumping back and forth or standing in ranks and seeming to irradiate the mound, but there was something else there that she did, and it almost made her heart stop.

The voice sounded reedy and distorted, like a Human voice heard by single-sideband transmission: artificial somehow, and quavering. "There can be no mistake," the red Bioroid said. "The creatures of this planet have attempted to disguise the Protoculture with a radioactive substance."

The alien mecha paced around the work area, fifty yards below, holding a strange circular instrument or tool in one mighty armored fist. At the time, Dana didn't question how she and Bowie heard and understood the words; it seemed that they were being amplified over a PA system.

"You will notify the mother ship that our calculations were correct," the red went on to a rank of three blues who stood at attention. "We will make further preparations to excavate."

But the red knew it wouldn't be as simple as that, and that the effort to regain the Matrix faced opposition more serious than mere Human interference. The three inorganic entities, the Protoculture wraiths the Masters had detected upon their arrival, had made their presence felt. Somehow, the guardians of the mounds were resisting the Bioroids' efforts to get a precise fix on exactly where the Matrix was, meaning that excavation using the

Masters' unsubtle techniques ran the risk of damaging or even destroying the last existing means of Protoculture production.

More, the wraiths exuded an air of arctic-cold confidence, an aura that the Plan, the great Vision, of the original Zor would not be derailed. The wraiths were shaped by the Protoculture, of course; even the Robotech Masters must proceed with caution.

Yet the wraiths had evinced no physical or PSI powers beyond that of a small confusion of the Bioroids' instruments. The red Bioroid could think of two ways to proceed: a gradual, almost surgical exhumation, or a brute scooping-up of the entire area of the mounds and everything around them for later dissection. Neither process could be undertaken while the local primitives were still capable of mounting resistance; that would risk destruction of the Matrix with a stray missile, energy barrage—any of a number of awful possibilities.

The red Bioroid awaited the Masters' commands while the trio of black apparitions within the mounds, created by the Matrix for its own purposes, following the instructions and the Vision of Zor, gloated, and mocked the Robotech Masters.

From the top of the cliff overlooking the invader operation, Dana and Bowie looked down with cold coursings of despair rippling through them. An enemy vessel larger than an assault ship, looking somehow industrial, utilitarian, hung with its lower hull a mere few dozen yards off the ground. Other Bioroids were moving heavy equipment around on pallets and sledges that never touched the Earth.

How could they have gotten past our sensors? Dana thought with a sinking feeling. *Earth is wide open to them!* She simply stored the references about Protoculture and excavation for her after-mission report; the intel analysts would have to deal with all that.

She and Bowie were lying on their stomachs, peering down at the demons'-foundry scene of the Bioroid mining. Dana debated between the urge to report this catastrophic alien beachhead at once and the awareness that every scrap of intelligence could be of pivotal importance—that another few moments of eavesdropping might yield the key to the whole war.

Training and textbook procedures won out for once. She had vital information to get back to headquarters; follow-up would be somebody else's problem. She reached out to give Bowie a silent, all-but-invisible contact signal, a code of grip-and-finger-pressure that would tell him it was time to leave the area quietly, then run like hell.

That was when the red Bioroid, halting, turned its lustrous blue-black faceplate up in the Humans' direction. Dana heard the words as clearly as if the stylized ornament in her hair were a real earphone: *I sense an enemy presence.*

The blues were alert at once. The red turned ponderously and stalked through the din and strobing of the work area, the great head craning to look up at their hiding place. "Geddown! Freeze!" Dana whispered, doing the same. They heard the resounding metal tread stop near the base of the cliff. *It seemed to emanate from this area,* the mind-voice said. *It would be advisable to have a look.*

A flood of light came from below. Against all training and every instinct save curiosity, Dana was moved by those same mysterious impulses to peer over the cliff's edge.

Bowie whispered, "What's goin' on, Lieutenant?" but she simply couldn't answer, transfixed by what she saw. Bowie eased up for a peek, too. He saw that Dana was transfixed, in some kind of daze.

The red Bioroid had halted and opened, its chest plastron swinging forward, pieces of the shoulder pauldrons and its helmet beaver swinging away, like an exploded illustration in a tech manual. Nestled within was a glowing orb, like a gunner's ball-turret, with a metal framing like lines of latitude and longitude, giving out a radiance even more intense than the searchlights'. The light from the orb grew brighter and brighter, then shot out long lines of shadow as something moved in its very heart. A tall, long-legged form emerged from the center of the unbearable incandescence.

Most of the Human race had been working on the assumption that these new invaders were like the Zentraedi, ten times larger than Human stature, and that the metal things the Earth was fighting were basically offworld giants in armor. That obviously wasn't true, and Bowie didn't know what to expect now. He was thinking along the lines of revolting, icky critters, when a young demigod stepped out to stand with one booted foot up on the edge of the open chestplate, surveying everything around him with an air of supreme hauteur.

The creature seemed to be male, and looked Human enough, though with an elfin air and long eyes and ears. The face was a chiseled archetype, ageless and slender, handsome as a Grecian statue. Masses of lavender ringlets tumbled around the being's head and shoulders. The limbs were long, too, but muscled and graceful; the torso was slender but powerful and well defined in the tight, shiny black costume the Bioroid pilot wore.

The outfit had a military look to it, with high, open collar, broad yellow belt, and scarlet demisleeves covering the forearms. At another time, the face would have been handsome, almost beautiful, Dana realized, but at the moment it was stern and watchful. She was having difficulty breathing, and it suddenly felt as if the air were thin, superheated, low in oxygen. She breathed short, quick breaths too rapidly, and watched that face.

Bowie gulped, then gasped, and that triggered a gasp in Dana. They seemed to be sounds too small to be detected in the noise of the alien work area, but somehow the red Bioroid pilot became aware of the observers, whether by hearing or some higher sense.

They heard his words quite clearly, though his lips never moved. *Just as I thought: there they are!* Then he spoke directly to them, mind to mind. *Do not attempt to escape! You will remain where you are!*

Lights! Sentries: take them! the willful demigod commanded his horde. Dana, faint and panting for breath, drew on every reserve of will as she fought the red Bioroid pilot's silent compulsion. Then she felt Bowie's hand close around her upper arm, pressing her ATAC arm brassard hard into the flesh just as the fully dilated searchlights swung round beams to converge on the troopers' hiding place, and it seemed to break the spell. The blues were pounding toward them, weapons coming to bear.

Dana and Bowie slid and churned and scrambled back down the incline, abrading hands and ripping uniforms, tumbling and skidding. But in time they reached the base, already up and running. They were two ATAC regulars in superb shape; ignoring the minor hurts, hurdling boulders, they were astraddle their cycles and gunning the engines in moments.

Behind them they could already hear the racket of preparations for the chase, like the baying of hounds. And the only word of encouragement Dana had left to give her blood brother, brother in tears and in arms and in peace, was a word used carelessly by others but emphatically in the 15th squad: "Faster!"

The cycles sprang away, trailing spumes of dust in the moonlight, nearly standing on their tails, and Dana felt the naked vulnerability any tanker would in that situation. Her thought, like Bowie's, was for the safety of speed, *speed* . . . but there was swift pursuit on her track already, and she knew better than virtually anyone else alive how fast those Hoverplatforms moved.

The aliens had turned the gleaming, enigmatic faceplates to Zor Prime, their leader, who screamed silently, *All Bioroids to your Hovercraft!*

Then the Hoverplatforms rushed out from the landing ship, in answer to the mind command, the blues thronging for battle, and the red Bioroid, with the hypnotic alien inside once again, leapt high to land on its skyriding platform with sinister grace. The red came after Dana and Bowie, a very Angel of Death.

The canyon was too narrow for evasions; Dana and Bowie went high and low, rode the highside of the stone walls, and let centrifugal force pull them down, over and up again to ride the opposite wall. They crisscrossed and shot along, all the time waiting for the shot that would end their lives; alien annihilation discs crashed around them. But there was no side street; it was a flat-out race. And the swift Hoverplatforms were erasing the cycles' lead at a fearsome rate.

"Hey, Lieutenant! These androids're gonna be right on our necks in another coupla seconds!" Bowie yelled over the rush of their passage.

Androids? Now, why did I assume they're clones? Dana wondered even as she reached down for the short energy carbine strapped into its scabbard beneath her saddle. With its wirestock folded, a Hovercyclist could fire it with one hand if the need arose.

"Well, how about a little target practice, Bowie?" she called back to him, trying to sound as if she didn't have a misgiving in the world.

Bowie didn't quite achieve a smile as more discs ranged around them, detonating. "Anything's better than this!" He started freeing up his own carbine.

They got ready to turn. "Don't fire until I do."

"You got it, Dana!"

They had ridden together and trained together enough to swing their cycles in tight bootlegger turns at almost the same moment, coming end for end and charging back at the onrushing Bioroids.

"Now!" Dana leaned to one side of her handlebars, steadied her weapon with both hands, and fired. The surprise move by the cycles caught the Bioroids completely off guard. In fact, the enemy firing stopped as the aliens tried to figure out what was happening.

And some incredible luck was upon her at that moment. The carbine was a powerful small arm, but nothing compared to weapons that had already failed to down Bioroids; nevertheless, the bolt hit a startled enemy mecha and knocked it off balance, so that it fell from its Hovercraft.

Dana swerved to elude the red, and drove for the hole in the invader formation left by the toppling of the blue. For a split-second she was among the huge offworld mecha, as a crashing shook the ground, then she was beyond. Dana waited for a disc to annihilate her, but none came.

She chanced a quick look back, and realized that Bowie wasn't with her anymore. She came through another sharp turn in a shower of dust and grit, and stopped short. Far back, the red Bioroid stood with one enormous, two-toed foot crushing the smoking remains of Bowie's cycle.

And, high aloft in the vast metal fist, it held Bowie. In the strange silence following the first passage-at-arms, he lifted his head and spotted her despite the knocking-around he had been through.

More, she could hear him. "Make a run for it, Dana! Save yourself!"

This, after she had led him into this horrifying mess. "Hang on!" she hollered, and pulled her cycle's nose up and around like a rearing charger. She roared straight at the gathered Bioroids.

Bowie screamed for her to turn back, but he could see that she wasn't about to. The red felt him struggle, and closed its grip until he couldn't breathe, his ribs feeling as though they were about to give.

Dana came racing directly at the red, which waited motionlessly. Dana saw in her mind's eye the unearthly eyes of the pilot. She leaned off to one side of the saddle, firing, praying for another miracle shot.

But this time a blue jumped into place in front of the red, to shield its leader and the prisoner with its own body. Two more leapt in to flank it, and the three laid down a murderous fire with their hand weapons. Dana rode straight into it, juking and dodging, triggering madly.

All three of the aliens began to get her range, their discs converging in a coruscating nova of destruction. It was so close that it jolted her from her bike, do what she might.

Bowie, straining, saw the Hovercycle go up in a deafening thunderball. He put everything he had into one last effort to escape, to get to Dana and, if she were dead, to somehow avenge himself. But the red closed its grip tighter and he slumped, unconscious.

CHAPTER
FOURTEEN

*Just like I tense up whenever somebody says the word "alien,"
there's a word that always gets Bowie sort of silent and thoughtful.
Even if—and I've seen this happen—somebody innocently mentions the
intermediate mode of a Veritech, Bowie sort of goes sphinx.*

And so, I react the same way, too, a bit. Nobody can say "Guardian" to me without conjuring up the image of General Rolf Emerson.

> Remark attributed to Lieutenant Dana Sterling by
> Lieutenant Marie Crystal

WHEN BOWIE CAME TO, HE WAS STILL BEING HELD BY THE
red. It was supervising from one side, as the blues picked through
the wreckage of Dana's cycle. There wasn't much left, and what
was was scattered wide. The Bioroids hadn't even been able to
find pieces of Dana.

At a silent signal from the red, the searching stopped. There
was no telling whether the Humans had reported the aliens' presence; the all-important mission to recover the Protoculture Matrix
took priority.

The Bioroids boarded their antigrav platforms and flew back to
the mounds, where strange lights still probed sky and ground.
Bowie lay helpless in the red's fist, weeping and swearing terrible
vengeance.

But from a cleft of rock, a battered figure pulled itself up to
watch the invaders go. Dana spat out blood, having bitten her own
lip deeply and loosened some teeth in the fall. Her body felt like
one big bruise. Fortunately, her tough uniform was made for this
kind of thing, and had saved her from having the flesh rubbed
right off her in the tumble. The many practice falls taken in training had paid off, too.

After she had been jolted from the cycle, the aliens had kept
firing at it, thinking she was still aboard, unable to see it well in
the midst of the explosion and raining debris. She managed to pull

herself to safety outside the area where they looked for her remains.

But she could feel no gratitude. "Bowie!" She tried to draw herself up, to follow after the Bioroid pack, but whimpered in sudden agony at the pain that shot through her shoulder.

Dana was brought before General Emerson without much cleaning up and only the most cursory debriefing. Whatever she had discovered was still going on, and time was all-important. Her left arm was in a sling; the medics said it wasn't a dislocation, but it was a painful sprain. She had survived the crash better than she had any right to.

Emerson put aside the dressing-down Dana had coming for disobeying orders; there were more important matters at hand. Besides, if it hadn't been for her curiosity, Earth might very well have remained ignorant of the alien landing until it was too late—if in fact it wasn't already.

"I've been informed that you've had a closer look at these alien Bioroids," Emerson said as soon as Dana saluted and reported.

"Yes, sir. In the wasteland north of Section Sixteen."

"And a Human being, or something *like* a Human being, was operating one?"

Dana couldn't hold back a little gasp, as a sudden vision of the red Bioroid pilot came to her. "That's the way it looked from where I was hiding, sir."

Rochelle turned to his superior. "General, Human or not, what would they be looking for out in that wasteland?"

"Could they be scavengers or something, looking for salvage?" Green interjected.

Emerson shook his head irritably. Green was a steady sort as a combat leader, but the suggestion was ludicrous. These invaders had come from an advanced culture with a highly developed technology, and everything about them suggested that they had an extensive technological and social support system behind them—at least until recently.

"No, that can't be the answer." He had read Zentraedi debriefing files as thoroughly as anyone. "They're in the service of the Robotech Masters."

Rochelle drew himself up. "Then, sir, I suggest we attack as soon as possible, before they become impossible to dislodge from their foothold."

Emerson shook his head again. "Not yet. First I want to know more about this situation, and about these Bioroids. And above all, I want to know what they're looking for."

Dana said plaintively, "But one of my men has been taken prisoner! Please, you have to let me go in there after him!"

"Permission denied." Emerson rose to his feet, no happier with the necessities of the situation than Dana was, but in a better position to see the overall picture.

"It was your decision to return to headquarters with this intelligence. It was the correct thing to do; we're fighting for Earth's survival. A lot of lives have been lost already, and more are certain to be before this thing is over. But our mission is to repel an alien invasion, do I make myself clear?"

He did, to all those listening. They were all soldiers in a desperate war, even Bowie, who meant so much to him.

But all Dana kept hearing were those words, *it was your decision.*

At the barracks she wandered back toward the ready-room, sunk in despairing musings, until she realized someone was blocking her way.

Angelo Dante leaned against one side of the doorframe, arms folded, his foot braced against the other. "Well, well! Aren't we forgetting a little something? Where's Bowie, Lieutenant? I hear he didn't make it."

Her face went white, then flushed angrily. She tried to move past, still feeling shame and failure at Bowie's capture. "Move it, Dante."

"I call that pretty tough talk for somebody who cut and ran and abandoned that kid out there like that."

Dana made a sudden decision and met Angelo's glare. "If I *hadn't* abandoned him, there wouldn't be anybody to go out and get him back, would there?"

With her foot she swept the leg supporting all his weight from beneath him; Angelo ended up on the floor with a yelp. "Got it?" she finished with a slow smile, shucking off the sling. Her arm hurt like blazes, but this was no time to be hampered.

Angelo was looking up at her with his mouth open, not sure if he was going to jump her and give her the drubbing she had coming, or congratulate her for what she seemed to be saying.

"Sergeant, it is my considered opinion that this squad needs some night training maneuvers."

He gave her a slow smile. "Like in that off-limits area?"

She stood there and gave him a wink even while she was saying, "I don't know what you're referring to, Angie. *Ten-hut!*"

The big three-striper was on his feet with machinelike speed. "Now, then," she went on. "This squad's gotten complacent, sloppy, and out of practice. Get me?"

"Yes, ma'am!"

"Consequently, you *will* pass on the order to scramble immediately. Tell 'em to stow the yocks and grab their socks, Sergeant."

The Bioroids' activities at the mounds had come to a standstill as the Robotech Masters weighed the problems posed by the wraiths.

Progress was hampered, too, because the red Bioroid was not on the scene. He had taken the prisoner into the forward command ship to examine the Human and see what could be learned. That had proved to be vexingly little; the creature was unconscious, and its thought patterns so unevolved that normal methods of interrogation didn't work.

Bowie slowly came back to life as he felt himself being jarred and shaken. He was still in the metallic grip of the Bioroid leader, being borne along a passageway to the sound of the massive metallic footsteps. Two blues walked behind. The place was stupendous, built to Bioroid scale.

All three mecha appeared red in the passageway's lighting. Bowie glanced around in punchy amazement; the place looked as organic as it did technological, some advanced mixture of the two. One area seemed to be composed of asymmetric spiderwebbing thicker than the thickest hawsers; the curved passageway ceiling had a vascular look, as though it were fed by blood vessels. Tremendous polished blue convexities in the wall might be darkened viewscreens or immense gemstones—Bowie couldn't even guess.

He strained at the grip, but it did no good. "C'mon, ya big ape! Lemme go! Yer crushin' me!"

The trio of Bioroids stopped before a triangular door even taller than themselves. The three door segments were joined along jagged seams, like a triskelion. As the door slid open, so did the red's broad chest and helm, exposing the glowing ball-turret and the pilot who sat there calmly, legs drawn up, looking remote and at peace.

Bowie snarled, shaking his fists. "Oh, so ya worked up the guts to show yourself, huh? Well, what happens *now*, Prince Charming? Afraid to let me go because you'd be gambling with your teeth?"

The red Bioroid pilot studied him as if he were something in a lab smear. Bowie fumed, "What's the matter, pretty boy? Can't you talk?"

The enemy spoke again in that eerie mental language. *Prisoner, you display much bravado. But like all primitives, you've yet to learn the value of silence.*

And the red pilot gave Bowie a quick lesson, tossing him into the compartment that had just opened up. The Bioroid had leaned down some way, so that Bowie wasn't maimed or killed. The fall stunned him, though, knocking the wind from him.

Door and Bioroid were already resealing by the time the captive got a little breath back. "That's right! You *better* hide in that tin can, you stinking coward!"

And then the door was shut. Bowie collapsed back on the deck, hissing with the pain he hadn't let his captors see. "Just you wait, pally!"

After a while he hauled himself to his feet. The compartment he was in was as big as his whole barracks complex back at the base; surely there must be some way out.

But a hurried search yielded little. The place was evidently a storeroom, but the crates and boxes bigger than houses were impervious to his efforts to open them. He could find no escape route, not even a Bowie-size mouse hole. The enemy had neglected to take his lockback survival knife from him, but there wasn't much it could do against the armored bulkhead all around him.

Then he gave more thought to the light far overhead. It was a triangular, grilled affair, and the light source seemed to be high above the mesh. It put him in mind of conduits and crawlspaces. In another moment he was shinnying up the side of a crate, ignoring the pain of his wounds and injuries.

It took him nearly twenty minutes of scrambling, leaping, and balance-walking among the containers and pipes and structural members, and he had to double back twice to try new approaches, but at last he came up under the mesh. He hoped against hope that he wouldn't hear the rumble of the ship's engines for just a while longer—that he could get out before the invaders got whatever they had come for and departed Earth.

He hesitated, the knife in his hand. But then he went ahead, to prize up the mesh and try his best to break free. As far as he knew, he was the only one left alive to sound the alarm to all Earth that the invasion had come. Then, too, there was Dana to avenge.

The instant the knifepoint dug into the seam of the mesh where it rested against its housing, there was an intense flash of light. Bowie didn't even have time to scream; the knife flew from his hand and he dropped.

"Sir, the sun's almost up out there and a recon drone got a look at the enemy position from high altitude," Rochelle reported. "They're just beginning to excavate at the site of the old SDF-1, but we have no idea as yet what they're after or why."

Emerson stretched, yawned, and rubbed his eyes. "We can't delay any longer. Whatever they're doing, we've got to see that they don't accomplish it. They started these hostilities; now it's our turn at bat. All right, you know what I want you to do. Proceed."

Rochelle, Green, Tessel, and one or two others snapped to attention. "Yes, sir!" Then they hurried off to begin implementing the op plan Emerson had approved during the hours of consultations and meetings.

Emerson was left alone to muse. *The only thing in that old wreck is useless, rotting Robotechnology. Well, one person's junk is another's Protoculture, I suppose.*

Something about that stirred a half-developed thought in the back of his brain. There would be an avalanche of operational decisions and problems coming down on him very soon; that was a hard and fast rule with any operation. But he shunted them aside for the moment, and punched up access to the UEG archives.

CHAPTER FIFTEEN

Dear Mom and Pop,

Things are still real quiet here, and my outfit is real rear echelon, so we're far away from the fighting, so I wish you two would stop worrying.

We've got a new commanding officer who's a woman, but she seems to be improving.

I know there's a lot of talk about the fighting right now, but don't sweat it; it's no big thing, and it'll be over soon, and then maybe I can get a furlough and come home for a while.

Say hi to everybody. I hope Pop's feeling better. The fruitcake was great.

Love,
Your son,
Angelo Dante

JUST ABOUT ALL THE OTHER SOUTHERN CROSS UNITS IN AND around Monument City had been mobilized during the night, and needed only the word to move out. The word was given.

This time, it had been decided, the TASC Veritechs, Tactical Air Force, and other flying units would stay out of it, at least for the time being. It had become obvious in the battle at Fokker Base that ground units like the ATACs were more effective against Bioroids in a surface-action situation.

Armored men and women, galvanized by the PA announcements, sprinted to their Hovertanks, troop carriers, and other vehicles. The elite MP shock troops in their powered armor suits, nonreconfigurable mecha as big as Battloids but lacking their Robotech firepower and adaptability, came marching out of their parking bays. Everywhere, the military was in motion, knowing that the enemy was now entrenched on Earth.

The Southern Cross began its deployment to draw a ring of

Robotech steel around Sector Sixteen. But there were already Human defenders on the scene.

Dana peered out from under the canopy of branches that camouflaged her Hovertank. The 15th was spread through a little woodlet at the base of a rise some distance from the SDF-1's final resting place.

She again wondered about the wisdom of riding in high-gloss armor in a high-gloss mecha; certainly, the polished surfaces reflected energy shots and offered protection in that way, but as every cadet learned through backbreaking work under the watchful eyes of exacting instructors, it made them awfully hard to hide.

Now, though, she was concentrating on two blue Bioroids who were standing sentry duty on the top of the rise. One thing about the Masters' fighting mecha: they didn't seem to give a damn about concealment.

And they didn't seem to think anybody else did, either; the blues held their hand weapons and searched the sky, giving only cursory attention to the ground. Dana figured that meant that battle to them was simply straightforward charge and countercharge, in spite of the crude infantry tactics they had appeared to use in the airfield battle.

The ATACs could get only a partial glimpse of what was going on at the excavation sight. It looked as if the labor mecha had been making test bores, and were now preparing to go at it full-choke. Dana hoped that would provide a little diversion, and cover the noise of the 15th's approach.

She counted eight blue Bioroids, spread fairly thin, guarding the part of the perimeter she planned to hit. Dana knew that a Bioroid had a lot more firepower than an ATAC, and more maneuverability if it got to its Hovercraft, but she was counting on surprise and accurate first-round fire for quick kills and a temporary advantage.

Her plan was less than subtle: a few members of the unit would make a dismounted scout and if possible get Bowie out without betraying their presence to the invaders. If that was unworkable, Dana and the 15th would burst through the perimeter, shooting up the place and inflicting all the damage they could, exploiting the edge that surprise would give them to fight their way to the forward command ship. Then the others would fight diversionary or holding actions as needed while she, Angelo, Sean, and Louie went after Bowie.

She had to admit that it wasn't the sort of thing Rommel or

Robert E. Lee might have come up with, but Sean was more or less content with it. She thought Patton might have approved.

Angelo sat cracking his knuckles inside their iron gauntlets. "When d'we attack, my proud beauty?" he said softly into his helmet mike.

Like the rest, Sean sat with faceplate open so that he could breathe fresh air as long as possible, gazing up at the Bioroids through his camouflage screen. He was chewing on a piece of wild mint. "Undaunted, we advanced, to serve the principles of freedom!" he quoted in his most dramatic stage whisper. Then he spat out the mint and closed his faceplate, figuring it was just about showtime.

" 'Forward through shot and shell, we went into the mouth of Hell,' " Louie added resignedly, lowering his visor, too. It fastened and sealed, and his armor was airtight. " 'And pers'nally, I felt unwell, but no one there could smell, or tell—' "

"Awright, *secure* that chatter!" Dana snapped in a harsh whisper. "What d'you think is happening here, an armored assault or a Shakespeare festival?"

Angelo was about to seal up, too. "Y'know, I've got one question: what d'we do if those 'roids spot us?"

"Pray you can shoot faster and straighter than they can." Dana sealed her helmet. "Let's move out, skirmishing order—"

"Watch it, Lieutenant! Up there!" Louie yelled, but Dana had seen the blue he spotted, centered the enemy in her gunsight reticle, and fired even before Louie had finished. Even though she fired with the less-powerful nose cannon of the Hovertank mode, she shot straight and first; the blast shook the Bioroid like a toy soldier, knocking it down for keeps.

Dana was already hovering her mecha on its foot thrusters, turning it end for end and going to Gladiator mode, as she called, "Thanks, Louie! I owe you one!"

Her seat had come around so that she was facing the enemy once again, but now the long barrel of the Gladiator's main battery poked in the direction of the invaders' perimeter. The 15th knew enough about the Bioroids' silent communications by now to be sure others were on the way. "Okay, let's go!" she called.

She launched herself into the air in Gladiator mode; the rest of the 15th followed, most in Hovertank, some mechamorphosing to Gladiator in midair. Two more blues showed up to take up firing stances; Dana nailed one while she was still in the air, and Angelo got the other.

"You go look for Bowie," Angelo called. "We'll keep the blue-birds of happiness busy."

"Check." She was preparing to hop again just when another pair of blues bounded into view. Dana and Angelo leapt their Gladiators away in different directions, avoiding their first salvo. Dana blew one away while Angelo maneuvered the *Trojan Horse* around toward the other's rear flank, traversing his barrel with the speed Robotech controls allowed. The alien mecha sought to spin and take out the Gladiator behind it, but Angelo was ready, and cut it in half with one shot. The Dana leapt *Valkyrie* again, to join him.

"You okay?" It had been a close one, like some oldtime gun-fight.

"Yeah," Angelo said lightly.

"We've got to get in closer!"

Hovertanks and Gladiators advanced in twenty-fifty-seventy-yard leaps now, not wanting to hurl themselves too high and so present a better target. More blues appeared to set up defensive positions; the mecha hammered and belched flame at one another. Concussions shook the ground.

"Units three, four, and five, cover the lieutenant's advance!" Angelo ordered. The ATACs went through a long-practiced ad-vance pattern.

There was a sudden cry over the net. A blue had peppered Lou-ie's area with raking fire, and there were smoking hotspots on the armor of the cockpit-turret of his tank, *Livewire*. Louie was screaming, arms thrown outward. Then he collapsed.

"Louie, what's wrong? You hit?" Angelo shouted over the net. The blue appeared to be surveying its handiwork, rising a bit to look down on the silent Gladiator. "Answer me, Louie!"

Louie, still unmoving, said, "Nah, I'm okay." As the blue rose up from cover a little, Louie straightened suddenly and jumped *Livewire* back, aiming the main battery as he did, greasing the en-emy neatly.

"But *that* clown didn't know it!" Louie finished proudly.

"No more stunts!" Angelo barked. "Just do what I tell you!"

More Bioroids had come up to reinforce the first, taking heavy losses because the ATACs had had time to reach secure cover from which they could fire. Things were settling into a vicious, close-range firefight.

"Move in now, Lieutenant," Angelo said, "but you'd better hurry."

* * *

In another part of the alien work area, back in Hovertank mode, *Valkyrie* wended closer to the giant ship's hull using all available cover. Her visor up, Dana studied the enemy ship. It wasn't a patch on the mother ships, but was still as big as the biggest Human battlecruiser. She tried to shake off the fascination of it, tried to fight off the fear that somehow her Zentraedi blood made her more vulnerable to these new enemies.

Then she nearly yelled aloud. *It's him!*

It came partly as shock, partly as something she had expected, and, deep down, even looked forward to—for reasons she couldn't analyze—to see the red Bioroid poised on an open deck high above. The Bioroid was open, and its tall, slim, deep-chested pilot waited in that characteristic pose of his, one foot on the open Robotech breastplate, his eyes closed as if he were listening intently.

She found herself short of breath, and gave out a low moan. *Mmmm . . .*

His eyes opened and his head came around until he was looking straight down at her. She heard that silent, internal voice of his again, *Hmmm . . .*

A fundamental recognition—something on profound levels to which she had little waking access—passed between Dana and the red Bioroid pilot. This time he shielded some of his thought from her: *This one is no ordinary primitive! She is Of the Protoculture! She has had open access to it; she has the power it gives!*

He watched her, unblinking, and made a sign of acknowledgment, a fey salute, hand going to brow, then cutting away. She heard the quavery mental voice in her head. *Know then, Primitive, that I am Zor Prime, Warlord of the Robotech Masters!*

Dana stared at him for a moment, then lowered her visor again. She sat looking up at him, and he stood gazing down. Neither moved.

Without warning a shot came from one side, a stray heavy-cannon blast from a Bioroid Hovercraft. It broke the spell; Dana maneuvered quickly, to make sure she wasn't in anyone's line of fire. When she glanced up again, the red Bioroid was diving down like a pouncing tiger, its hand weapon held out before it.

"Try again sometime!" Dana was already springing aside, going to Gladiator mode, sending up a hail of fire. The red flipped in midair, landed nearby, and fired back. The two mecha catapulted here and there, firing and jockeying for position.

The foe got three shots into the Gladiator's side in a line, but Dana had a target of her own. She missed taking the red's right arm off, but once again got the broader target, the big discus-shaped hand weapon, knocking it away through the air.

Let's see how you do without your big metal yo-yo!

But the alien recovered like a demon, throwing a punch, rocking the Gladiator back on its thrusters and suspension.

The red behemoth was about to throw itself on the Gladiator, when Dana pulled a move she had been saving for a special, desperate moment—this moment. Her Gladiator leapt high, to come down on the red's shoulders and head with all its weight, a staggering blow that sent the crimson mecha spinning and crashing onto its back.

Dana landed well, traversed her main battery, and fired, but the red was up, vaulting high once more, with astounding speed and agility. It landed close, launching a bombshell punch near her turret, sending the Gladiator to its knees.

The alien's metal fingers sank into the Gladiator's armor as the red lifted the Gladiator in an awesome show of strength, about to tear it to pieces. Dana had no angle with the main battery, but peppered away at the lustrous visor with her rapid-fire, quad-barreled secondaries as a distraction.

She wasn't dismayed at the turn of events though; this invader still had a lot to learn about the ATACs.

Now I've gotcha! She set the Gladiators thick, immensely powerful legs against the other mecha's torso, pushing off and firing thrusters at the same time. She launched herself free, nearly toppling the red again. "I'm tired of fooling around with you!" She summoned up her mecha's Battloid form.

Her landing sent shudders through the Earth she had come to defend. "Okay, Big Red! Time to settle this!"

The red was eager; it came through the air with a tackle so fast and strong that Dana couldn't counter it. She was flipped over backward, crashing against the side of the alien ship.

Inside, the sound of the impact and its vibrations made Bowie shake his head and open his eyes. It took him a few seconds to remember where he was and figure out what had happened. The charge from the mesh hadn't killed him, and somehow he hadn't fallen all the way to the deck. He lay on a monolithic crate a few yards below where he had been standing when the power surge hit him. He checked himself for broken bones, and found none. Then the ship shook again.

"What the blazes is going on here? Hey, if you're hauling anchor, *I want off!*"

* * *

Outside, the red swung a massive punch, but its timing was off. Dana ducked, and the unbelievable power of the Bioroid (plus some power, Dana was sure, that was the red's pilot's alone) let the great scarlet fist penetrate the alien ship's hull.

Dana reacted at once, bringing her Battloid's leg up to shove the Bioroid away sprawling. As she jumped her mecha to its feet, her external pickups registered a human voice, "Well, hi, Lieutenant!"

Somehow, she wasn't surprised; although the odds of finding him, especially like this, were so remote as to be absurd. But it all fit in with the feelings that had been going through her, and the odd sensation—of hidden forces at work—that had been building in her.

"Be with you in a minute, Bowie." She turned to deal with her opponent again.

"No sweat, Dana. Lay a few on him for me!"

But the Bioroid had regained its feet as well, and now came hurtling at her like a cross between a falling asteroid and a runaway freight train. Dana rolled and scrambled, and just avoided being trampled, her Battloid flattened. She heaved it to its feet, and decided to end the fight and get Bowie out of the ship, whatever it took.

Marquis of Queensberry rules seemed to be pretty well out the window anyway, so she didn't feel any guilt as she drew the battle rifle that had been the Hovertank's cannon moments before. The Bioroid didn't seem to know what to do. She fired from the hip, and the first shot blew the visor open.

The red flailed back and sank partway to the ground against the Masters' forward command ship. The ball turret within it was exposed amid smoking, fused components and bent armor. The shadowy form of the pilot lay inert and its pose suggested unconsciousness, or death. The red's knees trembled, then gave, and the crimson Goliath came down like a toppled building.

Bowie was straining at the opening the red's punch had made. "It's just too narrow, Lieutenant!"

Dana brought the cannon around. "Stand away!"

With a volley of shots she widened the hole so that three troopers could have walked abreast through it. It made the air of the compartment almost too hot to endure, to breathe.

He hurried to the opening, keeping clear of its glowing, molten edges. He gathered himself, leapt through. He landed on the back of the fallen Bioroid. When he reached the ground, Bowie smiled at Dana. "Thanks, Lieutenant."

"That's okay. It's nice and restful in the stockade; I could use a rest."

"If they need character witnesses, they'll probably make me appear for the prosecution, Dana."

CHAPTER SIXTEEN

One might have thought the Masters, with their lesser military strength, would have perceived threats to which the mighty Zentraedi were blind.

And the Masters thought they had: they addressed the "wraiths" within the mounds, and the mecha of the Human race. How the ghosts of Khyron, Azonia, and the rest must have laughed there, deep in Tellurian soil!

Major Alice Harper Argus (ret.), *Fulcrum: Commentaries on the Second Robotech War*

BACK AT THE COMMAND CENTER, COLONEL GREEN TURNED to Emerson. "We just got a sitrep from the advance elements of the attack force, sir. It says that Private Bowie Grant has already been rescued."

Emerson whirled from studying the tactical displays. "Explain."

"Well, it seems that Lieutenant Sterling mobilized her squad sometime last night and performed the rescue on her own this morning. But her troops are still engaged with the enemy, and our troops are moving in to reinforce. It seems we've seen only the first round; the enemy is regrouping for another."

Emerson glanced at the maps. "And what's their strength?" He wondered if Dana would be commended or shot this time—provided she lived through the morning at all.

"Roughly equivalent to ours, from all reports, sir," Rochelle supplied. "I'd say we're pretty evenly matched."

Sean Phillips had his visor thrown back. "C'mon, Dana, get moving! What's wrong?"

"You feeling okay?" Angelo asked anxiously.

But she was not. Moments before, triumph had seemed assured. The long, slanting rays of the morning sun reminded her that only a very short time had passed since her attack commenced. Then, before she could scoop up Bowie, her external pickups brought her the creaking of armor.

"I don't believe it!" She looked down in shock. "He's coming back for *more*? It's impossible!"

But the red fist had risen again to grasp the end of her rifle-cannon's barrel, bending it, dragging it down. The weapon was useless now; she released it, backing away, placing herself between the rising Bioroid and Bowie.

"Take cover, Bowie; the rest of you watch for other Bioroids! This one's mine."

Bowie dashed away as the red reached its feet once more. It trembled but moved purposefully and unstoppably. Dana backed up cautiously, her Battloid bringing its hand up for more close combat. She had made up her mind that she was going to deck this foe for good, rip that turret out of the enemy mecha and kill or capture its occupant, or die trying. The two armored titans maneuvered like wrestlers.

Okay, whoever you are! If you can go the distance, so can I! What she couldn't see was that within his turret, the pilot's eyes were closed and he looked for all the world as if he were unconscious or dead.

Just then a fusillade of shots ranged in nearby, blowing huge chunks of soil and rock high. More came in, bracketing the two duelists. Dana looked around. "What in—"

A face appeared on one of her control console displays. Nova Satori! "Lieutenant, I have an urgent message from headquarters. The enemy's regrouping for a massive counterattack. On the other hand, your reinforcements have arrived." She allowed herself a thin smile.

There were more cannonades from the bluffs and high ground all around the advance ship. Positions where blue Bioroids had entrenched themselves or established fire superiority were pounded and roasted, pieces of enemy mecha thrown high. Dana saw Gladiators, Hovertanks, conventional armor, and even some old-style Destroids and Raider X's. There were MP-powered armor, too, much like Battloids themselves. She wondered which one Nova was in.

"Looks like the cavalry arrived just in the nick of time, eh, Dana?" Nova added.

"We'll take care of the cleanup here, Lieutenant," the Strikeforce commander's voice came up over the net. "You and your squad can back off and sit this one out. We—Huh? *What's that?*"

He was looking up because the sun had been blotted out. Something huge had come down into the morning sky. It was a ship as big as a city, floating in with an appalling, slow sureness. And there were others, all having penetrated Earth's sensor defenses, all come to punish the impudence of the primitives below. The six gargantuan mother ships of the Robotech Masters closed in from all sides. The red Bioroid stood looking up at them reverently.

The Southern Cross soldiers gripped their weapons irresolutely, barrels realigned toward the sky, but seemed feeble and ridiculous against the immense power of the starcraft.

Suddenly, the mother ships began disgorging assault craft; the bottle-shapes, several from each mother ship, flashed down at their targets. MP-powered armor, Battloid, and the rest all were caught in intense strafing, with no air cover and little ground cover. But these Earth defenders all fired back, all stood their ground and fought. Men and women hurled defiance and blazing energy salvos back into the skies—and died.

The toll was terrible, even though the attack was short; a carpet of intense radiation blasts took out many of the mecha in the surrounding heights; only Dana and her troops, close to the advance ship, were relatively safe. Conventional APCs and tanks fared even worse, sitting ducks for the assault ships. Gladiators were putting up the strongest resistance; Dana saw two of them converge their fire to bring an assault ship out of the sky in a fiery crash.

Again she heard the quavering, inhuman voice of the red. "Retreat to the forward command ship." The blues followed it away in those kangaroolike, two-legged hops, up a ramp into the ship.

They're not getting out of here because they're outgunned, that's for sure! Dana realized. She was about to yell for everyone to run for it, when an area of cloud seemed to boil away before an intense ray of light, like a beam of supernova. It sprang down into the ground near one of the mounds, though not the one containing SDF-1.

There it ignited, or exploded. A white-hot infernal wind flew out from it, riding a shockwave, carrying before it mecha, powered armor, tracked vehicles, and armored infantry. It fragmented Earth's proudest war machines, tossing them like leaves before it. In moments the formidable attack force was reduced to stunned survivors, wounded, and the many, many dead.

But the Masters had calculated well. They knew a great deal

about the mounds now, knew that the Matrix would be safe for the time being—until they could return and deal with the wraiths.

Dana kept her head well down until the worst of the shockwave and heat had died away. Then she lifted her head, wiping dust from her visor, to see the forward command ship lifting away above her, moving to rejoin its mother ship. Far off to one side, a glowing crater hundreds of yards across gave testimony of the Masters' wrath.

She drew off the winged helmet tiredly, lowering it. It was a singular mercy to see Bowie wave exhaustedly from where he had taken refuge in Angelo's *Trojan Horse*.

Dana was filled with sorrow; nevertheless, she felt no guilt. Whatever the aliens wanted here, she and the others had kept it away from them.

But they'll come again. And then it'll be a fight to the death; we all know that now. A lot of good men and women died proving it today: this planet is ours! And now the Robotech Masters are going to pay!

And now she knew the name of her strangely familiar enemy: Zor.

In their great mother ships, the Robotech Masters pondered this latest development. The fleet of six huge ships withdrew to a geostationary orbit and remained there, silent and enigmatic.

Endless conferences took place between the Masters at their Protoculture cap and the Scientists, the Politicians, and other triumvirates at their lesser caps, and with Zor, their battlelord. The matter of the resistance of the Protoculture wraiths in the mounds was the prime source of discussion, but there were others.

For the time being there was no question of simply excavating the mound and taking the Matrix; the combined impediments of the wraiths and the Humans made that impossible. But the Masters insisted, and the Elders concurred with them, that the primitives *must* have some control over the incorporeal entities who guarded the mounds. Zor was tempted to disbelieve, but in the end agreed with their assessment when he recalled that the female he had battled was Of the Protoculture.

And yet, for reasons he could not explain to himself, he did not reveal this fact—kept all but the most perfunctory mention of Dana from his mind when reporting.

Several things became clear under the compassionless probing of the Masters: they could not take the Matrix by direct assault and dared not simply begin laying waste to the planet; their

Protoculture was in short supply, and their time was running out quickly.

Because their own Protoculture sources were shrinking, the Elders grew restive, demanding some resolution. Added to this was the fact that the Invid might become aware of the Matrix at any time, and intervene.

Using the splendid military skills and cruel, fanatic loyalty they had programmed into the last and finest of the Zor clones, Zor Prime, the Masters considered their next course of action.

A week went by.

In the UEG headquarters the military and civilian leaders of Earth's feudal government met in emergency session. They were desperate and short on sleep, and the observers who had come in from the east still had the stench of carnage and smoking ruin in their nostrils and on their clothes.

What constituted the core of the United Earth Government looked across the long table at its military hierarchy, some dozen men in a vaulted, gleaming hall. At a separate desk, facing the head of the table, sat Chairman Moran, who presided over the UEG. He was an elderly man of medium height and build, with silver-gray hair and mustache, dressed in civilian clothes adorned with the crest of the UEG. He had spent most of his life trying to reconcile the ideals of civilian freedom with the harsh necessities of military strength and preparedness.

The headquarters was a domed building of classic architecture, a new Versailles or Reichchancellory; within were fine furnishings and marble columns and rows of towering MP-powered armor to guard, but none of the men who ruled Earth took any pride or reassurance from those things today. They were disturbed and apprehensive as only the powerful, confronting an unexpected, greater power than themselves, can be.

Moran looked them over. "Gentlemen, many of you have already heard the news. This enemy military commander—Zor, or whatever his name is—has broken his self-imposed ceasefire. At oh-eight-hundred today, local time, he and his assault ships and Bioroids attacked and wiped out a training base in Sector Three. They leveled virtually every structure in that sector and killed nearly every living soul there."

The officers did know; they traded troubled glances, not knowing what to say. The attack had been so swift and merciless that there had been little time for counterattack.

"We've managed to keep word of this from getting out to the

general populace, but there have been rumors," Moran went on. "And we cannot afford a panic! Now, I want to know how this could have happened. Commander Leonard, how on Earth could we be caught so completely off guard?"

Supreme Commander Leonard, top-ranking officer in Earth's military, a big bear of a man with his shaven, bullet-shaped skull and flaring brows, stood.

He rose as if he were coming at bay before a pack of hounds, glowering at Moran and the others. "Sir, I wish I could explain how they neutralize or circumvent our sensors, but I can't. Our only viable response is to strike back at once, and hard! We drove them off before and we can do it again, until they stop coming back." He shook his big fist, a gesture he often used.

Inside, he knew a bitter frustration that Zand—Zand, who seemed to move in the shadows and had advised him so cannily before—could no longer be contacted. *Has Zand set me up?* Leonard wondered. But the man was Dr. Lang's heir on Earth, heir to the secrets of Robotech and Protoculture; elusive, furtive Zand, had sworn he was on Leonard's side. And so Leonard was determined to follow Zand's council and his own prejudices.

Moran looked to Emerson. "And what does the chief of staff have to say?"

Emerson came to his feet slowly, thinking. He didn't wish to contradict his superior, especially in that hall, but he had been called upon to speak his mind honestly. Certainly, Emerson thought that Leonard's characterization of the Masters as having been "driven away" was wide of the mark.

"Speaking candidly, sir," Emerson said, "we know next to nothing about Zor or the Robotech Masters' true capabilities. And until we do, I cannot recommend any mission that would risk our people and our ships and mecha."

Leonard, just about to sit down, slammed the table with his fist and rose up again. "Damn it, we're talking about the fate of the planet here, and about being wiped out sector by sector!"

Emerson nodded soberly. "I'm aware of that. But nothing will be gained by sacrificing our pilots to certain destruction with no hope of inflicting significant losses on the enemy."

Leonard sneered. "I won't stand for that kind of talk! You're impugning the courage and ability of our fighting forces!" Before Emerson could contradict, Leonard swung to Moran. "Those men and women have bloodied the enemy before, but good! If we let them take the offensive, they can finish the job!"

Emerson bit back his words as he heard Chairman Moran say, "Very well, Commander Leonard, prepare to attack."

Fools! thought Rolf Emerson even as he prepared to carry out the orders he was sworn to obey.

CHAPTER SEVENTEEN

TO: Supreme Commander Leonard
FROM: Dr. Lazlo Zand, Special Protoculture Observations and
Operations Kommandatura (Commanding)
Sir:

It is the conclusion of this unit that war against the Robotech Masters must be prosecuted as aggressively as possible, and that tactics used thus far (with particular emphasis on the Hovertank squads) still hold the best promise of positive results.

ONUMENT CITY DIDN'T FEEL MUCH LIKE A COMBAT zone even though all Earth was a combat zone now, Dana reflected as she led the 15th into the middle of the downtown area on Hovercycles.

Traffic was fairly heavy and the shops, arcades, nightspots, and theaters were all brightly lit. Streetlights, traffic signals, neon signs, and even park fountains were illuminated. *Why not?* she thought. *Blackout measures are useless for hiding targets from the Robotech Masters.*

And keeping people pent up inside didn't do any good, either; there had been plenty of shelters in Sector Three, or so the scuttlebutt ran, and it hadn't helped them at all. The only thing Civil Defense restrictions would do right now was cause panic.

And panic was what the 15th was there to prevent. They were on duty, but unarmed, looking more like they were out on an evening pass. The UEG had tried to suppress rumors of the atrocities in Sector Three, but there had been the inevitable leaks. Like a lot of other Southern Cross soldiers circulating through population centers this night, the ATACs were on the lookout for any crazy inclined to jump up on a street corner soap box and proclaim Judgment Day.

Well, it sure beats a twenty-mile hike with full field pack, Sean

Phillips decided, removing his goggles and readjusting his torso harness as the 15th parked their cycles side by side at the curb of a busy street. People were wandering by arm in arm, or window-shopping, taking in the sights. And there were women galore. "Well, men, this is going to be a true test of your character," he said, and got sly laughs from some of the guys.

"Ahem," said Dana, rising to face them. "All right, we start our patrols from here." She eyed them severely, then winked. "And don't do anything I wouldn't do, hmm?"

"Yes, ma'am," Sean said with a grin.

"Okay, I'll patrol the discos," somebody volunteered.

"And I'll start with that bar over there," another added with a goofy laugh.

"Yeah, you'll end with it, too," the first countered.

In another moment they were all splitting up to check out the area, all except Angelo, who gave a disgusted grunt. Duty was duty and playtime was playtime and the two shouldn't mix!

"Angie, why do I have the feeling you'd rather stay here and guard the horses?" Dana asked sweetly.

He crossed his arms and put his feet up on his handlebars. "Because you're a mind-reader, I guess."

That gave her a start, and she saw Zor's face again. *Maybe I am.* But she recovered and told her troops, "Right, move out."

Which they did with a will, whopping and laughing. "Idiots," Angelo snorted.

Is every attractive female in this town grafted to some civilian's arm? Sean thought as he made his way along. Then he saw her standing by a boutique window, looking at a coat. She was small and shapely, with auburn hair to her waist and yellow slacks that did nice things for her figure.

Sean squared his uniform as he went over. *Lady, this is your lucky night!* "You seem to like that coat a lot," he said. "I admire your taste." Actually, he scarcely glanced at it.

She turned in surprise. "What?" She looked him over and broke into a dimpled smile. "Will you buy it for me, hmm?"

This was more like it. The coat *was* nice, he guessed; all scarlet embroidery and white fur trim. "Well, now, I just might be persuaded—uh!" As he read the price tag and recalled that he was now a deuce private, he went pale. *Gah! That's more than I make in a year!*

"On second thought, red's not your color," he improvised. "Listen, why don't you and me go someplace and get ourselves a drink, yes?" He winked.

She made a wry face and removed the hand he'd settled lightly on her shoulder. "Thanks anyway. Maybe some other time." She said it walking.

"Sure, anytime you say!" he called after. *Maybe I sounded too insincere? Well, it's her loss.*

Two blocks away, Dana was looking into another boutique window, considering a nice little evening frock that looked just about right for her. A hand fell on her shoulder and she pivoted, ready to show some masher what Hovertank officers learned in hand-to-hand.

But she was facing a smug-looking Angelo Dante. "Time to spit on the fire and call in the hounds," he said. "We just got a general recall to base. Something big is up."

The 15th was back on standby alert, manning their Hovertanks and waiting. This show was reserved for the TASCs and the Cosmic Units.

Fokker Base had been rebuilt hastily. Barely twenty-four hours after the raid on Sector Three, the light of morning showed a half-dozen shuttles at the vertical and ready to launch. Final preparations were under way, and people were running for bunkers and observation posts.

The shuttles launched, the first battle wing of the planned strike. On the other side of the base, the Black Lions and the other Veritech outfits waited, the second battle wing. When the shuttles were away and clear, the VTs got the green light. With Maria Crystal leading, the fighters thundered down the runway to even the score with the Robotech Masters.

Leonard came into the command center to find Emerson bent over the illuminated displays. Leonard had regained his composure, especially in light of the fact that Emerson was his most capable subordinate. To put it more truthfully, over the years Leonard had garnered credit for many things that had been Emerson's accomplishments.

Leonard dropped a thick hand on the flared shoulderboard of Emerson's torso harness. "Believe me, Rolf, this is the only way."

Emerson studied him for a long time before replying, "I hope to God you're right."

* * *

The VTs went in first, loosing swarms of missiles at the enemy flagship, their sole objective. But the missiles were no sooner away than globes of light boiled out of the flagship, like enormous will-o'-the-wisps, bursting into hexagonal webs of pulsating light like gigantic snowflakes.

The snowflakes moved and drifted into position, intersecting the missiles' paths, and the Earthly ordnance detonated harmlessly against them. The other mother ships were silent and dark but for running lights, waiting.

Still more of the energy snowflakes came forth, until a net of them protected the flagship. The VTs swept around for another try, and this time beams from the chandelier-bulb cannon crackled across empty space. More than forty fighters were lost in the first ninety seconds of the massed attack on the flagship. Still the VTs swung around for another go, hoping against hope to get in under the hexagons and deliver a blow.

But they were flying straight into a murder machine.

"Attack groups two and eight have disengaged from the enemy," the flat, synthesized voice of the intel computer echoed in the command center. "Groups three, four, and seven report heavy losses. Other groups fail to respond to transmissions and are believed to have been totally destroyed."

Leonard turned to Emerson angrily but also, people in the command center could see, with a tremble of fear. "How can this be happening to us?"

Emerson chose to ignore him, except to observe, "So far we haven't even put a dent in them." He looked to Rochelle. "Any sign of a counterattack yet?"

"Negative at this time, sir. They're standing pat."

Emerson called for an update on losses. The computer printed out the awful facts and figures. Three quarters of the attack wings' forces were gone, immolated in a few minutes.

"All those men and women lost," Emerson murmured, scanning the list.

"It's—it's a disaster," Leonard said unsteadily. He turned and lurched toward the door.

Emerson didn't even bother to solicit Leonard's permission. "Call off the attack! All units disengage and return to base." Then he turned and glared at Leonard's back as the supreme commander exited.

* * *

Not far away, there was a different kind of battle being fought in the UEG's foremost Robotech research laboratory, in the military-industrial facility near the airbase. And this battle was turning, slowly, in the Human race's favor.

Dr. Miles Cochran and his colleague, Dr. Samson Beckett, were two of the hottest of the Robotech hotshots who had trained under Dr. Emil Lang and, later, Dr. Lazlo Zand. Now they pored over the remains of a downed blue Bioroid that lay on a worktable like the world's biggest cadaver awaiting the championship autopsy of all time.

Its guts were opened up and wired to every monitoring device the lab had. It looked like it was sprouting a garden of sensor wires, photo-optic lines, monitoring circuits, and computer links.

Cochran, a thin-faced, intense redhead, said, "I'm activating ultraviolet scanner, Sam."

Beckett, smaller and dark-haired, wearing tinted glasses was *ooh*ing and *aah*ing over the things he was encountering with his probes, but stopped to step back and watch.

The scanner came down to irradiate the Bioroid's entire form, passing from crown to toes, coordinating with readouts and analysis computers, scrutinizing every part of the shattered mecha.

The two went to the computer screens to see what they came up with. The data banks were linked in with recordings and sketches of the mecha the Southern Cross forces had fought thus far. The two watched the information and diagrams flash, the light reflecting off Beckett's glasses.

"What about the damage received?" Cochran asked. "See if you can get me a readout on that." Beckett bent to the task.

He got an integrated analysis of the internal structure of the mecha. There was severe mechanical damage because a leg had been ripped off in battle, but no physical explanation as to why all systems were so completely inert despite the Humans' efforts to activate them. Then they got the confirmation they were looking for.

"Definite traces of biogenetic material," Beckett said flatly.

"So there *was* something alive in there, something that escaped before the mop-up crew got to the scene, or self-destructed. Can you give us a look-see at what it was?"

"I can try." Beckett bent to his task again. The most powerful medical and genetic engineering programs were accessed, a stupendous amount of computer power. Alongside a detailed DNA blueprint, the computer drew up a human form. "Unbelievable," Beckett breathed.

"It's Human! Not simply *like* us, as the Zentraedi were, but *Human*!"

"But—it's from outside the Solar System!" Beckett was shaking his head. "Maybe . . . somehow they're from Hunter's SDF-3 expedition?"

It was Cochran's turn to shake his head. "No. But those ATAC tankers were right; they saw what they thought they saw."

Beckett removed his glasses. "God! Wait till Zand hears this! He'll freak!"

There was a chuckle from the darkness; Cochran and Beckett spun toward it even as they realized they knew who it was. "Perhaps that is too extreme a word, Samson. Let's just say that I'm—*pleased*."

Dr. Lazlo Zand came a little farther into the light, so that his eerie eyes could be seen. "And of course my little Dana was right! Of course your findings bear me out! The Protoculture weaves, it spins, it manipulates and *shapes*, young doctors! Its ability to shape mere machinery is nothing next to its ability to shape *events*!"

He stepped a little closer still, studying the Bioroid. He was a man of medium height, in unornamented UEG attire, his hair still unruly after all these years. His eyes seemed to be all iris, as Lang's had been ever since Lang had taken that Protoculture boost aboard the SDF-1 when it first landed. Only, in Zand's case, the transformation hadn't taken place until years later. He looked no less unearthly than a Robotech Master.

"You've done well, but now you must double-check your findings to be sure there is no error in your presentation when you take them to the UEG."

Cochran found his voice. How had Zand gotten into the lab? How had he known what Beckett and Cochran were doing there? They hadn't seen or had word of or about him in years. Yet, those weren't questions Cochran felt safe in asking, so he said, "Surely, Dr. Zand, you'll want to accompany us and elaborate on—"

"No!" Zand raised a warning finger. "No mention of me, understood? Good! Now, back to work, both of you." Zand turned for the door.

"But when will you—" Beckett began.

"When the time is right," Zand said, silhouetted against the light from outside, "you will hear from me again."

Emerson rested his chin on his interlaced fingers. "And so you're saying Zor is a Human being, and not a miniaturized Zentraedi?"

Beckett and Cochran nodded.

"Then Dana and Bowie were right," Emerson said softly, staring into space. "And we're fighting our own kind. Like brothers slaughtering each other."

Just then Rochelle buzzed Emerson with the final compilation of the battle casualties. Eighty-five VTs destroyed, seven damaged beyond repair; five shuttles destroyed, one damaged beyond repair. Two-hundred-seven pilots and aircraft crew people dead, another twenty ground support and two-hundred-odd civilians dead, the latter two figures from crashes of damaged aircraft. Eighty-seven missing in action and unaccounted for, presumed to be adrift in space, dead or alive.

In the ready-room at the 15th, for once the banter was all but nonexistent.

"Worst defeat of the war," Bowie said, stretching out the kinks that wearing armor always gave him, grateful to be back in a simple uniform.

"And that was only one ship," Sean reminded him.

"I tell ya, the VTs coulda got through if they hadn't've been called off," Angelo insisted. "Look what we did to those ali— those XTs on the Liberty mission."

Dana made no response to the fact that he hadn't used the word *aliens*, but she noticed that nobody in the 15th used it when referring to the enemy now. It moved her so, their literally unspoken support of her—she very warily felt them to be the family she'd never had.

Louie looked up from the calculations he was doing on a lap-size computer. "And I'm telling *you*, Angie, that that ship's design makes a frontal assault a complete impossibility."

Sean chortled. "I forgot: the professor, there, knows everything!"

Louie held his temper, used to this kind of flak. Bright and inventive enough for any tech school or advanced degree program, he had still opted for the ATACs. He liked being a corporal in a line outfit and, more to the point, the tinkering and computer hacking and equipment modifications he did were done without some frowning lab-coat type looking over his shoulder. He was also confident that the studying and research he did on his own, open-ended, put him way ahead of the people who had to complete course requirements in any school.

Dana put in, "But Zor's ship must have *some* weak spot."

Louie turned the dark-goggled gaze on her, nodding. "Exactly right. To start with, I figure that Zor's ship is not powered by an engine as we would recognize one."

"Huh?" Dana said. "Then how's it get around?"

"Well, it can travel between the stars by spacefolding, of course, like the SDFs and the Zentraedi," Louie explained. "And to get around over smaller distances, it has a more localized folding process, a sort of a twisting of opposing forces, like squirting a grape seed between your fingers."

Dana remembered some of the theory and jargon Louie had spouted in sessions past. "So, if you upset the hyper-balance, you've got yourself an unstable ship."

Sean caught her thoughtful tone and looked her over. "What exactly are you thinking about?"

She gave him a closed-face look. "Basic military strategy." She rose, took a few paces, then turned back to them. "C'mon, Louie, we've got work to do!"

CHAPTER
EIGHTEEN

Lazlo, my valued colleague,

It falls upon me to leave now with the SDF-3 expedition, and falls to you to stay, for reasons we both know.

But I ask you to keep in mind the fact that my Awakening to the Protoculture was in some measure accidental, while yours was fully aforethought, and that certain intents and purposes in you are at times very strong.

I exhort you to remember that you will be dealing with HUMAN BE-INGS, and to work contrary to their wellbeing will be in some measure, always, to work at cross purposes with the Protoculture. Please don't let the eagerness to plumb the depths of Protoculture distort your thinking.

Your friend,
Emil Lang

WHEN DANA APPEARED AT THE ROBOTECH RESEARCH LAB with Louie in tow, she had the impression that Drs. Cochran and Beckett were looking at her rather strangely, at least at first.

But she shrugged it off; research types were always off somewhere in a world of their own. Besides, Louie had them totally fascinated with his idea in short order. First thing she knew, Louie was sitting at Beckett's main computer terminal with the doctors looking on, bringing up diagrams and displays and equations and computer-generated images to explain and verify his analysis.

"It's only a theory, I admit," he said as the computer illuminated various parts of a grid-diagram of Zor's vessel. "But after all, no scans show any central power source, am I right?"

Cochran nodded, lower lip between his thumb and forefinger, staring into the screen. Louie went on. "But I, um, I accessed the intel computers and I found what's gotta be a bio-gravitic induction network."

The computer showed it, a convoluted array like a highway

system or blood vessels, picked out in neon red. "There seems to be some kind of perpetual bio-gravitic cycle; the Protoculture quanta are simultaneously attracted to and repelled by one another. Kinda like what's going on in the sun, if you want to put it that way, gravity and fusion fighting it out in a sort of equilibrium."

Dana tried to get a word in edgewise, but the three men were completely caught up in their tech-talk.

Beckett did sneak in a sidelong look at her, though. How had Dana, of all people, come to be the one to find this Louie Nichols, this gem-in-the-rough genius/weirdo? Of course it was again in total defiance of any coincidence, and Beckett had renewed awe for Protoculture's power to shape events.

"It appears to effect these two strong mega-forces," Louie said.

"Through phased bonding!" Cochran comprehended, grinning from ear to ear.

Dana was tired of hearing about the framistat field connected to the veeblefertzer anomalies. "So if we destabilize this equilibrium of yours, we'll knock the whole ship out of whack, right?"

They frowned at her coarse language, but Louie shrugged. "Yes. At least theoretically."

She looked to Cochran and Beckett. "Then you find the right spot and we'll see that the job gets done!"

Cochran hedged. "I don't think the chief of staff will choose you for the mission, Lieutenant. Not with your track record."

But inside he was wondering how Zand could let the girl run around loose like this, constantly daring aliens to shoot her cute blond head off. She was the very core of so much of Zand's work and planning.

Ah, but that's the heart of the matter, isn't it? he seemed to hear Zand lecturing. *It's Protoculture that shapes events, and living beings interfered with it or sought to hamper it only at their own peril.*

Zand, and even the great Lang, had realized this very early on; only by being observers of events and learning the innermost secrets of Protoculture—the ones that had died with the original Zor—could they ever hope to reach a point where they dared try to *manipulate* its greatest powers.

Dana was saying cheerfully, "Oh, I beg to differ. The Fifteenth is the perfect choice for this mission!"

Getting Bowie to agree to help her talk Emerson into letting the 15th take the mission was only slightly more difficult than getting a mule into high heels. But he saw that the rest of the 15th was all for it, so he gave in at last.

In Emerson's office, Dana, Bowie, and Louie held their collective breath while Emerson studied the data. "Sir, we've finally got the weapon we need to hit the Robotech Masters where it hurts," Bowie prompted.

Emerson brought his chair back around. "It's an insane mission. Hopeless. And we can't spare the pilots or VTs."

Dana gave him her best wide-eyed look. "But who said anything about Veritechs? Looks more like a job for Hovertanks, I was thinking, General."

Emerson moaned inwardly and wished for the days when he could paddle them when they had been bad and send them to bed without supper. And there had been quite a few of those.

But that was before the days when they were soldiers who had sworn an oath of duty. And before the days when the Robotech Masters had come to grind the Earth to rubble beneath an iron heel. "You think you can do it?"

Her gaze was level now, her nod slow and sure. "Yes, sir."

Emerson rose. "Good hunting, people."

Again the fighters went up, but this time they were as cautious as they could manage to be, firing from a distance, putting more emphasis on evasive maneuvers than on accuracy. Once more the glowing, throbbing hexagonal webs appeared. Dana thought how much like powerveined snowflakes they looked.

The snowflakes moved, as they had before, to supply coverage to heavily attacked areas, leaving others more lightly guarded. It was something intel had noted on the first assault; the time had come to use it.

The shuttle pilot flying the mission was a chill cube; when a stray Masters cannon round grazed the fuselage of his ship, he said offhandedly, "Just a flesh wound, pards. Goin' in."

He stood the ship on its side to make it between two of the spiral ziggurat megastructures on the deck below, then flew along a trench, well aware that a speed slow enough to make a combat drop was too slow to dodge enemy flak. He shrugged and kept flying. "Made it through," he thought to mention to the ATACs back in the drop bay, as if telling them that the mail had arrived.

"Outta the frying pan," Dana heard Sean mutter into his helmet mike. Then the pilot gave the order to open the drop bay door, and they were looking out at the onrushing techno-terrain of the mother ship's upper hull.

The Hovertanks' engines were already revving. The ATACs roared out in order, dropping into deployment pattern as they descended to the hull.

"Everyone accounted for?" Dana, in the lead, asked. She was trying to take in everything at once, looking for AA emplacements and other wicked surprises, spot her target, see how the battle was going, and make sure *Valkyrie* was functioning right.

Angelo, farther back, reported, "Roger that; everybody's in position, Lieutenant."

The ATACs barreled along, lining up on their leader according to assignment. "All right boys; you know the drill."

They did; it was Sterling-simple. They were to follow Dana's targeting program, pierce the hull, and expose that bio-gravitic network. Then they would concentrate fire, disrupt the energy highway system, and put the mother ship's lights out.

Unless any of ten thousand things went wrong. Bowie sang out a Southern Cross Army refrain, "Just another day in the SCA!"

They stayed in a long trench for cover, and had good luck for an astoundingly tranquil ten seconds before trouble reared its armored head. "Uh-oh, we got company," Sean noted. Four Bioroids had dropped down into the trench, far ahead, to block their way. Dana found herself holding her breath, wondering what color they were.

Well, if Big Red's in my way now, it's his tough luck! She made an obscene reference to what the Bioroids could go and do. "Forget 'em! It's that system we're after! Close up behind me!"

They did, and Dana hit emergency thrust. She dodged the enemy mecha's shots and was upon them before they got their bearings, bowling them over with the solid weight of her tank, not bothering to shoot. All were blues. The 15th howled like werewolves and followed her on toward the target.

"The shuttle got in under their defensive shields," Rochelle told Emerson. "We register a running firefight on the upper hull, sir."

Emerson inclined his head in acknowledgment but didn't take his eyes from the displays.

Bioroids closed in from both sides and behind, but none were on their Hovercraft, and so it remained a road-race. Trooper Thornton heard Sean's warning but couldn't dodge in time, and a wash of annihilation discs blew out and folded Bioroid hand in its nacelle under his tank's left rear armor skirt.

"Been hit, Lieutenant," Thornton drawled, trying for damage

control. But the decrease in speed let two Bioroids catch up to him; they dropped feetfirst onto his ship, disintegrating it in a fireball, and kept on coming.

"Louie! Battloid mode!" Dana called.

The Bioroids were fighting on their home ground, but the ATACs had the advantage of velocity, adrenaline, and a desperate need to carry out their mission. Dana and Louie mechamorphosed in mid-turn, and went rocketing back at the enemy as ultratech knights, weapons blazing. This time they used the main battery, the heavy Gladiator cannon that was usually stored in the Battloid's right arm but could be brought forth in extreme need. Everything around them seemed to be happening in slow motion.

They got the first Bioroid as it was still charging, the second and third when the enemy mecha stopped to shoot it out, and the fourth when it sought to withdraw and had its route blocked by a dikelike structural feature.

"Better luck next time," Dana bade the last to go, but as it went it toppled into a sort of utility groove. Its explosion set off another, greater one, and the groove became a crackling, Protoculture-hot version of an old-time blackpowder fuse.

Dana gasped as the eruption raced along the groove, sending up a curtain of starflame behind it, blowing armored deckplates high, moving as fast as any Hovertank. The racing superfuse reached a low, pillbox feature on the hull and went up like a roman candle.

"Louie, did we do it?"

Louie's helmet gave him a buglike look, but beneath it he was smiling wide.

"Yes, ma'am! We've found the bio-gravitic network!"

"Let's get it!" She raced in with a dozen and more Battloids covering and bringing up the rear, moving like veteran infantry, or SWAT cops. They fired with all the staggering power the Hovertanks could bring to bear; Bioroids, unused to such house-to-house, room-to-room type-combat, were at the disadvantage, and took all the losses then.

One Bioroid almost blasted Dana, but she stumbled out of its way and Angelo got the Bioroid instead, shooting it off a tall tower so that it fell a long way to the hull, somersaulting, like something out of an old western.

Dana came up with her Battloid's head hanging over the brink of a shaft exposed by the exploded pillbox. The shaft was so deep that she couldn't see the bottom.

"You found it, ma'am," Louie observed. "Down there's the processing field that manages the energy equilibrium. If we blow

up the equipment down at the field intersection locus, we'll destabilize this whole damn garbage scow."

Dana had regained her feet. "Let's do-it-to-it!" She studied the
diagram Louie was sending her, and armed the heavy missile she
was carrying for the purpose. All of them had one—just one
apiece—but Dana wanted this shot to be hers.

Nearby, the 15th was in a furious firefight with the Bioroids as
more and more enemy reinforcements showed up. The weapons
beams spat and veered, seeking targets; the annihilation discs flew.

Sean yelled, "Dana, we've got ya covered, but there're more
'roids crashing the party!"

"Hang on!" She adjusted the range on the missile, and its dial-
a-yield for maximum explosive force. Alien discs began ranging
in around her, and Louie turned the *Livewire* to give more covering fire. "Lieutenant, I really suggest you hurry!"

"Jump, all you guys! Go! Don't wait for me!" She released the
missile and watched its corkscrew trail disappear down into the
blackness. Then she turned to propel herself into space with
the strength of her Battloid's legs and the thrusters built into its
feet, breaking out of the surface gravity field around the upper
hull. She saw that the other Battloids were already in the air. As
she went, her instruments registered a direct hit.

The Bioroids were trying to shoot down the ascending Battloids
when the column of white light and raw destruction shot from the
shaft, like Satan's own artillery spewing forth. The Battloids were
already up and speeding away from it, but the Bioroids closing in
on the shaft to see what damage had been done got a final, hor-
rific surprise.

The gush of unleashed energy set off explosions in and around
the shaft; a dozen blues were whirled away like leaves in a hurricane, molten metal, dismembered by the force of the blast,
twisted into unrecognizable shapes as the volcano of energy blew
higher and higher.

"Looks like you knew what you were talking about, Louie,"
Sean said in a subdued voice, thinking what they were all thinking: the explosion surpassed all estimates and projections; if they
had hung around for another few seconds, the 15th would have
been history, too.

Then everybody was making ribald praise of the Cosmic Units
as the shuttle came into view, right on pickup vector. Dana looked
at the lapsed-time function on her mission displays and realized in
shock that the whole thing had taken only a few minutes.

"We see you, transport; get ready to take us aboard." Her elation was complete, for now.

Dana and the rest of the 15th, the Cosmic crews, and the TASC fliers could all see the secondary explosions ripping along the mother ship's hide as the ATACs dove aboard the shuttle. Furious fires burned out of control, becoming thermonuclear bonfires in the escaping atmosphere; the monster ship swung to in accordance with whatever motive forces it employed; its orbit decayed at once.

Dana watched over an optical pickup patched through from the shuttle bridge. She felt vast satisfaction, a quelling of her own fear and self-doubt.

Then the satisfaction retreated; the moment she touched down she would have to begin getting and training replacement personnel and mecha. It was plain the 15th would be needed again very soon.

Because the mother ship was beginning a long, controlled fall toward Earth.

"It's breaking up!" Emerson exclaimed, watching the relayed image.

"Only peripherally, sir," Tessel noted, reading another display.

"I never would've believed it," Rochelle commented quietly. He turned and called out a command, "Ready-reaction force, stand by for immediate deployment!"

"Once you have Zor's landing point plotted, seal it off and ring it in with defense in depth," Emerson instructed quietly. "Air, ground, subterranean listening equipment—everything!"

"Yes, sir!"

Emerson watched the listing mother ship, a wounded dinosaur helpless to stop its plunge. Bigger than a city, it settled toward a final resting spot in the hills above Monument City. Emerson wondered if that was by calculation. He was beginning to abandon all faith in coincidence.

The controlled crash didn't destroy the mother ship, nor did Emerson expect it to; that would have been too much to hope for. It loomed like a colossal glacier of metal, silent and challenging.

Very well, he thought. *Challenge accepted.*

He turned to Rochelle. "Oh, and Colonel."

"Sir?"

"Tell the Fifteenth to stand down for a little rest; they've earned it."

METAL
FIRE

FOR REBA WEST, JONATHEN ALEXANDER,
TONY OLIVER, AND THE DOZEN OTHERS
WHOSE VOICES BROUGHT THESE
CHARACTERS TO LIFE.

CHAPTER ONE

> *EXEDORE: So, Admiral, there is little doubt: [Zentraedi and Human] genetic makeup points directly at a common point of origin.*
> *ADMIRAL GLOVAL: Incredible.*
> *EXEDORE: Isn't it. Furthermore, while examining the data we noticed many common traits, including a penchant on the part of both races to indulge in warfare. . . . Yes, both races seem to enjoy making war.*
>
> From Exedore's intel reports to the SDF-2 High Command

NCE BEFORE, AN ALIEN FORTRESS HAD CRASHED ON Earth . . .

Its arrival had put an end to almost ten years of global civil war; and its resurrection had ushered in armageddon. That fortress's blackened, irradiated remains lay buried under a mountain of earth, heaped upon it by the very men and women who had re-built the ship on what would have been its island grave. But unbeknownst to those who mourned its loss, the soul of that great ship had survived the body and inhabited it still—an entity living in the shadows of the technology it animated, waiting to be freed by its natural keepers, and until then haunting the world chosen for its sorry exile. . . .

This new fortress, this most recent gift from heaven's more sinister side, had announced its arrival, not with tidal and tectonic upheavals, but with open warfare and devastation—death's blood-stained calling cards. Nor was this fortress derelict and uncontrolled in its fateful fall but driven, brought down to Earth by the unwilling minor players in its dark drama. . . .

"ATAC Fifteen to air group!" Dana Sterling yelled into her mike over the din of battle. "Hit 'em again with everything you have! Try to keep their heads down! They're throwing everything but old shoes at us down here!"

Less than twenty-four hours ago her team, the 15th squad, Alpha Tactical Armored Corps, had felled this giant, not with sling and shot, but with a coordinated strike launched at the fortress's Achilles' heel—the core reactor governing the ship's bio-gravitic network. It had dropped parabolically from geosynchronous orbit, crashlanding in the rugged hills several kilometers distant from Monument City.

Hardly a *coincidental* impact point, Dana said to herself as she bracketed the fortress in the sights of the Hovertank's rifle/cannon.

The 15th, in Battloid mode, was moving across a battle zone that was like some geyser field of orange explosions and high-flung dirt and rock—a little like a cross between a moonscape and the inside of Vesuvius on a busy day.

Up above, the TASC fighters, the Black Lions among them, roared in for another pass. The glassy green tear-drop-cannon of the fortress didn't seem as effective in atmosphere, and so far there had been no sign of the snowflake-shields. But the enemy's hull, rearing above the assaulting Battloids, still seemed able to soak up all the punishment they could deal it and stand unaltered.

An elongated hexagon, angular and relatively flat, the alien fortress measured over five miles in length, half that in width. Its thickly plated hull was the same lackluster gray of the Zentraedi ships used in the First Robotech War; but in contrast to those organic leviathan dreadnaughts, the fortress boasted a topography to rival that of a cityscape. Along the long axis of its dorsal surface was a mile-long raised portion of superstructure that resembled the peaked roofs of many twentieth-century houses. Forward was a concentrically coiled conelike projection Louie Nichols had christened "a Robotech teat"; aft were massive Reflex thruster ports; and elsewhere, weapons stations, deep crevices, huge louvered panels, ziggurats, onion domes, towers like two-tined forks, stairways and bridges, armored docking bays, and the articulated muzzles of the ship's countless segmented "insect leg" cannons.

Below the sawtooth ridge the pilots of the fortress had chosen as their crash site was Monument City, and several miles distant across two slightly higher ridges, the remains of New Macross and the three Human-made mounds that marked the final resting place of the super dimensional fortresses.

Dana wondered if the SDF-1 had something to do with this latest warfare. If these invaders were indeed the Robotech Masters (and not some other band of XT galactic marauders), had they come to avenge the Zentraedi in some way? Or worse still—as many were asking—was Earth fighting a new war with micronized Zentraedi?

Child of a Human father and a Zentraedi mother—the only known child of such a marriage—Dana had good reason to disprove this latter hypothesis.

That *some* of the invaders were humanoid was a fact only recently accepted by the High Command. Scarcely a month ago Dana had been face-to-face with a pilot of one of the invaders' bipedal mecha—the so-called Bioroids. Bowie Grant had been even closer, but Dana was the one who had yet to get over the encounter. All at once the war had personalized itself; it was no longer machine against machine, Hovertank against Bioroid.

Not that that mattered in the least to the hardened leaders of the UEG. Since the end of the First Robotech War, Human civilization had been on a downhill slide; and if it hadn't come to Humans facing aliens, it probably would have been Humans against Humans.

Dana heard a sonic roar through the Hovertank's external pickups and looked up into a sky full of new generation Alpha fighters, snub-nosed descendants of the Veritechs.

The place was dense with smoke and flying fragments from missile bursts, and the missile's retwisting tracks. As Dana watched, one pair of VTs finished a pass only to have two alien assault ships lift into the air and go up after them. Dana yelled a warning over the Forward Air Control net, then switched from the FAC frequency to her own tactical net because the real showdown had begun; two blue Bioroids had popped up from behind boulders near the fortress.

The blues opened fire and the ATACs returned it with interest; the range was medium-long, but energy bolts and annihilation discs skewed and splashed furiously, searching for targets. At Dana's request, a Tactical Air Force fighter-bomber flight came in to drop a few dozen tons of conventional ordnance while the TASCs got set up for their next run.

Abruptly, a green-blue light shone from the fortress, and a half second later it lay under a hemisphere of spindriftlike stuff, a dome of radiant cobweb, and all incoming beams and solids were splashing harmlessly from it.

But the enemy could fire through their own shield, and did, knocking down two of the retreating bombers and two approaching VTs with cannonfire. Whatever the damage to the bio-gravitic system was, it plainly hadn't robbed the fortress of all its stupendous power.

Dana's hand went out for the mode selector lever. She attuned her thoughts to the mecha and threw the lever to G, reconfiguring from Battloid to Gladiator. The Hovertank was now a squat, two-legged SPG (self-propelled gun), with a single cannon stretching out in front of it.

Nearby, in the scant cover provided by hillside granite outcroppings and dislodged boulders, the rest of the 15th—Louie Nichols, Bowie Grant, Sean Phillips, and Sergeant Angelo Dante among others—similarly reconfigured, was unleashing salvos against the stationary fortress.

"Man, these guys are tough as nails!" Dana heard Sean say over the net. "They aren't budging an inch!"

And they aren't likely to, Dana knew. *We're fighting for our home; they're fighting for their ship and their only hope of survival.*

"At this rate the fighting could go on forever," Angelo said. "Somebody better think of something quick." And everyone knew he wasn't talking about sergeants, lieutenants, or anybody else who might be accused of working for a living; the brass better realize it was making a mistake, or come evening they would need at least one new Hovertank squad.

Then Angelo picked up on a blue that had charged from behind a rock and was headed straight for Bowie's *Diddy-Wa-Diddy*. The attitude and posture of Bowie's mecha suggested that it was distracted, unfocused.

Damn kid, woolgathering! "Look out, Bowie!"

But then Sean appeared in Battloid mode, firing with the rifle/cannon, the blue stumbling as it broke up in the blazing beams, then going down.

"Wake up and stay on your toes, Bowie," Angelo growled. "That's the third time today ya fouled up."

"Sorry," Bowie returned. "Thanks, Sarge."

Dana was helping Louie Nichols and another trooper try to drive back blues who were crawling forward from cover to cover on their bellies, the first time the Bioroids had ever been seen to do such a thing.

"These guys just won't take no for an answer," Dana grated, raking her fire back and forth at them.

Remote cameras positioned along the battle perimeter brought the action home to headquarters. An intermittent beeping sound (like nonsense Morse) and horizontal noise bars disrupted the video transmission. Still, the picture was clear: the Tactical Armored units were taking a beating.

Colonel Rochelle vented his frustration in a slow exhale of

smoke, and stubbed out his cigarette in the already crowded ashtray. There were three other staff officers with him at the long table, at the head of which sat Major General Rolf Emerson.

"The enemy is showing no sign of surrender," Rochelle said after a moment. "And the Fifteenth is tiring fast."

"Hit them harder," Colonel Rudolph suggested. "We've got the air wing commander standing by. A surgical strike—nuclear, if we have to."

Rochelle wondered how the man had ever reached his current rank. "I won't even address that suggestion. We have no clear-cut understanding of that ship's energy shield. And what if the cards don't fall our way? Earth would be finished."

Rudolph blinked nervously behind his thick glasses. "I don't see that the threat would be any greater than the attacks already launched against Monument."

Butler, the staff officer seated opposite Rudolph spoke to that. "This isn't *The War of the Worlds*, Colonel—at least not yet. We don't even know what they want from us."

"Do I have to remind you gentlemen about the attack on Macross Island?" Rudolph's voice took on a harder edge. "Twenty years ago isn't exactly ancient history, is it? If we're going to wait for an *explanation*, we might as well surrender right now."

Rochelle was nodding his head and lighting up another cigarette. "I'm against escalation at this point," he said, smoke and breath drawn in.

Rolf Emerson, gloved hands folded in front of him on the table, sat silently, taking in his staff's assessments and opinions but saying very little. If it were left up to him to decide, he would attempt to open up a dialogue with the unseen invaders. True, the aliens had struck the first blow, but it had been the Earth Forces who had been goading them into continued strikes ever since. Unfortunately, though, he was not the one chosen to decide things; he had to count on Commander Leonard for that ... *And may heaven help us,* he thought.

"We just can't let them *sit* there!" Rudolph was insisting.

Emerson cleared his voice, loud enough to cut through the separate conversations that were in progress, and the table fell silent. The audio monitors brought the noise of battle to them once again; in concert, permaplas windowpanes rattled to the sounds of distant explosions.

"This battle requires more than just hardware and manpower, gentlemen. . . . We'll give them back the ground we've taken because it's of no use to us right now. We'll withdraw our forces temporarily, until we have a workable plan."

The 15th acknowledged the orders to pull back and ceased fire. Other units were reporting heavy casualties, but their team had been fortunate: seven dead, three wounded—counts that would have been judged insignificant twenty years ago, when Earth's population was more than just a handful of hardened survivors.

Emerson dismissed his staff, returned to his office, and requested to meet with the supreme commander. But Leonard surprised him by telling him to stay put, and five minutes later burst through the door like an angry bull.

"There's got to be some way to crack open that ship!" Leonard railed. "I will not accept defeat! I will not accept the status quo!"

Emerson wondered if Leonard would have accepted the status quo if he had sweated out the morning in the seat of a Hovertank, or a Veritech.

The supreme commander was every bit Emerson's opposite in appearance as well as temperament. He was a massive man, tall, thick-necked, and barrel-chested, with a huge, hairless head, and heavy jowls that concealed what had once been strong, angular features, Prussian features, perhaps. His standard uniform consisted of white britches, black leather boots, and a brown longcoat fringed at the shoulders. But central to this ensemble was an enormous brass belt buckle, which seemed to symbolize the man's foursquare materialistic solidity.

Emerson, on the other hand, had a handsome face with a strong jaw, thick eyebrows, long and well drawn like gulls' wings, and dark, sensitive eyes, more close-set than they should have been, somewhat diminishing an otherwise intelligent aspect.

Leonard commenced pacing the room, his arms folded across his chest, while Emerson remained seated at his desk. Behind him was a wallscreen covered with schematic displays of troop deployment.

"Perhaps Rudolph's plan," Leonard mused.

"I strongly oppose it, Comman—"

"You're too cautious, Emerson," Leonard interrupted. "Too cautious for your own good."

"We had no choice, Commander. Our losses—"

"Don't talk to me of *losses*, man! We can't let these aliens run roughshod over us! I propose we adopt Rudolph's strategy. A surgical strike is our only recourse."

Emerson thought about objecting, but Leonard had swung

around and slammed his hands flat on the table, silencing him almost before he began.

"I will not tolerate any delays!" the commander warned him, bulldog jowls shaking. "If Rudolph's plan doesn't meet with your approval, then come up with a better one!"

Emerson stifled a retort and averted his eyes. For an instant, the commander's shaved head inches from his own, he understood why Leonard was known to some as Little Dolza.

"Certainly, Commander," he said obediently. "I understand." What Emerson understood was that Chairman Moran and the rest of the UEG council were beginning to question Leonard's fitness to command, and Leonard was feeling the screws turn.

Leonard's cold gaze remained in place. "Good," he said, certain he had made himself clear. "Because I want an end to all this madness and I'm holding *you* responsible. . . . After all," he added, turning and walking away, "you're supposed to be the miracle man."

The 15th had a clear view of the jagged ridgeline and downed fortress from their twelfth-story quarters in the barracks compound. Between the compound and twin peaks that dominated the view, the land was lifeless and incurably rugged, cratered from the countless Zentraedi death bolts rained upon it almost twenty years before.

The barracks' ready-room was posh by any current standards: spacious, well-lit, equipped with features more befitting a recreation room, including video games and a bar. Most of the squad was done in, already in the sack or on their way, save for Dana Sterling, too wired for sleep, Angelo Dante, who had little use for it on any occasion, and Sean Phillips, who was more than accustomed to long hours.

The sergeant couldn't tear himself away from the view and seemed itching to get back into battle.

"We should still be out there fighting—am I right or am I right?" Angelo pronounced, directing his words to Sean only because he was seated nearby. "We'll be fighting this war when our pensions come due unless we defeat those monsters with one big shot; the whistle blows and everybody goes."

At twenty-six, the sergeant was the oldest member of the 15th, also the tallest, loudest, and deadliest—as sergeants are wont to be. He had met his match for impulsiveness in Dana, and recklessness in Sean, but the final results had yet to be tallied.

Sean, chin resting on his hand, had his back turned to the windows and to Angie. Long-haired would-be Casanova of the 15th and of nearly every other outfit in the barracks compound, he fancied conquests of a softer sort. But at the moment he was too exhausted for campaigns of any class.

"The brass'll figure out what to do, Angie," he told the sergeant tiredly, still regarding himself as a lieutenant no matter what the brass thought of him. "Haven't you heard? They know everything. Personally, I'm tired."

Angelo stopped pacing, looking around to make sure Bowie wasn't there. "By the way, what's with Bowie?"

This seemed to bring Sean around some, but Angelo declined to follow his comment up with an explanation.

"Why? He got a problem? You should have said something during the debriefing."

The sergeant put his hands on his hips. "He's been screwing up. That's not a *problem* in combat; it's a major malfunction."

Some would have expected the presence of the fortress to have cast a pall over the city, but that was not the case. In fact, in scarcely a week's time the often silent ship (except when stirred up by the armies of the Southern Cross) had become an accepted feature of the landscape, and something of an object of fascination. Had the area of the crash site not been cordoned off, it's likely that half of Monument would have streamed up into the hills in hopes of catching a glimpse of the thing. As it was, business went on as usual. But historians and commentators were quick to offer explanations, pointing to the behavior of the populace of besieged cities of the past, Beirut of the last century, and countless others during the Global Civil War at the century's end.

Even Dana Sterling, and Nova Satori, the cool but alluring lieutenant with the Global Military Police, were not immune to the fortress's ominous enchantment. Even though they had both seen the deadlier side of its nature revealed.

Just now they shared a table in one of Monument's most popular cafés—a checkerboard-patterned tile floor, round tables of oak, and chairs of wrought iron—with a view of the fortress that surpassed the barracks' overlook.

Theirs had been less than a trouble-free relationship, but Dana had made a deal with herself to try to patch things up. Nova was agreeable and had an hour or so she could spare.

They were in their uniforms, their techno-hairbands in place, and as such the two women looked like a pair of military bookends: Dana, short and lithe, with a globe of swirling blond hair; and taller Nova, with her polished face and thick fall of black hair.

But they were hardly of a mind about things.

"I have lots of dreams," Dana was saying, "the waking kind and the sleeping kind. Sometimes I dream about meeting a man and flying to the edge of the universe with him—"

She caught herself abruptly. How in the world had she gotten onto this subject? She had started off by apologizing, explaining the pressures she had been under. Then somehow she had considered confiding to Nova about the disturbing images and trances concerning the red Bioroid pilot, the one called Zor, not certain whether the MP lieutenant would feel duty-bound to report the matter.

Maybe it had something to do with looking at the fortress and knowing the red Bioroid was out there somewhere? And then all of a sudden she was babbling about her childhood fantasies and Nova was studying her with a get-the-strait-jacket look.

"Don't you think it's time you grew up?" said Nova. "Took life a little more seriously?"

Dana turned to her, the spell broken. "Listen, I'm as attentive to duty as the next person! I didn't get my commission just because of who my parents are, so don't patronize me—huh?"

She jumped to her feet. A big MP had just come in with Bowie, looking hangdog, traipsing behind. The MP saluted Nova and explained.

"We caught him in an off-limits joint, ma'am. He has a valid pass, but what shall we do with him?"

"Not a word, Dana!" Nova cautioned. Then she asked the MP, "Which off-limits place?"

"A bar over in the Gauntlet, ma'am."

"Wait a minute," said Bowie, hoping to save his neck. "It wasn't a bar, ma'am, it was a jazz club!" He looked back and forth between Nova and Dana, searching for the line of least resistance, realizing all the while that it was a fine line between bar and club. But being busted for drinking was going to cost him more points than straying into a restricted area. Maybe if he displayed the guilt they obviously expected him to feel . . .

"Where they have been known to roll soldiers who wake up bleeding in some alley!" Nova snapped. "If the army didn't need every ATAC right now, I'd let you think that over for a week in the lockup!"

Nova was forcing the harsh tone in her voice. What she actually felt was closer to amusement than anger. Any minute now

Dana would try to intervene on Grant's behalf; and Grant was bound to foul up again, which would then reflect on Dana. Nova smiled inside: it felt so good to have the upper hand.

Bowie was stammering an explanation and apology, far from heartfelt, but somehow convincing. Nova, however, put a quick end to it and continued to read him the riot act.

"And furthermore, I fully appreciate the pressure you've all been under, but we can't afford to make allowances for *special cases*. Do you understand me, *Private?!*"

The implication was clear enough: Bowie was being warned that his relationship with General Emerson wouldn't be taken into account.

Dana was gazing coldly at Bowie, nodding along with the lieutenant's lecture, but at the same time she was managing to slip Bowie a knowing wink, as if to say: *Just agree with her.*

Bowie caught on at last. "I promise not to do it again, *sir!*"

Meanwhile Nova had turned to Dana. "If Lieutenant Sterling is willing to take responsibility for you and keep you out of trouble, I'll let this incident go. But next time I won't be so lenient."

Dana consented, her tone suggesting rough things ahead for Bowie Grant, and Nova dismissed her agent.

"Shall we finish our coffee?" Nova asked leadingly.

Dana thought carefully before responding. Nova was up to no good, but Dana suddenly saw a way to turn the incident to her own advantage. And Bowie's as well.

"I think it would be better if I started *proving* myself to you by taking care of my new responsibility," she said stiffly.

"Yes, you do that," Nova drawled, sounding like the Wicked Witch of the West.

Later, walking back to the barracks, Dana had some serious words with her charge.

"Nova's not playing around. Next time she'll probably feed you to the piranhas. Bowie, what's wrong? First you louse up in combat, then you go looking for trouble in town. And where'd you steal a valid pass, by the way?"

He shrugged, head hung. "I keep spares. Sorry, I didn't mean to cause any friction between you and Nova. You're a good friend, Dana."

Dana smiled down at him. "Okay . . . But there's one thing you can do for me. . . ."

Bowie was waiting for her to finish, when Dana's open hand

came around without warning and slapped him forcefully on the back—almost throwing him off his feet—and with it Dana's hearty: "Cheer up! Everything's going to be fine!"

CHAPTER TWO

I wish someone would call time out,
They're welcome to disarm me,
We are the very model of
A modern techno army.

Bowie Grant, "With Apologies to Gilbert and Sullivan"

THIRTEEN, ROLF EMERSON SAID TO HIMSELF WHEN HE HAD completed his count of the staff officers grouped around the briefing room's tables. The tables would have formed a triangle of sorts, save for the fact that Commander Leonard's desk (at what would have been the triangle apex) was curved. This was also a bad sign. Ordinarily, Emerson was not a superstitious man, but recent developments in world events had begun to work a kind of atavism on him. And if Human consciousness was going to commence a backward slide, who was he to march against it?

"This meeting has been called to discuss strategic approaches we might employ against the enemy," the supreme commander announced when the last member of his staff had seated himself. "We must act quickly and decisively, gentlemen; so I expect you to keep your remarks brief and to the point." Leonard got to his feet, both hands flat on the table. His angry eyes found Rolf Emerson. "General . . . go ahead."

Emerson rose, hoping his plan would fly; it seemed the only rational option, but that didn't guarantee anything, with Chairman Moran holding Leonard's feet to the fire, and Leonard passing the courtesy along down the chain of command. *Brief and to the point,* he reminded himself.

"I propose we recommence an attack on the fortress . . . but only as a diversionary tactic. That ship remains an unknown quantity, and I think it's imperative we get a small scouting unit inside for a fast recon."

This set off a lot of talk about demolition teams, battlefield nukes, and the like.

Rolf raised his voice. "Gentlemen, the goal is not to destroy the fortress. We have to ascertain some measure of understanding of the aliens' purpose. Need I remind you that this ship is but one of many?"

Leonard quieted the table. Twice, Emerson had said *alien* as opposed to enemy, but he decided to address that some other time. Right now, the major general's plan sounded good. A bit risky, but logical, and he stated as much.

To everyone's surprise, Colonel Rudolph concurred. "After all, what do we know about the enemy?" he pointed out.

Leonard asked Rolf to address this.

"We have tentative evidence that they're Human or nearly Human in biogenetic terms," Emerson conceded. "But that might only apply to their warrior class. We *do* know that the Robotechnology we've seen them use is much more advanced than ours, and we have no idea what else they're capable of."

"All the more reason to recon that ship," Rudolph said after a moment.

There was general agreement, but Colonel Rochelle thought to ask whether a team really could penetrate the fortress, given the aliens' superior firepower and defenses.

"If it's the right team," Rolf answered him.

"And the Fifteenth is the one for the job," Commander Leonard said decisively.

Emerson contradicted warily: it was true that the 15th had had some remarkable successes lately, but it was still a relatively untested outfit, and there were some among the team who certainly weren't qualified for the job. . . .

But Leonard cut him off before he had a chance to name names, which was just as well.

"General Emerson, you know the Fifteenth is the best team for this job."

There was general agreement again, while Emerson hid his consternation. Dana and Bowie had entered the military because that was where they were needed, and a stint in the service was expected of all able-bodied young people. Emerson had encouraged Bowie to enter the Academy, because Dana had already decided to and because Emerson was well aware that that was what Bowie's parents would have wanted.

It was just bad luck that a war had come along. Perhaps it would have been better for Emerson to renege on his promises to the Grants, to have let the kid go off and study music, play piano in nightspots . . . maybe that way Bowie might have been the last piano player cremated by an alien deathray, or might have survived while the rest of the Human race hurled itself onto the pyre of battle to stop the invaders.

But Emerson didn't think Bowie would see things that way. Bowie had seen the invaders at far closer range than Emerson, and Emerson had heard and seen enough to know that Earth was in a win-or-die war.

Still, the idea of putting the 15th out on the tip of the lance yet again went against Emerson's sense of justice and of military wisdom; this was a commando job, not a tank mission.

Commander Leonard was well aware of Emerson's relationship to Bowie Grant; but promises or no promises, Bowie was a soldier, end of story. Leonard wasn't spelling all this out for everyone in the room, but Rolf had picked up the commander's subliminal message.

Rudolph and Rochelle also understood Rolf's predicament, but they, too, were resolute in their decision: it had to be the 15th.

"I suggest we prepare an options list," Emerson told the staff, "a variety of plans and mixes for the forces involved."

Leonard seemed to consider that. He addressed Colonel Rudolph: "Get together with the ATACs' CO and hammer out one scenario using the Fifteenth." He ordered Rolf to get the G3 shop to begin assembling alternatives.

Emerson acknowledged the order, relieved. But as the meeting broke up, Leonard pulled Rudolph aside, waiting until Emerson was gone.

"Colonel, I'm directing you to present this mission to the Fifteenth ATAC and Lieutenant Sterling as an order, not a proposal. We can't waste time dawdling." *And I can't waste time arguing with my subordinates, nor can I risk Emerson's resigning just now. My neck's on the block!*

Rudolph snapped to smartly. "Sir!"

The commander continued in a confidential tone. "We must put aside Rolf's personal matters and get on with the war."

* * *

"What d'ya think—that I'd *volunteer* us for this mission?" Dana said to her squad after the orders had come down from Headquarters. "Somebody has to recon that fortress—"

"And we're that somebody," Sean finished for her. "HQ wants to know who it's fighting."

"They'll be fighting *me* if this keeps up," Sergeant Dante threatened, clenching his big hands and adopting a boxer's stance.

The primaries of the 15th were grouped in their barracks ready-room, trying to find someone to blame for HQ's directive. Dana had already had it out with Colonel Rudolph, citing all the action the team had seen lately, their need for R & R, the sorry state of their ordnance and Hovertanks. But it all fell on deaf ears: when the supreme commander said jump, you jumped. With or without a chute.

"Hey, Sarge, I thought you *wanted* to keep fighting," Sean reminded him.

Dante glared at him. "I just don't like being used like a pawn in Leonard's game of 'name the alien.' We've gotta go out there and risk our lives to save their reputations."

"How *literary* of you, Angelo," Dana said sharply. "What the heck does *reputation* have to do with any of this?" She gestured out the window in the direction of the downed fortress. "That ship is at least a *potential* threat. What are we supposed to do—turn it into an amusement park ride?"

"How are we even going to get in?" Louie Nichols thought to ask.

The team turned to regard the whiz kid of the Southern Cross, waiting for him to suggest something. With his gaunt, angular face, top-heavy thatch of deep brown hair, and everpresent wrap-around opaque goggles, Louie came closer to resembling an alien than Dana herself. Some members of Professor Cochran's group actually believed that Louie had patterned himself after the infamous Exedore, the Zentraedi Minister of Affairs during the Robotech War.

"It's difficult enough analyzing their technology. But getting *inside* their ship . . . How are we supposed to pull that off?"

Angelo looked at Louie in disbelief. "Get in? How are we gonna get out, Louie, how are we gonna get *out*?! I don't think you realize there's a chance we may not return from this mission alive."

Sean made a wry face. "Pity . . . she's gonna miss me when I'm gone."

At the same time, Louie exclaimed, "Gone?!" Bowie asked, "Isn't that a song?" and Dana said, "Knock it off."

Sean acknowledged the rebuke with a bemused smile. "You're right," he told Dana. "This mission is more important than my miss. What's it matter, right? We're tough."

"That's the right stuff," Dana enthused. "And there's no other way to pull this mission off but to, well, to just *do it*!"

The sergeant was nodding in agreement now, wondering where his earlier comments had come from. If Dana the halfbreed could get behind it, he could, too.

"All right," he said rallying to the cause. "We'll make them rue the day they touched down on this planet."

The 15th had a little over twelve hours to kill, and sleep was out of the question. Dana had her doubts about giving anybody permission to leave the barracks, but realized that keeping them cooped up would only give them time to ferment and perhaps explode. She issued "cinderella" passes—good until midnight—along with dire threats about what Nova's MPs would do to anybody who screwed up in town or came back late.

Sean left to visit a good friend who found prebattle good-byes aphrodisiac. Louie Nichols sat down to tinker with his helmet video transmitters. Angie nursed drinks and cigars in the dark privacy of his own quarters. And Bowie Grant insisted on treating Dana to the finest beers to be had in Monument City.

Twenty minutes later, Dana and Bowie were lifting frosted, conelike pilsner glasses of pale, foamy beer and clinking them together in a toast to better times.

Bowie contorted his face for a clownish look. "I figured it was the least I could do after what you did for me yesterday."

As Dana lowered her glass her hand brushed something that he had slid over to her.

"What's this?" It was a gorgeous little blossom of delicate red, hot pink, and coral, and tones in between. "A flower?"

"An orchid, Dana. For good luck."

She pinned it ceremonially onto her torso harness, near her heart. "You're sweet, Bowie. And maybe too sensitive for this line of work. What d'ya think?"

Bowie drew a deep breath. "Well, I prefer music to space warfare, if that's what you mean. You know this wasn't my idea."

Dana looked hard at her handsome friend, thinking back through years of peaceful and playful memories, back to when their parents were still on-world—when her memory of them was still alive. . . .

She debated for a moment, then it occurred to her—as it did more strongly with each action she fought in—that for her, Bowie, the 15th, the Human race, tomorrow might be the last, for any or all of them.

Bowie had been making mistakes lately in a very uncharacteristic way. Dana was no shrink and she couldn't take away all Bowie's resentment of the military; but the way she saw it, it would be good for all concerned if he let off a little steam on some piano keys.

"So go find some piano in an on-limits place and play for the people," Dana said suddenly. "And quit gaping at me like that!"

Bowie's eyebrows beetled. "Don't put me on about this, Da—"

"I'm not putting you on. Just remember: I gave Nova my word; I'm responsible for you. Don't mess up or we both take a fall. And sign back in at the barracks *before* midnight, read me?"

"Roger that," Bowie said, and was gone.

Feeling a good two kilos heavier after knocking back several more glasses, Dana (Bowie's gift orchid boutonniered to her uniform) returned to the barracks compound, left her Hovercycle in the mecha pool, and elevatored to the 15th's quarters. She looked in on Louie, but decided not to take him from his gadgeteering, and made for the ready-room, where she found Angelo nursing a drink in the dark, silently regarding the distant fortress, a black shape all but indiscernible from the ridgeline's numerous stone outcroppings and buttresses.

The sergeant sat with his arms folded, legs crossed, a sullen but contemplative look on his face. He was unaware of Dana's presence until she announced herself, asking to speak to him for a moment.

"About tomorrow's reconnaissance mission," they said simultaneously. But only Angelo chuckled.

Dana had serious issues on her mind now, the success of the mission, the safety of her team. With a bit of luck Bowie would land himself in the brig and she would be able to scratch him from her worry list. Sean and Louie presented no problems, and either of them could handle the squad's grunts; but that left Angelo Dante.

"I know this doesn't have to be said but once," Dana went on. "But . . . I know I can depend on you, Angie. Just wanted you to know."

"Same here, Lieutenant. Don't worry; we're gonna kick some alien butt."

It was typical of Angelo to put it this way: at the same time he was deferring to her and questioning her command abilities. *Alien* was directed at her; the sergeant's unmasked attack on her mixed ancestry. But she had lived with the "halfbreed" stigma for so long that it hardly fazed her anymore. Who on Earth hadn't lost someone to the Zentraedi wars? And with all of her mother's people aboard the SDF-3 or the Robotech Factory Satellite now, she was in effect the unofficial scapegoat of the unspeakable crimes of the past. If only Max and Miriya had foreseen this; she would have preferred death to the purgatory of the present.

"I'm aware of my responsibilities," she told Angelo. "But I just wanted to say that this mission will fail even before it gets under way unless you and I can begin to trust each other."

She took the small orchid from her lapel, reached across Angelo, and dropped it in his Scotch and soda.

"Hey—"

"Tropical ice," she smiled down at him. "A little good luck charm for you, Angie—a peace offering. Do you like it?"

"I guess . . ." the sergeant started to reply, sitting up in his chair. But just then someone threw on the overhead lights. Startled by the intrusion, he and Dana swung around at the same moment to find Nova Satori and Bowie centered in the wide doorway.

"I put you in charge of Bowie and this is what happens?" Nova said, as the entry doors slid shut.

Dana met them halfway, sizing up the situation quickly and rehearsing her lines. She had certainly anticipated the arrival of these two, but not Bowie's disheveled appearance. His uniform was soiled and one of his cheeks looked bruised.

"Are you all right?" she asked him. "What's going on here?"

Bowie wore a distressed look, more genuine than yesterday's.

"I guess I did it again," he answered contritely.

"I ought to throw you *both* in jail," Nova scolded Dana. "He was in a barroom brawl." The lieutenant looked like her namesake, ready to incinerate whatever was in close proximity.

This time Nova herself had caught him red-handed, following him from the café and waiting until just the right moment to walk in on him. And now she had Dana just where she wanted her: of course Nova would agree to release Bowie to her custody once again, but this time there would be a price to pay—a first look at the results of tomorrow's recon operation for starters. With rivalry increasing daily between Leonard's army intelligence and the

Global Military Police, it was the only way Nova could count on getting the real dope.

Dana looked cross. "What was the fight about?"

"Ah, some loudmouth said no piano player is man enough to serve in the Hovertanks," Bowie admitted.

"That's a lot of rot!" Dana returned, back on Bowie's side all at once. "I wonder if *I'm* man enough?! I hope you taught him a lesson. I'm proud of you."

Nova expected as much, but played her part by growing angry.

"Go ahead, praise him, Lieutenant Sterling. You're digging his grave deeper."

"A soldier stands for something," Dana answered defensively. "What if somebody said no woman is good enough to be an MP—"

Nova wore a wry look. "Stuff the defense plea, Dana. Battles don't get won in barrooms, and merit doesn't get proven there either! What Bowie earned himself is a cell."

Unless we can cut a deal . . . Nova was saying to herself when Dana surprised her.

"All right then, take him away."

Both Bowie and Nova stared at her. The lieutenant's meticulously plucked eyebrows almost went up someplace into her hairline.

"Run him over to the guardhouse," Dana said evenly.

"B-but, Lieutenant, you can't be serious," Bowie burst out. Dana's verbal slap hurt more than that punch to the face. Even Angelo was stepping forward, coming to his aid, but Dana was unmoved.

"I have enough to handle without having to worry about an eight ball," Dana said, trying not to think about the orchid in the drink glass, so nearby.

Nova was watching these exchanges with her mouth open. She gulped and found her voice, hoping she could salvage something from this. "Dana, you'd better not be kidding—"

Dana shook her head. "I've failed somewhere along the line . . . It's your turn to take care of him now." She caught the hurt look that surfaced in Bowie's eyes and turned away from him, determined to finish this scene no matter what.

"I've got to be on that mission tomorrow," Bowie was pleading with her. "You said I was right to defend our honor, now you're taking away my chance—"

She whirled on him suddenly. "I've heard it all before, Grant! You should have thought of that before you went off to that bar!"

Bowie's eyes went wide. "But Dana . . . *Lieutenant* . . . you—"

"Enough!" Dana cut him off. "Private Grant, ten-*hut*! You will accompany Lieutenant Satori to the stockade."

Nova's puzzlement increased. *Where had this one gone wrong?* "You don't want to reconsider . . . ?"

"My mind is made up."

Nova made a gesture of exasperation, then smiled in self-amusement and led Bowie away.

"What made you do that?" the sergeant asked Dana after they left. Having recently caught a glimpse of Bowie's sloppiness in the field, he wasn't opposed to Dana's decision but wondered, nevertheless, what had motivated this sudden attack.

"Because I'm CO here," Dana said evenly.

CHAPTER THREE

Thrilled at having received word of the 15th's mission to recon the alien ship—it never even occurred to me that she might not return!—I was suddenly faced with a new obstacle: Bowie Grant was in the custody of the GMP. Dana's reactions to the fortress were of paramount importance, but I was equally interested in establishing the depth of her involvement with the young Grant. I asked myself: Would proximity to the Masters reawaken her Zentraedi nature to the point where she would abandon her loyalties to both teammates and loved ones? It was therefore essential that Grant accompany the 15th, and up to me to see to it that Rolf Emerson learned of Grant's imprisonment.

Dr. Lazlo Zand, *Event Horizon: Perspectives on Dana Sterling and the Second Robotech War*

THE PENETRATION OPERATION GOT UNDER WAY EARLY THE next morning. Coordinated air strikes would provide the necessary diversion, and, with a bit of luck, the breach the 15th was going to require in order to infiltrate its dozen Hovertanks. Tech crews had worked all night long, going over the complex mecha systems and installing remote cameras.

General Emerson was monitoring the proceedings from the situation room. Staff officers and enlisted-ratings were buzzing in and out supplying him with updates and recon data. There were never less than six voices talking at the same time; but Emerson himself had little to say. He had his elbows on the table, fingers steepled, eyes fixed on the video transmissions relayed in by various spotter planes over the target zone. Only moments ago a combined team of Adventurer IIs and Falcon fighters had managed to awaken the apparently slumbering giant, and an intense firefight was in progress on the high ground surrounding the alien fortress. Armor-piercing rounds had thus far proved ineffective against the ship's layered hull, in spite of the fact that the XT's energy shield had yet to be deployed. But Emerson had just received word that the air corps was bringing in a QF-3000 E Ghost—an unmanned triple-cannon drone capable of delivering Reflex firepower of the sort that had proved effective in earlier airborne confrontations.

The wallscreen image of the besieged fortress derezzed momentarily, only to be replaced by a bird's-eye view of the 15th's diamond-formation advance. Emerson felt his pulse race as he watched the dozen mecha close on the heavily fortified perimeter. It was ironic that his attempts to deescalate the fledgling war had resulted in the 15th's assignment to this mission to hell; but in some ways he realized the perverted *rightness* of it: Emerson literally had to put what amounted to his family on the line in order to convince the supreme commander to listen to him. And Dana and Bowie were just that—family.

So often he would try to run his thoughts back in time, searching for the patterns that had led all of them to this juncture. Had there been signs along the way, omens he had missed, premonitions he had ignored? When the Sterlings and Grants had opted to leave aboard the SDF-3 as members of the Hunters' crew, did it occur to them that they might not return from that corner of space ruled by the Robotech Masters, or that the Masters might come here instead? Emerson remembered the optimism that characterized those days, some twelve years ago, when the newly-built ship had been launched, Rick and Lisa in command. Rolf and his wife had taken both Dana and Bowie: After all, he had often watched over the kids while the Grants spent time on the Factory Satellite, and the Sterlings combed the jungles of the Zentraedi Control Zone—what used to be called Amazonia—for Malcontents; it seemed a perfect solution then that the kids should remain here while their parents embarked on the Expeditionary Mission that was meant to return peace to the galaxy ...

That Emerson had chosen to enroll both of them in the military had resulted in a divorce from his wife. Laura never understood his reasons; childless herself, Dana and Bowie had become her children, and what mother—what *parent*!—would choose to wish war on her offspring? But Rolf was merely honoring the promises he had made to Vince and Jean, Max and Miriya. Perhaps each of them did have a sense of what the future held, and perhaps they reasoned that the kids would have a better chance on Earth than they would, lost in space? Certainly they recognized why Rolf had decided to remain behind, just as surely as Supreme Commander Leonard recognized it. ...

Emerson pressed his hands to his face, fingers massaging tired eyes. When he looked up again, Lieutenant Milton, an energetic young aide, was standing over his right shoulder. Milton saluted and bent close by his shoulder to report that Bowie was in the guardhouse. It seemed that the GMP had caught him involved in a barroom brawl.

Rolf nodded absently, watching the displays, and thinking of a little boy who had cried so inconsolably when his parents left him behind. He wondered whether Bowie had purposely provoked a fight in order to absent himself from the mission. He had to be made to understand that rules were meant to be followed. The 15th had been chosen and as a member of that team he owed it to the others. Of course, it was equally plausible that Dana was behind this; she didn't seem to comprehend that her overprotectiveness wasn't doing Bowie any good, either.

"Tell Lieutenant Satori that General Emerson would consider it a personal favor if she could find a way to release Private Grant," Rolf told his aide in low tones. "Ask her for me to see to it that Bowie rejoins his unit as soon as possible."

The lieutenant saluted and left in a rush as Emerson returned his attention to the wallscreen's bird's-eye view of the 15th's advance, realizing all at once that Bowie's readdition to the team would raise their number to *thirteen*.

The terrain between Monument City and the fortress was as rugged as it came. What was formerly a series of wooded slopes rising from a narrow river valley had been transformed by Dolza's annihilation bolts into a tortuous landscape of eroded crags and precipitous outcroppings, denuded, waterless, and completely unnatural. Stretches of ancient highways could be seen here and there beneath deposits of pulverized granite, or volcanic earthworks.

Before dawn the 15th was in position just below the fortress's crash site, ringed as it was on three sides by pseudobuttes and tors. Dana had brought the column to a halt, awaiting the arrival of the Ghost drone. Quiet reigned on all fronts.

Cocooned in the mecha's cockpit, her body sheathed from head to foot in armor, she sensed a strange assemblage of feelings vying for her attention. By rights her mind should have been emptied, rendered fully accessible to the mecha's reconfiguration demands; but with things at a temporary impasse, she gave inner voice to some of these thoughts.

She knew, for example, that the thrill she felt was attributable to her Zentraedi ancestry; the fear, her Human one. But this was hardly a clear-cut case of ambivalence or dichotomy; rather she experienced an odd commingling of the two, where each contained a measure of its opposite. Her heart told her that inside the fortress she would encounter her own reflection: the racial past she had been told about but never experienced. How had her mother felt when going into combat against her own brothers and sisters? Dana asked herself. Or when hunting down the Malcontents who roamed the wastelands? No different, she supposed, than when a Human went to war against his or her own kind. But would it ever end? Even her fun-loving uncles—Rico, Konda, and Bron—were resigned to warfare in the end, telling her before they died that peace, when it came, would merely be an interlude in the War Without End. . . .

Beside her now, a Hovertank unexpectedly joined the 15th's front ranks, raising a cloud of yellow dust as it slid to a halt in the pebbly earth. Dana thought the Battloid's head through a left turn and almost jumped free of her seat straps when she recognized the mecha as Bowie's *Diddy-Wa-Diddy*.

"What in world are you doing here, Private?" she barked over the tac net.

"You tell me. Somebody sprang me."

"Good ole Uncle Rolf." She let the bitterness be heard in her tone. Emerson had undermined her command.

"That's the way I figured it," Bowie laughed. Then the laughter was gone. "And Private Grant is completely at your service. I've learned my lesson, Dana."

Rolf! Dana thought.

Infuriated, she began to hatch sinister plots against him, but the scenarios all played themselves out rather quickly. Rolf was thinking of Bowie's self-image, as always, and she couldn't help but understand. It was just that self-image wouldn't count for much if you didn't live to cash in on it. *Or would it? . . .* Senseless to debate it now, she told herself as the cockpit displays lit up.

"Then fall in, trooper!" she told Bowie.

"No more a' this eight-ball crap," Dana heard Angelo second over the net.

"I copy, Sarge," Bowie said.

Dana called in air strikes as the 15th got moving again, straight for the colossal alloy rampart that was the flagship's hull.

Scoop-nosed Tac Air fighters, Adventurers and Falcons, came down in prearranged sorties, dumping tons of smart and not-so-smart ordnance, strafing, braving the fire of the glassy inverted-teardrop fortress cannon. Warheads exploded violently against the ship's hull, summoning in return thundering volleys of pulse-cannon fire and an outpouring of Bioroids, some on foot, but many more atop ordnance-equipped hovercraft. Ground teams peppered the existing alien troops with chaingunfire, and the tac net erupted in a cacophony of commands, requests, praise, and blood-curdling screams.

While the two sides exchanged death, the Ghost drone dropped in on its release run. A nontransformable hybrid of the Falcon and the Veritech, the Ghost was developed in the early stages of Robotechnology as an adjunct to the transorbital weapons system utilized by the Armor series orbital platforms. It had undergone several modifications since, and the one in present use was closer to a smart bomb than a drone aircraft. Professor Miles Cochran's team had plotted an impact point toward the bow of the fortress, in the vertical portion of hull somewhat below the pyramidal structure known to some as Louie's "Robotech Teat."

ATAC Battloids took up firing positions and concentrated their total power on the predesignated section of the hull in an attempt to soften it up. Main batteries and rifle/cannon, and the multiple barrels of the secondaries, everything in the 15th cut loose, aimed at the one small section of offworld alloy. The air shimmered and cooked away; heat waves rose all around, and power levels in the ATACs dropped rapidly. Dana sweated and hoped that no assault ship or Bioroid came at them now, when the 15th's mecha must hold their positions until the breach had been made.

Sterling kept the 15th well back from the strike zone as the Ghost zeroed in. The craft fell short of its projected goal, but the ensuing explosion proved powerful enough to open a fiery hole large enough to accommodate a Hovertank, and no one could ask for more than that.

The ATACs lowered their weapons in a kind of shocked surprise.

"When we get back, I'll buy the beers!" Bowie said, breaking the silence.

Dana returned an invisible smile and thanked him, promising to hold him to his word. "All right, Fifteenth," she commanded over the tac net, "you know the drill!"

Protoculture worked its magic as Battloids mechamorphosed to Hovertank mode, reconfiguring like some exotic, knightly origami. Thrusters whined as the tanks floated into formation, forming up on Dana for the recon, and riding separate blasting carpets toward the jagged opening and the dark unknown.

Behind the visor of her *Valkyrie*'s helmet, Dana Sterling's eyes narrowed. "Now we take the war to *them!*" she said.

The Bioroids didn't exactly escort the 15th in, nor welcome them with open arms once they arrived. Dana raised the canopy of her mecha and gestured the team forward, ordering them over the net to maintain formation. She led them on a beeline to the breach, disc gun and cannon fire paving an explosive road for the Hovertanks, which continued to loose pulsed bursts in return. Miraculously, though, no one was hit and shortly the 15th found itself inside one of the fortress's cavernous chambers.

It was Professor Cochran's suggestion—based on a rather sketchy analysis of the fortress's infrastructure (which had led him to believe that much of the starboard holds were given over to defense and astrogation)—that the team swing itself toward the port side of the ship if possible. This quickly proved to be not only viable but necessary because the starboard section was found partitioned off by a massive bulkhead that would have taken another Ghost to breach. Consequently, the ATACs barely cut their speed as they advanced.

Three Bioroids suddenly appeared, dropping from overhead circular portals that simply weren't there a moment before—"They may as well have dropped in from another dimension," Louie Nichols would say later.

As annihilation discs flew past Dana's head, she trained the *Valkyrie*'s muzzle on the first of these and took it out with a faceplate shot; the alien seemed to absorb the cranial round silently, slumping down and shorting out as Dana sped past it. The other two were laying down a steady stream of crippling fire most of the team managed to avoid. But Dana then heard a terror-filled scream pierce the net and saw one of the 15th's tanks screeching along the vast corridor on its hind end. Dante was trying to raise Private Simon when the mecha barreled into one of the Bioroids and exploded. Dana and Louie poured plasma against the remaining one, literally blowing it limb from limb.

"Status report!" the lieutenant demanded when they brought the tanks to a halt.

The corridor, a good fifteen-meters wide, was filled with thick smoke and littered with mecha debris. The severed arm of a Bioroid lay twitching on the floor, leaking a sickly green fluid and a worm's nest of wires. Dana wondered what sort of reception HQ was receiving and tried without success to raise them on the radio. Display sensors gave no indication that the video units were incapacitated, so she swiveled the camera through a 360 for Emerson's benefit. Louie, meanwhile, launched a self-deployed monitoring unit.

It was Simon's mecha that had collided with the Bioroid. Fortunately, the private had bailed out at the last minute, his armor protecting him from the explosion and what would have been a full-body road rash. However, without the mecha, Dana informed him, he was going to be useless to the team.

"But why?" he was saying to her now. "It's not my fault my craft was disabled."

Sean, Road, and Woodruff had positioned themselves as a rear guard; Angelo, Bowie, and Louie were forward. Private Jordon and the rest of the team had dismounted and were grouped around Dana and Simon, the helmetless private looking small and defenseless in the vastness of the corridor. Jordon, who rarely knew when to keep his mouth shut, suddenly found it necessary to back up Dana's words to Simon.

"You just have to understand, Simon, we can't afford to jeopardize the mission by dragging you along with us."

Meanwhile, Dana had been trying to figure out just what she could do with Simon. They were a good half mile in, certainly not too far from the breach to have him leg it back, but what could he do when he got there? The skirmish was still in progress and he wouldn't stand a chance outside. He could ride second in one of the tanks, but Dana thought it was best to post Simon and one of the others here as backup. Jordon was as good a choice as any.

Jordon didn't take the news any better than Simon had, but Dana put a quick end to his protests. He and Simon were to wait for the team to return; if no one returned by 0600 hours they were to try and raise HQ and make their own way out of the fortress. In the meantime, Dana would see to it that Louie maintained radio contact with them every thirty minutes. With that, she regrouped the rest of the 15th and signaled them forward.

A substantial portion of their premission briefing had involved a thorough study of the archive notes left by the men who had reconned the first super dimensional fortress shortly after its fateful arrival on Earth. That group had been led by Henry Gloval and Dr. Emil Lang, and had also included the legendary Roy Fokker and the now notorious T. R. Edwards. But the 15th found little similarity between what they had read and what they were faced with now. For starters, the SDF-1 group had gone in on foot; but more important, this ship was *known to be armed and dangerous*. All Dana could do was keep proper procedure in mind and try to emulate Gloval's methodical approach.

As a group they continued at moderate speed along the dimly lit corridor, the height and width of which never varied. It was hexagon-shaped, although somewhat elongated vertically, a constant fifteen-yards wide across the floor—uniform blue outsized tiles—by some twenty-five yards high. The walls (paneled on the downward slope and strangely variegated and cell-like above) appeared to be constructed of a laser-resistant ceramic. There was no ceiling as such, save for a continuum of enormous tie beams, proportionally spaced, beyond which lay an impenetrable thicket of pipes, conduits, and tubing—an unending knot of capillaries and arterial junctures. But by far the most interesting objects in the corridor were the adornments that lined the upper walls of the hexagon—oval shaped, ruby-red opaque lenses spaced five meters apart along the entire length of the hall. Every twelfth medallion was a more ornate version, backed by a segmented cross with pointed arms. Twice, the 15th entered a stretch of corridor where these lenses found their match in similar convexities that lined the lower walls, but along one side only.

The team was moving parallel to the long axis of the fortress, one mile in when they reached the first fork, a symmetrical Y-shaped intersection at the end of a long sweeping curve, with identical corridors branching off left and right. The archway was lined with a kind of segmented trimwork that looked soft and inviting, but was in fact ceramic like the walls. Here, the servo-gallery above the openwork ceiling was bathed in infrared light.

Dana once again ordered them to a halt and split the team: the sergeant would take the B team—Marino, Xavez, Kuri, and Road—into the left fork; Dana, Corporal Nichols and the rest of the 15th would explore the right.

"We'll rendezvous back here in exactly two hours," she said to Angelo from the open cockpit. "Okay, move out."

Dante's group swung their vehicles out of formation and followed the sergeant's slow lead into the corridor. Dana gave a wave and the A team fell in behind her tank. Behind the 15th, unseen, three curious, Human-size figures stealthily crossed the corridor. One of them depressed a ruby-red button that seemed part of a medallion's design. From pockets concealed in the archway slid five concentrically-etched panels of impervious metal, sealing off the corridor.

Dana's group passed quickly through domed chambers, empty and discomforting, with riblike support trusses and walls like stretched skin. Beyond that was the selfsame hexagonal corridor and yet another Y intersection.

"Which way now?" Bowie asked.

Dana was against breaking the team up into yet smaller groups, but they had to make the most of their time. "Bowie, you and Louie come with me down the right corridor," she said after a moment. "Sean, you and the others take the left one—got it?"

While Dana was issuing the orders, Bowie happened to glance over his shoulder—in time to see what appeared to be the retreating shadow of a being of some sort. But the light here was so unsettling that he resisted alarming the others; his eyes had been playing tricks on him since they entered the fortress and he didn't want the team to think him paranoid. Nevertheless, Dana caught his sharp intake of breath and asked him what he had seen.

"Just my imagination, Lieutenant," he told her as Sean's group split off and moved their Hovertanks into the left corridor.

Dana also had the feeling that they were being watched—how could it *not* be so, given the techno-systems of the ship? But that was all right: *she wanted to be seen.*

The right corridor proved to be a new world: hexagonal still, but fully enclosed, with an overhead "bolstered" ridge and numerous riblike trusses. Gone were the medallions and ruby ovals; the walls, upper and lower, were an unbroken series of rectangular light panels. A new world, but a worrisome one.

Without success, Dana tried to raise Sergeant Dante on the net.

"I haven't been able to raise him, either," Louie said, a note of distress in his voice. "Do you think we should go look for him?"

Dana was considering this when the silence that had thus far accompanied them was suddenly broken by a distant sound of servo-motors slamming and clanking into operation. The three teammates turned around and watched as a solid panel began its steady descent from overhead.

The corridor was sealing itself off!

Ahead of them, a second door was descending; and beyond that a third, and fourth. As far as they could see, massive curtains of armor-plate were dropping from pockets built into the ceiling trusses, echos of descent and closure filling the air.

"Hit it!" Dana exploded. "Full power!"

The Hovertanks shot forward at top speed, barely clearing the first gate. They tore beneath a dozen more in the same fashion, seemingly gaining on the progression—three urban joyriders beating the traffic lights downtown.

Then all at once the progression shifted: up ahead of them was a fully closed gate. Dana, far out in front of Bowie and Louie, reached for her retro levers and pulled them home, favoring the port throttle so that the hind end of the tank gradually began to come around to starboard. There was no way in the world she wanted to hit that gate head-on. . . .

CHAPTER FOUR

*Initial analysis of the fruit [found aboard the alien fortress] revealed
little more than its basic structure—its similarities to certain tropical
fruits seldom seen in northern markets these days. But subsequent tests
proved intriguing: one taste of the fruit and a laboratory chimp soared
into what Cochran described as "a one-way ticket to reverie." And yet
it was not a true hallucinogen; in fact, molecular scans showed it to be
closer to animal than vegetal in makeup! . . . Several years would go
by before our questions would be answered.*

Mingtao, *Protoculture: Journey Beyond Mecha*

THE HUGE WALLSCREEN IN THE SITUATION ROOM WAS LITTLE
more than static bars and snow. A flicker of image enlivened it
momentarily, incomprehensibly, then there was nothing.

"We've lost contact with the Fifteenth," a tech reported to General Emerson.

"Increase enhancement," Rolf said sternly, bent on denying the
update. "See if you can raise them."

Haltingly a second tech turned to the task, well aware of what
the results would be. "Negatory," he said to Emerson after a moment. "I'm afraid the interference is overwhelming."

Colonel Anderson pivoted in his seat to face Rolf. "Should we
consider sending in a rescue team?"

Emerson shook his head but said nothing. *The loss of one team
would be enough . . . the loss of two loved ones, more than he
could bear.* He pressed his hands to his face, fearing the worst. . . .

The left corridor had led Sergeant Dante's contingent to an
enormous hold filled with a bewildering array of Robotech machinery.

"Where is Louie when you need him," Angelo was saying to
his men.

They had all dismounted from their Hovertanks and were

grouped together marveling at the chamber's wonders. The hold was simply too spacious to fathom, its distant horizons lost in darkness. Here was a massive cone-shaped generator, three hundred yards in circumference if it was an inch; there, a second generator harnessing and shunting energy the likes of which Dante had never seen—a raw subatomic fire that seemed to have a life of its own. Liquids alive as fresh blood pulsed through transparent pipes, coursing from generator to generator, machine to machine, while unattended display screens strobed amber-lit schematics to robot readers, communicating to one another through a cacophonous language of shrill sounds and harsh rasps.

There was no telling how high the hold went: indeterminate levels of conduits, tubes, and mains crisscrossed overhead, illuminated by flashes of infrared light projected by spherical anti-grav Cyclopean remotes—ruby-eyed monitors, ribbed and whiskered with segmented antennae.

"Look at the size of this place!" Private Road exclaimed. (Angelo couldn't wait to promote the guy just to put an end to the running joke.)

"Hold it down," said the sergeant. "Stay alert and keep your eyes peeled for anything that might be threatening."

"Threatening?" Marino asked in disbelief, his assault rifle welded to his hands. "This whole place looks pretty threatening to me, Sarge."

"Gimme hell anyday," Xavez seconded.

Dante whirled on both of them, raising his voice. "I said can it, and I'm not gonna tell you again! The next guy that speaks is gonna be in a sorrier scene than this! Now, spread out! But keep in sight of each other! We've gotta job to do."

High above them, one of the eyeball remotes blinked, fixing an aerial image of men and mecha in its fish-eye lens. That much accomplished, the device rotated slightly and emitted a patterned series of light.

On a gallery still higher up in the hold, the code was received by a shadowy creature, which acknowledged the signal and moved off into the darkness.

Private Road, meanwhile, had begun to edge away from the tight-knit group. There was no sense waiting around for the sarge to wrap up his lecture—they could recite it from memory by now, even the threats and imprecations. The private smiled in the privacy of his face shield and took a small step backwards. But suddenly something was taking him a step further: a vice had been clamped around his throat, shutting down his oxygen supply and crushing the nascent scream that was lodged in his throat. He could feel his eyeballs begin to swell and protrude as whatever had him increased the torque of its grip. He heard and felt the snap that broke his neck, the rush of death in his ears. . . .

". . . and I want you to sound off the minute you see anything suspicious," Angelo finished up. He had armed his weapon and was lowering his face shield when Kuri made a puzzled sound over the tac net.

"Hey Sarge, Road's gone."

Dante leveled his weapon and swung toward where he had last seen the private. Xavez and Marino exchanged wary looks, then followed the sergeant's lead.

"Road!" Dante called softly. He dropped his mask and called him again through the net. When there was no response, he gestured briefly to the team. "All right, don't just stand there: find him!" To Kuri he said: "See if you can raise the lieutenant."

Dante double-checked his weapon, thinking: *If this is Road's idea of a joke, they'll be calling him Dead-end from now on!*

Suddenly, without warning, the room was sectioned by laser fire.

"Stand clear!" Dana warned Bowie and Louie.

The two of them returned to their Hovertanks as Dana primed the laser and aimed it at the armored gate.

Dana's mecha had managed to stop just short of the thing, hind end almost fully around, two meters from collision. She had repositioned it in the center of the corridor now, thirty meters from the gate. The barrier was some sort of high-density metal, unlike the durceramic of the corridor walls, and Louie had every confidence that the laser would do the trick.

"Any luck raising Sergeant Dante or Jordon?" Dana asked Louie once more before targeting.

Louie shook his head and flashed her a thumbs-down.

"Even my optic sensor is out," he told her over the net.

That didn't surprise her, given the apparent thickness of the corridor walls and the fact that they were at least one-and-a-half miles into the fortress by now. Nor did the barriers come as any great shock; all along she had sensed that their progress was being monitored.

"Do you think they caught the others?" Bowie said worriedly.

"Your guess is as good as mine," she responded casually, and turned her attention to the laser. "All right then: here goes."

She depressed the laser's trigger; there was enough residual smoke in the corridor to give her a glimpse of the light-ray itself, but by and large her eyes were glued to the barrier. Louie had cautioned her that it would prove to be a tedious operation—a slow burn they would probably need to help along with an armor-piercing round—but Louie was not infallible: instead of that expected slow burn, the laser blew a massive hole in the gate on impact.

"Well that wasn't so bad," Dana said when the shrapnel-storm passed.

She reached for her rifle, dismounted the tank, and approached the gate cautiously. Beyond it was a short stretch of corridor that opened into what she guessed was the fortress's water-recycling and ventilation hold. What with the numerous shafts and ducts here, she reasoned she couldn't be far off the mark.

"What do you see, Lieutenant?" Louie asked from behind her.

Dana lifted her face shield. "Not much of anything, but at least we're out of that trap." As Bowie and Louie caught up with her, she cautioned them to stay together.

There were enough dripping sounds, sibilant rushes, and roars to make them feel as though they had entered a giant's basement. But there was something else as well: almost a wind-chime's voice, soft and atonal, all but lost to their ears but registering nonetheless as if through some sixth sense. It seemed to fill the air, and yet have no single source, ambient as full-moon light. At times it reminded Dana of bells or gongs, but no sooner would she fix on that, than the sound would reconfigure and appear harplike or string percussive.

"It's like music," Bowie said to a transfixed Dana.

The sound was working on her, infiltrating her, *playing* her, as though *she* were the instrument: her music was memory's song, but dreamlike, preverbal and impossible to hold. . . .

"Are you all right, Lieutenant?" Louie was asking her, breaking the spell.

She encouraged the tone to leave her, and suggested they try to locate the source of the sound. Louie, his face shield raised, ever-present goggles in place, had his ear pressed to one of the hold's air ducts. He motioned Dana and Bowie over, and the three of them crouched around the duct, listening intently for a moment.

"Maybe it's just faulty plumbing," Bowie suggested.

Louie ignored the jest. "This is the first sign of life we've encountered. We have to figure out where it's coming from and how to get to it."

Dana stood up, wondering just how they could accomplish that.

Excited by the discovery, Louie was firing questions at her faster than she could field them. She silenced him and returned her attention to the sound; when she looked up again, Louie was falling through the wall.

Sean and company—Woodruff and Cranston—were in what appeared to be some sort of "hot house," scarcely 200 yards from the water-recycling chamber (though they had no way of knowing this), but in any case separated from the lieutenant's contingent by three high-density ceramic bulkheads. "Hot house" was Sean's conjecture, just as recycling chamber had been Dana's, but it had taken the private several minutes to come up with even this description.

There was no soil, no hydroponic cultivation bins or artificial sunlight, no water vapor or elevated oxygen or carbon dioxide levels; only row after row of alien plants that seemed to be growing upside down. Central to each was an almost incandescent globe, some ten meters in circumference, tendriled and supported by, or perhaps suspended from, groupings of rigid, bristly lianalike vines. (Cranston was reminded of the macrame plant hangers popular in the last century, although he didn't mention this to the others.) The globes themselves were positioned anywhere from five to fifteen meters from the floor of the chamber, and below them, both still affixed to the stalks themselves or spread about the floor, were individual fruits, the size of apples but the red of strawberries.

The three men had left their idling Hovertanks to have a closer look. Sean had the face shield of his helmet raised, and was casually flipping one of the fruits in his hand, using elbow snaps to propel the thing in the air. Talk had switched from the plants themselves to the fact that the team had yet to encounter any resistance. No one had taken the dare to taste the fruit, but Sean had thought to stow a few ripe specimens in his tank for later analysis.

"It's crazy," the one-hand juggler was saying now. "They were awful anxious to keep us out of here in the first place, so why are they so quiet now?"

"Maybe we frightened them?" Cranston suggested. "Up close, I mean," he hastened to add after catching the look Sean threw him.

"W-w-what d'ya guys got against peace and quiet anyway?" Woodruff stammered.

Sean made a wry face. "Nothing, Jack. Except when it's *too* quiet, like it is right now. We just can't let ourselves be lulled by it, is all. Or else they'll be all over us." Sean held the fruit out in front of him and began to squeeze it. "Like this!" he said, as the fruit ruptured, releasing a thick white juice that touched all of them.

It was actually a hinged, polygonal section of wall that Louie Nichols had fallen through. And behind it were even stranger surprises.

At sight of the first of these—a rectangular vat filled with assorted body parts floating in a viscous lavender solution—Louie almost blew his breakfast, his eyes going wide beneath the tinted goggles. Bowie and Dana stepped in and followed his lead, registering their revulsion in stifled exclamations and sounds.

A five-fingered grappling claw was attached to the side of the vat, its purpose immediately obvious to Louie as he took in the rest of the room. Behind them was a conveyor belt, also equipped with a grappling arm, and a tableful of artificial heads.

"It's an assembly line!" Bowie said in disbelief. "And we thought these aliens were humanoid!"

"Mustn't jump to conclusions," Louie cautioned him, leaning toward the tank now and reaching forward to touch the arms and legs floating there. He was fully composed again, curious and fascinated. "These are android parts," he said after a moment of scrutiny, amazement in his voice.

Dana decided to risk another look and watched as the corporal pulled and probed at the ligamentlike innards of a forearm and the artificial flesh of a face.

"Incredible," Louie pronounced. "The texture is actually *life-like*. It isn't cold or metallic . . . They seem to have developed a perfect bio-mechanical combinant. . . ."

Bowie, feeling a little like a corpuscle in a lymph node, had wandered away from the vat to investigate the membrane walls of the room—any excuse to absent himself from Louie's continuing anatomy lesson. But even so, words from his science courses kept creeping into his thoughts: *cell-wall, vacuole, nucleus* . . . A minute later—during an elevator ascent through thin air—he would recall that *osmosis* was the last thing he had said to himself before being sucked through the wall. . . .

He also told himself that it was useless to struggle against this new situation: stepping off the radiant disk under his feet or propelling himself clear of the globe of soft light encompassing him seemed like risky ventures at the moment, and for all he knew this ride would land him outside the fortress, topside, smack dab in the middle of all that fighting and strafing, which was fine with him—

But all at once those dreams of an easy out came to an abrupt end, along with the disk itself. Bowie picked himself up off the floor—thankful there was one—and brought his assault rifle up, shouting demands into whitelight fog: "All right—what's going on here?!"

He was answered by the music they had heard in the water-recycling hold, who knew how many levels below him now. Only it was much more present here and, he realized, haunting and beautiful. He lowered the helmet's face shield and took one cautious step forward into the radiant haze, then a second and third. Several more and he began to discern the boundaries of the light; there was a corridor beyond, similar to those hexagonal ones they had already negotiated but on a smaller scale. The walls were textured, bare except for the occasional ruby-colored oval medallion, and the floor shone like polished marble. There was also a dead end to this particular windsong-filled corridor, or, as it turned out, a doorway.

Twin panels that formed the hexagonal portal slid apart as Bowie made his approach, revealing a short hall adorned with two opposing rows of Romanesque columns, medallioned like the walls. Overhead ran a continuous, arched skylight, hung with identical fixtures along its length—cluster representations of some red, apple-sized fruit. Shafts of sunlight danced along the hall's seamless floor.

Following the sound, Bowie turned left into a perpendicular hall, with curved sides and proportionately spaced rib trusses. The music was still stronger here, emanating, it seemed, from a dark room off to Bowie's right. Bowie hesitated at the entry, rechecked his weapon, and stepped through.

In the dark he saw a woman seated at a monitor—a curiously shaped device like everything on this ship, Bowie told himself—an up-ended clamshell, strung like a harp with filaments of colored light. The woman, on the other hand, was heavenly shaped: somewhat shorter than Bowie, with straight deep green hair that would have reached her knees if loosed from the ringlet that held it full halfway down her back. She was dressed in some sort of sky-blue, clinging chiffon bodysuit, with a coral-colored gauzelike cape and bodice wrapping that left one shoulder bare. She had her small hands positioned at the light-controls of the device when she turned and took notice of Bowie's entry. And it was only then—as her hands froze and the music began to waver—that Bowie realized she was *playing* the device: *She was the source of the music!*

He recognized at once that he had frightened her and moved quickly to soften his aspect, shouldering his weapon and keeping his voice calm as he spoke to her.

"Don't be scared. Is that better?" he asked, gesturing to his now slung rifle. "Believe me, you have nothing to fear from me." Bowie risked a small step toward her. "I just wanted to compliment you on your playing. I'm a musician myself."

She sat unmoving in the harp's equally unusual seat, her eyes wide and fixed on him. Bowie kept up the patter, noticing details as he approached: the thick band she wore on her right wrist, the fact that the hair bracketing her innocent face was cut short. . . .

"So you see we have something in common. They say that music is the universal language—"

Suddenly she was on her feet, ready to run, and Bowie stopped short. "Easy now," he repeated. "I'm not a monster. I'm just a person—like you." As he heard himself, he imagined how he must appear to her in his helmet and full-body armor. He rid himself of the "thinking cap" and saw her relax some. Encouraged, he introduced himself and asked for her name, tried a joke about being deaf, and finally dropped himself into the harp's cushioned, highbacked chair.

"I'm forgetting that music is the universal language," he said, turning to the instrument itself and wondering where to begin. "Maybe this'll work," he smiled up at the green-haired girl, who stood puzzled beside him, taking in all his words but uttering nothing in return.

Bowie regarded the ascending strings of light, marveling at shifting patterns of color. He positioned his hands in the harp, palms downward, interrupting the flow. As the tones changed, he tried to discern some correlation between the colors and sounds, thinking back to obscure musical texts he had read, the occult schools' approach to Pythagorean correspondences . . . Still he could make no musical sense of this harp. And it was soon apparent that the harpist herself could make no sense of Bowie's attempts.

"How long has it been since you had this thing tuned?" he said playfully, as the woman leaned in to demonstrate.

Bowie watched her intently, more fascinated by her sudden closeness than the richness of her music. But as her graceful hands continued to strike the light-strings, Bowie felt a soothing magic begin to work on him, eliciting feelings he could not define, other than to say that the harpist and her instrument were the source of them; that it felt as though *he could somehow be made to do the harp's bidding*.

"That's the most beautiful thing I've ever heard," Bowie said softly. "And you're the most beautiful thing I've ever seen."

She had scarcely acknowledged his earlier attempts at verbal communication, but this seemed to give her pause; she turned from the harp to stare at him, as though his words were music she could understand.

Then all at once the room was flooded with light.

Startled back to reality, Bowie leapt up from the seat, his helmet crashing to the floor, as a raspy synthesized voice said, "Don't make a move, Earthling."

Bowie reached for his rifle, nevertheless, snarling "trap" to both the harpist and the armored shock troopers who had burst into the room.

"Don't be a fool," cautioned the second trooper.

Bowie saw the wisdom of this and moved his hands clear of his weapon. It was difficult to know whether there were humanoids inside the gleaming armor worn by the aliens, but Bowie sensed that these troopers had been assembled from the android parts he had seen only a short time ago. This pair was human-size, armed with featureless laser rifles, and encased in helmets and cumbersome body armor, including long carapacelike capes that stood stiffly out behind them.

"Another move and it will be your last. You're coming with us—*now*. You, too, Musica."

Bowie turned at the sound of her name, and repeated it for Musica's benefit. He thought he detected the beginnings of a smile before one of the android's said: "All right, Earthman, come along quietly now"—as though lifting dialogue from an archaic motion picture.

Bowie sized up the two of them: They were side by side, perhaps three yards from him, gesturing with their rifles, but more intent on capturing him than blowing him away. Spying his helmet on the floor now, Bowie saw an opportunity and went for it. He took a step forward, as though surrendering to them, then quickly brought his right foot against the helmet, launching it square into the face of one of the androids, while pile-driving himself into the other one. The trooper took the full force of his blow and staggered backward but remained on its feet. Bowie was clutching the thing like a tackle when he saw that number one had come around and had the rifle leveled on him. He sucked in his breath and slipped out of the clutches of the second, just as number one fired, catching his companion through the face with several rounds. Both Bowie and the android were motionless for a brief moment while the weight of this reversal descended; then Bowie had his own rifle out front and put several rounds in the suddenly speechless alien. The trooper dropped to the floor with a thud.

Bowie turned to Musica and threw his shoulders back triumphantly. But this was no green-haired Rapunzel he had just rescued, and it didn't occur to him that he had just aced two of her people. Musica, her hands like nervous birds, was staring at him distressfully, backing slowly away, as if expecting the next round to come zinging her way.

Bowie finally realized what was going on and tried to persuade her that he had done her some sort of favor. "Don't tell me you're still afraid of me?" he said, putting his hands on her shoulders while she buried her face in her hands. "I saved you from those two, didn't I? Doesn't that prove I'm your friend?"

Musica was whimpering, shaking her head back and forth while he spoke; but still he went on: "Now all we have to do is get out of here. . . Can you show me the way?"

She finally succeeded in tearing herself away from him and began to run. Bowie was starting after her when all at once a blast rang out from behind both of them catching Musica unawares in the calf. Bowie caught up and supported her, thinking that she had been trying to warn him. He looked back toward the trooper who had loosed the shot: the android was on its knees now, but there would be no need for Bowie to waste a charge against it. In a second the thing was going to topple facedown of its own accord.

But again the mistress of the harp broke free and ran, this time through a blue and red triskelionlike doorway—some ultra modernist hexagonal painting that slid apart into three sections as she approached, and closed just as quickly behind her.

Bowie tore after her and found himself back in the columned hallway, but Musica was nowhere in sight. Then he chanced to look to the right and there she was: casually entering the hall from a perpendicular corridor.

"Well, that's better!" Bowie said smiling.

But off she went again and the chase was on.

"Take it easy," Bowie shouted after her, breathlessly. "You shouldn't be running on that wounded leg." What he really meant to say was that it wasn't fair of her to be outrunning him, but he was hoping that a demonstration of concern for her well-being might prove more effective than an admission of defeat. But then he noticed that her leg showed no signs of the wound he had definitely seen there only a minute before. And come to think of it, he found himself wondering: wasn't her hair more green than the blue he was seeing now?

The intersections and branchings grew more and more numerous, a veritable labyrinth of hexagonal corridors, polished replicas of the ones belowdecks, with medallioned walls and stark blood-red ceiling panels seemingly filled with axons and dendrites.

Bowie lost her in a maze of twists and turns. He stood still, breathing hard and fast, listening for any sound of her. But what he heard instead was the approach of something large and motorized. He brought his rifle off his shoulder and moved to the center of the corridor, waiting to confront whatever was about to show itself from around the bend.

CHAPTER FIVE

Did you ever see a dream walking?
Well, Bowie did.

Remark attributed to Angelo Dante

I N AN ORGANICALLY-FASHIONED CHAMBER LONG AGO GIVEN OVER to the demands of the Protoculture, the Masters observed the Humans who had been allowed access to their ship. The rubylike corridor adornments Louie had called medallions were their eyes and ears, and when the humans had strayed from these, the Masters had relied on intelligence gathered by their android troopers, the Terminators—the same armored beings who had almost gotten the drop on Bowie and were presently exchanging fire with Sergeant Dante's contingent, still trapped in the generator hold, one of their number already dead.

The trio of aged Masters was in its steadfast position at the shrub-sized mushroom-shaped device that was their interface with the physical world. In many ways slaves to this Protoculture cap, generations past the need for food or sustenance, the Masters lived only for the cerebral rewards of that interior realm, lived only for the Protoculture itself, and their fleeting contact with worlds beyond imagining.

But though evolved to this high state, they were not permanent residents in that alternate reality, and so had to compromise their objectives to suit the needs of the crumbling empire they had forged when control really was in their hands. This mission to Earth had proved to be as troublesome as it was desperate, a last chance for the Masters of Tirol to regain what they needed most—the Protoculture matrix Zor had hidden aboard the now ruined super dimensional fortress. The Masters were not interested in destroying the insignificant planet that had been the unwitting recipient of their renegade scientist's dubious gift; but neither were they about to allow this primitive race to stand between them and destiny; between them and *immortality*.

At this stage of the Masters' game there was still some curiosity at work: viewing the Earthlings was akin to having a look at their own past—before the Protoculture had so reconfigured fate—which is why they had permitted this small band of Terrans into the fortress to begin with. Earthlings had thus far proved themselves an aggressive lot: firing on the Masters when they had first appeared and goading them into further exchanges, as if intent upon ushering in the doomsday the Zentraedi had been unable to provide.

But perhaps this was but a measure of their stunted development? And this small reconnaissance party was nothing more than an attempt to determine exactly who it was they were up against. They were beginning to reason for a change, instead of simply throwing away their lives and resources, waging a war they were destined to lose in any case.

So, in an effort to glimpse the inner working of the Humans, the Masters had subjected the intruders to several tests. After all, they were not really to be trifled with, having in effect defeated the Zentraedi armada. They had even foiled the Masters own attempts to gain information about the Protoculture matrix by passive means, by accessing the information in the SDF-1's master-computer, which the Humans had named EVE.

The Masters had permitted the Terrans to enter through a lower level corridor that led to the mechanical holds of the ship. It had been interesting to note they had split up their team, showing that they did indeed function independently and were not in need of a guiding intelligence. There were also demonstrations of caring and self-sacrifice, things unheard of among the Masters' race. One group was currently battling Terminators in the generator hold—the troopers were ascertaining the strength of the Humans in close-fighting techniques; another group had wandered into the Optera tree room; while a third group had found the android assembly line.

One member of the latter group had actually conversed with Musica, Mistress of the Cosmic Harp, whose songs were integral in controlling the clones of the inner centers. But that Human was now reunited with his teammates, who at the moment were returning to their predesignated rendezvous point. The second group was also en route, and so the Masters passed the thought along to the Terminators that the skirmish in the generator room be called off, allowing the third group to follow suit. Once the Humans were regrouped, the Masters would initiate a new series of challenges.

General Rolf Emerson and Colonels Anderson and Green would have given anything for a glimpse at what was going on in the fortress. But the recon team was already an hour overdue and hopes for their safe return were sliding fast. In an effort to do *something*, Emerson had ordered a stepped-up assault on the fortress, in the hope of hitting it hard enough to shake the team loose—lost ball bearings in an old fashioned pinball machine. But instead of tilting, the fortress had merely upped the ante, filling the skies with Bioroids on their hover platforms and sending out ground troops to combat the teams stationed at the perimeter of the crash site. It had been a calculated gamble, but one that had not paid off.

The situation room was as busy as a hive, but the three massive screens opposite the command balcony told a woeful tale of defeat.

Emerson sat back into his chair to listen to the latest sitreps from the field, none of which were encouraging. A rescue ship sent to ATAC area thirty-four had been destroyed. Air teams were sustaining heavy casualties from the fortress's cannon fire. Bravo Fourteen had been wiped out completely. Sector Five had been overrun. A rescue squad was being summoned to Bunker niner-three-zero, where nearly a hundred men were trapped inside. Medics were sorely needed everywhere.

"Have you reestablished communications with Lieutenant Sterling yet?" Colonel Green asked one of the techs.

"Negative," came the reply. "But we're still trying."

Emerson caught Green's groaning sigh.

"Let's not give up on Lieutenant Sterling yet, Colonel," he told him, more harshly than was necessary. "She won't give up until she's succeeded in her mission."

Bowie, bareheaded and precariously perched behind and slightly above the pilot's seat of Dana's Hovertank, tried to fill the lieutenant in on his experiences since that elevator ride to Musica's harp chamber. He had never been too fond of Dana's reckless road tactics, and thought even less of them now that he had a chance to observe things from his friend's perspective. Dana was careening through the dark corridors at nearly top speed, not a care in the world as she twisted the *Valkyrie* through turns its gyrostabilizers were never meant to handle. The *Diddy-Wa-Diddy* had been left abandoned, set on self-destruct in the recycling hold. In an effort to take his mind off the very real possibility of a collision, Bowie continued his rundown of the events, even though there seemed to be a lot of discrepancies in his story.

"And you say she ran away after being shot in the leg?" Dana said skeptically.

"I know it sounds incredible, but I saw it with my own eyes!" Bowie replied defensively. "And she was one beautiful lady, too," he added wistfully.

Dana threw a knowing smile over her shoulder, forcing Bowie into paroxysms of fear as she took her eyes from the corridor.

"Maybe she was an android, Bowie."

"No way."

"Then my guess is she was a dream—after all, you claim that you felt yourself being taken up into the fortress and yet we found you on the same level we entered. We didn't take any elevator rides, Bowie, and we haven't seen a stairway yet."

"But I'm telling you I went *up*, Dana! I do know up from down, you know!"

Louie went on the external speaker: "Only when you're awake, Bowie, and I don't think you were. Think back to our briefing sessions and the notes from the Gloval Expedition into the SDF-1: when the captain's team exited the dimensional fortress they were certain that hours had gone by, and yet the guards who were stationed outside the fortress swore that only fifteen minutes had elapsed!

"It could be that there is some sort of lingering effect to hyperspace travel," Louie continued unchecked, "something we're not yet aware of. Maybe time actually occurs *differently* inside the fortress than it does outside. It's something I'm going to investigate someday."

The dark hallway was suddenly opening up and filling with light, and in a moment Dana and company found themselves on a polished floor as blue as the clearest of Earth's seas—an icelined canal of brilliant chroma, lined with a continuous wall of turreted and arcaded buildings. Reminiscent of ancient Rome, or Florence, before the destruction visited upon it during the Global Civil War, each structure was more than two hundred yards high, with curved, scalloped facades, ornately columned arcades crowned by friezes, and round-topped portals. Elsewhere, gracefully arched bridges crossed the solid canal, overlit by circular lights set high in the hold.

Stranger still, the hold was inhabited—by Humans.

"At least they look Human," Dana commented.

The aliens had all taken shelter under the arcades and were staring at the 15th's strange two-vehicled procession; but Dana didn't read actual fear anywhere, only an intense puzzlement, almost as though these people had no idea where they were, or what they were doing. Dress was uniformly practical, sensible, not so much fit for the Rome Dana had read about, but a Rome mock-up in the bowels of a spaceship. Shirt and trouser combinations of the same cut, the same fabric, individualized only by color or neckline, all with tight-fitting cuffs, blue, gray, gold.

Suddenly, Bowie yelled: "Lieutenant, stop the Hovertank—I just saw that girl!"

Dana and Louie cut their thrusters and the mecha settled to what seemed to be the street.

Dana wondered whether this was a show being put on for their benefit. She scanned puzzled faces in the unmoving crowds, looking for a green-haired girl.

"Are you certain it's her, Bowie?"

"I'm positive—she's one of a kind! I'd know her any—what?! It can't be! I'm seeing double!"

"Everybody here is either twins or triplets," Louie said, completing Bowie's thought. "They must be clones."

Dana followed Bowie's gaze and spied an attractive girl in chiffon, shoulder-to-shoulder with her identical twin. *Clones,* Dana said to herself. They had to be clones, like the Zentraedi. She thought back to what she knew of her people: how they had been grown from cell samplings of the Robotech Masters. How she herself had a part of this in her. And it suddenly occurred to her that these *clones* might very well be her sisters and brothers! Dana found herself looking around for someone who looked like her.

"Headquarters will be happy to find out that their advance intelligence reports were true," she heard Louie say.

Just then three armored shock troopers broke through the murmuring crowds, leveling laser rifles as they took up positions around the Hovertanks.

"Uh-oh—looks like we've got company!"

"Don't make a move!" one of the Terminators shouted.

"We've got you covered."

"See—there's that bad movie dialogue I told you about," Bowie said.

"Cowboys and Romans," Louie muttered. "What'll we do, Lieutenant—shoot it out with them?"

"No," Dana said quickly. "If we fire into this crowd we'll end up injuring a lot of innocent people. We'll just have to try to make a break for it! Better tell your girlfriends good-bye!" she aimed at Bowie.

The Terminators opened fire as the Hovertanks lifted off, mindless of the clones their stray shots cut down.

Valkyrie and *Livewire* sped off. In the rumble seat, Bowie clung to Dana's waist, staring back at the two Musicas, heedless of the white bolts of fire snapping at the Hovertank's heels.

"Boy, this mission's a washout," Cranston was saying to Sean. "I think those jokers abandoned ship when they saw us coming."

"I'm beginning to believe you're right, Cranston," Sean admitted, absently twirling his helmet in his hand, as he slowly guided the *Bad News* away from the corridor rendezvous point. Nothing much had happened since they left the hothouse, and when neither Dana nor Dante had showed up at the designated hour, he had decided to take Cranston and Woodruff into the corridor Dana's contingent was to investigate. "I've seen more action on a Sunday School picnic," he started to say. But something was approaching them fast from up ahead, coming in from the direction of the point.

Almost before Sean could bring his weapon into ready or issue instructions to his men, Dana and Louie came tearing by them without even stopping. Sean yelled, realizing if they hadn't seen them, it wasn't likely that they would hear him. But he called out anyway, worried all of a sudden about what it was that was chasing them.

And Dana's team pulled up short.

"Wow!" Dana exclaimed. "I was beginning to think we'd never see you guys again!"

Sean was puzzled by Dana's intensity. "Yeah, well I'm happy to see you, too, Lieutenant, but I wanna tell you, this is the dullest mission I've ever been on."

"Dull?!" Dana and her team all said at once, fixing Sean with a look he couldn't quite grasp.

"Yeah. We think the aliens abandoned ship or something."

Suddenly Dana, Louie, and Bowie were all talking at him in a rush. Grant was saying something about his having been transported by an invisible elevator to the arms of a beautiful green-haired woman he had jammed with, or something. But there'd been a chase a-and that was of course why they didn't have his Hovertank with them—because they didn't chance going back to pick it up—not that they could find their way there anyway. A-and then there was this population center they had just escaped from that looked like ancient Rome and was filled with nothing but identical clones and carapace-armored shock trooper androids. . . .

When it was over all Sean could do was exchange puzzled looks with his equally perplexed teammates.

"Well, we got to see the famous forest of light-bulb trees," he told Dana. "Guess the shock troops were avoiding us for some reason."

Just as Sean was saying this, Sergeant Dante's contingent—minus Road's Hovertank, and unfortunately, minus Road himself—hovered into view and joined them in the corridor. Dante told them of the firefight, how the aliens had crept up on them and pinned them down, only to back off unexpectedly at the last moment. . . .

He was in the middle of his explanation when the floor opened up underneath them. Nine Hovertanks and ten Humans plunged into the darkness.

"Is everybody okay? Bowie?" Dana called out into the blackness.

She knew she was wet and sticky, not from blood though, but from what she had landed in. Touching the stuff in the dark only led to more frightening images, so she groped in the opposite direction, wondering if she would stumble upon one of the Hovertanks. It would be a miracle if no one had been crushed under the falling mecha, and equally so if they all had as soft a landing as she had. There seemed to be some sort of weightlessness here—a dark and soggy lunar surface.

But one by one the teammates answered her.

"All present and accounted for. And apparently no injuries," Bowie yelled.

"Speak for yourself," Dana heard Louie say. "I've got enough bruises for the bunch of you."

"And I feel as light as a kitten in here."

"Where the heck are we, anyway?" Angelo asked. "And what's that rotten smell?"

"I've pulled enough K.P. in my time to recognize this smell

anywhere," said Woodruff. "I got no idea what these aliens eat, but this is their garbage, I'll stake my wad on that."

Sean, Marino, and Xavez all made sounds of disgust.

But it was Kuri that voiced the first *uh-oh* . . .

Machinery had been activated overhead, servos were coming into play and the sound was growing louder.

"Hey . . . wait a minute," Angelo said. "This must be a freakin' *compactor*! And guess who's about to be *compacted*?!"

"I *seen* this movie, Sarge!" Xavez was suddenly moaning. "What're they tryin' to play with our heads, or what?"

"Flatten our heads is more like it!" Kuri yelled from across the blackness.

"Echo readings indicate that there is in fact a massive plate descending on us," Louie reported calmly. "I calculate forty-eight seconds until we become tomorrow morning's breakfast crepes."

Dana heard two or three of her teammates pick up handfuls of the sludge and heave it in Louie's general direction. At about the same time Louie was hit and yelled, spitting words and whatever garbage had connected with him, Dana, who had been edging forward in the darkness, hands out front like a blind person, contacted one of the Hovertanks. From the feel of it, it had landed upright, and she quickly climbed aboard and hit the lights.

It was her first mistake.

Now everyone could see the sorry state they were in. They all looked around the room, and then up at the descending plate of the compactor. Yes, it was very much like a scene from a movie they had all seen.

"Lieutenant, you gotta get us outta here!" screamed Xavez.

"Stand back, everybody. I'm gonna blast us out of here."

"You can't, Lieutenant," Louie warned her. "These are high-density ceramic walls. They're laser resistant. I don't think it would be a good idea. If you remember that movie—"

"Then come up with a better idea, Louie. In the meantime, everybody hit the deck and hope for the best."

Hitting the deck meant diving back into the muck, but suddenly even that seemed preferable to feeling the heat of a richocheting plasma bolt.

"No-o-o!" yelled Louie once more before the end.

The bolt did just what everyone feared it would: it impacted against the wall to no effect and headed straight back from whence it came, narrowly missing Dana who ducked down into the cockpit at the last second, then caroming around the room like a homicidal billiard ball of energy, giving everyone an equal chance to dodge or be fried. Ultimately the crazed thing hit the floor of the chamber and exploded, right at the foot of Dana's mecha.

There didn't seem to be a hope that she had survived the shot. Where the Hovertank stood there was now only a huge garbage crater, smoking like a cookpot in hell. Blessedly the damn compactor had ceased its downward motion, and the hole was letting light into the room. They were all thinking that Dana had died for nothing, when suddenly they heard her voice rising from the hole. The garbage-spattered 15th grouped around the crater, peering in.

Dana was still seated in the mecha, which was now on the floor of a corridor that ran underneath the compactor. Several other Hovertanks had fallen with her, along with Xavez and Marino who were covered with grime and shaking like palsy victims.

"See—I knew it would work," Dana was saying unsteadily but knowingly. "The floor wasn't laser resistant."

No one bothered to tell her that the compactor had stopped on its own. One by one they lowered themselves through the hole, wiping off what garbage they could.

A corridor monitor blinked once and brought the reversed situation to the attention of the Masters. Things had not gone quite as planned, but the aged trio was willing to concede that no matter what happened, they were learning more about the Terrans and that was the purpose of the exercise—even though the female soldier had gotten a lucky break by finding her cannon round returned to the unprotected floor. And if anything, this only suggested that *luck* itself should be figured into the equation when dealing with this race.

The Masters' next plan was to separate this most fortunate one, the apparent commander, from her team, to see how the underlings would function without her. Just how much independent thought was available to them; how resourceful were they without adequate leadership?. . .

They had managed to retrieve seven of the nine remaining Hovertanks; two were so hopelessly mired in the garbage sludge that even the mecha's thrusters couldn't break the things free—not without a good deal more time than they had to spare.

The 15th was mounted in its mecha now, Bowie still riding behind Dana, Xavez behind Marino, Woodruff behind Cranston. The sergeant, Louie, Sean, and Kuri were back in their original units.

"You sure beat the odds that time, Lieutenant," Louie commented.

Dana adjusted her helmet and made a face as she picked sticky bits of refuse from the pauldrons of her uniform. "Let's not celebrate until we're out of here," she warned all of them.

"But which way?" Louie threw to the team. "Without our helmet monitors, we can't tell one direction from another. We've gotta be down at least one level, maybe two, and unless we can find a way up I don't know how we're gonna get outta this thing."

"Dead reckoning'll get us back to that hole; I'll bet I could find my way blindfolded," the sarge announced.

"We'll just blow our way out," Dana said. "We got in: we can get out. But stay alert . . . I've got that funny feeling that we're being watched again. . . ."

No sooner had she said it than something leapt at her from the corridor ceiling. She heard Sean's warning and the rapid report of his rifle—adrenaline coursing through her like high octane—and caught the movement of the thing peripherally.

Oddly, something said to her: *snake.* And when she raised her head to look back on the thing Sean's blast had downed, she realized that that image her mind's eye conjured wasn't far from wrong: it looked like an old-fashioned wire-coiled vacuum cleaner hose, only a lot wider, and capped with an evil-looking nipplelike device. In its final moments, before Sean's second round severed the thing's tubular body, the hose loosed a massive electrical charge that narrowly missed Dana's head and exploded against the far wall of the corridor. The hose spasmed around on its ruptured neck spewing a foul-smelling smoke but no more fire.

"Good shooting, Sean!" Bowie shouted.

Louie watched the techno-assassin flail about for a moment, then glanced down at his console, noticing instantly that the radio had begun to function again. He told the team, and they realized that they must be close to the exterior wall of the fortress. There was a good chance Headquarters was monitoring them once again.

"Good," Dana said, bringing the face shield down. "Let's move out."

"Stay together this time," Sergeant Dante hastened to add.

The Masters were no longer entertained by the shenanigans of their guests, and came about as close as they could to demonstrating real emotion. And emotion made it necessary for them to break their telepathic rapport and speak directly to the Terminator.

It was imperative that the Terrans not be allowed to leave the ship alive.

"See to it that all exits are sealed," said one of the Masters. "Move your sentries into corridor M-seventy-nine and use maximum force if necessary to prevent their escape."

"And see to it that Zor Prime is with your sentries," a second of the Masters thought to add, his voice betraying some ulterior motive.

Full out, the Hovertanks moved through the labyrinthine corridors of the fortress, their halogen lights piercing the darkness.

"Get ready," Dana told her teammates through the tac net. "It looks like we're going to have to fight our way out."

She hadn't actually seen anything up ahead, but as they ascended the ramp which returned them to the proper level, the mecha lamps illuminated a full line of Bioroids in the corridor ahead.

Zor Prime was leading them—the lavender-haired pilot of the red Bioroid, who had been haunting Dana's thoughts since the encounter at the Macross mounds. Diminutive against the fifty-foot high metal monsters behind him, the elfin alien was standing calmly at their fore and holding his hand up in a gesture that told the Humans to halt. When the Hovertanks accelerated instead, Zor's hand dropped decisively, a signal to his troops to open fire.

Dana tried to put the alien from her mind and called for evasive maneuvers. "Concentrate on tactical driving!"

The Bioroids opened up on the approaching Hovertanks with their disc guns, filling the corridor with white light and noise that could wake the dead. The Earth mecha weaved between hyphens of searing heat, criss-crossing in front of one another and returning fire to the wall of aliens standing between them and freedom.

Dana had a fleeting image of Zor as she swerved her Hovertank around him, unable to loose fire against him or run him over. But shortly there would be another image that would replace this last: In the dancing headlight beams the team saw two of their teammates sprawled lifeless on the corridor floor in puddles of their own blood.

Dana yelled: "It's Simon and Jordon! We can't leave them like this!"

Angelo disagreed. "It's too late to do anything for them, Lieutenant—we've got trouble up ahead."

A final Bioroid was standing guard at the exit. They certainly could have run it down without problem, but it would be a lot more profitable to take the thing alive.

Dana thought her tank through reconfiguration to Battloid. As she and Bowie rode up into the giant techno-warriors head, Dana readied herself at the controls.

"You can't take him alone," Bowie said. "He's too big!"

"He's not bigger than my Battloid," Dana reminded him. The Bioroid leapt, and Dana urged her mecha to follow. She thought the Battloid's metalshod hands into motion and grabbed the alien mecha by his pectoral armor.

Then the *Valkyrie* and its prize flew through the unmended opening. Dana didn't bother to look back.

CHAPTER SIX

I think I breezed through the rest of the recon in a kind of trance, my thoughts so wrapped around the Eureka! *Bowie's encounter with Musica had booted up in my mind. The Masters' fortress had defolded from its hyperspace journey with particles of the Fourth Dimensional Continuum still adhering to it, iron filings to a magnet—like memory itself, alive in the Human brain despite an elapse of chronological reckoning. Immediately I set to work on a new theory based on the hypothesis that time, like light itself, was composed of quanta—packets of stuff I then called* chronons. *What I eventually arrived at—years later—was nothing so much as a reworking of Macek's turn-of-the-century theorem (then unknown to me):* if you can take the time and travel, you can surely travel and take the time!

Louie Nichols, *Tripping the Light Fantastic*

Ten out of Lieutenant Sterling's original thirteen had returned from the reconnaissance mission; based on the casualties sustained by the ground forces and air support who had contributed to the penetration op, this proved to be on the low side average, and Dana found some comfort there. But it wasn't the numbers that remained with her, but the sight of Privates Jordon and Simon lying on that cold floor, bathed in the harsh light from her Hovertank, their lives flowing out of them. That, and the brief moments she and Bowie and Louie had spent in the Romanesque heart of the fortress. Were those twins and triplets Human clones, or had they been fashioned from the body parts Corporal Nichols had stumbled across during the mission? Her heart told her that they were clones, brothers and sisters to the Zentraedi half of her, but Headquarters wasn't interested in her *feelings*; rightly so, they needed concrete evidence, and the sad fact was that the monitoring devices had ceased to function early on. There was, however, the Bioroid Dana's mecha had spirited from the ship, and surely the pilot of that alien craft would lay all these questions to rest;

he or she wouldn't need to say a thing: it only remained to be seen whether the Earth Forces were up against androids or beings like themselves.

Dana had run these issues through her mind during the debriefing and since. Unable to sleep, she had left her bunk in the middle of the night. Sunrise found her and half the 15th in the barracks ready-room. They had all argued back and forth, unable to come to any consensus, so varied were their individual experiences inside the fortress. The squad was slated for patrol in less than an hour, and she desperately wanted to convince them that her instincts were correct.

"How can I be expected to shoot at people who might very well be my own relatives?" Dana had put to them finally. She had drawn her sidearm, and now had the distant, silent fortress bracketed in the pistol's sights. Sergeant Dante entered the room just then, and finding her thus, put a hand on her shoulder.

"I, uh, don't mean to interrupt," he said, out of real concern for the room's permaplas window.

Dana turned to dislodge his hand, and frowned as she reholstered the handgun.

"Target practice, eh? Too bad there's no aliens around to aim at."

Dana expected as much from Angelo. The mission had only served to convince him of the truth of his earlier beliefs: the aliens were nothing but bio-engineered creations that had been programmed for war. She knew that he felt the same about the Zentraedi, despite the fact that their *Humanness* had not only been proven, but was accepted by the very men and women who had once fought against them. Sean, Louie, and Bowie were acting like they weren't in the room.

"You're unbelievable, Sergeant," Dana said, disgust and disbelief in her voice. She looked to the others for support, but found none. She knew that Bowie agreed with her, especially now that he had had some sort of encounter of his own inside the ship, but he was too timid to make a stand. The vote was still out on Louie: like the staff at HQ, he was going to need clearcut evidence before saying anything. Sean, as always, had no opinion one way or another.

"I suppose you think we should shoot every alien on sight, huh? Would that make you happy?"

Angelo smirked. It was so easy to get to her. But that wasn't really his purpose; he merely wanted to get to the Human side of her. "Well, we'd be a lot safer, Lieutenant. And I don't think anybody on their side's gonna hesitate to fire at us."

Angelo had turned his back to her and was walking away, when a messenger entered unannounced through the room's sliding doors.

"Sir," the aide said stiffly, offering his salute. "General Emerson requests your presence. I'm to escort you and Corporal Nichols to Dr. Beckett's lab immediately."

Dana told the messenger to wait outside. She turned temporary command of the team over to Sergeant Dante, feeling as though she had lost a minor battle.

The Robotech Masters felt the same.

The three had summoned their Scientist and Politician triumvirates to the fortress command nexus after the Earthlings had made their daring escape.

"I expect a full report on damage to our ship and an update on the Micronian position," said the Master called Bowkaz. "Micronian" was a term the Masters used when speaking to any of their numerous clones, a holdover from Zentraedi times.

There was an unmistakable note of desperation in his voice, a fact that at once distressed and pleased the three Scientist clones—androgynous figures, with exotic features and long hair in brilliant colors.

"Most of the damage is isolated to the Reflex power modules," reported the honey-haired Scientist. "The Micronians will probably attack again. We should escalate our combat profile."

"How could the situation have come to this?" Dag asked rhetorically. Like his companion Masters he was hawk-nosed and liquid-eyed, monkish looking in the long gown whose triple collars mimicked the Flower of Life's tripartite structure. "It was never our intention to destroy the Micronians or their planet."

One of the young Politicians spoke to that. He resembled the Scientists in form and figure, save for the fact that he was dressed in togalike wrappings, and of course had been bio-engineered for political rather than scientific functions.

"The Micronians feel threatened by our presence here," he reminded the Masters now.

"But they must realize that our clones are not here to tamper with their civilization," said Shaizan, who was in many ways the Masters' true spokesman, most often called upon to communicate directly with the Elders of Tirol. "The true threat to both our races is the parasitic Invid, who will themselves come in search of the Protoculture."

Which was and was not true: but the Masters were compelled to make their clones feel that the journey to Earth was more noble than it actually was.

"We must complete our mission before the Invid arrive," Bowkaz countered. "The Micronians are dangerous and must be destroyed if they continue to obstruct us."

"I agree," Dag said after a moment of reflection. "The Micronian ignorance of our purpose and their inexperience with the Protoculture makes them a dangerous threat to our cause."

"And too many of our own Bioroid pilots have been severely injured to mount an effective attack against them at this time," Bowkaz hastened to add.

"Are our shields holding?" Shaizan asked of the Scientists.

Schematic representations of the fortress's energy system capabilities came to life on the oval-shaped screen that filled the interstices of the command center's neural-like structure.

"We estimate a functional capacity of only twenty percent," returned one of the Scientists. "Not even powerful enough to seal breaches in the fortress's hull."

"If we cannot leave and we cannot fight, then what option is left us?" asked a second.

The three Politicians and the three Scientists waited for the Master's pronouncements. Ultimately it was Shaizan who answered them.

"We must use the Micronians," he said somewhat haltingly. "First we will take some of their kind and subject them to a xylonic cerebral probe to determine whether or not we can turn them into Bioroid pilots. This will serve a dual purpose: First, it will allow us to strengthen our forces. Second, by allowing one of these reengineered pilots to be captured, we will be able to convince the Micronians that they have been manipulated into fighting their own kind. This will buy us the time we need to effect repairs or call in a rescue ship. In the meantime, we must reformulate our thinking and come up with a plan to secure the Protoculture matrix before it is too late."

The partially-dissected shell of the captured alien Bioroid lay on its back on a massive platform in Dr. Beckett's Defense Center laboratory. Colonels Anderson and Green, along with several forensic engineers and computer techs, were already in attendance when General Emerson entered with Dana and Louie in tow.

"I think you're going to find this very interesting," Beckett said by way of introduction.

He was a nondescript-looking man in his late thirties, with thick, amber-tinted glasses and a crisply starched white uniform he kept tightly fastened at neck and cuffs. Known for the yard-long pointer he was said to carry wherever he went, Beckett had little of Professor Cochran's savvy, and nowhere near the intellectual power of someone like Zand; but he was competent enough, and Louie Nichols let him ramble on for several minutes before saying anything.

"Let me start by saying that this thing is a complicated network of mechanical parts controlled by biological stimuli, the origin of which is uncertain at this time." Beckett used his pointer to indicate a control panel located below and to the left of the Bioroid's head. "However, we think that this module here acts as a sensor device, or overload circuit mechanism." He gave the panel several taps with the pointer.

"Then if you bypass that relay," Louie interjected, reaching for one of the Bioroid's sensor cables and coiling it around his forearm, ". . . ah, these should act like some sort of muscle."

Dana, who was standing next to the corporal, watched the arm of the Bioroid begin to twitch as Louie flexed the muscles in his forearm. Startled, she stepped back from the platform, worried that the thing was going to attack.

"Don't worry, Lieutenant," Louie said, full of confidence. "It's not going anywhere." He gestured to his forearm and once again flexed; the Bioroid's arm gave another shudder. "It's only responding to the stimulus I'm giving it."

"Like power-amplified body armor," Dana said, relaxing some.

"Bingo," said Louie, taking off his wrappings.

Emerson, Green, and Anderson looked to Beckett to elaborate. The doctor cleared his throat and said: "Yes . . . In many ways it functions rather like our own Veritechs, only in place of our sensor gloves and helmets, it seems to be directly attuned to its pilot."

Beckett instructed one of his techs to project the data he had prepared for the preliminary report. All eyes turned to the wallscreen above the forensic platform. Various schematic representations and readouts of the Bioroid's systems filled the screen as the Doctor spoke.

"It is indeed a type of armored suit that responds to the stimuli provided by a pilot. Through a complex network of bio-mechanical diodes, it actually interfaces with its pilot and carries out the pilot's commands in a matter of nanoseconds." Beckett paused as a new schematic assembled itself. "The difference here is that the pilot, too, seems to have been bio-engineered to interface with the mecha."

"So that's why they're so maneuverable," Dana said.

"Then this Bioroid is an extension of its pilot?" asked the bearded Green, still unsure what Beckett and this young corporal with the dark goggles were getting at.

"Exactly," the doctor said. "The circuits of the one *duplicate* the circuits of the other. We have yet to determine how such an imprint has been made possible, but there is no mistaking the accomplishment."

"But this is incredible," Emerson said. "You're suggesting a bio-mechanical lifeform."

Beckett shook his head. "A pilot *is* required," he started to say before Colonel Green broke in.

"What's the most effective way to stop these things once and for all?" the colonel demanded.

Dana, meanwhile, now had the cable wrapped around her own arm. If the Bioroid required a living pilot, then her case for the *Humanness* of the aliens was made. It would have been redundant to put *androids* in the Bioroids' cockpits. . . .

She tuned in for Beckett's response to Green's query, holding her tongue until the right moment. The doctor was once again tapping his pointer on the Bioroid's neck module.

"Well, considering what we now know about the design, I'd say the most effective shot would have to be placed in the area of this control mechanism."

Rolf Emerson now stepped forward, as if to silence everyone. "I'd like to have your input, Lieutenant Sterling. You and your team have engaged these things hand-to-hand, as it were. Did either of you observe any weak points in their individual defense systems?"

Dana shrugged. "I was too wrapped up in tactics to notice anything."

"Is the Bioroid equipped with any kind of microrecorder?" Louie asked Dr. Beckett. "Because if it is," he went on without waiting for a reply, "there must be some sort of internal damage-control monitoring system. . . . Our main computer could access the data and—"

"We've already seen to that, Corporal," Beckett interrupted, noticeably peeved. "Display the pertinent data," he said to the tech at the console.

"I think I know why these things have been so hard to stop," Louie muttered to Dana as new schematics scrolled across the wallscreen. "Display the damaged sections individually," he instructed the computer tech, stealing Beckett's thunder.

Louie stepped up to the screen and ran through an explanation of the data for General Emerson and the other brass, but it was Beckett who said: "The Bioroids are unaffected by direct hits unless you can destroy the cockpit."

"That's the way I read it," Louie seconded, no trace of competition in his voice.

"All right," said a pleased Colonel Anderson. "I'll make it a standing order to aim only at the cockpit."

It was the moment Dana had been worried about, the order she feared. "You can't do that, Colonel!" she blurted out, surprising all of them. "You'll be destroying the pilots as well as the Bioroids!"

Anderson seemed slightly bemused by the outburst. "Well I think that should be obvious, Lieutenant. The android pilot would be destroyed along with his machine. . . ."

"But they're *not* androids! It would make for a redundant system," she said, looking to Louie for help. She made mention of their experiences in the ship, the city of clones.

Green made a dismissive gesture. "But you have no proof that those, ah, *people* weren't simply androids. What about this android assembly line you claimed to have seen—"

"Exactly what do you know about the captured pilot?" Emerson asked Beckett. The doctor made a wry face and looked over to Green, who fielded the question, red-faced.

"I'm sorry to report that the pilot sustained some serious injuries as a result of our rather hasty efforts to remove it from the Bioroid. However, our medical teams are doing everything possible. . . ."

Green let his words trail off as a messenger entered the lab.

"General Emerson, your presence is requested in the war room. Commander Leonard is receiving a briefing on the captured alien pilot."

"How is the pilot?" Emerson asked.

Eyes-front, the messenger replied: "It stopped functioning over an hour ago, Sir. But the autopsy is complete."

General Emerson asked Dana to accompany him to the war room; it was the first time they had had a chance to talk in some weeks, but Rolf was careful to steer the conversation away from the issue of the aliens. He knew full well what must be going through Dana's mind, but there was as yet no proof about the nature or identity of the invaders. Rolf hoped that the briefing would put an end to this once and for all, and wondered what Dana's mother would have done. But then, had Admiral Hunter, Max, Miriya, and the others, not gone off on their Expeditionary Mission, none of this might be happening now. Miriya had turned against her own kind once before, and Rolf was certain that she would have remained on Earth's side in the present conflict.

Dana had to be made to realize that the Zentraedi were in no way connected with the Robotech Masters. Of course it was true that as clones of that very group there was blood between them, but the Zentraedi had gone off on their own; they had become their own people, and Dana was more than any other Zentraedi representative of this great change. There was no kinship between her and these clones the Robotech Masters had brought to Earth; there was only enmity between them; she had no brothers or sisters to that ship, any more than the people of Earth who had fought one another through the course of history felt blood between themselves.

The chiefs-of-staff were seated around that grouping of tables Rolf still wished triangular, with Leonard in his customary place at the curved apex, and Dr. Byron from Defense Medical standing off to his right. Byron was a tall man, whose head often appeared too small for his massive torso. He had sharp, pointed features, and a dark brown mustache that was a perfect inverted match for his arched and bushy eyebrows, giving his face a somewhat comic turn, at odds with the no-nonsense forcefulness of his personality.

Emerson and Sterling's entry had obviously interrupted the man. Rolf introduced Dana to Leonard and the staff, seeing the analytical glint in the supreme commander's eye now that he had a visual image of this person he had not seen in years, save for a brief handshake at the Academy ceremonies. But he was more than civil to Dana, complimenting her on the recon mission and the capture of the Bioroid.

Leonard bade Dr. Byron continue with his findings.

"First of all, we found something remarkable inside the pilot's body," Byron said, reading from his notes. "There was some sort of bio-electrical device implanted in its solar plexus. Subsequent analysis of this showed it to be similar to the animating chips used early on by Dr. Emil Lang's teams of Robotechnicians in the manufacture of Earth mecha."

Emerson's hand shot up. He gestured impatiently until Byron acknowledged him.

"I'm sorry to interrupt, Doctor. But was the pilot human or not?"

"Oh, definitely not human," Byron said, shaking his head.

Rolf heard Dana's heavy sigh of disappointment as the doctor continued.

"But I will say that it surpasses anything we ever attempted in the way of bio-mechanical creations. In fact, this animating device we found in the android's solar plexus is nothing if not akin to an artificial soul."

The supreme commander cleared his throat loudly. "Let's keep theology out of this," he directed at Byron. "Just stick to the facts, Doctor."

Byron winced at the rebuke and nervously adjusted the collar of his jacket.

"Our belief is that this race was forced to adapt to hostile environments as it began its expansion across the galaxy, and that an android bio-system was the natural outgrowth of this."

Leonard broke in again. "These aliens are not even the micronized Zentraedi we first thought, but an army of programmed androids in control of devastating bio-mechanical weapons. It's obvious to me that the Robotech Masters found it much easier to use androids than clones." He looked around the tables, then stood up, hands pressed to the table. "So much the easier for us, then. We are waging a war against an artificial lifeform, gentlemen, and we should have no qualms about destroying it—*utterly*."

Suddenly Dana was on her feet. "Commander, you're mistaken," she said. She raised her voice a notch to cut through the comments. "That Bioroid pilot may have been an android, but I believe that we're dealing with a race of living beings—not a soulless army of machines."

Byron narrowed his eyes and rocked forward on the balls of his feet. "My observations are completely documented," he countered. "What proof do you have to back up this absurd position?"

"I've had some first-hand experience in dealing with them," Dana shot back. But she now felt Rolf's hand tighten on her arm.

"Sterling, sit down!" he told her.

Leonard looked furious. "Look here, I'm familiar with your report, but it's possible you've misread your experiences, Lieutenant. The aliens could have implanted certain things in your mind. If they're capable of creating androids of this advanced form, who knows what else they're able to do?"

"No," Dana said back to him. "Why do you refuse to accept the possibility I might be right?!"

Leonard slammed his fist on the table. "Don't provoke us, Lieutenant. Quiet down at once or I'll be forced to have you removed from this session."

But Dana was on a roll, the persistent nature of her alien side well in control of her now. "You're fools if you refuse to hear me out!" she told the staff.

"Remove this insubordinate!" Leonard commanded. "I've heard enough!"

Two sentries had stepped in and taken hold of her arms.

But Emerson, too, was on his feet now. "Perhaps we should listen to her."

"I haven't got time for her disruptions," Leonard said stiffly.

Dana was pulled from the room, twisting and kicking, even breaking free of their hold once to call everyone an idiot. Rolf only hoped that Leonard was willing to overlook some of it. He sat down as a conciliatory gesture, exchanging looks with the supreme commander.

"Go on with your report, Dr. Byron," Leonard said after a moment.

Byron wrapped things up, losing most of the staff when he turned to technicalities.

Leonard cleared his throat.

"Gentlemen, it seems to me our course is clear: we must commit ourselves to the total destruction of these androids."

All but Emerson voiced their concurrence.

Leonard threw the chief of staff a dirty look as he stood up. "Do you have something to add, General?"

Emerson kept his voice controlled. "Only this: if these aliens possess any human qualities, we should try to negotiate. Fighting can't be the only alternative. Look what happened during the Robotech War—"

"Surely you don't believe that we could ever come to terms with a group of barbarians, do you Emerson?"

"That's probably just what Russo and Hayes and the rest of the UEDC said before Dolza's armada incinerated this planet," Rolf said with a sneer. "I believe *anything* is better than a continued loss of lives."

"Perhaps, perhaps," the supreme commander allowed. "But their advanced technology leaves us no other choice. Even if we *could* negotiate, we'd be doing so from a position of weakness, not strength, and that could prove fatal. It's out of the question! Now, will there be anything else from you, *General*?"

Leonard hadn't even heard him, Rolf said to himself as he took his seat. Worse, the commander was actually repeating the justification Russo and his doomed council had used before firing the Grand Cannon at an alien armada of over four million warships.

"No, Commander," Emerson said weakly. "Not now."

Someone will whisper the proper words over our graves.

CHAPTER SEVEN

Confronted with the issue of [Supreme Commander Leonard's] militaristic megalomania, we are tempted to point to the past and remind one another that history repeats itself. I know of no other statement that so demeans us as a planetary race. Since Humankind looked the Monolith in the face this authorless theory has been used to both excuse and justify our short-sightedness and shortcomings; to explain away our foolish actions and violent choices. But isn't it time that we asked ourselves why history has to repeat itself? Short of positing a new theory of reincarnation—with the same greedy men caught up in an eternal return to wage the same war over and over again—we are left in the dark. Certainly Leonard was being pressured by Chairman Moran, and certainly he had inherited the bloodstained mantle left behind by T. R. Edwards; but where are the actual chains, biogenetic or otherwise, that enslave him to history's dark flow? Perhaps we should look to the Robotech Masters for answers. Or the Protoculture itself.

Major Alice Harper Argus (ret.), *Fulcrum: Commentaries on the Second Robotech War*

"**T**HE OFFICERS ON THE GENERAL STAFF ARE NOTHING but a bunch of idiots," Dana reported to her teammates when she rejoined them in Monument Sector Five, a usually crowded downtown district of shopping and office malls that was all but deserted today.

With Angelo Dante in temporary command, the squad had just relieved the 14th squad Tactical Armored and already positioned their Hovertanks. Dana had roared up out of nowhere, executing a neat front leap from the nose of the *Valkyrie*, and immediately begun to regale them with an account of the briefing session with Commander Leonard. Both Sean and Angelo wondered to themselves what might be the outcome of Dana's being forcibly ejected from the war room; either one of them stood the chance of receiving a promotion if the lieutenant was busted because of her actions.

Louie waited for Dana to finish before telling her what he had learned at the forensic lab after she had left.

"We discovered that the relay we thought was a control device is actually some kind of sonic frequency receiver."

"So?" Dana asked him.

Louie adjusted his goggles. "So the Bioroid is probably controlled by a mixture of telepathic suggestion and signals from artificial sensors."

Dana's face fell. "You mean the Bioroids aren't controlled by the pilots? After I just shot off my mouth back there—"

"I'm sure they *can* be," Louie said encouragingly, "but not like we originally thought. It looks like some kind of higher intelligence may be controlling them by remote control."

"I don't get it," said Angelo, trying to scratch his head through his helmet.

"Someone or something is actually feeding instructions to the android pilots," Louie explained.

"They're not clones then?"

Louie shook his head.

Dana still refused to believe any of this. "Well, anyway," she started to say, "I told them. . . ."

All at once alert sirens were blaring throughout the city. Dana ordered everyone back to their Hovertanks (executing yet a second gymnastic leap as she mounted her own), and switched on her radio. The net was alive with a thousand voices, but she didn't need to try and make sense of the reports. One look up explained everything: the skies above Monument City were filled with the aliens' scarablike troop carriers.

"It's a full-scale enemy attack!" Sean said.

"If you have any alternative, don't shoot directly at their cockpits," Louie yelled before he threw himself into the Hovertank's seat. "We might be able to capture one!"

Hundreds of alien ships were closing on the city, but now, even higher overhead, appeared the telltale atmospheric streaks of Alpha fighters, breaking formation and falling in to engage their Robotech enemies. A hail of brilliant yellow fire, calculated to angle away from the city itself, was launched against the invaders, Skylord and Swordfish missiles and Teflon rounds impacting on the rust-colored crafts' armored hulls to little or no effect. The sky was lit up with tracers, dazzling crescents of light, and fiery explosions. But the troop carriers continued their attack, not only weathering the storm, but returning their own brand of hell fire as the Alphas completed their descent and dropped below them. The

four-muzzled guns of revolving undercarriage turrets spewed light
and death across the sky, taking down fighters faster than the eye
could keep track. Trailing tails of dense black smoke, Alphas
plunged uncontrolled toward the city, while others were simply
disintegrated in midflight. Pilots drifting homeward on synsilk
chutes were cut down as well.

"It looks like there's more than we can handle, Lieutenant,"
Angelo shouted over the net.

Dana said nothing. There had to be a way to disable those
Bioroids without harming the pilots, she thought. There had to be
a way—but *how*?

Now hatches on the side of the troop carriers sprang open.
Bioroids mounted on their Hoverplatforms were disgorged from
the ships in a seemingly unending line. They fell upon the city,
untouched by the Alpha fighters, outmaneuvering them in almost
every instance and bringing their own disc guns to bear against
them. The Bioroids fanned out over the city, as though searching
for something that had as yet eluded them. From every sector
came reports of their descent, but there was no clearcut sense of
their motive. They landed finally in unvarying groups of three and
spread through the city streets on foot.

Most of Monument City was packed away in the enormous underground shelters that had become as much a part of city life
since the Global Civil War as a Sunday stroll in the park. But, as
always, there were those who had opted to return home first to
salvage some precious knickknack, or make certain that family or
friends had already departed; and then there were the diehards
who simply refused, and the thrill-seekers who lived for this sort
of thing. And it was these last groups that the Bioroids moved
against, fulfilling the directives of the Masters to capture as many
Micronians as possible. Unseen by Dana and the rest of the 15th,
and as yet unreported by the Civil Defense networks, the Bioroids
were engaged in a novel form of looting: using their massive
metalshod fists to smash through the walls of dwellings and
shops, and grab in those same hands whatever Human stragglers
they could find, often unknowingly crushing them to death before
returning them to the troop carriers.

Ultimately the Bioroids entered the canyons of downtown and
found the 15th waiting for them.

Sean said, "Heads up, folks, here they come!"

"Have any bright ideas, Louie?" the sarge asked.

"Yeah, I do," the corporal answered, ignoring Dante's sarcasm.

"If you aim to either side of the cockpit, you can temporarily paralyze the pilot."

"Now why the hell would I want to do that, Nichols?!" Dante bellowed.

Dana cut into the tac net. "Angelo, just do as he says—it's important," she announced cryptically. "We've got to try to avoid hitting the pilots directly."

"Whose side are you on?" Dante got out just in time.

The Bioroids loosed plasma bolts from their Hoverplatforms top-mounted guns as they approached, one of the first shots finding Dante's mecha; the explosion threw the Hovertank fifty feet from its position in the center of the street, but the sergeant rode it out, reconfiguring to Gladiator mode during the resultant back flip and swinging the cannon around for a counterstrike. Dana had also reconfigured her mecha. She hopped the self-propelled gun over to Dante's new resting place, just as the sergeant blew one of the Bioroids from the air.

"Angelo, listen to me—I want you to try to shoot down their Hovercraft first."

"What are you up to, Lieutenant?" he fired back at her.

"Once you've got 'em off their Hovercraft," Dana went on, "shoot at their legs and put 'em out of commission." She was trying her best to make this sound appealing to Dante, but she could just imagine his face, screwed up in anger under the helmet.

The Bioroids were coming in low now, not more than ten yards off the ground, Bowie, Sean, and Louie a barricade they'd never get past. The 15th trio blew the Hoverplatforms out from under the attackers, even as explosions rocked the street all around them. Bioroids fell with ground-shaking crashes, while others decided to leap from their crafts and take up positions in recessed doorways and storefronts. Downtown became a war zone as both sides pumped pulsed fire through the streets. The sides of highrise buildings collapsed and cornices and friezes crumbled to the cratered street. Glass rained down in deadly slivers from windows blown out high above the fighting.

Dana ordered her team to reconfigure from Gladiator to Battloid for possible hand-to-hand encounters.

The street and surrounding area was pure devastation now, but the enemy had been held at the 15th's line. No one bothered to ask what the aliens were looking for, or where they hoped to get. Still in Battloid mode, the squad headed for the cover and continued to trade salvos with the entrenched group who had taken the far end of the avenue. Once again, Dana reminded them to go for the legs and not the cockpits. But this time Sean took issue with her.

"They can still blast us if we do that," he pointed out. "We've gotta take a chance and aim at an area near those cockpits, Lieutenant."

"They're androids, damn it, *androids!*" Angelo yelled over the net.

"I'm convinced they're *not*, Sergeant!"

"Well what's the difference whether they're androids or clones?!" Dante said as debris from a shattered store sign fell on him. He thought his Battloid through a front leap that took him clear across the street. "They're still *shooting* at us!"

"We've got to capture one!"

Without warning, a Bioroid appeared behind Dana's mecha and loosed a blast at her. She spun but not in time. Fortunately Angelo saw the move and managed to take the thing out, slugs from his chaingun tearing open the enemy's cockpit.

"So much for leg shots," Dante said.

"That's one I owe you," Dana responded tight-lipped.

Bioroids had taken to the rooftops and were pouring everything they had into the street. Troop carriers were dropping in to assist, and things quickly took a turn for the worse.

"We'll never be able to hold them!" Sean said, voicing what all of them were thinking.

But just as suddenly, the battle began to reverse itself, through no effort of the 15th. The Bioroids were returning to their Hoverplatforms and making for the scarab ships, seemingly in retreat.

Dante said as much over the net and ranged in the *Trojan Horse*'s forward viewfinder. One of the Bioroids had a civilian clutched in its hand. Dante turned and found another—the civilian limp, probably dead. Everywhere he looked now, he saw the same scene.

"They're taking hostages!" he told Dana. Traversing his cannon, he took aim on one of the Bioroids, muttering to himself, "You're a goner now, buddy. . . ."

But Dana positioned her Battloid in front of him, preventing a clear shot at his target.

"Angelo, stop! You'll kill the hostage—"

Two Bioroids blew the words from her, with shots that would have thrown her face-forward to the ground had Dante not been there to catch her.

"That's *two* I owe you," she said with some effort.

They both dropped their Battloids into a crouch and returned fire. Many of the Bioroids were left without Hovercraft and were obviously bent on going down fighting. There would be no captives here, just a scrap pile of mecha and android parts.

Dana did manage to blow the legs out from under one of their number, but a second later, the thing seemed to self-destruct. And when they did that, there weren't even *parts* left, just memories.

Further down the street the troop carriers were lifting off. The 15th was pinned down, unable to stop them. Still other carriers were landing close in to the fighting, picking up troops who would have been abandoned. *Could they be getting short of firepower?* Dana wondered.

The 15th pushed their line forward and took two more city blocks from the dwindling number of enemy troops. Then ultimately they found themselves firing on the carriers themselves as they were lifting off, presumably returning to the fortress.

"There they go," Dante said, laying his weapon aside. "I wonder what they're planning to do with all those hostages?"

"That's a good question, Sergeant," said Bowie.

"Yeah, a *real* good question," said Sean.

General Emerson and Commander Leonard watched the withdrawal from the central tower of the command center. Below, much of the city was in ruin; the sky above was smoke and orange flame.

"Negotiating couldn't have been worse than this!" Emerson said in disgust, turning away from the window.

"Don't make assumptions," Leonard told him from his seat. "Who's to say that if we had tried to sit down and reason with them the results would have been any different? We may have prevented a worse disaster."

Emerson was too frustrated to counter the remark.

A staff officer entered the room just then and Leonard got to his feet anxiously.

"Well, what's the figure?" he demanded.

"Over two hundred citizens have been kidnapped, sir. But the figure may go higher once all sectors have reported in."

"I see. . . ." Leonard said, visibly distressed. "In the official report, list them as casualties of the battle."

Emerson threw Leonard a look, which the commander took in stride. *Did the fool really expect him to tell the civilian population that the aliens were now taking people from their homes for some unknown purpose?*

"Yessir," the staff sergeant snapped.

"I don't know what they're up to," Leonard said under his breath. "But whatever it is, it won't work—not as long as I have a single man left to fight them."

CHAPTER EIGHT

Come on, people, we've done this before and we can do it again. There isn't one of us—except for the tots—who didn't see our homes and lives wiped out by the rounds and missiles of one faction or another. So, think back to those days, remember how we had to build and rebuild. And remember that we never lost sight of tomorrow. We can lean on each other and pull through this, or we can all retreat into our individual misery and lose everything. I'm going to leave it up to each and every one of you. But I know what I'm going to do: I'm going to roll up my shirtsleeves, grab hold of this shovel, and dig myself out of this mess!

From Mayor Tommy Luan's speech to the residents of
SDF-1 Macross, as quoted in Luan's *High Office*

THE HUMAN BOOTY THAT RESULTED FROM THE BIOROID RAID on Monument City was being housed in a massive stasis sphere inside the Masters' grounded flagship—a luminescent globe over fifty yards in diameter that had once been used to store the specimen clones derived from the cell tissues of the Tirolian scientist, Zor. Of the three-hundred-odd victims of the kidnapping foray, only seventy-five had survived the ordeal. These men, women, and children were drifting weightlessly in the gaseous chamber now, as the three Masters looked on dispassionately. The time had come to subject one of the captives to a xylonic cerebral probe to determine not only the psychological make-up of the Humans, but to ascertain their involvement with the Protoculture as well.

At the Masters' behest an antigrav beam retrieved one of the deanimated Earthling males and conveyed him to the mind probe table, a circular platform something like a light table, lit up by the internal circuitry of its numerous scanning devices. The subject was a young tech, still in uniform, his handsome face a mask of death. He was carefully positioned supine on the transparent surface of the platform by the antigrav beam, while the Masters took to the table's control console, a bowllike apparatus slightly larger than the xylonic scanner, its rim a series of pressure-sensitive activation pads.

"But can we extract the information we want from what is no doubt an inferior example of the species?" Bowkaz put to his companions. Their choice had been based on the fact that this one was clothed in an Earth Forces uniform; there had been captives of higher rank, but they had expired in transit.

"We will at least be able to determine the depth of their reliance on the Protoculture," Dag returned.

Six wrinkled hands were laid on the sensor pads; the combined will of three minds directed the scanning process. X-ray images and internal schematics of the Human were displayed on the control console's central screen.

"Their evolutionary development is more limited than we thought," Shaizan commented.

As the probes were focused on cerebral memory centers, video images replaced the roller-coaster graphics; these so-called mnemonic schematics actually translated the electroengrammic cerebral pulses into visual wave-lengths, permitting the Masters to view the subject's past. What played on the circular monitor screen were scenes that were to some extent archetypically Human: preverbal memories of infancy, recollections of school life, cadet training, moments of love and loss, beauty and pain.

The Masters had little trouble understanding the images of training and hierarchical induction, but were less certain when the scenes contained some measure of emotional content.

"Inefficient command structure and grotesquely primitive weapons system," Bowkaz offered, as military memories surfaced.

Now a fleeting image of a run through Earth's tall green grass, a companion alongside . . .

"Is this the specimen's female counterpart?"

"Most likely. Our previous studies have shown that the two sexes intermix quite freely and that the Earthlings apparently select specific mates. I believe that we are seeing an example of what might be referred to as the courting ritual."

"A barbaric behavioral pattern."

"Yes . . . The species reproduces itself through a process of self-contained childbirth. There is no evidence of biogenetic engineering whatsoever."

"Random . . . foolish," muttered Dag.

"But something about them is worrisome," said Shaizan. "It is no wonder the Zentraedi were defeated." He lifted his aged hands from the sensor pads, effectively deactivating the probe.

The young cadet on the table sat up, seemingly unaffected and reawakened; but there was no life left in his eyes: whatever was once his individual self had been taken from him by the Masters' probe, and what remained was empty consciousness, like a hand wiped clean of prints and lines, awaiting that first fold and flex . . .

"There is little chance of using these beings to pilot our Bioroids," Bowkaz pronounced. "The scanning process alone has destroyed much of this one's neural circuitry. We would need to recondition each of them to suit our purpose. . . ."

But if this part of their plan was foiled, it was at least encouraging to have learned that not all Humans had knowledge of the Protoculture, except in terms of its application to the enhancement of technology. They had not yet discovered its true value. . . .

" . . . And this is to our advantage," said Dag. "Ignorant, they will not oppose our removing the Protoculture matrix from the ruins of Zor's dimensional fortress."

"But we must prevent them from carrying out these attacks against us. Can they be reasoned with?"

Bowkaz scowled. "They can be threatened."

"And easily manipulated . . . I feel that the time has come to call down a rescue ship."

"But we are so close to our goal," Dag objected.

Shaizan looked to his companion. There was an unmistakable element of impatience in Dag's attitude, surely a contagion spread by the Earthlings who had been allowed to scout the fortress. Or perhaps by the very specimens the Bioroids had brought in. All the more reason to abandon the surface of the planet as quickly as possible.

"The time has come for us to activate Zor Prime and insinuate him among the Humans. The clone so resembles them that they will accept him as one of their own."

Bowkaz concurred. "We will achieve a two-fold purpose: by implanting a neuro-sensor in the clone's brain, we will be able to monitor and control his activities."

"And second?" Dag asked anxiously.

"The realization of our original plan for the clone: as the contamination takes hold of him, the neural imagery of Zor will be awakened. And once that occurs, we will not only know precisely where the Protoculture device has been hidden, but exactly how it operates."

Shaizan came close to smiling. "The Invid will be stopped and the galaxy will be *ours* once again."

Bowkaz looked at the Human subject, then the stasis sphere itself. "And what of these?" he asked his companions.

Shaizan turned his back. "Destroy them," he said.

"Specimen is in position and proton disposal is on standby," reported the bio-lab tech.

Commander Leonard stepped to the permaplas observation window and gave a last look at the alien android. It had been laid out on its back on a flyout platform central to the huge sanitization tank. Curiously, someone in forensic had thought to reclothe the dissected thing in its uniform. Consequently, this routine disposal was beginning to feel more like a wake than anything else, and Leonard didn't like that one bit.

The sanitization chamber resembled the sealed barrel of an enormous gun, its curved inner surface an array of circular ports linked by conduits to tanks of cleansing chemicals or particle-beam accelerators. No one had expected the supreme commander to drop by, and it was only happenstance that accounted for his presence—he and his retinue had been in the area and Colonel Fredericks of the GMP had invited him over to witness the process. Rolf Emerson was also present.

Leonard was just about ready to give the tech the go-sign, when Lieutenant Sterling came running in, urging him to wait, urging him not to give the signal.

"Commander," she said out of breath. "You can't just destroy him. He should be returned to his people. Perhaps we can bargain—"

Leonard was still burning from Dana's interruptions at the briefing, so he turned on her harshly now, gesturing to the lifeless form in the tank. "It's an unthinking piece of protoplasm even when alive, *Lieutenant!* Do you seriously believe that the aliens would bargain for *this*?!"

Rolf Emerson was ready to drag Dana away before she could respond, but she ignored his glare, even raised her voice some. "Why would 'unthinking pieces of protoplasm' bother to take Human hostages, Commander? Answer that!"

Leonard winced and looked around, wondering if anyone without a clearance had caught Sterling's comment. Fredericks understood, and stepped behind Dana, gently taking hold of her arms.

"Let me go!" Dana threw over her shoulder.

Fredericks backed off, then she said in low tones: "Calm down,

Lieutenant. There were no hostages taken yesterday, there were only casualties. And in any event, this matter has nothing whatever to do with you."

"Activate!" Dana heard the commander say. He had turned away from her, hands folded behind his back, silhouetted against the observation window now as a flash of bright light disintegrated the alien corpse. Follow-up chemicals poured from two ports removing any remaining traces of tissue.

Dana stood motionless; unresponsive to Leonard as he shouldered by her, dismissing her. Fredericks and Emerson closed in on her.

"Now then, Lieutenant," the GMP colonel began sinisterly.

"Will you take your hands *off* me?!" Dana yelled, twisting free of his grip.

Rolf stepped in front of her. "Dana," he said, controlled but obviously furious, "considering your past record, you risk a great deal by coming here like this. You know the punishment for insubordination is severe—and don't think for a moment that I'll intervene on your behalf."

"Yes, of course. Sir!"

Rolf softened some. "Believe me, I share your concern that Commander Leonard has been too resolute in this matter, but I'm in no position to debate his actions and neither are *you*. Do I make myself clear?"

Dana's lips were a thin line. "Clear, sir," she said stiffly. "Clear as day."

The 15th, like many of the other ATAC squads, had been assigned to mop-up duty. There were sections of Monument City untouched by the recent attack, but this was more than made up for by the devastation elsewhere. Still, it was business as usual for the civilians: thanks to Robotechnology, rebuilding wasn't the chore it would have been twenty years ago, even though there were relatively few mecha units given over to construction. Many wondered how Macross had been able to rebuild itself so often without the advantage of modern techniques and materials, not to mention modular design innovations. One would hear stories about Macross constantly, comparisons and such, but what always surfaced was a sense of nostalgia for the older, cruder ways, nostalgia for a certain *spirit* that had been lost.

Dana's generation didn't quite see things that way, however. In fact, they felt that Monument had *more* spirit than any of its prototypes. Whereas Hunter's generation had been brought up during an era of war—the Civil War, then the Robotech—Dana and her peers had enjoyed almost twenty years of peace. But they had been raised to *expect* war, and now that it was here, they simply did their part, then returned to the hedonistic pursuits that had always ruled them and provided them with a necessary balance to the dark predictions of their parents and elders.

In this way, mop-up operations were usually excuses for block parties. Civilians left the shelters and started partying as soon as they could, and the younger members of the Army of the Southern Cross were so easily distracted and seduced. . . .

"Get a move on, Bowie!" Dana yelled over her shoulder, as she leaned her Hovercycle into a turn.

Bowie was half-a-dozen lengths behind her, with power enough to catch up with her, but short on nerve. She had conned him into sneaking away from patrol for a few quick drinks at the club he frequented on leave. It was a crazy stunt to be pulling, but Dana was immune to his warnings. *What's the difference,* she had told him. *The High Command never listens to a word I have to say anyway, so why should I listen to them?*

Oh, he had argued with her, but as always she got the better of him.

"Hey, slow down!" he begged her from his cycle. "Are you crazy or something?"

It was a foolish question to be asking someone who had just walked out on patrol, so Bowie simply shook his head and gave the mecha more throttle.

The club (called Little Luna, an affectionate term for the Robotech Factory Satellite that had been in geo-synchronous orbit until the arrival of the alien ships) was SRO by the time Dana and Bowie arrived; it was body-to-body on the dance floor and tighter than that everywhere else. But Bowie enjoyed a certain cachet because he played there so often, and it wasn't long before they had two seats at the bar.

"Let me have a bottle of your best Scotch," Dana told the bartender. She asked Bowie to join her, but he refused.

"I don't know what's bugging you," he said, "but don't you think you might be going about this the wrong way? I mean, getting thrown in the brig isn't going to prove anything—"

Dana silenced him by putting her hand over his mouth. Her attention was riveted on someone who had just appeared on-stage.

"Ladies and gentlemen, boys and girls, haves and have-nots," the deejay announced. "George Sullivan!"

Bowie moved Dana's hand aside and leaned around her.

Sullivan was taking a quick bow for the crowd. He was a handsome man in his early thirties, on the old side for the following he enjoyed, and fairly conservative to boot. Clean shaven and wholesome looking, he wore his wavy brown hair in a kind of archaic pompadour, and liked to affect tailcoats with velvet lapels. Bowie could never understand his appeal, although he sang well enough.

"What a fox!" Dana commented.

Bowie made a face. "We jam together sometimes."

"You jam with that hunk? Bowie, I should have been coming to this club with you a long time ago."

Dana was too preoccupied to notice Bowie's shrug of indifference. "He's a newcomer." Sullivan had spotted Bowie and was leaving the stage and heading toward the bar, pawed at by some of the overeager. "He's coming over here," he told Dana quietly. "Don't make a driveling fool of yourself."

Dana's eyes lit up as Sullivan shook Bowie's hand. "I'm glad you stopped by, Bowie," Dana heard him say. "How would you feel about accompanying me on 'It's You'? I'm having some trouble with my romantic image."

Dana thought him even better-looking up close. And he smelled terrific. "That's hard to believe," she piped in.

Sullivan turned to her. "Have we met?" he said annoyed.

"This is Lieutenant Dana Sterling, George," said Bowie.

Sullivan stared at her: did his eyes narrow with interest just then, or did she imagine it, Dana asked herself? He was reaching for her hand. "A pleasure," she said, restraining herself from giving the masculine handshake she was accustomed to.

"*My* pleasure," said Sullivan, a bit too forcefully. He held on to her hand longer than he had to, communicating something with his eyes she could not fathom.

The three Masters stood before a towering curved wall of strobing lights and flashing schematics. Their hands reached out for the sensor pads of a control console.

"Vectors are coordinated," said number three. "Ready to override the Micronians' communications network."

"Let us begin immediately!" said Shaizan, aware too late of the haste implied by his tone. Bowkaz called him on it.

"Is this impatience? Now *you* are beginning to show signs of contamination!"

Shaizan growled slightly through clenched, vestigial teeth, yellow with age and disuse.

"Enough," said Dag, putting a quick end to the argument. "Commence override. . . ."

From his chambers in the United Earth Headquarters, Commander Leonard spoke with the Republic's prime minister via video-phone. A white-haired mustachioed politico who had served like Leonard under T. R. Edwards, Chairman Moran wore his badge of office on his right breast, and his sidearm to bed. He had learned tactics from Edwards, and that made him a dangerous man indeed.

"Your Excellency," Leonard said deferentially, "we must wait until we know more about the aliens before launching a preemptive strike. Frankly, my staff is split—"

"The final judgment is of course yours," the chairman interrupted. "But I hope you understand that it's becoming increasingly difficult for me to defend your inaction. If you're not up to it. . . ."

Leonard tried to keep his emotions in check as Moran left his threat unfinished. "I understand my obligations to the council," he said evenly.

Moran's head nodded in the monitor's field. "Good. I expect you to coordinate your attack plans as soon as possible."

The screen image de-rezzed and Leonard drew a hand down his face in frustration. *Curse Edwards for leaving me to this!* he said to himself.

But suddenly the screen was alive again; Leonard opened his eyes to wavering bars of static and multicolored contour lines. Then there was a voice attached to the oscillations—high-pitched and synthesized, though its message was clear.

"Consider this a final warning," it began. *"Interfere with our attempts to leave this planet and you face extinction."*

A second threat in as many minutes.

The monitor screen went blindingly white.

CHAPTER
NINE

Any assessment of T. R. Edwards's legacy must take into account the feudal structures his social and political programs fostered. It is not enough to say that the Council was organized along feudal lines; Human conventions and mores just as often reflect the nature of the ruling body as influence it. Feudalism ruled, both as political doctrine and spirit of the times, from the government on down to the constituency.

"Overlords," *History of the Second Robotech War, Vol. CXII*

DANA AND BOWIE SPENT TWO HOURS IN THE CLUB—TWO wonderful hours for Dana, talking with George, listening to him sing. He performed a medley of oldies, including several by Lynn-Minmei that were currently enjoying a revival. She sat at the piano, chin resting on her folded hands, while Bowie played and the audience applauded. And George sang for her. Afterwards he wanted to know all about her—Bowie, that dear, had often spoken of her to him—but he wanted to know more. All about her missions with the 15th, especially the recent one, when they had been responsible for bringing down the alien fortress. He let her go on and on—perhaps too far because of the Scotch she had consumed. But it had felt so good to get it all out, to talk to someone who was intensely interested in her life. In fact, he hardly talked about himself at all, and that was certainly something that set him apart from most of the men she met.

She was mounted on her Hovercycle now, waiting for Bowie to say his good-byes and join her for the return trip to the barracks. Back to the real world. However, it was a different world than the one she looked out on only hours ago; fresh and revived, suddenly full of limitless possibilities.

Bowie appeared and swung one leg over his cycle.

"I can't get that last song out of my mind," Dana told him,

stars in her eyes. "I've heard you mention George before, but why didn't you tell me he was so special?"

"Because I don't really know him that well," Bowie said. "He keeps to himself." He activated his cycle and strapped in while it warmed. "We better get a move on."

"Is he performing here again?" Dana wanted to know.

"Yeah, he's doing a set later tonight," Bowie returned absently. Then he noticed that Dana had switched off her cycle.

"Dana. . . ."

She was headed back into the club. "Don't worry about me. I just want to say good night. Take off. I'll catch up with you later."

Bowie sighed, exasperated, though he had little doubt she would catch up.

Dana went in through the stage entrance this time, noticing inside that some comedian had tampered with the sign above the door—instead of reading EXIT DOOR, it now read EXEDORE. The rear portion of the building was shared by an adjacent store, and there were numerous packing crates stacked here and there, and very little light. Dana called out to George in the darkness, and headed toward that meager light she could discern. Finally she heard the clacking of keyboard tabs and closed on that.

It was a small cubicle, brightly lit, with a cloth curtain for a doorway, and apparently served as both dressing room and office. George was seated at the desk, tapping data into a portable computer terminal. She called his name, but he was obviously too wrapped up in his task to hear her. So she waited silently by the door, wondering what he could be working on so diligently. Song lyrics, maybe, or a detailed account of the two hours they had just spent together. . . .

Dana looked again at the portable unit. There was something familiar about it. . . . Then she noticed the small insignia: the fluted column above the atomic circle . . . emblem of the *Global Military Police*!

Reflexively she drew in her breath and backed out of sight, hoping she hadn't tipped her hand. George had stopped. But then she heard him say: "Just as I thought . . . I suspected the enemy fortress had an outer hull weakness."

Pretty weird lyrics, thought Dana.

Cautiously, she peered into the room once again. Had she missed seeing someone, or was George talking to himself? Indeed, he was alone and a moment later gave voice to her worst fear:

"Now if I can just pry some more information out of the lovely

Lieutenant Sterling, maybe I'll be able to put my theories to the test."

A detailed account of their two hours, all right, Dana said to herself. Sullivan was a GMP spy. And what those double-dealers couldn't pull from HQ, they hoped to learn from her! *And she had told them!* All about the raid on the fortress, the recon mission, the bio-gravitic network ...

George muttered something, then surprised her further when she heard him say: "Oh, Marlene, if you were only here!"

She might have charged in at that moment if the stage manager hadn't appeared at the opposite door. "Five minutes," he told Sullivan.

Sullivan thanked the man and closed up the computer.

Dana backed away and ran to the exit door, her hand at her mouth.

The Masters were pleased with themselves, although each was now careful to avoid any displays that might be interpreted as emotional.

"Will they heed our warning?" Dag asked aloud.

"I can't believe they would be so foolish as to ignore it," said Bowkaz. He had been their voice to the Human commander.

Shaizan grunted. "All our questions will be answered soon enough."

"The time has come to signal the fleet."

Six hands reached forward to the console.

Dag removed his hands for an instant, breaking their link with the communicator. "Their behavior during the next few hours will indicate whether we have anything more to fear from them," he said darkly.

"Where have you been?" Angelo Dante said as Dana stormed into the 15th's barracks. The team was assembled in the rec room, talking tactics and stuffing their faces. Dana had heard warning Klaxons when she first entered the compound, but had no idea what they signaled.

"We've been looking all over for you, Lieutenant," from Sean now. "Where have you been?"

"Don't ask," Dana told them harshly. "Just tell me what's going on—are we slotted for patrol again?"

"Tomorrow morning," the sergeant explained. "Seems another enemy ship is on its way to Earth, probably to try and rendezvous with the grounded fortress. High command wants us there on the ground to meet 'em."

"They've already sent Marie up with a welcoming committee of TASC interceptors," Sean added. "Course they seem to forget we've got no way of fighting them until the bright boys down in data analysis give us some information."

Dana swallowed her initial surprise and smiled to herself.

"Sean, I've already taken care of that. I know where to get all the information we need."

They all froze, midaction, waiting for her to finish.

"That's right. I've got a way to get it straight from the GMP."

"What do they know that we don't know?" Louie asked her. "We're the ones who brought down that ship in the first place."

"But how do we know they didn't learn something from that Bioroid pilot?" Dana pointed out. "I find it awfully strange that he *expired*, just like that." She snapped her fingers. "They got something they're not telling us. Maybe they're even holding out on HQ. Why else would Fredericks have shown up at the zap tank? I'm telling you, the GMP is in on it."

"Even if you're right," Angelo said full of suspicion, "you and what army's gonna access that data?"

"Those files are top secret, eyes-only," Louie hastened to add.

"Come on," Dana laughed, throwing up her hands. "Give me a little credit, guys. One of their top agents is working for me— without his knowing it, of course."

It was enough to silence Angelo and tip the goggles off Louie's nose. Bowie and Sean just stared at her.

The song came back to her as she took in their looks.

> I always think of you
> Dream of you late at night
> What do you do
> When I turn out the light?

You spy for the GMP, geek, Dana answered herself and the song. *But now it's you who's lost, George Sullivan. . . .*

The following morning (while Dana showered away romantic feelings for George, decided that "Marlene" was probably some aging rock singer who wore too much makeup, and devised a plan to reverse the tables on suave Sullivan), Lieutenant Marie Crystal's TASC unit attacked the Earthbound fortress that had separated itself from the alien fleet to rendezvous with its grounded twin. Modified cargo shuttles had delivered the Black Lions to the edge of space and the assault was mounted with an absence of the usual preliminaries.

Leonard, Emerson, and the joint chiefs monitored the attack from the war room at Defense Headquarters.

"We're hitting them with everything we've got, but it's like water off a duck's back!" Leonard heard the lieutenant remark over the com net.

He would have been surprised to hear anything different; however, this was one time the chairman wasn't going to get the chance to accuse him of inaction. There was some hope early on that Crystal's squad could fell the fortress as Sterling's had the first, but apparently the aliens were quick to learn and not about to repeat mistakes: even if the Black Lions managed to disarm the defensive shields of the descending fortress, they would find the bio-gravitic reactor port sealed and unapproachable. And, as General Emerson had been quick to point out, having a second fortress crashland on Earth was not exactly optimum in any event. *Better to let them pick up their wreck,* Leonard said to himself as he studied the schematics on the situation board.

Leonard was trying hard not to think about the message that had been flashed across his monitor earlier that day, and had half convinced himself that it was an hallucination or the result of some plot hatched by Emerson's wing of the general staff meant to put him at further odds with Chairman Moran's Council.

"The assault group reports limited damage to the ship's superstructure," a controller reported now, "but the enemy's force shields remain intact and operational."

"The attack's having no effect whatsoever, Commander," Emerson said angrily.

Leonard adopted the same tone. "Then we'll destroy the grounded ship before this one can arrive to save it."

Emerson grinned wryly. *Just who was the commander kidding?* Perhaps he was uttering these absurdities for posterity, Rolf thought. *Leonard had the right idea,* they would say. *Leonard did everything he could.* Save for the fact everyone knew that the destruction of either fortress wasn't within their power. Nevertheless, the Tactical Armored units would be deployed to realize Leonard's grandiose lies.

Or at least die trying.

Dana had asked Bowie to find out where George lived. Her friend found it hard to believe that she could think about love at a time like this (*lust* was the term he actually used), but he relented and came through. She regretted having to keep him in the dark about her plan; however, she didn't want him going into battle with any more on his mind than was absolutely necessary.

Once again she put Dante in temporary command of the unit and set out on her private mission, trailing Sullivan from his low-rent apartment not far from the GMP ministry, to a grassy overlook in a restricted area on the outskirts of the city. It was a tedious challenge, since George had opted to hike to the spot. But once Dana was sure of his destination, she powered her Hovertank along the back roads that led to the overlook and arrived shortly after he did.

He was standing under perhaps the only shade tree on the entire ridgeline, his computer briefcase clutched in his left hand. "What in the world are you doing way out here?" he said, when she called to him from the mecha's cockpit. "Shouldn't you be with your squadron or something?"

"I couldn't bear to be away from you any longer," she told him dramatically. "And I was hoping I could get you to join my team . . . unless you have to report back to the GMP?"

George stepped back from the mecha as though he had been hit. Dana dismounted and told him not to worry about it—his secret was safe with her.

"But you used me," she said, unconcealed hurt in her voice. "And I want to know why. What are you trying to prove?"

Sullivan's face registered anger. "I'm not trying to prove anything." Then he closed his eyes for a moment and shook his head. "All right," he said after a moment. "But I've never told this to anyone."

Dana kept quiet while he explained. His sister had been a casualty of the first alien raid on Monument City, and Sullivan, then an HQ war department tech, blamed himself for her death—he had forgotten to pick her up after school and she had been caught up in the attack while waiting for him.

The sort of story Dana had heard all too frequently and become somewhat inured to, despite the sympathy she felt for him. One might as well blame chance or fate, she told herself as Sullivan continued.

He had deserted his post to visit her in the hospital and—though severely burned and not expected to last the night—she had spoken his name as if nothing had happened, assigning no blame and concerned that he would soon be alone in the world. That was when the military police had arrived on the scene; they had come to arrest him, but when they understood the depth of his grief they realized that he was someone they could use for their own purposes. He had been with them ever since, playing both sides of the fence whenever he could.

"So you've been waging a one-man campaign against your sister's murderers," Dana said when he finished.

"Whenever I can," he told her.

"Tell me one thing: does the GMP have new information about the fortress—vulnerable spots or weaknesses, some place we could hit them and incapacitate them?"

George nodded gravely, aware that he was breaking his security oath. "Yes. We have reason to believe that we do."

"And it's in that computer of yours?"

Again he nodded.

Dana smiled and took hold of his hand. "Well then, let's put what you've learned to good use." She led him back to the Hovertank and gestured to the rumble seat. "With your data and my firepower, we can send these alien invaders packing."

With annihilation discs raining down on them from all sides, the 15th was throwing everything they had against the enemy, often successfully when it came to downing trios of Hoversled Bioroids (especially in Dana's absence), but ineffectually in terms of their primary target—the fortress itself. Reports from Headquarters indicated that Crystal's Black Lion team had fared no better with the incoming ship, now visible in the explosion-filled sky above the angry ridgeline.

"These guys are slippery little devils!" Sean said over the net. "What does it take to nail them?"

"Keep your eyes open and I'll show you," Dante radioed back.

They both had their mecha in Gladiator mode, their cannons disgorging ear-splitting volleys without letup.

Dante ranged in his weapon and blew one of the airborne Bioroids to debris, just after it loosed a shot that managed to topple Sean's tank.

"Everything okay?" Dante asked when Sean righted the thing.

"I'll live, if that's what you mean."

"I was talkin' about the tank," the sergeant told him.

This from a guy he had once out-ranked, Sean muttered to himself. "Thanks for your concern, Sarge."

Then all at once Dana's *Valkyrie* was in their midst, oddly enough with a civilian passenger in the rumble seat. Bowie identified the stranger for the team and the tac net was nothing but

nasty comments for a minute or so. Sean got in the last word:
"Hey Lieutenant, I didn't know you went for thrill-freaks!"

"Just cut the chatter and give me some cover," Dana ordered.

Full-out, her tank was making directly for the fortress, un-
swerving in the face of the ground fire it was receiving from
Bioroid troops holding the perimeter. Sean watched her go airborne as the tank crested a small rise less than one hundred yards
from the ship, then lost her in the blinding flashes of plasma light
Alphas and Falcons were pouring against the fortress's defensive
shield.

A trio of Hovercrafts pursued Dana as she skimmed the tank
across the ship's armored surface, annihilation discs winging past
George's unprotected head as he studied the computer readouts.
Had her helmet not been essential for rapport with the mecha,
Dana would have handed it back to him.

"Have you coordinated the data yet?"

"It keeps shifting," he yelled into the wind.

"Keep trying," she urged him, piloting the tank through four
lanes of disc fire.

They had already made one pass over the fortress and she now
veered the tank around for a second, taking out a hovercraft as she
completed the break. There was no time to place her shots and
she was sorry for that; but if Sullivan's computer did its job, the
end would more than justify the means. Relying on the mecha's
lateral guns, her hands locked on the handlebar-like control and
trigger mechanisms, she thumbed a second and third Bioroid to
destruction.

Meanwhile the second fortress was eclipsing the sky overhead,
threatening to sandwich her small craft between it and the
grounded ship. Tactical units were loosing cannon rounds against
its plated underbelly, only adding to her predicament as the shells
often ricocheted and detonated along the Hovertank's course.
Dana had also noticed Logans overhead before the fortress
blocked her view; possibly the remnants of Marie Crystal's Black
Lion squadron.

"The vulnerable area will be exposed when the fortresses attempt a ship-to-ship link up," Sullivan said at last. "That'll be the
time to hit them!"

Dana looked up, trying to calculate how much time they had
left before the fortress rendered her and her new sweetie a memory. The ventral surface of the ship was an ugly sight, like the
mouth of some techno-spider about to devour them.

"I'm patching the information directly into your onboard computers, Dana. The rest is up to you."

"Leave it to me," she started to say, accelerating the mecha through the narrowing gap formed by the two ships. But suddenly a Hovercraft had appeared out of nowhere, raining rear energy hyphens at her. Then a Bioroid swooped in from her port side, forcing her dangerously close to some sort of radar glove, a small mountain on the hull of the ship. As she swerved to avoid it, she lost George.

She heard his scream as he flew out of the rumble seat, and craned her head around just in time to see him caught in the metalshod fist of a Hovercraft pilot.

Dana swung around hard, but lost sight of the alien craft. But Marie Crystal was on the net telling her that she had seen the near collision and had the enemy right in front of her.

Dana couldn't figure out what Marie was doing in the gap, but she didn't stop to think about it. She shot forward and attained the open skies again, scanning for Marie's Logan-mode Veritech.

Below her, one of her teammates had just reconfigured from tank to Guardian mode and loosed a bolt at one of the alien sky-sleds. Dana had a sinking feeling as she traced the shot's trajectory: it caught the Bioroid that was holding George, sending it careening into a fiery spin, and on a collision course with Marie's fighter.

Crystal broke too late, impacting against the out-of-control sled and falling into a spin of her own. Dana didn't know who to watch: the Bioroid holding Sullivan or Marie. Suddenly the tank that had fired off that fateful round—Sean's tank—was reconfiguring to Battloid, and leaping up to *catch* Crystal's ship. Despite her fascination, Dana involuntarily averted her eyes; but when she looked again, both Veritechs were reasonably intact.

Then all at once there was an explosion at nine o'clock. She turned, as her mecha was rocked by the shockwaves.

The Bioroid was history.

And George Sullivan was dead.

She screamed his name and flew into the face of the angry fireball, hoping, expecting to find who knew what. And as her scorched tank emerged she recalled his last words to her: *The rest is up to you.*

Inside the grounded fortress, the Masters watched a schematic display of their descending rescuer, a hundred yards overhead now and already extending the grapplers and tendrils that would secure the link-up.

"We are ready," Dag reported.

Shaizan nodded eagerly. "Good. Deploy the Zor clone toward their strongest defenses. . . . We must make certain that he is conveniently captured by the Micronians. . . ."

One minute Angelo Dante was sitting in the cockpit of the Gladiator doing his lethal best, and the next thing he knew he was airborne, turning over and over. . . .

He hit the ground with a thud that knocked the breath from his lungs and left him unconscious for a moment. When the world refocused itself, he recognized what was left of his mangled Hovertank, toppled on its side and burning.

Dante got to his feet, promising to tear the aliens apart, even as a sledded Bioroid dropped in for the kill. It was that gleaming red job, Angelo noticed, already outside himself and braving it out, the hero he was born to be. But just then a strange thing happened: a pinpoint blast from the fortress bull's-eyed the Hovercraft, sending sled and pilot into a fiery crash in the craggy outcroppings near the Earth Forces front lines.

Dante heard an atonal scream of agony issue from the craft as it fell.

"They shot down their own guy!" a puzzled Dante said out loud, figuring he would live to see another day after all. . . .

Dana tried to erase the fiery image of Sullivan's death as she piloted the Hovertank back toward the fortress once again. Split-screen data schematics were running parallel across the monitor screen of *Valkyrie*'s targeting computer, directing the mecha's weapons systems to the coordinates that would spell doom for the fortress. And by the look of things, there wasn't much time left.

With the rescue ship overhead now, the grounded fortress was actually lifting off, still the target of countless warheads that were exploding harmlessly against the alloyed hull—its complex network of close-in weaponry silent—and apparently drawing on all the reserve power available to it. The entire ridgeline appeared to be effected by its leave-taking; a deafening roar filled the air, and the ground was rumbling, sending rock and shale sliding down the steep slopes of those unnatural tors. Massive whirlwinds of gravel and debris spun from the underside of the ascending ship, as though loosed from traps set an eternity ago.

As Dana closed on the twin fortresses, she could see that four panels had opened along the dorsal side of the first, revealing massive socketlike connectors, sized to accept shafts—glowing like outsize radio tubes—that were telescoping from circular portals in the bulbous, spiny anchor shown by the second.

"Faster!" Dana urged her Hovertank, the cockpit screen flashing, the parallel series of schematics aligned. Then the mecha was suddenly reconfiguring to Gladiator mode, retroing to an abrupt halt, the cannon already traversing and ranging in. Having surrendered to the dictates of the computer, Dana could do nothing but sit back and pray that she had arrived in time.

The fortresses were linked in an obscene technomating, one atop the other, ascending and accelerating now, scarcely a three-meter wide gap between them.

Dana's mecha fired once, its energy bolt finding that narrow interface and detonating squarely against the link-up anchor. On all sides, explosive light erupted from the empty space between the ships, and the upper fortress seemed to shudder, list, and collapse over its mate.

But the ships continued to rise.

"It can't be!" Dana shouted over the net. "Why didn't it work?!" Even as she said it, though, she knew the answer. The computer was flashing its internal debriefing to her, but she didn't need to double-check the screen for what she knew in her guts: she had been a split-second too late, two hundred yards out of the required lethal cone.

Dana had one last look at the fortresses before they disappeared into battle clouds and smoke, a close encounter of the worst kind.

CHAPTER

TEN

I think I sensed something about the alien pilot even before Cochran turned to me with the results of his findings. Even now I can't say where that feeling originated or where my present thoughts are directed. I only know that the moment seemed full of import and grand purpose; something about the alien triggered a change in me that is beginning to overshadow my entire life.

From the personal journal of Major General Rolf Emerson

GENERAL EMERSON'S OFFICIAL CAR (A BLACK HOVERLIMO with large tail fins, a purely decorative vintage front grill, and an antique, winged hood ornament) tore from the Ministry's parking lot at a little after three o'clock on the morning following the lift-off of the enemy fortresses. Rolf was in the backseat, silent and contemplative, while his young aide, Lieutenant Milton, felt compelled to issue cautions. Monument City felt like a ghost town.

Emerson had logged two hours of sleep when the call from Alan Fredericks of the GMP had awakened him: something interesting had been discovered near the liftoff site—an alien pilot, alive and apparently well.

Rolf asked himself what Fredericks was up to: he had brought the alien to Miles Cochran's lab, and had yet to inform Commander Leonard of his find. With rivalry running high between the GMP and the militaristic faction of the general staff, Frederick's position was suspect. Perhaps, however, this was merely the GMP's way of making up for the hatchet job they did on the first captured Bioroid pilot. Emerson knew when he recradled the handset exactly what he could be setting himself up for but felt the risk justified. He had asked Colonel Rochelle to rendezvous with him at Cochran's lab, then called for his car.

"This is going to look suspicious, sir," Milton told him for the third time. "The chief of staff racing out of the Ministry in the middle of the night without telling anyone where he's going."

"I know what I'm doing, *Captain*," Rolf said brusquely, hoping to put an end to the man's ceaseless badgering.

"Yes, sir," the lieutenant replied, sullenly.

Emerson had already turned away from him to stare out the window once again. *At least* I hope *I know what I'm doing*, he thought. . . .

Rochelle, Fredericks, and Nova Satori were already waiting at Cochran's high-tech lab on the outskirts of Monument City. The good doctor himself, a bit of a privateer who walked that no-man's land between the GMP and the general staff, was busy keeping the Bioroid pilot alive.

Emerson stared down at the alien now from the observation balcony above one of the lab's IC rooms. Cochran had the handsome elfin-featured young android on its back, an IV drip running, a trach insert in its neck. The pilot was apparently naked under the bedsheets, and surrounded by banks of monitoring and scanning apparatus.

"Our last captive died through *official* mishandling," Rolf was telling the others, his back turned to them. "I want to make certain that doesn't happen again."

"Yes, sir," Fredericks spoke for the group.

Rolf swung around to face the three of them. "Who found him?"

Nova Satori, the GMP's attractive raven-haired lieutenant, stepped forward and offered salute. "I did, sir. Out where the fortress was."

Emerson's eyebrows beetled. "What were you doing out there, Lieutenant?"

Satori and Fredericks exchanged nervous looks. "Uh, she was looking for one of our agents," Fredericks said.

Emerson looked hard at the hawk-faced colonel. "And just what was one of your agents doing out there?"

Fredericks cleared his throat. "We're trying to determine that ourselves, General."

Satori related her brief explanation, purposely keeping George Sullivan's name out of it. But it was the singer/spy she had been looking for; more important, the terminal he'd been carrying when last seen—something Dana Sterling had better be able to account for. Nova had heard sounds coming from one of the downed Hovercrafts and upon investigation had discovered the alien pilot. He was ambulatory then, but collapsed soon after being taken into custody, as though someone had suddenly shifted him to standby mode.

"And he seems fluent in English," Nova concluded.

"All the more reason to let Cochran handle this personally," said Emerson. "And as of this moment I want an absolute information blackout regarding the prisoner."

Rochelle was saying little, waiting for Emerson to finish; but he now felt compelled to address the issue that had been plaguing him since the general's phonecall some hours before. It was a privilege of sorts to be included in Emerson's clique, but not if it was going to mean a court-martial.

"General," he said at last, "are you proposing that we keep this from Commander Leonard?"

Satori and Fredericks were hanging on Emerson's reply.

"I am," he told them evenly.

"Exactly *what* do you want us to do with the specimen?" Fredericks asked after a moment.

"I want you to run every test you can think of on him. I need to know how these creatures breathe, think, eat—do you understand me? And I need the information *yesterday*."

"Yessir," the three said in unison.

Just then Professor Cochran stepped into the observation room, removing his surgical mask and gloves, while everyone questioned him. He waited for the voices to die down and looked into each face before speaking, a slightly bemused expression on his face.

"I have one important fact to report straightaway." He turned and gestured down to the Bioroid pilot. "This *alien* . . . is Human."

The three Masters summoned their Scientist triumvirate to the command center of the newly ascended fortress. The Zor clone had survived and was presently in the hands of the Micronians. The functioning neuro-sensor that had been implanted in the clone's brain told them this much, although there were as yet no visuals. Schematics that filled the chamber's oval screen showed that some damage had been sustained, but all indications suggested it was nothing that need concern them. It was clear, however, that the Scientists did not share their Masters' enthusiasm for the plan.

"By capturing the Zor clone, the Micronians have played right into our hands," Shaizan said by way of defense. It was certainly unnecessary that he *explain* himself to the triumvirate, but it was clear that a certain rebelliousness was in the air, pervasive throughout the ship, and Shaizan hoped to lay some of that to rest. "They themselves will lead us to the Protoculture Matrix."

"And suppose the Micronians should attack us again?" the lavender-haired androgyne asked defiantly.

"One purpose of the neuro-sensor is to keep us appraised of all their military activities," Bowkaz told him, indicating the screen schematics. "We will have ample warning."

"Yes . . . and what happens if the Micronians should discover your *precious* neuro-sensor? What then?"

"Discover it?" Shaizan raised his voice. "That's absurd! Recording of the hyper-frequency of the device is far beyond the realm of their crude scientific instruments. The idea is ludicrous!"

The scientist scowled. "Let us hope so," his synthesized voice seemingly hissed.

Dana felt Sean's gentle tap on her shoulder and heard a forearm chord of sharps and flats. She opened her eyes to sunrise, distant crags like arthritic fingers reaching up into pink and grey layers of sky. She had fallen asleep at the ready-room's piano, although it took her a moment to realize this, head pillowed on forearms folded across the keyboard. Sean was standing behind her, apologizing for disturbing her, making some joke about her guarding the eighty-eights all night and asking if she wanted some breakfast. The rest of the 15th were scattered about the room, arguing and moping about by the looks of it.

". . . And who the hell was snoring all night?" she heard Angelo ask in his loudest voice. "Somebody sounded like a turbo-belt earth-mover with a faulty muffler."

Louie was off in a corner tinkering with some gadget that looked like a miniature Bioroid. Bowie was sullen-faced in another, distanced from the scene by earphones.

"I couldn't sleep a wink," Dana told Sean weakly. She remembered now that she had been thinking of Sullivan and his senseless death, been trying to peck out the melody of that old Lynn-Minmei tune. . . .

"You need to cut loose of that responsibility once in a while," the former lieutenant was telling her. "Let your hair down and have some fun, take life a little less seriously."

Dana got up, reached for the glass of juice she had left on top of the piano, and went to refill it at the dispenser. "There's a war going on, pal," she said, pushing past Sean. "Course you're not the first soldier I've run across who's found the call of the wild more attractive than the call of duty."

"Look who's talking," Sean laughed.

"I mean, I wouldn't want to think that the war was interfering with anything, *Private*."

"I don't let it cramp my style, Dana."

Style? she thought, sipping at the juice. *Let me count the comebacks to that one....* But as she said this to herself, fragments of last night's dream began to surface. There was George, of course, but then he became all mixed up with the images of that long-haired Bioroid pilot she and Bowie had crossed lasers with weeks ago—*Zor!* And then somehow her mother had appeared in the dream, telling her things she couldn't summon up now....

" . . . and I'm definitely not into hopeless romances."

Dana whirled, not sure whether she should be angry, having missed his intro; but she saw that Sean was gesturing to Bowie.

"Now here's a guy who was operating just fine up until a few weeks ago. Now he's out there where the shuttles don't run. And for a *dream*-girl at that!"

Bowie didn't hear a word of this, which Dana figured was just as well. Sean made a few more lame comments as he left the room. Dana went over to her friend and positioned herself where she could be seen, if not heard.

"Sean says you're upset," Dana said when he removed the headphones.

Bowie made a face. "What does he know?"

"It's that alien dame," said Sergeant Dante from across the room, his nose buried in the newspaper. "You better set your sights on something a little more down to earth, my friend."

Dana threw Angelo a look he could feel clear through the morning edition. "Just like that, huh Sergeant? He just snaps his fingers and forgets her."

"For cryin' out loud, she's an *alien*! . . . Uh, no offense, of course," he hastened to add.

"No offense taken," Dana told him. "I know your type can't help it. But I don't care if this girl Musica is 'Spiderwoman,' Angelo. You can't tell someone to just turn her heart on and off like a light switch."

"*Her* heart, Dana? *Her* heart?"

Dana had her mouth opened to say something, but she noticed that Bowie was crying. When she put her hand on his shoulder, he shrugged it off roughly, stood up, and ran from the room.

Dana started to chase him, but thought better of it halfway down the corridor. *Did her father have to put up with this from his squad?* she wondered. *Did her mother? And where* were *they,* she asked the ceiling—*where?!*

Lieutenant Marie Crystal had slept well enough, thanks to the anodynes she received at the base hospital after the crash of her ship. But the pills' effects had worn off now, and she couldn't locate a joint or muscle in her body that wasn't crying out for more of the same medication. She reached out for the bedside hand mirror and took a glance at her disheveled, pale reflection. Fortunately her face didn't look as bad as the rest of her felt. It was deathly hot and dry in the room, so she cautiously got out of bed, shaking as she stood, and changed out of the hospital gown into a blue satin robe someone had been thoughtful enough to drop by the room. She left it open as she climbed back under the sheets; after all, it wasn't as if she were expecting visitors or anything.

But no sooner had that thought crossed her mind when she heard Sean's voice outside the door. Having literally landed in the arms of the Southern Cross's ace womanizer was perhaps only a shade better than having piled into a mountain, but it was something she was going to have to live with for a while. She hadn't, however, anticipated that the trials were to begin so soon.

Marie ran a hand through her short, unruly hair and pulled the robe closed; Sean was running into some Nightingale flack at the door.

"Couldn't I just have five minutes with her?" Marie heard Sean say. "Just to drop off these pretty flowers that I picked with my own teeth?"

The nurse was resolute: no one was permitted to enter.

"But I'm the guy who practically saved her life! Listen: I won't talk to her or make her laugh or cry or anything—really—"

"No visitors means no visitors," the nurse told him.

Just whose side is she on? Marie began to wonder.

"Well isn't it just my luck to find the one nurse in this whole hospital who's immune to my many charms."

Now *that* sounded like the Sean Marie knew.

"Here," she heard him say now. "You keep the flowers. Who knows, maybe we'll just meet again, darlin'."

Marie's pale blue eyes went wide.

She was wrong: landing in the arms of his Battloid was *worse* than having crashed!

* * *

General Emerson was in the war room when Leonard finally caught up with him. He had been dodging the commander's messages all day, victimized by a dark premonition that Leonard had somehow learned about the alien pilot. And as soon as Leonard opened his mouth, Emerson knew that his instincts had been correct. But strangely enough, the commander seemed to be taking the whole thing in stride.

"I've been told that you're keeping a secret from me, General Emerson," Leonard began, with almost a lilt to his voice. "I thought I'd come over here and ask you myself: is it true that another Bioroid specimen had been captured?"

"Yes, Commander," Rolf returned after saluting. "As a matter of fact, Professor Cochran is running a complete series of tests on him."

Leonard suddenly whirled on him red-faced with anger.

"Just when were you planning to tell me about *him*, General?!"

Techs throughout the room swiveled from their duty stations.

"Or perhaps you were considering *keeping* this information from me!" Leonard was bellowing.

Rolf didn't even get the chance to stammer his half-formed explanation.

"I'm taking the prisoner out of your hands, General. He'll be analyzed by military scientists, not renegade professors, do you understand me?"

Rolf fought to keep down his own anger while Leonard stormed off, his boot heels loud against the acrylic floor in the otherwise silent room. "We mustn't let this prisoner be destroyed," he managed to get out without yelling. "We learned *nothing* from the last one. This time we must proceed impartially, and Miles Cochran's our best hope for that."

The commander had stopped in his tracks and swung around to face Emerson, regarding him head to toe before responding. And when he spoke his voice was loud but controlled.

"I'm sure our people could do just as well, General. But it seems to me that you've taken a personal interest in this prisoner. Am I correct?"

"I have," said Emerson, and Leonard nodded knowingly.

"Is there something more I should know about this particular *android*?"

Rolf was tight-lipped. "Not at the moment, Commander."

"Well then, since you're so ... *determined*. ... But keep in mind that this one is *your* responsibility, General. There are too many variables in this situation already."

Emerson saluted and Leonard was turning to leave, when all at once a novel blip appeared on the threat board. The power play forgotten, all eyes focused on the screen. Every terminal in the room was clacking out paper. Techs were hunched over their consoles, trying to make sense of the thing that had just appeared in sublunar obit *out of nowhere!*

"What is it?" demanded Leonard, his hands pressed to the command console. "Someone answer me!"

"A ship, sir," said a female enlisted-rating. "And it appears to be moving in to engage the enemy!"

CHAPTER ELEVEN

Major Carpenter and crew left today. "Lang's shot in the dark," as some are calling it. But I have already let it be known that the responsibility is mine, and one part of me is even envious of their leavetaking. Simply to attempt a return to Earth, to quit this malignant corner of space, this crazed and maniacal warfare against our own brothers and sisters and the unstoppable creatures borne of the Tirolians' savagery and injustice. . . . It is clear to me that my destiny lies elsewhere, perhaps on Optera itself, Lisa my life and strength beside me.

The Collected Journals of Admiral Rick Hunter

THE SHIP THAT HAD MATERIALIZED FROM HYPER SPACE AND created that blip on the threat board was long overdue in arriving in Earthspace. Ten years was hardly a measurable quantity by galactic standards; but to a planet brought once to the brink of extinction and now enmeshed in a war that threatened what little remained, ten years was an eternity—and the appearance of the ship a godsend. Unfortunately such feelings were soon to prove premature. . . .

Lost in space for the past five Earth-years—lost in corridors of time, in continuum shifts and as yet unmapped mobius loops—the cruiser had finally found its way home. Before that, it had been part of the Pioneer Expeditionary Mission—that ill-fated attempt to reach the homeworld of the Robotech Masters before the Masters' sinister hands reached out for Earth. The Mission, and that wondrous ship constructed in space and launched from Little Luna, had had such noble beginnings. The Protoculture Matrix thought to have been hidden inside the SDF-1 by its alien creator, Zor, had never been located; the war between Earth and the Zentraedi terminated. So what better step to take, but a diplomatic one: an effort to erase all possibilities of a second war by coming to terms with peace beforehand.

But how could the members of the SDF-3 have known—the

Hunters, Lang, Breetai, Exedore and the rest—how could they have foreseen what awaited them on Tirol and what treacherous part T. R. Edwards would come to play in the unfolding of events? Earth itself would have no knowledge of these things for years to come: of the importance of a certain element indigenous to the giant planet Fantoma, of a certain quasi-canine creature native to Optera, of a budding young genius named Louie Nichols. . . .

For the moment, therefore, the cruiser being tracked by Earth Defcon seemed like the answer to a prayer.

The ship was a curious, one-of-a-kind hybrid, fabricated on the far side of the galactic core by the Robotechnicians of the SDF-3 before the schism between Hunter and Edwards, for the express purpose of hyperspace experimentation: The SDF-3 hadn't the means to return to Earth, but it was conceivable that a small ship could accomplish what its massive parent could not. Those conversant with Robotech warship classifications could point to the Zentraedi influences on this one, notably the cruiser's sleek shark-like form, and the elevated bridge and astrogation centers that rose like a dorsal fin just aft of its blunted bow. But if its hull was alien, its Reflex power center was pure Terran, especially the quadripartite design of the triple-thruster units that comprised the stern.

The cruiser's commander, Major John Carpenter, had distinguished himself during the Tirolian campaign against the Invid, but five-years in hyperspace (was it five minutes or five lifetimes, who could say which?) had taken their toll. Not only on Carpenter, but on the entire crew, every one of them a victim of a space sickness that had no name except madness, perhaps.

When the ship had emerged from hyperspace and a vision of their blue-and-white homeworld had filled the forward viewports, there wasn't a crewman aboard who believed his eyes. They had all experienced the cruel tricks that awaited the unwary techno-voyager, the *horrors.* . . . Then they had identified the massive spade fortresses of the alien fleet. And there was no mistaking these, no mistaking the intent of the soulless Masters who guided them.

Carpenter had ordered an immediate attack, convinced that Admiral Hunter himself would have done the same. And if it seemed *insane*, the commander told himself as Veritech teams tore from the cruiser's ports—one relatively undersized ship against so many—one had merely to recall what the SDF-1 had done against *four million*!

Even the strategy was to be the same: all firepower would be concentrated against the flagship of the alien fleet; that destroyed, the rest would follow.

But Carpenter's crew put too much stock in history, which, despite claims to the contrary, rarely repeats itself. More important, Carpenter forgot exactly *who* he was dealing with: after all, these weren't the Zentraedi ... these were *the beings who had created the Zentraedi*!

In the command center of the alien flagship the three Masters exchanged astonished looks over the rounded crown of the Protoculture cap. Lifting their eyes to the bridge readout screens, the look the three registered could almost have passed for amusement: a warship even more primitive in design than those the Earth Forces had sent against them in the recent past had just defolded from hyperspace and was attempting to engage the fleet singlehandedly.

"Absurd," Bowkaz commented.

"Perhaps we should add *insult* to the list of strategies they have attempted to use against us."

"Primitive and barbaric," said Dag, observing how the fortress's segmented cannons were annihilating the Earth mecha, as though they were a swarm of mites. "We do them a service by obliterating them. They insult themselves with such gestures."

Behind the Masters the Scientist triumvirate was grouped at its duty station.

"We have locked on their battle cruiser at mark six bearing five-point-nine," one of them reported now.

Shaizan regarded the screen. "Prepare for a change in plans," he told the blue-haired clone. "Ignore the drones and deal directly with the cruiser. All units will converge on your coordinates. Our ship will hold the lead ... for the glory of the kill."

The techs, staff, and officers in the war room were still yahooing and celebrating the return of the Pioneer Mission. Supreme Commander Leonard had left immediately to confer with Chairman Moran, leaving General Emerson in charge of the surprise situation.

"Sir!" said one of the techs. "Pioneer Commander is requesting backup. Shall we scramble our fighters and Ghosts?"

Emerson grunted his assent and nodded, curiously uneasy, almost alarmed by the sudden turn of events. Was it possible, he asked as the techs sounded the call—the return of his old friends, a new beginning? . . .

Bowie and Dana, each cocooned in private thoughts, sequels to earlier interrupted musings, were in the 15th's rec room when they heard the scramble alert.

"All pilots to battle stations, all pilots to battle stations. . . . All ground crews to staging areas six through sixteen. . . . Prepare fighters for rendezvous with SDF-3 attack wing!"

Dana was on her feet even before the final part of the call, disregarding as always the particulars and details. Rushing past Bowie, she grabbed his arm and practically hauled him into the barracks corridor, where everyone was double-timing it toward the drop-racks and mecha ports. She hadn't seen such frenzy, such *enthusiasm*, in months, and wondered about the cause. Either the city was under full-scale attack or something miraculous had happened.

She saw Louie racing by and called for him to stop. "Hey, what's all the ruckus about?!" she asked him, Bowie breathless by her side.

Louie returned a wide grin, eyes bright even through the ever-present goggles. "It seems the cavalry's arrived in the nick of time! We've got reinforcements from hyperspace—the Pioneer's come home!"

Dana and Bowie almost fell over.

Something miraculous had *happened!*

"We need a miracle, John," Commander Carpenter's navigator said hopelessly. "We've thrown everything but the kitchen sink at them. Nothing's penetrating those shields."

The two men were on the bridge of the cruiser, along with a dozen other officers and techs who had wordlessly witnessed the utter destruction of their strike force. *That those men who had lived through so much terror should perish at Earth's front gate,* Carpenter thought, half out of his mind from the horror of it. But he was determined that their deaths count for *something.*

"Have the first wing make an adjustment to fifty-seven mark four-nine," he started to say when the cruiser sustained its first blow.

Carpenter was sent reeling across the bridge by the force of the impact, and several techs were knocked from their chairs. He didn't have to be told how serious it was but asked for damage reports nevertheless.

"Our shields are down," the navigator updated. "Ruptured. Primary starboard thrusters have all been neutralized."

"Enemy fortress right behind us, Commander!" said a second.

In shock, Carpenter glanced at the screens. "Divert all auxiliary power to the port thrusters! All weapons astern—*fire at will!*"

"What the devil's going on up there?!" Leonard shouted as he paced in front of the war room's Big Board.

Rolf Emerson turned from one of the balcony consoles to answer him. "We've lost all communication with them, Commander."

Leonard made a motion of disgust. "What about our support wing?"

"The same," Emerson said evenly.

Leonard whirled on the situation screen, raised and waved his fist, a gesture as meaningful as it was pathetic.

A radiant rash broke out across the pointed bow of the Masters' flagship, pinpoints of blinding energy that burst a nanosecond later, emitting devastating lines of hot current that ripped into the helpless cruiser, destroying in a series of explosions the entire rear quarter of the ship.

More than half the bridge crew lay dead or dying now; Carpenter and his second were torn up and bloodied but alive. The cruiser, however, was finished, and the major knew it.

"Ready all escape pods," he ordered, the heel of his hand to a severe head wound. "Evacuate the crew."

The navigator carried out the command, initiating the ship's self-destruct sequence as he did so.

"We're locked on a collision course with one of the fortresses," he told his commander. "Seventeen seconds to impact." Throwing a final switch, he added: "I'm sorry, sir."

"Don't apologize," Carpenter said, meeting his gaze. "We did what we could."

On a lifeless plateau above Monument City, Dana and Sean, side-by-side in the cramped forward seats of a Hovertransport, watched the skies. The rest of the 15th were not far off. Escape pods from the defeated Pioneer ship were drifting down almost lazily out of azure skies, gleaming metallic spheres hung from brightly colored chutes. Taking in this tranquil scene, one would have been hard pressed to imagine the one they had inhabited only moments before, the heavenly inferno from which they had been dropped.

Dana had learned the sad truth: it had not been the SDF-3 out there, but a single ship long separated from its parent. Like herself. The crew's last-ditch effort to hurtle the cruiser into one of the six alien fortresses had proved futile. Still, she had hopes that one among the valiant survivors who were now stepping burned and damaged from the escape pods would have some words for her personally, some message, even one five or fifteen years old.

Sean maneuvered their Hovertruck toward one of the pods that had landed in their area. Dana leapt out and approached the sphere, welcoming home its two bloodied passengers, and doing what little she could to dress their facial wounds. The men were roughly the same height, pale and atrophied-looking after their many years in space and badly shaken from their recent ordeal. The older of the two, who had brown hair, a wide-eyed albeit handsome face, introduced himself as Major John Carpenter.

Dana told them her name and held her breath.

Carpenter and the other officer looked at one another.

"Max Sterling's daughter?" Carpenter said, and Dana felt her knees grow weak.

"Do you know my parents?!" she asked eagerly. "Tell me . . . are they . . . ?"

Carpenter put his hand on her shoulder. "They were when we last saw them, Lieutenant. But that was five years ago."

Dana exhaled loudly. "You've got to tell me everything."

Carpenter smiled weakly and was about to say something more when his companion grasped him by the upper arm meaningfully. Again the two looked at each other, exchanging some unvoiced signal.

"Lieutenant," the major said after a moment. "I'm afraid that will have to wait until I speak with Commander Leonard."

"But—"

"That means now, Lieutenant Sterling," Carpenter said more firmly.

Supreme Commander Leonard hadn't logged many hours in deep space, but he was familiar enough with the ups and downs to recognize a case of vacuum psychosis when he saw it; and that's exactly what he felt he and General Emerson were up against while listening to the mad ravings of Major Carpenter and his equally space-happy navigator. In Leonard's office at the Ministry, the two men rambled on about the Pioneer Expeditionary

Mission, repeatedly referring to a schism among the Earth Forces—T. R. Edwards on the one side, Admiral Hunter and some group calling itself the *Sentinels* on the other. But in spite of it all, High Command's principal question had been answered: these aliens were indeed the Robotech Masters. They had abandoned their homeworld or Tirol and traveled across the galaxy to Earthspace; and it was beginning to seem obvious to Leonard that they had not come to *reclaim* anything, but to destroy the Human race and lay claim to and colonize the planet itself.

The two injured officers had concerns of their own, as anyone would after fifteen long years offworld, and the commander did his best to answer these without breaching security. He described the initial appearance of the Robotech ships; the fighting centered around the lunar base and space station *Liberty*; the voluntary disappearance of the Robotech Factory Satellite by the Zentraedi who operated it.

Leonard looked hard at the techno-voyagers after his brief summary of the past several months, hoping to return the topic to present mode.

"Naturally, we're *grateful* for what you attempted to do out there," the commander told them now. "But good god, man, what could you have been thinking of? *One* ship against so many! Why not have waited until the rest of the Pioneer Mission arrived?"

Leonard noticed Carpenter and the navigator exchange glances and braced himself for the worst. Carpenter was looking at him gravely.

"I'm afraid you've misunderstood us, Commander," the major began. "The Pioneer Mission will not be returning. Admiral Hunter and General Reinhardt can only offer you their prayers, and their firm conviction that the fate of Earth lies in good hands, with you and the valiant defense forces under your command, sir. But expect no assistance from the SDF-3, Commander, none whatsoever."

"And may God help them," the navigator muttered under his breath.

Leonard made a sound of disapproval.

"I wonder if there'll be anyone left on Earth to appreciate their prayers by the time they return from space," Rolf said, his back to the room while he watched a dark rain begin to fall on Monument City.

CHAPTER TWELVE

> *Of course, Cochran told me about the alien pilot. Emerson was a
> fool to believe he could keep this from me. He has no inkling of the ex-
> istence of the Secret Fraternity, that one which binds great minds to-
> gether, all petty loyalties be damned. . . . But I am thankful for his
> foolishness; it allows me a freer hand in these matters. Unfortunately,
> though, the pilot was moved before I could intervene. And now that I
> have learned his name, it is imperative that I get to him as soon as
> possible. If he is who I believe him to be . . . my mind reels from the
> possibility. In certain ways, I, Zand, am his child!*
>
> Dr. Lazlo Zand, *Event Horizon: Perspectives on
> Dana Sterling and the Second Robotech War*

IN THE NOW HEAVILY GUARDED LABORATORY OF MILES COCHRAN,
the Bioroid pilot who would come to be known as Zor Prime,
writhed in apparent agony, his lean but well-muscled arms straining at the ties that kept him confined to the bed. Masked and
gowned, Rolf Emerson, Nova Satori, and Alan Fredericks
watched with concern, while the professor monitored the captive's
vital signs from the sterile room's staging area. The fine-featured
young alien had come out of his coma three hours before
(prompting Emerson's second predawn visit to the lab), but
claimed to know nothing of his past or present circumstances.

"A most convenient case of amnesia," Fredericks suggested,
breaking the uneasy silence that prevailed when Zor's cries had
subsided some. "I think it's all too obvious that the creature is a
mole. These so-called Robotech Masters hope to infiltrate an
agent in our midst by the most transparent of ploys. A Bioroid pilot who suddenly has no memory of his past," the GMP man
scoffed. "Absurd. Not only that, but after-mission reports by the
Fifteenth Tactical Armor suggest that this particular Bioroid was
deliberately shot down by the enemy forces."

Rolf Emerson nodded his head in agreement. "I'm tempted to

agree with your assessment, Colonel. Still, there are ways we can use him—"

"How do we know he isn't one of our own hostages returned to us?" Fredericks interrupted. "Perhaps the aliens have sent us a brainwashed captive simply to convince us that we're waging a war against members of our own species?"

"General," Cochran spoke up, walking into their midst with an armful of diagnostic readouts. "Excuse me, Emerson, but please allow me to present my findings before you succeed in convincing yourself this pilot is an enemy plant."

"Go ahead, Doctor," Rolf said apologetically.

Cochran ran his forefinger down the data columns of the continuous printout sheet. "Yes, here. . . ." He cleared his throat. "Scans of the limbic system, extending along the hippocampal formation of the medial temporal lobes, fornix, and mammillary bodies, to the anterior nuclei of the thalamus, cingulum, septal area, and the orbital surface of the frontal lobes, most definitely point to diffuse cerebral impairment of the memory centers.

"It's quite unlike anything I've seen," he added, removing his glasses. "Inappropriate to classify as retrograde or anterograde, and, as it appears, only marginally posttraumatic. Closer to a fugue state than anything else, but I'd like to consult with Professor Zand before committing myself to any reductive explanation."

"Absolutely not," Emerson barked, stepping forward. "I don't want anyone else involved in this case, *least* of all Zand. Is that understood?"

Cochran gave a reluctant nod.

"Now what are our options, Doctor?" Rolf wanted to know.

Cochran replaced his eyeglasses. "Well, treatment varies with the subject, General. We might try hypnosis, of course."

"What about environmental manipulation?" Nova suggested. The GMP lieutenant looked over at the pilot. "His brain patterns are obviously abnormal, but they do appear to be stabilizing. Suppose we transferred him to another environment."

"Somewhere more *Human*, you mean," said Rolf.

"Yes."

"But who would supervise the treatment?" asked Fredericks.

"I would," Nova said confidently. "He doesn't seem to have a violent nature, and if the amnesia is genuine, he'll need someone to trust and confide in. . . ."

"It has been known to work. . . ." Cochran agreed.

"I think you're onto something, Lieutenant," Rolf said encouragingly. "But where do you suggest we bring him?"

"The base hospital," Nova answered. "We can secure a floor and gradually bring him into contact with the outside world." She gestured to the room's equipment banks and ob windows. "This place is simply too intimidating, too sterile."

"There's a reason for that," Cochran said defensively, but Emerson cut him off.

"I'm putting you in charge, Lieutenant Satori. But remember: the strictest security must be maintained."

Marie Crystal took a healthy bite out of a Red Delicious apple (from the fruit basket her squad had sent over, along with the flowers presently vased on the bedside table), and flipped through the pages of the glamour magazine she had purchased. It seemed a little bizarre—reading about projected fashion trends for the coming year when there was a war on—but she assured herself that it had probably always been thus: no matter how cruel the circumstance, the fundamental things applied. . . .

She was sitting crosslegged on the bed, the mag spread in front of her, an appealing portrait in dark-blue satin, when she heard a knock at the door.

"All right, c'mon out," a mock-stern voice threatened. "This is hospital security, and we know there's a perfectly healthy person in there."

There was no mistaking Sean's voice. She told him to wait a minute, stashed the magazine under the bed, and got back under the covers, clutching them tight to her neck and doing a reasonable impersonation of a patient.

Sean entered a moment later, flowers in hand. "Hi, Marie," he said, full of good cheer. "I thought I'd drop by and apologize for not coming sooner, but they've been keeping us pretty busy. . . . Who the heck brought you these?" he said of the squad's gift, pulling the yellow flowers from the vase and trashing them. He replaced them with his own bouquet.

Marie made a face behind his back and faked a small but agonized moan, subsiding to quiet whimpers as he turned to her.

"Hey, what's the matter?" he said, leaning over her now.

She came up hard and fast with a backhand as he was reaching out for her, slapping his arm away.

"Get away from me!" she growled into his surprised look. "What's the matter, you big jerk—you couldn't find any nurses to play with?"

Sean was open-armed, in a gesture of bewilderment. "Marie, you must have taken one on the head. I came to see *you*—"

"Just keep your hands to yourself!" she snarled, then groaned for real as a stabbing abdominal pain snuck up on her.

"My, my . . . you poor little darlin'," Sean teased. "You really are a credit to your uniform, the way you handle the *excruciating* agony. Or maybe I should say *lack* of uniform," he added, leering at her fondly.

Marie ignored the comment, not bothering to conceal her cleavage as she leaned up onto her elbows. "I'm faking it, is that it?" she said angrily.

Sean risked sitting on the edge of the bed, his hand stroking his jaw contemplatively. "No . . . Well, actually, the thought *had* crossed my mind." He folded his arms and sighed. "You know, looking back on it, I wonder what I was thinking when I *saved your life*."

Marie's eyes narrowed. "Looking for *gratitude*, Sean?"

"Aw, come on," he smiled. "Maybe just a little friendliness, that's all."

Marie's head dropped back to the pillow, eyes on the ceiling. "This whole mess should never have happened. It's all Sterling's fault I'm lying here like a lump."

"Calm down," he told her sincerely. "You can't blame Dana."

She turned on him. "Don't tell me what I can do ground-pounder! I hate the Fifteenth—the whole bunch of you."

Sean held up his hands. "Wait a minute—"

"Get out of here!" she yelled at him, the pillow raised like a weapon now. "Out!"

He backed off and exited the room without another word, leaving her to stare at the pink roses he brought and wonder if she had overplayed her hand a bit.

In the corridor outside Marie's room, Sean bumped into Dana, a bouquet in her hand and obviously on her way to pay a visit to the Fifteenth's newest enemy. Sean stepped in front of her, blocking her advance on Marie's room with small talk.

"And if you're here to see Marie, you can forget it," he finally got around to saying. "The staff didn't give the okay for her to have visitors."

Dana looked suspicious. "She was admitted days ago. Besides, they let *you* see her, didn't they?"

"Uh, they made an exception for me," Sean stammered as Dana pushed her way past him. "After all, I'm the guy who—"

"Does she still hate me?" Dana asked, suddenly realizing the purpose of Sean's double-talk.

Sean's forced smile collapsed. "Even worse. She's mad enough to say that she hates *me*! It'll probably blow over," he hastened to add. "But right now she kinda considers you responsible."

"Me?! Why?" Dana pointed to herself. "Jeez, *I* didn't shoot her down!"

"We know that," Sean said reassuringly. "She's just looking for someone to blame. And if she hadn't been trying to save that Sullivan dude . . ."

"Brother. . . ." Dana sighed, shaking her head.

They were both silent for a moment; then turned together to the sound of controlled commotion at the far end of the hospital corridor. A dozen GMP soldiers, armed and armored, were supervising the rapid transit of a stretcher to the elevator banks.

"What's all this about?" Dana wondered aloud.

"The place is crawling with Gimps," Sean told her. "I heard they cordoned off the whole ninth floor."

Dana snorted. "Leonard's probably here for his annual physical."

But even as she said it, something didn't sit well. Nonetheless, she gave a final look at the draped form on the stretcher and shrugged indifferently.

To avoid a scene like the one recently played in the war room, Rolf Emerson decided it best to inform Leonard of the new arrangements he had made for the alien pilot, who, shortly before being transferred to the base hospital, had given his name as Zor.

Zor!—the name Dana had mentioned in debriefing sessions following the rescue of Bowie at the Macross mounds. It had seemed coincidental then, but now , . .

Zor!

A name notorious these past fifteen years; a name whispered on the lips of everyone connected with Robotechnology; a name at once despised and held in the greatest reverence. Zor, whom the Zentraedi had credited with the discovery of Protoculture; Zor, the Tirolian scientist who had sent the SDF-1 to Earth, unwittingly ushering in the near destruction of the planet, the eclipse of the Human race.

Of course it was possible that Zor was a common name among these people called the Masters. But then again . . .

Emerson said as much to the commander when he reported to him. Leonard, however, was not impressed.

"I don't care what he calls himself, or whether he's Human or android," the commander growled. "All I know is that your investigation has thus far been fruitless. The man's name is no great prize, General. Not when we're after *military* data."

"Professor Cochran is confident that the change in environment will result in a breakthrough," Rolf countered.

"I want facts!" Leonard emphasized. "This Bioroid pilot is a soldier—perhaps an important one. I want him pumped for information and I frankly don't give a damn how that's accomplished."

Emerson held his ground. "All the more reason for caution at this point, Commander. His mind is fragile, which means he can either snap or become useful to us. We've got to find out what the Masters are after."

Leonard's fist came down on the desk. "Are you blind, man? It's obvious what they want—the complete obliteration of the Human race! A fresh planet to use for colonization!"

"But there's the Protoculture Matrix—"

"To hell with that mystical claptrap!" Leonard bellowed, up on his feet now, hands flat on the desk. "And to hell with caution! Bring me results, or I'll have that pilot's head, General—to do with as *I* see fit!"

The day's rain seemed to have scoured the Earth clean; there were even traces of redolent aromas in the washed air, sweet smells wafting in on an evening breeze that found Dana on the barrack's balcony. Strange to stare at the sawtoothed ridgeline now, she said to herself, the fortress gone but the harsh memories of its brief stay etched in her thoughts. The recon mission, a city of clones; then Sullivan, Marie, countless others . . . And presiding over all of it, robbing her of sleep these past few nights, the image of the red Bioroid pilot: his handsome, elfin face, his long lavender-silver locks . . .

Dana closed her eyes tightly, as though in an effort to compress the image to nothingness, atomize it somehow and free herself. It was worse now that she had gleaned some information about the Expeditionary Mission.

She might never see her parents again.

Silently, Bowie joined her at the balcony rail while her eyes were shut; but she was aware of his presence and smiled even before turning to him. They held each other's hands without exchanging a word, drinking in the sweet night air and the sounds of summer insects. There was nothing that needed to be said; since their youth they had talked about Max and Miriya, Vince and Jean, what they would do when the SDF-3 returned, what they would do if it never returned. They were close enough to read each other's thoughts sometimes, so it didn't surprise Dana when Bowie mentioned the alien girl, Musica.

"I know that the fortress represents the enemy," he said softly. "And I'm aware that I don't have much to go on, Dana. But she's not one of them—I'm sure of it. Something went off deep in my heart . . . and suddenly I believed in her."

Dana gave his hand a reaffirming prolonged squeeze.

Was *that* what her heart was telling her about the red Bioroid pilot?—that she *believed* in him?!

He had been moved; he knew that much. This room was warmer than the first, empty of that corral of machines and devices that had surrounded him. He also knew that there were fewer eyes on him, mechanical and otherwise. His body was no longer host to that array of sensor pads and transmitters; the vein in his wrist no longer receiving the slow nutrient flow; his breathing passages unrestricted. His arms . . . *free*.

Gone, too, were the nightmares: those horrible images of the mindless attack launched against him by protoplasmic creatures; the giant warriors who somehow seemed to have been fighting on his behalf; the explosions of light and a seering pain; the death and . . . *resurrection!*

Were they nightmares or was this something recalled to life?—something one part of him used to keep buried!

There was a female seated in a chair at the foot of his bed. Her handsome features and jet-black hair gave her an alluring look, and yet there was something cool and distant about her that overrode the initial impression. She sat with one leg crossed over the other, a primitive writing board device in her lap. She wore a uniform and a communicatorlike headband that seemed to serve no other purpose than ornamentation. Her voice was rich and melodic, and as she spoke he recalled her from the short list of memories logged in his virgin mind, recalled her as the one who had asked questions of him earlier on, before this sleep had intervened, gently but probing. He remembered that he desired to trust her, to confide in her. But there had been precious little to tell. Other than his name . . . his *name* . . .

Zor.

"Welcome back," Nova Satori said pleasantly when she noticed Zor's eyes open. "You've been asleep."

"Yes," he said uncertainly. His mind seemed to speak it in several tongues at once, but foremost came the one the female was versed in.

"Did you dream again?" she asked.

He shook his head and raised himself up in the bed. The female—*Nova*, he remembered—motioned to a device that allowed him to raise the head portion of the padded sleeping platform. He activated it, marveling at its primitive design, and wondering why the bed wasn't reconfiguring of its own accord. Or by a prompt from his thought or will . . .

"What's the last strong impression you remember from your past?" Nova asked after a minute.

For some unknown reason, the question angered him. But with the anger returned the dream, more clearly now, and it seemed to him suddenly that at one time he had been a soldier of some sort. He told her as much, and she wrote something on her notepad.

"And after that?"

Zor searched for something in his thoughts, and said: "You."

"Nothing in between?"

Zor shrugged. Once again the dream resurfaced. Only this time it was more lucid still. His very body was participating in the memory, recalling where it stood and how it felt. And with this came a remembrance of pain.

Nova watched him slide into it and was on her feet and by his side instantly, trying to soothe him, recall him from whatever memories were driving him into such unmitigated suffering and agony. She felt a concern that ran much deeper than curiosity or nefarious purpose, and gave in to it, her hand on his fevered brow, her heart beating almost as rapidly as his.

"Let go of it, Zor," she said, her mouth close to his ear. "Don't push yourself—it will all come back to you in time. Don't drive yourself to this!"

His back was arched, chest heaved up unnaturally. He groaned and put his hands to his head, praying for it to end.

"Make it stop," he said through clenched teeth. Then, curiously: "I promise I won't try to remember any more!"

Nova stepped back some, aware that he wasn't talking to her.

CHAPTER
THIRTEEN

He's the leader of a race of clones,
Who'd come to Earth to smash some bones.
He's the Bioroid with lots of fight,
The Disturber of your sleep at night;
He screams "Victory, bab-ee, victory!
I'm invincible, I'm somebody!"
Just get into a duel with—
the Crimson Pilot

"Crimson Pilot," music by Bowie Grant, lyrics by Louie Nichols

ANA LEFT THE WINDOWS OF HER ROOM OPEN THAT NIGHT, hoping that starlight and those redolent aromas would provide some soporific enchantment and ease her into sleep. But instead the light cast menacing shadows on the wall and the smells and sounds drove her to distraction. She tossed and turned for most of the night and just before sunrise lapsed into a fitful sleep plagued by nightmares that featured none other than the red Bioroid pilot. As a result she slept late. Upon awakening, still half in the grip of the night's fear and terror, she literally ran to the compound's battle simulator, where she chose land-based Bioroid combat scenario one-D-one-niner, and exorcised her demons by annihilating a holographic image of the crimson pilot, setting a new high score on the mecha-sized machine.

Entering her initials to the software package, however, was not prize enough to stabilize the circular pattern of her thoughts, and she carried a mixture of anger and bafflement with her for the rest of the day.

Sunset found her wandering into the 15th's ready-room, where Bowie was at the piano, vamping on the atonal progression of half-notes he had heard in Musica's harp chamber and finally been able to recall (and score). Angelo, Louie, Xavez, and Marino were lounging about.

"It's good to hear you playing again," Dana complimented him. She tried to hum the curious melody. "What is that?"

"It's as close as I can get to Musica's harp," he told her, right hand running through the modulating riff again. Bowie put both hands to it now, improvising an enhancement. "What kind of people can create music like this and still find it in their hearts to kill?"

"Don't confuse the people with their leaders," Dana started to say as Sean burst into the room. He made a beeline for her and was out-of-breath when he spoke.

"Lieutenant, you're not gonna believe this, but do *I* have a piece of news!"

"Out with it," she said, without a clue.

"I did some investigating and found out who the GMP have stashed away on the ninth floor of the medical center. It's a captured Bioroid pilot—a *red* Bioroid pilot."

Dana's mouth fell open. "Did you see him?"

Sean shook his head. "They've got him under pretty tight security."

"How did you find this out, Sean?" Bowie asked from the piano stool.

Sean touched his forefinger to his nose. "Well, my friend, let's just say that it pays to make friends with a cute nurse now and again. . . ."

Dana made an impatient gesture. "Do you think it's him, Sean—*Zor*, the one we saw in the fortress?"

"Don't know," he confessed.

"I've got to see him," she said, beginning to pace.

"Those Gimps might have some different ideas about that," Sean said to her back.

"I don't care about them," Dana spat. "I've got some questions to ask, and that Bioroid pilot's the only one capable of answering them!"

"Yeah, but you'll never get to see him," Louie Nichols chimed in.

Angelo had also picked up on the conversation. "I don't know what you've got in mind, Lieutenant, but I don't think it's a good idea to stick our noses where they don't belong."

"In any case," Louie pointed out, "he's probably been programmed against divulging information. It's not likely you'll get anything out of him."

"You're probably right," Dana agreed. "But I don't think I'm going to be able to get a good night's sleep until I confront him face-to-face."

Sean put his hands on his hips and thought for a moment. "Well, if it means that much to you, then let's do it. But how are we going to get in there?"

Dana considered this, then smiled in sudden realization. "I've got an idea," she laughed; then quickly added, "Fasten your seatbelts, boys—it's going to be a bumpy night!"

An hour later, a bogus maintenance transport was rumbling through the darkened streets of Monument City en route to the medical center. Louie had the wheel. Stopped at the gate, Angelo, riding shotgun, flashed a phonied-up requisition and repair order at the sleepy guard.

"Maintenance wants us to fix a ruptured ion gun in one of your X-ray scanning sequencers," the sergeant said knowingly.

The guard scratched absently at his helmet and waved the vehicle through. As it entered the underground garage, Louie said, "By the way, ion guns don't rupture."

"Rupture, shmupture," Angelo rhymed. "It got us in, didn't it?"

Louie steered the transport to a secluded parking area. Angelo hopped down from the front seat and threw open the rear doors: out stepped Bowie, Sean, Marino, and Xavez—all in coveralls and visored caps—and Dana, in a nurse's uniform that was at least three sizes too small for her and fit her like a second skin. Louie and Bowie immediately began toying with the hospital's phone and com line switches, while the rest of the men started to strip down. . . .

In Zor's ninth floor room, Nova put her clipboard aside to answer the phone. A nasal voice at the other end said:

"This is the office of Chief-of-Staff Emerson, Lieutenant Satori, and the general requests that you meet with him at the Ministry as soon as possible."

Nova frowned at the handset and recradled it. She apologized to Zor for having to leave so suddenly, and a minute later was on her way. . . .

Bowie, who had a reputation for vocal impressions, unpinched his nose and informed the team that Satori had taken the bait. The coveralls gone now, Angelo wore bedroom slippers and an unremarkable cotton terry robe. Marino and Xavez were dressed like orderlies. Sean was in his usual uniform.

"Okay," Dana told the sergeant, "make your move in ten minutes."

"I never missed a cue," Angelo promised.

Nova told the two GMP guards who were stationed either side of the door to Zor's room to keep their eyes peeled.

"I'll be back shortly," she said.

At the same time, someone pushed the buzzer outside Marie Crystal's seventh floor room. She was sitting in bed, reading a bodybuilding magazine, which she quickly hid from sight, slipping beneath the sheets as she did so and feigning sleep.

A moment later, the doors hissed open and in walked Sean.

Marie sat up, surprised. "What are you doing here at this time of night?"

Meanwhile, on the ground floor, Dana, toting a large shoulderbag (her nurse's cap in place), was escorting a stretcher to one of the elevators; the stretcher was borne by Xavez and Marino, both wearing surgical masks—to hide their smiles as much as anything else. They entered the car, pushing seven on the floor display, just as the adjacent elevator opened, allowing Nova Satori to step out.

Upstairs, Sean was down on one knee at Marie's bedside. "I got to thinking . . . you lying here all by yourself. I was worried about you."

"Oh, no kidding," she returned sarcastically.

"Seriously," he persisted. "It's a beautiful night, Marie. And I thought you might like to go up on the roof and enjoy it with me. A change of scenery, you know?"

Marie laughed. "Sounds great, but these doctors watch every move I make."

Sean stood up and lowered his voice conspiratorially. "How 'bout if I promised you you wouldn't get in any trouble?"

She threw him a puzzled look.

"I cleared it all with the administration," he said with elaborate innocence.

Marie couldn't help but be a little suspicious. "Why me, Sean?"

"Because you're so sweet and gentle," he flattered her. "I can't help myself!" Then all at once there was a light rap at the door and he seemed suddenly impatient. "Come on, get ready. Your limousine's here."

No sooner had Marie run a hand through her hair and cinched her robe, than the doors hissed open again. Two masked orderlies appeared bearing a stretcher.

Marie leaned back, startled and having second thoughts. "Sean, I don't know about this. . . ."

"What's the matter?" he said, coming over to the bed. "Let's not look a gift horse in the mouth." Without warning he pulled back the bed covers, and a second later, Marie found herself in his arms, being carried over to the waiting stretcher and those grinning orderlies. . . .

As soon as the 15th's trio had conveyed the stretcher a safe distance down the deserted corridor, Dana raced into Marie's room, doffed the starched cap, and opened the window. She leaned out and looked up: Zor's room was two stories directly above. From the shoulder bag, she retrieved a stun gun, a short coil of rope, and four climber's suction cups. She put her arm through the former, and strapped the cups to her knees and wrists. She tucked the stun gun into the uniform's narrow belt. That much accomplished, she climbed up on to the window stool and commenced her fly-crawl up the marble side of the building.

Reaching the ninth floor, she peered cautiously into the window, almost losing her grip when she saw Zor, the crimson pilot, sitting in the room's single bed, a uniform jacket over his shoulders. She lowered herself down when he seemed to sense her presence and turned to the window. She stayed that way for several seconds, then checked her watch. It read 9:29.

"Almost time," she said quietly, fixing a rope to the window's exterior frame. . . .

At exactly 9:30 a slippered and bathrobed Sergeant Dante stepped from one of the ninth floor elevators. Three GMP sentries were on him immediately.

"Get back in the elevator," one of them told him curtly. "This floor's closed to the public."

Angelo waited for the doors to close and then said: "That's all right, I'm allowed to be up here." He began to walk off nonchalantly. A second guard restrained him.

"Check this guy out with security," the guard ordered one of his companions. The man ran to the wall phone, but reported back with a shout that the line was dead.

Thanks to Louie's basement tampering, Dante thought.

"Lemme go, you guys," the sergeant protested to the two who had taken hold of his arms. "I tell ya, I'm here to see my wife!"

"Simmer down, pal," said the one on Dante's left. "We're going to go for a little walk. You coming quietly or do we have to drag you?"

Dante smiled inwardly and prepared himself for battle. . . .

In his room a short distance down the corridor, Zor heard the commotion and got out of bed to investigate. It was all the diversion Dana needed: she leapt in through the window, her stun gun in hand.

"Stop right there!" she told Zor, who was just short of the door. Zor turned and began to walk toward her, wordless but determined.

"Stay back!" Dana warned him, arming the gun and bringing both hands to the grip. "If you don't stop, I'll fire!"

But he was undeterred, one moment stalking her, and the next three feet over her head in a superleap that brought him down precisely on the gun. As it flew from her hands, Dana dropped back, adopting a defensive pose and waiting for him to come.

Zor leaned forward as if to step, but ducked adroitly as she came around with a roundhouse right. He threw himself against her midsection, taking her down easily and pinning her to the floor, his left hand clamped on her left wrist, his right forearm pressed to her throat, firm enough to strangle the breath from her.

"Why are you trying to kill me?" he demanded. "What have I done?!"

Dana gasped for air, managing to say: "You're responsible for killing men under my command!" *And more!*

She saw his eyes go wide in surprise, felt the pressure against her trachea lessen, and made the most of it, heaving up with her legs and throwing him over her head. But the nimble alien landed on his feet after a back flip, combat-crouched as Dana moved in on him.

He avoided her side kick and dropped to the floor, sweeping Dana's legs out from under her with his right foot. She came down hard on the side of her face and lost it for a moment. When she looked up, the alien had the gun trained on her.

"You're the one," Dana said, struggling to her feet. "The red Bioroid."

"What are you saying?!" He questioned her.

Dana had her fists clenched, her feet spread for another kata. "You're the one we saw at the mounds—the one who captured Bowie! And the one in the fortress!"

Zor relaxed his gun hand somewhat, his face betraying the bewilderment he felt. "Nova told me the same thing," he said with troubled brow. "What does it mean—*Bioroid?*"

Dana straightened from her pose. "Your memory only works when you're killing my men, is that it?!" she shouted. "I don't know why I'm even bothering with you, *alien!*"

Zor winced as though kicked. "Alien?" he seemed to ask himself; then: "I'm a Human being!"

Which he barely got out: Dana's powerful front kick caught him square on the chin and slammed him back against the wall. He still had the gun, but it was now hanging absently by his side.

"I was there when you crawled out of that Bioroid!" Dana seethed. "Don't deny it!" She stood waiting for him to get up, her hands ready; but the alien remained on his knees, blood running from his mouth.

"I won't," he said contritely. "But I wasn't responsible for what I was doing." Zor looked at her and said: "You've got to believe me!"

"Who made you do it?! Who are they?!" Dana demanded.

Resigned, Zor threw the gun at her feet. "Can't you see?" he said, full of self-disgust. "I've lost my memory. . . ."

Back at the elevators, Bowie Grant, in a white coat as large on him as Dana's nurse's uniform was small, had come to Angie's assistance. Not that the sergeant needed any: one guard was already unconscious, the one gripped in Dante's left arm well on the way, and the third was more than halfway there. Somehow, all of them had lost their helmets in the struggle.

"Ah, excuse me, Mr. Campbell," Bowie was saying in his best professorial voice. "Your wife's room is on the *eighth* floor."

Dante tossed the two sentries aside dismissively and went on to finish his scene with Bowie, playing to an all but unconscious house.

"So I made a mistake, Doc—is that any reason for these gorillas of yours to jump down my throat?!"

Bowie, too, was willing to play along, especially now that the three were coming around. "Calm down, Mr. Campbell. They were only doing their job. And you can hardly blame them for that, right?"

Angelo laughed shortly and let a whistling Bowie lead him away. . . .

The tune Bowie whistled was a strange one, with an unusual but haunting melody. It was Dana's signal to make her escape. She said as much to Zor who was now seated on the edge of the bed, his head in his hands.

"You can't remember anything at all?" Dana asked one final time.

"No, it's hopeless," Zor started to say but suddenly looked up at the sound of the whistled tune. "That music," he said anxiously. "What is that music?!"

Dana knelt beside him. "One of my troopers learned it from an alien girl on the fortress," she explained.

"Yes . . . I *remember*!" Zor exclaimed. "A girl named . . . *Musica*."

Dana gasped. "That's right!" *So Bowie's vision was real after all*, she said to herself.

"I'm not even certain how I know that," Zor shrugged. . . .

Elsewhere, Lieutenant Nova Satori was storming back to the med center elevators. "No one makes a fool out of me like that!" she seethed out loud when the car doors closed. . . .

"But this is great!" Dana was telling the alien, no longer anxious to leave the room. "It's starting to look like your memory's returning!"

Zor shook his head in despair.

And suddenly the doors hissed open.

Dana thought it might be Bowie and Angelo, but when she turned she found Nova Satori glaring at her.

"I'll have your bars for this, Sterling!" she heard the GMP lieutenant say. Dana took two quick steps and launched herself out the window, rappeling down to Marie's room with Nova's threats ringing in her ears.

CHAPTER FOURTEEN

Ironically, the man who could have helped most was also the one who could have done the most damage—Dr. Lazlo Zand, who emerges from his own works and those of numerous commentators as a kind of voyeur to Earth's ravaging by the Robotech Masters. His pathological manipulation of Dana Sterling has only recently come to light [see Zand's own Event Horizon*] and one understands completely why Major General Rolf Emerson was loath to involve the scientist in any of Earth's dealings with its new invaders. But it must be pointed out that only Zand, Lang's chief disciple, could have provided the answers to the questions Earth Command was asking. It is indeed fascinating to speculate what might have come from a meeting between Zand and Zor Prime.*

Zeitgeist, Insights: Alien Psychology and the Second Robotech War

OVA'S FIRST THOUGHT WAS TO HAVE DANA ARRESTED BY the GMP for knowingly violating security, tampering, or whatever trumped-up charges the boys at dirty tricks could dream up. But the fact remained that Dana's encounter with Zor had resulted in a breakthrough of sorts. When Nova had questioned him after Dana's swashbuckling escape from the ninth floor hospital room, it was evident that something within the alien had been stirred; he had at least partial recall of names and faces apparently linked to his recent past, perhaps while onboard the alien fortress itself.

Professor Cochran was already revising his initial diagnosis based on Nova's updated report; he was now rejecting the idea of fugue state and thinking more in terms of the retrograde type, or possibly a novel form of transient global amnesia. Brain scans done after the alien's fight with Lieutenant Sterling indicated that the limbic abnormalities detected earlier had lessened to some degree; but Cochran was still in the dark as to the etiology. He pressed Nova to openly call in Professor Zand, but Nova refused;

she promised him, however, that she would make mention of
Zand during her meeting with General Emerson.

The general was furious with Sterling for about five minutes.
After that, Nova could see that a new plan had come to him, one
that would place Dana Sterling at the very center of things. Nova
would retain control over Zor's debriefing, but Dana was to provide the stimulus.

Emerson explained all this to Dana scarcely a week after the
med center players had made chumps out of the GMP sentries.

Dana hadn't heard word one from Nova or High Command
during that time and had spent her idle moments preparing herself
for the brig, working her body to exhaustion in the barracks
workout rooms, and trying to make sense out of the conflicting
emotions she now felt toward the alien pilot. Zor had been spirited away from the base hospital and even Sean hadn't been able
to pry any additional information from the nursing staff.

So Dana was hardly surprised when the call came for her to report to General Emerson at the Ministry. But there were surprises
in store for her she couldn't have guessed at.

Rolf was seated rigidly at his desk when Dana announced herself and walked into the spacious office. Colonel Rochelle was
standing off to one side, *Zor* to the other. Dana offered a salute
and Rolf told her in a scolding voice to step up to the desk.

"I suppose there's no need for me to introduce you to Zor,
Lieutenant Sterling. It is my understanding that *you two have already met*."

Dana gulped and said, "Yes, sir. You see—"

"I don't want to hear your explanations, Dana," Rolf interrupted, waving his hand dismissively. "This issue's confused
enough already." He cleared his throat meaningfully. "What you
may or may not know, is that Zor is apparently amnesiac—either
as a result of the crash or perhaps through some neural safeguard
the Masters saw fit to include in their Human pilots. Nevertheless,
it is our belief that he can be brought through this. In fact, your
previous . . . *encounter* with him seems to have provided a start in
that direction."

"Uh, thank you, sir," Dana muttered, instantly wishing she
could take it back. Rolf's eyes were flashing with anger.

"Don't *thank* me, Lieutenant! What you did was unconsciona-
ble, and at some point you'll be expected to make amends for it!"
Rolf snorted. "But for the time being, I want to place Zor under
your personal direction. I want him to take part in the Fifteenth's
activities."

Dana was aghast. "Sir? . . . Do you mean? . . ." She looked over at Zor, struck by how terrific he looked in the uniform and boots someone had supplied him: a tight-fitting navy blue and scarlet jumpsuit, cinched by a wide, gold-colored belt, and turtle-necked, making his lavender locks appear even longer. His faint smile brought a similar one to her face.

"I think I understand the logic here," she said, turning back to Rolf. "A military assignment may jog his memory in some way."

"Precisely," said Rolf. "Do you think you can handle it, Dana?"

Again she looked over at Zor; then nodded. "I'm willing to try, sir."

"And what about your team?"

Dana thought her words out carefully before speaking. "The Fifteenth is the finest unit in the Southern Cross, sir. Everyone will do their part."

"And Bowie?"

Dana's lips tightened. Bowie would be harder to handle. "I'll talk to him," she told Rolf. "He'll come through, and I'm willing to stake my bars on it."

Emerson looked hard at her and said, "You are, Lieutenant."

When Dana had left the room with Zor, Colonel Rochelle had some things to say to Emerson, starting off by disavowing the entire project. "It's insane," he told Rolf, gesticulating as he paced in front of the desk. "And I want no further part of it. An alien pilot—an *officer*, at that—wandering around with one of our top units. . . . Suppose he *is* a mole? Suppose he's wired or rigged in some way we can't even fathom? We might just as well give the Masters an open invitation to have a peek at our defenses."

Emerson let him speak; Rochelle wasn't saying anything that Rolf hadn't already thought, feared, scrutinized, and analyzed to death.

"And why Sterling? She's a discipline problem and a—"

Rochelle cut himself off short of the word, but Emerson finished the thought for him.

"That's right, Colonel. She's half-alien herself. Part Human, part Zentraedi, and therefore the perfect choice in this instance." Rolf exhaled loudly, tiredly. "I know full well how risky this is. But this Zor is our only hope. If we can show him who we are, then perhaps he can become our voice to the Masters. If they're after what I *think* they're after, we've got to use Zor to convince them that we don't have it."

"The legendary Protoculture factory," Rochelle said knowingly. "I just hope you know what you're doing, sir."

Eyes closed, Emerson leaned back in his chair and said nothing.

* * *

"Our new recruit's a very skilled soldier," Dana told the assembled members of the 15th. "I can tell you that he was assigned to us personally by General Emerson himself, and that I have the utmost confidence in him."

The team, including a couple of greens fresh from the Academy, was gathered at ease in the barracks ready-room. Dana had been building up the new recruit for the past five minutes and Angelo for one was beginning to get suspicious. Especially with all this talk about having faith enough in the decision of High Command to accept a mission that seems somewhat extraordinary on the face of it.

"All right, you can come in now," the lieutenant was saying, half-turned to the ready-room sliders.

The doors hissed open and the lean, clean-shaven recruit entered. He was handsome in an almost androgynous way, above-average height, and affected a shade of light purple dye in his long hair. The yoke and flyout shoulders of his uniform were green to Dana's red, the cadets' yellow, and Louie's blue. Dana introduced him as Zor.

The name had no meaning to some of them, but Angelo gave loud voice to the sudden concerns of the rest.

"Is this *the alien*?!"

Dana said, "Zor is officially part of our unit."

Now everyone went bananas—all except Bowie, who Dana had spoken to beforehand and who was now gritting his teeth. Murmurs of disbelief and confusion swept through the ranks, until Dante angrily called them to a halt.

"Lieutenant, is this the real dope?" Corporal Nichols asked unconvinced.

"Blazing Battloids," Dana responded. "Do you think I'm making this *up*?"

Again the comments began and again Dante silenced them, stepping forward this time and fixing Zor with a gimlet stare.

"Lieutenant, I saw this alien *shot down by his own troops*! I saw it with my *own* eyes! The guy's a spy! What is it—too *obvious* for High Command to see that?! He's a damn *spy*!"

"No way I want him for *my* wingman," Sean called out.

"QUIET!" Dana shouted as things began to escalate. "Now, I'm still in command here, and I'm telling you that Zor is *officially* assigned to our unit! You let the general staff worry about whether or not he's a spy. It's our job to make him feel welcome and that's the long and short of it!" Dana stood, arms akimbo, with her chin thrust forward. "Any questions?" When no one spoke, she said: "Dismissed!"

All but Louie Nichols began filing out of the room, throwing hostile stares at the new recruit. The corporal, though, went over to Zor and extended his hand.

"Welcome to the Fifteenth," Louie said sincerely.

Zor accepted the proffered hand haltingly. It was easy enough to see where most of the team stood; but what was he supposed to feel toward those who were suddenly befriending him?

"So, big fella," Louie smiled. "You and Dana—you two getting along all right?"

The situation was, of course, *fascinating* to Nichols: the child of a bio-genetically engineered XT and a Human, now made responsible for an XT who might very well have contributed his own cellular stuff to the genetic slushpile. . . . Dana and Zor could be father and daughter, sister and brother, the possibilities were limitless. But what intrigued Louie even more was the idea that this *Zor* was related in some way to his Tirolian namesake—the genius who had discovered *Protoculture* itself!

The recruit Zor was puzzled by Louie's question; but Dana seemed to have seen through the corporal's friendly gesture.

"Don't you have something better to do?" she said leadingly. "Perhaps down in the mechanics bays or something?"

Louie took the hint and smiled. "Guess I could find *something* to do. . . . Later, Dana."

"And I'll thank you to address me in the proper manner from now on!" she barked as he was backing off.

Louie reached the sliding doors just ahead of Eddie Jordon, the younger brother of the private who had met such a cruel end during the fortress recon mission. Dana noticed the cadet add his own hostile glare to the pool before exiting, fixing Zor with a look that could kill.

They placed him in a small room, empty save for a single chair and dark save for the meager red light of solitary filament bulb. It was all so *alien* to him: these encounters, events and challenges. And yet one part of his mind was surely familiar with it all, directing him unthinkingly through the motions, putting words in his mouth, summoning emotions and reactions. But he was aware of the absence of connection, the absence of memories that should have been tied to these same encounters and emotions. A reservoir that had been drained, which they now hoped to refill.

Taken from the room he was left alone in the dark, although his senses told him that this area was much larger than the last, and that he was under observation. The slight one who had escorted him to this new darkness had strapped a weapon on him, and un-used laser pistol that somehow felt primitive and archaic in his grip. Again, the thought assaulted him that there was a kind of mindless redundancy at work here: *the weapon ought to be firing of its own accord,* adapting itself to his will, *reconfiguring....*

But all at once a spotlight found him, and he was no longer alone but at the center of a whirling ring of sequenced targets; and he understood that the nature of the test was to destroy each of these within a predetermined interval of time. Commands and countdowns were conveyed to him over an amplified address sys-tem he could not see, loud enough for him to hear through the padded silencers which someone had thought to place over his ears.

The black and white targets had been whirling faster and faster, but were now dispersing, abandoning the tight order of the circle for the safety of random, chaotic movement. A digital chronome-ter flashed in the background.

He spread his legs and clasped the weapon in both hands, empty of all thought and centered on picking out the sequenced target. As number one came in behind him, he crouched, turned, and squeezed off a charge, disintegrating the substanceless thing in a fiery flash. Number two flew in from his right and he holed it likewise, remaining in place for numbers three and four.

He risked a gaze at the numerical countdown and realized that he would have to press himself harder if he was to destroy all of them. His next blast took out two at once.

Now they were coming at him on edge, but still his aim proved true, as two, then three more targets were splintered and de-stroyed. He took out the final one with an overhead shot just as the countdown reached zero-zero-zero-zero.

As the room's overhead lights came on, Zor holstered the pistol and removed the safety muffs. Dana came running out of the con-trol booth, complimenting Zor on his score. Behind her, were sev-eral members of the 15th, sullen looks on their faces.

"I can't believe it!" Dana was gushing. "Where did you learn to shoot like that? You beat the simulator! No one's ever done that before! You're good, Zor; you're *really* good!"

Zor felt something akin to pride but said nothing. He heard one of the cadets say, "Yeah, too good."

He was young, on the small side, with dark brown bangs and

an immature but not unpleasant face. He had his arms folded across his chest, defiantly.

Eddie, Zor recalled.

"You can shoot all right, but what now, hot shot? You gonna destroy the Bioroids or us?"

Zor remained silent, uncertain.

"Can't hear you, big man!" Eddie taunted him. "What's the matter—cat got your tongue, tough guy?"

"Come on, Eddie," said Dana. "Lay off."

"*You* come on, Lieutenant!" the youth told her. "I don't buy this lost memory crap!"

Without warning Eddie drew his sidearm and leveled it at Zor, who stood motionless, almost indifferent. Dana had stepped in front of him, warning Eddie to put the gun away.

Instead the cadet grinned, said, "Here!", and gave the gun a sideways toss. Dana ducked, stumbling into Angelo's arms, and Zor caught the thing.

"And I don't think he's so tough, either!" Eddie said, walking away from all of them.

Dana drew herself upright and stared after him, hands on her hips. "Wise guy!" she muttered.

Zor looked down at the weapon, feeling a sudden revulsion.

The alien remained the outcast, but most of the 15th grudgingly grew to accept him. It seemed unlikely that he would ever be accepted as one of the team, but by and large the hostile looks had ceased. Except for Bowie and Louie, they all simply ignored him. Dana was a special case; her interest in Zor was certainly beyond the call of duty and especially worrisome to Sergeant Dante. There wasn't much he could do about it, but he kept his eyes on Zor whenever he could, still convinced that the Bioroid pilot was an agent of the Robotech Masters, and that this amnesia thing was spurious at best.

Only Sean was neutral on the issue of Dana's infatuation. It wasn't as if he hadn't given it any thought; it was just that he was too wrapped up in his own infatuation with Marie Crystal to pay it any mind. Ever since the night on the med center roof, Sean had been preoccupied with the raven-haired lieutenant, almost to the point of forgetting entirely about the other women in his life.

On the day Marie was due to be released from the hospital, Sean decked himself out in his fanciest suit and wiped the base florist clean of bouquets. He was on his way to see her, when Dana almost bowled him down in the barracks corridor. Sterling, too, was dressed to the nines: a skirt and blouse of pink shades, a white silk scarf knotted around her neck.

"Now listen, trooper," she laughed, "Marie's not going to be as easy as shooting down skylarks, do you get me?" She emphasized this by flicking her forefinger against one of the half-dozen bouquets he was carrying, shattering the petals from a rose blossom.

"Don't kid yourself," he joked back. "I shoot pretty well. . . . And what's with the civvies?" he said, giving her the once-over.

"Just a debriefing session with Zor," Dana told him, starry-eyed.

"Debriefing? In those clothes?"

"Yep," she nodded, checking her watch. "And I'm late! So tell Marie I said hi, and that I'll come and see her as soon as I can!"

With that, Dana was gone, leaving Sean to mutter in her wake: "A true space cadet."

Dana's idea of a debriefing session was to take Zor to Arcadia, Monument City's one and only amusement park. There they ate the usual junk food and fed credits to the usual games, but only Dana was interested in going on the rides. Zor watched her from the sidelines, as she allowed herself to be turned in circles in an endless variety of ways—upside-down here, centrifugally there, backwards, forwards, and sideways.

It amazed Zor that after all this she could still retain an appetite for the gooey sweets she favored; but then again, there was so much that was *uncommon* about her. At times he felt as though he knew her in some forgotten past that predated life itself, and was not so much a part of his amnesiac state, but had more to do with mystical links and occult correspondences.

For Dana it was much the same, only more so (as all things were with her). She recognized her infatuation and did nothing to repress or disguise it. Zor was supposed to be treated openly and honestly, and Dana didn't see why love couldn't jog his memory just as well as war might. On strict orders from General Emerson, she had yet to tell him of her mixed ancestry; but given his condition, the confession would have little impact in any case. So she simply tried to keep things fun.

At one point he suggested that they return to the base, but she vetoed it, pointing out to him that *she* was the one who was in charge.

"But I'm the one you're experimenting on!" he told her, making that sad face that made her want to hold and love him. In return, he caught the look on her face and asked if something was wrong with her.

"I think I'm in love," she sighed, only to hear him respond: "That word has no meaning for me."

It was a line she had heard often enough in the past; so she lightened up at once and convinced him to at least ride the Space Tunnel with her. He wasn't wild about the idea, but ultimately relented.

The Space Tunnel was Arcadia's main attraction; prospective dare-devils were not only required to measure up to a height line but practically submit a note from their physicians as well. It was a high-speed, grueling rollercoaster ride through tunnels that had been designed to play dangerous tricks with the optic and auditory senses. Riders found themselves harnessed side-by-side into two-person antigrav cars that were hurled into a phantasmagoric session with motion sickness and pure fright.

After Zor was made to understand that Dana's screams were the result of exhilaration and not terror, he, too, began to surrender to the experience. It was only when they entered the infamous swirling-disc tunnel that things started to come apart.

There was something about the placement of those light discs along the tunnel walls, something about their vaguely oval shape and curious concavity that elicited a fearful memory . . . one he could not connect to anything but horror and capture. It seemed to tug at the very fabric of his mind, rending open places better left sealed and forgotten. . . .

Dana saw his distress and desperately tried to reach for him; but she was held fast by both gee-forces and the harness mechanism itself. She could do nothing about the former but wait for a calmer point along the course; so in the meantime she went to work on the harness, pulling the couplers free of their sockets. Almost immediately she realized she had miscalculated: the car was accelerating into a full rollover and in an instant the shoulder harness was undone and she was thrown from the seat.

Zor saw her propelled to the rear of the speeding car, the shocking sight strong enough to overcome memory's hold. Except that it wasn't only Dana that he reached out for after he'd undone his own harness, but the radiant image of a woman from his past, a gauzy pink image of love and loss, not easily forgotten in this or any other lifetime.

Zor wrestled with the image of the woman for several days. He didn't mention it to Dana or Nova Satori, but it accompanied him wherever he went, his first clear-cut memory, seemingly a key to that Pandora's Box stored in his mind.

He was with the GMP lieutenant now, viewing a series of video images that were apparently supposed to have some meaning for him, but had thus far proven less than evocative. Tall fruit-bearing trees of some kind, tendrils wrapped around an eerily luminescent globe; protoplasmic vacuoles free-floating amidst a neurallike plexus of cables and crossovers; a round-topped armored cone rising from the equally armored surface of a galactic fortress ...

"We've been over and over these tapes, Zor," Nova said, illuminating the room with the tap of a switch. "What are you trying to do—drive us both crazy?"

Zor made a disgruntled sound. "I'm getting closer each time I look at these things. I can feel it, I can just *feel* it. I'm going to remember. *Something,* at least. I'll break through." Zor stroked his forehead absently, while Nova loaded a video cassette into a second machine. "Let's take a look at that first program again."

"What happens if you *do* regain your memory?" Nova asked him coolly. "Do you crack up or what?"

"Who would care, anyway?" Zor threw back.

Nova smiled wryly. "Maybe Dana, but she's about the only one."

The GMP lieutenant's attitude toward the alien had changed, although Zor was at a loss to understand it. He sensed that it had something to do with Dana, but didn't see how that might explain her sudden turnabout.

"Just play the tape," he told her harshly.

A red bipedal war machine Satori had called a Bioroid; other war machines in combat with Hovercrafts; *three identical mesas, round and steep-sided, crowned with vegetation and rising abruptly from a forested plain ...*

Zor stared at the scene, a sharp pain piercing his skull, words in an ancient voice filling his inner ears.

"Earth is the final source of Protoculture," the voice began. *"The basis of our power, the life's-blood of our existence. Our foremost goal is to control this life-source by recapturing that which was stolen from us, that which was hidden from us, that which we alone are deserving of and entitled to. . . ."*

Zor was on his feet, unaware of Nova's voiced concern. He saw three shadowy shapes arise from the mounds and disappear— creatures deliberately revealing themselves for his benefit.

Nova heard him groan, then scream in agony as he collapsed unconscious across the tabletop.

* * *

Professor Cochran was unavailable and Professor Zand was tabu; so Nova had to call in a relatively low-level GS physician on loan to the GMP from the defense department.

Zor was unconscious, though not comatose, writhing on the bed Nova and the doctor had carried him to in the military police barracks.

Dr. Katz and Lieutenant Satori were standing over him now; the doctor professionally aloof and Nova encouraged by the breakthrough but at the same time alarmed. Katz had undressed Zor and given him a sedative, powerful enough to calm the alien some but not strong enough to control the unseen horrors he was experiencing.

"Earth," Zor was groaning. "Earth, Earth is the source. . . . Earth! . . . Protoculture! We must have it! . . ."

"He's finally remembering," Nova said quietly.

Katz adjusted his eyeglasses and took a final glance at the bedside charts. "There is no apparent sign of brain damage. The sedative should take effect soon and last through the night."

Nova thanked him. "One more thing," she told him before he left the room. "You are now under top-security restriction. You haven't been here at all, you've never seen this patient. Is that understood?"

"Completely," said Katz.

Nova brushed wet bangs from Zor's feverish brow and followed the doctor out.

A minute after the door closed behind her, an electrical charge seemed to take charge of the sedated alien, starting in his head and radiating out along afferent pathways, forcing his body into a kind of involuntary stiff-armed salute. Zor screamed and clutched at the bed covers, his back arched, chest heaved up, but Nova and Katz were too far away to hear him.

CHAPTER FIFTEEN

Zor had sacrificed his life while attempting to redress some of the injustices his discoveries had brought about. It must have occurred to the Masters that his clone—properly nurtured, properly controlled to mimic the behavior of his parent/twin—would share the same selfless qualities. Just what the Masters had planned for Zor Prime after he'd led them to the Protoculture matrix is, and forever shall be, open to speculation.

Mingta, *Protoculture: Journey Beyond Mecha*

IN THE ROBOTECH FLAGSHIP, STILL HOLDING IN GEOSYNCHRONOUS orbit above Earth's equator, the three Masters were seated for a change. A spherical holo-field dominated the center of the triangle formed by their high-backed chairs, and in the field itself flashed enhanced video images of the world through the eyes of their agent, Zor Prime, electronic transcriptions of the data returned to them via the neural sensor implanted in the clone's brain.

"The poor blind fools actually believe they've captured a brain-washed Human," Bowkaz said acidly. "I expect the destruction of such a species will be no great loss to the galaxy."

Shaizan agreed, as an Arcadia image of thrill-seeking Dana appeared in the field. "They're like insects, but with emotions. Primitive, industrious, and productive, but frivolous. This immature female, for example. . . ."

"Hard to believe she's an officer," he continued, light from the holo-field sphere white-washing his aged face. "A commander of men and machines, leading them into war. . . ."

Another view of Dana now, as she appeared when seated opposite Zor at one of the park's picnic tables.

"And it seems that she is part Zentraedi," said Bowkaz, his chin resting on his hand.

Shaizan grunted meaningfully. "It doesn't seem possible, and

271

yet the sensors have detected certain bio-genetic traits. But the mating of a Zentraedi and a Human . . . how very odd."

"The clone has sensed something in this halfbreed, and that recognition has aroused him. Emotion is obviously the key to bringing back the memories of the donor Zor."

Again the sphere image de-rezzed, only to be replaced with those scenes Nova had recently shown Zor: the red Bioroid, battling mecha, and the three mounds.

"It is no wonder the clone experienced such agony," Dag commented, referring to this last holo-projection.

Under the man-made mounds were buried the remains of the SDF-1 and -2, along with Khyron's warship. The Masters felt certain that the Protoculture matrix was intact under one of these, and had gone so far as to investigate their hunch, but were stopped cold by the wraiths who guarded the device. The clone, of course, had led that particular operation.

"The clone is regaining his donor's memory of Protoculture," Bowkaz added knowingly. "Is it possible that he will tell them what he knows? Remember how he deceived us so many years ago; we must proceed with caution."

The sphere was a sky-blue vacuum now, a portrait of empty consciousness itself, interrupted at intervals by jagged eruptions of neural activity.

"Are you suggesting that we assume control of the clone?" Shaizan asked.

Bowkaz gave a slow nod, as one final image filled the sphere: the hostile faces of the 15th when Zor had first been introduced to them. "To avoid the risk of his being subjected to even more base emotions, I propose we begin immediately, if only to focus his mind on the Protoculture."

"Agreed," the other Masters said after a moment.

Nova's updated reports to General Emerson concerning Zor's identification with the Macross mounds and his ravings about Protoculture convinced Rolf that it was time to open up the case to the general staff. Commander Leonard agreed and an ad hoc interagency session was convened in the Ministry's committee room.

Emerson briefed the officers, and Leonard took it from there.

"The alien's flashes of memory tell us one thing: Earth is the remaining source of all Protoculture. If we can believe it, then this is the sole reason the Robotech Masters have not destroyed the planet."

No one at the table needed to be reminded that Protoculture had spared the SDF-1 from the Zentraedi in a similar fashion.

"But they will continue their attacks until they have accumulated every supply of Protoculture we have," Leonard continued. "This means that once they learn that the so-called factory was nothing but a legend, they will go after our power plants, our mecha, every Robotech device that relies on Protoculture.

"Therefore, our only hope for survival is very simple: we must attack first and make it count."

Rolf couldn't believe his ears. The idiot was right back where they were before Zor had even entered the picture.

"But Supreme Commander," he objected. "Why *provoke* an attack when we have something they would barter to get? Let's tell them we know why they're here and make a deal." Rolf raised his voice a notch to cut through the protests his proposal had elicited. "Zor can speak for us! We could get the word to them that we are open to negotiation!"

"Are you serious, General?" said Major Kinski, speaking for several of the others. "What do you propose to do—sit down and have a luncheon with the Robotech Masters?" He waved his fist at Emerson. "They won't deal; they haven't even made an attempt to communicate!"

Leonard sat quietly, recalling the personal warning the Masters had sent his way not long ago. . . .

"I'm quite serious," Rolf was responding, his hands flat on the table. "And don't raise a fist at me, young man! Now, sit down and keep quiet!"

"You heard him," Rochelle said to Kinski, backing Emerson up. Now it was Leonard's turn to cut through the protests.

"We're not in the deal-making business, gentlemen," he said stonily. "We're here to protect the sovereignty of our planet."

"How can you even *think* of negotiating with these murderous aliens?" asked the officer on Kinski's left.

Kinski's own fist struck the table. "A military solution is the only response. Our people expect nothing less of us."

Rolf laughed maniacally, in disbelief. "Yes, they *expect* us to bring the planet to the brink once more—"

"That's enough!" Leonard bellowed, putting an end to the arguments. "We begin coordinating attack plans immediately. This session is adjourned."

Emerson and Rochelle kept their seats as the others filed out.

* * *

Zor spent four days in the hands of the GMP and was then released to rejoin the 15th. Louie Nichols greeted him warmly when
he was returned to the barracks compound, desperate to show him
the scale replica of the red Bioroid he had finally completed.

"I made it myself," Louie said proudly. "It's just like the one
you wore in battle."

Zor stared at the thing absently and pushed his way past Louie.
"I . . . don't quite remember," he said gruffly.

"Hey, what's up?" Louie insisted, catching up with him. "I'm
only trying to help you remember what happened out there,
buddy."

"Sure," Zor mumbled back, moving on.

Louie would have said more, but Eddie Jordon had leapt off the
couch and was suddenly beside him, pulling the metal head off
the replica.

"Not so fast, hotshot," Eddie yelled. "I want to talk to you.
Turn around!"

Zor stopped and faced him; Eddie was hefting the heavy object,
tossing it up with one hand, threateningly. Louie tried to intervene, but the cadet shoved him aside.

"You're the cause of my brother's death!" Eddie declared angrily. "You're a liar if you tell me you don't remember! Now
admit it, *clone!*"

Angelo Dante was up on his feet now, warily approaching
Eddie from behind.

"Come on, Zor!" Eddie hissed into Zor's face, the robot head
still in his hand. "Tell me—just how much did my brother suffer?!"

Zor said nothing, meeting Eddie's gaze with eyes empty of
feeling, ready to accept whatever it was the cadet saw fit to deliver.

"You tell me about it!" Eddie was saying, angry but shaken;
taken over by the memory of loss and now powerless against it.
"I know you remember," he sobbed. "I just want to . . ."

Eddie's head was bowed, his body convulsed as the pain defeated him. Zor averted his eyes.

But suddenly the cadet's fury returned, cutting through the sorrow with a right that started almost at the floor and came up with
a loud *crack!* against Zor's chin. Zor fell back against the rec
room's bookshelves; he slumped to the floor and looked up at his
assailant.

"Feel better now?" Zor asked, wiping blood from his lip.

Eddie's face contorted in rage. He raised his right fist high and stepped in to deliver a follow-up blow, but Angelo Dante had positioned himself in front of Zor.

Eddie's fist glanced off the sergeant's jaw without budging the larger man an inch. Angelo frowned and said, "Don't you think that's enough?"

The cadet was both angry and frightened now. He looked past Angelo, glowering at Zor, and threw the robot head to the floor with all his remaining strength. Then he turned and fled the scene.

Angelo knuckled his bruised cheek. Behind him, Zor said, "Thanks."

"I won't stop him again, Zor," the sergeant said without turning around.

"I don't blame you," Zor returned, full of self-reproach. "I suppose I deserve a lot more than a few punches for what happened to his brother."

Dante didn't bother to argue the fact.

"You got that right, mister," he sneered, walking off.

Zor rode the elevator down to the compound's workout room; it was deserted, as he'd hoped it would be. He took a seat against the room's mirrored wall, regarding the many exercise machines and weight benches in bewilderment, then turned to glance at his reflection.

He had no memory of Eddie Jordon's brother, or of any of the evil deeds the team seemed to hold him responsible for. And without those memories he felt victimized, as much by his own mind as by the teams' often unvoiced accusations. Worse still, the more he did remember, the more correct those accusations appeared. Without exception his dreams and incomplete memory flashbacks were filled with violence and an undefinable but pervasive evil. *It must be true,* he decided. *I have killed other Human beings. . . . I'm a killer,* he told himself—*a killer!*

Zor pressed his hands to his face, his heart filled with remorse for wrongdoings as yet unrevealed. And how *different* this felt than the angry mood he had found himself in earlier the same day!

While he was on the way to the barracks from Nova's post, on the Hovercycle she had requisitioned for his use, Dana had ridden up alongside him, full of her usual optimism and what seemed to be *affection.*

"Have you remembered anything else?" she had asked him.

He practically ignored her.

"Why am I getting the silent treatment all of a sudden?" she had shouted from her cycle. "You've lost your recent memory, too? You've lost all respect for me?"

It was as though something inside him was *forcing* anger against her, irrational but impossible to redirect.

He had snarled at her. "I can't stand the constant interrogation, *Lieutenant. . . .*"

"So! There you are!" he suddenly heard from across the workout room. Dana was standing by the door, impatient with him. "I thought you were going to wait for me in the ready-room. I've been looking all over this place for you."

Zor squeezed his eyes shut, feeling the anger begin to rise in him again, dispersing the sorrow of only moments ago.

"I'm tired of this," he told her, trying his best not to betray the rising tide. "Please leave me alone, Dana."

Dana reacted as though slapped.

"I don't want you bothering me anymore." Something forced the words from his tongue. "And I don't want my memory back either, *understand?*"

"I don't believe what I'm hearing," she said, standing over him now.

Zor stood up and whirled on her. "I can't take this whole situation! If your people want what's locked up in my brain, tell them to *operate!*"

Dana's face clouded over. "You're really hurting me," she said softly. "I'm only trying to help you. I want us to keep being friends. Please . . . let me." When he didn't respond she risked a step toward him. "Listen to me, Zor. The past is the past. I don't care what you did. I only know you as you are now. And I think one part of you feels as close to me as I feel to you." She placed her hands on his shoulders and tried to hold his gaze. "Don't run away from this—we can win!"

"No!" he said, turning away from her. "It's over."

She took her hands off him and looked down at the floor. "Okay. If that's the way you want it, then that's it." Then her chin came up. "But don't come looking for me when you need help!"

Dana pivoted through a 180-degree turn and started off, her nose in the air. The room felt unfocused, and it was almost as if she didn't notice the large projection screen that had been positioned against the mirrored wall. Her foot slammed hard into one of the metal frame's support legs and she cursed loudly. But that wasn't enough for her. "You stupid thing!" she barked, and toe-kicked the tubular leg, knocking it free of the frame's weighted foot. The frame began to topple backwards, thick lucite screen and all, and everything seemed to hit the mirrors at the same time.

Instinctively, Zor had rushed forward, aiming to tackle her to safety; but two steps forward he caught sight of himself, reflected in each of the hundreds of mirror shards loosed from the fractured wall.

Past and present seemed to coalesce in that moment: Dana's frightened face became a dark silhouette, then transmutated into the visage of someone ancient and unmistakably evil.

Zzoorrr ... a disembodied voice called to him. *There is no place to run. You cannot escape us, you cannot get away....*

Now a hand as aged as that face pointed and closed on him open-palmed, and suddenly he found himself running through the curved-top tunnels of some twilight world, fleeing the grasp of armed guardians, caped, helmeted, and curiously armored. A trio of threatening voices pursued him through that labyrinth as well, but ultimately he outran them, launching himself through a hexagonal portal and secreting himself in a darkened room, filled with a heavenly music....

A green-haired woman sat at a harp, her slender fingers forming chords of light that danced about the room. He knew but could not speak her name. Likewise he knew that he had violated a tabu by visiting this place ... *those ancient ones who sought to control him, to keep him locked away and insulated; those ancient ones who sought to have him absorb a life* he had not lived!

Musica, the green-haired harpist told him....

But he had already moved behind her now, his arm across her neck. The Terminators had caught up with him, and he meant to use her as a shield, a *shield.* ... *They will not kill her* he told himself, as she quaked with fear in his arms. *She is one of them.*

But the Terminators had armed their weapons and were taking aim; and although he had pushed her aside and fled once more, they had fired—*fired at her.* ...

The world was blood-red. Someone was calling his name....

Dana was struggling beneath him; he had collapsed over her, shielding her from the glass but pinning her to the floor.

"Musica ..." Zor heard himself tell her, as she helped him get up. "When I first saw her, she was playing this beautiful music. Then I used her as a shield. ... I didn't think they'd kill her, but they did!"

Dana was staring at him, her eyes wide. "No, Zor, they didn't," she tried to tell him. "Bowie *saw* her—*alive!* It must have been a dream—"

Zor was up and walking away from her, fixed on his angry reflection in the shattered mirror.

"I have no memory," he declared, his azure eyes narrowed. "I'm an android. I did kill Eddie's brother, I'm certain of it."

He rammed his right fist into the mirror; then his left, tossing off Dana when she tried to restrain him. Again and again right and left, he punched and whaled at the broken glass, ultimately exhausting himself and reducing his hands to a bloody pulp.

"My god!" he howled. "The Robotech Masters! They must control me completely!"

Dana was leaning against his back, her hands over his shoulders, sobbing.

Zor's nostrils flared. "There's only one way to defeat them—I must destroy myself!"

"No," Dana pleaded with him. "There's always hope. . . ." She caught sight of the fresh blood dripping down the mirror and reached out for his hands. "Your hands!" she gasped. She pulled her kerchief out and wrapped it around his right, which appeared far more lacerated than the left. "Androids don't bleed," she said to him between sobs. "You're Human, Zor—"

"Without a memory? Without a will of my own?"

She wanted to say something, but no words came to her.

"I'm sorry, Dana," Zor told her after a moment. "I've said some terrible things to you. . . ."

"Let me help you," she said, looking into his eyes.

Zor pressed his forehead to hers.

Later, Zor marched determinedly down the halls of the Ministry, closing fast on the office of Rolf Emerson. Dana's help would be invaluable, but there were things he was going to have to do alone. To start with, he needed every scrap of information that was available on the Masters, on their fortresses and science of bio-genetic engineering, and Emerson was the only one who would have access to this.

At the office doors, he stopped and tried to compose himself; then lifted his bandaged hand to knock. He could hear voices coming from the other side of the door.

But something arrested his motion: answering the call of an unknown force, he stood silent and motionless at the threshold, eyes and ears attuned to a kind of recording frequency.

"But it's reckless for Leonard to press an attack now, General," Zor heard Rochelle say. "We aren't prepared."

Rolf Emerson said: "I know, but what can I do? Leonard has

most of the staff on his side. I'd hoped this wouldn't happen. I'd hoped to use Zor as a bargaining agent. . . . But instead, it's come down to all-out war."

For several minutes Zor listened at the door, while Emerson and Rochelle summarized the general staff's hastily coordinated attack plans. Then he turned away and walked stiffly down the corridor, his original motivations erased.

Unobserved at the far end of the corridor, Angelo Dante watched Zor leave; tight-lipped, the sergeant nodded his head in knowing confirmation.

The neuro-sensor implanted in Zor's brain now transmitted a steady supply of visual and auditory information, filling the flag-ship holo-sphere with new images that both troubled and enlightened the three Masters.

"Notice how the clone's rage interferes with our attempts to manipulate his behavior," Bowkaz pointed out, commenting on Zor's blood match with his own reflection. "This is worrisome."

"But even so," Shaizan countered, "the use of the clone goes well—even better than we had hoped." Emerson and Rochelle's exchange of attack plan data underscored the solitary image of a chevroned doorway. "It is interesting, though . . . the Micronians continue to delude themselves with plans of attacking our Robotech fortresses."

"I must say they have courage," said Dag.

Shaizan squinted at the holo-sphere's lingering transignal.

"One simple truth remains for the Micronians: we will annihilate every one of them. Annihilate them."

"Annihilate them," Bowkaz repeated.

"Annihilate them!"

CHAPTER SIXTEEN

"A-JACs, my butt! They're nothing but goddamned Protocopters!"

Remark attributed to an unknown TASC pilot

HE UNITED EARTH GOVERNMENT FLAG FLEW HIGH OVER THE copper-domed Neo-Post-Federalist Senate Building. Inside, Supreme Commander Leonard addressed a combined audience of UEG personnel, Southern Cross officers (Dana Sterling and Marie Crystal among them), representatives of the press, and privileged civilians, from the podium of the structure's vast senatorial hall. Behind him on the stage sat General Rolf Emerson, Colonels Rochelle and Rudolf, and the Joint Chiefs-of-Staff.

"We fully realize there has been much debate over the advisability of a preemptive strike against the alien fleet at this juncture. These concerns have been taken into careful consideration by the High Command of the Armed Forces. But the time has come to put an end to debate, and to unite all our voices behind a common effort.

"Proto-engineering has completed the first consignment of the new Armored Jet Attack Copters, henceforth designated as A-JACs. These will form the nucleus of the first assault wave. Your corps commanders will have your individual battle assignments.

"I know there isn't a single soldier in this hall today who isn't painfully aware of all the hazards that will certainly arise during the course of this mission, and there are still some who would advise against its undertaking. But the High Command has determined that we now have the capability of dealing a devastating blow to the enemy, and to do nothing in the face of this advantage is to admit defeat!"

Leonard's speech received less than enthusiastic support, except from certain members of the general staff and the militaristic wing of Chairman Moran's teetering legislature.

Emerson and Rochelle scarcely applauded. Leonard, the two had decided, was a megalomaniac; and the attack plan itself, utter madness.

Afterwards, in front of the building, where the press was all but assaulting Leonard's silver chariot limo, Marie Crystal maneuvered through the crowds to bring her Hovercycle alongside Dana's, just as the 15th's lieutenant was engaging her own mecha's thrusters. Though it was the first time the women had seen each other in several weeks, the reunion was hardly a happy one.

"Guess who's been assigned to the first wave?" Marie taunted her sometime rival. Recently given a clean bill-of-health by the med center staff, she had been reassigned to active duty and reunited with her tactical air squadron.

"Well aren't you the lucky little hotshot, Marie," Dana returned in her sarcastic best. "You're through licking your wounds, huh?" Dana never had paid her that visit—not after what Sean had reported of Marie's continuing quest for a scapegoat.

Marie's cat's-eyes flashed. "Believe me, I'm completely recovered," she told Dana, with a sly grin. "I never felt better in my entire life. But I think it's just *awful* that the Hovertanks won't be seeing any action this time around. Guess you'll be able to get some *training* done while we're gone—heaven knows you need it."

Dana let the remark roll off her back. "To be perfectly honest, I'm really not too unhappy about being grounded," she said in an off-hand manner. "You pilots'll have your hands full."

Marie sniggered. "It won't be that bad. At least this time we'll have a commander who knows what she's doing. Know what I mean?"

Dana frowned, in spite of her best efforts not to. "Oh, why don't you lose that line?" she snapped at Marie. "When are you going to realize that it wasn't my fault?"

Marie laughed, proud of herself. "Don't worry, I forgive you," she said, twisting the throttle and joining the exiting throngs. "So long," she called over her shoulder.

Dana was tempted to send some obscene gesture her way, but

thought better of it and reached down to reactivate the thrusters. No sooner had she armed the switch than Nova Satori wandered over.

"Make it brief, Nova," Dana began. "I have to meet Zor in fifteen minutes and he always starts worrying if I'm late."

Nova never had a chance to confront her face-to-face on the medical center stunt, and Dana was in no mood for an argument now. It had been settled officially, and she was willing to let it rest. Although Nova probably didn't see it that way.

"Zor's the very person I wanted to speak to you about."

"Well?" Dana said defensively.

"The GMP appreciates all you've done to help him regain his memory, but we feel there are some areas that only trained professionals can—"

"No!" Dana cut her off. "He's mine and I've promised to help him. These *professionals* you're so proud of will probably make a vegetable of him, and I'm not about to let that happen!"

"Yes, I understand your feelings, Dana," Nova went on in her even voice, "but this case requires some in-depth probing of the subject's unconscious mind." Nova glanced at her clipboard, as if reading from a prepared statement. "We've called a certain Dr. Zeitgeist, an expert in alien personality transference to—"

Dana put her hands over her ears. "Enough! You're giving me a monster migraine with all this psychobabble!"

Nova shrugged. "I'm afraid it's out of your hands, Dana. *I've* been assigned to supervise Zor's rehabilitation—"

"Over my dead body, Nova! All he needs is a little Human understanding—something you're in short supply of. Leave him alone!" Dana said, wristing the throttle, hovering off, and almost colliding with an on-coming mega-truck.

"Dana!" the GMP lieutenant called after her. *She's completely lost her objectivity,* Nova said to herself.

"I could just scream sometimes!" Dana said, bursting into the 15th's ready-room.

Cups of coffee and tea slipped from startled hands, chess pieces hit the floor, and permaplas window panes rattled on the other side of the room.

"What seems to be the problem, Lieutenant?" Angelo said, leaping to his feet.

"Nothing!" she roared. "Just tell me where Zor's hiding himself!" Dana's angry strides delivered her over to Bowie. "I thought I told you to keep an eye on him!"

Bowie flinched, stammering a puzzled reply and leaning back not a moment too soon, as Dana's fist came crashing down on the table in front of him. "I can't depend on you for anything at all!"

"Cool your thrusters, Lieutenant," Sean said calmly from the couch. "The patient's fine and we're keeping tabs on him, so simmer down."

"Well, where is he, Sean?" Dana said quietly but with a nasty edge to her voice.

Sean simply said: "He'll be back in a second," bringing Dana's back up once again.

"I didn't ask you for a timetable of his comings and goings, Private," she barked, hands on her hips. "I want to see him!"

"I think he'd rather you waited. . . ." Sean suggested, as she made to leave the room.

The ready-room doors hissed open. "Just tell me where he is."

"Men's room: straight down the hall, first door on the right."

Dana made a sound of exasperation, while everyone else stifled laughs.

"Any word on assignments from the war council?" Corporal Louie said, hoping to change the subject.

Angelo folded his arms across his chest. "Yeah, do we finally get permission to take care of the enemy this time or do we get held back again?"

Dana walked into their midst. "Well, if you really must know, the Supreme Command in all its infinite wisdom has decided to . . ." she let them hang on her words, ". . . keep us in reserve, of course."

Dana kicked Sean's legs out from under him as she paced past him, forcing him into an involuntary slouch before she exited the ready-room.

"This is getting kinda monotonous," Sean said with a grunt.

Angelo slammed his hands together. "Typical! Whoever makes these stupid decisions oughta be shot!"

Sean extended his legs, crossing his ankles on the table. "It's a crazy idea anyway. I'm telling you, the supreme commander's going nuts. He knows it's hopeless to try a frontal assault."

"The application of brute force is strategically wrong," Louie added, opposite Sean at the table. "We must fight with our intellect . . . By *developing* Robotechnology we stand a chance."

Time would prove him right, but just now Angelo Dante wasn't buying any of it.

"Forget all this machinery!" he counseled. "If they'd just give us a crack at 'em, we'd knock 'em outta the sky!"

* * *

Dana went up to her private quarters in the loft above the ready-room, the recent encounters with Marie and Nova replaying themselves in her memory; but these were the reworked and edited versions, now scripted with the things she should have said. She had convinced herself that Nova's spiel was nothing more than a transparent attempt to keep Zor all to herself. And that Marie would undoubtedly try to get her greedy little hands on him, too, once they met—which Dana planned to keep from happening.

She crossed the room and opened the wings of the three-paneled mirror above her vanity, regarding herself with as much objectivity as the moment allowed, sucking in her waist, patting her tummy, and striking fashion poses. She was pleased with her reflection, and decided that there was really nothing to be worried about. Nova didn't stand a chance of keeping Zor to herself. There was simply *no* comparison between Nova's cool prettiness and Dana's warm-blooded allure.

Zor had returned to the ready-room. Angelo was lecturing the others on what he planned to do once he got his hands on the enemy aliens, undisturbed by Zor's presence, actually *playing* to him at times. Zor took a seat across the room and tried to busy himself with a magazine, but his eyes refused to focus on the print; instead they seemed to *demand* that he concentrate his attention on the sergeant. . . .

But Dana's call broke the spell. "Zor, come up here!" she yelled from her quarters. He left the ready-room with the team's laughter at his back and climbed the stairs to the loft.

Dana was standing in front of her vanity when he entered, but what captured his eyes were the three *separate* reflections in the mirror above. Here was Dana in a red dress, Dana in a green pants suit, and Dana in an elegant old-fashioned gown. And yet the *real* Dana was in uniform!

Zor gasped and stumbled, feeling himself drawn once more to the edge of total recall—a dangerous precipice towering out of an absolute darkness.

"Dana . . . the mirror," he croaked, catching her by surprise. "That . . . *Triumvirate!*" He didn't know where the word had come from and was at a loss to explain it when she turned her puzzled face to him. "For a moment there were three different images of you in that mirror," he told her anxiously.

She made a wry face. "If you're going to start seeing things, maybe Nova's right and you do need professional help—"

"The Triumvirate!" he interrupted her. "It's starting to come back to me again. . . ."

A chamber filled with a swirling nebulous mixture of liquids and gases, a shape taking form amidst it all—gigantic, inhuman, devoid of all that life was meant to be . . . And now a triad of such chambers, but smaller, Human-sized, and within each, beings who shared a common face . . .

"The Triumvirate. . . ." he groaned, almost losing his balance. "Something to do with acting in groups of three."

Dana seemed almost disinterested in his distress; but in fact, she was beside herself with excitement. Zor had to be making reference to the same triplicate clones she, Bowie, and Louie had seen in the fortress. She was determined to keep Zor unaware of this; and just as determined to prove to Nova that she could handle the subject's unconscious as well as any Dr. Zeitgeist could. From now on it was going to be the kid glove treatment for Zor.

"Well, I have no idea what all that means," she said with elaborate innocence. "But it sounds just screwy enough to turn out to be important. I guess I'll let High Command know about it—even though they're going to think we're *both* crazy," she hastened to add.

At Fokker Field, Lieutenant Marie Crystal, already suited up in gladiatorial, tactical air combat armor, directed her TASC team to one of the score of massive battlecruisers that were positioned about the field in launch mode. Marie checked off names on the list she carried in her mind, as the flyboys rushed by her. Elevators carried them down to the field itself, where Hovertransports were waiting to ferry them to their destinations. In the distance, men and mecha were transferring themselves from transports to cruisers.

Over the PA the voice of a controller issued last minute instructions: *"Final loading of A-JACs in assembly bay nineteen. Transport commanders, signal when A-JACs are in place. . . . T minus ten minutes to attack launch . . . All pilots to standby alert. . . ."*

Marie checked her suit chronometer against the controller's mark and began to hurry her team along. "Come on," she told them, with a broad sweep of her arm. "Keep it moving! They're not going to wait for us!"

She leaned over the balcony railing to glance at the transports and happened to notice Captain Nordoff's Hoverjeep below. He looked up, spying her and waving his hand.

"We expect to see those A-JACs put through their paces up there!" he yelled.

Marie threw him an okay-sign and told her not to worry about a thing. "I only hope we don't get lost in the shuffle up there—I've never seen so many ships!"

"Just pray we've got enough, Lieutenant!" he said, and hovered off.

Marie straightened up from the rail and turned to find Sean alongside her, displaying his well-known roguish grin.

"Hello, *Private*," Marie said disdainfully.

"Hey, don't get personal," Sean laughed.

She turned her back to him. "What are you doing here, Sean? No hot date today? After all, the Fifteenth's not part of this action."

"Hey, don't say things like that, Marie," he said peevishly. "You're tearing me apart, you know that? I came here because I wanted to see you off. I care about you, in case you haven't guessed."

Marie looked at him over her shoulder. "Don't think that one night on the roof makes us an item, Sean," she warned him. "I trust you just about as far as I can throw you."

"*T minus six minutes to launch,*" the controller told them from the tower. "*All commanders to their posts. . . .*"

Neither one of them said anything for a moment; then Sean broke the silence with a quiet. "Be careful, okay?"

Marie's hard look softened. "I almost believe you really mean that. . . ."

"I, I mean it," he stammered.

Marie blew him a kiss from the elevator.

Elsewhere on the base, Zor stood alone, his azure eyes scanning the field, an unwitting transmitter of sight and sound. . . .

In the Robotech flagship, the three Masters watched over the Earth Forces base through the clone's eyes. The Protoculture cap was beneath their aged hands now as they readied their fleet for battle.

"This new armada is the single largest fleet they have yet dared to send against us," Bowkaz saw fit to point out, no suggestion of fear or anticipation in his deep voice.

"The more ships they employ, the greater our triumph," said Dag.

"Their armada will be destroyed and their spirit broken," Shaizan added. But suddenly there were signs of interrupted concentration in the transignal holo-image. "What is happening?" he asked the others.

Bowkaz repositioned his hands on the Protoculture cap, but the image of the prelaunch battlecruisers continued to waver and ultimately de-rezzed entirely. "Someone is interfering with the clone," he explained. "Distracting him. . . ."

While Dana had excused herself to notify Rolf Emerson of Zor's latest flashback, the alien himself had left the barracks. All at once compelled to visit the Earth Forces launch site, he had ridden his Hovercycle up to the plateau, and chosen a spot near the field that offered a vantage point for all the myriad activities taking place. In a certain sense he was not cognizant of where he was, nor what he was doing; and equally unaware that both Angelo and Dana, on separate cycles, had followed him there.

The sergeant had watched Zor for some time, wondering what his next move might be; but when he realized that the alien was simply staring transfixed at the prelaunch activities, he decided to move in.

"Just what the hell do you think you're doing up here, Zor?" he demanded, seemingly awakening Zor from a dream. "This sector's off-limits. And besides, you're supposed to be back at the barracks."

"I was trying to get a better view of the liftoff," Zor offered as explanation, although one part of him realized this wasn't true.

Angelo took a quick glance right and left; there was no one in sight, and Angelo was tempted to fix it so the alien would no longer be *capable* of moving around scot-free. Dante took a menacing step forward, only to hear Dana's voice behind him.

"It's all right, Sergeant, I'll vouch for him."

Angelo glared at Zor and relaxed some. Dana was marching up the small rise to join them, breathless when she arrived. She glanced briefly at Zor, then threw the sergeant a suspicious look.

"What did you have in mind, Angelo?" she asked him, her chin up.

Dante met her gaze and said: "Not a thing, Lieutenant."

Dana nodded warily. "I gave Zor clearance to go wherever he wants. I thought it might help him get his memory back."

"Or something," said Angelo.

Zor looked at both of them, beginning to feel the anger return.

Supreme Commander Leonard and his staff viewed the armada liftoff from command central's underground bunker. The darkly armored leviathanlike battlecruisers were underway, rising from the plateau base like a school of surfacing whales.

"Just look at them!" Leonard gushed, his eyes glued to the monitor screen. "How can they possibly fail?"

"Very impressive, Commander," said Rolf Emerson, giving lip-service to the moment. *I wish to heaven I shared your confidence,* he kept to himself.

Schematics of the attack force and the relative position of the Masters' fleet were carried to the oval screen in the flagship command center.

"Ah, here they come," said Bowkaz. "Like the proverbial moths to the flame."

"Is there no one among them who sees the stupidity of this?" Dag asked rhetorically.

"I will summon our defense force," said Shaizan.

But Bowkaz told him not to bother. "This won't require the rest of the fleet. One ship will be sufficient."

CHAPTER
SEVENTEEN

With Dana Sterling's penetration of the SDF-1 burial mound, Humankind [on Earth] had observed three separate stages of the Optera lifeform and still didn't recognize what they were seeing: Lynn-Minmei had watched Khyron ingesting the dried leaves, Sean Phillips had actually tossed the fruit of the tree in his hand, and Dana Sterling had seen the plants in full flower. All this intrigue centered on Protoculture, when the real treasure was in front of them all the time—the Flower of Life itself! ... Only one stage remained, but Humankind would have to await the Invid's arrival to glimpse it. In thinking about it, though, one might almost say that the Invid were the final stage!

Maria Bartley-Rand, *Flower of Life:
Journey Beyond Protoculture*

GENERAL LEONARD'S ATTACK PLAN WAS A BASIC ONE ("simple-minded," as Rolf Emerson would call it later): meet the enemy's six spade fortresses head-on with the more than fifty battlecruisers of the Earth Forces armada; use the new A-JAC gunships to confuse them; then, simply overwhelm them with superior firepower. Captain Nordoff would supervise the first-wave assault; Admirals Clark and Salaam would take it from there. There were no tactics built into the plan, no flanking or diversionary operations, no contingencies for possible setbacks. The attack, which Leonard had optimistically (and unrealistically) labeled *preemptive*, would render needless Angelo Dante's concerns that Zor might be an enemy agent; the Robotech Masters hardly needed the clone's eyes to see what was coming, and consequently they were more than prepared.

At a distance of 100 miles from the alien fortresses (which were still holding in geosynchronous orbit, some 47,000 miles above the Equator), Nordoff gave the order to open fire. Annihilation discs streamed from the cruiser's pulsed laser cannon like so many small golden suns—energy-Frisbees that to the last found their targets. But the enemy defense shields absorbed it all and gave every indication of being hungry for more. The great horned and spiked fortresses were not only left undamaged, but *untouched* as well.

Knowing how much was riding on the success of the first wave, Nordoff ordered his wing to maintain course and continue firing, even if that meant at point-blank range. An armchair tactician, Nordoff, not unlike Commander Leonard, refused to accept the fact that the fortresses were effectively invincible—this despite the projections and cautions of the Southern Cross's most brilliant minds. Even the 15th Squadron's downing of the alien flagship was now being reevaluated in terms of the Masters' own allowances and strategies.

At less than sixty-five miles the first-wave battlecruisers launched a second fusillade; but this time the annihilation discs were not absorbed: they were added to the fortresses' already immeasurably charged stockpiles and spit back. Radiant blue-white tentacles reached out from the lead fortress and grappled with one of the battlecruisers, probing indelicately for weak spots in its armored hull. Troops were caught unawares by the force, incinerated in a thousand flashstorms that swept through the ship, or sent spinning to vacuum death through ruptures which instantaneously bled precious atmosphere from the already scorched and scoured holds.

In the A-JACs launch bay aboard Nordoff's ship, Marie Crystal heard that what remained of the 007 was dead in space. She had been supervising the launch preparations for the choppers, but now ran from her post to one of the starboard cannon turrets, literally kicking the gunner from his seat to have a crack at the enemy herself. She had good friends aboard the demolished cruiser and wasn't about to allow their deaths go unpunished.

Once in the turret seat, Marie quickly removed her helmet and strapped on the weapon's sensor-studded targeting cap. As computer-generated graphic displays flashed across the helmet's virtual cockpit, she immediately realized why the first-wave had failed to cripple the enemy flagship: Nordoff and the other commanders were completely disregarding intel analysis reports concerning the fortresses' vulnerable spots. Concentrated fire directed at any one of these would circumvent the shields' absorption potential and allow pulses to penetrate to the hull itself.

Marie had been close enough to these things in the past to have committed their surface details to memory; in fact, during her recent hospitalization (when she wasn't glancing at muscle mags), she had done little else except replay the fortresses' topography over and over to herself. Ranging in the gun now, she felt as though she were directly over the fortress in her Logan and could place the shot precisely where she wanted it.

"Ah-ha! There you are!" she said out loud as the spot was centered in the cannon's reticle. Marie pulled home the twin handbrake-like triggers and loosed a full ten-seconds of plasma fire at the flagship, knowing almost before the fact that she had scored a direct hit.

In the flagship command center, the three Masters hardly reacted to news that one of the fortress barriers had been breached. Absorbing the energy discs delivered by the Terrans' cruisers had enabled them to leave their own plasma reservoirs untouched and therefore shunt would-be weapons system power to the fortresses' shields and self-restorative systems.

No sooner had Marie's well-aimed barrage holed the hull than new plating was already sliding into place to seal the breach.

Dag suggested that it might not even be necessary to fire on the Terrans; better to let them fall back in complete confusion, demoralized by their futile attempt.

But Bowkaz wanted to see concrete results.

The fortress fired back, taking out two more battlecruisers.

Dana and Zor had left their Hovercycles at the base and set out on foot for the grassy overlook high above Monument City. Dana had sent Dante back to command the 15th in her absence, ignoring his reminders that just because the ground-based tactical armored units weren't directly involved in the battle they were nevertheless still on standby alert. Not that he had expected her to abandon her pet project and return to the barracks; and the only reason the sergeant didn't bother to press his point (or, for that matter, inform Sterling's commanders) was that he felt a lot better off without the alien around—and that went for both Zor *and* Dana.

Dana was encouraged by Zor's most recent mention of "the Triumvirate" to resort to what she considered high-risk therapy now, and as they walked and talked, she was sorely tempted to confess her past to him, certain that he would then move even closer to recovering his own. It was of course a double-edged sword and she was aware of the ambivalence within her: on the one hand, Zor's memory could turn out to be the key that would unlock the mystery of the Robotech Masters and give Earth the data it needed to mount a proper defense, or, as Rolf hoped, engage in some sort of deal-making. But on the other, Dana liked having this past-less Zor by her side, this empty mind she could fill with the memories she wanted placed there; in a way there was something nurturing and maternal about the whole thing that went side-by-side with the more primitive feelings she had for Zor.

They had reached the flat grassy area now, lifeless crags and shale rivers ascending on three sides, with the last open to a spectacular view of the city, several thousand yards below them. Dana tried not to think about George Sullivan and the few moments the two of them had shared here.

The sky was not cloudless, but deeply sky-blue nonetheless, and the air was unusually warm, especially for this altitude.

Zor must have been aware of it, too, because he commented that it was hard to believe there was a war going on.

"It's so peaceful and quiet up here," she told him as they walked. "I always start thinking about where I grew up when I come up here ... the people I left behind."

It would have been better to tell him about where her *mother* grew up, she added silently. That would undoubtedly interest him a lot more than stories about Rolf's farm and the almost idyllic childhood she and Bowie had shared—until military school, that was, and Rolf's appointment to general and their move from New Denver to Monument City.

But Zor didn't ask for any specifics about that place; instead, he asked with a laugh: "Was one of the people you left behind a boyfriend?"

It sounded so ridiculous coming from him that for a moment she was certain he was joking with her. So she played cryptic to his question and said, "No, not really ..."

They were overlooking the city now, and Zor sat down in the tall grass to take in the view. "I wish I could remember where I grew up," he said wistfully. "I guess I'll never know what it's like to go home again."

"Well, the war will be over someday," she suggested. "You could think about starting a new home ..."

Zor had pulled up a long blade of grass and was chewing at one end of it absently. "No," he told her. "It's not as simple as that. A man without a past is a man without a home—now and always."

"But each day brings a little more of your past back to you," she reminded him encouragingly.

"That's true," he admitted haltingly. "I do remember something

about the Triumvirate and Musica . . . but mainly it's these terrible
visions about death and destruction. I know I was doing something important when the enemy attacked. And I get this feeling
that there were *giants* there to protect me . . . but after that, all I
can think about is bloodshed, devastation." Zor pressed the heels
of his hands to his temples. "If only I could remember where and
why that attack took place. But there's nothing there. Just a
blank."

"Don't put yourself through it now, Zor."

"And those strange mounds that Nova showed me before I
passed out . . ."

"Mounds?" Dana said all of a sudden. "You didn't tell me
about this!"

"That's when we weren't speaking. When I was staying at the
GMP headquarters."

"Of course! Why haven't I thought of this before?!"

Suddenly Dana had a flash of insight: the mounds, of course!
Zor had been there. There was no reason to think that the mounds
would do it for him after Bowie hadn't, but it was worth a chance.

Dana stood up, took hold of Zor's hand, and led him off in a
run.

Nearby, a curious animal poked its head from the tall grass.
From a distance it might have been mistaken for a small shaggy
dog; but up close several differences immediately presented themselves: the two knob-ended horns that rose from behind its
sheepdog forelock, the feet like soft muffins, the eyes that were
not of this Earth.

There was something about the creature's pose and expression
that suggested disbelief. It recognized its onetime female friend.
But it was the other human that captivated the creature's attention
just now: it was the being who had taken it from its homeworld.

The creature had almost run to this one, caught up in an in-
stinctual desire to be taken home. But instead, it followed the two
Humans from a discreet distance.

Nordoff had had a change of mind.

"A third of our battle fleet and nearly half our transports have
already been lost," he reported to the war room. "They're tearing
us to shreds! Sir, it's impossible for us to maintain battle formation. I suggest we withdraw immediately."

"Nonsense," said Leonard into the remote mike. "Why haven't
you brought the A-JACs to bear against the enemy, Captain?"

"We've been awfully busy just trying to *survive* up to this point," Nordoff returned. "Sir," he continued with greater emphasis, "the enemy has been dispatching our largest battlecruisers with regularity; I hardly think attack choppers have a—"

"Captain, this is a question for me to decide. Follow your instructions. Dispatch the A-JACs!"

Dana felt Bowie's presence essential; so she and the alien returned to the 15th's barracks and snatched Bowie from the ready-room before setting off for the place where Zor and Dana had first set eyes on each other, and where Bowie himself had been held captive—the burial site of the SDF-1.

Once again Angelo Dante didn't bother to protest, happy to be rid of the three of them, liabilities all. Now the sergeant said to himself, if he could only do something about Sean and a few of the others. But when he completed his mental list of rejects he found that he had eliminated all but one man from the 15th—*himself!*

Meanwhile, the therapist, her assistant, and their patient powered their Hovercycles to the top of the ridge and over the pass that linked Monument with what was once its sister city, Macross. There was no actual roadway left, but there were remnants of the original one, and the cycles easily allowed them to scramble around rough spots and landslide areas—both natural and deliberate.

Macross was theoretically off-limits to civilians and Southern Cross troops alike, although the site was in no way patrolled or otherwise kept under surveillance. It was a well-known fact that the final battle between the SDFs 1 and 2 and the Zentraedi warship manned by Khyron and his consort, Azonia, had left the area intensely radioactive. Whether this was still the case was top-secret and a question that could only be answered by Professor Zand or one of those few scientists who had served on the dimensional fortress and had not for one reason or another elected to accompany Lang, Hunter, and Edwards on the Expeditionary Mission to Tirol. In any case, the High Command didn't want anyone poking around: most of the usable mecha and Robotechnological marvels had been salvaged from the ship, but Lang had given strict orders that no one was to disturb the area. Hence, the two-fold purpose of the bulldozed mounds themselves.

The lakebed had dried up and the resultant bowl was now teeming with a wide assortment of vegetal and animal life, reminiscent of some of the atypical habitats that formed in the bottom of craters or calderas, like that of Ngorongoro in East Africa. And in the center of this were the three flat-topped mounds, steep-sided, with larger bases than crowns, capped with vegetation, and shrouded in mystery.

Dana brought the trio to a halt some distance from the mounds. She turned to glance at Zor, looking for any signs that might indicate familiarity or recall. But instead, Zor seemed puzzled and possibly spooked, as she herself felt.

"Well you know that 'military base' you keep dreaming about—the one that was attacked?" Dana began. "It occurred to me that this might be it. Bowie and I *saw* you here, Zor—we *fought* against you and your Bioroids *right on this spot!*" Dana looked apologetic. "I didn't want to tell you before, because Nova insists that I'm not to *plant* memories in your mind . . . but this place is so important. You actually held Bowie prisoner here, Zor. Don't you remember any of it?"

Zor was looking at Bowie for confirmation and receiving it; but even that had no apparent effect. Zor tightened his mouth and shook his head.

"There was a terrible battle fought here," Bowie added. "Between the Earth Forces and the last of the Zentraedi—a race sent here by your Masters to retrieve something they thought we had—something they believe we *still* have." Bowie gestured to the three mounds. "Underneath one of these are the remains of a ship that was probably sent to Earth from your homeworld, a planet called Tirol. By someone who you might even be related to—a being called Zor."

Zor listened without a word, as an animal might listen to Human speech: aware of the tone and even the words, but ignorant of the sense of it.

"My father's sister, my aunt, died here," Bowie said softly, his voice cracking. "Her name was Claudia Grant."

"I'm sorry for that," Zor returned. "And what was this thing you were supposed to have that my Masters are still so desperate for?" he asked them.

Dana spoke to this, shrugging first, to indicate her limited knowledge of these things. "Some kind of generator. Something that has to do with Protoculture—the sort of *fuel* that drives our mecha and permits our Veritechs to transform."

"To reconfigure," Zor said, at the edge of something. He absently gnawed at his lower lip. "Protoculture . . ." he said thoughtfully. "I don't know . . . It does seem familiar; but I don't recall anything."

"Well since we're here, let's poke around some," Dana proposed. "Maybe we'll find something to jog your memory. I mean, if you feel up to it . . ." she thought to add.

"Of course I am," Zor assured her, straightening himself in the cycle's seat. "I'll investigate the mound on the left."

"I'll take the right one," Bowie said eagerly.

Dana smiled and worked the mecha's throttle. "Okay. Then let's get cracking!"

Zor and Bowie hovered off and she did the same, heading for the center mound, which up close proved to be somewhat larger than the others. But like them, it had the same atmosphere of enchantment and eerieness lingering about it, the same profusion of shrubs, saplings, and underbrush growing from crevices in its steep sides.

Out of sight the pollinator watched her, and began to head toward the same mound.

She saw nothing that might indicate a way into the mound and considered attempting to power her cycle up the sides for a look at the top; but first decided to circle around the thing once or twice to see what she could find. Just shy of completing the circle she found what she was looking for: something like the mouth of a cave, large, dark and fanged by stalactite-like deposits. She called out for Bowie and Zor to join her, and in moments they were by her side.

They dismounted their cycles and made their way up to the mouth of the opening, scrambling over rocks and through the barbed and tenacious growth that covered the mound's inclined lower base. At the mouth, Bowie bravely stepped in, and stood for a moment in the darkness waiting for his eyes to dark-adapt.

"It looks like it goes all the way in," he told Zor and Dana.

They followed. Even Zor seemed to have misgivings. "Let's be careful," he told Dana. "We don't know *what* we might find in here."

"Now, when have I not been careful?" She laughed, hopping over a rock at the entrance and starting in, passing Bowie by.

It wasn't a natural opening in the side of the mound; it appeared to have been excavated. Dana began to wonder whether looters had worked over the sites during the past fifteen years.

They moved cautiously through the darkness, alert to distant sounds.

"It's like a tomb in here—all this place needs are a few mummies," said Bowie.

"Stop that," Dana told him. "I'm scared enough already."

As they penetrated further, one thing was immediately obvious:

although there were indeed organic deposits growing from the ceiling of the cave (some twenty yards high) and vines and what-not clinging to the walls, the cave was in no way natural—they were actually inside an enormous corridor. Exposed panels and circuitry, rusting structural members and bulkheads confirmed this much.

But there were live things in the corridor as well, as Dana was soon to find out.

Without warning, a group of bats flew straight at them out of the darkness. Dana screamed, launched, and latched herself onto Zor's arm, instantly regretting her show of weakness.

She reached up to find his mouth in the darkness, angrier when she felt a smile there.

Zor laughed and insisted that they keep going.

They moved along the corridor for another fifteen minutes, following it along a gentle arc; then there was light ahead of them—what appeared to be a free-standing monolithic light bar, but was in fact a narrow opening in the wall of the corridor, permitting light to issue forth from somewhere deeper inside the mound.

Zor volunteered to take the point on this one, feeling as though he was indeed approaching something that would lead him to clues of his real origins and past. He seemed to know this place somehow, the feel of these corridors. It was not quite the same as the picture his mind drew of it, but familiar nevertheless. In a strange way, he felt that he knew this place as one would a home.

The opening was just large enough to slip into, but it required that he keep his shoulders pressed flat against the wall. It had to be a ventilation shaft or accessway that was not meant to be walked.

Dana and Bowie stuck close. "Can you see?" Dana asked Zor. "Are we almost at the end?"

"A little more . . ." he told her.

And all at once they were through the breach and inside an enormous chamber. Below them was what seemed to be an excavated pit. Rough staircases had been cut into the dirt and debris that settled into the place when the roof caved in possibly a decade or more ago. Shafts of sunlight poured in through openings in the crust above, along with vines and the off-shoots of trees.

But the pit itself was what struck them: from a viscous-looking organic soup all but bubbling in the bottom of the cauldron, grew an orderly pattern of strange, unearthly green stalks, blossoming with fragrant buds and tripetaled flowers even as they watched. Overhead, light, mist, and bioenergy given off by the plants conspired to form what looked to be an arrangement of power coils.

"This place is unbelievable," said Dana. "It's throbbing with power . . . and those plants . . . What on Earth are they?"

"It's like some kind of greenhouse," Bowie suggested.

The trio made their way down the roughly-hewn staircase until they were standing at the very edge of the cauldron. The plants swayed, as though moved by some wind only they could detect. More, they seemed to be communing with each other, issuing a song that circumvented normal Human hearing. Dana felt compelled to reach out toward one of the flowers, just to stroke the velvety surface of its petals . . .

"No, don't touch that!" Zor yelled.

But it was too late. The flower seemed to meet Dana's hand halfway and attach itself to her. She felt no pain from this, but Zor's yell had startled her so, that she quickly snatched her hand away.

Bowie was aghast. "The plant sensed you, Dana! Did you see it move toward you?"

Zor was now standing transfixed by the scene, mesmerized by the shafts of dazzling light and something that played at the edge of his memory.

"The Triumvirate! . . ." he said suddenly. "Look at these flowers—they grow in threes!—the *three who act as one*! Once again, the same thing I saw in my dream."

Dana tried to coax more from his tortured mind. "Could those things be related somehow?"

"Do you think maybe these plants are what the Masters are trying to get their hands on?" Bowie asked.

Zor shook his head, eyes shut tight. "I don't know . . . But I do know that these flowers aren't what they seem. They're some kind of dreadful mutation, feeding off a source of incredible power. They're definitely a new form of life, unlike any that we've ever seen."

Dana turned to regard the cauldron, the writhing plants, their siren song . . .

"I don't like this at all . . ." she said warily.

Zor concurred. "Neither do I," he told her. "I feel this cavern is full of emanations of great strength. It's as if these plants were calling out . . . making contact with something far away. My past is buried here somehow. But how can I expect anyone to believe this?"

"We'll bring the Supreme Commander here and show it to him—he'll have to believe you then!"

"Oh, terrific!" Bowie exclaimed. "Can you imagine what he'd say to that—'You expect me to believe this balderdash about flowers and strange emanations?' ... *That's* what he'd say! He'd think we're crazy, Dana."

Dana took a deep breath and reached for Zor's hand.

General Emerson and Colonel Rochelle sat silently in the war room. The assault had proved to be a total disaster, to men and mecha alike. Dozens of battlecruisers had been lost, along with an untold number of the A-JACs the supreme command had put so much faith in.

Nova Satori was with the two men; she had volunteered to get some coffee for all of them, and was returning with steaming mugs when ground-base com acknowledged an incoming message from Lieutenant Sterling. Emerson had the techs patch the transmission through to the command balcony, and in a moment Dana's face filled the monitor screen.

"First of all, sir ... I'm fully aware that I disobeyed orders."

"So, what else is new?" Nova muttered behind the general's back.

Dana caught the comment and replied to it. "I'm sorry, Nova, but I have Zor with me and we've just paid a visit to the site of the SDF-1. General, I hope you're not too angry with us."

Depleted of emotion, Emerson simply snorted. Besides, he had interesting news of his own to report—perhaps the only good news that had come from the battle.

"Lieutenant," he began. "We've just received a transmission from Marie Crystal. She was in direct contact with the enemy and her visual evidence seems to bear out that theory of yours regarding the trichotomous pattern of the aliens' behavior."

"I can't take credit for it, sir. It was Zor's idea. Is Marie all right?"

"Our losses were disastrously heavy ... But I've been informed that Lieutenant Crystal is now safely back aboard. She and the entire first assault wave have disengaged and are withdrawing toward the dark side of the moon. However, I regret to say that the attack has been something of a fiasco."

In another part of the UEG headquarters, Leonard was receiving the most recent battle update.

"Supreme Commander," a tech reported from the monitor, "the first assault wave has fallen back in disarray."

"Well then, we'll demonstrate that we have more where that came from," Leonard growled.

"Sir? . . ."

"Mobilize the second assault wave. Order them to rendezvous with the remaining operational units of the first wave and prepare for a combined attack against the enemy."

The tech went wide-eyed with disbelief. "Another frontal assault, Supreme Commander?"

Leonard ran a thick hand across his bullet-shaped skull and nodded gravely.

"And this time, we'll fight to the very last Human life!"

THE FINAL
NIGHTMARE

CHAPTER ONE

Many women were often in the thick of the fighting during the First Robotech War. They served splendidly and gallantly. But they were usually restricted to what the military insisted on calling "non-combat roles," despite the great numbers of them killed as a direct result of enemy action.

By the time of the Second Robotech War, with the Earth's resources depleted and its population drastically reduced by the First, sheer necessity and common sense had overcome the lingering sexism that had kept willing, qualified women off the front lines.

Nevertheless, the Robotech Masters' onslaught quickly had Earth on the ropes. It is instructive to consider what the outcome would have been if the Army of the Southern Cross had faced the planet's second invasion without half its fighting strength.

Fortunately for us all, that is not what happened.

Betty Greer, *Post-Feminism and the Robotech Wars*

LIEUTENANT MARIE CRYSTAL MADE A WILLFUL EFFORT TO face the camera now as she had faced enemy guns yesterday.

She drove back her bone-deep exhaustion, the pain of battle injuries, and the despair of a desperate situation that even the light lunar gravity couldn't alleviate. She intended to finish her report with the clarity and precision expected of a Tactical Armored Space Corps fighter ace and the leader of the TASC's vaunted Black Lions. . . .

And maybe, after that, she could collapse and get a few minutes' sleep. It seemed now that she never wanted anything *but* sleep.

In the wake of the disastrous all-out attempt to destroy the Robotech Masters' invasion fleet, Marie had to shoulder even more responsibility. The chain of command had been shot all to hell along with the Earth strikeforce itself.

Admiral Burke was dead—diced into bloody stew by an exploding power junction housing when the blue Bioroids cut the strikeforce flagship to ribbons. General Lacey, next in line, lay with ninety percent of the skin seared off his body, teetering between life and death.

The senior officer, a staff one-star, was still functional, but he had virtually no combat command experience. The scuttlebutt was that he was being pressured to let somebody else run the show. An implausibly successful Bioroid sortie and the resultant hangar deck explosion on board the now-defunct flagship resulted in Marie being named the new flight group commander.

She went on with her after-action report to Southern Cross military headquarters on Earth.

"Our remaining spacecraft number: one battlecruiser, two destroyer escorts, and one logistical support ship, all of which have suffered heavy damage," she said, looking squarely into the optical pickup. "Along with twenty-three Veritech fighters, twelve A-JACs combat mecha, and assorted small scout and surveillance ships. At last report we have one thousand, one hundred sixteen surviving personnel, eight hundred and fifty-seven of them fit for duty."

Fewer than nine hundred effectives! Jesus! She pulled at the collar ring seal of her combat armor, where it had chafed her neck. She couldn't recall the last time she had been able to strip off the alloy plate and get some real rest. Back on Earth, probably. But that was a lifetime ago.

"As I stated previously, deployment of the enemy mother ships, and their assault craft and Bioroid combat mecha, made it impossible for the strikeforce to return to Earth. Since we were also cut off from L5 Space Station Liberty, and were forced to take refuge here at Moon Base ALUCE, we are making round-the-clock efforts to fortify our position against an enemy counterattack. Major repairs and life-support replenishment are being carried out as well, and civilian personnel have been placed under emergency military authority."

It all sounded so crisp, so can-do, she thought, trying to focus her eyes on her notecards. As if everything were under control, instead of at the thin edge of utter catastrophe. As if the survivors were an effective fighting force instead of a chewed up, burned-out bunch of men and women and machinery. As if the attack hadn't been the most insane strategy, the worst snafu, the most horrifying slaughter she had ever seen.

Recording her stiff-upper-lip report, she felt like a liar, but that was the way Marie Crystal had been taught to do her duty. She wondered if the brass hats at Southern Cross Army HQ back on

Earth would read between the lines—if that pompous, blustering idiot, Supreme Commander Leonard, had any idea how much suffering and death he had caused.

She yanked her mind off that track; feeling murderous toward her superiors would not help now.

"Our medical personnel and volunteers from other strike-force elements are tending to the wounded in the ALUCE medcenter. But facilities are extremely limited here, and I am instructed to request that we be permitted to attempt a special mission to ferry our worst cases back to Earth."

What could she add? There was the natural Human impulse to tell the goddamn lardbutts in their swivel chairs how much hell she had seen. There was the desire to see someone capable, someone like General Emerson, for instance, march in before the United Earth Government council and charge Leonard and his staff with incompetence. There was an inner compulsion to tell how futile it felt, preparing the civilian ALUCE—Advanced Lunar Chemical Engineering—station for a last stand, and getting the VTs and other mecha ready to sortie out again if the need arose.

Forget it; shoot 'n' salute, that was a soldier's duty. Maybe a miracle would happen, and the mysterious aliens who called themselves the Robotech Masters would cut ALUCE and the strikeforce a little slack. If the Humans could just have a few days to get themselves back into some kind of fighting shape, that would change the mix a lot. But Marie had her doubts.

"This completes the situation report. Lieutenant Marie Crystal, reporting for the Commander, out." She saluted smartly, her mouth tugging in a faint, ironic smirk.

The camera tech wrapped it up. "We'll transcribe it and send it out in burst right away, ma'am." She took the cassette of Marie's report.

The Robotech Masters had been having more and more success interfering with the frequency-jumping communications tactics the Humans had been forced to use. To avoid any interference, the report would be sped up to a millisecond squeal of information. Hopefully it would get through.

And when they get it, what then? Marie wondered. *We might be able to sneak one shipload of WIAs back, but for the rest of us there's no way home.*

In the headquarters of the Army of the Southern Cross, Supreme Commander Leonard studied the tape. The smudged and hollow-eyed young female flight lieutenant reeled off facts and figures of bitter defeat with no expression except that last up-curling of one corner of her mouth.

"Mmm" was all he said, as Colonel Rochelle turned off the tape. "We received this transmission from ALUCE eight minutes ago, sir," Rochelle told him. "Nothing else has gotten through the enemy's jamming so far. Looks like they're onto our freq-jumping stunt. The people down in signal/crypto are trying to come up with something new, but so far the occasional odd message is all we can really hope for from Stikeforce Victory."

Leonard nodded slowly, looking at the huge, gray screen. Then he whirled around and threw himself into a seat across the conference table from Major General Rolf Emerson.

"Well, Emerson! How about that!" Leonard pounded his pale, soft, freckled fists the size of pot roasts on the gleaming oak. "It would appear that our little assault operation wasn't a complete failure after all, eh?"

Everyone in the room held their breath. It was a well-known fact that Emerson had opposed the mad strikeforce scheme from the outset, and that there was no love lost between the Supreme Commander and his chief of staff for Terrestrial Defense, Emerson. And everyone had watched Emerson grow grimmer and grimmer as Marie Crystal delivered her casualty report.

Now Emerson looked across the table at Leonard, and more than one staff officer wished they had had time to get a little money down on the fight. Leonard was huge, but a lot of it was pointless bulk; there was some question about how much real muscle was there. Emerson, on the other hand, was a ramrod-straight middleweight with a boxer's physique, and few of the men and women on his staff could keep up with him when it came time for calisthenics or road drill.

Not a complete failure? Emerson was asking himself. *God, what would this man call "failure"?*

But he was a man bound by his oath. A generation before, military officers had violated their oaths. They had served grasping politicians—most tellingly in the now-defunct USA—and that had led to a global civil war. Every woman and man who had sworn to serve the Southern Cross Army knew those stories, and knew that it was their obligation to obey that oath to the letter.

Emerson stared down at his fingers, which were curled around an ancient fountain pen that had been a gift from his ward, Private First Class Bowie Grant. He worried about Bowie only slightly more than he worried about each of the hundreds and thousands of other Southern Cross Army personnel under his command. He worried about the survival of the Human race and that of Earth more than he worried about any individual Human life—even his own.

Emerson gathered up all of his patience, and the perseverance for which he was so famous. "Commander Leonard, the ALUCE base is a mere research outpost, with civilians present. Aside from the fact that by the standards of the Robotech war we're fighting, ALUCE is tinfoil and cardboard! I therefore presume you're not seriously thinking of fortifying it as a military base."

It was as close to insubordination as Emerson had ever permitted himself to go. The silence in the Command Briefing Room was so profound that the roiling of various stomachs could be heard. Through it all, Emerson was locked with Leonard's gaze.

The Supreme Commander spoke deliberately. "Yes, that is my plan. And I see nothing wrong with it!" He seemed to be making it up as he went along. "Mmm. As I see it, a military strikeforce at an outpost on the moon will enable us to hit those alien bastards from two different directions at once!"

A G3 staff light colonel named Rudolph readjusted his glasses and said eagerly, "I see! In that way, we're outflanking those six big mother ships they've got in orbit around Earth!"

Leonard looked pleased. "Yes. Precisely."

Emerson took a deep breath and pushed his chair away from the oak table a little, as though he was about to face a firing squad. But when he came to his feet, there was silence. All eyes turned to him. The general feeling was that no one on Earth was more trusted, more committed to standing by his word, than Rolf Emerson.

No one could be relied upon more to speak the truth into the teeth of deceit.

And this was certainly that moment. "ALUCE is a peaceful, unreinforced cluster of pressurized huts, Commander Leonard. I don't think that anything the strikeforce survivors can do will make it a viable military base. And it's my opinion that by provoking the enemy into attacking it you'll be throwing away lives."

So many staffers inhaled at the same time that Rudolph wondered if the air pressure would drop. Leonard's face flushed with rage. "They've already mauled our first assault wave; it's not a question of provocation anymore. *Damn* it, man! This is war, not an exercise in interstellar diplomacy!"

"But we haven't even *tried* negotiating," Emerson began, a little hopelessly. An over-eager missile battery commander named

Komodo had fired on the Robotech Masters before any real attempt could be made to contact them and learn what it was they wanted. From that moment on, it had been war.

"I'll have no insubordination!" Leonard bellowed. To the rest of the staff he added, "Mobilize the second strikeforce and prepare them to relieve our troops at Moon Base ALUCE!"

Outside the classified-conference room, a figure clad in the uniform of the Southern Cross's Alpha Tactical Armored Corps—the ATACs—moved furtively.

Zor still didn't quite understand the half-perceived urges that had brought him there. It was a familiar feeling, this utter mystification about who he was, and what forces drove him. It was as though he moved in a fog, but he knew that somewhere ahead was the room where all Earth's military plans were being formulated. He must go there, he must listen and watch—but he didn't understand why.

Suddenly there was a bigger figure blocking his way. "Okay, Zor. Suppose you tell me just what the hell you think you're doing here?"

It was Sergeant Angelo Dante, senior NCO of the 15th, fists balled and feet set at about shoulder width, ready for a fight. His size and strength dwarfed Zor's, and Zor was not small. Dante was a career soldier, a man of dark, curling hair and dark brows, not quick to trust anyone, incapable of believing anything good of Zor.

The sergeant grabbed Zor's leather torso harness and gave it a yank, nearly lifting him off his feet. "What about it?"

Zor shook his head slowly, as if coming out of a trance. "Angie! Wh—how did I get here?" He blinked, looking around him.

"That's my line. You're sneakin' around a restricted area and you're away from your duty station without permission. If you don't have a pretty good explanation, I'm gonna see to it your butt goes into Barbwire City for a long time!" He shook Zor again.

"Oh, Zor! There you are!" First Lieutenant Dana Sterling, commanding officer of the 15th, practically squealed it as she rounded a corner and hurried toward them. Angelo shook his head a little, watching how her smile beamed and her eyes crinkled as she caught sight of Zor.

Like her two subordinates, she was dressed in the white Southern Cross uniform, with the black piping and black boots that suggested a riding outfit. She barely reached the middle of Angelo's chest, but she was, he had to admit, a gutsy and capable officer. Except where this Zor guy was concerned.

She rushed up to them and grabbed Zor's hand; Angelo found himself automatically releasing his captive. Dana seemed completely unaware that she had blundered into the middle of what would otherwise have been a fight. "I've been looking for you *everywhere*, Zor!"

Zor, still dazed, seemed to be groping for words. "Just a second, Lieutenant," Angelo interrupted.

But she was tugging Zor away. "Come along; I want to ask you something!"

"Hold it, ma'am!" Angelo burst out. "Why don'tcha ask pretty boy here what he's doing hanging around a restricted area?"

Dana's expression turned to anger. Like the sergeant, she had tracked down Zor with difficulty, but she wouldn't let herself think badly of her strange, alien trooper. She shot back, "What are you, Angie, a spy for the Global Military Police?"

Angelo's black brows went up. "Huh? You know better than that! But somebody has to keep an eye on this guy. Or don't you think what he's doing is a little suspicious?"

Dana rasped, "Zor's suffering from severe memory loss. If he's a little disoriented at times, that just means we should show him a bit of compassion and understanding!"

She slipped an arm through Zor's, clasping his elbow. Angelo wondered if he were going crazy; wasn't this the same alien who had led the enemy forces in his red Bioroid? Didn't he try to kill Dana, as she had tried to kill him, in a half-dozen or so of the most vicious single combats of the war, her Hovertank mecha against his Bioroid?

"I'll speak to you later, Sergeant," Dana said, dragging Zor off.

Angelo watched them go. He had gained a lot of respect for Dana Sterling since she had taken command of the 15th, but she was only eighteen and, in the sergeant's opinion, still too impulsive and too inclined to make rash moves. He tried to suppress his sneaking suspicion as to why she was so protective of Zor—so *possessive*, really.

But one indisputable fact remained. No matter how loyally Angelo tried to discount it, Dana herself was half alien.

CHAPTER TWO

I could never figure out why Leonard, who hated anything alien, would tolerate that wacky experiment where Zor was thrown in with the 15th ATAC—especially since a female halfbreed was CO. One day, I remember, Leonard had been grumbling about putting Zor back into lab isolation and dissecting him.

Ten minutes later the phone rang. Leonard didn't say much in that conversation—it was real brief. And whatever he heard through the earpiece had him sweating. Right after that he dropped the topic for good.

I happened to see the phone logs for the afternoon over at the commo desk a little later. The call had come from Dr. Lazlo Zand, who ran Special Protoculture Observations and Operations Kommandatura. I did my best to forget I'd ever seen that log.

Captain Jed Streiber, as quoted in "Conjuration,"
History of the Robotech Wars, Vol. CXXXIII

HE REVENGE OF THE MARTIAN MYSTERY WOMEN?"
Zor echoed Dana.

"Right!" she said excitedly. "Everybody says it's a dynamite movie. You'll love it! And it won't cost you anything 'cause I've already got the tickets!" She showed him the pair of ducats.

They were sitting in a little park outside the big, imperial-looking building that housed Alpha Tactical Armored Corps HQ. Birds were singing, and a fountain splashed nearby. "As a matter of fact, they're hard to come by, and the scalper charged me *plenty* for these!" She frowned a bit, wondering if she was making a fool of herself.

Zor gave a thin smile. "Well then, how can I refuse, Lieutenant?"

An officer in the 10th squad who had seen the movie last night had said that it was romantic as well as exciting. Dana liked the idea of seeing a movie about alluring, captivating alien women with Zor.

She rushed on, "I don't know *what* I would have done if you hadn't said yes!" Then she stopped, looking perplexed. "Only—now I'm not sure what I ought to wear. . . ."

Zor watched her as she deliberated, certain that no matter what she decided to wear she would look beautiful. He tried to sort out the conflicting emotions and veiled impulses that kept him in a state of confusion much of the time. Zor wondered if these feelings for his lieutenant were what the Human beings called love.

In a geostationary orbit some 23,000 miles above the Earth hung six stupendous mother ships—the invasion fleet of the Robotech Masters.

In the huge flagship, which still bore the scars of battles with the Human race both in space and on the surface of the planet, stood the Triumvirate of Masters. They looked down from the vantage point of their floating Protoculture cap—the enormous, humplike instrument that gave them total control of superhuman mind powers and abilities.

Like virtually all members of their race, the Triumvirate of Masters functioned as a triad, each standing upon a small platform attached to the hovering cap. They were males, with hawklike faces that wore perpetual scowls. The severity of their faces was emphasized by scarlike V's of tissue under each cheek. All of them were bald- or shave-pated; their long, fine hair fell below their shoulders. They wore monkish robes, their wide, floppy collars suggesting the tripartite blossom of the Invid Flower of Life.

The Masters usually mindspoke through direct tactile contact with their Protoculture cap, but they chose now to say their words out loud. Shaizan, who was often the spokesman for the Triumvirate, said, "So, you're saying our Bioroid clones are limited in their effectiveness?"

Looking up at him was a triad of Clonemasters, two males and a female, standing under their own, smaller Protoculture cap. All were tall, pale, and slender. They wore tight-fitting clothes vaguely suggestive of the early Renaissance.

Both males wore full blond-brown mustaches and mutton chops, and one of them had a beard; the androgynous-looking female wore her long blond hair in a simple style. The minor differences between them only served to emphasize their sameness of body and features.

The leader of the Clonemaster triumvirate nodded. "Precisely. Their current cerebral composition makes them undependable. They perform adequately as shock troops, but in order to deal with an Invid attack, we'll need clones much more tightly mindlinked to our triumvirate."

And they all knew that the need to deal with the savage, relentless Invid might come soon. The Flower of Life had bloomed on Earth, and where the Flower bloomed, the Robotech Masters' mortal enemies, the Invid, were bound to appear in short order.

It was all so frustrating to the Masters, even though they didn't reveal any emotion. They had traveled for nearly twenty years—across the galaxy—in search of the last Protoculture Matrix in existence. They were determined to find that source of power that could return them to their rightful place as lords of all creation. And yet, although they were near their prize, they were unable to claim it because of the stubbornness of the primitive Humans below. Unbeknownst to the inhabitants of Earth, the Matrix, sealed under one of three mounds on the outskirts of Monument City, was going to seed.

The Masters' calculations showed that the Protoculture would soon shift from a contained mass, kept in the prefertilized state in which it exuded its incredible and unique forces, and convert into the Flowers of Life that the Invid ingested to sustain themselves.

But the Humans weren't the Masters' only opposition; they weren't the most formidable enemies. The mounds were guarded by invisible Protoculture entities—three strange, mysterious, and sinister wraiths.

The wraiths had manifested themselves once—or rather, they had *permitted* the Masters to perceive them. They were cloaked and cowled fire-eyed specters—ghosts whose power stymied the Masters' efforts to find out *exactly* where the Matrix lay. Without that information, it was impossible for the Masters to use simple brute force to rip the Matrix from the mounds; that would risk damaging the thing they had come so far to retrieve. The Masters weren't sure yet what other powers or designs the wraiths might have.

And now, to complicate matters further, local perturbations were hampering the performance of the Masters' cloned slave populace. "Yes, that might be our problem with Zor Prime," Shaizan was saying. "We've had some trouble with him, almost from the first moment when he was set down among the Humans. His neuro-sensor has been malfunctioning."

Not that Zor Prime, cloned from tissue samples of the slain original Zor, greatest genius of his race and discoverer of Protoculture, hadn't been of some use. Divested of his memories, the clone had been dispatched among the Terrans as an unwitting spy, so that the Masters could see through his eyes and hear through his ears.

The Masters were also hoping that the trauma of being among the local primitives, and being on the planet to which the original Zor had dispatched the Protoculture Matrix so long ago, would spur Zor's memory. Perhaps they could get Zor Prime to tell them why the Matrix had been sent, precisely where it was, and how to get it back from both the Humans and the invisible wraithlike Protoculture entities who guarded the mounds that hid it.

Dag, second among the Masters, had a slightly more prognathous jaw than the others. He said, "It seems the Human behavioral dysfunction known as *emotions* may be responsible for this malfunction."

Bowkaz, third of the Masters, nodded, his brows nearly meeting as his frown deepened. "Yes. These *emotions* destabilize the proper functioning of the healthy brain and the rational mind."

"What is your will then, Masters?" asked Jeddar, leader of the Clonemaster triumvirate—their chief slaves—bowing humbly before them.

"Hmmm," Shaizan said, gazing down on him. "You would like our permission to carry out this plan of yours, no doubt."

The Clonemaster kowtowed. "Yes, my lord. We believe it will be our key to a quick, decisive victory. We only need your approval."

The Masters touched hands to their Protoculture cap. Wherever one of the nailless, spiderlike hands touched a mottled area of the mushroom-shaped cap, the mottled area came alight with the power of Protoculture. The Masters swiftly and silently came to a consensus.

The barracks housing the 15th squad, Alpha Tactical Armored Corps—ATAC—was a truncated cone a dozen stories high, of smoky blue glass and gleaming blue tile (the most modern of polymers) set on a framework of blued alloy. It was a large complex even though it only served as housing and operational facility to a few people; much of the above-ground area was filled with parts and equipment storage and repair areas, armory, kitchen and dining and lavatory space, and so on. In many ways it was a self-contained world.

At the ground and basement levels were the mecha servicing and repair stations, and the motor stables filled with parked Hovercycles and other conventional vehicles, along with the giant Hovertanks—the 15th's primary mecha.

Up in her quarters, Dana wasn't thinking about any kind of machinery just then. Agonizing over what to wear for her date with Zor, she flung every skirt, dress, and blouse in her closet in different directions, draping them with lingerie.

There was, no doubt, something in the regs about officers dating privates, but Zor was a different case. He had been placed with the 15th in the hope that military service would help him recover his missing memory, and that exposure to Earth-style social interaction and bonding would sway him against his former Masters.

When it came to social interaction, Dana was more than ready. It wasn't just that Zor was dreamy looking and a little disoriented. There was also the fact that he was alien, as was Dana's mother. She sometimes wondered if it was blood calling to blood.

Long before she had actually seen him, Dana had felt inexplicable emotions and experienced strange Visions bearing on the red Bioroid Zor piloted. Something within drew her to Zor.

Now, as she hurried into the unit ready-room, which doubled as a rec room during off-duty hours, she tried to set all that aside and concentrate on having a good time.

Decked out in a frilly skirt and silk blouse, she was all set to yell *Hi Zor! I'm here!* Only—it wasn't Zor she found there.

Squad Sergeant Angelo Dante stepped away from the autobar (it was after duty hours, and the cybernetic mixologist would dispense alcohol to troopers who were certified off-duty) and strolled over toward her. "Well, well! Aren't *we* looking awfully chic tonight?"

She tried to act nonchalant; she wanted to enjoy herself with Zor and not start off the evening with another row with Angelo. "Have you seen Zor around?"

In the days before the First Robotech War (after which an almost medieval cluster of the city-states had banded in a loose hegemony to fill the vacuum of world rule and form the United Earth Government—the UEG) soldiers had had less autonomy and more discipline, so the old salts liked to say. If so, she would have welcomed a reversion to those old days.

If she kicked Angelo's feet out from under him and mashed a coffee table over his head, Southern Cross Command might not consider the act a necessary disciplinary measure and it could cause sociodynamic strains. Besides, Angelo was awfully tough.

Dana restrained herself, but resolved to command his loyalty— even if it meant inviting the very big, very strong, and quick NCO to step downstairs to the motor stables and have it out—before another day passed. There was no way *two* people could run a Hovertank squad, or any other unit.

Angelo smiled spitefully. "Yeah. I bet if he had seen you in your prom queen rig, he would have never asked Nova out tonight."

"Nova? Nova Satori?"

Angelo buffed his nails on his torso harness. Dana considered decking him; he was large, but she was used to fighting for everything she had ever gotten, and if she could get in the first shot . . .

"Uh-huh," he said. "Let's see now: something about dinner, and the theater afterwards."

He backed away suddenly as she came at him with clenched fists, ready to spit brimstone and, he could see from the way she held herself, do some damage.

She was raving. "That no-good two-timer! That sneaking *alien*! He's getting more Human every day!"

Angelo was fending her off. "Well now, ma'am, maybe all he needs is a bit of compassion, remember?" That was what she had said to *him*, back when Angelo was about to take Zor's face off.

"You're enjoying this, huh?" she seethed at him. Then she had an image of suitable revenge. She held up the two movie tickets. "Well, I guess *you'll* just have to escort me, big boy!"

Angelo's face fell and he made some odd sounds before he found the words. "Uh, ah, thanks, Lieutenant, but I'll pass—"

"You ain't reading me, Sergeant! It's an order!"

The Clonemasters' update was even more bleak than had been anticipated.

"My lord, our reservoirs of Protoculture power are running dry. The effects of this are being felt throughout the fleet. Our new clonelings are lethargic and unresponsive; the effectiveness of our weapons is limited; and our defensive shields cannot be maintained full-time. If we do not secure a large infusion of Protoculture, we are doomed."

As Jeddar spoke, the humpish Protoculture cap of the Masters showed them, by mind-image, the deteriorating situation in all six of the enormous mother ships. Where the Protoculture energies had once coursed through them like highways of incandescence or arterial systems of pure, god-like force, those flows were now reduced to unsteady rivulets. It was like looking into one huge, dying organism.

* * *

Elsewhere in the colossal flagship, six clones—two triumvirates—faced off, five against one.

On the one side was Musica, ethereal weaver of song, Mistress of the Cosmic Harp, whose melodies gave shape and effect to the mental force with which the Clonemasters controlled their subjects. She was pale and delicate looking, slender, with long, deep green hair.

To one side were her two clone sisters, Octavia and Allegra, both of them subdued and frightened by the very idea of *discord*. And across from Musica was the triumvirate of Guard leaders: tall, fit, limber military males who were now unified in their anger as much as in their plasm.

Lieutenant Karno spoke for them. His long hair was a fiery red; he spoke with uncharacteristic anger, for a slave of the Masters. "Musica, it is not your place to decide how things shall be!"

Another, Darsis, looking like Karno's duplicate, agreed, "It has been decided for us and you have no say in the matter!"

Sookol, the third, added, "That is our way, as it has been since the beginning of time!"

Musica, eyes lowered to the carpeted deck, trembled at the heresy she was committing. And yet she said, "Yes, I know that. We've been chosen for each other as mates, and we must resign ourselves to it. But—that doesn't change the fact that we are strangers, we Muses and you Guards."

Karno's brows knit, as if she were speaking in some language he had never heard before. "But . . . what does that matter?"

Musica gave him a pleading look, then averted her eyes again. "I want so much to accept the Masters' decision and believe that it is right, but something very strange within me keeps saying that the Masters cannot be right if their decision makes me feel this way."

" 'Feel'?" Karno repeated. Could she have contracted some awful plague from the Humans when the primitives from Earth managed to board the flagship for that brief foray?

Darsis and Sookol had gasped, as had Allegra and Octavia. "It's madness!" Sookol burst out.

Musica nodded miserably. "Yes, feelings! Even though we've always been told that we're immune to them, I'm guilty of *emotions*."

Madness, indeed.

She saw the repulsed looks on their faces as they realized she was polluted, debased. But somehow it didn't change her determination not to surrender these new sensations—not to be cleansed of them, even if she could.

"I know I should be punished for it," she declared. "I know I'm guilty! But—*I cannot deny my feelings!*" She broke down into tears.

"What's—what's that you're doing?" Darsis asked, baffled.

"I think I know," Karno answered tonelessly. "It's a sickness of the Earthlings called 'crying.' "

If it was a sickness, Musica knew, there was no question about who had infected her with it. It was Bowie Grant, the handsome young ATAC trooper who she had met when his unit staged a recon on board the flagship.

Instead of a mindless primitive in armor, he had turned out to be a sensitive creature. Bowie was a *musician* and he sat down at her Cosmic Harp and played tunes of his own devising—beautiful, heart-rending compositions that bound her feelings to him. *New* songs—songs that wouldn't be found in the approved songlore of the Masters. He had shown an inexplicable warmth toward her from the very start, and he quickly drew the same from her.

Now Musica found herself sitting at her Harp, playing those same airs, as the other five looked on in shock.

Bowie, do you feel this way about me? How I wish we could be together again!

CHAPTER
THREE

There was never any other child born on Earth from a union of Zentraedi and Human. I made sure of that, with the powers at my command. Because, of course, I immediately knew that Dana was the One; Dana was all that was needed. And the plan went forward.

Dr. Lazlo Zand, notes for *Event Horizon: Perspectives on Dana Sterling and the Second Robotech War*

LIEUTENANT NOVA SATORI TOOK A PRECISE SIP OF WINE, THEN consulted the heavy chronometer on her wrist. "Zero hour."

Across from her, Zor gave her a puzzled look. "Something important?"

Although he was good at fighting, there were still so many things he simply didn't understand. Was he, in the terms of this "date," behind schedule somehow? Was he late in initiating the curious physical interchanges the barracks braggarts always talked about? Was there some accepted procedure for abbreviating the preliminaries? Perhaps he should begin removing garments—but whose?

Nova stared at him. "Well . . . don't tell Dana or anyone else, but the relief force is just lifting off for the moon."

Nova couldn't for the life of her figure out why she was telling him, except that she liked one-upping Dana. She couldn't really put a finger on why she had come along with him to the restaurant either, except that she felt drawn to him—almost against her will.

When Zor was first captured, Nova was responsible for his interrogation. She had felt that he was an enemy then and was suspicious that that still might be the case. But there was something *singularly* attractive about him. He had an agelessness about him even though he looked young, a serenity even though he was tormented by his missing memory, as though he were a part of her. It was as if he, as the expression went, had a very *old soul*.

Zor was thinking along quite different lines. Nova's mention of Dana reminded him that he was supposed to have gone to the movie with her. It had completely slipped his mind; he wondered if bit by bit he was losing all memory functions.

Some curiosity—more of a compulsion, actually—had made him ask Nova to dinner. He hoped that she could tell him more about himself; he might even be able to recover a part of his lost self. But there was more to it than that, motivations Zor Prime couldn't fathom.

He studied Nova, an attractive young woman with a mantle of blue-black hair so long that she had to sweep it aside when she sat down. Like Dana, she wore a techno-hairband that suggested a headphone. Her face was heart-shaped, her eyes dark and intense, lips mobile, bright, expressive.

"Earth calling Zor." She chuckled, breaking his reverie.

"Eh?"

"Promise not to mention it, I said. Dana's got an awful temper; she's going to split a seam when her precious 15th squad gets left out of another major operation!"

"Don't worry. I won't tell her."

Nova shrugged to indicate that it really wouldn't be *so* bad if Dana found out from him and learned that he had found out from Nova.

She said, "No one's supposed to know the relief force is on its way until tomorrow. I really shouldn't have told *you* about it."

The vague compulsions in Zor suddenly coalesced, and he found himself asking, "How many ships are going? How are they planning to get past the enemy?"

It would all be revealed tomorrow anyway, and Nova's tongue had been loosened by the wine with which Zor had been plying her. "Well, I heard that—"

"So! there you are!" Dana howled, rushing toward the table. The pianist stopped playing and silverware was dropped by startled diners.

Angelo Dante followed, embarrassed. *The Revenge of the Martian Mystery Women* had been a debacle, animated camp moron-fodder instead of the sizzling interplanetary romance-comedy-adventure Dana was under the impression they would be seeing. Apparently the officer who had told Dana about it was jazzing her. Angelo had laughed so maniacally that she had slugged his arm and dragged him out of the theater. Then she set out on a mission of revenge.

Now, she set her fists on her hips and glared daggers at Zor. "Just who the hell d'you think you are, you double-dealing dirtbag, standing me up so you can take out something like *her*?"

Zor looked very confused and almost queasy. Nova said, "I don't think I like the sound of that last part."

"You're not *supposed* to, you tramp! It was an *insult*!"

Angelo managed to intervene just as Nova was about to vault across the table for a go at Dana, who was waiting to clean Nova's plow before going on to put Zor in traction.

"Now calm down, ladies!" He looked to Zor for assistance; the maître d' was already headed their way. "Hey, Zor, you just gonna sit there like a vegetable or what?"

Zor tried to put his thoughts in order. He couldn't remember why it had been so important to get Nova to tell him those secrets about the relief expedition. Now that Dana had interrupted everything, he could barely recall the impulse that had made him ignore his date with Dana.

"I—I'm so sorry." He got to his feet unsteadily. "I don't feel well. . . ." He lurched from his place, and headed for the door.

"Damn chicken! Come back and die like a man!" Angelo fumed, for he felt that he was about to meet his own fate.

Outside, Zor stopped to catch his breath, leaning on a railing overlooking a garden near the restaurant's entrance. He heard Nova's voice in his head again, "The relief force is just lifting off for the moon."

But then there was another voice, a cold one, speaking directly to his mind. It filled him with terror and hate, and he saw an image of an ax-keen, angry face set against a collar that looked like the Invid Flower of Life.

It said, *Message received and understood.*

At Fokker Aerospace Field, on the outskirts of Monument City, the last units of the emergency relief force were lifting off. The larger warships were being helped aloft by the brute power of a dozen flying tugs. The tugs released their cables as the warcraft climbed above Earth's gravitational grip.

They formed up, making their way out beyond the atmosphere, moving at flank speed, maintaining communications silence. Their ascent was masked by the bulk of the Earth for the time being. Since the Robotech Masters couldn't maintain geostationary position over Monument City and still guard access to Luna, the expedition would have an element of surprise.

To someone of an earlier day, the giant battlecruisers would have resembled prenuclear submarines, complete with conning towers, and bulky thruster packages attached to their sterns. Their estimated time of rendezvous with the units from ALUCE station, barring trouble, was in just under six hours.

At Moon Base ALUCE, Marie Crystal began organizing things for the evacuation, with brave words to the wounded about how they would be on Earth by the next morning.

Home, she thought, and thought, too, of a certain deuce private—formerly a First Lieutenant—in the 15th squad, ATAC. *Sean, Sean! To be with you again!*

Jeddar, group leader of the Clonemasters, glared at Musica sternly. "What exactly is the meaning of this behavior?"

"Do you realize that you're jeopardizing the very existence of our people?" added bearded Ixtal, the other male in the Clonemaster triumvirate.

Tinsta, the tall, androgynous female, commanded not unkindly, "Child, explain yourself."

Allegra and Octavia watched the scene, not daring to say a word. They had already concluded that they would never be able to comprehend Musica's new, aberrant behavior. They were frightened to death of being contaminated or punished for what their triad-sibling was doing. Off to one side, Karno and the other Guard clones looked on.

Musica sounded as if she was ready to weep again, something with which Allegra and Octavia were becoming uncomfortably familiar. "I'm sorry! I wish I could explain! I don't *mean* to be disobedient, really I don't!"

"Your mate has been selected, Musica," Tinsta said. "And he is Lieutenant Karno. You will submit to this decision."

"The survival of your own people requires it." Jeddar pressured her.

She shook her head, her long, deep-green hair swinging around her face, moaning, "No . . . no . . ."

"Yes!" Jeddar shot back. "Disobedience cannot be tolerated!"

Musica, moaning, seemed to undergo some sort of seizure. Then she slumped to the deck. Her sisters rushed to kneel by her. The Clonemaster triumvirate gaped; finally Jeddar found words. "This is far worse than I had imagined."

"Has she ceased to live?" Lieutenant Karno asked numbly.

Jeddar replied, "She has fallen into what the Humans call a 'faint.' " A cold current rippled through him. Until this moment, he had been *sure* that his Robotech Masters ultimately would be victorious. But as Musica now knew emotions, so did Jeddar begin to know the meaning of doubt.

Everything was on schedule, and the relief force was expecting rendezvous with Marie's contingent, when the chilling news came.

"Enemy ships spotted at mark seven niner, closing on us fast!"

General quarters sounded, armor-shod feet pounding the deck as men and women rushed to battle stations. Cannon and missile tubes were run forth from their turrets as the rust-red, whiskbroom-shaped assault ships of the Robotech Masters plunged at the relief force.

Fast-moving and mounting formidable firepower, the assault ships dodged the Terrans' shot patterns and began scoring hits almost immediately. Hulls were penetrated by fusion-hot lances of energy; there were explosions and explosive decompression in the breeched warcraft. Southern Cross soldiers died in flames, in whirlwinds of shrapnel, and in vacuum.

Battlecruiser number three, the *Austerlitz*, disappeared in a furious fireball. Other vessels were taking heavy damage. The Terrans had been taken by surprise, and no one could answer the question, *How could this have happened? How could they have been waiting for us, as if they knew we were coming?*

But the Humans struggled to throw up a screen of AA fire, bring damage under control, and simultaneously launch mecha of their own. In moments the A-JACs, rotors folded for space combat, howled forth from the battlecruisers to engage in battle.

As soon as the A-JACs began their counterattack, the hatches opened in the sides of the assault ships, and enormous Bioroids rode forth to give battle on circular antigrav Hovercraft. The Bioroids deployed for the fight, looking like vaguely human-shaped walking battleships. They swarmed angrily, outnumbering the Human mecha.

"Air Cavalry One to Lieutenant Crystal," the call came over the command net. "I'm breaking radio silence to request immediate assistance. We are under heavy attack and request immediate assistance."

Marie, on the bridge of the destroyer escort *Mohi Heath*, saw the worried look on the face of Lieutenant Lucas, the Aircav commander. She opened her headset mike to transmit. "Roger, Aircav One; we're on our way."

The ships of the patchwork evacuation force went to maximum speed. Marie threw the headset aside and ran for her own A-JAC, and the rest of her TASC outfit, the Black Lions, hot-scrambled.

The Bioroids were enjoying good hunting.

The relief expedition was short on mecha, since so many had been committed to the first strikeforce and many more had to remain behind to guard Earth. So, the enemy assault ships stayed back and let the clone-operated Bioroids ride their Hovercraft, and slaughter the enemy.

The relief force A-JACs and others fought valiantly, but the sheer unevenness in numbers became apparent at once. Bioroids blazed away with the weapons mounted in the control stems and platform bows of their Hovercraft, and with the disc-shaped handguns that were as big as fieldpieces. A-JACs blazed into explosive death one after another.

Lieutenant Lucas, his unit half gone, was calling to ask permission for a hasty withdrawal; there was no point in throwing away Earth's valuable mecha. Then, suddenly, there was a blue Bioroid on his tail, the gun in its control stem spewing annihilation discs. Lucas only had a split second to wonder who would take over (his exec being dead already) and to hope that the strikeforce somehow would survive.

But then the Bioroid disappeared in a flaming ball of gas, and a strange A-JAC bearing a rampant black lion came zooming past. "Crystal, this is Lucas! Crystal, is that you?"

"Looks like this time the settlers have come to rescue the cavalry," she said. She added to her own outfit, "Okay, boys; let's wrassle 'em around some."

But that was already happening. Marie Crystal's Black Lions had come in on the enemy's rear flank, undetected, and hurled themselves into the furious dogfight. They had already changed the odds; within seconds they were turning the kill ratios around. Before fifteen seconds passed, eight surprised Bioroids had been shot to fragments or utterly destroyed.

But the enemy seemed determined to stand its ground, as it were, and fight. The Lions, having been mauled so badly on their first assault only days before, were more than willing to oblige.

Dogfight? Rat race? *Oh, yes!* Marie thought. *Now you pay! And if somebody asks who your accountants are, you just say, "the Black Lions"!*

The engagement got even hotter. Marie did a classic "Fokker Feint," flamed a blue, then raised Aircav One again. "Lieutenant Lucas! Now's your chance! Head for ALUCE base!"

It was too sensible a suggestion for Lucas to argue with; the units still on the moon would need the relief force, and Marie's pilots were keeping the enemy busy. Lucas disengaged his A-JACs even as the relief warcraft made their way past the distracted Bioroids to recover Aircav One and its birds on the fly. He headed for ALUCE at top speed.

Some of the enemy tried to give chase, and Marie led several of her A-JACs to stop them. She decided to change the mix a bit, and went to Battloid mode. Other A-JACs followed suit, screaming after the enemy with back and foot thrusters blaring.

The A-JACs launched missiles, and three more Bioroids got waxed. The rest broke off their chase, to turn on their tormentors. Aircav One and the rest of the relief force were already disappearing for their rendezvous with Luna.

The Black Lions hit the Bioroids with everything they had, driving them back, until Marie judged that the evacuation force had enough of a head start. With the enemy ranks drastically thinned out and their attack broken, the A-JACs got in a final barrage that blew one of the invader assault ships to atoms. As before, destruction of their field-command nerve center confused and demoralized the Bioroids; the A-JACs took advantage of that to break contact and return to their convoy at max thrust.

Soon Earth loomed huge and blue-white before them.

CHAPTER
FOUR

Very well; I can't stop you. Take the Protoculture from me! Seal my fate, and seal your own as well!

The original Zor to the Lords of Tirol

THE ROBOTECH MASTERS' ANGER WAS NOT ASSUAGED BY their warriors' excuse that Zor Prime had mentioned nothing of a second force coming from Luna to catch the Bioroids in a pincer. If the Masters were not so short of functioning servants, many clones, both in the command structure and in the ranks, would have been deactivated and sent to reclamation.

The Clonemasters cut short the reports and turned to one another, as they waited fearfully. "Well then," Dag said to the Clonemaster group leader, Jeddar, "I presume that is all the evidence we need. We know we can no longer depend on Zor Prime's transmissions."

Jeddar bowed. "That is correct, Master. He has been overexposed to the emotional contagions of Humanity. But there is a matter of more immediate concern."

"And that is?" Bowkaz demanded, looking down at him.

"Taking Musica as an example," Jeddar responded, "we are seeing an upsurge in emotionality and counterproductive behavior similar to what we now know happened to the Zentraedi giants when *they* tried to recover the Protoculture Matrix."

Shaizan declared to the other Masters, "It seems to me that the time has come to begin all-out production of our Invid Fighters."

The Masters' Invid Fighters were different from the mecha of the same designation once used by the Zentraedi giants. But like the Zentraedi's, the Masters' Invid Fighters—more commonly referred to as the Triumviroid—were the most powerful mecha in the Masters' inventory. The clone/fighting machine system had been developed rather recently—by their stagnated standards—and incorporated certain characteristics of the savage Invid with whom the Masters had fought a long and unrelenting war.

The reason there were not more Triumviroids in the Masters' forces was because their production was so costly. But the Masters now faced the choice of either losing the war or launching a crash program to create a fighting force of Invid Fighters—even if it meant cannibalizing their conventional blues, combat vessels, and their own instrumentality.

The Robotech Masters were also constantly aware that their *own* masters, the Triumvirate of the Elders, waited far across the dark lightyears, expecting results. Nearly all of Tirol's remaining resources had been thrown into this expedition to obtain the last Matrix; the Elders, who were left in the shambles of their empire with a mere handful of clones, expected results—and were impatient.

The decision didn't take the Masters long; they lusted for the power of the Protoculture Matrix more than any vampire ever thirsted for lifeblood. They desired immortality and feared death with a terror greater than any short-lived Human or clone could ever imagine.

The Robotech Masters turned to their slaves and nodded as one.

Supreme Commander Leonard let Marie make her brief report. Leonard was more pleased with the battle as a propaganda victory and a bolster to his influence with the UEG council than he was with it as a military success. But he was pleased with that aspect of it, too—his loathing of aliens bordered on the psychotic.

After she was dismissed, Marie stepped back into the corridor only to discover Dana, Angelo Dante, and Sean Phillips coming toward her.

Marie was still dressed in smudged battle armor, dirty and weary, but she didn't let that stop her from crying out his name and running toward him, as he hurried to embrace her. "Oh, Sean, *Sean,* you came!"

He was the same as she had pictured him a thousand times since leaving Earth, the smiling, roguish ladykiller of the 15th. Sean had been its commanding officer not too long ago, with Dana his untried executive officer fresh out of the Academy. But a certain scandal concerning a colonel's daughter had gotten Sean busted to deuce private in the Hovertank outfit he had formerly commanded.

The romance started when he saved her life during a firefight. Marie had been very wary of his advances at first, refusing to be one more notch on his bedpost. They had fought like alley cats. But in time she had come to believe his declarations of love, and let herself admit that although she had never been in love before, she was now.

"Darlin', I thought maybe we'd lost you," he grinned, to hide all the worrying he had been doing. Sean was used to being the reckless swashbuckler, going into danger while a woman kept the light in the window, not vice versa.

Then he held her at arm's length again, and saw her eyes brimming. "Marie, what's wrong?"

She didn't let herself surrender to tears. But after the long, exhausting mission, the death and the killing, shouldering all burdens and enduring sleeplessness while sustaining the morale of all around her, she laid her head against his chest and let her breath go, running her fingers through his hair. "Oh, Sean, I—I wasn't sure you really ... *really* cared—"

He hugged her and rubbed her alloy-clad back, while the others cleared their throats and turned to look at something else, anything else. Then he held her face in his hands to gaze into her eyes. "It's you and me, Marie Crystal. From now on. Always."

In the conference room, Supreme Commander Leonard turned to his subordinates.

"The relief force has the materials and know-how to turn ALUCE into a strategic military base. With it, we will be able to attack the enemy on two fronts."

But Leonard knew he couldn't afford to fight a two-front war, one against those obscene alien invaders and one against the damned meddling council. However, he had come up with what he considered a brilliant strategy for solidifying his place as Supreme Commander: eliminate the one man who could conceivably be tapped to replace him, and whose military genius threatened to eclipse his.

He turned to Major General Emerson with a fulsome smile. "And Rolf, I have a great little surprise for you."

Emerson, already three steps ahead of Leonard, resigned himself. *He's got my range and coordinates this time.*

* * *

The 15th was on stand-down, relaxing in the ready-room, when Louie Nichols charged in with his news.

Bowie Grant sat at the piano, playing sadly and brooding over Musica, as he had since he first met her. He had thought of and discarded a hundred plans for getting back to her somehow, for being with her, for finding some kind of life together with the Mistress of the Cosmic Harp. She had enthralled him—magicked an enchanted ring round his heart, so that he could think of nothing and no one else. If he had taught her what love was, she was also teaching him, even—*especially*—in their separation.

Louie Nichols burst in, babbling and running around in such a lather that Dana, Angelo, and the rest thought they were going to have to kneel on his chest to get him to spill out what he knew. It sounded as if he was about to begin blubbering, but it was hard to tell with Louie because he always wore big, square, tinted tech goggles, day and night.

"Well," he managed at last, "they've appointed a new commander to take charge of ALUCE and open the second front."

Sean stared at him. "Yeah, so? Who is it?"

Louie worked himself up to answer. "Leonard's sending General Emerson!"

Bowie had been playing softly. Now he brought his fingers down hard in discord. The Robotech Masters seemed to have some kind of pipeline into Southern Cross plans, and everyone knew how high the casualties would probably run at ALUCE.

Emerson was supervising the organization of a new expedition to ALUCE. With the original reinforcing group fortifying the lunar base, it was time to get more personnel, combat units, and equipment up there, to expand preparations for the second front.

He heard a scuffle behind him, and his name being called. He turned from his contemplation of the intense activity all across Fokker Base, the readying of the strikeforce he now commanded. His adjutant, Lieutenant Colonel Rochelle, was struggling to hold back Lieutenant Dennis Brown, a TASC Veritech pilot who had once served as aide to Emerson.

"Brown, we've heard enough out of you!" Rochelle was yelling.

Brown thrashed, trying to break loose. "But it's a suicide mission, General Emerson! They're trying to get rid of you!"

"As you were!" Emerson hollered, and Brown and Rochelle subsided. Emerson went on, "It's not for me to second-guess my orders, Lieutenant, nor is it for you. We give orders and see that they're obeyed; we obey the orders that are given us. We see to it that we don't violate the oath we've sworn, not for any personal loyalty or preference. There's no other way an army can function. Thank you for your concern, but if you don't return to your post at once, I'll have no choice but to have you placed under arrest."

Rochelle and Brown had released one another. The lieutenant saluted. "Yes, sir."

"One more thing," Emerson snapped. "No operation under *my* command has ever been or will ever be a suicide mission. I'd have thought you knew me better than that. Dismissed."

Dana found that Bowie simply refused to talk about his godfather being posted to ALUCE. Bowie seemed determined to have the world think he cared nothing about General Emerson.

It was Emerson who had insisted Bowie serve time in the Southern Cross Army, as Bowie's parents had wished it, Emerson claiming that it had nothing to do with personal feelings or his affection for Bowie. Now it was Bowie's chance to hide behind a soldier's code, and the rest of it, to shield his sorrow. Dana, with little choice, let it be so.

At the Global Military Police headquarters, a round-the-clock screening program consumed everyone's time, especially Nova's. The high command was determined to plug the leak in its system. Endless computer reviews and field reports were the order of the day. Anyone who had access to classified information and particularly those who had access to long-range communications gear were being scrutinized.

After all, how else could an espionage agent get the word across tens of thousands of miles of empty space?

Zor got off the shuttle bus across the street from GMP headquarters only to find Angelo Dante standing next to a jeep, waiting for him.

"I keep asking myself, 'Now, why's ole Zor-O so eager to see Nova?' " Angelo said, blocking his way. "And what d'you think crossed my mind? Why, Nova's with GMP! Maybe that's why you're bringing her a present, hey?"

Angelo reached to grab the object Zor had tucked under one arm. It turned out to be a classified looseleaf binder whose title sent Angelo's eyebrows high. *"An Intelligence Overview on the ALUCE Base?"*

Angelo grabbed Zor's torso harness again, just as he heard a

Hovercycle flare to a stop at curbside behind him. He heard Dana yell, "Sergeant Dante! Let him go!".

Angelo did, as she stalked over to him. "Now hold on a minute, Lieutenant—"

She yanked the binder out of his hands. "You *will* stop harassing this trooper, Sergeant! Grow up and quit playing GMP spy! Now, get lost!"

Angelo's face was a purple-red. He cared passionately about his world and its people and their survival, of course, and his duty. But there was more to it than that.

Why should I care if this guy uses Dana and wrecks her life? It's her own fault and she's just a snotty, pushy teenage know-it-all anyway! Okay, so she's proved she's got what it takes to lead the 15th, but why should I care if she gets what she's got comin' for getting this weird crush on Zor-O?

He thought all that looking down into the pug-nosed, freckled face and regretted making such a jackass of himself at the movie. Without warning, he found himself wondering what it would feel like to hold her tenderly, the way Sean had embraced Marie Crystal the other day. Then Angelo Dante violently suppressed the thought.

"Yes, ma'am," he said through clenched teeth. He saluted, about-faced and marched to the jeep. Tires chirped as he accelerated away from the curb.

Dana handed the binder back to Zor without even looking at the cover. "Here. Sorry about that, but Angie's such a—"

"Thank you." Zor took the classified book, turned and went up the steps toward the main entrance, barely having registered her presence.

"Hey!" She started after him, but just then a hand closed around her elbow.

If she had been only a little hotter under her high military collar, she would have turned around swinging. But she reconnoitered first, and saw who it was. "Captain Komodo!" she said in bewilderment. "What's the matter, sir?"

Komodo was a man of about five-ten, with a powerful build, of Nisei descent. Just now, he was sweating and a little wild-eyed. "Lieutenant, I need a favor!"

Most people in the Southern Cross knew who Komodo was. After the Robotech Masters' first attack on Moon Base One, Komodo had violated Emerson's ironclad wait-and-see orders to launch missiles at them, ending Emerson's hopes for negotiations.

Emerson had wanted him court-martialed for firing the goading shot in a war nobody wanted, but Leonard, ever the alien-hater, had had Komodo decorated for prompt and brave use of personal initiative, and transferred to fire control on a battlecruiser. Still, the word on the scuttlebutt grid was that Komodo regretted what he had done and he had made mention of his wish to redeem himself.

Now Dana let herself be pulled off to one side by the captain, not sure how anything fit together with anything else anymore.

In a small park near GMP headquarters, Komodo finished, "So I thought you could help me, Lieutenant."

Dana looked him over carefully. "And Nova's the one for you, huh?" According to the captain's story, he had only talked to her a few times, and always in the line of duty. *But when did love ever let reality stand in its way?* she sighed to herself.

Captain Komodo chuckled self-consciously. "I'm assigned to go with General Emerson to ALUCE," he explained.

"And you figure you might not make it back, so you want her to at least know you exist before you go?" Dana said with a blunt, uncharacteristic *need* to hear his answer.

She paced a few steps up and back while Komodo gave a sighing laugh and admitted, "I suppose she could never want *me*."

"Let's have no defeatist talk, Captain!" Dana responded.

Maybe Komodo could serve as a distraction and pry Nova and Zor apart—and maybe not. Still, it was the only card she had to play, short of letting Angelo—who seemed to despise the alien for reasons she couldn't understand—put Zor in Intensive Care.

She took Komodo's arm. "You can't give up the ship before you've fired your first salvo, Captain." They both laughed, walking back toward the GMP HQ.

They left the trees just in time to see Sean Phillips go racing by at the wheel of a jeep, at breakneck speed. He was roaring with laughter, and Marie Crystal, in the ninety-percent seat, was laughing, too, one arm around his shoulders. He turned a corner on two wheels.

"There's living proof, Captain," Dana said, frowning. "If *that* sorry sack can win a female heart, *anybody* can." Her words didn't seem to fortify Komodo.

The appalling workload at GMP and the presence of Colonel Fredericks, her CO, had kept Nova from seeing Zor when he showed up to return the ALUCE documents. So, Zor had left the binder for her, wrapped in plain paper, and she had claimed it when at last she knocked off for a few hours' sleep.

Somehow, she couldn't see what she was doing as compromising Southern Cross secrets. She did not even *think* of Zor as a security risk. She could only think of those huge, oblique, elfin eyes, the face like a classical sculpture's, the tumbling lavender locks of hair that fell past his shoulders, the hypnotic fascination he held for her.

At the door of her billet in the Bachelor Officers' Quarters, she found a lush bouquet of pink, black, and red roses, wrapped in silver-and-black striped metallic paper. The sight of them took all her fatigue away.

Nova Satori pulled them close to her body, inhaled them, and carried them into her billet. That scent—she drew it in deeply and wished she could lose herself in it, could live in the Heart of the Rose forever. To be with Zor, somehow, someday, seemed so hopeless.

I thought love was supposed to make you happy?

In the dimness of a bend in the hallway, Dana patted the sweating Komodo's shoulder, as they watched Nova's door close from their concealment.

"That completes the first part of the operation, Captain: the softening-up process!"

Inside her rooms, Nova set down the ALUCE binder and the roses side by side. There was a note in the flowers, printed in block letters: FROM AN ADMIRER.

She held up the other note she had gotten that day, the one Zor had tucked into the ALUCE book. *I can't begin to thank you, Nova. Every bit of information you give me restores more of my memory, more of me.*

Then she realized all at once that she had violated the regulations she was sworn to enforce. *What have I done?*

So the screwball contredanse continued. Dana tried to convince Komodo that his flowers were the cause of the lovesickness he saw on Nova's glum face. Meanwhile, Nova determinedly snubbed Zor and resisted his every effort to get in touch—yet she felt dangerously drawn to him.

It had Nova so distracted that she screwed up, and flagged a VT pilot named Dennis Brown—a former aide to Emerson's, yet!—who had been scheduled to go to ALUCE and was now held back as a security risk.

She hunted the lieutenant down out on the flight line to apologize. He merely shrugged it off. He looked her over for a few moments and decided she could be trusted to hear the truth.

"Maybe it's all for the good. You have the computers and you aren't blind, Nova. Leonard's weeding out all the officers who aren't loyal to him personally, like some Roman emperor sending all his rivals off to distant provinces. Thanks to you, though, at least one of us'll be here to keep an eye on things: me."

He really *was* thanking her! Nova summoned up a grateful smile and resolved to bury Brown's name and file where few in the GMP would ever notice it.

At the far end of the flight line Dana, watching from behind a shuttle's huge tire, whistled. "Man, that Nova knows how to play the field!" Captain Komodo fought off an attack of terminal disheartenment.

CHAPTER FIVE

*SPECIAL PROTOCULTURE OBSERVATIONS AND OPERATIONS KOMMANDATURA
(DESIGNATION—"JAMES" PERSONNEL ONLY)*
*In view of the adverse relationship between Major General Emerson
and certain members of this unit, the transfer of the Singularity
Effect—generating equipment to his flagship will be effected in such a
way as to preclude all mention of or reference to the origins of the
aforementioned equipment.*

(signed) Zand, Commanding

THE 15TH'S READY-ROOM WAS DARK. MOST OF THE TROOPERS were out on pass or on ATAC guard duty or dozing. A few, like Robotechnofreak—another term for it was "mechie"—Louie Nichols, were taking care of maintenance or tinkering with their Hovertanks down on the motorstable levels.

Bowie Grant sat playing the piano softly. Sometimes he went into the melodies he had played for Musica, and the ones she had played for him. But tonight he kept coming back again and again to the ones Emerson had taught him as a child, when the General introduced him to the piano and fostered Bowie's love of music. Bowie played his own compositions, the early ones that had made Emerson so proud. There was no one in the dimness of the ready-room to hear the music, or to see his tears.

Below, though, in a long, black military limousine parked under the open windows of the ready-room, there was an audience.

Major General Rolf Emerson sat in the back seat with the window down, listening. He didn't recognize the alien tunes, though he suspected what they meant; he knew each note that Bowie played from their shared past, however, and understood those completely.

Emerson's efforts to contact his ward had been rebuffed, and the general respected Bowie's right to be left alone.

Perhaps I never should have made him enlist; perhaps he

shouldn't have had to serve, Emerson reflected. *But then, it would be a better Universe if none of us had to. But it's just not that kind of Universe.*

"That's enough. Take me back," he told his chauffeur, hitting the button that raised the window.

Take me back . . .

This time it was a *cascade* of roses, tumbling down onto Nova in a fragrant red avalanche the moment she opened the closet in her billet to hang up her cloak. Suddenly she wasn't bone-tired anymore, not even with the liftoff of Emerson's strikeforce less than forty-eight hours away.

She let the roses shower around her, giggling and gasping, and tried forlornly to understand all the conflicting emotions and impulses that were starting her own private war. She was knee-deep in flowers.

There was a note taped to the shelf: *Depot 7 at 2100.*

At the elegant Pavilion du Lac, Marie Crystal pushed away her fourth sidecar. *If Prince Charming doesn't get here with the carriage soon, Cinderella's gonna be too stinko to care!*

Might even serve him right, she thought. She had blown half her savings on a drop-dead white satin evening gown, and the most expensive perfume she could find. Her walk was very different than it was when she was in uniform; she had seen men panting, admiring. And rather than cut a swath through the local male wildlife, here she sat, waiting for her Romeo.

She went out onto the balcony to get a little fresh air, sighing in the moonlight, thinking of Sean, smelling the orchids there.

She had been shot out of the sky and he had mechamorphosed his Hovertank, risen up in Battloid mode to catch her burning, falling Veritech. He had sworn he would love her, and no one else, evermore. Had held her to him as his Battloid had held her VT to it. Had made her love him.

You beast! You toad! I've never been in love before . . .

Below, hiding behind a column on the portico, Sean grinned and got ready to go surprise her.

Marie had shown up early for their dinner date, and she had decided to see how long it would take her to lose patience. It hadn't taken long; he was barely late at all. *But I've kept her waiting long enough,* he thought guiltily, and got ready to run up the steps to her.

A voice behind him called, *"Seanie?"*

It was Jill Norton, an old flame, all decked out like a green-sequined sea goddess, throwing herself at him to hug him. "It *is* you!"

She locked her lips to his, and he had to wrestle her in order to crane his head around and look up at the balcony. Marie was giving him the kind of stare that preceded homicides.

Just like Cinderella, Marie lost a glass slipper on the winding stairs. In fact, she lost both of them. She pushed her way in between Sean and his latest trollop, about to leave, but spun around suddenly and grabbed him by the front of his suit.

Before he could move, she kissed him as hard as she could—she put all her love and all her wanting and all her hurt into it. Sean was starting to think he might survive the encounter when she pushed him away and rocked him with a slap that almost took his head off.

In the poorly lit corner of Depot 7, Dana practically had to put an arm-bar on Komodo to get him to show himself and approach Nova. As he walked over, he kept turning around to make sure Dana was still in the shadows for moral support.

However, his worst fears came true when he turned to Nova and got a backhanded fist, knuckles cocked, that sent him whirling onto the cold duracrete facedown.

"Stay away from me, Zor!" she shrilled. "You hear me, Zor?" But inside, she feared that she might really have hurt him.

Komodo pushed himself up partway. "Lieutenant Satori, I hear you." He wiped blood from his mouth.

"Oh my god! Captain Komodo!"

He levered himself up. "Zor, eh? Now I get it!" He lurched off into the blackness, sobbing, running nearly doubled over, as if she had given him some eviscerating wound.

She looked around and saw Dana standing, a small pale figure, under a nearby worklight. "I might've guessed, Sterling. Now do I have to part that little blond puffball hairdo with a loading hook, or are you going to tell me—"

She was interrupted by her own wrist comset. The only way she had been able to get some time to herself for the depot rendezvous had been to sign out for a purported tour of the GMP patrols, to check up. So she was on duty.

"Lieutenant Satori, we have a report of an individual, thought to be a woman, driving very erratically and recklessly in a military jeep."

Nova was on her Hovercycle and away before Dana could get

a word in edgewise. Dana went and vaulted into the getaway jeep that was waiting, Lieutenant Brown behind the wheel. Dana knew Brown from his brief instructor days at the Academy, and Brown was an old close friend of Komodo's.

Accosted by Komodo, Brown had explained why Nova had come to see him: not a matter of passion, but rather of apology. Then, he joined in on the plot to get Komodo and Nova together, and volunteered to act as chauffeur.

"Go!" Dana howled, pointing at Nova's disappearing Hovercycle as it vanished through the loading bay doors.

"Don't turn on the light, Zand. Just sit down."

Rolf Emerson's voice was soft in the darkness of the office in Southern Cross HQ, but it still filled Zand with fear. How had he gotten in? Not only were there guards and surveillance equipment, but Zand himself had hidden powers that should have prevented any such unpleasant surprise.

And yet, there stood the Chief of Staff for Terrestrial Defense, in the glow spilling into the darkened office from streetlights and moonlight. "I won't stay long," Emerson added. "Just close the door, sit down, and listen."

Zand did, leaving his office dark. He thought about sounding an alarm; Emerson certainly outranked him, but this kind of unauthorized visit was nothing that even a general's stars would justify. However, there were old animosities between the two, nothing Zand would like to have brought to light. And so he sat, waiting.

"I'm leaving in the morning; you already know that, no doubt," Emerson said, sounding tired. "I just wanted to say this—"

Suddenly he was at Zand's side, his strong hand around Zand's throat. Emerson shook him like a rag doll as the Robotech scientist made strangling sounds.

"You *will* leave Dana alone while I'm gone, do you hear me? If I come back to find that you've tried anything, *anything*, I'll kill you with this same hand and let the Judge Advocate court-martial me."

For all his mild appearance, Zand could easily have shaken off the grip of virtually anyone else; the Protoculture powers he had given himself through dangerous experimentation made such physical tricks simple.

But for some reason, Zand's enhanced powers simply didn't work on Emerson. It was as if the general was immune to Zand's abilities. Emerson knew very little about Protoculture; he had no conscious access to its vast gifts. Emerson had no idea that he was throttling a superman.

He shook Zand. "Do you hear?" Zand managed to nod, breath rattling. Emerson let him go. There would be fearsome bruises on his throat by daylight.

The last time Zand felt Emerson's grip on his throat was thirteen years ago. That was at night, too, when Emerson burst into Zand's lab upon discovering that Zand was running bizarre experiments on the daughter left behind by Max and Miriya Sterling. He was exposing Dana to Protoculture treatments and substances from some strange alien plant. Emerson had heard it had something to do with activating the alien side of her mind and genetic heritage. The general was Bowie's guardian, but had been a good friend to Dana's parents.

Zand had believed he would die that night, that moment; Emerson's strength seemed illimitable. Or perhaps it was simply that none of Zand's acquired powers worked in Emerson's presence? Zand avoided him from that time to this moment, and Emerson had made sure, no matter where he was or what he was doing, that Dana was beyond Zand's reach.

Gasping and wheezing, rubbing his throat, Zand tried to make some sense of it. How could a mortal like Emerson block the Shapings of the Protoculture this way? *And in such complete ignorance of what it was that he was doing?* It was as if the overwhelming frustration of it all was some tithe Zand had to pay to win that ultimate triumph, that incredible prize, that he saw promised to him by the Shaping.

It was even more humiliating that Emerson didn't even *realize* with whom he was dealing. To Emerson, Zand was some half-demented Protoculture mystic from R&D, who had deviated from the saner paths followed by Dr. Lang, and ended up deranged.

"I know you've been keeping tabs on her through back-channels and informants," Emerson said quietly. "Don't ever do it again. If I have to come and see you a third time, Doctor, it will be *to take you off the roll call for good!*"

Zand didn't even realize that Emerson had moved away from him until he heard the door open and close. The heir to Emil Lang's Protoculture secrets, and master of new, more perilous secrets of his own, massaged his tortured windpipe. One thing was clear: Emerson was an obstacle that would have to be dealt with first.

Dana Sterling was vital, because she stood at the center of all Zand's star-spanning schemes.

* * *

Marie wove her jeep through the streets and byways of Monument City.

What a little idiot I've been! I knew what Sean was like. I heard all the stories, yet I still believed he'd change just for me!

She ignored lights, ignored speed limits, ignored all peril to herself and others, sideswiping whoever didn't stay out of her way. The night and imminent death drew her on.

Her jeep bounced through an alley and onto an access road that would take her to the cliff overlooking the city. She wasn't thinking clearly about what she would find there, but something told her it would be better than what she was feeling now, and she liked the feeling of the accelerator under her stockinged foot. She only wished she were in her mecha.

It took her some time to realize that a GMP Hovercycle and a jeep were behind her. Over a loudspeaker Nova Satori's voice was commanding her to halt.

Marie stepped on the accelerator.

As the chase barrelled out onto the cliff headland, Nova tried to sideswipe her to a halt. Marie's jeep jounced off a rock, and slewed at the cycle. Marie had an instant's view of Nova's terrified face as she fought her handlebars. Marie hit the brakes and over-corrected, and her jeep went sliding toward the cliff, tailgate foremost.

But Dennis Brown was there first, with Dana belted in the rear and covering her eyes. The VT pilot brought Marie to a stop by letting Marie's jeep slam taillights-first into his own, broadside. The two vehicles plowed along in a spume of dust; Brown's left front wheel went over the edge, and the undercarriage grated along.

The jeep tottered there, but held. Dana and Brown sighed simultaneously. Marie hung against her steering wheel, crying like a lost child.

Dana, Brown, and Nova were still trying to sort things out when the distant sirens and flashing lights caught their attention.

Brown *tch*ed. "It'd sure be bad for morale if we let the Gimps find the hero of the TASCs in this condition." He lifted Marie out of the jeep gently and set her down on the ground.

"But—Lieutenant Brown!" Nova objected, as he slipped behind the wheel of Marie's jeep.

"It's simple," he said, revving the engine. "Frustrated pilot bumped from big mission gets hands on jeep and whiskey, *understand?*"

Nova did; she owed him one. It would be just as he said. "It means the brig, you know."

Brown shrugged at Nova. "A couple days. They need me in my VT too much to do more. Besides, I've got nothing better to do with my time."

He winked at her. "Come down 'n' see me once in a while, huh?"

Then he eased the jeep back and headed off in a spray of gravel. Leaving a high plume of dust and grit, slewing and running flat-out, it wasn't hard for him to catch the posse's attention; the strobing lights and wailing sirens followed Dennis Brown away into the night.

Dana tried to decide what to do or say, with the perplexed Nova to one side, the curled-up, weeping Marie on the other.

In the invasion flagship, the Robotech Masters watched their new production line of Invid Fighters being put through its paces. The mecha resembled oldtime naval mines, spined spheres that looked as much biological as technological. They seemed to be grown of mismatched horn, chitin, and sinew.

The Invid Fighters performed their maneuvers flawlessly. They evaded the fire of multitudes of gun turrets, and when the command came, they turned devastating fire on the turrets with pinpoint accuracy.

"And when they conjoin, they will be an undefeatable Triumviroid," Bowkaz said.

Jeddar of the Clonemasters made his abasing bow. "A Triumviroid, yes, Master. Self-contained and capable of performing the three basic functions of combat: data accumulation, analysis, and response, all within milliseconds."

The very essence of Robotechnology. *Logic dictates that these mecha cannot be defeated!*

A weapon as perfect as we ourselves, the Robotech Masters shared the cold thought.

Dawn had brought a break in the clouds; final preparations for the launch of Emerson's strikeforce were being made, last matters on the checklists were ticked off.

Captain Komodo led his unit out at a run. He had indulged his grief and put aside his humiliation; now it was time to discharge his duty, to live up to his oath of service. But a voice calling his name made him stop short as the rest ran on to the personnel elevator that waited to take the battlecruiser's crewpeople to their assignments.

Dana caught up, breathless. "I just want to . . . say, I'm sorry, sorry about—"

He gave her a smile. "Forget it, Dana. Thanks for everything."

The silence that followed was awkward, as they listened to announcements and instructions for everyone who was going to hurry, and for everyone else to get clear. Dana and Komodo groped for something to say to each other.

Then a hand reached out to touch Komodo's armored shoulder. "Captain . . ."

Komodo, pivoting to see Nova Satori standing at his side, looked like a deer caught in headlights. She took his gauntleted hand in both of hers. "I just wanted to say—be sure to come back safely."

It took him a few starts to answer. "Nova, yes! I will!" He turned, dashing to catch up with his command. "Don't worry about that!"

Dana figured Nova was still not in love with Komodo. But what did that matter when a person might die—when a whole world might?

Dana was about to bury the hatchet with Nova, to tell her what a decent thing that was to do, when both were distracted by another lift-off drama.

"Marie! Come back!"

But Marie Crystal already had a head start, and even weighted by her combat armor she got to the elevator well ahead of Sean Phillips. And anyway, Sean had been caught by Angelo Dante, who gathered him up practically under one arm, and dragged him back.

Angelo hollered at his onetime CO, "Be a man, for god's sake! She's got more important things on her mind, idiot!"

But Sean struggled free at the last moment, as the countdown went for zero and ground crews and PAs bellowed at the ATACs to get to shelter. Sean dashed for the elevator, but he was too late. The doors closed just before he got there. Marie watched emotionlessly—or did she? Just as the closing doors took her from him, her stone-face expression seemed to change.

Sean curled up inconsolably on the hardtop, and let Angelo, Dana, and Nova lift him up and bear him away.

In the ready-room, Bowie was by himself again at the piano. He played the songs Emerson had taught him, and the ones he himself had composed early-on.

He heard the first rumbles of prelaunch ignition reverberate across the countryside and the city, as his godfather and guardian readied for battle.

The battlecruisers, destroyer escorts, and other combat ships rumbled and flamed and rose, shaking the ground. The thunderclaps of their drives echoed across Monument City. Dana, Sean, Nova, and Angelo watched the strikeforce draw lines of fire into the blue.

The tumult and the glare of it filled the ready-room windows; Bowie hit a last, hateful note, then sat staring at the keys.

CHAPTER
SIX

It is, perhaps, some ultimate universal justice on the behalf of intelligence (as opposed to physical strength or predation skills) that the secrets of the Universe are open only to those who have left certain outdated belief systems behind.

Or, maybe it's one big—how do the Humans say it?—one big gag.

Exedore, as quoted in Lapstein's *Interviews*

T HE ROBOTECH MASTERS, IN THEIR FLAGSHIP, WERE AWARE of the impending launch of Emerson's expeditionary force; this time there would be no surprises, and the Earth would be dealt a final, crushing blow.

It was imperative that Earth be destroyed not only because the constrained seeds of the Flower in the Matrix below were beginning to sprout into actual blossoms, but also a new and more dangerous element had entered their equations.

The Robotech Masters, nailless hands touching their Protoculture cap, contemplated the cloud of interstellar gas that, in astronomical terms, was so close. To an Earthly observer it would simply be a curiosity, a spindrift that had wandered Earth's way from some impossibly distant H II region. Its aberrant motion could be attributed to a close encounter with a far-off mass of dark matter or to galactic streaming dynamics. The oddities in its internal movements and constitution would be chalked up to some natural phenomenon of density waves.

Just another collection of whorls and billows of dust and phosphorescent gas; just another emission nebula.

But the Robotech Masters knew better and had good reason to be afraid. It was an Invid Sensor Nebula, searching for Protoculture and/or the Flower of Life. The Invid would be coming soon, and so the Masters' time was short.

Long ago, the Invid had been a peaceful species, living out their lives on idyllic Optera, ingesting the Flower and, with the powers it gave them, rejoicing in their contemplation of the Universe. Then Zor, the original Zor, had come to live among them, to learn. He saw in their almost photosynthetic biological processes a by-product that, when isolated, gave him the key to ultimate power: Protoculture.

The infinitely metamorphic Invid were the Apple of Temptation to him, harboring ultimate secrets. Zor was the same to them—especially to the Invid Queen, revealing to them the two-edged bane/blessing they had never conceived of: passion, love.

He understood that the key to the power of the Flower was the Invid Queen. Zor, consumed with the hunger for knowledge, used her, barely knowing what it was he was doing, and set the course of a tragedy that would stretch across eternity.

The Invid Queen, the Regis, became infatuated with Zor. This infatuation would bring a universe crumbling down with no promise of what would rise from the ashes. Love and Protoculture, Protoculture and love; they were locked forever after in a pattern of exaltation and disaster.

Zor's superiors on Tirol, his homeworld, immediately understood the more obvious implications of Protoculture—its power to penetrate spacetime, to impart vast mental powers, its connection to the fundamental shaping force of the Universe. Like all leaders, they lusted for power; naive Zor was no match for them . . . at least at that point.

Using rudimentary powers derived from the more malign aspects of Protoculture, the overlords of Tirol banded together to subdue Zor mentally, to place an irresistible Compulsion on him. At their direction, Zor stole as many of the Flower seeds as he could from his Optera hosts.

Under his Masters' enslavement, he betrayed the Invid hivequeen, who had taken on a form like his own. Zor left the Regis loveless and full of hate—she who had literally *transfigured* herself, loving Zor so. The rest of Optera Zor laid waste, so that the Flower of Life would never grow there again.

Love and Protoculture; Protoculture and love.

Conquest and dominance were the companion cravings of the Tirolean tyrants' Protoculture addiction. Their giant, cloned Zentraedi worker-menials were transformed into conquering legions; Zor became their savant-slave. He shaped the Protoculture Matrices, and went forth to seed the Flower of Life on other worlds, so their seeds could be harvested for more Matrices.

The overlords of Tirol were transmogrified into the Robotech Masters. Their own race became to them mere objects, plasm to be reshaped and put to the use they chose.

Meanwhile, the Invid, changed by their hatred and suffering, burst forth from Optera to seek the Flower of Life wherever the Masters seeded it, and to slay the Robotech Masters and their servants wherever they found them. The Invid began reproducing with monocellular speed, becoming a teeming horde that daunted even the Masters. A stupendous war roiled across galaxies, but the Masters were content that in time they would win.

The Masters, however, in their arrogance, had forgotten Zor's original exposure to the secrets of Protoculture on Optera, and the expansion of his mental gifts. Little by little, Zor was making patient, microscopic progress against the Compulsion by which the Masters held him.

His breakthrough came in the form of a Vision of what was to be, given to him by the Protoculture. He saw a small, blue-white, unimportant world. A world where Humanity would ultimately obliterate itself, and all life on the planet, in a Global Civil War. There *was* an alternative. It would involve great hardship and suffering for the Human race, but at least it offered a chance for racial survival.

The Vision showed Zor a possible future, wherein a great cyclone of mindforce a hundred miles wide rose from Earth and, high above the planet, transformed itself into a Phoenix of groupmind. The Phoenix spread wings wider than Earth, and with a single cry so magnificent and sad that it wrenched Zor's mind free of the Masters' domination, the bird soared away to another plane of existence.

Zor was then free to work his act of defiance. He dispatched the SDF-1 to Earth, hiding it from the Masters, even as he gave up his life to an Invid attack in a death he had foreseen in his Vision. The last Matrix by which new Protoculture could be produced was gone; the others had all been used up or destroyed in the course of the war, and only Zor had the secret of their creation.

The Robotech Masters, regarding with arctic dread the roving Sensor Nebula that was one of the Invid's coursing bloodhounds, knew little about the original Zor's motives, and nothing of his Vision. They only knew that their fanatic enemies would find them bereft of Protoculture's powers, helpless, unless the Masters triumphed soon on Earth.

And that demanded as a first step the quick and utter destruction of Emerson's expeditionary force.

Aside from some oddities noted in the peculiar nebula drifting so close to Earth, there was nothing to report, the techs said. Emerson worried nevertheless.

The enemy fleet still hung in distant orbit, permitting the expedition room for passage. Emerson's force had already passed the enemy's optimal point for launching assault ships to intercept and engage him. Soon the Humans would be past their closest approach to the invaders, and would be hightailing for Luna. He kept his escort forces deployed and ready for battle, even as his command passed through the leading edge of the nebula.

Once out of the nebula, past the point of greatest proximity to the enemy, the crewpeople began to breathe easier. But Emerson grew even more vigilant.

The Robotech Masters gathered vast amounts of data through their Protoculture cap. "The Humans must be relieved to have passed their zone of likeliest combat without a confrontation," Shaizan conjectured.

"Prepare to destroy them," he sent out the command.

"What're you trying *now*, Louie?" Dana asked the lanky corporal as he bent over the training simulator's guts.

"I'm gonna win back those two beers I owe you," Louie said smugly, fooling with the systemry there, changing some connections, putting in a special adaptor. "You're in for a surprise."

Dana scoffed, "C'mon, Louie! You can't beat a born warrior like me, even with a lot of mechie tricks."

At least he never had yet, even on the *Kill Those Bioroids!* program that he himself had designed for the simulator. She was happy to let him keep trying though; hand-eye training never hurt. She was just sorry the simulator, in the canteen at the local Southern Cross service club, wasn't set up more like a Hovertank's cockpit-turret, or that she hadn't been able to beg, borrow, or steal a simulator for the 15th's ready-room.

The thinking caps did the bulk of the controlling for Robotech mecha, but the tankers inside still had to know their instrumentation the way a tongue knew the roof of its mouth. At the 15th, as in TASC and other units, mock-ups of the cockpit layouts of the particular mecha used by the individual outfit were pasted up in the interiors of lavatory stalls so that the soldiers sitting there could refresh their memorization of their instrumentation during what the brass euphemistically called "available time."

Now Louie, making a final adjustment said, "That's what *you* say." He climbed into the simulator and shocked her by taking off the big, square, dark tech goggles that he wore almost constantly—even in the shower and often when sleeping. It gave his face an open, surprised look.

Dana wasn't sure what to think. Louie was undoubtedly a maverick technical genius. Word was that he had passed up numerous offers for advanced study or research assignments because he liked the action in Hovertanks, but also because he preferred to tinker and modify without somebody breathing down his neck.

Certainly, he had been responsible for one of the major victories of the war when his analysis of the Masters' flagship's power and drive systems permitted the 15th to disable it and bring it down. Even though the other ships had retrieved it and guarded against any recurrence, nothing was taken away from that spectacular success. And *still*, Louie had refused transfer to Research and Development or some think tank.

Now he put aside his goggles and pulled on a wraparound visor, a black and glittering V shape, like something a sidewalk cowboy might wear downtown.

Two jumpsuited technical officers in a nearby booth, discussing Emerson's mission in low tones, suddenly became aware of a furor near the simulator, with TASC pilots and ATAC tankers and others crowding around, exclaiming and cheering. They went over and saw a tall, skinny corporal in black shades blowing away computer-modeled Bioroids with a speed and accuracy unlike anything simulators—or even real mecha—had ever approached.

As the two officers began shouldering their way through the crowd, the kid was waving an adaptor cartridge around and explaining that it was computer-enhanced targeting linked into his glasses, a step up from even the thinking caps.

"I call it my Visual Trace Firing System, or VTFS," Louie was telling them all proudly. "Or if you prefer, my 'pupil pistol.'"

"Mind if I see it?" said one officer, holding out a hand for the cartridge. Louie was instantly wary, and Dana looked the two over as well.

"Major Cromwell, Robotech R&D," the officer said. He indicated his companion. "And this is Major Gervasi. I think we can use this system of yours in our simulation training. We'll help you upgrade it and give you advice, assistance, and technical resources. Is this the only copy?"

"N-no," Louie admitted, a little uncertain.

Cromwell slipped the cartridge into the shoulder pocket of his jumpsuit. "Fine. If you don't mind, we'll have a look at this one, then. Can you be in my office tomorrow at thirteen hundred hours?"

While stuttering that he could, Louie handed over the visor as well. Dana decided that she couldn't pull rank on two majors, especially ones who worked for the top-secret R&D division.

But more than that, she was experiencing strange sensations, something to do with the mention of research, of Robotechnology, and thus of Protoculture. Something about Protoculture and experimentation . . . It gave her a queasy feeling, sent a jolt of fear zapping through her, brought not-quite-perceived, evil memories. . . .

But she shook it off as Cromwell walked away telling Louie, "We're looking forward to working with you."

Dana smiled affectionately at the goofily grinning Louie. "My brainy boy!" she said.

Outside the service club, Gervasi said to Cromwell, "Good work, Joe. Just what we need, out of nowhere!"

Cromwell nodded. "Send word up the back channels to Leonard and Zand right away. 'Rolling Thunder' is about to get the green light."

Emerson's force was very close to the moon when the Masters' fleet appeared like ghosts all around them, not on the monitors one second, hemming them in the next.

It was what the general had feared. The Masters had penetrated Earth's detection systems before; measures to counter that capability just hadn't worked, and the invaders had bided their time until they could use the tactic to best advantage. That time was now, with the expedition out of combat formation and deployed for lunar approach, with no way back and no way forward.

Emerson was reordering the disposition of his units even as the alien mother ships disgorged scores of the whiskbroom-shaped assault craft. With his battlecruiser *Tristar* at the center, Emerson prepared to fight his way through to ALUCE.

Blue Bioroids came in at the Humans like maddened automaton hornets. The call went out for the A-JACs to scramble, and the expedition's ships began throwing out a huge volume of fire to clear the way for them and hold the Bioroids off.

Once more, Marie Crystal led her Black Lions out in the A-JACs. She was all combat leader, all Robotech warrior now, the regret and hurt from Sean's betrayal savagely thrust aside. Leave love for fools, and let Marie Crystal do what she did best!

The Bioroids and the A-JAC's swirled and struck, lighting an unnamed volume of space with thermonuclear lightning and sunfire. The killing began at once, the casualties piled up.

Marie skeeted a Bioroid right off its Hovercraft, so that the circular platform went on, unguided, heading for infinite space. She went to Battloid mode, ordering others to do the same, changing tactics abruptly and taking advantage of the foe's brief confusion.

Assault ships swept in, to hammer away at the larger expeditionary vessels and be volleyed at in reply. Hulls were pierced through and through; blasts claimed Human and clone alike. Space was a maelstrom of plasma-hot beams and blowtorching drives and the ugly flare of dying ships.

Professor Miles Cochran gathered up all of his nerve to ask, "Dr. Zand, the Invid Nebula is so appallingly dangerous—it might even take hostile action against Emerson's force. Are you certain we shouldn't give him some inkling of that? Perhaps it's not too late. . . ."

There had been a tremor in his voice; he couldn't help it. Cochran began to tremble as Zand turned that eerie stare upon him there in the grandiose, forbidden sanctuary of the Kommandatura in a Robotech-rococo chamber deep in the Earth. Zand's eyes were all pupil, with no iris or white at all; his was a gaze no one could meet for long.

Even more unnerving than his eyes was the power radiating from him, which intimidated his handpicked disciples. The power of Protoculture. The outside world might see him as a slightly odd-looking researcher, the UEG's top scientific officer and adviser—a man of normal height and build with an unruly forelock, who dressed in a somewhat rumpled uniform. An egghead. But the seven men and one woman seated around the table knew differently.

The group met in a vaulted room that mixed the technological with the mystical. Side by side with the latest computer equipment and with Zand's own systemry were musty copies of the *Necronomicon* and *The Book of James*, along with talismans and gnostic paraphernalia. There was an enlargement of a satellite photo of the mound in which the wreckage of SDF-1 was buried. Zand sat at the head of the black obsidian table staring at Cochran.

He said, almost delicately, "Do you think I expunged all mention of the Invid, the Matrix, and the Flower of Life from every record but our own just so that you could go blurting it to Leonard and his military imbeciles? Or the fools at UEG? Have I wasted so much time on you?"

Cochran fought against a years-long habit of obedience to Zand, of self-sacrifice to the transcendent plan the scientist had enacted. He and the few others who sat there—Beckett, Russo, and the rest—were the only ones on Earth aside from the man himself who knew just how much Zand had altered the course of history.

"Confrontation is the whole point of the Shaping, don't you see?" Zand went on. "War is the whole point. Do you think Dana Sterling's dormant powers will be released by anything short of the Apocalypse?"

Data on the Invid and the Matrix and the rest of it, gathered from the Zentraedi leaders Exedore and Breetai, and from Captain Gloval, Miriya Sterling, and a few others, had been kept under tightest restrictions. Once Lang, Hunter, and the rest left Earth on the SDF-3 mission, it hadn't taken Zand long to see to it that everyone who knew about that information either joined his cabal, or died.

"The Protoculture's Shaping of history is moving toward a single Moment," Zand reminded them all. "And that Moment is near; I can *feel* it. I shall take ultimate advantage of that Moment. Nothing will be allowed to stop it."

Cochran, a thin-faced, intense redhead, swallowed. He had a brother in Emersons' strikeforce—who probably would soon become a casualty of the Shaping, but Cochran knew that would not matter to Zand.

To make him feel even more uncomfortable, Cochran was seated next to Russo. Russo was the former senator and head of the United Earth Defense Council. He was the man whose ambitions and prejudices had made him, more than any other Human being, the source of the misjudgments and errors that had cost Earth so terribly in the First Robotech War.

Russo had no ambitions now; he was barely alive. He was a vacant-eyed, doglike slave to Zand, very much a creature of the shadows, like his master.

Cochran managed, "I just thought—"

"You just thought to interfere with the Shaping so that your brother would be out of danger?" Zand cut in. "Don't look so surprised! Why do you think your attempts to get him a transfer all failed? It was because I was giving you a test, a test of loyalty. You wavered, and so you failed. Kill him."

The last words were soft, but they brought instant action. Russo was out of his seat in an instant, pouncing on Cochran. Beckett, on the other side—Cochran's colleague and friend since college—didn't hesitate either, helping Russo bring Cochran to the floor.

Zand's other disciples threw themselves into the fray, terrified of failing this newest test. Even matronly Millicent Edgewick was there, kicking the doomed man. Zand sat and watched, nibbling dried petals of the Flower of Life.

Cochran went down, his chair overturned. His screams didn't last long.

CHAPTER
SEVEN

*The generals who let us die
so they can shake a fist—
They'd none of 'em be missed,
they'd none of 'em be missed!*

Bowie Grant, "With Apologies to Gilbert and Sullivan"

OWIE WAS TINKERING WITH THE KEYS AGAIN, TRYING NOT to think about the strikeforce expedition. "Doesn't that get boring?" Sean asked, leaning on the piano.

"Not really."

"I don't mean you, Bowie; I mean *those* two."

He pointed toward Dana and Louie, who were toiling over a simulator that looked as if it had been stripped, components lying everywhere. Why they had chosen the ready-room to work in instead of one of the repair bays or maintenance workrooms was still unclear, except perhaps the fact that Dana kept trying to entice people into volunteering to help.

Dana had commandeered the simulator from the canteen on authority from R&D, and neither she nor Louie had slept that night. On the other hand, as of yet no R&D support troops had shown up.

"I'm starting to wonder if that Cromwell really wants Louie's gizmo for simulation training," Sean murmured.

"I just—like machines," Louie was expounding to Dana, as he reassembled things. "They expand Human potential and they never disappoint you, if you build 'em right. Somebody with the right know-how could create the ideal society. Unimpeded Intellect! Machine Logic!"

"I didn't know you were such a romantic," she said dryly. *Ideal society? Boy, what a mechie!*

Louie wanted to run the final test, but Dana pulled rank and he yielded amiably. She pulled on a visor, hopped into the simulator, and the computer-modeled slaughter began. It was a quantum leap from the old thinking cap; her score soared.

Elsewhere, the *Tristar*, Emerson's flagship, was fighting a desperate diversionary action, luring the main body of the enemy's forces one way so that the more badly damaged expedition ships could try to limp to ALUCE.

"We can't take much more of this pounding!" Green growled, as the *Tristar* was jarred again by enemy fire.

"I know," Emerson said calmly. "Get me a precise position fix and tell the power section we'll need emergency max power in two minutes."

"Sir," Rochelle said and bent to the task. Green turned a silent, questioning look on the man he had served for so long.

"We're going to generate a singularity effect," Emerson said. They all knew he meant use of the mysterious "special apparatus" given him by R&D in a cryptic transfer that, rumor had it, could be traced to Zand himself.

The idea was to create a small black hole where the ship was, the ship itself being yo-yoed momentarily into another dimension. The singularity would then pull in and destroy everything in close proximity to it. The untested theory and some of the apparatus came from Dr. Emil Lang's research on the now-destroyed SDF-1.

"And then the enemy becomes a brief accretion disc, gets sucked into the singularity, and vanishes forever," Green muttered. "Perhaps."

"We try it or die anyway," Emerson pointed out. To underscore that, another enemy salvo shook the *Tristar*.

Power readings seemed insane, violating all safety factors and load tolerances. Emerson had a microphone in his hand.

"Lieutenant Crystal, you and the other TASCs will lure all enemy forces as close to the *Tristar* as possible, and be ready to get clear on a moment's notice, in approximately six minutes, do you copy?"

"You heard the man," Marie told the Lions.

It was the weirdest mission she had ever been on: sting and run, get the enemy assault ships and battleships and 'roids chasing you. Juke and dodge to keep them from shooting your tail off;

somehow keep them from engaging and diverting or delaying you. Protect your teammates but keep moving; do your best to ignore the heavy losses suffered by pilots who had been forbidden, in effect, to turn and give battle. And watch the time diminish down to zero.

As the timer wound down, the area around the *Tristar* was thick with dogfighting mecha, the biggest rat race of the Second Robotech War. The enemy forces were hitting Emerson's flagship almost at will, and it couldn't last much longer.

Then Marie heard Emerson's order to get clear; the A-JACs cut in all thrusters and headed away, leaving the field to the milling Bioroids and combat vessels.

Emerson watched the indicators and, when it was time, he threw the switch. Crackling energy wreathed the battlecruiser, seeming to crawl around it like superfast serpents. The tremendous discharge expanded to form a sphere just big enough to contain the ship. The Bioroids' emotionless faceplates were lit up by the radiance of the blaze.

There were cosmic fireworks, then nothing to see as the lightshow was engulfed by the Schwarzchild radius. The Bioroids and vessels closest to the vanished flagship were destroyed by tidal forces. The invaders were sucked into nullset-space.

Those slightly farther away were helpless to escape becoming accretion material, whirling down to and over the event horizon after their fellows. The Masters' mightiest assault force was gone except for a little quantum leakage.

Marie was waiting for the *Tristar*, praying that the last and most critical part of the operation wouldn't be a disaster, when cannonfire rocked her A-JAC. "Damn!" she yelled, pushing her stick up into the corner for a pushover, *imaging* the aerocombat move through her horned helmet even though she was in airless space. *There was one battleship left!*

The other A-JACs scattered as the enemy drove in at them, putting out a fearsome volume of fire with primary and secondary batteries. It was obviously damaged—and so had moved too slowly to be drawn within the deadly radius of the singularity effect.

Now it was practically on top of the Lions, still capable of doing fatal damage to the *Tristar*, should Emerson's ship reappear and be taken by surprise. Marie gave quick orders, and the Black Lions went at the enemy dreadnought like wolves after a mammoth, biting, ripping, coming back for more even though they suffered heavy losses—and luring the battlewagon into position.

But the clones weren't blind to what had happened to the rest of their battle group and fought to keep clear. The Masters' battleship put its remaining power into a run for safety.

But it found another vessel blocking its way. Although the *Salamis* was shaking with secondary explosions and seemed more holes than hull, it closed in on the alien, firing with the few batteries still functioning.

The captain of the *Salamis* and most of its officers were dead. Captain Komodo was now in command, and he knew he rode a death ship. His engines were about to go, and there was nothing he and his crewpeople could do but make it count for something.

Salamis rode its failing drive straight into the enemy's fire.

All engine readings were far into the red; the destroyer-escort trembled. "I love you, Nova," Komodo whispered.

Salamis vanished in brilliance.

"Okay! Everybody run for it!" Marie commanded. The A-JACs heeded her, zooming away in all directions.

Marie was beginning to think she had miscalculated. Maybe she misjudged the spot or perhaps Emerson simply wasn't coming back. Then an enormous globe of ball-lightning leapt into existence near the enemy, and cometlike sparks flew outwards from it.

Even though the explosion of Emerson's reentry was nothing like the release of energy the decay of a natural black hole would have produced, it was enough to vaporize the enemy battlewagon. In another moment *Tristar* floated alone in space, as Marie laughed aloud and Emerson prepared to rejoin the expedition's main force.

Supreme Commander Leonard put on a self-satisfied look as he passed word of Emerson's victory along to the UEG council, taking as much of the credit for himself as he possibly could. But inside, he seethed. He must have victories of his own!

When he was back in his offices, though, a phone call brought welcome news that turned his day around.

"That was Cromwell from R&D," said his aide, Colonel Seward. "They've completed modifications on that targeting system they got from the trooper in ATAC. Mass production and retrofitting have already begun; they've got their special units on it now."

Then we can start preparation for my attack plan! Leonard exulted. He said to his gathered staff, "Gentlemen, the time has come to strike the telling blow, and capture or destroy the enemy flagship, using both Earth-based forces and the ALUCE contingent.

"Inform General Emerson I want him back here on Earth A.S.A.P. He'll be my field commander on this one."

Run the gauntlet again, Rolf! Your luck has to give out sometime!

"Listen up, everybody!" Dana's tone was so upbeat that the 15th knew this briefing wasn't just some joystick info-promulgation. They gathered round her, there in the repair bay.

When she had them quieted down from the usual griping and groaning about being interrupted, she motioned to Bowie and said, "Your friend Rolf—that is, Chief of Staff Emerson—has arrived at Moon Base ALUCE with his expeditionary force."

She saw Bowie's breath catch, but then, with deliberate effort, he put on a bored expression. "Oh, yippee-pow. Now we can do some more fighting."

"What's it all mean for us, Lieutenant?" Angelo broke in, seeing that Dana was vexed by Bowie's reaction and wanting to keep things on track.

That somehow triggered the strac side of her personality, the hardnose officer so unlike the wild rulebreaker. She put on her best CO expression and said tightly, "Squad Fifteen, Alpha Tactical Armored Corps, will stand-to and make ready to participate in an all-out assault on the enemy flagship to take place in approximately forty-eight hours, Major General Emerson commanding."

She let the gasps and exclamations go on for a few seconds, then cut through them. "*As you were!* Fall out and follow me."

Grumbling, they hopped onto the drop-rack, the conveyor-beltlike endless ladder that carried them down to the motor pool levels to their parked Hovertanks. As soon as they jumped clear of the drop-rack, they saw that someone else had been at work there—at work on their own sacrosanct mecha, in violation of every ATAC tradition.

Odds and ends of components and machinery and one or two forgotten tools were lying around. They gave her betrayed looks, knowing now why they had been given other work details to keep them all off the motor-pool levels.

"They've all been retrofitted and augmented by R&D for extended space combat capability," she recited the briefing that had been given her. "Get used to them. You'll find instruction manuals and tutorial tapes in each tank. We will all run individual in-place drills and dry-fire practice from now until chowtime."

The 15th was only grumbling a little now, because they were fascinated with what had been done to their vehicles. The mecha's lines had been changed only a little, but the 15th could see that the detection and targeting gear was newer and more compact, more long-range. Life-support and energy systems were smaller and much more effective, too. The space saving was mostly due to upgraded firepower and thicker armor.

They spread out, looking admiringly at the tanks but not trusting them yet. Dana herself was uneasy about this sudden mucking around with the 15th's mecha, but she had her orders, and she thought that everything might go all right.

"Good; you're here," someone said behind her. She turned, and found herself facing Lieutenant Brown, decked out in his tailored TASC uniform. "Looks like it's gonna be fun, doesn't it?" he added.

"You're coming along on this party," Dana said, not making it a question.

Brown's handsome face twisted into a droll smile. "Gotta prove I'm not a screwup, don't I?" He looked around and spotted the *Livewire.* "Hey, Louie! Congratulations; I heard you're the one who dreamed up the new targeting systems."

Dana turned, saw that Louie was hunkered over the control grips and computer displays in his cockpit-turret. He didn't respond to Brown's hail. She turned back to the TASC flyer. "Y-you mean the simulator gizmo?"

"They told me it was for simulation training," Dana heard Louie's trembling voice. He was still bent over his controls, his back to them.

Sean was lounging in his tank, the *Bad News*, reveling in its now-enhanced power, checking out the VFTS "pupil pistol" target acquisition and firing system. "First-round kill every time," he assessed; Louie heard him, and groaned aloud.

"Shut up, Sean!" Dana screamed at him, her voice almost breaking.

Something snapped inside Bowie. What if the Robotech Masters had run short of fighters in the wake of Emerson's apocalyptic victory? What if Musica or someone like her was sealed into the ball-turret control module of the next blue Bioroid to find itself in his gunsight reticle?

"I'm through with this!" Bowie howled, veins standing out in his neck and forehead. "There're Humans like us in those Bioroids and *they're not our enemies*! And we're not theirs, can't any of you understand that?"

Dana started to calm Bowie down, but before she could get out more than a few vague, soothing words, she heard a rattle and felt waves of superheated air behind her. Dana and the rest of the 15th turned around and saw Louie Nichols with a thermo-rifle in his hands, its bulky power pack lying on the permacrete at his feet.

His eyes were unreadable behind the dark, reflective goggles, but he was trembling all over. "Those bastards from R&D never even asked me; they just lied, picked my brain, and did what they were planning to do all along. Like *we're* the clones; like *they're* the Robotech Masters!"

He shot a lance of brilliance at the motor-pool wall in a test-burn; alloy melted and small secondary fires started. He figured he had enough power in the rifle to burn the cockpit out of every tank and then go hunting for Cromwell and Gervasi.

"Like we're a bunch of experimental animals," Louie cried at his squadmates desperately, swinging the thermo-rifle's bell mouth this way and that to keep them all back.

He had joined the Southern Cross because he believed in it, but the mind and the products of the mind belonged to the individual, to do with as the individual saw fit; that was the first order of his convictions. Or else, what was the point of all this fighting? Why were the Human race and the Robotech Masters not one and the same?

"We're not just slaves or puppets or lab animals!" Louie shrieked, and put another spear of furnace-hot brightness into a partition, melting it, setting it alight, to keep back an overeager PFC who had been edging toward him.

Lab animals, the phrase registered in Dana and lodged there, because it set off images and reflexes on the very limits of the perceivable. *I know what it feels like to be one!*

Angelo started for the corporal one small step at a time. "Louie, the balloon's already up. Emerson and the rest go, whether we do or not. All you can do this way is give the goddamn aliens a better edge."

Dana winced at the *aliens* reference and leapt forward to shove Angelo aside, the strange evocations of Louie's words still moving her. She leveled her gaze at berserker Louie.

"Go ahead, Louie." She jerked a thumb at the tanks. "Flame 'em all."

Angelo was making confused, contrary sounds. She went on, "If you can't do it, then I will!" She walked in Louie's direction, only slightly out of the path of the thermo-rifle's tracer beam. The beam wavered on her, away, and back.

Then she was before him, and he turned the nozzle aside. "They lied to us," Louie said, lowering the barrel.

"I know," she answered gently, taking the weapon from him and turning it once again on the tanks.

Angelo stepped into her line of fire. "You swore an oath!"

"So did they, Angie," she said evenly. Dana turned to burn her own Hovertank, *Valkyrie*, first. But she found another figure in her way. Zor gazed at her through the heat waves of the thermo-rifle's pilot.

"I understand this war from both sides; maybe I'm the only one who ever will," he told her. "And humanity mustn't lose, it *mustn't lose*, do you hear me? Listen, all of you: I know what the Bioroid clones feel when they die. I've died before—and I'll die again, as we all will. The difference is in how we'll *live*, don't you see? And for that, I'm willing to fight. And even to kill.

"Dying is a natural thing, sometimes it's even a mercy. But living as a slave—that can make dying seem like a miracle."

He was before her now, almost whispering the words. Dana turned the muzzle of the thermo-rifle up toward the ceiling. Zor pried it from her fingers and deactivated it, just as Louie ran from the motor pool.

"The war must end, *but the Robotech Masters must not win*," Zor said to them quietly, putting the rifle aside.

CHAPTER EIGHT

Hwup! Twup! Thrup! Fo'!
Alpha! Tact'l! Armored! Corps!
If yo' cain't git yo' mind tame,
Better play some other game!

Marching-cadence chant popular among
ATAC drill sergeants

IN THEIR FLAGSHIP, THE ROBOTECH MASTERS SHOWED NO SIGN OF
their dismay as the Clonemasters assessed the damage they had
suffered in Emerson's doomsday victory.

Many of their combat vessels and blue Bioroids were gone,
along with much of the materials that were to have gone to mecha
construction. "We have begun emergency production of the new,
augmented Triumviroid mecha, my lord," Jeddar was saying,
"giving each the power of an Invid Fighter. It lies within our ability to produce many of these and they are superior to anything the
Humans can field."

The Masters studied the Triumviroid, a red Bioroid similar to
the one Zor Prime had piloted. With one of the horned
Triumviroid Invid Fighter spheres in each ball-turret control module, they would have, in effect, hundreds of Zors—hundreds of
duplicates of their most capable fighter and battle lord.

"This is our crowning achievement." Dag leered, studying the
enormous fists and weapons. "Utterly invincible."

Bowkaz pronounced his evaluation, "The Humans' Battloids
will be worthless against it."

And Shaizan contributed, "Finally, the Protoculture will be
ours."

The gleaming red armored immensity of the straddle-legged
Bioroid loomed above them, so massive that it seemed it could

tear worlds apart. The Masters were sure that they were destined to succeed.

There was, however, a tacit silence among them on the matter of the *Humans'* aspirations, which might be contradictory.

The ALUCE forces had rested, repaired their mecha and licked their wounds. At Emerson's order, they lifted off again, to rendezvous with him for what the Human race hoped would be the knockout punch of the war.

Earth and the moon shook to the drives of Southern Cross battleships; the Black Lions and some twenty-five thousand other soldiers looked to their weapons and waited and wondered whether this would be the day they died.

At Fokker Base, Marie Crystal, who had come with Emerson on his harrowing broken-field run back from the moon, prayed for her own soul and those of all the men in her unit. Then she rose, armored like Joan of Arc, and got ready to lead them forth to slay and be slain.

In a mess hall near a launch pad at Fokker Base, there was little for the 15th to do except sit and wait. Their tanks were already loaded, nobody seemed to feel much like talking, and the squeaking and scraping of body armor was the only sound. Serenity seemed to be inversely proportionate to rank: Dana felt the weight of the world on her shoulders, while the latest transferees were trying to bag a few z's on the floor.

They had been listening to the Bitch Box—the PA speaker—drone on for hours. Who was supposed to go where, cautionary notes about final maintenance—and more ominously, chaplain's call and final offers from the Judge Advocate General's office to make sure wills and deeds were in order.

Dana looked out the mess hall window, at the scarred, alloy-plowed spot on a distant hillside where the Robotech Masters' flagship had crashed a lifetime—a month?—before.

"C'mon," she murmured to the PA. *I don't mind dying, but I hate to wait!* "Let's get this turkey in the oven!"

Sean, wandering past seemingly by accident, patted her glittering steel rump. "Easy, skipper."

She spun on him and would have taken a swing at him if he had been closer. Did he think she was so incapable that she needed *his* imprimatur to run her squad? Dana didn't have time to think of anything more subtle or telling, so she barked, "Squelch it, dipstick!"

They were both sweating, teeth locked, ready to punch each other for no good reason—except that they were about to go into battle, to shoot or perhaps be shot by total strangers.

Bowie bounded to his feet, despite the weight of his armor. "Stop it. We only have one enemy, and that's the Robotech Masters. We should be thinking about that." He said it with the uncomfortable knowledge that he couldn't even take his own advice; he, too, was preoccupied, but in a very different way.

Angelo was checking over the mechanism on his pistol. "Think, schmink! Why don'tcha all quiet down and think *mission*?"

"Angelo is right," Zor said quietly.

Louie snorted, "That's easy for you to say, Zor. But us Humans get emotional, especially when it comes to gettin' killed."

Zor didn't rise to the taunt. "You're right: I'm not Human. I wish I could remember more than I do, but I recall one thing clearly. I was far less than I am now, when my mind was ruled by the Robotech Masters.

"I want to destroy them to make sure that never happens to me or anyone else. I'd gladly give my life to ensure that. If you knew what I was talking about, you all would, too."

Nobody said anything for a few seconds. They had all been in combat too many times to have much tolerance for gung-ho speeches, but something quiet and sure in Zor's voice kept them from mocking him.

"I'm impressed," Angelo said, to break the silence. There were a few grunts and nods of the head, about as close as the 15th could come to wild applause at a time like this.

In their flagship, the Masters gazed down at the Scientist triumvirate. "We observe the Humans' preparations," Shaizan said. "And their apparent intention to use such crude tactics is difficult to rationalize. Do you detect any indication that they are preparing to fight the Invid Sensor Nebula should it attack them?"

The Scientists floated close on their satellite Protoculture cap. Elsewhere in the cavernous compartment, the Clonemasters, Politicians, and other triumvirates stood on their drifting caps and watched silently.

Dovak, leader of the Scientists, answered, "According to our monitorings and intercepts, they plan nothing against the Nebula, but they *are* mounting an all-out offensive against *us*."

The Masters pondered that. Perhaps the primitives below were ignorant of the danger of the Invid. But that hardly seemed likely, especially since the Zentraedi who had defected to the Human side in the First Robotech War would have been well aware of it, and of the Nebulae. Perhaps the Humans were hoping for aid from the Invid.

If so, they hoped in vain; the Invid had a mindless hatred of any species but their own.

In any case, the Humans plainly would not constitute a buffer or third force should the Invid arrive; their civilization and perhaps all life on their planet—except the Matrix—would in all likelihood simply be swept away.

And if they weren't ready for the Invid and in control of a replenished Matrix by then, the Robotech Masters would be destroyed as well.

Finally the orders came. Dana grabbed up her winged helmet with its long alloy vane like a Grecian crest.

"All right, Fifteenth! Saddle up! C'mon, *move out!*"

Out on the launch pad, Nova managed to steal a few moments from the frantic activity of ensuring a trouble-free embarkation, to meet with Lieutenant Brown.

"I was sorry to hear about poor Komodo," he told her. "I know it was awkward for you but—you made him happy, Nova. Don't ever regret that, no matter what."

She had almost decided not to meet Dennis, fearing that her farewell might be a jinx. She struggled to say something.

"Just take care of yourself until I see you again," he smiled.

"Isn't that *my* line, Dennis?" She felt as if she might start shivering.

He shrugged his armored shoulders. "Nothing to worry about. 'Just another day in the SCA.'" The stock Southern Cross Army crack didn't sound so light, though.

She had a hard time understanding just how she had come to care so much for him, especially in the midst of all the craziness about Zor and the sadness over Captain Komodo. At first it had to do with her guilt over messing up his clearance. Later she admired him for the way he took the fall for Marie Crystal's stunt-driving exhibition, and for his role as getaway driver in Dana's demented matchmaking scheme.

But there was something more to it than that, something that had to do with the indestructible good humor with which he faced every misfortune. She just felt that in some ways he was a kinder, a better person—more compassionate—than she could ever pretend to be.

The warning hooters were nagging. "Gotta go," he said.

He turned to leave, but she caught his wrist. "Dennis, be careful. Do that for me?"

He nodded with a handsome grin. "Count on it. See you soon."

She nodded, watching him as if he were some apparition. She couldn't quite work up the nerve to tell him, *Come back safe to me, because I seem to have fallen in love with you.*

He was trotting toward his transport, and she had to hurry to reach a bunker. Drives boomed again, and the next phase of the Second Robotech War began in earnest.

The forces from ALUCE came on, unopposed. The Masters refused to react to Humanity's drawing gambit, and played a waiting game. Earth's strikeforce positioned for attack.

Dana found Bowie down in the cargo hold where the 15th's Hovertanks were secured for flight. It took some prompting to get him to open up, but when he did the words came out in a flood.

"Since I met Musica and Zor, I just can't feel the same about fighting those Bioroids! The people in them just aren't to blame! It's like one of those ancient armies where they drove innocent captives in first, to be slaughtered, to gain a tactical advantage!"

"Bowie, I understand. There's nothing wrong with what you're feeling—"

She had put a hand on his shoulder but he shook free, batting it aside. "I'm right on the edge, Dana, and I haven't got my mind right, don't you understand? I can't handle it anymore! I'll let you all down!"

That was serious talk, because everyone in the 15th knew—as all soldiers know—that you don't take that hill for the UEG council, the Promise of a Brighter World, or Mom's fruitcake. No; you do it for your buddies, and they do it for you.

"Bowie, we've always been straight with each other, and I'm telling you: I get those same feelings, too."

"But Dana, that doesn't tell me how to deal with it! Ahhh! So, there it is. Nothing you can do about it, Lieutenant. I'm gonna have to sort this one out for myself."

"I'm only part Human," she blurted. "I, I guess I'm *related* to Zor and the rest, in a way. I don't like the idea of killing any of the clones, either. But Bowie, *think about the alternative. Remember what Zor said!*"

She threw her arms around his shoulders, pressing her cheek to him. "We can't let that happen to Earth, Bowie," she whispered, "and we can't let that happen to the Fifteenth."

A few weeks before, the Masters' fleet would have disintegrated the impudent Human attack. Now it fought for its life, its energy reservoir failing to a point where the battle was horribly even and attrition seemed to be the not-so-secret weapon.

Terran energy volleys and alien annihilation discs cross-hatched, thick as nettles, as the Human strikeforce closed in.

The 15th cranked up and sealed their armor, preparing to follow Dana's *Valkyrie* into the launch lock. They got word that their tactical area of responsibility—their TAOR—had been increased by 50%, because the 12th squad had been blown to bits along with everyone else aboard the battlecruiser *Sharpsburg* when enemy salvoes found it.

The earth fleet threw everything it had at the enemy, but the news that came to Emerson, watching stone-faced from his flagship, was bad.

"Missiles, solids, energy—nothing seems to be doing them much damage, sir," Green told him.

There was no sign of the hexagonal "snowflake" defensive fields the Masters had used before, but what Green said was undeniably true. Ordnance and destructive force equivalent to a good-size World War was being tossed at the lumbering invaders, to no avail.

"It might be some kind of shield we haven't seen before, or it might just be their hulls," Emerson replied. But there wasn't much room for fancy changes of plan or pauses to consider now; the huge operation was, by its own size and weight, all but unstoppable.

"Press the attack," Rolf Emerson forced himself to say, trying not to think of the casualties but only of what would happen to Earth if he and his fleet failed. He had seen excerpts from Zor's debriefing, and the monitoring of Zor's comments about life under the Robotech Masters.

"Hit them harder," Emerson said, "and get ready to send in the fighters, then the tanks."

Going in close, risking the furious-bright particle beams of the teardrop-shaped invader batteries, the Earth ships poured down torrents of fire at them. Tube after tube of the heavier missiles, Skylords and such, gushed forth flame and death; racks of Swordfish and Jackhammers emptied, only to be reloaded for another fusilade.

Marie Crystal, ready to lead the TASCs out, sent a silent thought to Sean, to take care of himself.

A close, highly concentrated missile barrage that cost the Terran forces a destroyer escort and the crippling of a frigate somehow opened a gap in the alien flagship's hull. It happened just as the 15th was about to leave the launch lock, and their mission changed in a moment.

There was little G3 operations could add to the standing orders. *Get inside there and disable them! Distract, neutralize!*

The Hovertanks, compact as enormous crabs or turtles with all appendages pulled close, dropped on the inverted blue candleflames of their thrusters.

The rent in the enemy's upper hull was as big around as the 15th's barracks; a gaping, irregular hole, sides fringed with twisted, blackened armor seven yards thick, streaming black smoke and atmosphere like a funnel. It was slightly forward and portside of one of those mountainous spiraled ziggurats Louie insisted on calling "Robotech Teats."

It would still be a tight squeeze for a whole Hovertank squad, and Dana didn't like the idea of being crowded together fish-in-a-barrel style. But there was no telling when the gap would be closed by some repair mechanism, no time to pause and reconsider. At her order, the ATACs dropped slowly toward the hole, for a close pass before paying their housecall.

No Bioroids anywhere, Dana registered.

I don't like it, Angelo told himself.

"A different tactic now. How strange," Shaizan said, sounding more puzzled than perturbed.

Dag turned away from the crystalline pane, where he had been observing the Hovertanks. "This is an unexpected opportunity," Dag said, as the descending mecha swung slowly past the ruptured hull behind him.

"Yes; I believe it is time to test the new Invid Fighter," Shaizan concurred.

Dag turned and barked, "Scientists! Quickly!"

That triumvirate, having been high among the looping arteries and carryways of the ship's control systemry, descended now on their cap. "Yes, Masters?"

"Deploy our Triumviroid Invid Fighters against those Human mecha out there at once."

"At once!" The Scientists soared off to obey.

Bowkaz, watching the 15th come around for another close pass, closed his thin, atrophied hand into a fist, the spidery fingers unaccustomed to such a strong gesture. "Amazing! These missing links actually think they can triumph against *us*!"

In a large compartment in the flagship, an infernal fantasy landscape had been created. The transluclent pink room consisted of high-arching carryways and Protoculture arteries, with clusters of globes that resembled grapes, of all things, at their intersections.

Far below the energizing and monitoring systemry, the Invid Fighters reared, standing in threes, insects by comparison but cyclopean giants in terms of the war raging on the outside.

The Bioroids' chest plastrons were open, shoulder pauldrons raised, helmet beavers lifted to expose the ball-turrets in which their pilots would sit, in yogi fashion.

Dovak's voice came, "Vada Prime, triumvirates of the Invid Fighters, to your mecha! Haste! The Human prey is near!"

Light poured in from the arch intersections where the grape clusters hung; it illuminated triads of young male clones, the Vada Prime, red-haired but bearing a strong resemblance to the original Zor. They stood, back to back, where the extended chest plastrons of the mecha met like lowered drawbridges.

"Prepare for utilization against the Humans and their blasphemous concepts, their individuality! Obliterate them!"

"Three will always be as one!" one Vada leader chanted. That was the essence of the Invid Fighter systems: the transference of power, awareness, thought—Protoculture energy—back and forth among the members of each triune unit and its mecha, on a millisecond basis. This occurred so that each machine and pilot would be triply effective in the telling moments of combat, which were themselves relatively few.

"One for three and three for one. In thought, action, firepower, and reaction," Dovak intoned. "Remember this, Vada Prime!"

The Vada Prime clones retreated to their globular control sanctuaries, and prepared to hunt down the Hovertanks.

Dana led the 15th in a low approach vector, ready to go down into the hole in the enemy flagship's hull, hoping things went better than they had the last time the 15th entered the Masters' metal homeworld.

But things became complicated even before the tanks could enter; giant figures on Hovercraft rose up out of the smoking abyss of the hull breech. Dana couldn't help but feel dismay when she saw what was ahead. Red Bioroids!

Three, four—six that she could see, and perhaps more in the smoke. She tried not to surrender to despair. *Six red Bioroids!* "New targets ahead," she said, trying to sound confident.

The 15th bore in at the Triumviroids, the downsweep of their front cowlings and the halogen lamps tucked beneath them giving the tanks the look of angry crabs about to settle a grudge. The tanks broke right and left and up and down; they needed maneuvering room.

The enemy split up and jumped them, firing from weapons in their control stems, and from the disc handguns, lashing streams of annihilation discs this way and that. Dana saw what she feared: they were all as fast and deadly as Zor was, operating in perfect coordination. She fought her recurring image of a complete rout.

Three of them went for a tank that had gone low, like cowboys chasing a wandering heifer, bringing their discus sidearms to bear. Dana saw with a start that the Hovertank was Zor's *Three-In-One*.

CHAPTER
NINE

The politicians who kill troops
But leave no babe unkissed!
They'd none of them be missed,
They'd none of them be missed!

Bowie Grant, "With Apologies to Gilbert and Sullivan"

DANA YELLED, "ZOR, GET OUT OF THERE!"

Zor had the presence of mind to retro, rather than try some fancy maneuver or an uneven firefight. The reds' shots stitched the flagship's hull, passing through the airless spot where Zor would have been. He escaped with only a spider-webbing of his canopy, the effect of a grazing shot.

"That was close, but I'm all right," he said calmly.

An A-JACs unit had found a bowside cargo lock blasted open by another Terran barrage; the mechachoppers zipped in at it like angry wasps, under the same romp-and-ruin orders as the ATACs.

The command came to the Vada Primes from Dovak: "A new enemy combat group is attempting to enter the flagship. Readjust battle plan and destroy them at once."

It took the A-JACs a fatal few moments to realize that they were being attacked by mecha far superior to their own.

One A-JAC was blasted as soon as it came in, going up like a Roman candle. A second, already standing by the opened hull, was riddled and fell apart in fragments. The reds came in, maneuvering and firing in perfect cooperation. The A-JACs' counterfire had no effect on the Triumviroids' battleshiplike armor.

"We're no match for them in these A-JACs!" Lieutenant Brown

yelled to the few survivors left in his team. "Everybody pull back! Evasive maneuvers!"

Dana had her own plan of action. She sent her *Valkyrie* leaping high, imaging a change, her helmet sensors picking up the impulses and guiding her tank through mechamorphosis.

Components slid, reconfigured, rearranged; the tank went to Battloid mode. It stood in space, a Robotech Galahad, taking as its rifle the altered cannon that had rested along the tank's prow moments before. She landed on the hull to make her stand, feet spread, rifle/cannon strobing. Angelo and Bowie landed next to her in the same humanoid mode.

Three reds swept in in echelon, their fire well coordinated, promising to sweep the Battloids before them. Angelo remembered what he had learned about the blue Bioroids. He stopped pouring out heavy fire and took deliberate aim.

He hit the lead Triumviroid's faceplate; it shattered, spilling atmosphere and ruin. The thing's Hovercraft began to waver gently, and the red itself went immobile.

"I got one! Hey Lieutenant, go for their faceplates!"

But as Dana looked around to see what was going on, the red's ball turret exploded, the body of its Vada Prime pilot tumbling out into vacuum, breath and blood stolen away in a red mist.

They're humanoids, she saw. *They look . . . just like Zor.*

But she said, "You all heard Angie! Faceplates! And make every shot count!"

Bowie prepared to fire, but a vision of Musica came to him, and he froze. Three more reds came in low over a hull projection, firing so as to scatter the gathering Battloids, and one burst knocked Bowie's tank from its feet.

Dana and a trooper named Royce were almost shoulder to shoulder, putting out a heavy volume of fire, to cover him. The red broke off and banked away.

"You all right, Bowie?"

His Battloid began to lumber to its feet. "I think so."

"Then start shooting, god damn you! Bottom line: *They're* programmed to destroy *you.*"

Sean was isolated, his fireteam partner just a conflagration and a memory, the enemy closing in. "Somebody get these 'roids offa me!"

The answer came in the form of an angel of death; the Triumviroid so close to nailing him flew apart in a coruscating detonation. He picked himself up off the hull to see an A-JAC hovering loose. "Huh? I'm dreaming! I'm dead!"

Marie Crystal was on the 15th's freq. "Neither, hotshot."

"Marie?"

"That's right, Phillips, you lucky swine you. You're about four hundred yards from your squad, at one hundred seventy degrees magnetic. Get back to 'em and stay alert! I ... I don't want to lose you, Sean."

"I won't forget you said that. And I won't let you. What d'you wanna name our first kid?" She could hear the smugness in his voice but didn't mind a bit. His Battloid dashed away at top speed as Dana rallied her command.

Marie switched off her mike. "I won't forget," she whispered. Then she broke left, to try to help suppress the murderous AA fire from the teardrop cannon.

The interior of the flagship was a Hovertank job, and A-JACs, Veritechs—no other mecha had any place in it.

Dana and the first of her 15th leapt right down into a cobra pit.

Her transmissions were patched directly through to Emerson; the ATACs were Earth's best hope now. "General, we're pinned down in the entrance gap by heavy fire from red Bioroids! We're about at a standstill and request assistance—A.S.A.P.!"

Emerson was out of his command chair. "We've got to force the enemy mecha back and make that entrance bigger. Any suggestions?"

Green was giving him a dead-level look. "Ramming them is the only way, Rolf."

It didn't even take Emerson a second to make up his mind; Earth could never mount another assault like this, and it was make-or-break time. "Then make ready to use this ship as a battering ram at once."

Emerson's crew acted instantly, and *still* it looked as though it wouldn't be soon enough.

If the enemy mother ship's fire had been as intense as it was when the Masters first arrived in the Solar System, the Human battlecruiser would have been holed and immolated as soon as it came close to the invader. But great hunks of armor and superstructure were blasted away from the enemy ship, and Emerson's flagship was able to stay on course, bearing down on its enemy.

And it provided a welcome diversion, permitting Dana's troops to break contact with the devilishly fast and powerful Invid Fighters and scatter. Even the Triumviroids' power wasn't enough to stop the heavyweight Earth dreadnought.

The wedge-shaped bow drove into the long rift in the invader; the impact sent Bioroid and Battloid alike sprawling and bouncing across the hull. Dana had no idea what power it was that generated gravity on the surface of the enemy ship, but she was grateful for it then—grateful not to be sent spinning into infinite blackness.

With the outer armor breached, the battlecruiser experienced less resistance from the mother ship's internal structure. Bulkheads and decks and vast segments of systemry were crushed or bashed aside as secondary explosions foamed around the cruiser like a fiery bow-wave.

Then Emerson's ship was through, having lengthened and deepened the hull breach to three times its former size, all the way through to the mother ship's port side. As the battlecruiser lifted clear, more explosions from the alien lifted the armor even further, as if peeling back aluminum foil.

Dana got word from the cruiser that the entryway was clear, and for the moment the reds were nowhere to be seen. She hated the thought of leading her command down there where so many explosions had already gone off, but this was the only chance to go through the opening.

."Let's do it, Fifteenth! Follow me!" The 15th, all in Battloid mode, dashed toward the opening, huge metal feet pounding against the hull, rifle/cannon ready. Angelo was close behind Dana, and then Bowie. Sean Phillips, Zor, Louie Nichols—those were all of the squad that got through.

Several others were annihilated right at the verge of the gap. Still more raced for cover. The sum accomplishment of the biggest Human offensive of the Second Robotech War was to get exactly one officer and one NCO and four enlisted men of ATAC aboard the enemy command vessel.

Aboard his flagship, Emerson was hoping he had given the 15th the margin it needed. No other mecha had succeeded in reaching a position that would allow them to board, and, for the time being at least, none seemed likely to.

Emerson was calling for more diversionary strikes, to keep the Masters busy and eliminate as many red Bioroids as possible, when his flagship was battered by another massive volley.

Colonel Green picked himself up off the deck, checked the incoming reports and called to his commanding general, "It's *an-*

other alien mother ship, sir!" He checked damage readouts. "And we're in no shape to take 'em on, Rolf!"

After the battle and the ramming, Emerson knew that was only common sense. But he said, "The battle plan does not allow for withdrawal at this time—"

A second barrage, even stronger than the first, rattled them all around like dice in a cup. Emerson saw that it wasn't just *one* mother ship coming to the rescue, but at least three. There was no choice; his forces would be utterly obliterated if he didn't at least fall back to regroup.

And there was no time for an extraction mission to recover the 15th; it was committed. Its few young troopers were very likely the last, best hope of Earth.

Marie, back aboard her attack transport to rearm and refuel, heard the announcements and commands over the PA and went cold, as the Earth fleet began to break off contact and withdraw. *Oh, Sean!*

The 15th spotted the two Triumviroids in the corridor ahead of them before the reds spied the 15th. The ATAC Battloids charged almost shoulder to shoulder, unavoidably bunched up, putting out the heaviest volume of fire they could.

A strange thing happened; the enemy mecha whirled and froze. ATAC rifle shots spattered their torsos and faceplates, blowing them out, and the Triumviroids dropped like puppets whose strings had been snipped. The ATACs had had the advantage of numbers and surprise, but it was still a remarkably easy win in comparison to the harrowing battle on the outer hull.

The 15th never even broke stride, but charged on further into the ship, weapons ready. But even as Dana leapt her Battloid over one red's body something occurred to her. *Two—there were only two this time.* And the reds had been working in threes up above. Presumably there was at least one more around down here, perhaps damaged or crushed by Emerson's ramming maneuver.

She had no time to pursue the thought, though, as she led her squad along a curvy passageway built to mecha scale. The deck and bulkheads seemed unremarkable here, but the overhead looked like a big, metallic neural network. No time to stop and study, however.

"Must be kinda familiar, huh, Zor-O?" Angelo taunted. "Which way d'we go?"

"I wish I knew, but I don't remember, Sergeant," Zor answered, unruffled.

"I'll just bet ya don't, alien!"

Dana snapped, "Knock it off, Dante! Stay sharp, *all* of you!"

The warning was well timed. A moment later, a diamond-shaped hatch slid open before them and three Triumviroids leapt into the opening.

But the 15th was so juiced up on adrenaline and the heat of battle that they opened fire instantly. For some reason these enemy mecha, too, were slow in responding, and with their faceplates shot out, they went over like bowling pins.

"Shoot for the faceplates, that's their weak spot!" Dana confirmed, as the ATACs rushed the hatch, covering one another. "If y'get one or two away from the third, it slows them down; if you get a trio, hit them at *exactly* the same moment. Looks like that overloads 'em somehow."

"They have discovered an inherent weakness of our Invid Fighter," Shaizan said tonelessly. It seemed that the single-thinking Human animals were a match for the Three-Who-Act-as-One.

Dag said, "Then, we must reactivate Zor Prime's programming, and resume full command of his mind and actions."

A perfect solution. There could be no chance of malfunction, since Zor was so close to the Protoculture cap.

Bowkaz touched his long, nailless fingers and his palm to a mottled patch of the cap, and the patch shone with radiance. "It is done."

"Lieutenant, somethin's wrong with Zor!"

It was odd to hear concern in Angelo's voice.

Dana and the others stopped and pounded back to where Angelo's Battloid faced Zor's, which stood stiff as a mannikin.

The power of Protoculture coursed through Zor's brain, taking control of every corner of his mind in moments.

Dana shook the paralyzed Battloid a little. "Zor, what's wrong? Are you hit? Answer me!"

Suddenly the *Three-in-One* lashed out, grabbing the enormous alloy fist of Dana's *Valkyrie* in its own, bending it in a take-away hold, threatening to rip it off.

Angelo yelled, "Zor, that's enough!" He had his rifle up, but Dana was in his line of fire.

She worked a quick hand-to-hand trick, rotating her mecha's

wrist out of the grip and yanking herself free. "What's gotten into you?"

But Zor's Battloid was already running in the other direction, off toward a side passageway.

Dana only had a second to decide, and no time to sort through her various motives. A part of her simply could not bear to see Zor go off, perhaps blanked out again or suffering some mental seizure, to be captured or slain. Furthermore, he was an important resource to her mission and to the Southern Cross, perhaps her best hope of doing her job in the mother ship and getting her unit out alive.

But she couldn't risk her whole squad trying to tackle one berserk trooper. "Angelo, come with me! The rest of you set up security here and maintain radio contact!"

They had barely started to chase Zor when another threesome of the reds tried to block their way. Dana felt sure the Triumviroids were covering Zor's escape, that he had given them the order to do so.

Dana managed a broken-field run through them, but Angelo took one out with a shoulder block, slamming it against the bulkhead, as the disc guns opened up and the rifle/cannon replied. The passageway was an inferno of close-range firing.

Sean yelled an obscenity as he, Louie, and Bowie set up the heaviest fire they could, distracting the enemy from Dana and Angelo. The Triumviroids seemed to hear an unspoken order, and turned their attention on the remaining troopers. The mecha blasted at each other, blowing holes in deck and bulkheads, brilliant spears of novafire skewing across the small distance separating them.

CHAPTER TEN

You look at us and ask why we are slaves. But we look at you and wonder why you are not. What hideous mutation has given you the curse of free thought, and taken away your peace of mind forever?

Remark of an anonymous clone to
ATAC trooper Corporal Louie Nichols

THIS PLACE COULD BE ROMAN! DANA THOUGHT, LOOKING around the compartment into which Zor had disappeared.

It was like some vast gathering hall or ballroom. There was invader systemry around the bulkheads. But set all around the hall/compartment were what seemed to be marble columns in the classic style, supporting entablatures with carved friezes. The ceiling was a smooth dome of polished stone. It made no sense to her, and she had no time to puzzle over it all.

"Zor! Zor, please come out!" The design of the bulkheads was so strange, she couldn't tell what might be a hatch or place of concealment; the columns were too small to offer a Battloid cover.

"We're your friends, Zor!"

Angelo's *Trojan Horse* came double-timing up, having hung back to cover their rear. "Lost him, huh?"

"I saw him come in here."

Angelo raised his weapon. "He can't be trusted. He betrayed us." The punishment for treason in wartime or desertion under fire was obvious. "And I'm gonna give him what he's got coming."

It was also obvious that Zor wasn't going to willingly show himself, but Angelo had his own straightforward solution for that. "Gladiator mode!"

The sergeant imaged the transformation through his spike-topped thinking cap, and his *Trojan Horse* went through mechamorphosis.

Angelo opened fire, hitting one of the columns dead center. It broke into a shower of stone splinters and dust, collapsing and breaking into a thousand fragments. He traversed the barrel and let off another round, blowing chunks from the ceiling.

"C'mon, Zor! *Show yourself!*"

He was right, Dana saw. All her anger at the Robotech Masters welled up; what right did they have to live in such beauty, slave keepers that they were? She went to Gladiator as well, and together she and Angelo Dante stomped about the hall, firing, demolishing the gorgeous entablatures and columns.

Then at random she fired at another bulkhead of rectangular metal. The rectangle crumpled and fell, revealing a space beyond. The hatch fell and through the smoke and flame stepped one lone red Bioroid.

"Zor!" Dana knew it had to be him. All her anger was gone in a moment, and the terrible thought that she had lost him again, perhaps forever, to the Masters, brought out the other side of her personality. Forgetting everything, she hiked herself up out of her seat, and leapt to lower herself from her cockpit-canopy. "Zor!"

"Lieutenant!" Angelo's first impulse was to fire for effect, but before he could do anything, she was in too close, nearly at the Bioroid's feet, arms held up to it imploringly.

"Oh, Zor," she cried forlornly. "Don't you remember me? Have they taken that from you, too?" But the great discus-shaped handgun in the red fist swung to bear on her.

Angelo locked down his controls and rose, to drop from his tank. He couldn't start a firefight and he wouldn't leave Dana to be captured or killed. He chose not to question his own motives as he ran to stand at her side, but he knew loyalty and duty were not his only ones.

Dana was so young and beautiful, so filled with a fighter's spirit. . . . In his whole life, he had met only a handful like her: good soldier, reliable companion . . . someone you could *trust*, could *count on*. In Angelo's vocabulary, those words meant everything.

Zor's voice came to them without benefit of their headphones. It sounded, once more, as it had when Dana had first seen him revealed, near the burial mound of SDF-1. His mindspeech was thin and reedy, higher than it had been a few moments ago, and sounding like someone talking on the inhalation rather than the exhalation.

"Do not move. Surrender or you will be instantly destroyed."

"Zor," she murmured, distraught. "What have they done to you?"

Then light broke from the Bioroid as its head swung back. Its chest and shoulders opened outwards, to reveal the ball turret within it. That, too, opened—and Zor uncurled from a fetal position, seemingly given birth, in blinding glory.

He stood to regard them with contempt, mindspeaking to them. "You have fallen into this trap much more easily than I would have thought, Lieutenant Sterling. You and your command are now captives of my lords, the Robotech Masters."

"I cannot understand the extraordinary influence the female Micronian exerts over Zor Prime's mental functions," Dag told his two counterparts. "Exposure to her emotions is causing departures from several of the clone's cognitive schemata, even here at the center of our power."

"But our control module is at maximum energization," Bowkaz pointed out. "We have near-total manipulation of Zor Prime. Clearly, it will suffice. What are emotions, after all, but primitive behavioral residue?"

Zor had retreated back into his control sphere, and the discus handgun remained pointed at Dana and Angelo. The two ATACs had removed their helmets and stood looking up.

"Zor, I have to talk to you!" Dana tried again. "You remember me, don't you?"

There was no response, but Angelo noticed that, suddenly, the pistol was wavering. From the shadowy figure of Zor, curled up again in his globe, there was no movement. Dana started walking toward the Bioroid's foot.

"Look out, Dana! He's gonna shoot!" Angelo tackled her just as the titanic handgun fired; the annihilation disc missed, as the two ATACs fell headlong together, but Angelo was quick to understand that it would have missed anyway.

Another blast superheated the deck nearby, but at that range it should have been dead center. Dana and Angelo looked up to see the red's armor re-securing, closing protectively around the ball turret. The red moved spasmodically; more rounds blasted into the deck at random.

Angelo made his decision and ran for his tank. The red continued its disoriented firing, seemingly in conflict with *itself*, until it noticed his main battery coming to bear on it. Dana was just far enough out of the way. Angelo fired, but the Bioroid ducked,

barely in time. Zor fell aside as the deckplates beneath his feet
leapt up in fire from the sergeant's second shot.

Within his Robotech womb, Zor sweated, moaning, in his
trance. He fought himself even more determinedly than his
Bioroid fought Angelo, but the internal combat wasn't going well.

Dana swung to Angelo. "You'll never stop him that way!
Switch to Battloid mode! And *don't hurt him!*"

Who's she think I am, Wyatt Earp? Angelo wondered. *What'm
I supposed to do, wing that goddamn 'roid?* But he went to
Battloid and fired his rifle/cannon from the hip. The red dodged,
but more slowly.

"Zor's brainwaves indicate a deviance," Bowkaz observed.

Behind him, Myzex, group leader of the Politician triumvirate,
spoke from his triad's Protoculture cap. "His exposure to Human
influence may have produced an adverse effect on his anterior
brain structure."

Dag half turned to the politicians. "You suggest an awakening
of dormant racial memory?"

"Possibly, my Master."

Perhaps this was the breakthrough the Masters had hoped for!
It might be that emotions were the missing key to the recovery of
Zor's mental gifts and, possibly, even to the Inheritance of Acquired Knowledge capacity they had hoped to channel into him by
use of their artificial psi abilities. The I.A.K. and the recovery of
the original Zor's secrets, a new Matrix—a universe-spanning
realm belonging to them alone—it was suddenly all possible.

"The Human disturbance and distraction must be eradicated at
once," Shaizan decreed.

Suddenly Zor barreled past Angelo before the sergeant could
get off a shot, bashed through another hatch, and disappeared
down a passageway.

"Angelo, stay down!" Dana yelled.

"What happened?" Angelo was shaken badly; he had thought
his number was up. "He had me dead to rights; why didn't he nail
me?"

"I don't know," Dana said, heading back to the *Valkyrie*. "But
we have to find Bowie and the others before the aliens do."

Aliens.

The firefight in the passageway was successful for the 15th.
The ATACs used what they had learned about the Triumviroids'

weaknesses. Without Dana around to object, they had done some fast, straight faceplate-shooting, and even Bowie, seeing that his squadmates' lives were on the line, had made his choice and taken his stand.

But as they stood in the smoking aftermath of the firefight, they had realized that it was time to lie low for a while. They had withdrawn to a nearby recycling plant—a gigantic compartment full of moving conveyor belts and organic-looking reclamation equipment. Hopefully Dana would follow their transceiver signals.

Sean picked up two signals that got stronger, until they had to be right in the compartment. He looked up to see two Hovertanks shake loose of the debris and scrap on a ten-yard-wide belt high overhead, and descend on gushing thrusters. Angelo and Dana landed amid a shower of junk and garbage, Dana crying, "Look out below!"

" 'Bout time, Lieutenant," Bowie commented dryly.

There were no guards or surveillance devices that they could see. Dana and Angelo and the others hid their tanks in the dark reaches under a big overhead, then the 15th gathered around to do some improvising.

It was clear that they couldn't rely upon Emerson's return anytime soon, and to simply run riot would be to make it just a matter of time before the Triumviroids converged to wipe them out.

"So, what we gotta do is locate the flagship's command center or bridge or whatever they call it around here, then come back with the tanks and take it by force. Everybody, shuck your armor; this is a recon job."

"Secret agent time," Sean sighed. "And where d'we look, in a ship five miles long?"

"The logical place, in view of their setup and systems, is the center of the ship," Louie said. They began climbing out of their armor and checking their small arms.

The ATACs wanted to pack all the weapons they could, but Dana nixed the idea. A lot of throw-weight would only attract attention, and if they got into a situation wherein a few pistols and a rifle wouldn't suffice, they weren't likely to get out of it at all.

Another conveyor belt took them past an entrance decorated with a marble arch. They hopped off there, went along a corridor lined with meticulous, hand-done stonework. Angelo, walking point, found himself looking out on a scene that resembled a cross between the Roman Senate and the Borgias' waiting room. There was the same gorgeous artistry, and gleaming floors underfoot.

Clones were moving around in small groups, their pastel clothing running toward togalike affairs, or tights with short mantles.

"What's it look like out there?" Dana wanted to know, just behind Angelo but unable to see around him. "Are any of those guards nosing around, or can we keep moving?"

"All I can see are civilians, I guess," he whispered back. He held his tanker's carbine high and moved a step further.

Dana came up and peered out, then told her men, "They don't look like the type to ask questions, out there. We'll just mingle, and make our way along."

"Nothing ventured—" Louie resigned himself.

But the inhabitants of the ship *did* seem quiet, subdued—almost lethargic. The ATACs moved out along an upper thoroughfare that overlooked public gathering places and quiet quadrangles.

They had only gotten a few steps when Dana and Louie saw a small surface-effect runabout headed their way.

Everybody else caught the signals and warnings except Sean, who had been traipsing along more or less on the heels of three attractive females who walked in a bunch. By the time he realized what was happening, the others had taken cover. He was in no position to bolt and decided, in typical fashion, to strike up a casual chat with the gals.

"Um, 'scuze me, Miss—" He tugged her elbow; all three turned as one and went *"Hmm?"* in those eerie, indrawn-breath voices. The runabout of guards was cruising closer.

Sean made idiotic stammerings about having met them before someplace, and maybe they should all do lunch. He laughed unconvincingly, slipped them a couple of winks, sweated.

They were actually quite fetching, triplets with hair dyed orange, blue, and pink to differentiate themselves. They looked at him and listened for a few moments. Sean tried to maintain eye contact and yet watch the guards' slow cruising progress.

Orange Hair turned to her sisters. "This clone's condition is remarkably degenerative, don't you agree?"

"Note the spasmodic facial expressions: neurological breakdown," Blue Hair agreed gravely.

"Let us try to determine the nature of his malfunction before he destabilizes completely," Pinkie put in.

Before Sean could get over his astonishment, they were gathered around him, prying open his mouth, spreading his eye wide to study it, thumping his chest—*feeling him up.*

He had left his torso harness back with his armor, and the three Clonehealers somehow had his tunic open and down around his waist, pinning his arms, and were tripping his feet out from under him in matter-of-fact fashion. He had been walking point, and so he wasn't even carrying a gun.

Their deliberate proddings and pokings sent him into a ticklish laughing fit. *Please, whatever gods there be: Don't let Marie find out about this!*

Dana rushed to the rescue, pushing the women aside. "All tarts pile off!"

"These clones are obviously all infected," said Orange Hair. She raised her voice. "Guards! Seize these clones immediately!"

The runabout came end for end and the guards came roaring back.

"Split up!" Dana cried. "They can't follow us all!" She vaulted a railing with Bowie and Louie bringing up the rear. "Meet back at the tanks!" She ran off down glossy black steps that were mirror-bright and five yards wide.

Angelo dragged Sean to his feet, but realized he had left their tanker carbines leaning against the wall. And there was no time to go for them; shots were ranging around them. They dashed off along the upper thoroughfare; the runabout was following them.

"Y'can't palm yourself off as an *alien*, ya ragweed!" Angelo panted.

"Aw, write it home to your *mother*, Sergeant!" Sean snarled back. They ducked into the first alley they came to. The guard craft stopped and a cop triumvirate piled out to continue the chase on foot.

The cop/guards split up to search a loading dock at the far end of the alley. Sean and Angelo popped out to jump the middle one, the sergeant punching the lone clone *hard*, making sure he wouldn't get up again. Sean grabbed the guard's short, two-handed weapon to cut down another guard. He pivoted, he and the third guard drawing a bead on each other at the same moment.

CHAPTER ELEVEN

I think the real change in Dana began the first time she had to write one of those letters that starts, "As commanding officer of the 15th squad, ATAC, it is my sad duty to inform you . . ."

Louie Nichols, *Tripping the Light Fantastic*

USICA CARESSED THE RAINBOW-BEAM STRINGS OF HER Cosmic Harp, evoking from it sad tonalities. She had no heart for the tunes the Masters would have her play. The acoustics of her darkened hall made it sound like a cathedral.

Her sisters Allegra and Octavia approached, and she resigned herself to yet another disagreement over her new-found defiance. But Allegra said, "A band of alien soldiers has invaded the core district. We thought you would want to know."

Musica caught her breath. "Have they been injured? Captured?"

Allegra spread her hands in a gesture to show that she didn't know. "Karno and his men have started an all-out search for them. They will be found."

Musica sprang to her feet and walked away. "Don't go!" Octavia called after. "It's too dangerous!"

"I must be alone for a while," Musica said over her shoulder. She thought, *No harm must come to him! Oh, Bowie!*

"You mean your units have permitted the enemy primitives to get away?" Mega, androgynous female of the Politician triumvirate, demanded.

The guard group leader conceded, "Only temporarily, Excellency. But they cannot evade us for long, or escape the ship."

She gave him a frigid glare. "Your incompetence will be punished."

Louie, Bowie, and Dana were not the best mix of talents and traits.

They found what looked like a dormitory, then had to dive under the bedlike furnishings when they heard voices. Peeking out from under the beds, they watched as the Clonehealers (who had been accosted by Sean and had accosted him in return) entered, discussing the matter of the alien invaders.

"I cannot wait to sanitize myself," Spreella said, pulling off her robes, "from the pollution of contact with them." All three undressed, to the ATACs' vast interest, and lay down on beds. Projectors of some kind automatically swung into place. Lights beamed down on the clones and put them instantly to sleep. Little ring-auras danced over them.

A few seconds later, the troopers were wearing the togas, hoods pulled up. They ventured out again, and moved across a rotunda in what looked to Dana like Romeo and Juliet's old neighborhood, except that there were no trellises, no flowers or plants of any kind.

More guard runabouts appeared. The three ducked into the first door they came to and found themselves in a place that made them think of a cocktail lounge. It had softly lit art-shapes of glassy blue panes, and gently turning, unearthly mobiles. There was soft music from something that reminded Bowie a little of a flute. They sat nervously at a table and a female clone placed a strange drinking cup before each of them.

"Drink this, then step through that door to the bioscan chamber," she said, and moved on. Everyone else was downing the same purplish stuff; it smelled fragrant.

They were all thirsty, and hadn't been able to find anything like a public fountain or even a tap. They downed the stuff; it was delicious, a real pickup. Not beer, but not bad, and it cut their thirst.

Dana decided to have a look through that door. "Bioscan chamber" sounded like something the brass hats would want to know about. They went through the door, pistols ready in their belts.

A female nurse-technician clone was there, and the three were directed to put their feet on lighted markers inside capsulelike structures. The nurse manipulated a control component that resembled a small, halved Protoculture cap set on a pedestal, its flat face covered with alien instrumentation that looked like the detailing of a mecha.

Rays played over them, and the nurse informed them that although their dysfunction was far along, there was hope for them. Their mental readouts gave the clone particular alarm.

Bowie and Louie looked like they wanted to bolt, but Dana had the feeling that they were close to something vitally important about the Masters' self-contained world. She followed as the nurse led them into the next and far larger chamber.

The place seemed to be filled with a strange blue mist, a large compartment with scores of glassy, coffinlike containers in rows. Long, transparent cylinders descended from apertures in the ceiling to cast pale light. There were more of the control modules set here and there among the scores of shimmering coffins. The ATACs could see still forms in the glassy caskets.

"Looks like we've found the morgue," Dana murmured.

"These conversion stabilizer units will remedy your malfunctions," the nurse explained. She was used to clones being disoriented when they came to her, but she wondered if these particular three were beyond help. "Observe how this unit is now in complete harmony with his environment."

She referred to a male clone who was revealed as his sarcophagus lid rose. He sat up, blinking, on his elbows.

"His structure was stabilized by this treatment and a simple bio-energy supplement," the nurse went on. "You will now drink these."

She was talking about a sluggish looking stuff in three more drinking vessels that had come down on a floating table. Something in Dana was drawn to the idea of *taking an alien elixir*, of finding out what the strange sleep brought. It triggered some deep memory. She yearned to comply, even while the Southern Cross lieutenant in her knew it would be madness.

The nurse was doing something at a wall unit. Louie suddenly yelled, "Look out, Lieutenant!"

Dana turned. The just-awakened clone was lurching toward her, arms outstretched. He didn't look very stabilized to Dana; he looked like something out of a horror movie, pale and hollow-eyed, the living dead.

Their systems aren't functioning up to par, I guess, Louie thought.

Dana, filled with revulsion, screamed for the thing to stay back and hurled her drinking vessel at it; the glass missed and smashed into a control module. Liquid splashed, the module began sparking and sputtering, and the lights started dimming and brightening.

"More trouble," Louie observed; the see-through caskets' indicators and controls were going haywire. The lids were rising; the clones rose from their resting places.

"Oh, great! The whole graveyard's coming to life!" Bowie yelled.

Dana showed her teeth to Louie with a hunting cat's ferocious mien. "*Here's* your ideal society, Louie! *Here's* your machine dream, your Empire of Unimpeded Intellect!" She seemed about to pounce on him. "Well? How d'you like it?"

The nurse was shrilling something about third stage alerts and out-of-control clones. The three ATACs didn't realize that she meant *them*, not the late risers.

She must have put in a call already, though, because the troopers heard running footsteps coming toward them. Three guards with the submachine gun–looking weapons appeared in a doorway.

"Use the zombies for cover and head for that other doorway!" Dana shouted. Bowie and Louie followed her, weaving among the sluggish, confused clones. Dana was hoping the guards would be busy rounding up the blitzed-out sleepwalkers, but the cop/clones gave chase instead.

The three ATACs ended up out on what appeared to be a public transport platform, like a subway station. Dana, in the lead, took a turn and kept sprinting. They wound through sideways and almost tripped over a parked, unattended runabout.

Dana jumped in, determined to get it working; she hit controls at random and it tore away into the air, leaving Bowie and Louie behind.

Everything she did seemed to make it worse, and in moments she had another guard runabout pursuing her. Dana rode over the rotundas and through the passageways, coming close to crashing every two or three seconds, somehow managing not to kill astonished clones, trying to get back to her squadmates.

She heard the pursuing runabout careen out of control and crash into a wall. As she zoomed out of an alley, Dana's own vehicle tried for a wingover, and she went flying. Resigned to death, she had her fall broken by some kind of awning, and slid through as it ripped. She fell on her rear end on some kind of big disposal chute. It disposed of her, down into a steeply pitched shaft, just as she heard her stolen runabout explode against a distant ceiling.

Her funhouse ticket was good for another ride; she went screaming down into darkness. She came sliding down across an arrival stage, losing speed and uniform fabric and skin, and went shooting off, to bounce off something soft and land in a heap.

"Where did *you* come from?" a calm male clone voice asked.

Dana, rubbing her butt and groaning, turned and said, "You wouldn't believe it."

She found herself looking at a slender, graceful clone with long, straight, steel-gray hair and a very young face. "I am Latell, of the Stonecutters," he said, rising from the peculiar-looking pallet on which he had been sitting and coming to kneel by her. "Are you badly hurt? Is there anything I can do?"

She looked around her. The room suggested a Roman bath converted to use as a clone hospital, but here the beds had no lids. Around the room, the Masters' slaves were lying down or sitting, looking very torpid. "Well, you could tell me what this place is."

"Why, this is the district interim center for purging and replacement."

So, she was at yet another clone spa. "Purging of what?"

He tilted his head, studying her. "The personal consciousness of those who must be rehabilitated, naturally."

A male clone nurse appeared, a twin of the one who had tried to serve Dana the mickey. "You two! Your rest period is now terminated. Resume training."

Latell snapped to attention, then drew the truculent Dana to her feet, afraid that she was so destabilized as to risk punishment. Dana saw it wasn't time to start a dust-up, and let Latell lead her away.

He took her to a chamber where dozens of people—that was how she thought of them—were standing two or three apiece at glowing projection tanks. The clones studied abstract shapes and symbols and hypnotic patterns, which changed and shifted, the clones staring down at them with intense concentration.

"Why are *you* here, Latell?"

"I was found guilty of individual thought," he confessed to her. "And you?"

"Uh, the same."

He looked infinitely sad. "But they've allowed you to keep your permanent body," he observed, too polite to point out what a nonstandard body it was—so rounded and with such an odd voice. "Not the normal procedure at all."

"It's, ah, part of an experiment, Latell."

They were at one of the pool tables. Latell was gazing down at the shapes there, brow furrowed. The shapes began changing, multiplying, going do-si-do. "I'm afraid I must confess: *my* reprogramming efforts haven't been entirely successful—oh!"

He was staring disappointedly at the lightshapes. "The trainer is having no effect. I still have individual thought patterns."

She looked him up and down. "What's so bad about that?"

"You know as well as I. Unstable minds cannot be tolerated—"

He was interrupted as a nearby female slumped against her pool table–trainer and fell to the floor. Dana rushed to her, trying to revive her without success.

She looked around. "Somebody give me a hand, here!"

A female who was twin to the one Dana cradled said frostily, "That is forbidden. Her body will have to be replaced."

So, when one member of the triumvirate got out of whack by the Masters' standards, he or she was either fixed, or replaced. And the triumvirate went on.

Dana showed her teeth in a snarl. "What are you, Human beings or cattle?"

Human? She could hear the word ripple through them with a shiver of disgust. The clones left their trainers and began to converge on her. Latell dragged Dana to her feet, though she fought him.

"You've gone too far," he said. "You must leave."

"Idiots!" she was screaming. "Can't you see what they're doing to you?" Was this how Zor would end his days? But he had been a freethinking Human! To come to this . . .

The nurse had reappeared, with a twin. "This one requires a body replacement. Yes. You, come with us."

The clone grabbed her and Dana let out her rage in the form of a quick footsweep and a shoulder block. The nurses went flying in either direction.

She seized Latell's wrist. "C'mon. I'm getting you outta here." He didn't resist. He was doomed, whatever he did, and in addition found her fascinating.

Angelo and Sean had guard uniforms to wear over their Southern Cross outfits (though Angelo's was strained to its limits, to say the least), and guns and a runabout, but with the action over, they were at a loss as to what to do next. Parked in a deserted upper-tier plaza, they worried and debated.

A plate on the runabout's dash came alight and a voice said, "Unit thirteen, return to Main Control. Prepare for Override Guidance to return you to Main Control."

Sean checked over his stolen weapon. "Get ready, Angie. We just got our ticket to the target."

Stolen vehicles were the order of the day, only natural for a stranded Hovertank unit. Bowie and Louie had heisted themselves a vanlike craft, and techmaster Louie had quickly figured out how to drive it.

They cruised slowly, hoping to spot one of the others and to get their bearings on either the control center or the tanks. Bowie, riding shotgun, abruptly yelped, "Louie, pull over! Stop!"

"Hah? Whatsamatter? Whatsamatter?" But he did as the other asked. Bowie leapt out and went running after Musica, who had been wandering along as if in a daze.

Louie shrugged. "Why not? We got nothin' better to do."

At Musica's direction, the three drove to the weirdest place they had yet seen in the mother ship. It was like some underground grotto or an ant's orchard.

Glowing spheres, some of them fifty feet across, were *growing* there—at least that was what it looked like. The spheres were held by a network of vinelike growths, alien lianas four and five feet thick, which sprouted dense crops of translucent hairs the width of hawsers.

The vines traveled up to the roof and down to the floor in clusters, where they were rooted in the soil. There, smaller spheres sprouted on single vines, with spores of the mature forms growing in the middle.

Bowie sat and Musica knelt, each looking off in the opposite direction at the tree-broad base of one of the rootvines. Louie waited in the van, some distance off.

"Everyone is looking for you," she was saying. "I was so afraid you'd been hurt or captured."

"It almost happened. It still could, but now I don't care."

She turned to him. "Why do you say that?"

Without looking at her, he reached out to close his hand around her pale, slender forearm. "Now that I've found you again, nothing else matters to me."

She said haltingly, "It's very strange to me, but I feel the same way. And the odd yearning—that peculiar disquiet in me is no longer there when we are together."

"We belong together."

"I would be happy to remain this way for the rest of time, Bowie."

He was about to reply in kind when a harsh voice cut through the peace. "Do not move, Micronian! Stand slowly!"

Bowie found himself gaping at Karno and two others more or less just like him, and the big dark muzzles of their guns.

CHAPTER
TWELVE

When the Robotech Masters first appeared, the Factory Satellite sent itself off on a far, SDF-style orbit. It went to Code Red and manned battle stations. It issued heartening war bulletins.

No wonder the situation got so crazy. Southern Cross had forgotten the lessons of terrestrial wars, and nobody had warned us that we might see the enemy as Human beings.

Louie Nichols, *Tripping the Light Fantastic*

"MUSICA, MOVE AWAY FROM THE ALIEN AT ONCE," commanded Darsis. More guards with their guns leveled appeared from among the massive vines.

"He is an enemy of our people," Karno stated. But Musica defied him, moving to stand between Bowie and the Guards, arms spread.

"You musn't hurt him, Karno! I forbid it! He's done you no harm!"

She forbids? The insanity of it boggled Karno's brain.

Darsis frowned. "Anyone shielding an enemy of the state will be punished! Now, stand aside, Musica!"

The Guards were in a quandary, though; Musica was far too vital to the Robotech Masters and their hold over the population of the ships to simply shoot, and she knew it. It was a situation the Guards had never encountered before.

They were saved from the inconvenience of thinking by the revving of a van engine. Louie came hot-tailing at the Guards, yelling for Bowie to make a break. Karno and his men got a few rounds into the van, but then had no choice but to hit the dirt or scatter.

They were up again right away, firing into the vehicle's stern, and it arced toward the ground leaking smoke into the distance.

Louie managed to get out of the van and saw the Guards racing after him. He turned to go, but realized there was a beeping in his pocket.

He pulled forth one of his gadgets, studied it, smiled broadly, and raced off to make his escape.

Bowie, going for cover in the midst of a tangle of the colossal vine-roots, skidded to a stop. More guards emerged from it, hemming him in against those pursuing him.

Louie shook off his hunters and followed his gadget; it didn't take very long to find what he had detected. Some sixth sense comprehension of systemry and Robotechnology led him to a vaulted compartment in what had to be the center of the flagship. To his amazement, it was unguarded. What he found there left him speechless.

In the center of the vastness was a device the size of an upright shuttlecraft. Top and bottom were sawtoothed halves, as if a cylinder of taffy had been sawn apart and stretched. What hung between them was—

Whaaa-at? Louie asked himself, dumbfounded. It looked like a single braided mass of fibrous tissue, red, black, pink, and yellow like some textbook illustration of a muscle. But pieces hung from it, curled and kinked in the way of sprung wires peeling from a cable, or fibers of steel wool.

The whole circular chamber was lined with instruments stretching up and up out of sight. The central device itself was orbited by slow-moving amoeboid shapes of pure blue-white light.

What an amazing creation! The flagship's control nexus.

Louie still had the alien energy-burpgun he and Bowie had managed to steal. He worked it as if he had been using one all of his life, preparing to empty it in one blast, without regard to his own survival.

Destroy this, and the Robotech Masters are finished. And there wasn't even anybody around to put him in for a posthumous medal, oh well. . . .

He decided to start high and blast a vertical cut in the thing. No sooner had he opened fire than jagged lightning broke from one of the amoeboid shapes. The weapon was suddenly giving out heavy voltage. He managed to let go before his heart was stopped, and it was levitated away high into the air.

From the central tissue mass, a hundred ghostly ribbons of force, or ectoplasmic lariats, were dropped. They wound around Louie and squeezed his breath from him, sending an awful surge of energy through his body. He was lit up like a Christmas tree ornament. One of the less fortunate martyred saints.

Word went out that the Living Protoculture had captured its assailant. The search for the other raiders intensified.

Dana didn't want to hear or see any more.

Latell had taken her past too many glassy spheres filled with bubbling fluid. In them, naked, wired-up clones wearing helmets floated, dead to the world. One of those clones was supposed to be the *actual* Latell the Stonecutter, or perhaps the embodiment of the triumvirate of Stonecutters, but then who was this talking to her?

This time, the guards who showed up didn't do much talking. The doors parted and three charged in shooting. The first few rounds shattered the container of Latell's "original body." The Latell she had been *talking* to gave a grievous moan as she pulled him behind the other containers and apparatus for cover.

The clone-fetus, slick with fluids, looked at Dana. Then its eyes rolled up into its head and it expired there among the shards of its container.

Something in her snapped, and several objects on which she could vent her rage were right close to hand. The guards weren't really much as soldiers; apparently all they had ever had to do was keep docile slaves in line and now and then round up some extraordinarily aberrant one. Invaders were all but unknown, and the upshot was that the guards' combat skills weren't nearly so well-honed as Dana's.

She came flying at them from behind a pillar of support equipment, shrieking a *ki-yi* that froze them. She took out the first with the sword edge of her right foot, and that only fed her hatred. The second, too close to get clear, tried to swing the butt-plate of his weapon into her face. She ducked, and then broke his neck.

She bent down to pick up the weapon he had dropped, but the third had fallen back against the hatch to spray energy bolts in her direction, forcing her to throw herself back. Latell managed to find her among the disintegrating containers and sputtering power lines, and together they crawled off through a side hatch as still more guards appeared and converged on them.

The guards cornered them in the next compartment, a sort of nursery for infants. *Why would the Masters need infants,* it occurred to her, *when they can grow clones to adulthood* in vitro*?*

Latell palmed a tiny device to her. "This is a maintenance sensor; it will lead you to the control center. Destroy the center!"

Latell tried to push her to cover, tried to block the way. He was a dysfunctioning slave of no importance; the guards shot him down.

There was no place to run away. Dana cradled his head in her lap. He achieved a thin smile. "Please do not feel badly, Sister. You are Freedom, and my life was not worth the living."

And so the clone Latell the Stonecutter died.

The firefight in the power-relay area was one of the more interesting fights of Angelo Dante's life, although it did threaten to fix things so he would never collect any of his retirement pay.

Still, he and Sean had good cover. They had taken out a lot of guards already, and there was still some chance they could get free. Angelo stood and sprayed shots at the enemy. If the ATACs were pinned down, so were the guards, who had learned better than to try to rush the Human marksmen across the yards of open space.

Then the sergeant realized that Sean wasn't firing. He was about to holler something suitably crude and insulting when he felt a tug at the sleeve of his stolen guard uniform.

Angelo whirled to see ten, eleven, perhaps a dozen of the runabouts in an arc behind him, all crowded with guards and officers who had drawn a bead on him and Sean.

"Don't think I'll forget your face, slimeball, 'cause *I won't!*" Angelo growled as the guard thrust him headlong onto the detention cell floor. Sean, who had been more resigned and reasonable, disembarked from the elevator with his hands behind his neck. The elevator doors closed.

Dana, sitting on a sleeping shelf with her knees drawn up, simply looked at the two new arrivals. Louie didn't even look. Bowie knelt by Angelo's side. "You okay, Sarge?"

Angelo nodded, springing up and shrugging Bowie off, stretching and flexing his ample muscles. "Yeah. Gang's all here, huh?"

Dana grunted. They were all there, stripped of weapons and disguises, dressed in their ATAC uniforms.

"And we failed our mission," Angelo went on, as bitter at himself as at any of them or at fate. "We lost!"

Now Dana *did* look up, to fix him with her stare.

"Only round one," she said.

Gazing down on the captive specimens through their Protoculture cap, the Robotech Masters were taken aback, in spite of the information and insights they had gained through Zor Prime.

"Most interesting," Shaizan said. "They show no fear of their captivity, only anger that they have failed, and an illogical unwillingness to face reality."

There was an unspoken consensus among them: there were terrible, unsuspected powers in the one-mindedness and emotions of the Micronians.

Powers upon which a universe could turn.

It didn't take long, in a little bowl-shaped, inescapable confinement some fifteen feet across at floor level, for the ATACs to get on each other's nerves.

A crack from Angelo about Zor's spying. A hurt objection from Dana that she had no way of knowing. A blithe comment from Sean that love was blind, followed by Dana kicking Sean's feet out from under him, then both of them ready to twist each other's bones loose, and the others diving in to break it up.

"Fascinating. The Earthlings have a pronounced tendency to turn upon one another in confinement," Shaizan remarked.

Dag said, "They are too primitive to comprehend that what we are doing will ensure *their* survival as well as our own." It did not need to be added, of course, that that survival would be as a slave species. The Masters considered their slaves greatly honored, Chosen.

"If the Invid obtain the Protoculture Matrix before we do," Bowkaz put to words what they all knew, "it will in all likelihood mean the eradication of the entire Human species."

"The last part of that statement is not an entirely unpleasant prospect," was Shaizan's rejoinder.

"As to the prisoners," Dag went on, "my suggestion is that the five of them should be reprocessed as new biogenetic material for our cloning vats straight away."

"No—all but the female," Dag corrected. "According to our measurements, her intellect and biogenetic traits are extremely contrary to Human norms. Dissection and analysis are in order."

"I say it might be more efficient and safe simply to destroy them all," Bowkaz said.

Jeddar, group leader of the Clonemasters—whose triumvirate floated nearby on its cap—took the extraordinary step of interjecting a comment. "Excuse me, my Masters, but we propose that you delay these actions until we've reprogrammed Zor Prime's memory, restoring full awareness to him."

Tinsta, the female of their triad, continued, "His experience on Earth has increased his bio-energy index above that of any other clone, even far above precious Zor clones.

"We believe it has something to do with his prolonged exposure to Human emotions. We think that these emotions maximize certain aspects of clone performance. But we cannot be certain until further—eh?"

A message was being broadcast over the ship's annunciator system. "Attention, all sectors. This is Clone Control. Quadrant four reports that Zor Prime is missing. Repeat, Zor Prime has left his assigned sector. All guard units begin search pattern sigma. Security leaders contact Clone Control at once."

Musica's attempts to drown her grief in her songs were unsuccessful. Even the accompaniment of her sisters on spinet and lute couldn't lift her spirits or erase the image of Bowie from her mind's eye.

At last she hit a dissonant note and turned to them. "I am sorry, sisters, but there come upon me now times when I wish we weren't always together—the Three-Who-Act-as-One. I find myself wondering what it was like *before* the time of the triumvirates, when each individual was able to act independently."

Allegra and Octavia showed their revulsion, crying out at her to be still, but she went on. "A time when we were capable of feeling pleasure, pain, happiness, even loneliness! I wonder what it is like to love."

She bent over her Cosmic Harp, face buried in her hands.

The words of three guards, making a sweep through the chamber, brought her up sharply. In answer to Allegra's question, they explained about the escape of Zor Prime and their search.

I know what I must do now, Musica realized.

Zor Prime wandered aimlessly through the various districts of the flagship's residential sector. He hadn't evaded the search by any conscious effort; he was too disoriented for that.

The ancient stone buildings seemed to fade in and out, to be replaced by scenes of Monument City, so that part of the time he thought dazedly that he was back on Earth. The sun seemed too bright and hot, too intense, overhead. Often he saw Dana coming toward him, beckoning, laughing, so desirable. . . .

A patrolling guard runabout failed to spot him because a veiled figure pulled him back into the darkness of an alley. Zor shook off his trance and saw Musica lower her veil and look up at him hopefully.

So many half images and confused memories assailed him that he lost balance and fell to his hands and knees on the gleaming terrazzo flooring. "Why is my mind so full of nightmares?"

"You are the clone of the original Zor," she said. "In a way, it might be said that you are the only *true* Robotech Master."

With her help, he found the strength to rise again. But just then a bright ray struck him from behind, and he fell once more. Standing behind him were guards, and the Clonemasters, on an antigrav platform.

"It was only a low-gain destabilizer," Jeddar told Musica. "We need the clone for a little while longer."

CHAPTER THIRTEEN

Dear Mom & Dad,

Everything here remains quiet, as always, and I don't know why you two keep insisting there's bad war news. Take it from me. As I wrote you before, I'm in a rear-echelon unit that hardly ever sees any action at all. So I hope you'll excuse me for asking you both to kindly quit worrying. Especially with Pop in the condition he is in.

I'm sorry I missed Christmas. There's always next year, after all. I think I might be able to pull a furlough soon, with things being so dull around here and all.

Thanks for the fruitcake; it was great.

Love,
Your son,
Angelo Dante

THE ORDER OF THE DAY WAS EXECUTION, AND THE CLONES with the rifles weren't listening to any ATAC objections about the Geneva Convention. Dana and her squadmates had no room to try anything in the cell; they marched out with hands behind their heads, as per instructions.

Surrounded by guards, the troopers were marched through the detention center and into a side corridor. Without warning, the clones' exacting schedule was interrupted.

A driverless runabout with its engine shrilling came zooming at the lead guards. The triad was knocked high in the air with bone-breaking force, Dana just barely managing to pull back out of the way. In a shower of sparks and metal fragments, the runabout overturned and shrieked to a stop upside down. The first guards were crunched to the floor as the troopers jumped the other three, who seemed paralyzed by what had happened.

It was a short fight, Sean ramming an elbow back into one rear guard's throat, Angelo crashing the heads of the other two together like cymbals. Even as the 15th was rearming itself from the selection of weapons lying around, Musica came running toward them. "Bowie!"

Louie was delighted to find that one of the guards was carrying the pulse-grenade that he himself had been carrying when he'd been captured. *Okay, Living Protoculture; let's just go another round, what d'ya say?*

In the Memory Management complex, Zor rested, strapped to a padded slab, at an acute angle, nearly standing upright. He was still unconscious, his head encased in a helmet like a metal medusa.

Technician clones were moving precisely, ensuring that no mistake would be made. Zor's original memories, as servant to the Masters, Bioroid warrior, battle lord of the fleet, must be restored to him and integrated with the memories of his time among the Humans. Then the totality of his memory would be comprehensible, and would be shifted to storage banks for further study. The lump of tissue that was the last Zor clone could be disposed of.

Jeddar watched the preparations with satisfaction. He would have been less happy had he seen what was transpiring on an upper tier of the chamber.

On a glass-walled observation deck, a big forearm locked around a guard clone's throat, and the guard was silently removed from active duty. Angelo resisted the temptation to dust off his palms.

Dana and the 15th looked down on the demons' workshop below. She saw what they were doing to Zor and almost gave out a yelp, but Louie shushed her, as he studied the instruments and machinery. He adjusted his tech goggles to detect energies on very subtle levels and looked the lab over like a sniper studying the landscape through a nightvision device.

"Screwy operation," Sean said wryly.

"But convenient," Louie countered. "See those gauges over there? When they hit the top, Zor's memories will all be back in his brain."

Louie indicated a bank of three stacked rectangles. The first was filled, all glowing blue; the second was filling, as if it were a resplendent blue thermostat marking a sudden, incredible heat wave.

The techs had to pry Zor's jaws apart and wedge a mouthpiece between them as the indicators rose. As the third stack filled, he began to convulse. Louie had to hold Dana back from hurling herself through the glassy pane of the observation deck to intervene.

At last a tech clone pronounced, "Full reinstatement of memory is now complete. Reintegration of memory will begin at once—" He was cut off by an intense barrage from above. The tier window and much of the complex's apparatus was shot to bits. Before anybody there could react, the ATACs had dropped to the main floor and had the clones covered.

"Don't anybody move," Dana warned. They could see from her eyes what would happen if they did.

Jeddar and his Clonemasters were more astonished than afraid. This was, after all, their first close encounter with Humans. Behind the raiders came Musica, and Karno was visibly shaken to see her, breathing her name.

In another second, Louie and Angelo freed Zor from his restraints and cranial wiring. The big sergeant got the unconscious clone over his shoulder with ease. As much as Angelo might have berated Zor, Dana noticed that now he glared around furiously at the creatures who had tortured him.

The troopers were so busy making sure that no one on the scene made any hostile moves that they missed the slight motion it took Jeddar to press a button on his wristband. A moment later, a door snapped open and three more guards leapt into the opening.

Everyone opened fire simultaneously, and those guards who were already in the lab took the opportunity to spring for cover, as did the Clonemasters, the ATACs, and Musica. The energy bolts crashed and flashed; the air began heating up at once. Shots set off eruptions of power from the complex's systemry.

"I believe you've gone mad, Musica!" Karno called to her over the din of the firefight. "What have these monsters done to you to make you a traitor to your own kind?"

Musica, flustered, didn't know how to explain except to say, "Zor is their friend; they're saving him!"

Then Bowie was towing her along. "We're getting out of here!"

Intense fire from the 15th had cleared the doorway; three guards lay dead or dying there. With practiced calm and precision, the five troopers fired as they moved. The remaining enemy had no choice but to keep their heads down, only able to risk the occasional shot.

There was another runabout outside the complex; in a moment, the escapees were roaring away, with Dana and Sean keeping up a high volume of fire to make sure no one followed or tried for a parting shot.

Released from the grip of the mind apparatus, Zor began to stir, then came around. Dana was overjoyed and stopped shooting long enough to gush about how happy she was, but Angelo, at the controls, growled, "*Secure* that hearts-and-flowers crap! We've still gotta find ourselves a way outta this joint, remember?"

At that moment three red Bioroids appeared, skimming along close to the ceiling of the high central passageway in which the runabout was traveling. Angelo managed to dodge their first bolts, nearly smearing the vehicle along the nearby wall, then made a desperate turn into a side way, losing the enemy mecha for the moment.

"We've got to get back to the Hovertanks!" Dana yelled over the wind of their passage.

"I'm workin' on it, ma'am."

She consulted the tiny sensor Latell had given her. "Take that next right!" Perhaps they could retrace their steps from the control center, which Musica had pointed out along the way.

They slewed and hairpin-turned and blasted along, coming around a corner only to run head-on into another triad of guards. Disinclined to stop, Angelo gritted his teeth and slammed into them, hurling two to either side, slamming the middle one to the floor.

But the impact made the runabout defy its controls. It hit a stanchion, bounced back the other way while Angelo fired retros desperately, then hit the floor surface and slowly upended. Its occupants were spilled out and it came to a final rest with a clang and crunch.

Dana shook her head, looking up. Directly before her was an open hatchway, and beyond—"Look! It's the central control area!" The housing in which the Living Protoculture was situated was closed, protecting it.

For the moment.

They heard Hovercraft approaching and scattered to find concealment in the center. In another few seconds, the three reds settled in for a landing, dismounting and scanning the area.

Seeing the Bioroids sparked something in Zor's still-disorganized memory. He turned to Musica, who crouched with him under a huge conduit. "Why did the Masters send me to Earth in the first place?" he whispered. Somehow he knew that she, Mistress of the music that was part of the Masters' power over their realm, could answer.

She looked at him with infinite sadness. "You were their eyes and ears. You were sent to Earth as a spy," she mouthed the words more than whispered them. "They planted a neuro-sensor in your brain. You weren't even aware of what you were doing, Zor!"

The entire center, the entire ship, began thrumming with a peculiar vibration, something that made their hair stand on end. The Bioroids cocked their heads, registering it.

"It's a battle alert," Musica mouthed to the ATACs. "Your forces must be attacking us!"

"Time to make our move," Dana said. "We take out this control center, whatever it costs, understood? Otherwise Emerson won't have a chance." With a little luck, Louie could figure out some way to put it out of commission. But first the reds had to go.

The 15th troopers fanned out, firing at the Bioroids, dodging from cover, heading for the Living Protoculture. They kept close to the systemry, shooting from its protection. The enemy mecha seemed reluctant to fire, enduring the minor consequences of the small arms fire rather than risk damaging the ship's core. One was angling for a clear shot at them; Louie reluctantly used his pulse grenade on it, but only staggered it instead of putting it out of the fight.

Only Zor and Musica remained behind, she stunned by what was happening, he immobilized by surfacing memories. Then Zor found himself remembering, remembering much. His gaze traveled to the 15th's commanding officer.

Dana...

He knew what he had to do. He crept away to one side, getting clear of the shooting.

At the same time, Musica was coming to a decision. *There isn't much time. The ship will be destroyed soon. I must get to the barrier control!*

She raced for the stairs that wound up around the housing that protected the Protoculture. Bowie, seeing her go, yelled her name and sprinted after.

Musica ran like a deer up the broad steps. But she was in the open, and a Bioroid risked a shot as she neared the top. At the same moment, a bolt from Angelo's weapon hit the red's discus gun; its discharge hit the housing near Musica, missing her, but dazing her and damaging the housing.

In a moment, Bowie was at her side. "Bowie, the barrier! It *must* be deactivated!"

He nodded, and sprang up the last few steps to the control panel she had been trying to reach. The 15th was pitching at the reds with everything they had, and the damage to the housing kept the reds from attempting another shot at Musica or Bowie.

At her direction, he pushed a button, pulled down on the gleaming lever that appeared in response to that. A world-shaking hooting rose above the first alarms and even the firefight. "Hurry!" she called to him. "We must go!"

The Bioroids were at a terrible disadvantage since it was forbidden by the unseen Masters to fire any shot that might endanger the ship's systemry. The ATACs had been quick to exploit this fact; five rifles were a lot of firepower if the users knew where to aim, and the troopers had had plenty of practice at hitting faceplates.

As Bowie helped Musica down from the steps, the last Bioroid tottered backward and came to rest leaning against the bulkhead. The fugitives raced into the passageway, but another trio of reds dropped from nowhere, blocking their way. The rifles were all but exhausted, and there was no hiding behind systemry now. The leader took dead aim with its discus handgun—

The gun and the arm blew apart in an eruption that almost knocked them flat on their backs. Jetting down the passageway behind them came a well-remembered red on its Hovercraft.

"Go get 'em, Zor!" Dana cheered.

Zor was still the greatest battle lord in the enemy fleet. He dodged the other reds' blasts deftly, firing with great accuracy all the while. He leapt his mecha from the Hovercraft, and let the saucer-platform crash into them, destroying his opponents in a collision that half-deafened the fugitives.

Zor's Bioroid landed with a deck-shaking impact. "Dana, you and the others go ahead; the Hovertanks are that way, through there. I'll stay here and delay any further pursuit." His voice was the voice of the Zor they had served with, not the eerie, indrawn-breath voice of the Master's slave.

"*Huh!*" Angelo said, with something like approval.

"We'll be waiting for you," Dana said somberly.

There was no other option; the escapees dashed on. Zor turned to wait patiently. It didn't take long; three groups of Triumviroids raced into view on Hovercraft. Zor took aim and began firing.

Astoundingly, the tanks were just as the 15th had left them.

"But what good'll they do us?" Angelo asked, as the squad fired up their mecha. "There's no way we can reach Emerson on just tank thrusters!"

"Don't you think I know that?" Dana snapped. With their

mecha in tank mode, the 15th followed her as she tried to retrace the route she had taken on her first evasive dash with Bowie and Louie.

At last she found what she was searching for, a sort of cul-de-sac compartment piled high with salvaged components and disabled equipment. It was obvious that a lot of repair work was done there as well.

The tanks stopped, cannon trained on the only hatchway. The troopers rose to stand in their cockpit-turrets. Dana pointed to a rank of Hovercraft that had seen better days.

"Louie, you've got to find us the five best out of those, and make sure they'll get us to Emerson."

Easy for you to say! he thought. Was she crazy, or just ignorant? "Lieutenant, I—"

"I don't want to hear it! I'm not talking about winning a Formula X race; we'll only need them for a few minutes. If we're not back with the fleet by that time, it won't make any difference."

Aboard his flagship, Emerson had long since reached the conclusion his subordinates were warily expressing. The Earth forces were going at the Masters with hammer and tongs once more, but couldn't take the beating they were getting for much longer.

There was no sign of the 15th and no radio contact. Emerson ordered that the fleet prepare to withdraw, that the A-JACs prepare to return to their transports. When Lieutenant Crystal objected, he dressed her down brusquely, and reiterated his orders.

But the whole time, he thought, *Bowie. Dana.* And he knew the other names as well.

CHAPTER FOURTEEN

Bowie, life in danger with you is
so much more than
Life without you would be
even if death strikes its chord

Musica, "End of the Old Songs"

WHILE LOUIE DID HIS WIZARD-OF-ROBOTECH NUMBER, Dana and the others, with Musica's help, discovered the controls that opened the shaft overhead. The ATACs redonned their armor, and Bowie made sure his canopy was tight; Musica had no other protection.

In Battloid mode, the 15th boarded the Hovercraft. Dana's *Valkyrie* reached out a huge finger to flick a Bioroid-scale switch. The shaft hatch opened, triggering the closing of emergency doors in the passageway leading to the cul-de-sac. The 15th rose amid a storm of junk and debris hurled upward by the escaping atmosphere.

It was the first and last time such an unlikely combination of Robotechnology took place. Weaving through volleys from their own forces, the ATACs started their survival run. There was still no sign of the red Bioroid, and it was too late to turn back.

Unstoppable, unbeatable, Zor not only sent his opponents reeling back, but actually fought his way forward towards the control center.

Knowing all the Triumviroids' weaknesses, he was also their superior in experience and speed and adaptability, master of virtuoso tactics they had never even had time to learn. He had left a trail of death and destruction through the flagship's passageways.

Now Zor stood before the Living Protoculture, which still hid within its armored cylinder. He knew, though, that it was too weak to defend itself, depleted and wounded by the battle raging through the ship. He felt that it sensed its impending destruction.

I betrayed my friends. Just as it happened so long ago, with the Invid! Am I damned, doomed to live this agony over and over? The red Bioroid raised its discus weapon and aimed at the cylinder. Fire and smoke rose around it.

And now my only way to redeem myself is by betraying my people. Everything I touch turns to ashes. So be it.

Dana, good-bye!

He triggered the weapon just as the cylinder slid open, and the Living Protoculture lashed out in a last desperate effort to save itself.

The explosion was bigger than anything ever seen from a mother ship before; an entire section of the stupendous vessel was simply vaporized, its edges pushed outward as the Main Control section detonated.

"You stupid alien," Dana said in a small voice, looking back at it. "You said you'd catch up."

"I'm truly sorry, Dana," Angelo fumbled, not used to soft words. "I—I know you were fond of him. And he liked you a lot, I could tell."

Sean was already in contact with Emerson's fleet. The 15th hadn't beaten the clock by much; they just about had enough time and fuel to catch the withdrawing strikeforce.

Louie also watched the explosion. He adjusted his tech goggles, trying to see what information they might offer. He did a slight double take, changed magnification and spectrum bands, and looked again. "Lieutenant? I think you better check this out."

It was beginning to be visible to the naked eye against the glare of the explosion so close behind it—a form resolving itself into a red Bioroid on a Hovercraft.

"It's him!" Dana's heart had never been so full. At first it looked as if Zor was helping along a wounded red, but then they saw that he had his Battloid clasped to him.

"Whaddaya know," Angelo drawled. "He even brought along a change of clothes."

Zor, racing to overtake them, wondered about the ways of fate, and the Shapings of the Protoculture. The last effort of the living mass that served the Masters had only contained the inevitable explosion for scant seconds—enough time for him to retrieve his tank and find a Hovercraft and flee.

But he was still an alien in a strange land. He wondered if what waited ahead would be any better than what he left behind.

The Masters knew their flagship was doomed.

Invader assault ships, forward command ships, and the other smaller craft that were berthed in the Masters' flagship took aboard as many clones as they could in the little time they had left. But because the Masters were impatient to get to safety and unwilling to risk themselves or their possessions for the sake of unstable clones, many were left behind. And so they abandoned their faithful slaves.

In one evacuation ship, Allegra and Octavia clung to each other, Karno staring out of the viewport furiously as explosion after explosion rocked the flagship.

Musica! the two sisters sent out the silent, plaintive cry.

In the cockpit of the *Re-Tread*, Musica gasped. But when Bowie asked what was wrong, she just shook her head and said it was nothing.

"The whole thing's gonna blow!" he yelled excitedly.

She turned in time to see blue, concentric rings leap out from the flagship. Then a star grew from it, hurling forth a gaseous cloud.

Farewell, my sisters, she thought, as the 15th got ready to link up with Emerson's fleet.

While Emerson elected to withdraw to the ALUCE base with the main body of his command, damaged vessels and as many of the casualties as possible made a run for Earth. One such vessel was the one that happened to have picked up Dana and her companions.

In the tremendous confusion, it wasn't hard to smuggle Musica to a place of temporary safety, but that left the problem of Fokker Base, and debarkation. Fortunately, the rest of the 15th, having been separated from them, were on another ship, bound for ALUCE base with Emerson's main force, leaving fewer to keep the secret. Surprisingly, Angelo was loudest among those voices raised to protect the Mistress of the Cosmic Harp.

"We can't let the GMP get her! Remember what they did to Zor, all that testing and probing and scanning, like he was some kinda animal?" It was already a matter of barely spoken agreement that there would be no mention to Southern Cross Command of Zor's temporary defection, at least for the time being.

Dana was calmer. "Don't worry; anybody who messes with Musica is going to have to mess with us first."

"Blast him!" Leonard bellowed in Southern Cross Army HQ. "I question Emerson's commitment! I question his sanity!"

It was all for the benefit of UEG observers who were on the scene; Leonard knew his words would reach Moran and the rest of the council promptly. "The enemy fleet still has five fully operational mother ships, and yet he withdraws!"

But Leonard was upset for another reason. Now he could no longer fall back on Emerson's genius and leadership. There was no one to whom he could delegate authority; the defense of Earth, the responsibility and the culpability, fell squarely on him. He was unsure now; his attitude toward Emerson's absence in the field was very different.

Zor had passed out just after being brought aboard the transport and had suffered the injuries to justify it. Dana had no choice but to turn him over to a med team and hope he would keep the secret of what had happened in the flagship, as the 15th would keep it.

The ambulance with Zor in it had barely pulled away when Nova Satori showed up. "Welcome back, Dana. What—what did they say about Zor?"

They hadn't spoken to one another since Komodo's death. They felt uneasy in each other's company.

"He'll recover. Listen, Nova, I'm really busy right now, so if you don't mind . . ."

That kind of evasiveness from the 15th's CO set off alarm bells in Nova's head. *Now* what were these eight balls up to?

Musica held back panic, enclosed by armor that seemed ready to crush her, fearful of what life among Humans might hold. Oddly enough, it wasn't any of those, or the danger of exposure, that beset her the worst just then. Instead, it was a comparatively little thing, the sickly-sweet, rubbery smell of the ATAC helmet's breather mask; she was nauseous, not sure how long she could control herself. The 15th, long since oblivious to the smell, had forgotten how it sometimes affected boot trainees.

She did her best to be brave, but wasn't sure she was up to it.

* * *

"Looks like somebody else took a hit, too." Louie and Angelo, suit helmets doffed, were carrying the stretcher themselves. As they passed Nova, they both suddenly put on expressions more appropriate to a poker game than a homecoming.

Nothing they could say could keep Nova from getting to the stretcher, throwing back the blanket. Dana sighed, and took off the reclining trooper's helmet when Nova threatened to do it herself.

Sean Phillips smiled up at her. "Shrapnel, right in the big toe, can ya believe it? But I still qualify for a medal and recuperative leave, and it *does* smart, and—"

Nova upended the stretcher and walked away. Dana was yelling at the few 15th troopers around her—her core group—to get busy and off-load the Hovertanks, and she even gave Sean a swift kick. Then she barked at another, "You, too! Hurry along there, Private Doppler! Double time!"

Then they had disappeared back into the transport. Nova stalked away angrily, but stopped suddenly. " 'Doppler' ?"

Minutes later, GI personnel staff was confirming that the only Private Doppler was a 15th trooper who had died during the assault that had temporarily brought down the mother ship, weeks before.

Who could Dana be hiding, if that's what she's doing? The only possibility seemed too farfetched. Even Dana wouldn't be *that* crazy.

"Here: Lemme take a look at you." Dana felt only mild jealousy that Musica looked better in one of her outfits than Dana herself.

Musica turned 180 degrees self-consciously. Her green hair would fit in with current Earth fads; caught back as it was in a heavy clip, nearly reaching her waist, it was gorgeous. "But— these garments expose my legs."

"With legs like yours, Musica, I wouldn't let it bother you. See for yourself, in the mirror."

Musica did, pulling at the puffy sleeves of the pink blouse, the hem of the full skirt. "Why is it whenever *I* wear something like that it makes me look about ten years old?" Dana wondered aloud.

They decided to let Bowie enter at last and cast his vote. It took him a while to find words, and when he did all he could say was, "I'll write a song about it." Musica's face shone.

Angelo called from the hospital to tell them Zor was being released. The rest of the 15th was in one of the ships that had gone to ALUCE with Emerson, and had been seconded to the 10th ATAC squad, another Hovertank unit. Since the 15th was badly under strength, it wasn't on alert or standby; Dana decided that a party was in order.

"Get Zor over to the Moon of Havana by eight, okay, Angie? We'll meet you there."

It was good to be alive.

In the mother ship to which the Masters had withdrawn when their own flagship was atomized, Allegra and Octavia were thrust into a detention area.

They were still in shock. Muse clones simply weren't treated this way!

But they saw that much had changed, and this wrath of the Masters was only part of it.

Deprived of their instruments and, in Musica's absence, a vital part of themselves, they trudged into the cheerless and impersonal holding area. The clones confined there were dispirited and lethargic.

The two Muses huddled together in a corner, fearful of what might come next. "It's all because of Musica," Allegra said bitterly. "She abandoned us and betrayed her own people! They can't understand that her sins aren't ours, so they've cast us away in here!"

"Allegra—"

But she cut Octavia off. "I feel—" Allegra made a vague, angry gesture, to express the rage for which she had no word.

"Musica is our sister; we three are one," Octavia said soothingly. But she was troubled. Didn't Allegra see that she was falling victim to the same malady that had claimed Musica? Apparently, the sickness called "emotion" had more than one symptom.

The party started with a toast to the ATACs who had been killed or wounded in the battle. Then, one to the members of the 15th who had been redeployed to ALUCE. After that, life, love, and happiness were the subjects. The ATAC troopers had no urge to toast victory or rehash the battle—it was time to forget the war for a while.

The manager gave the 15th a great table, a circular banquette. Soon Bowie was at the Moon of Havana's piano. Musica sat, absorbed in his playing. And the songs he played were new, like nothing she had ever heard or thought of before! And he was *making some of it up as he went along!* These Humans were truly astonishing.

Things were going fine until they realized Nova Satori was

standing in front of their table. Dana couldn't think of anything to do but invite her to sit down.

Nova sat, and turned to Musica. "I don't believe we've met. I'm Lieutenant Nova Satori of the GMP. You are . . . ?"

Musica looked nervously to Dana for rescue. "Friend of Bowie's," Dana replied. "We haven't been able to get her to say 'boo' all night. Another musician—plays the ukulele or something like that, I think he said."

Nova was about to press Musica some more, when Dana interjected, "What d'you hear from Dennis, Nova?"

That shook Nova off the track. "I—he's part of the force that went to ALUCE with General Emerson. He, he got in touch on a back-channel and said he's all right."

Before Nova could go back to her interrogation, Bowie finished a number and the crowd's uproar drowned her out. Bowie was forced to do an encore. Musica floated on the sounds he made, but she couldn't help thinking, *If my sisters were here, we would play them music of great beauty, too!*

She was suddenly filled with emptiness. She hung her head, shaking it so that the green hair swayed. "Oh, sisters, forgive me!" She said it low, so the policewoman wouldn't hear.

"No, Musica," Zor, next to her, countered quietly. "Betrayal cannot be forgiven. I am beyond forgiveness and so are you."

His memories were merging, surfacing, becoming available to his conscious mind. He was becoming the original Zor, with all the regrets and despair. He was thinking, too, of that awful final moment, when he destroyed the flagship, and the deaths of uncounted defenseless clones—no, *people!*

Angelo didn't interfere for the moment. He saw how living among Humans was both a joy and a torment to Musica, a lot like a kid's story he remembered, *The Little Mermaid*. Funny how that just popped up; he hadn't thought of it for decades.

Sean grabbed the shoulder of Zor's torso harness. "Hey, modulate, there, trooper!" But Zor wrenched himself loose and strode from the nightclub.

Musica, watching him go, began to slump into a faint. Sean and Louie were quick to catch her. As tactical withdrawals went, dropping off Musica at her nonexistent apartment was a little thin, but it was all Dana could come up with.

Nova watched the 15th leave, just barely having kept them from sticking her with the check. *Go ahead and play out your hand, Dana. You haven't got much left.*

CHAPTER
FIFTEEN

Hey, Billy!
You said you owed me one, and if I needed a favor, just ask.
Okay.
Things are a little tight right now, and living on deuce private's pay is tougher than I remembered. You and I know each other, so you'll forgive me if I call the debt in.
Things've gotten strange here, but when was it otherwise? By the way: that kid they gave my 15th squad to? She could've been worse.
Anyway, I'm gonna need some money and I'm gonna need some favors. We've got the Plague of Love around here.

Your old pal,
Sean Phillips

NEAKING MUSICA BACK ONTO THE BASE AND THE BAR-racks compound wasn't too hard. The ATACs were a little worried about Nova, but they forgot about that when they saw Bowie and Musica embrace.

It's a good thing we've got some vacant quarters available, Dana thought. She was thinking more and more these days of how well Sean adjusted to losing his commission and hoped she could be as upbeat once they busted her. Bowie and Musica's being together seemed, against all expectation, like something that justified that risk.

Then a commotion off to one side had the rest realizing that Zor had wandered off and Angelo had followed. "What d'ya *mean*, you shoulda stayed on the mother ship?"

Zor was leaning against a tree, eyes to the grass, arms folded. He answered in a low voice, "It was where I belonged."

"And you'd've been killed." Angelo's fists were on his hips. He didn't look aside as the other ATACs and Musica came up.

"That's exactly my point. Besides, then I'd merit a hero's fu-neral, isn't that right? A golden opportunity for you to display those precious emotions of yours—weeping for the fallen comrade, and all that."

Angelo felt betrayed. He had doubted Zor from the beginning, had seen him turn traitor—then come back to his senses and fly right again. He had carried Zor over his own shoulder, saved Zor as Zor had saved him.

Zor was one of the 15th, and it wasn't something Angelo granted lightly. And now Zor was spurning that, making a fool of the sergeant.

But worse, infinitely worse, Zor was saying that Angelo *liked* grieving for dead buddies, got some kind of sick charge out of the most wrenching pain the sergeant knew. It insulted Angelo and, more, made a sham of the deaths of brave men and women.

One minute a red tide was rising up Angelo's neck and face; the next, Zor was flat on the ground with a split lip.

Dana knew words weren't going to do much good, so she got in Angelo's way and threw a straight right to the sergeant's sternum. It was like punching a bus tire, but it halted him—more through shock than pain.

"Get up. You ain't hurt. Yet," Angelo told Zor.

Zor rose, rubbing his jaw. "So I'm to be happy that I'm alive to go out and kill or be killed again tomorrow?"

Dana pushed Angelo away when he would have gone at Zor again. "Back off! That's an order!" She could hear Musica running off, sobbing, and Bowie going after her, but Dana had no time for that lesser crisis at the moment.

She turned to Zor. "You think it's going to make you feel better to get us to hate you? It won't! Quit punishing yourself and quit trying to get Angie to do it for you! Whatever's in your past is over with! And besides, you had no control over what you did; we all know that. Zor, it's time to let all of that go, and begin again."

He looked down at her as if seeing her for the first time: just an uncivilized Micronian, scarcely more than a wild animal by the standards of the Robotech Masters. Where was she finding these words? What were the sources of this wisdom?

But his inner torment gave him the strength to resist her. "Begin what? Dana, *it will always be the same! This incarnation, like all the others. That is my punishment! I can't even trust my own mind and I'm tired. I'm so tired of it all!*"

He didn't even know why he had escaped the flagship's destruction at the last moment; some survival reflex had taken over. He had begun regretting it at once.

He brushed past them. When Angelo snarled some objection, he shot back, "Just leave me alone! It's my problem, and I'll deal with it."

"Bowie, I'm so sorry. I feel that this is all my fault," Musica said, tears rolling down her face.

"Sorry that we survived, Musica? Sorry that you and I are together?"

"Oh, no! But—why am I so unhappy? Why is there pain all around us?"

"Because our people are at war. But we can't let that keep us from loving each other!"

He took her in his arms. She was slightly taller, laying her head on his shoulder. "You and I will be different," he told her. "We'll be an island of peace in the middle of all this hatred and misery. We'll have each other."

"Her name is Musica. You'll find her at the barracks of the Fifteenth ATAC squad."

Nova couldn't believe what she was hearing; she looked at the phone handset as if it were an alien artifact. Around her, the bustle and buzz of Global Military Police HQ seemed to fade. "You mean the girl I saw at the Moon of Havana?"

"I suggest you apprehend her as soon as possible," the firm male voice said, "before she manages to—"

"Just hold on. Who *is* this?"

"Can't you guess, Nova?"

"*Zor?* Listen, what's this all ab—"

But he had hung up.

Dana, deciding it was time to make more concrete contingency plans, was about to knock at the door of her own quarters when she stopped, transfixed.

It was a sound so ethereal that at first she didn't recognize it as a Human voice. Then she knew Musica was singing, and that the Muse herself was an instrument as hypnotic and magnificent as the Cosmic Harp. The notes soared, evoking emotions both familiar and unknown.

> "come, let me show you
> our common bond
> it's the reason that we live
> Flower, let me hold you

> we depend upon
> Power that you give. . . ."

She sang of the galaxies, of the depths, of the long story of the eons, and Dana found herself seeing stars swarm before her eyes. Musica's voice moved her with powerful tidal forces of feeling, giving her Visions.

She sensed a great epoch unfolding, something about Zor and a frightening but tragic alien race and—things just beyond the realm of her perception.

> "we should protect the seed
> or we could all fade away
> Flower of Life
> Flower of Life
> Flower. . ."

Outside, Zor turned to hear the siren song. Then he continued on his way to await Nova.

Dana saw worlds from other star systems. She saw wonders and horrors. It seemed that the voice coming from the other side of the door had split into three, harmonious and almost identical, flawlessly matched and perfect.

She saw something from her own dreams and visions: a triad of three-petaled flowers of a delicate coral color, drifting through the air, trailing long stamens. The flowers themselves grew in a Triumvirate. One drifted past, brushing her cheek. She looked down at it in amazement, where it rested on the corridor floor.

The song faded; the Flower disappeared. Even as Dana blinked herself back to full awareness, many of the things she had envisioned faded from her memory, and she was left with vague shadows of recollection.

She lunged into her quarters. Bowie was still on the bed, Musica by the window.

"What was that?" Dana burst out. "Musica, you sang something about—the Flower of Life, was that it?"

"Yes, Dana. That is right."

Dana turned to Bowie. "I'm *sure* that's the flower we found in the ruins of the SDF-1! The day we sneaked in there, remember? Those plants that moved by themselves?"

How could he forget? It was like some malign greenhouse, something that didn't belong on Earth, that belonged on no sane world. "And you think there's a connection?" He didn't sound excited about it, just alarmed.

"Could that be it, Musica?" Dana asked. "Could that be what the war is all about?"

"The Robotech Masters have not given it to me to know that, Dana, but for your sake, I hope there are no Flowers of Life here. They are often accompanied by great evil."

Louie Nichols burst into the room. "Read it and weep! Nova's downstairs with a bunch of GMP gorillas and she wants to see you, Dana."

It'll be all right," Dana told the frightened Musica and the grim Bowie. "C'mon, Louie; let's go see what the Gimps want."

"Unauthorized person in the barracks?" Dana gave Nova her best wide-eyed look. "What makes you think there's one around here?"

"Zor told me."

The odds looked bad. The GMP apes were armed, and outnumbered the unarmed ATACs. *Maybe there'll just be time for Angie to finish what he started on Zor.*

Zor, for his part, stood studying the floor, ready to accept their loathing—anticipating it. Dana wondered if Zor's treachery was committed to make it easier for him to end his own life or perhaps, commit some even worse betrayal.

Dana turned back to Nova. "She saved our lives. When it comes right down to it, Musica saved the whole fleet."

"Tell it to the brass."

"Sure, Nova, while they're busy sticking electrodes in her ears and trying to light her up like an arcade game. Would it help to tell you she and Bowie love each other?"

Dana knew it wouldn't—not now, with all the GMP goons standing around as witnesses. But she wanted Nova to know just how much harm she was doing, every bit of it.

"I always thought, as Gimps went, you were the exception to the rule, Nova, but I see now: you fit in just fine! C'mon; let's go."

Dana turned to lead Nova and her squad upstairs. She had hoped she could hide Musica until Rolf Emerson could get back from ALUCE and intercede. All that was hopeless now. Maybe Dana could go outside the chain of command, appeal directly to the UEG council? Her career was over either way.

Zor was standing near the stairs. Dana gave him one brief, chilly glance. "You had the chance to do something good and kind for a change. It might have made up for a lot of the stuff that's torturing you so, did you ever think of *that*?"

Zor put on a sardonic look, but what she had said went through him like a dagger of ice.

Nova got her troops ready, and they went through the door of Dana's quarters in a SWAT-style rush, guns ready. The balcony door was open, the curtain wafting gently on the night breeze.

The Gimps searched the place just to be sure, but it was easy to see their hearts weren't in it; they hardly even busted anything up.

Dana stood looking out at the night and wondered where Bowie and Musica could possibly find refuge in such a world.

Bowie got them over a compound wall and across a road, yanking her into the bushes out of the sudden glare of a GMP patrol's headlights. They plunged deeper into the forest.

They ran through the darkness hand in hand; her feet were cut and bruised, branches and rocks seemed to lie in wait for her. But she didn't complain; Bowie had enough to worry about as it was.

Musica had lived her entire life in the confined structures of the Robotech Masters and she fought back the agoraphobia that beset her now. The darkness made that a little easier, but she wondered how she would cope when the sun came up again.

An abrupt glare turned the whole world black and harsh white. A sound like the end of the Universe, coming with a concussion that shook the ground, made her lose balance again. She was sure that the GMP had used some sort of ultimate Robotech weapon, that the final battle with the Masters had come, or that the Earthlings were willing to wipe out an entire region of their planet to make sure she was dead.

Bowie helped her up. "Just thunder and lightning," he said. "Harmless electric discharge." *Unless it hits us, or a tree near us,* he amended to himself, but there was no point in worrying her. They ran on.

A winged creature of some sort gave a hateful caw and took to the air on the next lightning strike. And then, astoundingly, droplets of freezing-cold water were falling on Musica from out of the sky. She knew about condensation in a cerebral way, but this was her first experience with it.

It seemed a planet that was infinitely cruel; it seemed she had followed Bowie Grant into hell. But her hand was in his, and she recalled how bleak and pointless life without him had been. She steeled herself and went on.

"Don't expect us to do your dirty work for you," Dana told Zor in the unit ready-room, as the torrential rain struck the windows. "If you want to be punished, go do it yourself."

She didn't know what to feel about him anymore. There was still, somewhere, the love she felt for him, the yearning to stand by him and to take away the pain. But he had shown that he was just too good at keeping anyone from doing that. Dana wasn't quite ready to let him have the victory of making her hate him, but she despaired, feeling that soon he would win.

"At least he remembered his duty, Lieutenant," Nova said as she entered, shaking rainwater off her cloak. Her Gimps were still beating the bushes for the two fugitives, but she knew it was in vain; this called for more extreme measures.

Zor took advantage of the distraction to wander out, as Dana and Nova faced off. Dana was mounting some good arguments on Musica's behalf, but Nova cut through it with the news that the ATAC commanding general had granted Nova temporary operational control of the 15th.

"At first light, you and your unit *will* begin search operations, apprehend Grant and the alien, and place them under close arrest, is that clear enough for you, Sterling? In the meantime, I will consult with the Judge Advocate General's office with regard to court-martial proceedings against you and your men."

Just when Musica had resigned herself to dying at Bowie's side in the endless forest, lights appeared ahead—an outlying army equipment storage facility. Bowie left her for a moment, disappeared into the rain, and came back mounted on a Hovercycle.

He pulled her on, and they jetted off through the driving rain, headlights coming alight behind them as jeeps took up a pursuit. It was a mad chase over benighted roads that even the cycle's headlights couldn't seem to light. Bowie's major advantage was that mud and slick road conditions didn't matter much to a surface-effect vehicle.

But Musica was unused to riding and couldn't help him by leaning correctly on the turns. They got a lead on the posse, staying ahead by one or two bends in the road, but just about the time he was assuring her that he was a past master at Hovercycle racing, he snagged a branch and almost rammed a tree.

As it was, they slewed through a screen of bushes, and he laid the sky-scooter down in a not-quite-controlled fall that sent them both tumbling.

It turned out to be a blessing in disguise, because the pursuing jeeps roared on by. Bowie crept over to where Musica lay and couldn't breathe until he saw that she was all right.

He got her under the shelter of a tree, the lightning having stopped. The rain was letting up a bit; he drew her to him, opening his jacket, trying to warm her.

"Bowie . . ." She sounded so exhausted. "Lying here like this, I can feel your heart beating against mine. It's such beautiful music; I wish we could stay like this forever."

He felt such fear for her, such apprehension about the future, the pain of the fall, and the cold and damp of the night. It astounded him how much of that suffering and unhappiness she took away with a kiss.

"Zand, I haven't the time for—"

"Yes, you have, Mr. Chairman." Zand didn't move out of Moran's way. "I'll be brief."

Even with the flock of squawking flacks and bureaucrats trailing him, waiting for the chance to get the ear of the chairman of the UEG, Moran didn't brush Zand aside.

He saw by the look in Zand's strange, liquid-black eyes that the Robotech genius wouldn't stand for it. Moran made a casual-seeming gesture of the hand; in seconds, his security people had the followers fended back, and Moran, Zand, and Zand's aide were ushered into an empty conference room.

Zand saw no reason for preamble. "There's word that an alien woman has been smuggled back to Earth and that your people are looking for her so that you can use her as a peace envoy. Don't do that, Mr. Chairman."

Chairman Moran—white haired, white-mustached, kind old Uncle Pat, as some commentators called him—frowned. "That's not for you to say."

Zand's vacuous-faced, unobtrusive aide had taken a seat off to one side. Now Zand shot him a look. Russo leapt to his feet. Suddenly, instead of a vacant-eyed hound, he was once more the senator, the kingmaker and wheeler-dealer he had been back in the days of the old UEDC, despite the persona that fooled younger people.

" 'Lo, Patrick," he said. "You know what the boss, here, wants." It was as if he were still wearing pinky rings, and carrying a long Havana cigar. "Listen: You've gotta start following that party line, fella."

Zand concealed his own fascination with Russo's transformation. In the wake of the terrible attack of Dolza, at the end of the war with the Zentraedi (but before the attack of Khyron), Russo had simply been listed as missing and presumed dead.

It was Zand's good luck to discover him in a refugee center: the man who knew most of the secrets of the Earth's government, and had leverage against so many rulers and would-be rulers. Zand's Protoculture powers put Russo under his control with a mere pulse of thought.

Russo was still talking in that back-room-boys voice. "Paddy! Patto! We're not asking you *not* to make the offer, fella! We're just asking you, man to man, to hold off a while."

"We don't have a while—" Moran began.

"There's time." Russo said, a little more sternly. "Time for Doc Zand, here, to get a better deal! But if *you* wanna play hardball, *we* can play hardball."

Moran was looking at him, but not saying anything. Russo went on, "Those fingerprints are probably still on file in the vaults down in Rio, Pat; I think *they* survived the war. And what about that prosecutor? D'you think his skeleton is still there?"

Zand silently congratulated himself on having salvaged what was left of Russo's brain and the body it came in. The kingpin of prewar politics was a henchman devoutly to be grateful for.

"How wouldja like the opposition party to force a confidence vote?" Russo hinted darkly. Zand was pleased with the look on Moran's face.

"Not now. We could have peace, I think—"

Russo almost pounced at Moran. "You still can, Pat! We're not saying you can't! We're just saying: Give us until tomorrow. Is that so much to ask? The peace you make could be better than anything you ever imagined! My friend, if you want your place in the hist'ry books, this is the time to be brave!" Russo subsided just the right amount. "But you gotta play along."

Moran was lost in thought for a second; his opposition would certainly be able to call for a vote of confidence if Russo's secrets were made known. Now, of all times! *How did I get involved in such terrible things,* Moran wondered a little dazedly, *trying to do good?* "Very well, but only twenty-four hours."

He touched a timer function on his watch; the twenty-four hours began.

"You'll never regret it, Paddy," Russo said. Moran made a non-committal sound and moved for the door.

With his hand on the knob, he swung around to Zand, indicating Russo. "Keep that thing away from me, is that understood?"

Zand snapped his fingers, but more importantly, sent out a mental signal. The thing that had been Senator Russo went blank-faced again and sat down in the nearest chair.

Moran gave a fatigued, grudging nod, and went off to stick his finger, his head, his body into the hole in the dike.

CHAPTER SIXTEEN

Little Protoculture Leaf,
Waiting for our palates,
Where will you take us?
Flower of Life!
Treat us well!

Ancient song of the autotones of Optera

HOVERTANKS WERE NOT THE SORT OF TRANSPORTATION APpropriate to stalking fugitives in the wilds, so the 15th took out two jeeps and got ready to go afield.

There was something like a picnic air to it; any break from combat and combat alert was to be enjoyed, and nobody really thought Dana was going to hand Bowie and Musica over to the GMP, although no one was sure what she *would* do. So they loaded up the jeeps with weapons, field gear, rations, detection equipment, commo apparatus, and the rest.

At Louie Nichols's tentative inquiry as to whether or not she had any idea where Bowie might go, Dana hedged. But she declared, "We play this one by the book. Isn't that what we've always done?"

Well, no, it wasn't—her words didn't reassure them, but her sly wink did. The ATACs were a lot happier—except for Angelo—as they set off, just as the sun came above the horizon.

Above them, Zor watched their departure from the ready-room. At the command of the SCA brass, he was ordered not to accompany the hunters. He thought about the wording of the order, as the jeeps disappeared.

From her vantage point nearby, Nova Satori studied the route the 15th was taking, and revved her Hovercycle.

* * *

Protoculture was accessible to the Masters only through the Matrices and the power-supplying masses the Matrices produced. The germinal stage of the Flower of Life was contained in a balance something like that between fusion and gravity in the core of a star.

But eventually, the urge of the Flower of Life to bloom overcame any means of prevention ever devised, and that was happening now. Making matters far worse was the disaster of the loss of the flagship and its Protoculture mass.

The Robotech Masters' options had all been used up; they would have to strike, all-out, at once, or lose the means to strike at all.

"And that is my decision, approved by the council," Supreme Commander Leonard was saying. "We'll launch a final, no-quarter offensive against the alien fleet commencing at thirteen hundred hours today."

All preparations had been made in secret. No one pointed out any of the hundred strategic inadequacies in the plan; at Moon Base ALUCE, Emerson heard the news through a direct commo link to the command center, but made no comment.

"We will drive them from our skies forever or die trying," Leonard finished.

Long, slanting rays of sunlight wakened Musica. She shivered a bit, lying on Bowie's jacket with her own dew-covered one over her, but the day was already becoming warm.

She heard a melodious sound and opened her eyes. On a large open area of water nearby—a smallish lake, but much bigger than anything she had ever seen before—an egret swept in low for a landing. Smaller birds trilled to one another in a natural symphony that delighted and amazed her.

Bowie wasn't next to her. Rubbing her eyes drowsily, she looked around for him and saw the tree under which they had taken shelter the night before. A thrill ran through her as she remembered what had happened between them then, the most beautiful music of all.

The clouds were all gone, making way for a clear blue sky; moisture dripped from the leaves and the air was filled with the scent of renewal. *How could I have thought this planet so awful? It's beautiful, it's magic—oh, I have so much to learn!*

Then she spied him and heard him. Bowie was working on the

Hovercycle with tools from its small kit. "Just about ready to go," he said when she called out to him, then he stopped, taking a longer look at her. "You're even more wonderful to look at in the morning than you are at night."

"So are you, Bowie."

In another few minutes they were on the cycle and racing down the road. Musica had never felt so free, so deliriously happy.

Bowie got his bearings, and turned his course for his objective. Soon, the mound that was the burial cairn of SDF-1 came into sight.

Veritechs were launched from Fokker Base while A-JACs were trundled into the transports for the assault. Hatches were run back from missile silos as ground armored and artillery units deployed to defensive positions against enemy counterattack.

"General Emerson, you are aware that the enemy is on the move with his entire fleet, preparing to attack Earth?"

Emerson looked at Leonard's sweating face on the screen. "Yes, sir." Was aware of it, had expected it, and had marshaled all the moon's forces to try to help cope with it.

"You will move at once with all units under your command and engage the enemy, blunting his attack and otherwise bringing your total force to bear against him," Leonard ordered. "You will under no circumstances break off contact or withdraw; you and your contingent are totally committed, do I make myself clear?"

A death warrant wasn't too hard to read. "Yes, sir."

When Leonard signed off, Emerson turned to Colonel Green. "Find Rochelle, please—oh, and Lieutenants Crystal and Brown—and meet me in my office. Pass the word to stand ready; we'll be launching in ten minutes."

Sean was at the wheel, Dana in the 90% seat, lost in thought.

Louie pulled up even with them so that Angelo could yell, "You can stop worrying about what you wanna do with them when you find 'em!"

He was holding a pair of compu-binoculars and he jerked a thumb toward the road behind. "We got a little tail with GMP plates on it. Hovercycle."

"Nova!"

Sean didn't seem disturbed. "Want to lose her? Fasten your seatbelt, ma'am." He tromped the accelerator, and Louie did the same.

* * *

At the base of the mound, Musica said, "Are you sure this is the right one? The one where you saw the Flowers of Life?"

There were two others. Under one rested the SDF-2, and under the other the remains of the battlecruiser of Khyron the Backstabber.

"This is the one, I'm certain," Bowie said. Somewhere deep within were the remains of Admiral Henry Gloval, enlisted-rating techs Kim Young, Sammie Porter, and Vanessa Leeds, and Bowie's aunt, Commander Claudia Grant—five names that rang in Earth history.

"Bowie, this place frightens me." The mound was a high, Human-made butte scraped together from the surrounding countryside to cover the radioactive remains of Earth's onetime defender. The short half-life radiation was safer than it had been fifteen years before, but it still wasn't a place in which to linger long. Still, they had to do what must be done.

"Trust me," he said, taking her hand again. They entered the cave-tunnel he and Dana had found some weeks before.

A few yards in, they made their way over a rock and into an underground corridor. It was a prefab walkway that had been dropped in along with so many tons of rubble and building materials in the frantic effort to seal up the radiation.

It took several reassurances from Bowie to make her believe the bats, spiders, and other creatures rustling around her or scuttling overhead wouldn't hurt her.

The burial material that had been piled here so long ago had been originally slated for installation in a new government building. Ageless, round Buddha-like faces gazed out at the explorers from each pour-formed block. Mushrooms, moss, and fungus were in abundance. Water seeped from the ceiling and walls, to form brackish, vile-smelling pools.

Bowie felt his way along one wall, fingertips brushing through the slime, as Musica clung to his elbow. In time, they spied a light ahead and quickly went toward it.

It was an exit to the space in the center of the mound. Just as they were about to go through, a gust of golden dust, fine as fog, hit them.

"Wha—" Bowie's head reeled and he went to one knee.

"Bowie! What's wrong?" She knelt down next to him.

He shook his head, clearing it. "Just dizzy for a second."

"The Flowers! It must be the Flowers of Life!" She looked out at the open space in the center of the mound. "Bowie, we've come too late!"

Something was strobing and gleaming up ahead; she ran toward it, leaving it for him to catch up. He tottered through the doorway and stood reeling as if he had taken a punch.

Above them glowed something that reminded him of a kid's diagram of an atom—a complex assemblage of ring orbits that glistened in rainbow colors. It was two hundred feet across, hanging unsupported near the ceiling of the place; it seemed to be playing notes like a delicate carillon.

But he only had a moment to gape; Musica gave a woeful cry. "It's just as I feared! We're too late!"

They were looking down into a vast circular pit like a transplanted rain forest, in a shallow soup of nutrient fluids. There the Flowers of Life flourished in their triads, some open to show their triple structure. Most of the buds were still closed in shape like a twisted, elongated teardrop, a shape that made Bowie think at once of the shape of the mother ships' cannon. Among them, too, blew the golden pollen.

As they watched, more of the buds burst open, spewing forth the golden smoke. But sporangial structures in the Flowers also cast forth seeds like miniature parasols, which drifted toward the ceiling, defying gravity and air currents. It was like a gentle rain of glowing dandelion seeds in reverse.

Bowie tried to remember his botany classes and make some sense of it. The Flowers looked like some kind of angiosperm, producing the golden pollen, and yet they cast forth spores, like gametophytes. He couldn't guess what their alien life cycle might be like, or how it fit in with this Protoculture business.

She pointed to the tiny, drifting parasols, which looked like seeds to Bowie, but which she insisted on calling spores. "The Invid will sense this, no matter where they are. They're probably on their way here even now."

"The Invid? Who're they?"

"The enemies of your people and mine!" That was true enough, though it didn't *tell* the truth, but it was all that she had been taught.

There was a rustling and a series of shallow little sounds, as if something alive was moving around somewhere in the mass of Flowers. Bowie strained to see what it was, or hear it again, but could detect nothing.

Musica went down closer to the vast growing place, sandal heels slapping. He followed, calling for her to be careful.

He had never been sure of exactly which part of the SDF-1 this open space corresponded to—hangar deck, or Macross City compartment?— but he was beginning to suspect he knew.

The plants were growing so thickly that their stems were compressed into a mass that seemed to move and twist of its own volition. He looked up and saw that, while the quickened spores drifted up seeking release through a chimney-like opening at the top of the mound, something seemed to be confining them to the cavern. Perhaps there was still hope.

He looked again to the shining, chiming energy rings, listening to their song. There was something, something he seemed to remember. . . .

He tried to get his bearings again, having been told since the time he was a kid just how the SDF-1's last battle had been fought, how it had crashed, and in what mechamorphosis configuration. And then it hit him.

"I, I know where we are, Musica. This is the power section, where the sealed Robotech engines were, the engines that not even Doctor Lang dared to open."

He gripped her excitedly, pointed to the shining orbits. "This is the Protoculture Matrix! The one that the Zentraedi came and attacked Earth to get in the first place!"

The one that Lang and Exedore and Gloval and the others thought had disappeared along with the spacefold equipment, after the catastrophic jump to Pluto's orbit; the last Protoculture Matrix created by Zor. The only one in existence.

He knew the history of that war better than almost anyone, because he had seen copies of excerpts from his aunt's diary that were still circulated in the family, even though the originals were classified. He knew that once, a truce had been declared between SDF-1 inhabitants and Zentraedi, the ship had been scoured for any sign of the Matrix, and none was found.

But he had already learned from Musica that the Protoculture had its own Shapings, its own destinies to weave. Surely, hiding in the enormous sealed engines and turning aside sensor emissions or fooling passive sensor equipment would be a small marvel compared to the other things it had done. And there, hanging above Bowie, singing to itself, was the collection of interlocked rings that was the manifestation, on this plane of existence, of the Protoculture Matrix.

And though he didn't realize it, he and Musica were being watched. The triumvirate of wraiths that guarded the mounds was attentive to what was transpiring, though the trooper and the Muse had no idea they were there. The hour of the wraiths' long-awaited liberation was close at hand.

Bowie gripped Musica's shoulders. "This is the Protoculture Matrix! We've found what they've been looking for, what they've been fighting over for twenty years!"

She moved to put her arms around him, to lay her head against his shoulder. "Yes, but we found it too late."

"It can't be! We've got to think of something!"

"Oh, Bowie . . . if you had any idea what the Invid are like, how horrid they are—"

Pebbles knocked loose from a ledge higher up in the cavern. Bowie looked up to find that the 15th had followed him and, after getting lost, somehow ended up there. "Dana, I'm warning you: We're not going back."

"We're not here to bring you back, numb-nub!" she grinned.

When his squadmates made their way down to him and he explained what he had found out, Bowie had the dubious fun of watching them all fish-mouth in shock. He was more than passingly interested in Dana's response, though; this wasn't just some new kink in the war, to her—it was a part of her heritage, a part of herself.

She breathed the golden clouds, looking out on the coral triads of the Flowers of Life. She felt a strangeness—not a dizziness or faintness, but something closer to the opposite: as if she were being galvanized on some subcellular level.

Nova stole forward through the gloom, on the path the ATACs had taken. She had her sidearm out and was alert to every sound; something behind her made her turn.

Zor pushed the pistol barrel aside gently but firmly, as if he were dealing with a child and a child's toy. His eyes glowed in the darkness. "You won't be needing that. Come."

He set off for the light of the cavern. "You, you followed me?" she said.

"Yes. Now it is you who must follow *me*."

Musica and the 15th heard a groan and looked up to see Zor, muscles tensed in agony, hands clenched in the long lavender hair, gazing madly at the drifting spores. Next to him stood Nova Satori.

Nova managed to pull herself together a bit. "I'm here to take Musica back to headquarters," she managed shakily, then cast another frightened look at Zor.

"No, you're not," Dana answered.

Nova plunged down the steps that connected her level with the one below. But when she was halfway there, Zor, remaining where he was, let out a tormented howl.

"This plant is responsible for my becoming the monster I am!" He gasped for breath, staggered for balance there at the brink of the ledge.

He was only dimly aware of them all staring up at him. The scent of the spores and the presence of the Matrix forced his memories to merge and open themselves to him with the same compulsion that made the Flower of Life blossom. He stared out into the resplendent rings of the Matrix, his creation.

"I stole the secret of Protoculture from the Invid, and betrayed them. I was betrayed in turn, and my contemporaries became the Robotech Masters." He went down on all fours at the very lip of the drop.

"But I broke free of their will at last! I thwarted them! And they've brought me back as a clone, again and again, hoping I would give them my great secret. *But they won't have it!*"

"I don't know about that," Bowie yelled back in the echoing chamber, "but this is all something the Invid want"—sweeping his hand at the Flowers of Life—"and *they're on their way!*"

That seemed to jolt Zor back to a measure of reality. Nova continued her descent of the steps. She couldn't understand how she had ever felt drawn to Zor, felt such attraction to him; some alien trick perhaps? The thought made her all the angrier.

"We can sort all of that out later. Musica is still my prisoner, and I'm taking her back with me." Nova came to the bottom step.

Dana stepped to block her way. "Sorry, Nova. No."

CHAPTER
SEVENTEEN

And the mountains in reply
Echoing their joyous strain

Prewar Earth hymn

THE ROBOTECH MASTERS HAD DEPLOYED THEIR ASSAULT
ships and command ships and lesser warcraft. Blue and red
Bioroids were set to fight, mindlessly, in a *Götterdämmerung*.

Emerson's fleet was coming at flank speed, to hurl itself on the
invaders' rear. In an order that had his staff gulping, Emerson
directed that his *Tristar* flagship lead the attack. The equipment
that had let him work his singularity ploy was fused and useless;
this battle would be toe-to-toe.

As Emerson's battle-weary elements threw themselves into a
last, almost spasmodic attack, the Masters' advance faltered. Virtually everything in the Southern Cross capable of getting off the
ground rose from Fokker and a dozen other bases, braced for the
Twilight of the Robotech Gods.

Marie Crystal and Dennis Brown led their A-JACs forth, and
the Triumviroids thronged to meet them. The Earth mecha did
their best to use the tactics that were successful against the invaders for the 15th. Dreadnoughts lit the eternal night with cannon
salvoes. Missiles left their ribbontrails.

Nova ignored Zor's attempted intercession. "I'll expect you all
to remember your oaths of service," she said, sweeping her eyes
across the 15th. She gave Bowie Grant a particularly fixing stare;

he was the key to it all. If she could get him to see past his deluded attraction to the clone woman, the whole affair would be resolved peacefully. If not . . .

"I'm not part of the military anymore," Bowie said stubbornly, squeezing Musica's hand.

"General Emerson is," Nova invoked the name. "And *he's* fighting with everything he's got to save this planet."

"I don't care!" Bowie burst out. *"Musica's my friend—not my prisoner or my enemy, and not yours either, do you hear me? Why can't you leave us alone?"*

Nova saw that all the ATACs quietly agreed—even the normally duty-bound Dante.

"Is love so difficult for you to understand, Nova?" Dana asked angrily. "Why d'you always have to be so coldblooded?"

The question rocked Nova a little, almost as if Dana had struck her. She had felt like an outsider all her life, the more so when she had joined GMP. The bewildering attraction she had felt for Zor, and then the sudden absence of it; the slow warming to Dennis Brown; the pity she held for Captain Komodo, because she knew how it felt to be rebuffed—those were things she didn't dare inspect too closely.

She drew her sidearm, holding it close to her hip and leveling it at them.

"It's my duty, that's why," she told Dana. "And for me, Earth comes first. And the Human race. I'm taking Musica back, whether some of you get hurt or not."

It was all too melodramatic, Dana thought, even as she got set to play out her role. Bowie had stepped into the line of fire, shielding Musica, and Musica was already making timid but determined insistence that he move aside, to avoid bloodshed.

The rest of the 15th reacted to the appearance of the pistol with predators' reflexes, shifting weight, edging this way and that slightly, barely seeming to move their feet. They turned their bodies side-on to Nova to minimize their target silhouettes, bracing to take her.

"What happened to all that *talk* back at GMP headquarters, Nova?" Bowie challenged, holding Musica back. "Honor. Freedom. Defending Human ideals and our way of life. You said you could be a friend to anyone who valued those things.

"Well, *this* is my life." He put his arm around Musica's waist. "D'you really have it in you to be a friend?"

"I—" Nova had forgotten those talks, an attempt to win over a friend in the enemy camp of the 15th. It had started out as a turning operation, at Colonel Fredericks's direction. But it ended up with her actually feeling something for the maverick trooper private, if only an unspoken sympathy for his confusion, his alienation. And then he was also Claudia Grant's nephew.

Nova had the flash of memory again, not clear but *strong*.

It was Christmas in rebuilt Macross City, the Christmas that would see Khyron's sneak attack. Little Nova Satori was out with her older sister and her sister's friends, caroling, as the snow drifted down. They happened upon a tall, regal black lady, beautiful as a Snow Queen, who looked very sad.

But when she spoke to them, Nova's sister recognized the lady's voice, as all the older girls did. Back on the SDF-1, hers had been the PA voice that so often restored hope in the midst of war; told the people where to go and what to do; gave the world calm; transmitted courage.

She was Commander Claudia Grant. The chorus of little girls gathered close in a ring around her and sang, the best they ever sang. There was no question about what carol it would be:

"An-gels we have heard on high!
Sweetly singing o'er the plain!"

They all wanted to *be* Commander Grant; Commander Grant wanted them to be more. She'd hugged them all to her and wept.

"—I'm a friend. . . ." Nova managed, not sure what she was saying. Her training and the pistol gave her command of the situation: She knew what moves to make and procedures to follow, even what tone of *voice* she ought to be using at this point to ensure that Phillips and the others didn't try any of their absurd heroics.

She had singlehandedly managed situations against even greater odds, against truly ruthless and evil people, and that last part was the glaring incongruity. She was disarmed of her greatest weapon: the conviction that she was totally in the right. And all her other resources, powerful though they were, began to fail her.

When Zor's big hand closed over the weapon and took it from her, Nova barely registered it through the sudden numbness she felt. "You won't need this," he said in an almost conversational tone. She could have had the pistol back at once, by using an infighting trick; she didn't.

Nova shook herself loose of the paralysis, the realization that she couldn't fire at these people, that her oath conflicted with the ideals it was supposed to uphold.

She looked to Zor. "But—isn't she one of the clones? Zor, they did such terrible things to you—"

Zor was shaking his head, the lavender curls swaying. "She is a Muse, the very soul of harmony. She is vital to the Robotech Masters, however. Look!"

Nova and the others followed Zor's pointing finger. They were watching the great mass of the Flowers of Life, hearing the tonalities from the Matrix that were so like the Muse's songs. "From the Protoculture all life flows. Once the clones have been quickened, it is the playing of Musica and her sisters that keeps them docile and obedient. That tells them, in effect, who they are."

"And now, she's learning to play the songs of Humankind," Louie Nichols said quietly, the words forming a core of argument there at the very center of Nova's decision. There was too much happening for her to consider the fact that it was an amazingly profound thing for such a mechie—as she had always thought of him and his ilk—to put forth.

And if Fredericks and Leonard and the UEG got their hands on Musica? They would pull her every which way like a wishbone—cruelty was one of their first resorts. Musica embodied the hope of peace, but Nova dreaded to think what her songs would sound like once she had been put into the United Earth Government's mill.

"We have to move quickly," Nova said. "I commoed for a flying squad of GMP officers; it'll be here any time now."

"We've gotta get out of here!" Dana snapped. Emerson was in battle, and there were few others she could trust. But the world was wide, much of it unpopulated, and a Hovertank squad mounted plenty of firepower. They would have to lay low, try to get to someone sane. Perhaps they would have to contact the Robotech Masters as well, and force some kind of ceasefire. Then a truce; then peace.

She threw aside her oath in that moment; the other party—the UEG and, by extension, the Army of the Southern Cross—hadn't kept its end of the bargain. She sensed that her ATACs stood with her, as did Nova and Musica.

Peace renegades! It sounds so weird, she thought.

"Your officers won't make any moves without instructions from you," Zor, who knew from experience, reminded Nova. "We must move calculatedly, but very quickly now."

He showed no emotion as Dana clapped her hands and began

organizing the escape, somehow drawing Nova into her little band as if the GMP lieutenant had always been an ally. That instinctive talent for commanding loyalty and cooperation must be something Dana had inherited from both her warrior-woman Zentraedi mother and her ace-of-aces Human father, Zor reflected in passing.

Suddenly there was that sound again, the one Bowie had heard before, as if something was moving among the mass of Flowers. They all heard it, as they heard a sudden, high, playful sound, like a cross between a small dog's yip and the tones that came from the Matrix.

"*Polly!*"

Dana was on one knee, beckoning to him, and Bowie groaned. "I should've known." Nova and the others stood trying to fathom their latest marvel.

The little creature looked a low-slung white dog or mophead, some kind of crypto-Lhasa apso with a sheepdog forelock, until one noticed the knob-ended horns and feet something like untoasted muffins. He showed a miniature red swatch of tongue and yipped again, running to her.

"You *know* this thing?" Angelo demanded, scratching his head.

Bowie answered for Dana. "All her life. Her godfathers introduced her to him. Only—*I* never believed in Polly till now, never saw him. I, uh, always thought he was imaginary."

Dana was nuzzling and laughing, hugging the little beast. A *Pollinator*, her three unlikely, self-appointed godfathers, the former Zentraedi spies Konda, Bron, and Rico had called him. Three-year-old Dana had given him his shortened name right then and there.

She had quickly learned that Polly was a magical beast who came and went as he willed; no walls or locks could hold him. He showed up very rarely and went his way when he wished, simply vanishing while she was looking the other way. In her whole life, she had seen him perhaps seven or eight times. He never changed, or seemed to grow older.

"A Pollinator, yes," Zor said, looking down. "And now you know what he pollinates." *She's been tied to all this since she was a child—perhaps before her birth. Dana, Dana: Who are you?*

Dana couldn't picture Polly buzzing around like a bee there in the Flower mass, but obviously *something* had been at work. She let the little creature lick her cheek again, then stood up with him in her arms, petting him.

"What're you all staring at? Let's go!"

Zor looked to the Flowers of Life that would no doubt be detected by the Invid. He still couldn't recall everything, but one thing, he knew:

The Masters' power must be broken. The original Zor was not altogether responsible for what had happened once he beguiled the Invid Regis. Perhaps I am not either, though I am him and he is me.

But it lies within my power to do what must be done. Let this be the lifetime when at last I accomplish it!

The fighting raged around the five great surviving mother ships of the Masters' fleet. The Humans were proving to be enemies even more terrible than the teeming Invid.

But that was not the worst news. Optical relays showed an invader in the realm of their Protoculture masses, a thing to be feared more than any Invid or Battloid.

It was small and white, yipping and chasing its own bedraggled tail among the storage canisters. A Pollinator.

The Masters knew better than to waste time attacking it. Try to stab the wind; shoot a bullet at the sun.

The Masters accepted the devastating news with the same emotionless reserve they had always displayed. To say it was stoicism would have been inaccurate. It would have implied they had some other mode of behavior.

The dissipation of Protoculture made itself felt not only in the declining performance of the Masters' Robotechnology, but in the failure of judgment, dispiritedness, and lack of coordination of the clones themselves. Never had the Masters' own—the primary—Protoculture cap been so weakened.

Even now, whole masses of Protoculture were transforming, all through the fleet, into the Flowers of Life, just as was happening below.

Their unspoken conference was short. Shaizan gave the order. "Transfer all functioning clones and all Protoculture reserves to Our flagship. Set automatic controls on an appropriate number of combat vessels to land them on the Earth's surface, and fuel them for a one-way voyage. Process as many clones as is feasible to serve as mindblank assault troops."

The Scientist bowed his head, swallowing his objection. The clones were mere plasm, subject to the dictates of the Masters. Who dared declare things otherwise?

Even if it meant genocide . . .

* * *

Allegra and Octavia had not so much adjusted to their reduced status as gone into a sort of lasting shock that insulated them from it. Even though they were Muses, Musica and her Cosmic Harp were the key to their triad's power and effect. Without her they were all but useless to the Masters. Since being interned, they had seen the horror of reduced Protoculture and the *dissonance* of Musica's absence all around; they had become desensitized to it.

But a new flurry of activity roused them a little. The most ambulatory of the malfunctioning clones were being injected by guards, shunted along in a torpid line, at the end of which was a door. None who were passed through that door returned.

Antipain serum, the words came quietly among the despondent prisoners near them; Allegra looked to Octavia. They both knew what that meant: clones who would be all but immune to normal sensation once the drug took effect—who would be aggressive, terrible antagonists. Their minds would be blanked to anything but fighting, until they were blasted apart or until the drug burned up their physiology completely.

"Mindblanked assault troops," a voice said. Octavia turned to see who it was, and gasped.

In the advance stages of Protoculture deprivation, the clone had become a crone, witchlike, nodding out the last moments of her life.

She gazed, glassy-eyed, at the other clones being injected. "Sacrifices on the altar of war. That is the Robotech way."

Resistance from the mother ships seemed to be failing, but Marie Crystal kept herself from any hope or distraction, dodging through enemy fire and preparing for another run. At Emerson's order, she began to consolidate elements of the various shattered TASC units.

But we better get some help soon, she thought, *or that's all he wrote.*

"General, you *have* to commit all your reserves *now*," Emerson's image said to Leonard.

The supreme commander kept his face neutral. "Current tactical trends preclude that at this time."

So much easier than saying "screw you," Emerson thought, as his flagship shook to a Bioroid assault and the guns pounded.

"There'll be no other chance!" he roared at Leonard. "Move now, you fool!"

Leonard's wattles shook with his anger. "You dare give *me* orders? Carry out your mission!"

He had barely broken the connection, and was picturing Emerson's imprisonment for insubordination under fire, when an aide leaned close to say, "Enemy assault ship descending for landing, sir, about five miles outside the city limits."

Leonard turned back to raise Emerson again. There must be no more penetration of Earth's defensive forces, whatever it took.

Predictably, Emerson claimed that the order was unworkable, was simply contradictory to reality. Leonard let him go on, and then hit him with a blow he had been saving until the battle was over.

"Carry on! Oh, and it may interest you to know that your ward, Private Grant, has deserted in the company of an enemy agent. The GMP is hunting him even now."

Emerson wanted to cry out in grief, to insist that it had to be a mistake or that Bowie had been brainwashed. But he saw Leonard was enjoying it too much to be persuaded of anything Emerson might claim.

Emerson broke the commo connection and began redeploying his remaining forces for a direct assault on the only remaining mother ship.

On Earth, Leonard exulted that he had managed to give Emerson such agonizing news when the man couldn't even spare a moment for regret or memory or worry.

But he didn't have long to enjoy it. An appalling new enemy teemed from the assault ships that were slipping through, to wreak havoc in Monument City.

Assault ship hatches dropped open, even as Leonard watched from his tower, and the mindblanked assault troop clones charged forth like insane demons.

CHAPTER
EIGHTEEN

It's ironic that the SDF-3 expedition was on its way to find the Robotech Masters to strike a diplomatic accord, at exactly the time the Masters were on their way to Earth. Ships passing in the night, in truth.

There are those who lament the fact because they believe the second war could have been averted. I do not share this view. Do Humans, mining for precious gems, make deals with the monkeys whose jungle they invade?

The Masters were arrogant in a way that, in Humans, would certainly be diagnosed as psychotic. They were as single-minded as the mindblanked clone troops they were forced to use in their final offensive.

Major Alice Harper Argus (Ret.), *Fulcrum: Commentaries on the Second Robotech War*

"DOESN'T EVEN FAZE 'EM," AN INFANTRYMAN GRIT-ted over his tac net. He put another burst into the alien, and this time the raving, long-haired wildman in offworld uniform went down.

But not for long. The thing got up again, hollow-eyed, skin stretched tight across its face, leering like a skeleton. It raced at him with unnatural speed and dexterity, firing some kind of hand weapon. The grunt flicked over from teflon-coated slugs to energy and held the trigger down, until the zombie was burning chunks of debris.

But all at once another zombie reared up, grinning, to bear him over and grapple hand to hand, not skilled but as unrelenting as a mad dog. They pressed rifles against one another. Only the infantryman's armor kept him from having his throat bitten out.

Everywhere it was the same. Only a few Southern Cross units had been deployed here to Newton, to guard against a landing at the outmost perimeter of Monument City. The grunts were badly outnumbered by the Living Dead. What had happened among the defenseless civilians, the soldiers could not bring themselves to think about.

The zombies kept coming even after their weapons were exhausted, trying to grapple hand to hand, wanting only to kill before they themselves died from the supercharged overdoses they had been given. In time, the Human survivors rallied near the town's central plaza. They formed a tiny square of fifteen men and women, one rank standing and one kneeling.

Like something from a nineteenth-century imperialist's fantasy, the square fired and fired on all fronts as the damned rushed in at them. Time and again the tremendous firepower of modern infantry weapons cleared the area, and each time more mindblanked assault clones stormed forth, some still firing but most not, their weapons exhausted.

At times it was hand to hand; body armor gave the infantry a powerful edge. But each time they drove back their foes, a new wave came to crash against them.

The square shrank to a triangle, eight desperate men and women. And then, high above, cross hairs fixed on them.

It was regrettable that two assault ships' cargoes of mindblanked clones had been mistakenly disembarked in the target population center. But such things were unavoidable, given the haste of the operation and the unreliability of some of the crew clones.

Still, the demonstration of Robotech Master power had to be made as ordered, even at the cost of a few expendable null sets.

From a third assault ship, a beam sprang down and the entire middle of Newton disappeared in a thermonuclear inferno. Friend, foe, civilian—all vanished instantly, as blast and shockwaves spread holocaust.

Leonard heard the news without showing any response, cold as a Robotech Master. The technical officers clamoring at him with their assorted explanations of how the alien ray worked, some claiming it was a new development, others disputing it, were of no importance, and he waved them aside.

Two towns had been utterly destroyed, but that was of no importance to him; Leonard knew as well as anyone that Monument City might very well be next, and it had no defense. There was no time to consolidate forces in the UEG capitol, but he gave the command that it be done nevertheless.

An aide tapped his shoulder tentatively, *"We're receiving a communication from the Aliens!"* The face of Shaizan appeared on the primary display screen before him, Bowkaz and Dag standing behind and to either side.

They knew his name. "Commander Leonard, we are now capable of destroying your species with very little effort. You will therefore surrender and evacuate your planet immediately."

Leonard looked at the screen blankly. Evacuate? He had once read a war college projection that if spacecraft production were to continue at full speed and the birth rate were suddenly to drop to zero, such a thing might be possible in another ten years or so. As it was, the aggregate space forces of Terra *before* the current battle wouldn't have had a hope in hell of carrying out such a mission.

But where was the Human race supposed to go? A few frail Lunar and Martian colonies, and several orbital constructs were the only alternatives, unless the Masters meant to help, which they manifestly did not.

That left an instant for Leonard to marvel at how the Masters overestimated the Human race in assuming *homo sapiens* could pull off such a miracle. But again, it was more likely that the Masters simply didn't care; maybe "evacuation" only meant, to them, the escape and preservation of the power structure—the government.

Thoughts and evaluations boiled in Leonard's mind then: perhaps it *would* be possible to take the very most essential personnel—himself chief among them, of course—and thus avoid total annihilation.

As he was studying the Masters' sword-sharp faces he heard Shaizan say, "Within thirty-eight of your hours. Else, we shall have no option but to slay you one and all."

Leonard's fists shook the desk with a crash, as he stood. "Now you listen: this world has been ours, from the time our species stood up straight to use its hands and its brains! Through every disaster and our own wars and the ones you and your kind waged on us! *This world is ours!"*

He was shaking his bunched fists in the air before him, speaking an unprepared speech for once. Then he realized, with surprise, that a few of the men and women around him were nodding their heads in agreement. He had come to think of himself as a man who could never have the heartfelt support of those around him.

He was thinking along new lines when Bowkaz, speaking up, dashed his hopes. "Leonard, this is an ultimatum—a fact of life—

not a suggestion or a mere threat. The Invid, our bitter enemies, will soon confirm the presence of Protoculture on your planet."

"They will come," Dag said. "And, it seems, there will be more war. You can leave or you can be crushed between; there is no third way. Go, and leave this matter to us."

Leonard resisted the urge to duck offscreen to consult with his advisers and image-makers, or break the connection. But pride made him stand there, as the Masters knew by now that it would, protecting to the last his Lone Warrior, his Gunfighter-Patton-Caesar persona.

But the self-preserving side of his mind was making very, very fast calculations. If only a portion of the Human race were to survive, it was his duty to rule them.

"Impossible," he told Shaizan, hoping the word didn't sound too tremulous. "More time!" Leonard added. He grabbed a figure from the air, "At least seven days!" There was something Biblical about it, but nothing workable.

Shaizan raised his arm, but Leonard couldn't see that he, like his triad mates, was touching the Protoculture cap.

"Forty-eight of your hours, and no more," Shaizan decreed. He cut off Leonard's objections. "And after that, *no life on Earth.*"

The screen de-rezzed, then went clear. Leonard turned to his nearest subordinate, saved from an agonizing decision because the Masters had insisted on the impossible. "Reconsolidate all units in the area of Monument City and prepare for an all-out assault."

There were only a few tentative hesitations; all of them jumped-to when he bellowed, "Do it now! On the double!"

They were compliant because no other attitude was tolerated in Leonard's inner circle, and so there was no contradiction. They scurried.

Leonard reflected, *We whipped the Zentraedi and we can whip these Robotech Masters! And the Invid, whatever in hell they are!*

Men and women prepared as best they could: Some children were shielded or remanded to shelters by their elders, but many found a weapon and got ready to be part of the final battle.

There was a brief calm in the wake of the beams, something to savor even though it wasn't meant to be savored. Soon, the sky split apart again.

The holding action fought by the *Tristar*, Emerson's flagship, was the sort of thing children's stories and patriotic poetry are made of. Emerson himself would have given anything not to be there, or at least not to be the last living crewmember among the dead.

But that was how it had happened. An enemy blast took out virtually all the bridge systemry and killed the senior gunnery commander who had been standing between him and the nearest explosion. But he had taken shrapnel and the command chair under him was stained with his blood. His head had been rocked against his headrest at an angle where the padding was of little help, dazing him.

Emerson felt infinitely tired and regretful—regretful that he had never spoken his heart to Bowie; that he had lost the battle; that he had made such a mess of his marriage. More than anything, he was regretful that so many lives had been or were about to be sped into the blackness.

Smoke roiled from the control panels in a bridge that would soon be a crypt. Emerson's head lolled back and he had only an instant to recall something he had read in Captain Lisa Hayes-Hunter's war-journal, *Recollections*.

It was getting harder to think, but he pulled the quote together by an act of will. *Why are we here? Where do we come from? What happens to us when we die?* Questions so universal, they must be structured in the RNA codons and anticodons themselves, it seemed to Emerson.

He had no answers, but expected to shortly. He was pretty sure those answers would be as surprising to the Robotech Masters as they would be to dead Terran generals.

Then he was blinking up at Lieutenant Crystal and Lieutenant Brown. Emerson couldn't imagine how they could have landed their craft on the critically damaged *Tristar*. He couldn't decide if they were real or not. But the agony he felt as they dragged him over to an ejection module convinced him it was all real, and even revived him a bit.

Dennis Brown didn't quite know what to say to Marie; the whole Emerson rescue had been so improvised, and they had only gotten to know one another as unit commanders. Sitting crowded into the little alloy-armored ball with the injured general made things different, somehow awkward. But there had been no time to get back to their mecha, and anyway both craft were so badly damaged that the ejection capsule was the better bet.

"Looks like we made it," he ventured, as the *Tristar* began to blow to pieces behind them, jolting the metal sphere along on its shockwave.

She considered that. "Yes," Marie hedged.

But then they saw that they had been premature; the maw of an enemy cruiser, one of the last still functioning, came at them like the open mouth of a shark, like something out of a nightmare.

They were swallowed up.

At some point, Dana looked down and the Pollinator was no longer frisking along behind; she was used to those sudden disappearances, but wondered if she would ever see him again.

The 15th and its friends and allies, having made it to the top of the mound that buried the SDF-1 and every vital secret of Protoculture, looked down at a circus of light and sound. The GMP appeared to have gotten there first, with troop carriers, giant robots, and crew-served weapons. There was an energy cordon farther out, and a lot of activity at the foot of the mound. In the distance, cities burned and smoke went up in mile-wide clouds where the enemy had struck. For some reason the GMP troops, following Colonel Fredericks's orders to recapture the aliens at all costs, were forgotten or couldn't be reached by Southern Cross brass desperate for reinforcements.

As Zor thought about the madness of it all, Dana thought about Zor and how very badly she needed to understand him and understand herself. As the eight who stood there dealt with their wildly varying thoughts and memories and impulses, another shadow crossed the land.

They all looked up, as did the Gimps below, to see, hovering above, a cinnamon-red, whiskbroom-shaped Robotech Master assault ship.

Karno and his triad mates were gazing into an enormous lens. "There rests the last Protoculture Matrix," Karno said in his single-sideband voice. "But who are those, atop the mound?"

Theirs was the ship and the mission for which all the rest were providing a distraction. The last thing they had expected was to find the mound surrounded by combat units.

It was all very confusing. There was no sign of the three frightful Protoculture wraiths, no least indication of any counteraction, and that was enough to make anyone knowledgeable in the ways of Protoculture cautious.

But *this*? As the focus zoomed in, Karno saw his onetime fiancée, Musica, the latest of the Zor clones, and six Earth primitives ranged about at the brink of a cliff.

"Zor is with them," Darsis observed with a dispassion worthy of the Elders themselves.

"Even Musica," pronounced Karno, forcing himself to match that proper tone, willing to die before admitting the hot, hateful feelings coursing through him.

Dana looked at Zor in surprise, as he stepped to the brink and addressed the empty air. "If you attack, we will destroy all that is here. Flowers. Protoculture. Muse. All.

"Go to your Robotech Masters! Tell them this war must end. You in the depths of your ignorance, you and your Masters: it is time for you to learn how to learn."

Zor was intent on the ship, but Nova looked at him wonder-ingly, and had misgivings. What if, somehow, he wasn't bluffing?

The godlike voice from the assault ship gave the Humans a start, but Musica and Zor were braced for it. "We will be back," it said, as flames rose from alien strikes all around, all the way to the horizon and beyond. The assault ship lifted away, for space and the flagship.

Nothing Nova had ever been taught quite served in analyzing what had come to pass. She, too, set aside her oath of allegiance as Dana had, silently but finally. "Zor, the Flowers—the Masters . . . you remember now!"

He made the barest of smiles. "Yes, but only in fragments." He turned the smile on Dana. "It's all beginning to coalesce in my mind now, and Musica is the key!"

Dana's back went stiff. *And that's all, huh? Musica?* Ignoring everything Dana had . . . *Ah, hell!*

Zor started giving orders, and Nova for one seemed to be ready—*willing*—to take them. Zor outlined his plan to have Angelo, Sean, and Louie infiltrate the GMP perimeter and come back with the 15th's Hovertanks tandem-towed.

Dana walked over to the ventlike opening in the mound, watching the minute parasol spores bump against some invisible barrier and float back down, to rise and bounce again. She couldn't sort out for herself the reason why there was such immense fascination in it for her. She resolved that, if they lived, she would make Zor explain.

Zor looked up at Earth's sky, while Bowie hugged Musica to him. Some people were fleeing Monument City, terrified of another on-slaught of the destructive rays or the arrival of the Bioroids.

Last of a long line of one selfsame entity, heir to brilliant mas-tery of the Shaping forces of the Universe and to every misdeed of his predecessors, Zor Prime sniffed the breeze.

And now the war ends, he promised himself, promised all Cre-ation.

CHAPTER
NINETEEN

This sudden shifting of focus, from Matrix to Muse—and Zor Prime—is bewildering only to those who haven't familiarized themselves with the subtler powers of Protoculture.

From a distance, we can see it, of course, and feel smug in our overview. If the players on stage that day were mystified and even illogical, who can fairly blame them? The Shaping of the Protoculture had the world in its teeth and was shaking it.

S. J. Fischer, *Legion of Light:*
A History of the Army of the Southern Cross

THE CAPTIVES COULD SEE THAT IT WAS A VERY HIGH SPACE. The multicolored invader lightstructure, as faceted as a stained glass chandelier and as big as a Hovertank, was hanging unsupported very high above them.

It looks like—radioactive diamond; a crystallized thought—I dunno, Emerson thought woozily, as Brown and Marie tried surreptitiously to hold him upright on the couch.

"Well?" Dag repeated. "Will you make your species see reason, and surrender?"

Emerson took a breath and looked again at the three strange beings who floated before him on the Protoculture cap's small standing platforms. Would Leonard have gone insane right on the spot? It was intriguing to consider, but not very helpful.

" 'Surrender'?" Emerson repeated the word tiredly, feeling the wounds on his face and neck, and in his side. "Haven't you arrogant ghouls learned *anything* about the Human race yet? Your Zentraedi came after us, and now you come after us—*sss*—"

Emerson hissed in pain, going a little faint but coming around almost at once. Lieutenant Crystal wedged up against him, propping him up so that Emerson hadn't teetered. Good soldier!

"—after us," Emerson resumed, stiffening his spine. "But you

444

don't seem to realize: *It doesn't make us weaker; it makes us stronger!*"

Dag looked down on him. "A great pity; our information led us to hope that you are seeking the same peaceful settlement as we—that our goal was the same."

Emerson shook off his fatigue and pain. How old *were* these apparitions, these seeming Grim Reapers before him? *How many Protoculture-grown Dorian Gray portraits in the old closet?* he speculated, then pulled himself together. It was no time for whimsy.

"Nice try," Emerson shot back, "but you know as well as I do that you opened fire on us first. You never *tried* to negotiate."

"Regrettable," Dag parried, "but we respect you as we do other intelligent beings who have the same Human form as we, the same biogenetic structure—even a kindred intellect."

"That so?" Marie glowered up at the Master from beneath her long black brows. "Then why haven't you called off your Bioroids?"

"You're liars, the whole pack of you," Emerson told the Masters.

Shaizan's eyes opened wide with his surprise and displeasure. "Truly, you are stupid creatures!"

Emerson smiled mirthlessly. "Map reference point Romeo Tango 466-292; that's where you intend to make your initial landing, right? *That's* how stupid we are. And you're going to see more mecha and more fighting-mad Human beings than you could've dreamed of in your worst nightmares!"

It was only a wild guess on his part, based on repeated alien activity there, and those last transmissions from Leonard's staff before commo was knocked out on *Tristar*. The gambit was worth a try, Emerson had decided. Earth's defenses were nearly finished, but perhaps the Masters didn't know that, and Emerson's words would throw them off balance for a bit.

And, terrible as the aliens' new beam weapon was, they would not use it on the mounds, that much was obvious; they didn't want to destroy the mounds, didn't *dare* to, or they would have done so long ago. It was tragic irony that, now that the Human race finally knew something about the Masters' original, bewildering demand, the Masters had upped the ante. Emerson saw, just as Leonard had, that there was no way to evacuate the Earth, and no place to go even if such a thing were possible.

"And we know about the Protoculture," Marie was saying, even though the intelligence report on the 15th's discoveries inside the flagship, and analysis of the Masters' transmission to Leonard, had been very sketchy.

"We know that if you don't get it, you die," Brown added.

That gave the Masters pause again, and the captives had the impression the invaders were in silent conference once more. After a moment, Bowkaz said, "Tell us just how much you people know of us, of our history."

"We know about your weak points," Emerson answered. "The Earth is ours, and nobody's taking it away from us or making us leave it! But if you'll agree to a ceasefire, then perhaps we can help each other. We can stop this war."

"The Invid are coming, do you not understand what that means?" Shaizan demanded. "You will all be wiped out!"

"We cannot allow your stubbornness or the fate of one tiny world to endanger the establishment of our Robotech Universe," Dag said.

"Your small-mindedness merely illustrates how primitive you are," Bowkaz added.

Emerson laughed madly, so that Marie and Brown feared for a moment that he had snapped. Then the general met the Masters' glares with one of his own. "Then, so be it."

An area of mottling on the mushroomlike cap grew bright, and Bowkaz put his palm to it. The cap spoke so that the Humans could hear as well, "I am receiving information on Zor Prime.

"Zor and the Human military unit in which he served are now at the site of the buried Protoculture Matrix. Musica is with him, but she is no longer connected to the Cosmic Harp; she has given her loyalty to Zor and the Humans."

"Bowie!" Emerson murmured. "I knew you were no deserter, son."

Shaizan turned back to Emerson. "Our reprieve is withdrawn! Your Earth has just run out of time!"

Sean and the others had simply slipped back to their concealed jeeps, put on combat gear, then made their way back through the GMP lines as if they were a recon unit going to the rear to make a report. Passwords given to them by Nova made it easy. No one thought to question them with the Masters' attacks and the chaotic situation in Southern Cross HQ.

The return trip was in some ways easier, the piloted mecha lifting the unpiloted ones over the GMP perimeter. The Gimps were hesitant to shoot at friendly forces without specific orders, until it was too late.

Now the 15th stood around their Hovertanks, watching smoke rise from the blasted Monument City, which had taken scattered beam hits but not the sort of all-out, fused-earth attack that had claimed Newton.

"Bowie, I'm so ashamed," Musica said, tears wetting her cheeks, as they saw the ragged lines of survivors making their way from the city.

"It's not your fault," Bowie told her, holding her to comfort her.

She looked up at him, trying to smile. "The harmony is strong, between you and me. I feel your joys and sorrows; they are my own." Being close to him was so wonderful, a divine gift of happiness that shored her up in the horror that was around them.

Off to one side, Dana asked Nova quietly, "Do you think Zor knows what's going to happen next? That he sees the future?" It was no time to voice a more personal question to herself, *And, have* I? All her dreams and Visions crowded so close about her.

Nova considered that. "What are you saying?" The results of her interrogations and observations were inconclusive but—if Zor *did* have some sort of precog powers, perhaps the Human race could turn them to good use.

Dana was looking at Zor, who stood alone, watching the pyre that was Monument City. "He doesn't want to help Musica," Dana faced the truth. "He wants revenge, and he wants to die more than he wants to live, I think." Her voice caught a little; she still loved him.

Zor studied the destruction and suffering before him, standing near the *Three-In-One*; Dana had supposed he named his tank that because of its three configurations, but understood now that it was some deeper memory that had moved him to do so. Zor was repeating the silent vow as if it were a mantra, *This time they'll pay! This time I'll stop them!*

That was when he heard the crackle of Shaizan's voice over the cockpit speaker of Sean's Hovertank, the *Bad News*. "Zor! Traitor! Are you there?" Sean nearly jumped out of the tank like an ejecting pilot.

Zor was in the cockpit of his *Three-In-One* in an instant, hands on the control yoke grips. "I hear you."

Somehow, the Masters had contrived to send their image over the tank's display screen. "You are aware that the Protoculture Matrix is undergoing degradation, as the Flowers bloom." It wasn't a question. "And by now, the Sensor Nebula has surely alerted the Invid."

Zor looked at his onetime Masters. The words made bits of

memory and realization fall into place. "I—yes. But I also know that *I* control the key to this planet's survival. I dictate the terms."

"We are of the opinion that you are mistaken," Shaizan replied. "Watch closely, and you will see."

The other ATACs were watching on their own screens, with Musica looking over Bowie's shoulder and Nova over Dana's. They saw Rolf Emerson, teeth locked in pain, with Marie and Brown trying to comfort him.

"Emerson," Bowie said numbly, while Sean whispered Marie's name like a hopeless prayer, and Dana heard Nova breathe, "Dennis."

Then the Masters were onscreen again. "These three men will be released when you return Musica and remove your troops from this area."

Men? Sean Phillips found a second to think, wondering if they had gotten a good look at Marie. *I suppose everybody in armor looks the same to them but—maybe these vampires aren't as smart as everybody keeps tellin' me they are. Anyway, if that's what it's like to be immortal, they can keep it!*

"Do you find this acceptable?" Shaizan continued. "We trust that we need not mention the alternative."

Zor fought down his fury long enough to ask, "What are your conditions?"

"You will be picked up, and we will exchange prisoners onboard our mother ship." The Masters disappeared from the screen.

Zor lowered himself from his tank wearily and had barely begun, "I do not wish for the rest of you to be invol—" Bowie hit him with a shoulder block, driving the bigger Zor up against the armored side of *Three-In-One*, trying to choke the life out of him.

"They're not getting Musica! I'll kill you!"

Zor grimaced, trying to twist free, but didn't strike out at him. "Then stay here and do nothing, and watch your good friend be killed! The techniques of the Masters can be more cruel than anything you can conceive of!"

Dana was dashing to intervene, but somehow Musica got there first. "Stop it, Bowie!" He had no choice but to risk harming her or back off. He let go his grip on Zor.

"I will not permit you all to suffer because of me," she told Nova and the 15th. "I will go back."

Before Bowie could object, Dana said, "She's right. Saddle up, Fifteenth! C'mon, what're you all gaping at?"

Nova was the one among them most distanced from Emerson's

predicament. The fate of a few Human beings, even a flag-rank officer and two TASC fliers, was insignificant against the survival of the Human race and its homeworld; everyone who took the Southern Cross oath understood that. Shaping strategy and policy on the basis of hostages and emotional responses led to disaster; it had been one of the major contributing factors to the Global Civil War.

Marie thought about her pistol again, but realized that events had gone too far for that, and that she must see things through along with Dana's ATACs. Protoculture seemed to have some barely hinted-at power to shape events, and she could only hope that the benign side of that mystical force was working now, because Fate had the bit in its teeth.

"There's no telling what'll happen," Dana was telling her men. "We'll have to play it by ear. But this thing isn't about Southern Cross or the UEG anymore. I don't think even the mound, here, is as important now. This thing is between us and the Robotech Masters."

In the wake of her experiences on the flagship and her exposure to the spores, pollen, and Flowers below, and to Musica's song, something in her was coming fully to life—was flexing its powers like a butterfly emerging from its cocoon and pumping out its wings.

Dana didn't know exactly how, but she knew the words were true. "Maybe this was always meant to be, right from the start."

The contact broken, the Masters easily reached an unspoken consensus: Musica was critical to their plans, and there was no longer any need for the others—not even Zor. Furthermore, there were disturbing things about the halfbreed lieutenant, Sterling; some genetic throw of the dice had embued her with insights and an affinity for the Protoculture that made her dangerous. It was best that she and her unit be terminated as soon as possible; the Masters could tolerate no rival in the matter of the Protoculture.

The units encircling the mounds simply held their fire as a flotilla of a dozen assault ships came low to pick up the Hovertanks. Hopelessly outgunned, the GMP troops breathed a universal sigh of relief when the invader craft lifted away.

In due course the 15th came forth to form a spearhead on the huge hangar deck: Dana's *Valkyrie*, Angelo's *Trojan Horse*, Bowie's replacement tank, the *Re-Tread*, which had taken place of his *Diddy-Wa-Diddy*, abandoned on an earlier sortie aboard a mother ship. Sean's *Bad News* and Louie Nichols's *Livewire* completed the roster.

There were ranks of clone guards with rifles aimed at them, rabbits policing the wolves. But the ATACs only watched and waited, the tanks' headlights and downswept hoods making them appear to be glowering.

When Dana had looked the place over, she switched her mike to an external speaker and announced, "First of all, we want to see Chief of Staff Emerson."

There was some conferring among the invaders. Finally they opened ranks and the Hovertanks fell in to follow a guard runabout, moving into the vaulted passageways of the residential district, so much like those of the Masters' original flagship.

Guards stood on ledges all along the way. Dana wondered if they realized they were scarcely more than so many pop-up targets before the armor and firepower of the Hovertanks. They didn't seem worried, and that worried her.

But while she didn't have words to explain it, *something* told her that what she was doing was right, that against all logic, what she was doing was what she *should* be doing. Again she felt connected to something much greater than herself, and breathed a quick prayer that it wasn't some kind of self-delusion. It was nothing but faith, really, but if she had understood her Academy philosophy courses, what cognitive process wasn't?

The guard runabout stopped at a bulkhead hatchway as big as a hangar door, and the tanks settled in behind it, idling.

"From this point, Musica and two others may continue, but no more. The exchange will be made at once."

Dana stood in her cockpit-turret, taking up her tanker's carbine and slinging it over her armored pauldron. Her winged helmet, with its crest of bright metal, and her flashing armor seemed to daunt the guards a little. "That's you and me, Bowie." She couldn't figure out why the Masters weren't luring Zor in, too.

"Right." Behind Bowie, Musica rose to her feet, to show that she was ready.

Valkyrie and *Re-Tread* were escorted among more of those stone-faced corridors Dana remembered so well, and through more technological-looking passageways as well. At last the runabout leading them stopped, and the tanks settled to a halt. At Dana's signal, Bowie and Musica dismounted to join her, both ATACs carrying their carbines. They were led to a triskelion hatch that rotated open.

Emerson looked up with a resigned smile. "It's you." Dana

knew some of it was for her, but most of the general's warmth was for Bowie.

"Rolf," Bowie said simply.

"General Emerson!" Dana strode over to him, carbine still at sling-arms, as Dennis Brown and Marie Crystal helped him to his feet. "You're wounded."

She could see there wasn't much she could do with her combat med kit that Brown and Crystal hadn't already done with theirs. "It's nothing serious," the general told her, a lie and they both knew it. "I'm glad you're here, Dana."

Then he turned to Bowie, who stood rooted. "Good to see you, soldier."

Bowie inclined his head to his guardian. "Pleasure to be here, General." But his eyes danced behind his helmet visor, and Dana took an instant from her scheming and calculating to be glad. Whatever had gone wrong between the two had somehow been made right again.

Dana was figuring the best order of march, meaning to use Musica as insurance—something Musica had already agreed to—when there was a muffled cry. Dana whipped around, the carbine slung down off her shoulder butt first and the muzzle coming up, to see Musica being borne back, wrenched from Bowie's grasp, and carried through two firing ranks of clone guards. The guards had appeared from nowhere, their backs to what she had assumed was a solid wall—she had fallen for an old trick. The ranks closed, and the guards assumed firing stances.

"Dana!"

Sean had never quite heard that tone in Angelo's voice before, but there wasn't much time to stop and reflect on it. Sean himself had been preoccupied, worrying about Marie.

But Dana had left her mike open, and there was no mistaking the sound of a firefight or the lieutenant's yell for reinforcements.

"I'll come with you!" Angelo roared, as the tanks' thrusters blared. Nova, riding with him, was all for that, thinking of Dennis Brown.

Sean automatically reverted to a command voice, even though the big sergeant now outranked him.

"You know your orders! Hold this position! And you, too, Louie; you've got to secure the escape route!" Sean fired up *Bad News* and bashed through the hatch before him while Angelo was still making strangled objections.

It wasn't too hard to find the way; Dana and Louie each had a transponder in their armor's torso-instrumentation pack. Then, Dana's vanished from the display screen.

But Bowie's still functioned, even though Sean couldn't raise him or the lieutenant over the radio. Sean had clones ducking low every which way, indifferent to their puny small arms fire, laying out an occasional burst just to keep them discouraged.

The race to get there seemed to take forever. Dana's signal was dead and she might be, too; and Marie was in there, along with the others. . . .

He bashed through a final hatch like an iron fist through rice paper, holding fire because he didn't know. where friend or foe might be. Energy bolts began coming his way at once.

Still he held fire, trying to get his bearings. It was a singular piece of discipline; as someone in an earlier war had remarked, you would shoot your own mother if she happened to charge across your field of fire in battle.

Bad News settled in for a low hover, as a triad of guards concentrated their fire on it. Sean would wonder later if the clones had any real idea of warfare, would feel as though he had simply executed them. But in the heat of the moment, seeing there were no friendlies near, he laid out a single bolt from the cannon and was on the move even while the immolated bodies were turning to ash.

He was too zoned-up for combat to feel sorry for them; there was only one thing he cared about, and the voice Sean heard then sent waves of relief and joy pushing through him, remarkable in their intensity.

"You took your time getting here!" Marie scolded from behind a fluted column, snapping off judicious shots with a fallen guard's rifle.

"But my heart was with you all the while. Believe me, my little pigeon!"

The romance had started, for him, as just one more conquest. *When did she come to mean everything to me?* Sean couldn't help wondering, even while trying to keep his mind on business.

Maybe it was because Marie Crystal wasn't dazzled by him, having more than enough medals and decorations of her own; or maybe it was bound up in that spooky destiny stuff Dana kept yammering about and Sean refused to accept. Most likely, if he and Marie lived to be together again and spent their whole lives that way, they would *still* never figure it out, he decided.

He thought all that in a tiny slice of time, pivoting the *Bad News* and laying out heavy suppressive fire, blowing beautiful friezes to cinders and fountaining tiles from the deck to keep the enemy's head down.

The clones didn't seem to care about their own lives. Some stood right up into the fire and shrapnel; their small arms counterfire was radiant dotted lines running at every angle across the compartment.

CHAPTER TWENTY

Emerson! Shoulderer of sorrow!
Champion of the light! Although—
It wasn't given him to know that
Until his work was done

Mingtao, *Protoculture: Journey Beyond Mecha*

ROLF EMERSON LOOKED UP, CLUTCHING HIS WOUNDED ARM to him, to see Bowie and Musica sheltering in the lee of a column not far away, and a guard clone angling to get a clear shot at them from behind.

Dispassion and logic were no part of it; Emerson was sprinting headlong through the gauntlet of weapon blasts before rationale had any chance to come to bear. The space between his cover and Bowie's column was fairly safe; the shots were well directed by then. Emerson launched himself through the air just as the clone pressed his cheek against the stock of his rifle for maximum accuracy, down on one knee.

There was a split-second image of Musica's face, frightened, worried for *him*, Emerson could see.

So beautiful, it occurred to the general as the charge hit his back. *Perhaps she's the better part of us all; we must listen to her*.

The bolt hit him squarely in the back, vaporizing flesh and singeing bone, setting his tunic afire. The next thing he knew, he was in Bowie's arms and the clone rifleman had been mowed down by Dana's fire.

Sean was walking his tank's secondary-battery fire back and forth in the compartment; most of the enemy withdrew and the rest died. In moments, the violent echoes gave way to silence.

Bowie threw his helmet aside, kneeling to gather Emerson into his embrace, smelling the charred flesh. "Rolf. Father . . ."

Emerson found his hand, gripped the cold alloy. "I heard your music. The night before they sent me to take over ALUCE base,

I stood under the barracks window and listened to you play. It was beautiful, Bowie; you have a gift."

"I wasn't—I haven't—" Bowie wanted to talk about love and found only apologies on his lips, and knew there was no more time.

Emerson's hand squeezed the metal-sheathed fingers. "You and Musica . . . it's such a *good* thing, Bowie. You must both teach it. Son."

Emerson was still alive for another few seconds, though he would never speak again. He looked up over Bowie's shoulder to see Dana with her helmet faceplate open. Her armor was seared where the enemy bolt had burned out her transponder, but failed to wound her.

She might have even more to teach than Bowie or Musica, it occurred to him. Dana gave him a nod, knowing words wouldn't serve. Then she slipped away out of sight, rifle held at high port.

Emerson saw with some surprise that the world wasn't going dark, the way traditional lore said it would. Instead, the range of his vision and perception went out and out, encompassing things wonderful and terrible, things defying all description—a terrible beauty beside which mortal life seemed a lesser matter.

There was a celebration of light around him, and he threw himself forth willingly. The Universe embraced him, opening all secrets, answering every question.

In his protected sanctum, Dr. Zand, monitoring the battle through technical relays and paths of information of his own, suddenly straightened as if he were about to suffer a stroke. But he relaxed again in a moment, breathing raggedly.

He grasped the front of Russo's tunic. "Emerson is dead! The Moment comes! Gather my special equipment!" He sent the smaller man on his way with a shove.

As Russo slunk away, Zand began unbuttoning his uniform jacket. Nevermore would he wear false colors! It was time to garb himself in more fitting vestments.

Today a new Universe begins!

Nova was wearing a spare suit of ATAC armor, a thing with long horns that had originally belonged to Cutter, who had died in that first assault on the mother ship. She looked a little like a metallic steer, gazing back in the direction from which the two tanks—formerly three—had come on their rescue mission.

"I don't see Zor anywhere," she leaned down to tell Angelo Dante. "He's sneaked off somewhere."

In another part of the mother ship, Zor stepped his red Bioroid forth, stalking the passageways, willing to die so long as he could work his revenge. For a moment the image of Dana's face was before him, for no reason he could name, but he thrust it aside and went on again, the ultimate intellect, bereft of any thought but revenge.

"Sarge, these passageways all look the same to me!" Louie called over the tac net. "How'll we ever find them?" Some new interference was jamming all long-range commo and even blotting out Bowie's transponder.

"We keep lookin'," Angelo said. Damn Phillips anyway, for not marking his trail!

Just then figures came dashing and dodging from a side passageway up ahead, fire ranging all around them from behind. "It's Lieutenant Crystal and Lieutenant Brown!" Louie yelled.

Bowie and Musica came close after, ducking for cover at either side of the passageway, as the two TASC pilots did. Intense fire from the guards splashed from the bulkheads. The guards' counterattack was so sudden and determined that the Humans had been forced to leave Emerson's body behind.

Sean's holding action back in the "senate" chamber wasn't keeping all the guards pinned down. More showed up, from the other direction, with a clear line of fire. But before they could cut down their prey, a sustained burst from a Hovertank's secondary batteries felled them all in a squall of blazing rapid-fire bolts.

Bowie and the others turned and, stunned, saw Dana drift her *Valkyrie* to a stop, its quad-barrels sending up shimmering heat waves.

Bowie was momentarily confused. Hadn't *Re-Tread* and Dana's tank been parked in the *other* direction? He hadn't seen her slip away while Emerson lay dying, to make an almost suicidal dash for her mecha.

Now she jumped up in her cockpit and fired with her carbine, afraid that the heavy guns might hit friend as well as foe. A last guard pitched from a ledge just above her friends' heads. Then she whirled and fired into a guard runabout that was bearing down on her from the opposite side; the runabout's windshield melted and the little vehicle rolled, throwing guards every which way, and plowed to a stop.

Sean fought his way free and caught up, as Angelo, Nova, and Louie came to a stop with blaring retros. While Dennis Brown and Bowie supported Sean in holding back the guards who had chased them from the "senate," Marie Crystal jumped into the runabout and got it started up.

Musica, Bowie, and Brown piled in. Marie gunned away, convoyed by the four Hovertanks. It was only then that Dana realized Zor was missing.

The decision had been made to strike, the Humans' determination to fight notwithstanding.

"We must consolidate our strength," Dag declared. "Eliminate all clones functioning beneath an efficiency factor of eighty percent." The other four mother ships and most of the combat vessels were almost useless for combat now, depleted as they were; the flagship was the only remaining hope.

Jeddar started to object. He knew that the Master didn't mean simply denying the clones Protoculture, but also to eject them from the flagship.

"They may not *submit* to elimination, m'lord," Jeddar pointed out.

"Then confine them for the moment!" Shaizan lashed out. "And get ready to dispose of them. Begin the assault on the buried Matrix below!"

Even the fanatic loyalty of the guard clones failed before the massed firepower of the tanks; in time the running firefight became an unchallenged withdrawal. Dana couldn't believe the Masters didn't have more of their Triumviroids around—but why weren't they using them?

The ATACs had lost their bearings, and even Musica couldn't tell where they were. They burned through hatches, and came at last to a hangar deck where whiskbroom-shaped assault ships were ranked side by side.

There was only time for brief kissing and hugging—passionate between Sean and Marie, more reserved but plainly heartfelt between Nova and Dennis—before the question of how to get out alive took center stage.

Marie and Dennis weren't sure if they could fly an assault ship; planetary approaches in an unfamiliar spacecraft were a lot different from joyrides in a guard runabout.

"See what you can do," Dana said, revving *Valkyrie*. "I'm going back for Zor."

Angelo felt like tearing out his hair. "Lieutenant, this just ain't fair! It ain't *army*!"

"I'm not working for the army anymore, Angie," she threw back, the tank pivoting on its thrusters. "If I'm not back in twenty minutes, go on without me."

She was scarcely gone when Bowie and Musica went to stand before the sergeant hand in hand. "I'm going back, too," Bowie announced. "Musica says her people are in terrible danger."

"I can sense it," she explained. "My sisters and I are linked—are one."

Bowie touched her shoulder gently. "It's all right; we'll find them." Perhaps this was part of the teaching that Rolf Emerson had said he and Musica must do; in any case, Bowie knew he couldn't abandon Musica's people.

Suddenly, Nova stepped forward, letting go of Dennis's hand. "I'll go with you. Dana's right: We're not working for the army anymore, and it's time for the dying to stop."

Then Brown joined her, and Marie; Angelo Dante surrendered to the inevitable. The flying officers outranked him, but that meant nothing since this was a Hovertank operation. "Sean, you 'n' Lieutenant Crystal stand pat here with *Bad News* and hold this position! See if you can figure out how to fly these things. Rest of ya, do me a favor and try not to screw up."

The Southern Cross had rallied everything it had, mobilizing reserves and arming any willing civilian, no questions asked. Cops, students, robots, convicts, bureaucrats, homemakers, kid gangs—the Human race readied its remaining resources for a last-ditch stand.

What regular forces there were would go out and meet the approaching flagship head-on; the rest would wait, to fight it out on home soil if that was what it came to.

Supreme Commander Leonard heard details of the hasty preparations, then dismissed his staff for a moment to see to a matter of personal readiness. Opening his desk drawer, he checked to make sure that the charge in his pistol was full.

He burned again with his loathing of the aliens. Leonard tucked the gun into his tunic and closed the drawer. He had no intention of letting those monsters take him alive.

It smashed its way through a stone partition and came face to face with three red Bioroids. Perhaps they recognized Zor's mecha as that of their onetime battle lord, or perhaps not; it made no difference.

Even if they had been operating at peak efficiency, the Triumviroids would have found Zor a formidable opponent. But they were depleted—scarcely any kind of match for him at all.

He dropped them with fast, accurate shots from the thick, discus-shaped handgun his Bioroid carried, its muzzle bigger than a howitzer's. But as he stepped into the compartment, three more reds dropped from above, springing their ambush.

Zor proved how experience counted; his Bioroid held up a great slab of stone to shield itself from the ambushers' fire, then blazed away in response, leaping high. He dropped one, two, three, holed through at the point where their operating clones sat curled in the control spheres.

Zor broke into yet another compartment only to see a high ledge lined with Triumviroids, dozens of them, waiting for him. Here and there were armed guardsmen, looking like insects among the mecha.

"Take me to the Masters!" he commanded. "I mean you no harm; my business is only with them."

He saw Karno, standing to one side, drop his arm in signal. Zor's Bioroid's external sound pickup caught the shouted order, "Fire!"

Zor's red ducked aside, as the blasts volleyed in all directions, ricocheted from bulkheads or penetrated them, lanced through the deck and overhead. A secondary explosion from a weakened power routing system knocked the mecha sideways.

He was momentarily in the cover of the hatchway frame, rolling and about to surge to his feet again, his red's armor striking rooster tails of sparks from the deckplates.

Karno reached out to pull a long lever nearby. "We knew you would come."

There were carefully planned explosions, and the overhead gave way; tons of metal and conduits and organic-looking Protoculture systemry landed on him like a cave-in, pinning him. At the same time, the bulkhead collapsed, tearing aside, leaving him exposed to his enemies' fire.

Karno looked down on Zor, not with the dispassion of a cloned slave, but rather with the cold hatred he had felt since losing Musica. Emotions were seeping throughout the servants of the Masters, unstoppable and often unrecognized.

"You're a fool, Zor," Karno snarled, "if you believe you have the power to stand against us! Now that this lunatic quest of yours has failed, I am instructed to offer you one final chance to repent, and rejoin us." The tone of his voice made it clear that Karno offered reconciliation unwillingly. He would much rather give the order to fire again.

Zor's red managed to lever itself up. But despite all its immense strength, it still couldn't fight its way clear of the pinning wreckage.

Zor looked into the muzzles that had been brought to bear on him, his red's gleaming black visor panning slowly, and said, putting weight behind each word, "Never. I won't stop until I end the Masters' tyranny or they end *me*."

Karno nodded, not unhappy with that pronouncement. "It shall be as you wish it." He raised his hand again to give the signal to resume firing, and the fetal clones curled in each Triumviroid's control sphere sent out commands of readiness, preparing to shoot Zor's mecha to incandescent bits.

"And so passes the very last of Zor." Karno hissed out the words, looking like a handsome young demigod turned angel of death, signal arm ready to fall.

But like a wash of pure light, an enormous bolt from a Gladiator's main battery came through another gap in the bulkheads, sending one Triumviroid leaping off the firing ledge in a volcanic blast. The Gladiator, standing in the smoking breach, traversed its great gun to blast another enemy, and then another, like clay pipes in a shooting gallery.

The lack of Musica's harmonics and the decline in Protoculture energy had the clone operators at a level of functioning that was near failure. Instead of firing back, they awaited orders, or turned and collided with each other, or merely stood waiting to die—except for the one or two who shot, inaccurately. Karno was enough of a realist to flee through a side hatchway, seething with the need to slay, to avenge himself—reverting to a level as primitive as that of any primate, without realizing it, because his intellect fed him justifications.

CHAPTER
TWENTY-ONE

When I was a little kid, after my parents left in SDF-3, I had three godfathers for a while. Maybe you heard about them, the ex-Zentraedi spies—Konda and Bron and Rico.

They knew I was half Zentraedi and that I had no close family after my folks went, so—they appointed themselves.

What I'm getting at is, they were kinder to me than anyone ever was. They had loved three female techs who were killed in the SDF-1, and I suppose to some extent I was the Zentraedi-Human kid they never had.

And when I was—I don't know, twelve or so, I guess—they got very ill. I found out later that the doctors said it was something that came from being reduced to our size in the Protoculture chambers. What I didn't know was that there was a possible cure, but it would only work on a full-size Zentraedi. But they stayed Human-size, so they could look after me.

They died on the factory satellite within weeks of each other. So what I'm saying is, don't ever ask me if I'm ashamed of being half alien, or ask why I'm willing to grant Zor the benefit of the doubt. A lot of people think courage is something you can only prove on the battlefield, and love is something noisy and—what's the word I'm looking for? Demonstrative.

But aliens taught me differently.

Dana Sterling, in a remark recorded by Nova Satori

ANA FIRED AGAIN, THEN SAW THAT THE TRIUMVIROIDS were making no meaningful resistance, and ceased fire; her war wasn't with mind-enthralled, blameless clones anymore.

She operated controls and imaged with her winged, crested helmet. *Valkyrie* pivoted end for end, changing, rearing up, and in an instant she was an armored Goliath, holding a rifle the size of a field piece.

Something about the mechamorphosis made some of the reds react, it seemed; they were in motion again. She laid out a few rounds to keep their heads down, but suddenly they moved with more purpose. Dana leapt to crouch by Zor's red Bioroid, partly shielding it with her own Battloid, pouring out covering fire.

"Zor, stay down!" She shot from the hip, and a red that had been about to nail Zor went down in a subsidence of ripped armor and glowing components. But others stirred, raising their discus pistols shakily.

More reds were being brought back under control, getting ready to take up the attack once more. *Valkyrie* swung its weapon back and forth, Dana was well aware that so many Triumviroids, even hindered as they were, would shortly prevail unless she did something. She fired with one hand, trying to drag Zor free with the other. A red tromped over to a point on the ledge behind her, ready to shoot directly down.

Zor's red's arm pulled free and swung its weapon; fierce artificial lightning crashed, and the red above toppled from the ledge, even while others staggered to move into positions of advantage.

"Thank you for saving my life, Dana," Zor said, a little numbly. "But I must go on alone."

Dana dismissed the matter of who had saved whom from what in the time since she had first seen him. Each had spared the other in combat; did that count as a higher form of rescue?

Anyway, there would be better times to sort all that out; the problem was living to see them. "No way, trooper!" She was helping his mecha to its feet, pulling wreckage off it, supporting it. "It's my fight, too."

It is, in some ways I can explain, and others that—I just can't, yet.

Then he was up, and the red Bioroid and the blue-and-white Battloid were pounding along the passageway shoulder to shoulder, so that the deck alloy gonged. "Be warned: I mean to confront the Robotech Masters and destroy them," he said.

"Long as you don't destroy *yourself* at the same time. Or me," she cautioned. He heard her concern for him in her tone; and in the midst of his killing wrath, he felt a calm, clear sanity flowing from her to himself.

But a hatchway loomed up before them just then. "Look sharp, now," she said.

They took it ATAC style, poised to either side with their backs against it, like infantry in house-to-house fighting, or SWAT cops going in. Another red's shots fireballed through the hatchway past them.

Zor waited for the right moment, went through the hatchway

firing, bent low, and rammed his foe shoulder-on. Dana followed, waiting for a clear shot.

"There are my people! Oh no, no . . ."

Musica was nearly collapsed against a crystal concavity of a viewport taller than herself, seemingly close to a faint. Bowie, Angelo, and the others halted in some confusion, not sure what she meant and thoroughly spooked by the abandoned residential district around them.

The Humans had been forced to leave their tanks behind, to pass through the tight confines of the Human-scale areas. They were armed and armored, though.

The other troopers set up security and fingered their rifles, as Bowie caught Musica just before she slumped. She was again wearing the ceremonial vestments of her office—the blue tights and torso-wrapping, the cold alloy ring around her neck with its arrowheadlike emblem.

She had found the clothes in an empty guard command center and, for some reason, insisted on changing into them while the ATACs searched nearby. But there had been no sign of her sisters and her people.

Bowie couldn't help worrying about the ceremonial clothing. The Masters had brought it with them from their other flagship and held it ready. Zor had been compelled to turn traitor; must Bowie fear such a thing from Musica?

Now, though, the riddle of the missing clones was answered, and the answers made a horrifying sense. "They *are* outside the ship!" Musica added in a small, forlorn voice. She had sensed it, but the enormity of such a thing, the sheer incomprehensibility of it, had kept her from considering it seriously.

The troopers gathered around Musica and saw what was going on. There were many ships, drifting close by because the Masters' new flagship hadn't finished its waste disposal yet; every viewport and dome in the inert combat vessels out there was crammed with motionless, seemingly sleeping clones.

Louie Nichols looked out at it all and thought, as his stomach turned, of an animal gnawing its own leg off to escape a trap's iron teeth. What the Masters had done was infinitely worse. *God, it's all stripped away! Compassion . . . mercy.*

The pure intellect and the rational organization of society—this is where they point. Dana was right. He teetered a little, then caught his balance, and looked around to see if anyone else had noticed. But they were all transfixed.

Nova Satori looked out at the sight, rocked with surprise at herself because, until this awful moment, she had never really been able to bring herself to think of the aliens as Human beings. She had never thought of them as creatures with souls, all Zor's appeal and powers of persuasion aside. But she gazed upon genocide and knew she had been blinding *herself*. It hadn't taken so very much ordi-psych indoctrination or so very many pep talks from Supreme Commander Leonard and Colonel Fredericks to set her attitudes in concrete.

Now, though, those were wiped away. There were people out there who needed rescue.

There were other castaways, set adrift in spacesuits and smaller craft. *Now why didn't those Masters just space 'em?* a practical side of Angelo wondered. *Why leave 'em safe and sound, as it were?* Maybe the Masters meant to come back and reclaim their slaves, if the Masters won.

But the ATACs intended to see to it that the Masters didn't win. "Are they alive?" Bowie asked, gripping Musica by the shoulders.

"Yes, but doomed. Cut off from the Protoculture and the Masters' will."

And from the music of the Cosmic Harp, she admitted to herself. The Cosmic Harp was nowhere to be found; perhaps it had been destroyed in the first flagship. She was cut off from it forever, a pain as sharp as any physical wound.

"A rescue mission would be just about impossible," Louie said in his best mechie, noncommittal voice. But within, he was plotting his own personal vector along new grids, and changing parallax. There were more spacecraft in the mother ship. *Maybe, sometimes, trying the impossible is the whole point.* "Maybe we can—"

Musica cut him off. "Allegra! Octavia! My sisters are nearby!" Her eyes rolled up so that only the whites showed, and Bowie had to bear her up.

He held her close, so that he breathed her sweet breath, almost tasted it. "Are they alive?"

Blue-haired Allegra, sundered from the harmonies upon which she and her Muse sisters had lived as upon food, drink, and the air they breathed, found a troubling and yet comforting new orchestration in ministering to those around her who were suffering. She hadn't known she knew how to do it, and yet the harmonies assured her, *conducted* her through every movement.

Now she was cooling the brow of a feverish stonemason clone with a damp cloth, feeling Octavia's gaze upon her.

Allegra, kneeling there by the stone bench that had been made a sickbed, said, "His bio-index has fallen too low, and his own reserves are gone. I'm afraid there is no hope for him." The clone was pale white, sweat slick along his face and neck, long hair damp and clinging, and yet his skin was cold.

But Octavia told Allegra, "There is always hope!" and wondered where the certainty, the rightness of the words that made them a new harmony, had come from. All the old certainties had been burnt away, but in the ashes she was finding bright, warming determination that had yet to find its form.

Allegra looked at her dubiously. "I wish Musica would come." They sensed that she was near, ever the centerpiece and the wellspring of their power.

"Without the eternal Song of Musica's Harp," the stonemason clone who rested under Octavia's dove-gentle hand said, "I have no will left to live."

How much harder do you think it is for me? she thought.

"You must not say that!" Octavia found that her voice had become harsh, a commanding note a Clonemaster might use, or even a Robotech Master. "We must learn to live on our own."

The words and the very wisdom of them had come unbidden. Suddenly there was a current of awareness in the big holding chamber, which lifted the clones' lassitude and fed power back to her. Some shackle she had never felt, even though it had confined her life and her art, had been broken. But the rightness of what she had said was a clarity that she couldn't deny or stifle, a pureness of a profound inner music she had never heard before.

A tech clone stood up next to his pallet, nearby. Weaving as he stood, he got out, "We know nothing of the Dead Life, the Life of the One. We only know the triumvirates, and now the triumvirates are no more."

Octavia didn't realize she was moving, as she stood up and gathered her half-shawl, the words flowing to her as notes from some new, unsuspected song. "Then it's time for us all to learn a new way to live. Musica is willing to stand on her own two feet and survive."

Whence come these thoughts? she belabored herself, brain roiling. Perhaps some had been transferred to her by the link with Musica, and there was the breakdown of the Masters' power, the depletion of the Protoculture, and the silence of the Cosmic Harp. The suspect sources were many.

But the central melody of it, Octavia somehow knew, came from within: a music long subsumed by the narrow, repetitive themes the Masters had forced the Muses to play.

"We still may be rescued, or save *ourselves*," Allegra added. Octavia was shocked at first, but then felt more sisterly to her than she ever had.

But Allegra's patient hiked himself up on his elbows, feverish, to say as if in some fortune-telling trance, "Even if we *are* rescued, who among us could live a life so forlorn? A life where the triumvirates are broken apart? We are *parts*, we are not *whole*!"

Octavia didn't know how to answer that, exactly; she hadn't the right words in her vocabulary, or the right notes in her music.

And yet, bringing all her will to bear, she knew in a revelation as bright as a mountain sunrise that he was wrong.

From Earth rose every remnant of its military striking power. Nothing that could conceivably reach the approaching Masters was left behind; men and women readied for battle and took strength from a source greater than the Protoculture.

They were willing to die for their families and children and planet, if that be the price, so long as the Masters died as well. And if the Masters meant to end life on the planet then *all*, invader and defender, would die alike.

The beings who had ruled galaxies, and meant to rule all the Universe, wouldn't have understood that sense of fatalism no matter how it was phrased.

Again, that terrible Human advantage had come into play. The Masters proceeded, as they always had, upon logical conclusions; the creatures Earth had bred rose up, in a manner that swept those calculations away, to stand and fight.

Just then a minor sub-subentity, an artificial intelligence construct of the Protoculture cap, reported to the Masters that there was no rational explanation as to why these creatures had not either totally destroyed themselves, or become a slave culture (a stagnant one, the subentity would have pointed out, if the Masters had created it to be more candid) like the Robotech Masters' clones. The concept of a third alternative had simply never been considered before.

Zor, Zor . . . you sent your dimensional fortress to no random world! Earth was a deliberate choice for the centerpiece of this great War, wasn't it? Some least-constrained part of the Master's unified consciousness whispered the insight, a death-dry croak that sent panic all through them and made the cap pulse like an alarm beacon.

Then they had it back under control again, and themselves as well. "The Micronian fleet is advancing, m'lords." Jeddar said, head bowed low, frightened by his own boldness in interrupting them but frightened even more by the long barracuda shapes of the Terran warships.

Then Shaizan, Dag, and Bowkaz were alert once more, eyes so bright that it seemed rays of divine wrath might shoot forth. The Masters had shaken off or put down every misgiving. If there was some small voice within their communal mind that persisted in faint, tormented murmurs of mortality, it was altogether drowned out in their drumming mental din of conquest.

Or at least, *almost* altogether; none of the three would dare admit he heard it.

Shaizan sent out the command, "Let half of our remaining attack forces go forth to engage this enemy fleet. The remainder will descend to the planet and retrieve the Protoculture Matrix."

The other mother ships were all but useless, as were the combat craft and clones and mecha remaining to them. But the Protoculture cap told them the resources still available to the Masters in their flagship would more than suffice.

As long as the Matrix was recovered, any and all losses suffered would be negligible. But if the mission failed, such sacrifices would be immaterial: the Robotech Masters themselves would have no hope of survival.

Shaizan touched the Protoculture cap again, so that the Masters were gazing down on a scene of the three mounds near Monument City. Sensors indicated that the aura of protection generated by the guardian wraiths below was weakening. As the energy of the last Matrix began to fail, the powers of the wraiths diminished. There was yet a tiny, unique window of opportunity. The Protoculture cap had already gotten a precise fix on the Matrix's location, like seeking out like, across the negligible distance between planet and space.

Shaizan had activated another mechanism. Like magic, a circular gap appeared in the deck behind them, and from it rose a glassy sphere a yard in diameter. They turned to regard it.

Within it was the last major Protoculture mass left to them, not a Matrix that could perpetuate itself and spawn other Matrices, but still a power source of vast potency. It was a tangled collection of vegetable-looking matter, glowing and flickering, sending out concentric waves of faint blue light in a nimbus. It was far different from the huge mass Louie Nichols had seen and by which he had been captured; this one was uncontaminated and unbloated.

It was contained in a clear canister only a little larger than and the same shape as an earthly hurricane lantern, with flat metal discs of systemry at either end. The container and the globe around it rested on a stem of metal that was grown around with leaved creepers of a Flower of Life stem.

Ranged around the compartment were other such vessels, the Flowers within them now blooming—the masses useless, their remaining power shunted into the single remaining viable one.

Its power, too, would soon show signs of atrophy, but it would serve. The three looked on it silently, thinking greedy thoughts of the vast energies waiting for them on Earth, exulting in the contemplation of the absolute tyranny they could establish.

"Our victory is within reach," Shaizan said aloud, and the words had a death-knell echo in the chamber.

"I shall *never* allow that victory!" a new voice cried, a ringing challenge. The Masters whirled, shocked.

CHAPTER
TWENTY-TWO

Lazlo, my dear friend,

Comes now a parting of the ways; you know our quandary. Max and Miriya Sterling will not consent to bringing their child, Dana, along on the SDF-3 expedition for fear that the Shaping endangers her, and for mistrust of me, I suspect. It may even be that Jean and Vince Grant leave their little boy behind for kindred reasons.

Of course, you will be monitoring Dana's progress and seeing to her welfare and education; that is a given. But I warn you to do nothing, nothing, to harm her. The scales of the Protoculture, we know, often take a long time to come back into balance, but ill is always paid for ill, and good for good, despite your ponderings.

Parents are a fearsome breed anyway; how much more so, Earth's greatest Robotech ace and the battle queen of the Zentraedi?

While we may look to the Shaping for certain protection, do not make the mistake of forgetting that there are Powers far and above anything we see in the Protoculture.

Your colleague,
Emil Lang

SO, ZOR PRIME, YOU HAVE FINALLY COME," SHAIZAN managed to say. "We have been expecting you, and you have not disappointed us."

And they had expected him, but not quite like this. How had he survived the Triumviroids? He was armored, though unhelmeted, and had a Southern Cross assault rifle leveled at them. Dana was backing him up, the stock of her tanker's carbine clamped against her hip, muzzle swinging a bit to keep them all covered.

Still, the Masters were little dismayed. In the final analysis wasn't Zor one of them? The Protoculture's intoxicating effect on them, the rush of its sheer power, made them sure that if they offered to share it with the clone, he would be theirs. The halfbreed enemy female was of no real importance.

"So—you know why I'm here?" Zor asked, eyes narrowed.

Shaizan nodded serenely. "But of course. Your purpose has always remained the same—through *every incarnation*."

"You are the embodiment of the original Zor," Bowkaz added, "creator of the first Protoculture Matrix, the Master responsible for our race's ascendency."

The words had Dana reeling; she had good reason to know some of the Masters' works. "You mean . . . Zor also developed the Zentraedi people?"

Dag studied her. "Zor was the prime force behind *all* the advancements of our race." He sensed that Zor Prime hadn't yet recalled all the things the Masters and their Elders had done to the original Zor. If he had, Dag thought, the clone would have entered firing.

Dana studied Zor Prime, reincarnation of the man who had created her mother's race—he who was therefore, at least in part, her own creator as well. She looked back to the Protoculture mass, and wondered if it was the key to everything: the war, peace, and her own origins and destiny.

"But his most important discovery—the one from which our lifeblood flows—is the Protoculture that makes possible eternal life," Shaizan was saying.

Zor, though, was shaking his head angrily, eyes squeezed to mere slits, breathing hard. "No! I was never a Master, never one of you! And the Protoculture hasn't brought life; it has brought only death!"

He brought the assault rifle level with his waist and fired, the weapon burping brief meteoric bursts that blew open a half-dozen of the canisters of degraded Protoculture mass along the wall. It showered the deck with nutrient fluids and the raveled, dripping Flowers of Life, their soaked petals and spores, their intertangled roots and blossoms.

"I will end this here and now!" he screamed, turning the barrel on his onetime Masters.

In spite of their calm greeting, the Masters hadn't thought to confront Zor at this moment, in this situation. It was suddenly clear that he was too overwrought to listen to reason or blandishment. The accursed Human emotions had thrown the Masters' calculations awry yet again.

Shaizan stepped from the Protoculture cap to stand protectively near the resplendent globe that held the remaining mass. Zor must be kept at bay, until the help that had already been silently summoned could arrive. "Surely you are not prepared to destroy your most precious creation, the embodiment of all your hopes and dreams. Without it, your own species and the civilization you founded will die."

Shaizan himself felt a strange ripple coursing through him. He felt as if he needed biostabilization and longed for contact with the Protoculture cap, but there was no time for that in this crisis. He could see that both Dag and Bowkaz were experiencing the weird perturbations, too.

"My civilization is *already* dead!" Zor hissed, and opened fire again, bolts chopping at the spilled, saturated Flowers, sending up steam and burning blossoms and bits of glowing deckplate.

Zor felt as if he were made of pure rage. Strange, that beings as emotionless as the Masters should find it so easy to use emotions to their own ends—to torment him and manipulate him so with guilt and sorrow—to batter down his resolve. They made it so hard to think clearly, and unclear thought could only work to their benefit.

Then, all at once, the scent of the Flowers came to him. The aroma summoned up a memory as clear and substantial as diamond, though it was a memory inherited from a Zor who had died long ago. He recalled how he had plumbed the mysteries of Protoculture, and why, and the tragedies of that great undertaking. He recalled, too, that he had never intended his discoveries to be used for the ends to which the Masters had put them. He saw that the civilization—if that was the word for it—around him was *their* perversion, their responsibility, not his.

And he saw, in an almost preternatural calmness, that it didn't lie within his power to *change* the Masters' civilization, only to *stop* it.

Zor brought his weapon around and blasted the base of the sphere. The glassy material shattered, in big fragments and infinitesimal ones, like the end of some Cosmic Egg. Shaizan bent aside, shielding himself with his hands.

A secondary explosion in the systemry under the Masters' last Protoculture mass shot the hurricane-lantern canister into the air, as if a child had launched a tin can with a firecracker.

Trailing wires and dendrites, it turned slowly end for end. Unused to physical action, Bowkaz still sprang from his standing place at the cap to catch it before it shattered against the deck.

But Zor was pivoting, livid with anger. Perhaps he would have fired at *anybody* who came into his sights then—even Dana. Certainly, he shot Bowkaz, the impact of the blasts sending the Master back, setting his monkish robes on fire, his Flower of Life–shaped collar flopping, to fall to the deck.

But while Zor was distracted, firing at the Master, Dana was in motion, slinging her carbine over her shoulder and leaping high. It wasn't so different from football or volleyball, but it was the best save she had ever made. She had always been athletic, but a desperation to save what might be her own personal salvation and the key to the war made her faster and stronger than she had ever been before.

And yet, even while she hurled herself up for the catch, gauntleted hands closing in, she could hear the one called Dag actually screeching, "Do not touch the terminals!"

She had no choice; Dana caught it as best she could, and as her hands closed over the discs of systemry at either end of the canister, there was a bright discharge. She wailed, a long, sustained sound, as an absolute-zero shock of energy pulsed through her, and time seemed to slow.

She could see every detail of the vegetable mass in the canister. It was really very beautiful. Unhurriedly—though she could sense, somehow, that it was happening very quickly—the little twisted buds that reminded her of the mother ships' cannon began to open.

Sheets of crackling energy raged and swept through the compartment, throwing out harsh shadows one moment, then making her and Zor and the Masters all transparent as X rays the next. Bowkaz had barely begun to fall, but his fall was stopping, making him seem to her to hang in midair, contorted with pain from Zor Prime's shot.

The canister and its Protoculture mass glowed like a star. Shaizan, watching, registered *Impossible*! The Masters, in concert with their Protoculture cap, might have been able to work something like that effect, but no unaided entity—not Elder, Master, clone, Zentraedi, or Human—could so evoke the power of the Universe's most potent force.

But Dana heard. Somehow, as if from far away, she heard Shaizan's thought-speech, *The Flowers have blossomed!*

Far below, Flowers began opening faster and faster, as the three enigmatic entities set to guard and watch over the matrix by Zor sensed what had happened in the mother ship. The three wraiths began to gather themselves, depleted as they were, for their final task.

Zor felt himself engulfed in a quicksand of time dilation; he began to mouth a cry that echoed Dana's, a cry that seemed to stretch to Forever. And still the canister poured its full energies into Dana Sterling, who hung in a split-instant's graceful pose, high in the air with the Masters' last Protoculture mass radiant between her hands. . . .

With no sense of transition, she found herself awakening on a green field lush with the pink Flowers of Life. She still wore her armor; she looked around at hills and vales, not sure that they were of Earth, though she saw the wind-blasted crags and what seemed to be rusting Zentraedi wrecks in the distance. She had barely begun to wonder how she had come to be there when she realized she wasn't alone.

"Huh?"

There were dark, cloaked figures standing back at a slight remove—female, she thought, feeling a bit drifty, though she couldn't quite be certain. Each of the dark figures held one of the three-stemmed Flowers of Life, the three-that-were-one.

But there was someone else, kneeling right before her, a compact, blond young woman in gauzy pink robes, clutching a bouquet of the Flowers, wearing a necklace something like Musica's. The woman had a roundish hairdo and an upturned, freckled nose; she was calm and yet there was a sense of life and gusto to her that made her very winsome.

Dana gave her head a slight shake and realized that she was looking at herself. And she realized that she, like this image of her, held a Flower of Life.

She levered herself up and saw that there were more of the dark figures, standing silently—making no move as yet—clutching their Flowers, forming a ring around Dana and her doppelgänger. Dana realized that she wasn't armed, but somehow the fact didn't bother her, and she felt only peace and a yearning to have her questions answered.

Then the kneeling image of herself suddenly shifted, separating out to either side so that there were three, smiling their mysterious smiles at her.

The triumvirate! She sat bolt upright, recalling what had happened—grasping the canister—and looking at the Flower in her hand.

The discharges released the Zentraedi side of my mind! I'm seeing those other sides of me that would have come to life if I were part of a triad!

She suddenly felt terribly alone. She had never known her family, never known much about her mother's race, had grown up cut off from most of the knowledge of self that people around her so took for granted.

And here was not just one other Dana, but three. A chance for a closeness and unity, a companionship, beyond anything Humans knew. No surprise, it occurred to her, that it was the first thing her expanded powers of mind had summoned up from the vast reservoir of the Protoculture.

But even as she was about to embrace her sibling-clones, something held her back. The image came to mind of Musica, and of the sad scenes in the mother ships of the Masters. She remembered the antiseptic cruelty of triumvirate life and the obscene murder of the clone Latell.

She still couldn't understand or see clearly who those shrouded entities were, gathered around her, but perceived that they were listening closely, were attentive to her response. Dana felt that some crucial judgment was hanging in the air.

But it didn't take a lot of soul-searching. She had seen all the sorrows of the submerged personalities of the triumvirates. She looked to her potential otherselves again. Their stares were somehow malign now, and hungry—as if they wanted to devour her, to subsume her in themselves and bury forever the personality that had grown up, for good or ill, as Dana Sterling.

Dana hurled the Flower to the ground; it shattered and disappeared like a de-rezzing computer image. "I am *not* a part of your triumvirate! I am an *individual Human being!*"

The triplicate visions moaned in concert—hollow sounds like the far away wails of tortured children. They seemed to turn to smoke, becoming vacant-eyed ghosts that were rent in the wind like spindrift, their Flowers dissolving as well.

The dark listeners evaporated, too, with thin, pipe-organ howls like mourning specters, resigned to their eternal fate. They faded, now part of a reality that would never come to be.

Dana was on her feet. The green had vanished, and she ground herself in a bleak and blasted setting, lifeless as any lunar crater but still recognizably an Earthscape.

She threw the words out angrily. "I reject the horrors of your civilization!" She wasn't sure if she was talking to the Masters, or the Protoculture, or her own Zentraedi heritage. "I reject your values and your beliefs!"

Who is there to hear? she wondered, and yet she knew she wasn't going unheard. "I'm an individual, a free Human being of the planet Earth!"

It came to her that she was standing in a place of scattered Human bones, a skull nearly beneath her feet. There was no stirring of air, no hint of life, anywhere across a limitless plain covered with ash and roofed over by low clouds that might have come from some planetary cremation.

Is this it? Is this the future of both civilizations? Suddenly she was running, calling for help in a bleak landscape that even denied her echoes.

Her foot turned on a shattered skeleton, and she fell headlong. But as she fell, the ash smothering her, clogging her throat and nostrils, she heard somebody calling her name.

She shook her head to clear it, but when she looked up, she was in some strange, kinder place. There was the blue and green of growing things, but not any that she could identify. The smell of life and the clarity of the air made her gasp, though.

"Dana, wait for me! I'm coming!"

There were low crystal domes of the Flowers of Life before her, and a starlit sky with no constellation she could recognize. Somewhere there was ethereal music that reminded her of the Cosmic Harp's, and a little girl was dashing toward her.

"I—I'm not going anywhere," Dana said dazedly.

She was ten or so, Dana guessed, a black-haired, sprite-like thing with huge dark eyes, wearing a short, flowing garment of gold and white. Her tiny waist was encircled by a broad belt, her wrists and throat banded by the same red-brown leathery stuff. She wore a garland of woven Flowers of Life in her hair, and carried another.

"Who *are* you?" Dana got out.

The child stopped before her, "Your sister, Dana! That other daughter of Max and Miriya Sterling! I was born a long, long way from Earth, and I've come to warn you. Oh, Mother and Father will be so glad to know I've *finally* made contact with you!"

"I'm glad, too," Dana said haltingly, praying it wasn't just some hallucination. "But what are you supposed to warn me about?"

"The spores, Dana."

This, even while the girl pressed the Flower of Life into Dana's armor-clad hands. "I've come to bring you these Flowers and to warn you about the spores."

"Please—" Dana couldn't bear it, was afraid the thought of the Flowers and the Protoculture and the rest of it would shake her loose from this Vision or contact or whatever it was. "Let's not talk about that. Tell me about *you*! What's your name?"

The little girl was giggling. But then she turned and raced away in the direction from which she had come. Dana was left to yell, "Hey! Please come back! I want to know more!"

Two more shadow-figures had appeared, a man and a woman, graceful beings whose figures were indistinct in the way of this strange half world. A cape billowed around the woman, and there was something familiar about the way the man had his arm around her, two presences Dana had felt before.

The child went running toward them, and they opened their arms to her. As the three apparitions looked to her, Dana heard voices she knew, speaking without speech.

The spores, Dana! Beware the spores, and the Invid!

"The—the what?" She felt dizzy. Her own memories and old tapes of Max and Miriya Sterling told her that she was truly hearing her parents' voices—or rather, their thoughts.

Beware the Invid! They will come in search of the spores!

She had a million things to ask them and to tell them, but the contact seemed to be growing weaker, for when the mind-message came again, it was faint.

Time grows short. So much has happened since our last contact with Earth, so many astounding things! Your powers are awake now, and they are growing! Use them cautiously; we of the Sentinels are only beginning to understand the true nature of Protoculture.

The Sentinels? Dana wondered at the sound of the words.

And then she heard her sister's voice. *We love you, Dana! We love you very much!*

We love you very, very much, daughter, her parents added, as the voices faded.

"Oh, I—I love you, too! And I miss you so!"

Then the shadow figures were gone, and she was left to hope they had heard her, as the pink petals of the Flower of Life drifted around her.

CHAPTER TWENTY-THREE

I lie down at night with my children safely asleep and my dear wife beside me and send up a—one hopes, modest—prayer to the One. And the prayer is thanks.

But, oh! Those days! How I would love to have lived them, even if it were only to be slain on the first!

Isaac Mandelbrot, *Movers and Shakers: The Heritage of the Second Robotech War*

OR CROUCHED NEAR DANA'S BODY, GLARING UP AT THE IMages of the two surviving Robotech Masters.

He still held his weapon, but it would do him little good; Shaizan and Bowkaz had struck the moment Zor turned aside to shoot down the android shock troopers they had summoned. That had been the work of mere seconds, but in that time, as Zor stood straddling the unconscious Dana, the Masters had recovered the last Protoculture mass and made their escape, protected by the powers of the cap.

But they had sent back the mind-projected simulacra to deliver their death warrant. Zor heard Dana begin to stir, but felt little relief; his hatred of the Masters was too all-consuming for him to feel any gentler emotion.

Dana raised her head groggily, hearing the one called Shaizan saying, "All those who stand against us shall perish! Soon we will have the Matrix, and be all-powerful once more. Therefore, surrender to us and be spared, Zor."

She saw the two Masters, but realized that she could see *through* them, as though they were made of stained glass.

Zor threw his head back and spat, "Your perversion of the Protoculture only proves how little you truly know about it. Do

477

you think such things can go unpunished? No! And I'll never rest until there has been vengeance."

Dana had hauled herself to her feet, mind still whirling with the things she had seen and heard in her trance. But she drew a deep breath and said, "I'll be right behind you, Zor."

That seemed to bring him out of his seizure of blind rage. He turned and put his hand on her shoulder. "Thank you. Thank you many times over, Dana. For showing me kindness and . . . for caring for me. For helping me become whole again, and free myself."

He smiled, but it was bittersweet, as he shouldered his weapon. "I only wish you were safely out of here."

He indicated the compartment's hatch. "That's one barrier we could never burn through with hand weapons, and the Masters have sealed us in—given the ship's systemry an order through their Protoculture cap. We're trapped."

"Are you sure? It's worth a try, anyhow." She crossed to it. "Maybe we can short-circuit it, or something."

He was about to tell her that the Protoculture didn't work that way, that there was no hope of countermanding the Masters' instruction to it, when the hatch opened to her touch at the controls.

Zor Prime looked at her, open-mouthed. *"By the Protoculture!"* he whispered. *"Who are you?"*

She shrugged. "I'm only beginning to find out. In a lot of ways, we're the same. Now, how do we find those two and stop them?"

He had the rifle off his shoulder again. "Rest assured: we will find them."

"Musica's come!" Octavia rose from her ministrations to a dying clone, and Allegra did the same. Already, in the Muses' minds, there were the unheard harmonies of their triumvirate.

Musica appeared a moment later, leading the ATACs and Nova Satori and Dennis Brown. The Muses were reunited in a three-cornered embrace. "I'm so happy you both are still alive!" Musica said. "Many of our people have been set adrift in space."

Bowie had come up behind her. "We've got to get out of here. The guards are headed this way!"

The Muses turned to their people, the three voices raised in urgent singsong, beseeching them to get up, to follow, and escape.

The phlegmatic clones didn't seem to hear, at first, but in moments the 15th troopers were tugging them upright. Dante's voice came in a roaring counterpoint, getting more of the clones moving the way only an experienced NCO could; he was perfectly happy frightening and intimidating people, if it was for their own good.

Nova, too, helped roust the Masters' slaves. She no longer looked on them as the enemy or soulless biological units; she had changed, just as the others had changed in this last stage of the Second Robotech War. Coming across the tiny infant clone that Dana had seen on the 15th's last foray aboard a Master ship, she saw no one else was looking after it and so gathered it up in her arms, calling on the adults to follow her lead.

In seconds, scores of clones who had been resigned to death were up and active. Hope, and the example of Musica and her sisters, filled the emptiness that had afflicted the clones when the Masters discarded them.

The patchwork Terran attack fleet moved in, deploying its combat forces, and opened fire. A-JACs, VTs, and other combat craft raked the mother ships with energy weapons and all the ordnance they could carry. Triumviroids swept out to meet them, fighting with a furious disregard for their own survival.

The Human battlecruisers let loose their volleys; missiles and cannon blasts lit the scene. Warheads blossomed in hideous orange-red eruptions. The Robotech Masters' Flower bud–shaped guns answered, filling that volume of the void with their eerie green electric-arc effects and white-hot volleys.

With power so low, though, the Masters couldn't afford to generate their snowflakelike defensive fields, and so the battle was a slugging match. The four remaining mother ships, drained of the Protoculture reserves, were sitting ducks for the Human gunners. Pass after pass by the mecha and broadsides from the heavier craft inflicted heavy damage on the mightiest machines of the Masters' Robotechnology. But what the Humans didn't realize was that they were wasting valuable time and effort on targets of no importance—on targets that contained only a few barely functioning zombies.

The Masters' flagship was far more effective, taking a heavy toll on its attackers and sustaining little damage. The Southern Cross forces, unaware that they had been out-flanked, decided to concentrate on eliminating the other mother ships first. They would deal with the flagship once the rest of the invasion fleet had been destroyed.

One mother ship flared, and minutes later, another, their power systems rupturing and yielding up their remaining energy in explosions that expanded them and rent them apart.

Another mother ship, drifting, began the long crash-plunge into the Earth's atmosphere. Mecha and heavy craft raced after, trying desperately to shoot it to bits. The impact of an object that large could work more damage than any other blow the Masters had yet struck; Humanity had learned that with the SDF-1's crash, so long ago.

It was then that the first reports came through of the massive, renewed attack on Earth itself.

The Triumviroids dropped in waves on Monument City, Fokker Base, and a half-dozen other strategic objectives in the region of the mounds. Southern Cross mecha and defense forces barely had time to brace themselves before the countryside became a ghastly killing ground.

Reds whirled and swooped on their Hovercraft, strafing and spreading death and destruction. Outnumbered, the Humans fought grimly to make every death count, but still the uneven score mounted in the enemy's favor. All the volunteers and final reserves went into action. The death toll mounted and mounted.

Triumviroids met their end, too, in staggering numbers; it mattered little to the Masters if their mecha-slaves were wiped out to the last one. The Matrix was the only important thing now. Neither side gave quarter or asked it.

In his office high up in the Southern Cross headquarters, Supreme Commander Leonard looked down on the flaming graveyard that was Monument City.

Colonel Seward implored again, "Sir, the defense forces are simply outgunned and outnumbered! Monument City's doomed! We have no choice but to evacuate!"

Seward knew there was at the moment another flight of assault ships coming in at the city from the north. It might already be too late. For some reason, the enemy hadn't seemed to have understood that the slim white towers were the nerve center of the Terran military. But with the enormous volume of communications traffic now being channeled directly there, and the obvious disposition of surviving forces to protect it, even the aliens would realize it was a prize target.

Seward fidgeted, wanting to run. Good career moves might justify a certain recklessness, but all the threat-evaluation computers agreed that staying in the HQ was suicide. And Seward had no desire for a posthumous medal, no matter how high.

But Leonard didn't seem to see things that way. He stood,

bulky and stolid as a stone, his back to the staff officer, watching as the city burned.

Even as Seward was begging for Leonard to see reason, alien sights were ranging on the white towers. Slim, gleaming pillars suggesting Crusaders' pennons and medieval ramparts, the HQ structures were an easy target to spot. Targeting computer gunlock was established almost instantly.

"Go if you want," Leonard said brusquely. "I'm staying here until this battle is over."

It wasn't an act of bravery or loyalty. He knew he had made a terrible blunder, answering the alien feint with the bulk of his forces. His hatred of all things unearthly, the loathing born in the terrible injuries he had taken in combat against the Zentraedi, had blinded him to everything but the chance for revenge.

He seemed bigger than life to the people around him, but the damage done him—to his body and thus to his spirit, his mind— that day the Malcontents were crushed, almost thirteen years earlier, was beyond any healing.

From the moment when Leonard had overridden Emerson's wait-and-see policy, when the Masters first showed up, things had gone from bad to worse. Leonard had long since admitted to himself that Rolf Emerson was the better strategist and tactician by far, the better general even in terms of commanding his troops' loyalty. But—*damn it*! The man had no true appreciation of the danger of these aliens, of *all* aliens!

Seward saw further argument was useless, and started for the door. His rationalization was that he was carrying Leonard's last dispatch, but in fact he was deserting his doomed post. The Southern Cross was finished.

Leonard let him go, waiting to die. Better that way, rather than to live, being known as the man who had lost Earth to obscene monsters from another star.

Leonard didn't have long to wait; the first salvoes hit while Seward was still in the doorway, a massive strike that lit the sky and shook the ground. The proud white towers of the Southern Cross were blackened, as concrete went to powder and structural alloys melted at the peripheries. At the centers of the hits, there was complete destruction. For Leonard, it was the end of an inner agony that had lasted decades; for the Human race, his death came too late.

* * *

The 15th had picked up more of the refugee clones, hundreds of them, until Angelo Dante began wishing somebody a little more suited to the mass escape was in charge—say, somebody who could part the Red Sea, for instance.

But there wasn't; even Lieutenant Satori was less qualified than he to lead a combat operation like this. *Just a big, dumb career sergeant waiting around for his pension,* he thought, *who happened to get his turn in the barrel at the wrong time. Just bad luck; drive on, ATACs!*

Going back for the tanks was out of the question. The 15th had to move onward, as fast as possible, and give their trust to luck.

"This hatch leads to an assault ship docking area," the clone who was guiding him said, crouched on the ladderway under an oblong metal slab. "I think it is the one you wanted."

Dante was hunkered down next to him, studying the hatch. Spread out behind him on the ladderway and the drawbridge-like catwalks leading to it were the murmuring, frightened clones marked by the Masters for mass extermination. Nova and the rest of the 15th were spread out through the crowd, trying desperately to keep the people from panicking.

People, Dante sighed to himself. Hell, no denying it: that was the way the ATACs had come to think of them. And ATAC-15's line of work was *not* letting innocent people be slaughtered.

Angelo gripped his rifle and awkwardly changed places with the clone, then eased the hatch up for a look. The place was empty, as far as he could see; more to the point, there were three or four of the whiskbroom-shaped assault ships waiting there, parked in a row. The hatchway was in a passageway leading to the hangar deck, which was at a slightly lower level.

He couldn't believe the ships hadn't been committed to the battle, but he didn't have time to question the gift from above. What he didn't realize was that the combat craft ferried in from the other, abandoned mother ships were so many that the Masters couldn't man them all with the functioning clones and mecha left to them. *Not much choice; this's the only chance we're gonna get.*

He couldn't see Sean Phillips around anywhere, though. Maybe this *wasn't* the right hangar. Nevertheless, it would have to do.

Angelo knelt in firing position by the open hatch, waiting for the snipers to smoke him. But when that didn't happen, he turned to face the anxious clone looking up at him.

"Get 'em all up here now, and start boarding 'em. Tell 'em to hurry, but keep the noise down."

The word was passed. The first of the refugees began pouring up out of the hatch and making their way, at Angelo's direction, down the passageway, gathering in it and awaiting the run for the ships.

He looked this way and that constantly, swinging his rifle's muzzle, even though he knew an ambush at this point would probably be the end of it. And it would save the army at least one pension, god*damm*it all!

But as he tried to help people up through the hatch with one hand and guard at all points at the same time, help arrived. Louie Nichols came up, dark-goggled and very matter-of-fact, taking up a kneeling firing stance at the other side of the hatch. Bowie, having sealed the lower hatches behind them, was next, covering another field of fire, with Musica and her sister Muses flocking after. Angelo began to feel better.

Still the clones poured in, filling the area between the deck-level hatch and the much bigger one through which they would have to race for the assault ships. Nova Satori emerged, still clutching the baby, but with her pistol in the hand that held it, the other hand free to grip the ladder-well railing. Dennis was right behind, with one of the short two-hand weapons.

Hundreds came up; Angelo was sweating not just for the time when he could kick the hatch shut and seal it with a few shots, and get the hell out of the mother ship, but for the moment when he could turn his problems over to some brass hat. Anybody who wanted responsibility for this many lives had to be some sorta egomaniacal helmet case.

He was just thinking that when he heard the mewing of alien small arms, in the direction of the large hatch at the end of the passageway.

There wasn't much room for stealthy approach in the bleating press of the frightened mob, but Angelo went bulling through them, holding his weapon high in the hope that it wouldn't be jostled and torn from his grip. Forging his way to the front of the crowd, he noticed that Louie and the others were doing their best to follow, but lacked his size and sheer strength.

The bodies of three clone refugees, two males and a female, lay dead on the deck.

There were huge containers and crates at that end, and ledges near the hatch. Now clone guard riflemen stood all along those, as the lights came up. "Stay where you are!" a clone voice was saying, in that trembling single-sideband quaver of the true Masters' slave.

Angelo heard somebody say, "Huh?" beside him, and realized

that Louie Nichols was there, somehow, swinging the sights of his rifle to cover the left, leaving the right to Angelo, just like a drill.

"Make no move, or you will be shot." The lights brightened. A triad of clones marched in lockstep from behind one pile of cottage-sized crates, and Angelo couldn't even tell which one was talking—or maybe they *all* were—when they right-faced and glared at the escapees. "Everyone in this room, go back or be exterminated."

"Karno," Bowie heard Musica say. And Allegra added, "We're trapped here."

The Muses looked at their selected mates: Karno, Darsis, and Sookol, as alike as they could be without being one person. Musica said, "Karno, how can you *do* this? We all have a right to live!"

Darsis spat, "How *dare* you speak of rights, you who have betrayed the triumvirate? Traitors to our society and our way of life! All of you will return to your appointed places immediately, or be shot down where you stand!"

The crowd let out a concerted moan at that, but they didn't withdraw. They were creatures who knew logic—at least—thoroughly, and they saw that there was no survival in that direction, either. The ATACs and Nova were moved by something less subject to rational analysis, but they all stood shoulder to shoulder.

CHAPTER TWENTY-FOUR

Alpha! Tact'l! Armored! Corps!
Yo' ain't goin' home no more!
Yo' want comforts, yo' want millions?
Shoulda stayed wit' the civilians!

ATAC marching cadence

"**N**O ONE WILL BE LEAVING HERE," NOVA PRO-
nounced the words slowly and carefully. Bowie noticed how open
the words were to several different interpretations.

Nova patted the small bundle of the clone infant. She had
tucked her sidearm in its holster, turning her hip away from the
clones' sight, but was ready to grab it out if things came to that.
Dennis was edging her way.

She was also drawing the guards' attention. She had noted that
Louie Nichols was holding a shock grenade behind his back, fid-
dling with it by feel while he watched Karno and the rest,
readying to toss it. Nova readied herself to dive for cover, taking
into account the fact that no harm must come to the baby if she
could help it.

"These are not your slaves!" Musica cried. "These are individ-
uals, whose freedom of choice has made them free of your society. Now, stand away!"

"Then you will die, you who disrupt our lives!" With that,
Karno brought up his weapon, as did Sookol and Darsis, and
opened fire. At that moment, the young man who had acted as
guide for Angelo threw himself in front of Musica. He took the
five rounds of the firefight, all at once and all in one tight
group.

The ATACs were standing straddle-legged, firing back at almost point-blank range, in the same second—all except for Louie,
who slid the shock grenade the guards' way and hollered, "Get
back!"

Refugee clones in the first rank fell like scythed wheat, but the ATACs' fire cut into the enemy guardsmens' ranks at once, and all the clones' accuracy was lost. Enemy shots rebounded from the troopers' armor, and the tankers laid down a suppressing fire that had the guardsmen ducking for cover.

The detonation of the shock grenade was like a freeze-frame of the guards' postures, lasting only a fraction of a second. Its blast sent them somersaulting and flying, while the refugees and the Humans scuttled for cover, and the ambushers struggled to regain the offensive.

Musica, crouched behind one structural frame, cradled to her the youth who had guided Angelo and taken the rounds meant for her. "Why did you . . . ?"

"You are the soul of us all. You are the hope of us all." The eyes rolled up in his head, showing only white, and the breath rattled from him.

She laid his head down gently, then rose and stepped back into the passageway, into the fairway of the firefight, the various beams and bolts and streams of discs bickering back and forth. "Karno! Stop this at once!"

Bowie, pinned down, couldn't reach her, but screamed at her to get to cover. Karno, crouched to fire from cover, bawled, "Musica, the Micronians have cast a spell over you!"

"That's not true! I've freely chosen a new way of life—*ahh!*"

There was no telling if the beam that seared her arm was from friend or foe. She went on through locked teeth, "The truth is . . . we are all free beings. With free will. *And you know that!*"

"You speak lies!" he shrieked. "You're bewitched!"

"Got any brilliant inspirations?" Louie asked Angelo, as they squatted in the lee of a huge packing crate.

"We *could* send 'em candy and flowers an' say we won't never do it no more," Angelo allowed, then snapped off another round. "Or, pray for a miracle—"

Just as he was saying that, the bulkhead was punched inward, one of the more curious coincidences of the war. It was as if one of those ancient beer-can openers was broaching a cold one, only the opener was a stiff-fingered shot by a Battloid.

The Battloid, having followed their transponders, peeled back the bulkhead like wrapping paper and stood into the gap. Smoke curled around it and the guard clones shrank back in hysteria, forgetting their attack. A voice amplified to Olympian volume rang, "So for *this* you stood me up at our rendezvous?"

"Meant to drop ya a note, Phillips," Dante admitted. "But I got real distracted."

"No excuses!"

Where he might have used the towering mecha's weapons to wipe out every enemy there, Sean instead chose to chastise them. He had seen enough war, seen enough slaughter and, more to the point, sensed that a few more incidental enemy KIAs wouldn't influence the outcome of things. He had no heightened senses or Protoculture powers, just simple Human intuition that the outcome of the war—the very core of it—had nothing to do with scoring a few more clone body counts.

The colossal Battloid brushed a flock of guards into a wall; most of the others broke and ran, dropping their weapons. Among those downed was the Guard Triumvirate.

Angelo led the refugees the other way, toward the assault ships. But Karno reared up and spied Octavia, who had been promised to Sookol so long ago by the Masters. She looked so like Musica.

Karno dragged himself up and dug out his sidearm, to shoot her as she dashed by. She screamed and fell, Bowie and Musica turning back to help her.

Sean turned his Battloid and brought up the Cyclopean foot. Even as Bowie and Musica were carrying Octavia to cover, Karno screamed. The last thing the clone ever saw was the bottom of the foot of the Battloid-configuration Hovertank *Bad News*, 15th squad, Alpha Tactical Armored Corps.

Bowie knelt in the lee of the alloy container while Musica sought to comfort her sister.

Octavia's hand caressed her cheek. "It's all right, Musica—I know my spirit and my songs will live in you!"

"We're still . . . as one," Musica struggled.

"Yes, I know, though greater things are in you now, such greater things! But to the end of space and time—we three are one . . . always . . ."

And she was dead. Bowie tugged at Musica's arm because a sudden rush by counterattacking guards might put Musica in jeopardy before Sean's Battloid could make them see reason and drive them back.

The counterattack was repulsed, not much of a job for a mecha that had the firepower of an old-time armored troop. Sean's *Bad News* burrowed through a bulkhead like a big, glittering badger, and opened the way for the refugees, who went spilling into the assault ship hangar deck. "There; that oughta do it; everybody into the troop carriers!"

* * *

As planned, the battle on and just over the planet's surface and the decoys that were the surviving mother ships had led most of the Earth forces away from the flagship. Those that were left were of no importance. The Robotech Masters' last functioning mother ship closed in to execute the final portion of its mission.

Three segmented metal appendages, like huge blind worms, extruded themselves from the underside of the flagship and met, their completed instrumentality throwing out a light as bright as a solar prominence. A beam sprang down to penetrate one of the mounds below, and the second, and the third, with zigzagging sensor bolts.

Inside the Masters' ship, engines of raw power were brought into play. The distortions and occlusions of the Protoculture wraiths could not stand before that raw power, and the Masters saw at last where their target lay.

The three wraiths looked upward. Their hour was nearly sped; there was no resisting the focused might of the mother ship.

At the touch of the Masters' might, the mound covering the SDF-1 shuddered, then began to split open, as the Flowers of Life stirred, and the spores bobbed upward. Rock ground against rock, and tremendous volumes of soil were shifted with ease. The mound itself was split in half and pulled apart by the invaders' awesome instrumentality. As the gap widened, trees, boulders, and dirt from the mound's flat top rained down onto the wreckage below. In the place of the relatively small opening that had been above the Matrix garden, there appeared a rift that exposed the entire wreckage of the SDF-1.

The guardian Protoculture wraiths released the hold they had maintained on the spores for so long; the spores began drifting up toward the sunlight and the winds of Earth.

The Masters, studying their operations with satisfaction, watched the mound split open and willed their great ship to speed to it, for the extraction of the Matrix. There was time to save enough of it to provide them with sufficient new Protoculture to rebuild their galactic empire.

They were no longer on their floating cap, since its systemry had to be merged with that of the ship itself for this crucial function. Instead they stood on a circular antigrav platform, nearly at floor level. Without Bowkaz, it was less crowded than they were used to. Shaizan held the canister with the last mass once more, waiting for the moment when its total power must be brought to bear.

"Soon even the Invid will not dare stand against us," Shaizan declared. He turned to issue another order to the Scientist triumvirate, whose members stood nearby, supervising the mission, gathered around a big control module in the middle of the chamber.

But the opening of a hatch behind them made Shaizan and Dag whirl. Zor Prime entered, with the clone guard they had posted held in an armlock, his rifle aimed at them with his free hand. Dana followed, holding her carbine.

"Masters, heed me: the moment of retribution has come. Now you pay for all the evil you've done!" Zor Prime thundered.

Shaizan seemed almost sad. "Will you never understand, Zor? It is much too late." He gestured to the screens, which showed the opened mound, and Monument City in flames. "In moments, we will have the Matrix back, at last. You cannot stop us."

Dana snarled, "We're *not* going to let you snakes have that Matrix. It's too powerful!"

The Masters were mystified as to how Zor and the female had escaped; it was, perhaps, some effect from the sundering of their Triumvirate, Dag and Shaizan concluded.

Dana brought the carbine up and aimed it at the Scientist clones, clicking off the safety. "Stop the machines."

Dovak, the triumvirate leader of the Scientists, protested, "Impossible! They cannot be stopped now; they've been given final instructions!"

Dana decided to find out, with a few well-placed bursts into the controls—perhaps even into the clones, if they didn't see reason. But just then, Zor shoved her aside. Energy bolts blazed through the spot where she had stood, splashing molten droplets and sparks from the bulkhead.

The Masters' antigrav platform was rising, and from an energy nozzle on its underside, a stream of shots raged at the interlopers. Zor had dived for cover, hurling the guard against the bulkhead and the clone dropped, stunned. Rolling, Zor fired back, and Dag clutched his midsection, slumping, crying out in pain and hysterical fear of death.

Dana fired, too, but her shots at the weapon nozzle and the platform's underside didn't appear to be doing much good. Then she hit a hornlike projection, and the platform rocked, smoking and crackling with powerful discharges, and fell back to the deck.

The platform came straight at them, and Dana and Zor threw

themselves to either side. Somehow, Shaizan, still cradling the canister to him, gained control at the last moment and managed to leap free, before the platform went on to plow into the Scientist clones and their control module. They screamed, transfixed in horror, as the platform crashed down on them and their control module ruptured, spilling out furious energy surges.

By the time Zor and Dana got back to their feet, Shaizan was already at another hatch, clinging to the Protoculture mass. Zor screamed, "Master, you can't escape me!" but the tripartite hatch closed behind Shaizan.

As they were rushing to catch up, Dana heard some monitoring system shrilling in alarm. A voice simulacrum wailed, "Warning! Warning! Guidance systems off-line! Power systems failing! Crash alert! Impact in three point five five units!"

Dana looked at the display maps, and saw the projected point of impact: it looked to her like Monument City. She wasn't aware that the city had already been shot to ruins by the Triumviroids.

"We've got to stop it, or it'll kill everyone in the city! Zor, there's got to be a manual control system!"

He shook his head slowly. "We must get Shaizan to release his hold over the systemry first."

He started for the hatch with Dana sprinting along behind. "Then we have to capture the last one alive!"

In fear of his life, Shaizan ran as he hadn't run in an age. Fright gave him more strength than he had ever thought possible, and the pumping of adrenaline in his system felt savage, bewilderingly primitive, after a long sedentary life.

But he was the quarry of young people in top condition; they soon caught up with him, in an ejection capsule access deck not far from the bridge. Zor saw Shaizan ahead and stopped to take up a firing stance. "Stop, I command you!"

"Zor, *don't!*" But before Dana could strike down the rifle barrel, Zor fired. Shaizan dropped in a swirl of robes; somehow, the canister remained intact.

Zor went to look down at the old man. Somehow, death had taken away the constant anger of the Master's visage, and he was nothing but a frail, infinitely tired-looking creature with a smoking hole in him, head pillowed on a collar resembling the Flower of Life. How could these creatures have lived so long and thrived on the Protoculture without understanding its Shapings—without foreseeing this day?

"It's over now," Zor said, more to himself than to Dana.

"What d'you mean, 'all over'?" Dana barked. "This ship's gonna demolish the city!"

"The Masters brought their own punishment down on themselves, by their misuse of the Protoculture," he told her, putting a hand on each of her armored shoulders. "And I was the instrument of that punishment, ordained by the Shaping."

"But what about *my* people? It's not fair to punish them for something they didn't do—*mmmmm* . . ."

He leaned forward to put his lips to hers. Their mouths locked, they kissed for what might have been seconds or centuries. When they parted a bit, he smiled at her tenderly, and she was astounded to see from his eyes that—

He—he loves me!

Zor had her back in his arms, was lifting her off the deck. "Do not worry about your people, Dana. I will allow no harm to come to them."

She felt like relaxing, just letting him carry her where he would; like going limp and simply trusting him. But some inner, independent part of her made her start to object. Just then, she realized that he was setting her down into the cocoon padding of an ejection capsule.

"Good-bye, Dana."

At first she had thought he was going to join her inside—that they would cast aside the armor of war and never wear it again. And she had been working up the self-discipline to make sure everything really *was* all right before she took her own armor off, though the temptation was great.

But instead, he drew back, and she was so astounded that she sat frozen while the hatch of the little superhard alloy sphere closed and secured. All at once she was staring at him through a viewport. His smile was wistful, as he made some adjustment to the locking mechanism, and it gave a loud click. He smiled at her again, fondly but mournfully.

"*Zor!*" She was pounding at the viewport and trying to work the locking controls, but it did no good. He disappeared from view. She was still struggling to get free, crying, shouting his name, when the capsule gave a lurch, moved by the transfer servos, preparing for ejection.

CHAPTER
TWENTY-FIVE

They give you clothes, they're free with guns,
And trainin', food and lodgin',
But tell me: what career moves
Can come from bullet dodgin'?

Bowie Grant, "Nervous in the Service"

ARGE, WE'RE PICKING UP SOME KINDA EJECTION capsule launch from the mother ship," Louie Nichols reported, sitting beside Angelo at the controls of the liberated assault ship.

Behind them, refugee clones were crowded in tightly, frightened, but used to the discipline of the Masters and so obediently quiet. Angelo, sweating over the controls, snapped, "So what? Maybe it's somebody makin' their own getaway. It sure ain't a raidin' party or a Bioroid."

That was true, and it was unlikely that there were many combat forces left in the mother ship, or that they would do the Masters much good even if they could get to the Earth's surface. For some reason, the Bioroid-pilot clones and other fighters of the Masters' invasion force had, according to the transmissions the escapees were monitoring, suddenly become almost totally ineffective. The attacking enemies' ability to fight, their very *will* to fight, seemed to have simply vanished, and Earth's ragtag defenders were counterattacking everywhere, a complete rout.

Something occurred to Angelo. "Get on the military freqs and find somebody who's in charge," he told Louie. "Tell 'em we got an airlift of refugees comin' down, and to hold their fire. Tell 'em . . . tell 'em these people here ain't the enemy."

Louie threw him a strange smile. "Hear, hear, Angie."

He felt Bowie, who stood behind him, clap him on the back,

and felt Musica's light touch at his shoulder. Then Angelo pronounced a few choice army obscenities, the ship having wandered off course. He was no fly-boy and even the coaching of experienced clone pilots didn't make it much easier to herd the alien craft along.

"Everybody keep still and lemme drive," Angelo Dante growled.

Within the mother ship, Zor's red Bioroid stomped back toward the command center, its discus pistol clutched in its gargantuan metal fist. Below the ship, the mounds hove into view.

I cannot undo the damage I've done. Across a hundred reincarnations; across a hundred million light-years. And yet: I'll make what restitution I can.

The Invid would not have Earth.

Below, the Protoculture wraiths sensed Zor Prime's coming, all in accordance with the Shaping that had given the original Zor his vision and set the course of the Robotech Wars, so long ago and far away.

The wraiths summoned up the strength that was left to them, for their final deed. The rainbow-rings of the Matrix were dimmer now, but still dazzling, still playing their haunting song. As the wraiths tapped its power, the Matrix flared brighter.

Dana's efforts to contact Zor with the capsule's little commo unit had drawn no response. Now she blinked at the bright sunlight, as the hatch opened and the fragrant air of Earth drifted in.

The capsule had landed at the crest of a low foothill across the plain, just within view of the SDF-1's gravesite. She already knew from the capsule's crude monitoring equipment that the mother ship had followed her down through the atmosphere, headed for the mounds.

Dana drew herself out of the capsule and saw the five-mile length of the Masters' last starship come in to hover over the resting place of the SDF-1. "Zor. Don't—please!"

There is no other way.

Zor's red raised its discus pistol. The destruction of the mother ship directly over the mounds would ensure that the Flowers of Life and their spores would be completely obliterated, and spare the Human race the slaughter and ruin of an Invid invasion. Some spores had already drifted free of the mound, though instruments weren't clear as to why that hadn't happened before; there were completely unique and unprecedented Protoculture aberrations down there, and no time to analyze them. But that didn't matter now. The radius of the blast would get all of them.

Now!

The red fired its pistol at carefully selected targets; it was easy for him to find the vulnerable points in the systemry the original Zor had conceived. In moments the entire ship was a daisy chain of ever increasing explosions, ripping open its hull, gathering toward that final, utter detonation.

He thought he would be swallowed up by grief in those last moments, to see only the ghosts of the victims, and the shadows of the suffering he had caused. Unexpectedly, though, Zor Prime's last thoughts were of the thing that had made this last incarnation so different from the rest, and let him free himself.

Dana, I love you!

Dana shrieked at the exploding ship, knowing it would do no good, until the explosions reached a crescendo. "Stop! Zor, there must be a better way—"

Then she threw herself to shelter behind the grounded, armored capsule and wept, face buried in her arms.

In the mounds, the wraiths gathered all their remaining energy, and contained the explosive force of the mother ship.

Zor's calculations were entirely correct, insofar as they went. The self-destruction should have vaporized the mounds and wiped out the curse that was the blooming Flowers, the drifting spores.

But the Shaping of the Robotech Wars had been set long before. Earth was to be saved from destroying itself in a Global Civil War and, at the same time, serve as the focal point that would let a tremendous wrong be righted. The time for the righting of that wrong had not yet come to pass, though the stage was now set.

And so the wraiths dampened the blast of the exploding starship. The Matrix flared like a nova, sang a single piercing note, and released all its power upward. The wraiths used it to muffle the blast in an unimaginable contest of warring forces, and won.

Still, the mother ship was blown to fragments and, even as Zor Prime soared to a higher plane of existence, freed at last of the cycle of crime and guilt in which he had been caught since his first terrible transgression, the fragments began to fall.

Even a small piece of the mother ship was enormous, and not

all of the explosive force had been contained. Housings and armor and structural members pelted the plain and the mounds, raising huge puffs of dust, opening the mound even further; the explosive force caught the rising spores and sent them high and wide, to ride the winds of the world. Ripping down into the garden that had been the last Matrix, the blasts freed a hundred thousand times as many more, and sent them wafting, lifting petals and even whole plants, gusting them forth.

The winds that came from the Protoculture detonation behaved unlike normal air currents. It was as if they had been given a purpose, dispersing the spores, *sowing* them, taking many into upper airstreams that would bear them far—would seed the face of the planet with them.

The wraiths looked upon their work and upon the Earth that the Shaping had made their home for so long. They had been given life, of a sort, by the Protoculture, taking power from the masses within the wreckage of SDF-1, SDF-2, and Khyron's downed battlecruiser.

But now their part in the Shaping was over, and the Matrix's last energy was used up; it was gone forever. They began their return to nothingness, making sure that the residual Protoculture around them underwent conversion to the Flowers of Life.

Dana watched the drifting pink petals, the swirling spores. *The Invid are coming!* Her parents' warning was right, and nothing could stop this species that even the Masters held in dread.

Three shadows loomed up out of the mounds, growing, but becoming more and more tenuous as they did. Dana, her senses expanded by her exposure to the Matrix and even more so by the jolt from the canister containing the Masters' last mass, knew that the phantasms would do her no harm.

She was so preoccupied, thinking about her family, about the Masters' words and Zor's, that she didn't hear the stealthy footsteps behind her, covered as they were by the moan of the winds. The projectile took her at the base of the skull, where her armor offered no protection. She went down.

"You *saw* them!" an eerie voice said. It sounded Human but had some of the sepulchral emotionlessness of a Robotech Master's. "Without instruments or sensors, you *saw* the Guardians of the Mounds!"

She lay on her side, dazed, unable to move though she was fully conscious. She realized she had been shot with some kind of paralyzing agent. A moment later, two peculiar men came into view.

One she recognized, and the sight of him almost stopped her heart. Zand, heir to Dr. Lang's secrets. He was wearing gleaming angelic robes, shiny metallic stuff, cut somewhat in the fashion of the Robotech Masters' monkish ones, and his collar was shaped like the Flower of Life. That alone told Dana what was happening, and the danger she was in.

Zand had gone completely insane and saw her as his passport to divine powers.

Along with Zand was a stout, vacant-faced little man with a pencil mustache, so different from the pictures in the history books that Dana didn't recognize him until Zand turned to say, "Russo! Bring the equipment." The scientist tossed aside the tranquillizer gun indifferently.

Russo scuttled away. Dana knew there was no aircraft or surface vehicle around; she had seen none on landing. Had they simply been sitting out here, *waiting?* She couldn't figure out how Zand had foreseen that she would be where she was. Perhaps his powers were *already* greater than hers.

Russo returned with devices like nothing either Earth's Robotechnology or the Masters' had ever produced. It seemed to be all crystal nimbuses and rainbow whorls, humming faintly like the Matrix.

Zand smiled like a fiend. "Much more compact than anything you'll have seen even in the mother ships, I'll bet. Those were crude toys compared to this."

He was assembling it in some fashion she couldn't quite follow. "I've had plenty of time to study the Matrix, you see. Years!" The apparatus seemed to shift and fold, as if it were moving among dimensions. Its aura had a fractal look to it.

Zand laughed a bit. "The Masters and the Human race, destroying each other over a mere *Matrix!* When the *real* crux of the matter is *you*, Dana—and your Destiny, which is to yield up your powers to me!"

He reached out to touch something like a node of pure light against her forehead. It clung there, and she felt an utter cold, even through the numbness. "Your powers will grow. They will see *beyond* the Protoculture! They will be matchless! But," his mouth flattened grimly, "they'll do all that as *mine*, once I've taken them from you."

He looked around. "Where is the Protoculture cell?"

When Russo gave him a blank look, Zand lashed out and sent him sprawling. Russo crawled and flopped away, whimpering like a whipped hound, to return with a prism perhaps a foot long, slender and glowing.

Dana fought against her paralysis, but couldn't shake it or defy it. Zand had planned it well. He had foreseen this day with powers of his own. As he took the Protoculture cell and prepared to shift Dana's gifts to himself, she had a moment to wonder: what, then, of her Vision, the Phoenix?

Her own life, she knew, was over. Zand was about to take something that was so much her essence that she would die like a withered husk without it.

He had mated the prism with the rest of his strange device. "So much Protoculture in one place," he smiled. "It took a long time to gather, even for *me*, diverting military supplies. But it's the power I need to draw your powers from you to me."

The device shone brighter, Russo was groveling, crouched with his face in the sand. Zand's strange voice was exalted. "First the power of the Protoculture fills me, then the powers of Dana Sterling! The Masters promised me that I would be wed to the power of the Flower, and I shall!" The light was unbearable.

Zand seemed to swell and grow. Dana feared what the Universe was in for, with Zand striding across it like a god.

Just then she heard a bark.

Polly! In her paralysis, she couldn't even say it.

The Pollinator came traipsing up and sat down, head canted to one side, tongue lolling, to consider Zand. He barely registered the XT creature, though, because something was terribly wrong with him.

His enlarged form was vibrating. Soon he was contorting, convulsing, his device flashing like a lighthouse in an earthquake. Russo had thrown himself flat, covering his head with his hands, wailing.

Dana had a sense that the last of the wraiths was vanishing away. And with them, the last of the Matrix, as well as the last of the Protoculture in the area, was being *transformed*.

Zand voiced a howl of agony and fright so ghastly that she was to remember it all her days. The light engulfed him. Still the Pollinator sat and watched. The Protoculture in the Matrix had been changed to the Flowers of Life. . . .

Perhaps it was the discharge of so much Protoculture. In any case, Dana felt the world slipping away, and saw the old Vision once again, the Phoenix. Only, this time she saw Zor, too. It was given to her, in that trance, to know why the Robotech Wars had come to be, and what the ultimate outcome was—just what the Phoenix was.

Just as the blinding light faded, Dana found that she could move a little. Either Zand had underestimated the dosage or her expanded powers were helping. Dana, Polly and the whining Russo gazed on what had appeared in Zand's place.

In a way, he got his wish, was Dana's first coherent thought.

There had never been, nor ever would be again, one to match it, the biggest Flower of Life that ever was. It stood rooted in the sand, spreading its petals, a coral-colored tripartite beauty. Of Zand there was no sign except, perhaps, in the shape and detail of the central blossom; it might only be her imagination, or it might be that she saw his face there.

Of his fantastic device, nothing remained.

She found she had the strength to rise, but came only to her knees, swaying. She heard a cry and looked up to see Russo, shrieking and screaming, running off down the hill like a crazed ape. He was headed directly out into the wastelands; she let him go.

Dana dragged one foot to her, until she was on one knee, the spores drifting about her. The odd thought struck her that perhaps Zand's fate was some lesson from the Protoculture, some chastening, to balance the power she had been granted.

She found herself humming, then realized it was a seventeenth-century hymn her father had loved and her Zentraedi mother had approved of as holding much and proper wisdom; so Rolf Emerson had told her, when Emerson taught it to Bowie and Dana. As a little girl she had taught it to Konda, Bron, and Rico, and they had insisted that what was in the words and the tune was nothing less than universal truth:

> Lead kindly, Light,
> Amid the encircling gloom
> Lead Thou me on,
> The night is dark and I am far from home
> Lead Thou me on,
> Keep Thou my feet
> I do not ask to see the distant scene
> One step enough for me

CHAPTER
TWENTY-SIX

Now our slaves, the Robotech Masters, are passed away
Now all our Protoculture balefires burn low
Now the Shapings turn; we surrender the stage to Invid and Human
Our cold light leaves the Universe
We see at the last that
Those who remain behind know no fear of the darkness
And we ourselves learn
What it is to weep

Death song of the Robotech Elders

DANA GATHERED POLLY UNDER ONE ARM AND WALKED tiredly back to the escape capsule. Russo, already a mile away, was barely visible as a mad figure capering and lurching into the wastes. The Pollinator licked her face.

A thin whine of engines caught her attention, and she looked up to see an assault ship coming in at her, flying unsteadily, seemingly about to go into a nosedive.

She threw herself flat, expecting the worst, but somehow the vessel righted itself enough for a jouncing set-down right near her. She remembered that she was unarmed, but she had no place to run and was too tired and battered to feel fear—thought that, perhaps, she would never know it again.

But when the assault craft's hatches opened, instead of letting forth attack teams of Triumviroids, it yielded her own 15th squad, along with Nova, Musica, and a bunch of clones.

"Damn it, Phillips!" Angelo Dante was seething. "I'd like to see you make a better landing with an XT ship! We walked away from it, didn't we?"

"All I said was," Sean replied in a blasé voice, "that I could do better with boxing gloves on. Hey, Dana! You made it!"

The refugees stayed back, but her squadmates and Musica and

Nova clustered around her, along with Marie Crystal and Dennis Brown. She blinked at him. "How did you find me?"

"Picked up your voice transmissions from the escape capsule," Angelo said. "But then, all of a sudden, the engines and all the systems quit. We had to land on emergency power."

"Ya shoulda let Marie and Dennis take over," Sean snorted.

But Dana was shaking her head. "No, Angie couldn't help what happened. It's the Protoculture—there was nothing he could do." Angelo looked at her strangely, not used to having her defend him.

There was still Protoculture power supplies on Earth, she knew, outside the radius of effect of the wraiths' transformation. Enough to animate mecha for a transition period. But there would be no new Matrices, no new sources.

"The war's over, Lieutenant," Bowie told her happily. "The enemy mecha stopped fighting, and the clones just want peace."

"That's . . . that's great, Bowie." He didn't understand why she sounded like she was about to start bawling. People noticed the Pollinator, but hesitated to ask about it. They saw the huge Flower that had been Zand, but they were used to seeing the triad plants by now, and even such a huge one was far down on the list of topics of discussion.

"Where's Zor?" Musica inquired timidly, fearing to hear the answer.

Dana pointed to where the mushroom cloud of spores and petals still rose up and up, funneled into the higher atmosphere, sent on their appointed way by those strange winds. "He died trying to save Earth."

Musica was shaking her head slowly, looking at the pink petals and tiny spores that filled the sky like a blizzard. "But in vain. Now the Invid come. Oh poor, poor Zor!" Bowie slipped his armored arm around her.

Nova drew a deep breath and declared, "Well, then! We've got to get back and report to whoever's in interim command! We have defenses to set up, plans to make—" She looked a little funny acting military with the infant still in her arms.

But Dana was shaking her head, too. "You do what you have to. I'm through with war." She already saw where her new course lay.

She had beheld something greater than herself, greater than the Human race or any other corporeal race. She understood at last the Vision that had filled her dreams all her life. She knew that there was no way to oppose or derail the Shaping, though there was much more suffering and strife ahead. She recalled that magnificent, infinitely sad Phoenix of racial transfiguration, and the recollection took away some of her sorrow.

"What d'you mean? You think you can hide from what's coming?" Nova snapped. "There's nowhere to run, Dana." The 15th and the others were looking at her worriedly, too, afraid that what she had been through had pushed her over the edge.

"What's going to happen on Earth will go beyond armies, beyond Protoculture," she told them calmly. "The next Robotech War will be the last, but I've had enough. I'm going to find my parents, and my sister. They're with a group that includes Admiral Hunter and Admiral Hayes, who've parted ways with the original SDF-3 expedition. They're trying to establish a new, positive force, the Sentinels. I'm joining them."

Everybody was babbling at once, but Angelo Dante held stage center by dint of his overwhelming voice. "Even if you weren't crazy, Dana, there's no way to get there! All the Robotech Masters' starships were blown to smithereens, and Earth ain't got no more." He looked toward the flaming remains of Monument City and Fokker Base. "And ain't likely to for a long, long time."

The Pollinator let out a playful yip and he reached out unconsciously to pet the thing, barely aware that Polly was there.

Dana puzzled for a microsecond, but her new powers offered up the answer at once, like some unfailing databank. "Before too long, another expedition will arrive, carrying word from the SDF-3, like Major Carpenter's ships did.

"By then, I'll be ready with the fuel and charts and everything else I need to take one of his ships and find my family and the others. Any of you who want to come are welcome."

They didn't have to ask if she meant to get the starship by legal means; the world was in ruins and all chains of command shattered. All the military certainties were swept away.

And, somehow, nobody thought to scoff at her, not even the aloof, skeptical Nova. The way back to what they had known was shut to them forever; within seconds they were all telling her she could count them in. All save one.

"Wish you the best of luck," he said, then shrugged a little. "You follow your own instincts, Dana, but somehow I figure my place is here. I think Earth's gonna need me."

She accepted that, knew that special knowledge was given where it was needed, and that she was far from unique in that regard. "If it's what you want, Louie."

Louie Nichols gave his patented clever-funny smirk. "There's still a lot of things I want to know, and I can only find 'em out *here*. And besides, well—don't laugh!—but maybe I've got my *own* part to play." He adjusted the big, dark tech goggles self-consciously.

Nobody laughed. There would be months, perhaps years, of preparation yet—in a world half in ruins—and only Dana had any coherent idea of what was to come. But somehow there was, on the crest of the little hill, a feeling very much like what the sundering of the Round Table must have felt like.

ATAC squad 15 (Hovertanks) turned to get the refugees formed up for the long hike back to Monument City; the assault ship would never rise again. There were already the pairings of Bowie and Musica, Sean and Marie. And now, Nova Satori stayed close to Dennis Brown; the looks they exchanged spoke eloquently.

Dana, sitting on a rock, was stripping off the armor that she hoped never to have to wear again. The spores still drifted everywhere. A sudden loneliness had come over her; there was so very much to do yet, and no one could possibly share her knowledge and her responsibilities—no one could ever understand her longing. She let go a long breath.

Something blocked the low, orange rays of the sunset from her. Angelo Dante stood there, stretching and scratching, having ditched his own armor, wearing a pack made up of most of the usable things he had managed to scare up in the assault ship. The weight of it didn't seem to bother him. He was adjusting his rifle sling.

He didn't seem to have a care in the world. "Lieutenant—Dana—you're still callin' the shots. I got 'em ready; you move 'em out."

Before she knew it, she was on her feet, arms thrown around him. About her had spun the symmetries and vectors of the Second Robotech War; she alone had the powers of mind that would let a leader perform the job she had to do now. But her nineteenth birthday was still three weeks and three days away.

Angelo patted her back and spoke more softly than she had ever heard him. "There, there, now, ma'am: we can't *all* be sergeants. But as officers go, I've seen worse than you. Dana, all we need is someone to show us the way."

She knew he didn't mean the way to Monument; the flames would do that. She surprised herself as much as him by pulling his head down to her and kissing Angelo Dante hard.

Then she let him go, took the sidearm from his belt and stalked off to the front of the disorderly mob while he was still recovering and turning to glower at the ATACs, who had seen what happened but kept discreet silence.

Dana saw that the 15th had gotten all the emergency supplies and lights, water and rations from the assault ship and even from her own little escape capsule. She tucked Angelo's pistol into her belt and noted with approval the order of march, weakened or older refugees surrounded by stronger ones who could help at need.

Not that she thought there would be much call for it; the route was pretty straightforward and unobstructed, and the clones who had been so lethargic before now seemed somehow more vital.

She was about to call for a start when there was a little yipping sound nearby. Dana had put Polly down while stripping off her armor; she had assumed that he had disappeared. But he was practically sitting on her feet.

"Polly. In for the distance, are you, hmm?"

The Pollinator showed her a red postage stamp of tongue. She looked back to see that the 15th had the refugees formed up for the march. Angelo winked and gave her a look she hadn't seen from him before. She wondered whether or not she would, at some point, return it; she had a feeling she might.

Later.

First Lieutenant Dana Sterling, 15th squad, Alpha Tactical Armored Corps, gave hand and voice signals, and all the rest began moving. The Pollinator fell in to waddle along beside.

ATACs and TASCs, GMP and clone refugees followed her down the slope and the Pollinator capered around her feet, as darkness came across the sky. They looked for her to point the way.

DEL REY® ONLINE!

The Del Rey Internet Newsletter...
A monthly electronic publication, posted on the Internet, GEnie, CompuServe, BIX, various BBSs, and the Panix gopher (gopher.panix.com). It features hype-free descriptions of books that are new in the stores, a list of our upcoming books, special announcements, a signing/reading/convention-attendance schedule for Del Rey authors, "In Depth" essays in which professionals in the field (authors, artists, designers, salespeople, etc.) talk about their jobs in science fiction, a question-and-answer section, behind-the-scenes looks at sf publishing, and more!

Internet information source!
A lot of Del Rey material is available to the Internet on our Web site and on a gopher server: all back issues and the current issue of the Del Rey Internet Newsletter, sample chapters of upcoming or current books (readable or downloadable for free), submission requirements, mail-order information, and much more. We will be adding more items of all sorts (mostly new DRINs and sample chapters) regularly. The Web site is http://www.randomhouse.com/delrey/ and the address of the gopher is gopher.panix.com

Why? We at Del Rey realize that the networks are the medium of the future. That's where you'll find us promoting our books, socializing with others in the sf field, and—most important—making contact and sharing information with sf readers.

Online editorial presence: Many of the Del Rey editors are online, on the Internet, GEnie, CompuServe, America Online, and Delphi. There is a Del Rey topic on GEnie and a Del Rey folder on America Online.

Our official e-mail address for Del Rey Books is delrey@randomhouse.com (though it sometimes takes us a while to answer).

By
✄ JACK McKINNEY ✄